A STAINLESS STEEL TRIO

Tor Books by Harry Harrison

Galactic Dreams
The Jupiter Plague
Montezuma's Revenge
One Step from Earth
Planet of No Return
Planet of the Damned
The QE2 Is Missing
Queen Victoria's Revenge
A Rebel in Time
Skyfall
Stainless Steel Visions
The Stainless Steel Rat Goes to Hell
The Stainless Steel Rat Joins the Circus
Stonehenge
A Transatlantic Tunnel, Hurrah!
50 in 50
A Stainless Steel Trio

The Hammer and the Cross Trilogy

The Hammer and the Cross
One King's Way
King and Emperor

A STAINLESS STEEL TRIO

A Stainless Steel Rat Is Born

The Stainless Steel Rat Gets Drafted

The Stainless Steel Rat Sings the Blues

HARRY HARRISON

A Tom Doherty Associates Book
New York

This is a work of fiction. All the characters and events portrayed in these novels are either fictitious or are used fictitiously.

A STAINLESS STEEL TRIO

This book is printed on acid-free paper.

Edited by Patrick Nielsen Hayden

Book design by Jane Adele Regina

A Tor Book
Published by Tom Doherty Associates, LLC
175 Fifth Avenue
New York, NY 10010

www.tor.com

Library of Congress Cataloging-in-Publication Data

Harrison, Harry.
A stainless steel trio / Harry Harrison.—1st ed.
p. cm.
"A Tom Doherty Associates book."
ISBN 0-765-30277-2 (alk. paper)
1. DiGriz, James Bolivar (Fictitious character)—Fiction. 2. Science fiction, American.
I. Title.

PS3558.A667 A6 2002
813'.54—dc21

2001059610

First Edition: June 2002

Printed in the United States of America

0 9 8 7 6 5 4 3 2 1

Contents

Introduction

If you are new to the world of the Stainless Steel Rat, I bid you welcome. There are now ten novels that have been published in the series that features this protagonist. All this mighty effort, all the acres of trees turned to paper, all of the twenty-three translations into different languages, all of this can be dated back to a single short story that was published in *Analog* some years ago. This story, and another short story following the adventures of the same character, were eventually incorporated into a novel by the same name.

What—or who—exactly is this rust-free rodent? He is a man, not a rat, although he firmly believes that just as there are flesh-and-blood rats in wooden houses today, so will there be stainless steel rats in the future, when the world will be all metal and concrete. In human terms, this means that there will always be individuals who are a part of society—yet separated from it.

When Kingsley Amis read the first Stainless Steel Rat novel, he said, "Well, Harry, you have written the first picaresque science-fiction novel." I nodded sagaciously—and at the first opportunity rushed to my dictionary.

Picaresque 1. *of or relating to a type of fiction in which the hero, a rogue, goes through a series of episodic adventures.*

Well, that is a fair enough description. My hero is alone against the universe, with every man's hand—if not every woman's—turned against him. He is without the law, verily a law unto himself, with a strict sense of morality. Aren't the two mutually incompatible? No, as you will soon discover.

This character first appeared in *The Stainless Steel Rat*. But you will not find that novel here. Instead, you will be introduced to James diGriz, sometimes called Slippery Jim, as a young man, perhaps even a callow youth, because I realized, as the number of these books grew, that I was intrigued as to where this brash and very successful character had come from. How had he grown up among peaceful, law-abiding citizens and become, what many might call, a crook?

As the author, I thought that I knew. But I wanted these thoughts amplified on paper, then expanded into a novel. After all, if I care, certainly the readers would be concerned as well. They were! They greeted the first prequel with happy cries.

Let me explain the term "prequel." We all know that a sequel is a novel that continues a previously related story. Well, a prequel takes the same idea—

only turns it the other way around. It takes place earlier in time in the character's life than the first novel—even though it is written after the first novel. In my case, I wanted to flesh out my character, to know him a bit better. Therefore *A Stainless Steel Rat Is Born*. (A title that won a prize from the *London Times Literary Supplement* readers as the most incredible book title of the year.) And what jolly fun it was to explore my hero's youth! The only problem was that I could not get all the new material into one book.

So, *The Stainless Steel Rat Gets Drafted* followed soon after. The draft, a fate that befell me during World War II, filled me with a great deal of empathy for my character. That the future will re-create the past, I do not doubt. Nor that the military, as long as they are in existence, will be stupid, arrogant, bull-headed, wrong-headed, and all of the other wholesome adjectives. So Jim has survived birth, survived the army, and is ready to march into his picaresque future.

Well . . . not quite. He still had not gained his complete rattish personality, was still a bit incomplete in certain ways. What was to be done? Fill in the gap, of course, with *The Stainless Steel Rat Sings the Blues*. Yes, he does sing, along with his friends. There was even a cassette recorded of the music he composed. Life imitates art. Art enriches life.

So here you are: three novels neatly bound inside a single cover so that, if the weather is bad, this volume will enable you to not leave the house for a week or more. Depending, of course, on how fast you read.

Read and enjoy—for you have set your feet upon the path of the righteous rat.

Life will never be the same again.

HARRY HARRISON

A Stainless Steel Rat Is Born

Chapter 1

As I approached the front door of The First Bank of Bit O' Heaven, it sensed my presence and swung open with an automatic welcome. I stepped briskly through—and stopped. But I was just far enough inside so that the door was unable to close behind me. While it was sliding shut I took the arc pen from my bag—then spun about just as it had closed completely. I had stop-watched its mechanical reflex time on other trips to the bank, so I knew that I had just 1.67 seconds to do the necessary. Time enough.

The arc buzzed and flared and welded the door securely to its frame. After this all the door could do was buzz helplessly, immobile, until something in the mechanism shorted out and it produced some crackling sparks, then died.

"Destruction of bank property is a crime. You are under arrest."

As it was speaking, the robot bank guard reached out its large padded hands to seize and hold me until the police arrived.

"Not this time, you jangling junkpile," I snarled, and pushed it in the chest with the porcuswine prod. The two metal points produced 300 volts and plenty of amps. Enough to draw the attention of a one-tonne porcuswine. Enough to short the robot completely. Smoke spurted from all its joints and it hit the floor with a very satisfactory crash.

Behind me. For I had already leapt forward, shouldering aside the old lady who stood at the teller's window. I pulled the large handgun from my bag and pointed it at the teller and growled out my command.

"Your money or your life, sister. Fill this bag with bucks."

Very impressive, though my voice did break a bit so the last words came out in a squeak. The teller smiled at this and tried to brazen it out.

"Go home, sonny. This is not . . ."

I pulled the trigger and the .75 recoilless boomed next to her ear; the cloud of smoke blinded her. She wasn't hit but she might just as well have been. Her eyes rolled up in her head and she slid slowly from sight behind the till.

You don't foil Jimmy diGriz that easily! With a single bound I was over the counter and waving the gun at the rest of the wide-eyed employees.

"Step back—all of you! Quick! I want no little pinkies pressing the silent alarm buttons. That's it. You, butterball—" I waved over the fat teller who had always ignored me in the past. He was all attention now. "Fill this bag with bucks, large denominations, and do it *now*."

He did it, fumbling and sweating yet working as fast as he could. The customers and staff all stood around in odd poses, apparently paralyzed with fear. The door to the manager's office stayed closed, which meant that he probably wasn't there. Chubby had the bag filled with bills and was holding it out to me. The police had not appeared. There was a good chance I was getting away with it.

I muttered what I hoped was a foul curse under my breath and pointed to one of the sacks that were filled with rolls of coins.

"Dump out the change and fill that too," I ordered, sneering and growling at the same time.

He obeyed with alacrity and soon had this bag stuffed full as well. And still no sign of the police. Could it be that not one of the moronic money employees had pressed the silent alarm button? It could be. Drastic measures would have to be taken.

I reached out and grabbed up another bag of coins. "Fill this one as well," I ordered, slinging it across to him.

As I did this I managed to get the alarm button with my elbow. There are some days when you have to do everything for yourself.

This had the desired effect. By the time the third bag was full, and I was staggering towards the door with my loot, the police began to appear. One groundcar managed to crash into another (police emergencies are pretty rare around these parts), but eventually they sorted themselves out and lined up outside, guns ready.

"Don't shoot," I squeaked. With real fear, because most of them didn't look too bright. They couldn't hear me through the windows but they could see me. "It's a dummy," I called out. "See!"

I put the muzzle of the gun to the side of my head and pulled the trigger. There was a satisfactory puff of smoke from the smoke generator and the sound effect of the shot was enough to make my ears ring. I dropped behind the counter, away from their horrified gaze. At least there would be no shooting now. I waited patiently while they shouted and cursed and finally broke down the door.

Now, you might find all of this puzzling—if so I do not blame you. It is one thing to hold up a bank, another thing still to do it in such a manner that you are sure to be caught. Why, you might ask, why be so foolish?

I'll be happy to tell you. To understand my motives you have to understand what life is like on this planet—what *my* life has been like. Let me explain.

Bit O' Heaven was founded some thousands of years ago by some exotic religious cult, which has happily since vanished completely. They came here from another planet; some say it was Dirt or Earth, the rumored home of all mankind, but I doubt it. In any case, things didn't work out too well. Maybe the endless labors were too much for them—this was certainly no picnic-world in the early days. As the teachers at school remind us as often as they can, particularly when they tell us how spoiled the young folk are these days. We manage not to tell them that they must be spoiled as well because certainly nothing has changed here in the last thousand years.

In the beginning, sure, it must have been rough. All of the plant life was pure poison to human metabolisms and had to be cleared away so edible crops could be grown. The native fauna was just as poisonous, with teeth and claws to match. It was tough. So tough that ordinary cows and sheep had a shockingly short life expectancy. Selective gene manipulation took care of that and the first porcuswine were sent here. Imagine if you can—and you will need a fertile imagination indeed—a one-tonne angry boar hog with sharp tusks and a mean disposition. That's bad enough, but picture the creature covered with long quills like an insane porcupine. Odd as it sounds, the plan worked; since the farms are still breeding porcuswine in large numbers it *had* to have worked. Bit O' Heaven Smoked Porcuswine Hams are famed galaxy-wide.

But you won't find the galaxy rushing to visit this piggy planet. I grew up here, I know. This place is so boring even the porcuswine fall asleep.

The funny part is that I seem to be the only one who notices it. They all look at me funny. My Mom always thought that it was just growing pains and burnt porcuswine quills in my bedroom, a folk remedy for same. Dad was always afraid of incipient insanity and used to haul me off to the doctor about once a year. The doctor couldn't find anything wrong and theorized that I might be a throwback to the original settlers, a loser in the Mendelian crapshoot. But that was years ago. I haven't been bothered with parental attention since Dad threw me out of the house when I was fifteen. This was after he had gone through my pockets one night and discovered that I had more money than he did. Mom agreed fervently with him and even opened the door. I think they were glad to see the last of me. I was certainly too much of an irritation in their bovine existence.

What do I think? I think it can be damn lonely at times, being an outcast. But I don't think I would have it any other way. It can have its problems—but problems have solutions.

For example, one problem I licked was getting beat up all the time by the bigger kids. This began happening as soon as I went to school. I made the mistake at first of letting them know I was brighter than they were. Bam, a black eye. The school bullies liked it so much that they had to take turns to beat up on me. I only broke the punishment cycle by bribing a university physical education teacher to give me lessons in unarmed combat. I waited until I was really proficient before fighting back. Then I creamed my would-be creamer and went on to beat up three more of the thugs one after another. I can tell you, all the little kids were my friends after that and never tired of telling me how great it looked to see me chasing six of the worst ruffians down the block. Like I said, from problems come solutions—not to say pleasures.

And where did I get the money to bribe the teacher? Not from Dad, I can tell you. Three bucks a week was my allowance, enough to buy maybe two Gaspo-Fizzes and a small sized Get-Stuffed candy bar. Need, not greed, taught me my first economic lesson. Buy cheap and sell dear and keep the profits for yourself.

Of course there was nothing I could buy, having no capital, so I resorted to not paying at all for the basic product. All kids shoplift. They go through the phase and usually get it beaten out of them when they are detected. I saw the unhappy and tear-stained results of failure and decided to do a market survey as well as a time and motion study before I entered on a career of very petty crime.

First—stay away from the small merchants. They know their stock and have a strong interest in keeping it intact. So do your shopping at the large multis. All you have to worry about then are the store detectives and alarm systems. Then careful study of how they operate will generate techniques to circumvent them.

One of my earliest and most primitive techniques—I blush at revealing its simplicity—I called the book-trap. I constructed a box that looked exactly like a book. Only it had a spring-loaded, hinged bottom. All I needed to do was to push it down on an unsuspecting Get-Stuffed bar to have the candy vanish from sight. This was a crude but workable device that I used for a good length of time. I was about to abandon it for a superior technique when I perceived an opportunity to finish it off in a most positive manner. I was going to take care of Smelly.

His name was Bedford Smillingham but Smelly was the only name we ever called him. As some are born dancers or painters, others are shaped for lesser tasks. Smelly was a born snitch. His only pleasure in life was ratting on his schoolmates. He peeked and watched and snitched. No juvenile peccadillo was too minor for him to note and report to the authorities. They loved him for this—which will tell you a lot about the kind of teachers we had. Nor could he be beat up with impunity. His word was always believed and it was the beater-uppers who suffered the punishment.

Smelly had done me some small ill, I forget exactly what, but it was enough to stir dark and brooding thought, to eventually produce a plan of action. Bragging is a thing all boys enjoy, and I achieved great status by revealing my book-shaped candy bar collector to my peer group. There were oohs and ahhs, made more ooh and ahhish by portioning out some of the loot free for the taking. Not only did this help my juvenile status—but I made sure that it was done where Smelly could eavesdrop. It still feels like yesterday, and I glow warmly with the memory.

"Not only does it work—but I'll show you just how! Come with me to Ming's Multistore!"

"Can we, Jimmy—can we really?"

"You can. But not in a bunch. Drift over there a few at a time and stand where you can watch the Get-Stuffed counter. Be there at 1500 hours and you will really see something!"

Something far better than they could possibly have imagined. I dismissed them and watched the Head's office. As soon as Smelly went through the door I nipped down and broke into his locker.

It worked like a charm. I take some pride in this since it was the first criminal scenario that I prepared for others to take part in. All unsuspecting of course. At the appointed time I drifted up to the candy counter at Ming's, working very hard to ignore the rentaflics, who were working equally hard pretending they weren't watching me. With relaxed motions I placed the book atop the candies and bent to fix my boot fastener.

"Nicked!" the burlier of them shouted, seizing me by the coat collar. "Gotcha!" the other crowed, grabbing up the book.

"What are you doing," I croaked—I had to croak because my coat was now pulled tight about my throat as I hung suspended from it. "Thief—give me back my seven-buck history book that my Mom bought with money earned weaving matts from porcuswine quills!"

"Book?" the great bully sneered. "We know all about this book." He seized the ends and pulled. It opened and the look on his face as the pages flipped over was something sweet to behold.

"I have been framed," I squeaked, opening my coat and dropping free, rubbing at my sore throat. "Framed by the criminal who bragged about using that same technique for his own nefarious ends. He stands there, one Smelly by name. Grab him, guys, before he runs away!"

Smelly could only stand and gape while the ready hands of his peers clutched tight. His schoolbooks fell to the floor and the imitation book burst open and disgorged its contents of Get-Stuffeds upon the floor.

It was beautiful. Tears and recriminations and shouting. A perfect distraction as well. Because this was the day that I field-tested my Mark II Get-Stuffed stuffer. I had worked hard on this device which was built around a silent vacuum pump—with a tube down my sleeve. I brought the tube end close to the candy bars and—zip!—the first of them vanished from sight. It ended up in my trousers, or rather inside the hideous plus-fours we were forced to wear as a school uniform. These bagged out and were secured above the ankle by a sturdy elastic band. The candy bar dropped safely into it, to be followed by another and yet another.

Except I couldn't turn the damn thing off. Thank goodness for Smelly's screaming and struggling. All eyes were on him and not me as I struggled with the switch. Meanwhile the pump still pumped and the Get-Stuffeds shot up my sleeve and into my trousers. I turned it off eventually but if anyone had bothered to look my way, why the empty counter and my bulging-legged form would have been a might suspicious. But thankfully no one did. I exited with a rolling gait, as quickly as I could. As I said, a memory I will always cherish.

Which, of course, does not explain why I have now, on my birthday, made the major decision to hold up a bank. And get caught.

The police had finally broken down the door and were swarming in. I raised my hands over my head and prepared to welcome them with warm smiles.

The birthday, that is the final reason. My seventeenth birthday. Becoming seventeen here on Bit O' Heaven is a very important time in a young man's life.

Chapter 2

The judge leaned forward and looked down at me, not unkindly.

"Now come on, Jimmy, tell me what this tomfoolery is all about."

Judge Nixon had a summer house on the river, not too far from our farm, and I had been there often enough with his youngest son for the judge to get to know me.

"My name is James diGriz, buster. Let us not get too familiar."

This heightened his color a good deal, as you might imagine. His big nose stuck out like a red ski slope and his nostrils flared. "You will have more respect in this courtroom! You are faced with serious charges, my boy, and it might help your case to keep a civil tongue in your mouth. I am appointing Arnold Fortescue, the public defender, as your attorney. . . ."

"I don't need an attorney—and I particularly don't need old Skewey who has been on the sauce so long there isn't a man alive who has seen him sober. . . ."

There was a ripple of laughter from the public seats, which infuriated the judge. "Order in the court!" he bellowed, hammering his gavel so hard that the handle broke. He threw the stub across the room and glared angrily at me. "You are trying the patience of this court. Lawyer Fortescue has been appointed. . . ."

"Not by me he hasn't. Send him back to Mooney's Bar. I plead guilty to all charges and throw myself on the mercy of this merciless court."

He drew in his breath with a shuddering sigh and I decided to ease off a bit before he had a stroke and collapsed; then there would be a mistrial and more time would be wasted.

"I'm sorry, judge." I hung my head to hide an unrepressed smile. "But I done wrong and I will have to pay the penalty."

"Well, that's more like it, Jimmy. You always were a smart lad and I hate to see all that intelligence going to waste. You will go to Juvenile Correction Hall for a term of not less than—"

"Sorry, your honor," I broke in. "Not possible. Oh, if I only had committed my crimes last week or last month! The law is firm on this and I have no escape. Today is my birthday. My seventeenth birthday."

That slowed him down all right. The guards looked on patiently while he punched for information on his computer terminal. The reporter for the *Bit O' Heaven Bugle* working just as hard on the keys of his own portable terminal at the same time. He was filing quite a story. It didn't take the judge long to come up with the answers. He sighed.

"That is true enough. The records reveal that you are seventeen this day and have achieved your majority. You are no longer a juvenile and must be treated as an adult. This would mean a prison term for certain—if I didn't allow for the circumstances. A first offense, the obvious youth of the defendant, his realization that he has done wrong. It is within the power of this bench to make exceptions, to suspend a sentence and bind a prisoner over. It is my decision . . ."

The last thing I wanted to do was hear his decision now. Things were not going as I had planned, not at all. Action was required. I acted. My scream drowned out the judge's words. Still screaming I dived headlong from the prisoner's dock, shoulder-rolled neatly on the floor, and was across the room before my shocked audience could even consider moving.

"You will write no more scurrilous lies about me, you grubbing hack," I shouted. As I whipped the terminal from the reporter's hands and crashed it to the floor. Then stamped the six-hundred-buck machine into worthless junk. I dodged around him before he could grab me and pelted towards the door. The policeman there grabbed at me—then folded when I planted my foot in his stomach.

I could probably have escaped then, but escape at this point wasn't part of my plan. I fumbled with the door handle until someone grabbed me, then struggled on until I was overwhelmed.

This time I was manacled as I stood in the dock and there was no more Jimmy-my-boy talk from the judge. Someone had found him a new gavel and he waved it in my direction, as though wishing to brain me with it. I growled and tried to look surly.

"James Bolivar diGriz," he intoned. "I sentence you to the maximum penalty for the crime that you have committed. Hard labor in the city jail until the arrival of the next League ship, whereupon you will be sent to the nearest place of correction for criminal therapy." The gavel banged. "Take him away."

This was more like it. I struggled against my cuffs and spat curses at him so he wouldn't show any last moment weaknesses. He didn't. Two burly policemen grabbed me and hauled me bodily out of the courtroom and jammed me, not too gently, into the back of the black Maria. Only after the door had been slammed and sealed did I sit back and relax—and allow myself a smile of victory.

Yes, victory, I mean that. The whole point of the operation was to get arrested and sent to prison. I needed some on-the-job training.

There is method in my madness. Very early in life, probably about the time of my Get-Stuffed successes, I began to seriously consider a life of crime. For a lot of reasons—not the least of which was that I *enjoyed* being a criminal. The financial rewards were great; no other job paid more for less work. And, I must be truthful, I enjoyed the feeling of superiority when I made the rest of the world look like chumps. Some may say that is a juvenile emotion. Perhaps—but it sure is a pleasurable one.

About this same time I was faced with a serious problem. How was I to prepare myself for the future? There had to be more to crime than lifting Get-Stuffed bars. Some of the answers I saw clearly. Money was what I wanted. Other people's money. Money is locked away, so the more I knew about locks the more I would be able to get this money. For the first time in school I buckled down to work. My grades soared so high that my teachers began to feel there might be hope for me yet. I did so well that when I elected to study the trade of locksmith they were only too eager to oblige. It was supposed to be a three-year course, but I learned all there was to know in three months. I asked permission to take the final examination. And was refused.

Things were just not done that way, they told me. I would proceed at the same stately pace as the others and in two years and nine months I would get my diploma, leave the school—and enter the ranks of the wage slaves.

Not very likely. I tried to change my course of study and was informed that this was impossible. I had *locksmith* stamped on my forehead, metaphorically speaking of course, and it would remain there for life. They thought.

I began to cut classes and avoid the school for days at a time. There was little they could do about this, other than administer stern lectures, because I showed up for all the examinations and always scored the highest grades. I ought to, since I was making the most of my training in the field. I carefully spread my attentions around so the complacent citizens of the city had no idea they were being taken. A vending machine would yield a few bucks in silver one day, a till at the parking lot the next. Not only did this field work perfect my talents but it paid for my education. Not my school education of course—by law I had to remain there until the age of seventeen—but in my free time.

Since I could find no guidelines to prepare myself for a life of crime, I studied all of the skills that might be of service. I found the word *forgery* in the dictionary, which encouraged me to learn photography and printing. Since unarmed combat had already stood me in good stead, I continued my studies until I earned a Black Belt. Nor was I ignoring the technical side of my chosen career. Before I was sixteen I knew just about all there was to know about computers—while at the same time I had become a skilled microelectronic technician.

All of these were satisfying enough in themselves—but where did I go from there? I really didn't know. That was when I decided to give myself a coming-of-age birthday present. A term in jail.

Crazy? Like a fox! I had to find some criminals—and where better than in jail? A keen line of reasoning, one has to admit. Going to jail would be like coming home, meeting my chosen peer group at last. I would listen and learn and when I felt I had learned enough the lockpick in the sole of my shoe would help me to make my exit. How I smiled and chortled with glee.

More the fool—for it was not to be this way at all.

My hair was shorn, I was bathed in an antiseptic spray, prison clothes and boots were issued—so unprofessionally that I had ample time to transfer the lockpick and my stock of coins—I was thumbprinted and retinapixed, then led to my cell. To behold, to my great joy, that I had a cellmate. My education would begin at last. This was the first day of the rest of my criminal life.

"Good afternoon, sir," I said. "My name is Jim diGriz."

He looked at me and snarled. "Get knotted, kid." He went back to picking his toes, an operation which my entrance had interrupted.

That was my first lesson. The polite linguistic exchanges of life outside were not honored behind these walls. Life was tough—and so was language. I twisted my lips into a sneer and spoke again. In far harsher tones this time.

"Get knotted yourself, toe-cheese. My monicker is Jim. What's yours?"

I wasn't sure about the slang, I had picked it up from old videos, but I surely had the tone of voice right because I had succeeded in capturing his attention this time. He looked up slowly and there was the glare of cold hatred in his eyes.

"Nobody—and I mean *nobody*—talks to Willy the Blade that way. I'm going to cut you, kid, cut you bad. I'm going to cut my initial into your face. A 'V' for Willy."

"A 'W,'" I said. "Willy is spelled with a 'W.'"

This upset him even more. "I know how to spell, I ain't no moron!" He was blazing with rage now, digging furiously under the mattress on his bed. He produced a hacksaw blade that I could see had the back edge well sharpened. A deadly little weapon. He bounced it in his hand, sneered one last sneer—then lunged at me.

Well, needless to say, that is not the recommended way to approach a Black

Belt. I moved aside, chopped his wrist as he went by—then kicked the back of his ankle so that he ran headfirst into the wall.

He was knocked cold. When he came to I was sitting on my bunk and doing my nails with his knife. "The name is Jim," I said, lip-curled and nasty. "Now you try saying it. Jim."

He stared at me, his face twisted—then began to cry! I was horrified. Could this really be happening?

"They always pick on me. You're no better. Make fun of me. And you took my knife away. I worked a month making that knife, had to pay ten bucks for the broken blade. . . ."

The thought of all of the troubles had started him blubbering again. I saw then that he was only a year or two older than me—and a lot more insecure. So my first introduction to criminal life found me cheering him up, getting a wet towel to wipe his face, giving him back his knife—and even giving him a five-buck goldpiece to stop his crying. I was beginning to feel that a life of crime was not quite what I thought it would be.

It was easy enough to get the story of his life—in fact it was hard to shut him up once he got in full spate. He was filled with self-pity and wallowed in the chance to reveal all to an audience.

Pretty sordid, I thought, but kept silent while his boring reminiscences washed over me. Slow in school, laughed at by the others, the lowest marks. Weak and put upon by the bullies, gaining status only when he discovered—by accident of course with a broken bottle—that he could be a bully too once he had a weapon. The rise in status, if not respect, after that by using threats of violence and more than a little bullying. All of this reinforced by demonstrations of dissections on live birds and other small and harmless creatures. Then his rapid fall after cutting a boy and being caught. Sentenced to Juvenile Hall, released, then more trouble, and back to Hall yet again. Until here he was, at the zenith of his career as a knife-carrying punk, imprisoned for extorting money by threat of violence. From a child of course. He was far too insecure to attempt to threaten an adult.

Of course he did not say all this, not at once, but it became obvious after endless rambling complaints. I tuned him out and tuned my inner thoughts in. Bad luck, that was all it was. I had probably been put in with him to keep me from the company of the real hardened criminals who filled this prison.

The lights went out at that moment and I lay back on the bunk. Tomorrow would be my day. I would meet the other inmates, size them up, find the real criminals among them. Befriend them and begin my graduate course in crime. That is surely what I would do.

I went happily to sleep, washed over by a wave of wimpish whining from the adjoining bunk. Just bad luck being stuck in with him. Willy was the exception. I had a roommate who was a loser, that was all. It would all be different in the morning.

I hoped. There was a little nag of worry that kept me awake for a bit, but at last I shrugged it off. Tomorrow would be fine, yes it would be. Fine. No doubt about that, fine. . . .

Chapter 3

Breakfast was no better—and no worse—than the ones I made for myself. I ate automatically, sipping the weak cactus tea and chewing doggedly at the gruel, while I looked around at the other tables. There were about thirty prisoners stuffing their faces in this room, and my gaze went from face to face with a growing feeling of despair.

First, most of them had the same vacuous look of blank stupidity as my cellmate. All right, I could accept that, the criminal classes would of course contain the maladjusted and the mental mud walls. But there had to be more than that! I hoped.

Second, they were all quite young, none out of their twenties. Weren't there any old criminals? Or was criminality a malfunction of youth that was quickly cured by the social adjustment machines? There had to be more to it than that. There had to be. I took some cheer from this thought. All of these prisoners were losers, that was obvious, losers and incompetents. It was obvious once you thought about it. If they had been any good at their chosen profession they wouldn't be inside! They were of no use to the world or to themselves.

But they were to me. If they couldn't supply the illegal facts that I needed, they would surely be able to put me in touch with those who did. From them I would get leads to the criminals on the outside, the professionals still uncaught. That was what I had to do. Befriend them and extract the information that I needed. All was not lost yet.

It didn't take long for me to discover the best of this despicable lot. A little group was gathered around a hulking young man who sported a broken nose and a scarred face. Even the guards seemed to avoid him. He strutted a good deal and the others made room around him when he walked in the exercise yard after lunch.

"Who is that?" I asked Willy, who huddled on the bench next to me, industriously picking his nose. He blinked rapidly until he finally made out the subject of my attentions, then waved his hands with despair.

"Watch out for him, stay away, he's bad medicine. Stinger is a killer, that's what I heard, and I believe it too. And he's a champ at mudslugging. You don't want to know him."

This was intriguing indeed. I had heard of mudslugging, but I had always lived too close to the city to have seen it in action. There was never any of it taking place near enough for me to hear about, not with the police all around. Mudslugging was a crude sport—and illegal—that was enjoyed in the outlying farm towns. In the winter, with the porcuswine in their sties and the crops in the barns, time would hang heavy on their agrarian hands. That was when the mudslugging would begin. A stranger would appear and challenge the local champion, usually some overmuscled ploughboy. A clandestine engagement would be arranged in some remote barn, the women dismissed, moonshine surreptitiously brought in plastic bottles, bets made—and the barefisted fight begun. To end when one of the combatants could not get off the ground. Not a sport for the squeamish, or the sober. Good, hearty, drunken masculine fun. And Stinger was one of this stalwart band. I must get to know Stinger better.

This was easily enough done. I suppose I could have just walked over and spoken to him, but my thought patterns were still warped by all of the bad videos I had watched for most of my life. Plenty of these were about criminals getting their just deserts in prison, which is probably where I originated the idea of this present escapade. Never matter, the idea was still a sound one. I could prove that by talking to Stinger.

To do this I walked, whistling, about the yard until I was close to him and his followers. One of them scowled at me and I scuttled away. Only to return as soon as his back was turned, to sidle up beside the head villain.

"Are you Stinger?" I whispered out of the side of my mouth, head turned away from him. He must have seen the same videos because he answered in the same way.

"Yeah. So who wants to know?"

"Me. I just got into this joint. I got a message for you from the outside."

"So tell."

"Not where these dummies can hear. We gotta be alone."

He gave me a most suspicious look from under his beetling brows. But I had succeeded in capturing his curiosity. He muttered something to his followers, then strolled away. They remained behind but flashed murderous looks at me when I strolled in the same direction. He went across the yard towards a bench—the two men already there fleeing as he approached. I sat down next to him and he looked me up and down with disdain.

"Say what you gotta say, kid—and it better be good."

"This is for you," I said, sliding a twenty-buck coin along the bench towards him. "The message is from me and from no one else. I need some help and am willing to pay for it. Here is a down payment. There is plenty more where this came from."

He sniffed disdainfully—but his thick fingers scraped up the coin and slipped it into his pocket. "I ain't in the charity business, kid. The only geezer I help is myself. Now, shove off—"

"Listen to what I have to say first. What I need is someone to break out of prison with me. One week from today. Are you interested?"

I had caught his attention this time. He turned and looked me square in the eye, cold and assured. "I don't like jokes," he said—and his hand grabbed my wrist and twisted. It hurt. I could have broken the grip easily, but I did not. If this little bit of bullying was important to him, then bully away.

"It's no joke. Eight days from now I'll be on the outside. You can be there too if you want to be. It's your decision."

He glared at me some more—then let go of my wrist. I rubbed at it and waited for his response. I could see him chewing over my words, trying to make up his mind. "Do you know why I'm inside?" he finally asked.

"I heard rumors."

"If the rumor was that I killed a geezer, then the rumor was right. It was an accident. He had a soft head. It broke when I knocked him down. They was going to pass it off as a farm accident but another geezer lost a bundle to me on the match. He was going to pay me next day but he went to the police instead because that was a lot cheaper. Now they are going to take me to a League hospital and do my head. The shrinker here says I won't want to fight again after that. I won't like that."

The big fists opened and closed when he talked and I had the sudden understanding that fighting was his life, the one thing that he could do well. Something that other men admired and praised him for. If that ability were taken away—why they might just as well take away his life at the same time. I felt a sudden spurt of sympathy but did not let the feeling show.

"You can get me out of here?" The question was a serious one.

"I can."

"Then I'm your man. You want something out of me, I know that, no one does nothing for nothing in this world. I'll do what you want, kid. They'll get me in the end, there is no place to hide anywhere when they are really looking for you. But I'm going to get mine. I'm going to get the geezer what put me in here. Get him proper. One last fight. Kill him the way he killed me."

I could not help shivering at his words because it was obvious that he meant them. That was painfully clear. "I'll get you out," I said. But to this I added the unspoken promise that I would see to it that he got nowhere near the object of his revenge. I was not going to start my new criminal career as an accomplice to murder.

Stinger took me under his protective wing at once. He shook my hand, crushing my fingers with that deadly grip, then led me over to his followers.

"This is Jim," he said. "Treat him well. Anyone causes him trouble got trouble with me." They were all insincere smiles and promises of affection—but at least they wouldn't bother me. I had the protection of those mighty fists. One of them rested on my shoulder as we strolled away. "How you going to do it?" he asked.

"I'll tell you in the morning. I'm making the last arrangements now," I lied. "See you then." I strolled off on an inspection tour, almost as eager to be out of this sordid place as he was. For a different reason. His was revenge—mine was depression. They were losers in here, all losers, and I like to think of myself as a winner. I wanted to be well away from them all and back in the fresh air.

I spent the next twenty-four hours finding the best way out of the prison. I could open all of the mechanical locks inside the prison easily enough; my lockpick worked fine on our cell door. The only problem was the electronic gate that opened out into the outer courtyard. Given time—and the right equipment—I could have opened that too. But not under the eyes of guards stationed in the observation booth above it right around the clock. That was the obvious way out, so it was the route to be avoided. I needed a better idea of the layout of the prison—so a reconnoiter was very much in order.

It was after midnight when I eased out of my bed. No shoes, I had to be as quiet as possible, so three pairs of socks should do the job. Working silently, I stuffed extra clothing under the blankets so the bed would look occupied if one of the guards should look in through the barred door. Willy was snoring lustily when I clicked the lock open and slipped out into the corridor. He wasn't the only one enjoying his sack time and the walls echoed with *zzzz*ing and gronking. The nightlights were on and I was alone on the landing. I looked over the edge carefully and saw that the guard on the floor below was working on his racing form. Wonderful, I hoped that he had a winner. Silent as a shadow I went to the stairs and up them to the floor above.

Which was depressingly identical to the one below: nothing but cells. As was the next floor and the one above that. Which was the top floor so I could go no higher. I was about to retrace my steps when my eye caught a glint of metal in the shadows at the far end. Nothing ventured, as the expression goes. I scuttled past the barred doors, and the—hopefully—sleeping inmates, to the distant wall.

Well, well, what did we have here! Iron rungs in the wall—vanishing up into the darkness. I grabbed onto the first one and vanished up with them. The last rung was just below the ceiling. It was also just under a trapdoor that let into the ceiling above. Metal, with a metal frame—and locked securely as I discovered when I pushed up against it. There had to be a lock, but it was invisible in the darkness. And I had to find it. Looping one arm through the iron rung I began to run my fingertips over the surface of the door in what I hoped was a regular pattern.

There was nothing there. I tried again, changing hands because my arm felt like it was being dragged from its socket—with the same result. But there *had* to be a lock. I was panicking and not using my brain. I fought back my rising fears and stirred up my brain cells. There must be a lock or seal of some kind. And it was not on the trapdoor. So—it had to be on the frame. I reached out slowly, ran my fingers along the sides of the frame. And found it at once.

How simple the answers are when you ask the right questions! I eased the lockpick from my pocket and slipped it into the lock. Within seconds it had clicked open. Seconds after that I had pushed the trapdoor up, climbed through, closed it behind me—and sniffed appreciatively of the cool night air.

I was out of prison! Standing on the roof, yes, of course, but free in spirit at least. The stars were bright above and shed enough light so I could see across the dark surface. It was flat and broad, bordered with a knee-high parapet and studded with vents and pipes. Something large and bulky occluded the sky, and when I worked my way close to it I heard the dripping of water. The water tank, fine, now what was visible below?

To the front I looked down into the well-lit courtyard, guarded and secure. But what was the back like?

Far more interesting, I assure you. There was a straight drop of five stories to a rear yard, which was feebly illuminated by a single bulb. There were waste bins there, and barrels, and a heavy gate in the outer wall. Locked, undoubtedly. But what man had locked man could unlock. Or rather I could. This was the way out.

Of course there was the five-story drop, but something could be worked there. Or perhaps I could find another way into the backyard. Plenty of time to run through the permutations of escape, six days yet. My feet were getting cold and I yawned and shivered. I had done enough for one night. My hard prison bunk seemed very attractive at this moment.

Carefully and silently I retraced my steps. Eased the trapdoor shut above me, checked to see that it was locked, went down the ladder and the stairs to my floor. . . .

And heard the voices ahead. Loud and clear. The loudest of all being my dear cellmate Willy. I took one horrified look at the open door of my cell, at the heavy boots of the guards there, then pulled myself back and ran up the stairs again. With Willy's words ringing like a tocsin of doom in my ears.

"I woke and he was gone! I was alone! Monsters ate him or something! That's when I started shouting. Save me, please! Whatever got him came right through the locked door. It's gonna get me next!"

Chapter 4

Anger at my cretinous cellmate warmed me; the imminence of my capture instantly chilled me again. I fled unthinkingly, away from the voices and commotion. Back up the stairs, one flight, another—

Then all the lights came on and the sirens began to wail. The prisoners stirred and called out to one another. In a few moments they would be at the cell doors, would see me, would cry out, guards would appear. There was no escape. I knew this, yet all I could do was run. To the top floor—then past the cells there. All of which were now brightly lit. I would be seen by the prisoners as I went by them, and I knew for certain that I would be ratted on by whichever juvenile delinquent spotted me. It was all over.

Head high, I walked past the first cell and glanced in as I passed.

It was empty. As were all of the other cells on this floor. I still had a chance! Like a demented ape I swarmed up the iron rungs and fumbled my lockpick into the lock. There were voices below me, getting louder, and footsteps as well as two of the guards ascended the stairs that faced away from me. But all that one of them had to do was turn his head. And when they reached the floor I would be seen at once.

The lock clicked open and I pushed and swarmed up through the opening. Flat on the roof I eased the door down. Seeing two fat guards through the opening just turning my way as it shut.

Had they seen it closing? My heart thudded like an insane drum and I gasped for air and waited for the shouts of alarm.

They did not come. I was still free.

Some freedom! Depression instantly clutched and shook me. Free to lie on the roof, to shiver violently as the perspiration began to dry, free to huddle up here until I was found.

So I huddled and shivered and generally felt sorry for myself for about a minute. Then I stood and shook myself like a dog and felt the anger begin to rise.

"Big criminal," I whispered aloud, just to make sure that I heard. "Life of crime. And on your first big job you let yourself be trapped by a knife-wielding moron. You've learned a lesson, Jim. May you someday be free to put it into practice. Always guard your flanks and your rear. Consider all the possibilities. Consider the fact that the cretin might have woken up. So you should have coshed him or something to make certain of his sound sleep. Which is certainly water over the dam. Remember the lesson well, but look around now and try to make the best of this rapidly disintegrating escape."

My options were limited. If the guards opened the trapdoor and came up to the roof they would find me. Was there any place to hide? The top of the water tank might offer a temporary refuge, but if they came this far they would certainly look there as well. But with no way to get down the sheer walls it offered the only feeble hope. Get up there.

It wasn't easy. It was made of smooth metal and the top was just beyond my reach. But I had to do it. I stepped back and took a run, leaped, and felt my fingers just grasp the edge. I scrabbled for a hold but they pulled loose and I dropped heavily back to the roof. Anyone below would have certainly heard that. I hoped I was over an empty cell and not the hall.

"Enough hoping and not enough trying, Jim," I said, and added a few curses in the hope of building my morale. I had to get up there!

This time I retreated to the far edge, the backs of my knees against the parapet, taking breath after deep breath. Go!

Run up, fast, the right spot—jump!

My right hand slapped against the edge. I grabbed and heaved. Got my other hand up there and pulled mightily, scraping and bruising myself on the rough metal, hauling myself up onto the top of the tank.

To lie there breathing heavily, looking at a dead bird not a foot from my face, vacant eyes staring into mine. I started to pull away when I heard the trapdoor slam heavily back onto the roof.

"Give me a push up, will you? I'm stuck!"

By the wheezing and grunting that followed I was sure that this had to be one of the fat guards that I had seen on the floor below. More gasping and puffing heralded the arrival of his adipose companion.

"I don't know what we're doing up here," the first arrival whined.

"I do," his companion said quite firmly. "We're obeying orders, which never did no one no harm."

"But the hatch was locked."

"So was the cell door he went through. Look around."

The heavy footsteps circled the roof, then returned.

"Not here. No place to hide. Not even hanging over the edge because I looked."

"There is one place, one place we haven't looked."

I could feel the eyes burning towards me through the solid metal. My heart had started the drumbeat thing again. I clutched at the rusty metal and felt only despair as the footsteps crunched close.

"He could never climb up there. Too high. I can't even reach the top."

"You can't even reach your shoelaces when you bend over. Come on, give me a lift up. If you boost my foot I can reach up and grab on. All I got to do is take a look."

How right he was. Just one look. And there was nothing I could do about it. With the lethargy of defeat possessing me. I lay there, hearing the scratching and the curses, the overweight puffing and scrabbling. The scratching grew close and not a foot before my face a large hand appeared, groping over the edge.

My subconscious must have done it because I swear there was no logical thought involved. My hand shot out and pushed the dead bird forward, to the very edge, below the fingers—which descended and closed on it.

The results were eminently satisfying. The bird vanished, as did the hand, followed by screams and shouts, scrabblings, and two large thuds.

"Why did you do that—?"

"I grabbed it, uggh—oww! My ankle is broke."

"See if you can stand on it. Here, hold my shoulder. Hop along on the other foot, this way. . . ."

There was plenty of shouting back and forth through the trapdoor while I hugged myself with relief and pleasure. They might be back soon, there was that chance, but at least the first round was mine.

As the seconds, then the minutes, moved slowly by I realized that I had won the second round as well. The search had moved away from the roof. For the moment. The sirens cut off and the bustle moved down to the ground below. There were shouts and the slamming of doors, racing of engines as cars moved out into the night. Not soon after—wonder of wonders—the lights began to go out. The first search was over. I started to doze—then jerked myself awake.

"Dummy! You are still in the soup. The search has been made, but this joint is still sealed tight. And you can bet your last buck that starting at first light they will go through every nook and corner. And will be up here with a ladder this time. So with that in mind it is time to move."

And I knew just where I was moving to. The last place they would look for me this night.

Through the trapdoor one last time, and down the darkened corridor. Some of the inmates were still muttering about the events of the night, but all of them appeared to be back in their bunks. Silently I slipped down the stairs and up to cell 567B. Opening it in absolute silence and closing it behind me the same way. Past my stripped bunk to the other bunk where my fink friend Willy slept the sleep of the unjust.

My hand clamped his mouth shut, his eyes sprang open, and I exacted primal and sadistic pleasure by whispering in his ear.

"You are dead, you rat, dead. You called the guards and now you are going to get what you deserve. . . ."

His body gave one gigantic heave then went limp. The eyes were closed. Had I killed him? At once I regretted the bad taste of my little joke. No, not dead, passed out, his breathing light and slow. I went to get a towel, soaked it in cold water—then let him have it right in the mush.

His scream turned to a gurgle as I stuffed the towel into his mouth.

"I'm a generous man, Willy, that's how lucky you are. I'm not going to kill you." My whispered words seemed to reassure him because I felt the tremble in his body subside. "You are going to help me. If you do that you will come to no harm. You have my word. Now prepare to answer my question. Think carefully about this. You are going to whisper just one thing. You are going to tell me the number of the cell that Stinger is in. Nod your head if you are ready. Good. I'm taking the towel away. But if you try any tricks or say anything—*anything*—else, why then you are dead. Here goes."

"*. . . 231B . . .*"

This same floor, good. The towel went right back in. Then I pressed hard behind his right ear, applying continuous pressure to the blood vessel that leads to the brain. Six seconds unconsciousness, ten seconds death. He thrashed then went limp again. I released my thumb on the count of seven. I do have a forgiving nature.

I used the towel to clean my face and hands, then groped for my shoes and put them on. Along with another shirt and my jacket. After that I gurgled down at least a litre of water and was ready to face the world again. I stripped the blankets from the beds, bundled them under my arm—then left.

On tiptoe, as silently as I could, I slipped down to Stinger's cell. I felt immune, impervious. I realized that this was both foolish and dangerous. But after the traumatic events of the evening I seemed to have run out of fear. The cell door opened beneath my delicate touch and Stinger's eyes opened as well when I pushed his shoulder.

"Get dressed," I said quietly. "We're getting out now."

I'll give him this much—he didn't bother asking questions. Just pulled his clothes on while I took the blankets from his bunk. "We need at least two more," I said.

"I'll get Eddie's."

"He'll wake up."

"I'll see he goes back to sleep."

There was a murmured question—followed by a solid thud. Eddie went back to sleep and Stinger brought over the blankets.

"Here's what we do," I told him. "I found the way up to the roof. We go there and knot these blankets together. Then we climb down them and get away. Okay?"

Okay! I had never heard a more insane plan in my life. But not Stinger.

"Okay! Let's go!"

Once more up the stairs—I was really getting pretty tired of this—and tired all over as well. I climbed the rungs, opened the trapdoor, and pushed the blankets through onto the roof when he passed them up to me. He didn't say a word until I had closed and sealed the door again.

"What happened? I heard you got away and I was going to kill you if they ever brought you back."

"It's not that simple. I'll tell you when we get clear. Now let's start tying. Opposite corners lengthwise; we need all the length we can get. Use a square knot like you learned in the Boy Sprouts. Like this."

We knotted and tied like crazy until they were all connected, then took the ends and pulled and grunted and that was that. I tied one end to a solid-looking pipe and threw the bundle of blankets over the side.

"At least twenty feet short," Stinger said, scowling down at the ground. "You go first because you're lighter. If it breaks with me at least you got a chance. Get moving."

The logic of this could not be argued with. I climbed up on the parapet and seized the top blanket. Stinger squeezed my arm with an unexpected show of emotion. Then I was climbing down.

It was not easy. My hands were tired and the blanket fabric hard to grip. I went down as quickly as I could because I knew that my strength was running out.

Then my legs scrabbled at empty air and I had reached the end. The hard floor of the courtyard appeared to be very far below. It was difficult to let go—or rather really very easy. I could hold on no longer. My fingers opened and I fell—

—hit and rolled and sat on the ground gasping for breath. I had done it. High above I could see the dark figure of Stinger swarming down the rope, hand over hand. Within seconds he was on the ground, landing light as a cat beside me, helping me to my feet. Half-supporting me as I stumbled to the gate.

My fingers were trembling and I couldn't get the lock open. We were painfully visible here under the light and if any of the guards glanced out of a window above we were trapped. . . .

I took in a long, shuddering breath—then inserted the picklock once again. Slowly and carefully feeling the grooves on the interior, turning and pushing.

It clicked open and we hurled ourselves through. Stinger pushed it silently shut, then turned and ran out into the night with me right at his heels.

We were free!

Chapter 5

"Wait!" I called after Stinger as he pelted down the road. "Not that way. I've got a better plan. I worked it out before I was sent up."

He slowed to a halt and thought about this and slowly made up his mind. "You called the shots OK so far. So what we gonna do?"

"For openers—leave a trail that they can follow with sniffer robots. This way."

We left the road and cut through the grass and down to the nearby stream. It was shallow but cold and I could not suppress a shiver as we waded across. The main highway ran close by and we headed that way. Crouching low as a heavy transporter thundered by. For the moment there was no other traffic in sight.

"Now!" I called out. "Straight up to the road—then right back down walking in your own footprints."

Stinger did what he was told, backtracking with me to the stream and into the frigid water again.

"That's smart," he said. "The sniffers find where we went into the water, where we came out—and follow us to the road. Then they think that a ground-car maybe picked us up. So what comes next?"

"We go upstream—staying in the water—to the nearest farm. Which happens to be a porcuswine farm. . . ."

"No way! I hate them mothers. Got bit by one when I was a kid."

"We have no other choice. Anything else we do the fuzz will pick us up at daybreak. I can't say I love the porkers either. But I grew up on a farm and I know how to get along with them. Now let's move before my legs freeze off at the ankles."

It was a long, cold slog and I could not stop the trembling once it began. But there was absolutely nothing else to do except push on. My teeth were rattling in my head like castanets before we came to the brook that bubbled down through the fields to join the stream that we were wading in. The stars were beginning to fade; dawn was not too far away.

"This is it," I said. "The stream that we want. That chopped tree is my landmark. Stay right behind me—we're very close now." I reached up and broke off a dead branch that overhung the stream, then led the way. We waded along until we reached a tall, electrified fence that spanned the stream. It could be clearly seen in the growing light. I used the branch to lift the bottom of the fence so Stinger could crawl under, then he did the same for me. As I stood up I heard the familiar rustle of large quills from the oak grove nearby. A large, dark form separated itself from the trees and moved towards us. I grabbed the branch from Stinger and called out softly.

"Sooo-ee, sooo-ee . . . here swine, swine, swine."

There was a bubbling grunt from the boar as it approached. Stinger was muttering under his breath, curses or prayers—or both—as he stood behind me. I called again and the great creature came close. A real beauty, a tonne at least, looking at me with its small red eyes. I stepped forward and raised the branch slowly—and heard Stinger moan behind me. The boar never moved as I poked the stick behind its ear, parted the long quills—and began to scratch its hide industriously.

"What are you doing? It'll kill us!" Stinger wailed.

"Of course not," I said, scratching harder. "Listen to it?" The porcuswine's eyes were half-closed with pleasure and it was burbling happily. "I know these big porkers well. They get vermin under their quills and can't get at them. They love a good scratch. Let me do the other ear—there are nice itchy patches behind the ears—then we can go on."

I scratched, the boar moaned happily, and dawn crept up on us. A light came on in the farmhouse and we knelt down behind the porcuswine. The door opened, someone threw out a basin of water, then it closed again.

"Let's get to the barn," I said. "This way."

The boar grumbled when I stopped scratching, then trotted along behind us, hoping for more, as we skulked across the farm. Which was a good thing since there were plenty more of the spiky porkers on all sides. But they moved aside when the kingpig approached and we proceeded in stately parade to the barn.

"So long, big feller," I said, giving a last good scratch. "Been nice knowing you." Stinger had the barn door open and we slipped inside. We had just slid the bolt again when the heavy wood trembled as our overweight companion leaned against it and snorted.

"You saved my life," Stinger gasped. "I'll never forget that."

"Just skill," I said humbly. "After all, you are good with fists—"

"And you're great with pigs!"

"I wouldn't have phrased it *exactly* that way," I muttered. "Now let's get up into the hayloft where it is warm—and where we won't be seen. There is a long day ahead of us and I want to spend as much of it as I can sleeping."

It had been quite a night. I burrowed into the hay, sneezed twice as the dust got into my nose—then must have fallen instantly asleep.

The next thing I knew Stinger was shaking me by the shoulder and sunlight was streaming between the boards in the wall. "Cops is here," he whispered.

I blinked the sleep from my eyes and looked through the crack. A green and white police floater was hovering outside the farmhouse door and two uniformed pug-uglies were showing a sheet to the farmer. He shook his head and his voice was clear above the farmyard sounds.

"Nope. Never seen neither of them. Never seen a soul in a week if you want to know. Fact is, kind of nice to talk to you fellers. These guys really look nasty, criminals you say . . ."

"Pops, we ain't got all day. If you didn't see them they could still be hiding on your farm. Maybe in your barn?"

"No way they could do that. Them's *porcuswine* out there. Most ornery critters in creation."

"We still got to look. Orders are to search every building in the vicinity."

The policemen started our way and there was a screech like an insane siren and the thud of sharp hooves. Around the corner of the barn—quills rattling with anger—came our friend of the night before. He charged and the police dived for their floater. The angry boar crashed into it, sending it rocking across the yard with a great dent in its side. The farmer nodded happily.

"Told you weren't no one in the barn. Little Larry here, he don't cotton onto strangers. But drop by anytime you're in the neighborhood, fellers. . . ."

He had to shout the last words because the floater was heading west with Little Larry in snorting pursuit.

"Now that is what I call beautiful," Stinger said, awe in his voice. I nodded silent agreement. Even the dullest of lives contain moments of pure glory.

Enough fun; time to work. I chewed on a straw and stretched out on the warm hay. "Porcuswine are nice when you know them."

"The police don't seem to think so," he said.

"Guess not. That was the best thing I ever saw. I don't exactly get along with the police."

"Who does? What you got sent up for, Jimmy?"

"Bank robbery. Did you ever hold up a bank?"

He whistled appreciation and shook his head *no*. "Not my style. I wouldn't know what to do first. Mudslugging's my style. Ain't been beat in nine years."

"Knocking around the way you do you must meet a lot of people. Did you ever meet Smelly Schmuck?" I extemporized rapidly. "He and I did some banks in Graham State."

"Never met him. Never even heard of him. You're the first bank robber I ever met."

"Really? Well, I guess there aren't that many of us these days. But you must know some safecrackers. Or groundcar thieves?"

All I got for my efforts was another shake of the head. "The only time I ever meet guys like you is in jail. I know some gamblers; they go around the mudslugging fights. But they're all two-buckers, losers. I did know one once who swore he knew The Bishop, long time ago."

"The Bishop?" I said, blinking rapidly, trying to sum up what little I knew of the ecclesiastical hierarchy. "I don't go to church much these days. . . ."

"Not that kind of bishop. I mean The Bishop, the geezer used to clean out banks and things. Thought you would have heard of him."

"Before my time, I guess."

"Before everyone's time. This was years ago. Cops never got him, I hear. This two-bucker bragged he knew The Bishop; said that he had retired and was lying low. He must of been lying, two-bucker like him."

Stinger knew no more than this and I hesitated to pump him too hard. Our conversation died away and we both dozed on and off until dark. We were thirsty and hungry, but knew that we had to remain under cover during daylight. I chewed on my straw and tried not to think of large beers and bottles of cold water, but thought about The Bishop instead. It was a thin lead, but was all that I had. By the time the sun went down I was hungry and thirsty and thoroughly depressed. My prison escapade had turned out to be a dangerous fiasco. Jails were for losers—that's about all I had found out. And in order to discover this fact I had risked life and limb. Never again. I took a silent oath to stay away from prison and the minions of the law in the future. Good criminals don't get caught. Like The Bishop, whoever he might be.

When the last trace of light was gone from the sky we eased the barn door open. A bubbling grunt reached our ears and a great form blocked our exit. Stinger gasped and I grabbed him before he could flee.

"Grab a stick and make yourself useful," I said. "I'll teach you a new skill."

So we scratched like crazy under the creature's quills while it grunted with pleasure. Trotting behind us like a pet dog when we finally left. "We got a friend for life," I said as we slipped out the gate and I waved goodbye to our porcine pal.

"Those kinds of friends I can live without forever. You figure out what we do next?"

"Absolutely. Advance planning, that's my middle name. There is a siding down this way where they transship from the linears to trucks. We stay away from it because the police are sure to be there. But all the trucks take the same road to the highway where there is a traffic control light. They have to stop until the highway computers see them and let them on. We go there—"

"And break into the back of one of the trucks!"

"You're learning. Only we get one in the right lane going west. Otherwise we end up back in the fine city of Pearly Gates and right after that in the prison we worked so hard to get out of."

"Lead the way, Jim. You are the brainiest kid I ever met. You're going to go far."

That was my expressed wish and I nodded quick agreement. I was just sorry that he wasn't going too. But I didn't want to live with some far-off yokel's life on my conscience—as much as he might deserve a little agro. But Stinger planned far more than that. I could not be party to a killing.

We found the road and waited in the bushes beside it. Two trucks rumbled up together—with the lights of another one following. We stayed out of sight. First one, then the second pulled out and headed east. When the third slowed down to stop for his turn, lights came on. West!

We ran. I was fumbling with the locking bar when Stinger shouldered me aside. He hauled down and the door swung open. The truck started forward and he pushed me up into it. He had to run as it started its turn—but grabbed the sill and pulled himself up with a single heave of those mighty arms. Between us we got the door closed but not sealed.

"We done it !" he said triumphantly.

"We certainly did. This truck is going in the right direction for you—but I have to get back to Pearly Gates as soon as the heat dies down. In about an hour we'll be passing through Billville. I'll leave you there."

It was a quick trip. I swung down at the first stop for a light and he gripped my hand. "Good luck, kid." he called out as the truck pulled away. I couldn't wish him the same.

I dug out a buck coin as the truck rumbled way. And made a mental note of its registration number. As soon as it was out of sight I headed towards the lights of a phonebox. I felt like a rat as I punched the buttons for the police.

But, really, I had no choice.

Chapter 6

Unlike the hapless Stinger, I had a careful escape plan worked out. Part of it was a literal misdirection for my late partner. He was not really stupid, so it shouldn't take him very long to figure out who had blown the whistle on him. If he talked and told the police that I had returned to the fine city of Pearly Gates—why that would be all for the better. I had no intention of leaving Billville, not for quite a while.

The office had been rented through an agency and all transactions had been done by computer. I had visited it before my hopeless bank job, and at that time had left some supplies there. They would come in very handy right now. I would enter through the service door of the fully automated building—after turning off the alarms by using a concealed switch I had been prudent enough to install there. It had a timer built into it, so I had ten lazy minutes to get to the office. I yawned as I picked the lock, sealed the door behind me, then trudged up three flights of stairs. Past the dull eyes of the deactivated cameras and through the invisible—and inoperative—infrared beams. I picked the lock of the office door with two minutes to spare. I blanked the windows, turned on the lights—then headed for the bar.

Cold beer had never tasted better. The first one never even touched the sides of my throat and sizzled when it hit my stomach. I sipped the second as I tore the tab on a dinpac of barbecued ribs of porcuswine. As soon as the steam whistled through the venthole I ripped open the lid of the stretched pack and pulled out a rib the length of my arm. Yum!

Showered, dipilated and wrapped around a third beer, I began to feel much better. "On." I told the terminal, then punched into the comnet. My instructions were simple; all newspaper records on the planet for the last fifty years, all references to a criminal named The Bishop, check for redundancies around the same date and don't give me any duplicates. Print.

Before I had picked up my beer again the first sheets were sliding out of the fax. The top sheet was the most recent—and it was ten years old. A not too interesting item from a city on the other side of the planet, Decalogg. The police had picked up an elderly citizen in a low bar who claimed that he was The Bishop. However it had turned out to be a case of senile dementia and the suspect had been ushered back to the retirement home from which he had taken a walk. I picked up the next item.

I tired towards morning and took a nap in the filing cabinet, which turned into a bed when ordered to do so. In the gray light of dawn, helped by a large black coffee, I finished placing the last sheet into the pattern that spread across the floor. Rosy sunlight washed across it. I turned off the lights and tapped the stylo against my teeth while I studied the pattern.

Interesting. A criminal who brags about his crimes. Who leaves a little drawing of a bishop behind after scarpering with his loot. A simple design—easy enough to copy. Which I did. I held it out at arm's length and admired it.

The first bishop had been found in the empty till of an automated liquor store sixty-eight years ago. If The Bishop had started his career of crime as a teenager, as I have done, that would put him in his eighties now. A comfortable age to be, since life expectancy has now been pushed up to a century and a half. But what had happened to him to explain the long silence? Over fifteen years had passed since he had left his last calling card. I numbered off the possibilities on my fingers.

"Number one, and a chance always to be considered, is that he has snuffed it. In which case I can do nothing so let us forget about that.

"Two—he could have gone offplanet and be pursuing his life of crime among the stars. If so, forget it like number one. I need a lot more golden bucks, and experience, before I try my hand on other worlds.

"Three, he has gone into retirement to spend his ill-gotten gains—in which case more power to him. Or four, he has changed rackets and stopped leaving his spoor at every job."

I sat back smugly and sipped the coffee. If it were three or four I had a chance of finding him. He had certainly had a busy career before the years of silence; I looked at the list with appreciation. Plane theft, car theft, cash theft, bank emptying. And more and more. All of the crimes involving moving bucks from someone else's pockets to his pockets. Or real property that could be sold quickly, with forged identification, for more bucks. And he had never been caught, that was the best part of it. Here was the man who could be my mentor, my tutor, my university of crime—who would one day issue a diploma of deviltry that would eventually admit me to the golden acres I so coveted.

But how could I find him if the united police forces of an entire world, over a period of decades, had never been able to lay a finger on him? An interesting question.

So interesting that I could see no easy answer. I decided to let my subconscious work on this problem for a bit, so I pushed some synapses aside and let the whole thing slip down into my cerebellum. The street outside was beginning to fill up with shoppers and I thought that might be a good idea for me as well. All the rations I had here were either frozen or packaged, and after the sludgy prison food I felt the urge for things that crackled and crunched. I opened the makeup cabinet and began to prepare my public persona.

Adults don't realize—or remember—how hard it is to be a teenager. They forget that this is the halfway house of maturity. The untroubled joys of childhood are behind one, the mature satisfactions of adulthood still ahead. Aside from the rush of blood to the head, as well as other places, when thoughts of the opposite sex intrude, there are real difficulties. The hapless teenager is expected to act like an adult—yet has none of the privileges of that exalted state. For my part I had escaped the tedious tyranny of teendom by skipping over it completely. When not lolling about in school or trading lies with my age group, I became an adult. Since I was far more intelligent than most of them—or at least I thought that I was—adults that is, I had only to assume the physical role.

First an application of crowsfooter around my eyes and on my forehead. As soon as this colorless liquid was applied wrinkles appeared and the calendar of my age rushed forward a number of years. A few wattles under my chin blended in well with the wrinkles, while the final touch was a nasty little moustache. When I pulled on my shapeless under-office clerk jacket, my own mother would not have recognized me if she had passed me in the street. In fact this had happened about a year ago and I had asked her the time and even then no spark of recognition had brought a glint to her bovine eyes. Taking an umbrella from the closet, since there was absolutely no possibility of rain, I stepped from the office and proceeded to the nearest shopping mall.

I must say, my subconscious was really working fast this day, as I shortly found out. Even after all the beers I still had a thirst. That dry stay in the barn had left its mark. Therefore I turned smartly under the platinum arches of Macswineys and marched up to the serving robot that was built into the counter. The plastic head had a permanent grin painted on it and the voice was syrupy and sexy.

"How can I be of service, sir or madam?" They could have spent a few bucks on a sex-recognition program I thought as I scanned the list of TUM-CHILLER YUMMY DRINKS on the wall.

"Let me have a double-cherry oozer with lots of ice."

"On the way, sir or madam. That will be three bucks, if you please."

I dropped the coins in the hopper and the serving hatch flipped open and my drink appeared. While I reached for it I had to listen to a robotic sales pitch.

"Macswineys is happy to serve you today. With the drink of your choice I am sure you would like a barbecued porcuswineburger with yummy top secret sauce garnished with sugar-fried spamyams. . . ."

The voice faded away from my attention as my subconscious heaved up the answer to my little problem. A really simple and obvious answer that was transparent in its clarity, pristine pure and simple. . . .

"Come on, buster. Order or split, you can't stand there all day."

The voice graveled in my ear and I muttered some excuse and shuffled off to the nearest booth and dropped into it. I knew now what had to be done.

Simply stand the problem on its head. Instead of me looking for The Bishop I would have to make him look for me.

I drank my drink until my sinuses hurt, staring unseeingly into space as the pieces of the plan clicked into place. There was absolutely no chance of my finding The Bishop on my own—it would be foolish to even waste my time trying. So what I had to do was commit a crime so outrageous and munificent that it would be on all the news channels right around the planet. It had to be so exotic that not a person alive with the ability to read—or with a single finger left to punch in a news channel—would be unaware of it. The entire world would know what had happened. And they would know as well that The Bishop had done it because I would leave his calling card on the spot.

The last traces of drink slurped up my straw and my eyes unfocused and I slowly returned to the garish reality of Macswineys. And before my eyes was a poster. I had been staring at it, without seeing it, for some time. Now it registered. Laughing clowns and screaming children. All rapt with joy in slightly faulty 3D. While above their heads the simple message was spelled out in glowing letters.

SAVE YOUR COUPONS!!
GET THEM WITH EVERY PURCHASE!!
FREE ADMISSION TO LOONA PARK!!!

I had visited this site of plastic joys some years before—and had disliked it even as a child. Horrifying rides that frightened only the simple. Rotating up-and-down rides only for the strong of stomach; round-and-round and throw up. Junk food, sweet candy, drunk clowns, all the heady joy to please the very easily pleasable. Thousands attended Loona Park every day and more thousands flooded in on weekends—bringing even more thousands of bucks with them.

Bucks galore! All I had to do was clean them out—in such a very interesting way that it would make the top news story right around the planet.

But how would I do it? By going there, of course, and taking a good hard look at their security arrangements. It was about time that I had a day off.

Chapter 7

For this little reconnaissance trip it would be far wiser for me to act my age—or less. With all the makeup removed I was a fresh-faced seventeen again. I should be able to improve upon that; after all I had taken an expensive correspondence course in theatrical makeup. Pads in my cheeks made me look more cherubic, particularly when touched up with a bit of rouge. I put on a pair of sunglasses decorated with plastic flowers—that squirted water when I pressed the bulb in my pocket. A laugh a second! Styles in dress had changed, which meant that plus-fours for boys had gone out of fashion, thank goodness, but shorts were back. Or rather a reprehensible style called short-longs, which had one leg cut above the knee, the other below. I had purchased a pair of these done in repulsive purple corduroy tastefully decorated with shocking-pink patches. I could scarcely dare look at myself in the mirror. What looked back at me I hesitate to describe, except that it looked very little like an escaped bank robber. Around my neck I slung a cheap disposable camera that was anything but cheap, disposable—or only a camera.

At the station I found myself lost in a sea of lookalikes as we boarded the Loona Special. Screaming and laughing hysterically and spraying each other with our plastic flowers helped to while away the time. Or stretch it to eternity in at least one case. When the doors finally opened I let the multichrome crowd thunder out, then strolled wearily after them. Now to work.

Go where the money was. My memories of my first visit were most dim—thank goodness!—but I did remember that one paid for the various rides and diversions by inserting plastic tokens. My father had furnished a limited and begrudging number of these, which had been used up within minutes, and of course no more had been forthcoming. My first assignment then was to find the font of these tokens.

Easily enough done, for this building was the target of every prepubescent visitor. It was a pointed structure like an inverted ice-cream cone, bedecked with flags and mechanical clowns, topped with a golden calliope that played ear-destroying music. Surrounding it at ground level and fixed to its base was a ring of plastic clown torsos, rocking and laughing and grimacing. Repellent as they were, they provided the vital function of separating the customers from their money. Eager juvenile hands pushed buck bills into the grasping palms of the plastic punchinellos. The hand would close, the money vanish—and from the clown's mouth a torrent of plastic tokens would be vomited into the waiting receptacle. Disgusting—but I was obviously the only one who thought so.

The money went into the building. Now I must find where it came out. I strolled about the base and discovered that the regurgitating dispensers did not quite girdle it. To the rear, behind the concealment of trees and shrubs, a small building snuggled up to the base. I pushed my way under the shrubs and found myself facing a private policeman stationed beside an unmarked door.

"Get lost, kid," he said sweetly. "Employees only."

I dodged around him and pushed against the door—and managed to photograph it at the same time. "I gotta go to the bathroom," I said crossleggedly. "They said the bathroom was here."

A hard hand pulled me away and propelled me back to the shrubbery. "Not here. Out. Back the way you came."

I went. Very interesting. No electronic alarms and the lock was a Glubb—reliable but old. I was beginning to like Loona Park after all.

It was an excruciating wait until dark when the park closed down. Out of boredom I sampled the Glacier Ride where one hurtled through mock ice caverns with Things frozen into the ice on all sides—though they occasionally lunged out at the screeching riders. Rocjet Rovers was equally bad, and in the name of good taste I will draw the curtain down over the heady joys of Candyland and the Swamp Monster. Suffice to say that the time did arrive at last. The token dispenser closed down an hour before the park shut. From a nearby vantage point I watched with avid interest as an armored van took away a great number of solid containers. Even more interesting was the fact that when the money went—so did the security. I imagine that the logic behind this was that no one in their right mind would want to break in and steal the tokens.

So I wasn't in my right mind. As darkness fell I joined the exhausted celebrants as they staggered towards the exits. Except that I didn't get that far. A locked door at the rear of Vampire Mountain unlocked easily under my gentle ministrations. I slipped into the darkness of the service area. High above me, pale fangs shone and fake blood dripped; I felt very comfortable indeed tucked in behind a coffin filled with dirt.

I let an hour go by, no more. This should clear the employees out of the way but still leave enough revelers in the streets outside the park so that my disgusting outfit would not be noticed when I finally made my exit.

There were guards about, but they were easily avoided. As I had expected, the Glubb opened easily and I slipped quickly inside. The room proved to be windowless, which was fine since my light would then not be seen. I switched it on and admired the machinery.

A simple and clean design—I appreciate that in machinery. The dispensers were ringed about the walls. Silent now, but still obvious in their operation. When coins or bills were inserted they were counted and passed on. Machines above released the measured amount of tokens into the delivery chutes. Beside them pipes sprang out of the floor and terminated in a bin above—undoubtedly they were filled from underground conveyors that returned the tokens ready for redispensing. The bucks, untouched by human hands, were being conveyed through sealed and transparent tubes to the collection station, where the coins fell into locked boxes. They were not for me since they were too bulky to move easily. But, ahh, the bills, they were far lighter and worth far more. They slipped along the chutes until they dropped gracefully through an opening in the top of a safe. An operation that appeared to be relatively secure from light-fingered employees.

Wonderful. I admired the machinery and thought about it, then made notes. The dispensers had been manufactured by a firm by the name of Ex-changers, and I took pix of their trademark on the machines. The safe was a secure and reliable brand that easily yielded to my ministrations. It was empty of course, but I had expected that. I made a note of the combination, then opened and closed it a number of times until I could do it with my eyes closed. A plan was taking shape in my head and this was to be an integral part of it.

Finished at last, I slipped from the building without being seen, and with little more effort escaped from the park to join the frolicking throngs. They were less boisterous on the return journey and I only had to use my spray-glasses twice. I cannot describe the relief I felt when I finally staggered through the office door, stripped off the outlandish garb, then buried my nose in a beer. Then, metaphorically of course, I put my thinking cap on.

The next weeks were busy ones. While I worked at the equipment I needed for my operation I followed the news accounts closely. One of the prison escapers, after a fierce struggle, had been recaptured. His companion had not been found, despite the help rendered by the one who had been caught. Poor Stinger; life wouldn't be the same for him once the will to fight was taken from him. However life would still be the same for the man he had planned to kill so I did not feel too sorry for Stinger. And I had work to do. Two things to do in tandem; plan the robbery—and lay the trap for The Bishop. I am proud to say that I accomplished both with some ease. After this I waited until there was a dark and stormy night to visit Loona Park again. I was in and out as quickly as I could, which was some hours since there was a good deal of work to be done.

After that it was only a matter of waiting for the right time. A weekend would be best, with the tills overflowing. As part of my plans I had rented the garage quite legally, but had stolen the small van most illegally. I used the waiting time to repaint it—a better job than the original if I must say so—to add new identification numbers, and to fix nameplates to the doors. At last Saturday came and I had to work hard to control my impatience. To pass the time, moustached and crowfooted, I enjoyed a good and leisurely lunch, for I had to wait until late afternoon, when the coffers would be full. The drive into the countryside was pleasant, and I reached my appointed spot at the appointed time. Close to the service entrance to the park. I had some apprehension as I pulled on the skintight and transparent gloves—but the feeling of anticipation was far greater. With a smile on my lips I reached out and switched on the apparatus fixed underneath the dash before me.

An invisible radio signal winged out and I tried to visualize with my mind's eye what happened next. Fast as light to the receiver, down the wires to its target—which was a tiny charge of explosive. Not much, just a carefully measured amount that would destroy the latch on one of the token dispensers without rupturing the tube at the same time. With the latch destroyed, a steady stream of colored plastic wafers should now be rattling down into the dispenser, filling it and flowing over—gushing on in a never-ending stream. What a benefactor I was! How the children would bless me had they but known my identity.

But that wasn't all that was going to happen. For every minute now another radio signal pulsed out of my transmitter, another latch was destroyed, another gusher of tokens spouting forth each time that this happened. Another and then another. At the proper moment I started the van's engine and drove to the service gate of Loona Park, opened the window, and leaned out above the sign on the door that read EX-CHANGERS DISPENSING MACHINES.

"Got a radio call," I said to the guard there. "You got some kind of problem here?"

"No problem," the guard said, heaving the gate open. "More like a riot. You know where the building is?"

"Sure do. Help is on the way!"

Though I had visualized the effects of my unexpected largesse, I quickly discovered that reality far surpassed my wildest expectations. Screaming, cheering kiddies rushed about laden with tokens, while others fought for places around the gushing dispensers. Their happy cries were ear-splitting and the attendants and guards could do nothing to stop their wave of exuberance. It was slightly less crowded on the service road, but I still had to drive slowly, hand on the horn, to make my way through the stragglers. Two guards were pushing kids back through the shrubs when I drove up.

"Got some trouble with the dispensers?" I asked sweetly. The guard's snarled response was lost in childish cries of delight, which was probably all for the best. He unlocked the door and all but pushed me and my toolbox through.

There were four people there, struggling ineffectually with the machines. They could not be cut off since I had taken the liberty of shorting the switchbox. A bald-headed man was working on an armored cable with a hacksaw and I made tsk-tsking sounds. "That is a recipe for suicide," I said. "You got a four-hundred-volt line in there."

"Can you do anything better, buster," he snarled. "They're your damned machines. Go to work."

"I shall—and here is the cure."

I opened the sizable toolbox, which contained only a shining metal tube, and took it out. "This will do the job," I said, turning the valve at the top and hurling it from me. The last thing I saw were their eye-popping expressions as the black smoke billowed out and filled the room—blocking out all vision completely.

I had been expecting it; they had not. The toolbox was in my arms as I took four measured paces in the darkness and fetched up against the side of the safe. Any noises I made were drowned by their shouts and screams and the constant chugging of the token dispensers. The safe opened easily, the lid of the toolbox fit neatly against the lower edge. I leaned in, felt the mounds of bills, then swept them forward into the waiting container. It was quickly filled and I snapped it shut. My next task was to make sure that the right person took responsibility for this crime. The card with its inscription was in my top pocket. I slipped it out and laid it carefully in the safe, which I then locked again to make absolutely sure that my message would be received and not lost in all the excitement. Only then did I pick up the now-heavy toolbox and stand with my back to the safe, turning and orientating myself.

I knew that the exit was there in the darkness, nine easy paces away. I had taken five when I bumped into someone and strong hands grabbed me while a hoarse voice shouted in my ear.

"I got him! Help me!"

I dropped the box and gave him exactly the help he needed, running my hands up his body to his neck and doing all the right things there. He grunted and slid away. I groped for the box—for a panicky moment I couldn't find it. Then I did, clutched the handle, and seized it up and stood. . . .

And realized I had lost all sense of direction during the fracas.

My panic was as dark as the smoke, and I shook so hard that I almost dropped the case. Seventeen years old and very much alone—with the unknown world of adults closing in upon me. It was over, all over.

I don't know how long this crisis lasted, probably only seconds, although it seemed infinitely longer than that. Then I grabbed myself by the metaphorical neck and shook myself quite hard.

"You wanted it this way—remember? Alone with everyone's hand turned against you. So give in to them—or start thinking. Fast!"

I thought. The people screaming and banging all about me were no help or threat—they were as confused as I was. All right, hand outstretched, go forward. Any direction. Reach something that could be identified by touch. Once this was done I should be able to work out where I was. I heard a thudding ahead, it had to be one of the dispensers, then I bumped into it.

While at the same moment a draft of air touched my face and a familiar voice called out close by.

"What's going on in here?"

The guard! And he had opened the door. How very nice of him. I moved along the wall, avoiding him easily since he was still shouting in the darkness, then followed the billowing smoke out into the light of day. Blinking at the brightness and at the other guard who was stationed just before me, grabbing me.

"Just hold it right there. You ain't going nowhere."

He could not have been much wronger, I mean grabbing onto a Black Belt like that. I eased him to the ground so he wouldn't hurt himself when he fell, threw the box into the van, looked around to see that I was totally unobserved, closed the door, started the engine, then drove slowly and carefully away from fun-filled Loona Park.

Chapter 8

"All fixed, everything just fine back there," I called out to the guard and he nodded while he pulled the gate open. I drove off in the direction of the city, slowly around a bend—then turned sharply inland on an unpaved road.

My escape had been as carefully planned as the theft. Stealing money is one thing; keeping it is another altogether. In this age of electronic communication a description of me and the van would be flashed around the planet in microseconds. Every police car would have a printout and every patrolman verbal warning. So how much time did I have? Both guards were unconscious. But they could be revived, could pass on the information, a phone call would be made, warning given. I calculated that this would take at least five minutes. Which was fine since I only needed three.

The road wound up through the trees, made a final turn—and ended in the abandoned quarry. My heart was thudding a bit since I had to take one chance in this operation. And it had worked—the rental car was still here, just where I had left it the day before! Of course I had removed some vital parts from the engine, but a determined thief could have towed it away. Thank goodness that there was only one determined thief around.

I unlocked the car and took out the box of groceries, then carried it to the van. The side of the box swung down—revealing an empty box. The protruding tops of packets and containers, just the glued-together tops of packets and containers. Very ingenious, if I say so myself. Which I have to, since no one else knows about this operation. Money into box, close box, put in car. Take off work clothes, shiver in the cool breeze as I throw them into the truck. Along with moustache. Pull on sports outfit, actuate timer on thermite charges, lock van, get in car. Simply drive away. I had not been observed so there was no reason at all now why I shouldn't get away with my little adventure. I stopped at the main road and waited for a clutch of police cars to go roaring by in the direction of Loona Park. My, but they were in a hurry. I turned onto the road and drove slowly and carefully back to Billville.

By this time the van would be burning merrily and melting down to a pool of slag. No clues there! The van was insured by law so the owner would be reimbursed. The fire would not spread—not from the heart of the stone quarry—and no one had been injured. It had all worked well, very well.

Back in the office I heaved a sigh of relief, opened a beer and drank deep—

then took the bottle of whiskey from the bar and poured a stiff shot. I sipped it, wrinkled my nose at the awful flavor, then poured the rest of the drink into the sink. What filthy stuff. I suppose if I kept trying I would get used to it someday, but it scarcely seemed worth the effort.

By now enough time should surely have elapsed for the press to have reached the scene of the crime. "On," I called out to my computer, then, "Print the latest edition of the newspaper."

The fax hummed silkily and the paper slid into the tray. With a color pic of the money fountain operating at full blast on the front page. I read the report with a glow of pleasure, turned the page, and saw the drawing. There it was, just as they had found it when they had finally opened the safe. A drawing of a bishop with a line of chess notation written below it.

R—Kt 4 X B

Which means in chess notation Rook to square Knight 4 takes Bishop.

When I read it the warm glow of pleasure was replaced by a chill of worry. Had I given myself away to the police? Would they analyze the clue and be waiting for me?

"No!" I cried aloud. "The police are lazy and relaxed with little crime to keep them on their toes. They may puzzle over it—but they will never understand it until it is too late. But The Bishop should be able to work it out. He will know that it is a message for him and will labor over it. I hope."

I sipped at my beer and had a good worry. It had taken me tedious hours to work out this little mind-twister. The fact that The Bishop used a chess bishop as his calling card had led me to the chess books. I assumed that he—or she, I don't believe that anyone had ever determined The Bishop's sex, although it was assumed the criminal was male—cared about chess. If more knowledge was needed he could consult the same books that I had. With very little effort it could be discovered that there are two different ways of noting chess moves. The oldest of them, the one that I had used, named the squares of the file after the piece that sat at the end of the file. (If you must know, "ranks" are the rows of squares that stretch from side to side of a chessboard. "Files" are the rows that stretch between the players.) So the square on which the White King sits is King 1. King 2 would be the next one up. If you think that this is complicated don't play chess—because this is the easiest part! However there is a second form of chess notation that assigns a number to each of the 64 squares on the board. So Knight 4 can be either 21, 8, 22, or 45.

Confusing? I hope so. I hope the police never think it is a code and get around to cracking it. Because if they do I am cracked as well. This little bit of chess movement contains the date of my next crime, when I am going to "take bishop," meaning take The Bishop card to a crime. Meaning also I am going to take credit for being The Bishop. Also meaning I am taking The Bishop to the cleaners.

I have the scenario clear in my mind. The police puzzle over the chess move—then discard it. Not so The Bishop in his luxury hideout. He is going to be angry. A crime has been committed and he has been blamed. Money has been taken—and he doesn't have it! My hope is that he will worry over this chess move, see it as a clue, scribble away at it, and eventually solve it.

By thinking about the fact that Knight is a homonym for night. Night three—what can that mean? The third night of what? The third night of the Modern Music Festival in the city of Pearly Gates, that is what. And this third night is also the forty-fifth day of the year, which is—that's correct—also known as Knight 3 in one of its four permutations. With this added verification The Bishop would be sure that some crime would take place on the third night of the Festival. A crime involving money of course. My mental fingers were crossed in the hope that he would be more interested in me than in informing the police in advance about the crime.

I hoped that I had struck the right balance. Too complex for the police, but capable of solution by The Bishop. And he had exactly one week to solve it and come to the Festival.

Which also meant that I had one week to hype myself up and depress myself down, get too much sleep—then not enough sleep. And take pleasure only in the construction of plans and apparatus for this bold foray into the pockets of the public.

On the night in question it was raining heavily—which suited me perfectly. I turned up the collar of my black coat, jammed my black hat down on my head, then seized up the black case that held the musical instrument. A horn of some kind. This was made obvious by the swollen shape at one end, where the case swelled out to accommodate the bell. It might be a crumpaphone or even a dagennet. Public transportation took me close to the stage entrance to the theater. As I walked the rest of the way I soon found myself braving the elements among other black-garbed, instrument-bearing musicians. I had my pass ready, but the doorman just waved us through and out of the rain. There was little chance that anyone would question my identity because I was only one of 230. For tonight was the premier of what was sure to be a head-destroying piece of so-called music modestly entitled *Collision of Galaxies*, scored for 201 brass instruments and 29 percussion. The composer, Moi-Woofter Geeyoh, was not known for the delicate dissonances of her compositions. The choice of this piece of music had also made this the night of my choice; even reading the score gave one a headache.

There was a shortage of dressing rooms for the musical multitude and they were milling about all over the place emitting lost noises. No one noticed when

I slipped away, drifted up a back staircase—and let myself into a janitorial broom closet. The service staff had long departed so I would not be disturbed—other than by the music. Nevertheless I locked the door from the inside. When I heard the sounds of tuning up I took out my copy of the score of *Collision*.

It started out calmly enough—after all, the galaxies had to get on stage before they could collide. I followed the score with my finger until it reached the red mark I had placed there. The score folded neatly into my pocket as I carefully unsealed the door and looked out. Corridor empty, as it should be. With steady tread I walked down the corridor, the floor of which was already beginning to throb with impending galactic destruction.

The door was labeled PRIVATE—KEEP OUT. I took the black mask from one pocket, removed my hat and pulled the mask on, extracted the key to the door from another. I did not want to waste time with lockpicks, so had made this key when I had scouted this location. I hummed along with the music—if that could be said to be possible—with the key in the lock. At the correct destructive crash I opened the door and stepped into the office.

My entrance had to of course been unheard, but my movements caught the older man's eye. He turned and stared, and the pen he had been using dropped from his limp fingers. His hands reached towards the ceiling when I drew the impressive—and fake—gun from my inside pocket. The other and younger man could not be threatened and dived to the attack. And continued to dive unconscious to the floor, knocking over and breaking a chair on the way.

None of this made a sound. Or rather it made a lot of sound, none of which could be heard over the music that was now rapidly working itself up to a crescendo that would drown out the crack of doom. I moved fast because the really loud parts were coming close.

I took two pairs of handcuffs from a coat pocket and locked the older man's ankle to his desk, then pulled his arms down before they got tired. I next secured the sleeping dreamer the same way. Almost time. I took the plastic explosive from another pocket—yes, there *were* a lot of pockets in this garment, and not by chance either—and slapped it to the front of the safe. Right over the time lock. They must have felt very secure here with their careful arrangements. All the night's ample receipts had been locked away in the safe in the presence of armed guards. To remain locked and secure until the morning when other armed guards would be present when it opened. I pushed the radio fuse into the explosive, then retreated across the room until I was out of the line of fire along with the others.

Every loose object in the room was bouncing in time with the music now while dust rained down from the ceiling. It still wasn't time. I used the opportunity to rip out the phones by their roots. Not that anyone would be talking on a phone until after the concert.

There it was—almost there! I had the musical score in my mind's eye and at the instant when the galaxies finally impacted I pressed the radio actuator.

The front of the safe blew off in silent motion. I was stunned by the musical catastrophe way up here in the office—not by the explosion—and I wondered how many of the audience had gone deaf in the name of art. My wondering didn't stop me from shoveling all the buck bills from the safe into my instrument case. When it was filled I tipped my hat to my prisoners, one wide-eyed, one unconscious, and let myself out. The black mask went back into its pocket and I went out of the theater by an unwatched emergency exit.

It was a brisk two-block walk to the underpass entrance and I was just one other figure hurrying through the rain. Down the steps and along the corridor, to take the turning that led to the station. The commuter trains had left and the corridor was deserted. I stepped into the phone booth and made my unobserved identity change in exactly twenty-two seconds, precisely the rehearsed time. The black covering of the case stripped away to reveal the white covering of the case inside. The flared bell-shape went too. That had been shaped from thin plastic that crunched and went into a pocket with the black cover. My hat turned inside out and became white, my black moustache and beard disappeared into their appointed pocket so that I could shed the coat and turn it inside out so that it too, that's right, became white. Thus garbed, I strolled into the station and out the exit along with the other arriving passengers, to the cab rank. It was a short wait; the cab rolled up and the door opened. I climbed in and smiled appreciatively at the shining skull of the robot driver.

"Mah good man, tay-ake me to thu Arbolast Hotel," I said in my best imitation Thuringian accent—since the Thuringar train had arrived at the same time I had.

"Message not understood," the thing intoned.

"Ar-bo-last Ho-tel, you metallic moron!" I shouted. "Ar-bowb-bo-last!"

"Understood," it said, and the cab started forward.

Just perfect. All conversations were stored in a molecular recorder for one month in these cabs. If I were ever checked on, the record would reveal this conversation. And my hotel reservation had been made from a terminal in Thuringia. Perhaps I was being too cautious—but my motto was that this was an impossibility. Being too cautious, I mean.

The hotel was an expensive one and tastefully decorated with mock arbolasts in every corridor and room. I was obsequiously guided to mine—where the arbolast served as a floor lamp—and the robot porter glided away smarmily with a five-buck coin in his tip slot.

I put the bag in the bedroom, took off the wet coat, extracted a beer from the cooler—and there was a knock on the door.

So soon! If that was The Bishop he was a good tail, because I had not been aware of being followed. But who else could it be? I hesitated, then realized that there was one certain way to find out. With smile on face, in case it was

The Bishop, I opened the door. The smile vanished instantly.

"You are under the arrest," the plainclothes detective said, holding out his jeweled badge. His companion pointed a large gun at me just to make sure that I understood.

Chapter 9

"What . . . what . . ." I said, or something very like this. The arresting officer was not impressed by my ready wit.

"Put on your coat. You are coming with us."

In a daze I stumbled across the room and did just as he commanded. I should leave the coat here, I knew that, but I had no will to resist. When they searched it they would find the mask and key, everything else that would betray me. And what about the money? They hadn't mentioned the bag.

As soon as my arm was through the sleeve the policeman snapped a handcuff on my wrist and clicked the other end to his own wrist. I was going nowhere without them. There was little or nothing I could do—not with the gun wielder three steps behind us.

Out the door we went and along the corridor, to the elevator, then down to the lobby. At least the detective had the courtesy to stand close to me so the handcuffs were not obvious. A large black and ominous groundcar was parked in the middle of the no-parking zone. The driver didn't even bother to glance in our direction. Though as soon as we had climbed in and the door closed, he pulled away.

I could think of nothing to say—nor were my companions in a conversational mood. In silence we rolled through the rainy streets, past police headquarters, which was unexpected, to stop before the Bit O' Heaven Federal Building. The Feds! My heart dropped. I had been correct in assuming that breaking the clues and catching me had certainly been beyond the intelligence of the local police. But I had not reckoned upon the planetary investigation agencies. By hindsight—which is not very satisfying—I saw my error. After years of absence The Bishop strikes again. Why? And what does the bit of chesswackery mean? Put the cryptologists on it. Oho, a bit of bragging, scene and date of the next crime revealed. Keep it Federal and out of the hands of the local and incompetent police. Watch the cash with the most modern of electronic surveillance techniques. Track the criminal to see if others are involved. Then pounce.

My state of black depression was so great that I could scarcely walk. I swayed when our little procession stopped before a heavy door labeled FEDERAL BUREAU OF INVESTIGATION, with DIRECTOR FLYNN in smaller gold letters beneath it. My captors knocked politely and the doorlock buzzed and opened. We filed in.

"Here he is, sir."

"Fine. Secure him to the chair and I'll take over from here on out."

The speaker sat massively behind the massive desk. A big man with sleek black hair, who was made even bigger by the enormous quantity of fat that he was carrying around. His chin, or chins, hung down onto the swelling volume of his chest. The size of his stomach kept him well back from the desk, upon which the fingers of his clasped hands rested like a bundle of stout sausages. He returned my shifty gaze with his steady and steely one. I made no protest as I was guided to the chair, dropped into it, felt the handcuffs being secured to it, heard footsteps recede and the door slam.

"You are in very big trouble," he intoned.

"I don't know what you mean," I said, the impact of my innocence lessened by the squeak and tremor of my voice.

"You know full well what I mean. You have committed the crime of theft tonight, purloining the public purse donated by stone-deaf music lovers. But that is the least of your folly, young man. By your age I can tell that you have also purloined the good name of another. The Bishop. You are pretending to be something that you are not. Here, take these."

Purloined a good name? What in the galaxy was he talking about? I snatched the keys out of the air by reflex. Gaped at them—then gaped even more broadly at him as I tremblingly unlocked the cuffs.

"You are not . . ." I gurgled. "I mean, the arrest, this office, the police . . . You are . . ."

He calmly waited for my next words, a beatific smile on his face.

"You are . . . The Bishop!"

"The same. My understanding of the message concealed by your feeble code was that you wanted to meet me. Why?"

I started to rise and an immense gun appeared in his hand, aimed between my eyes. I dropped back into the chair. The smile was gone, as was all warmth from his voice.

"I don't like to be imitated, nor do I like to be played with. I am displeased. You now have three minutes to explain this matter before I kill you, then proceed to your hotel room to retrieve the money you stole this evening. Now the first thing that you will reveal is the location of the rest of the money stolen in my name. Speak!"

I spoke—or rather I tried to speak but could only sputter helplessly. This had a sobering affect. He might kill me—but he was not going to reduce me to helpless jelly first. I coughed to clear my throat, then spoke.

"I don't think that you are in too much of a hurry to kill me—nor do I believe in your three-minute time limit. If you will cease in your attempts to bully me I shall try to tell you carefully and clearly my motives in this matter. Agreed?"

Speaking like this was a calculated risk—but The Bishop was a game player, I knew that now. His expression did not change, but he nodded slightly as though conceding a Pawn move—knowing that he still had my King well in check.

"Thank you. I never thought of you as a cruel man. In fact, when I discovered your existence, I used you as a career model. What you have done, what you have accomplished, is without equal in the history of this world. If I offended you by stealing money in your name I am sorry. I will turn all the money from that robbery over to you at once. But if you will stop to think—it is the only thing that I could do. I had no way of finding you. So I had to arrange things so that you could find me. As you have. I counted upon your curiosity—if not your mercy—not to reveal my identity to the police before you had met me yourself."

Another nod granted me another Pawn move. The unwavering barrel of the gun informed me that I was still in check.

"You are the only person alive who knows my identity," he said. "You will now tell me why I should not kill you. Why did you want to contact me?"

"I told you—out of admiration. I have decided on a life of crime as the only career open to one of my talents. But I am self-trained and vulnerable. It is my wish to be your acolyte. To study at your knee. To enter the academy of advanced crime in the wilderness of life with you on one end of the log and me on the other. I will pay whatever price you require for this privilege, though I may need a little time to raise more money since I am turning the receipts of my last two operations over to you. There it is. That is who I am. And, if I work hard enough, you are whom I wish to be."

The softening gaze, the thoughtful fingers raised to chin meant I was out of check for the moment. But the game wasn't won yet—nor did I wish it to be. I wanted only a draw.

"Why should I believe a word of this?" he asked at last.

"Why should you doubt it? What other possible reason could I have?"

"It is not your motives that disturb me. I am thinking about the possibility of someone else's, someone in a position of police responsibility who is using you as a pawn to find me. The man who arrests The Bishop will rise to the top of his chosen profession."

I nodded agreement as I thought furiously. Then smiled and relaxed. "Very true—and that must have been the very first thing to come to your mind. Your office in this building either means that you are high in the ranks of law enforcement, so high that you could easily find out if this had been the plan.

Or—even more proof of your genius—you have ways and means of penetrating the police at any level, to fool them and use them to actually arrest me. My congratulations, sir! I knew that you were a genius of crime—but to have done this, why it borders on the fantastic!"

He nodded his head slowly, accepting his due. Did I see the muzzle of the gun lowered ever so slightly? Was a drawn game possibly in sight? I rushed on.

"My name is James Bolivar diGriz and I was born a little over seventeen years ago in this very city in the Mother Machree Maternity Hospital for Unemployed Porcuswineherders. The terminal I see before you must access official files at every level. Bring up mine! See for yourself if what I have told you is not the truth."

I settled back into the chair while he tapped commands on the keyboard. I did nothing to distract him or draw his attention while he read. I was still nervous but worked to affect a surface calm.

Then he was done. He leaned back and looked at me calmly. I didn't see his hands move—but the gun vanished from sight. Drawn game! But the pieces were still on the board and a new game was beginning.

"I believe you, Jim, and thank you for the kind words. But I work alone and wish no disciples. I was prepared to kill you to preserve the secret of my identity. Now I do not think that will be necessary. I will take your word that you will not look for me again—or use my identity for any more crimes."

"I grant your requests instantly. I only became The Bishop to draw your attention. But reconsider, I beg of you, my application for membership in your academy of advanced crime!"

"There is no such institution," he said, hauling himself to his feet. "Applications are closed."

"Then let me rephrase my request," I said hurriedly, knowing my remaining time was brief. "Let me be personal, if I can, and forgive any distress I may cause. I am young, not yet twenty, and you have been on this planet for over eighty years. I have been only a few years at my chosen work. And, in this brief time, I have discovered that I am truly alone. What I do I must do for myself and by myself. There is no comradeship of crime because all of the criminals I have seen are incompetents. Therefore I must go it alone. If I am lonely—then dare I even guess at the loneliness of your life?"

He stood stock-still, one hand resting on the desk, staring at the blank wall, as through a window, at something I could not see. Then he sighed, and with the sound, as though it had released some power that kept him erect, he slumped back into the chair.

"You speak the truth, my boy, and only the truth. I do not wish to discuss the matter, but your barb has been driven well home. Nevertheless what is, will be. I am too old a dog to change his ways. I bid you farewell, and thank you for a most interesting week. Been a bit like old times."

"Reconsider, please!"

"I cannot."

"Give me your address—I must send you the money."

"Keep it, you earned it. Though in the future earn it under a different identity. Let The Bishop enjoy his retirement. I will add only one thing, a bit of advice. Reconsider your career ambitions. Put your great talents to work in a more sociably acceptable manner. In that way you will avoid the vast loneliness you have already noted."

"Never!" I cried aloud. "Never. I would rather rot in jail for the rest of my life than accept a role in the society I have so overwhelmingly rejected."

"You may change your mind."

"There is no chance of that," I said to the empty room. The door had closed behind him and he was gone.

Chapter 10

Well, that was that. There is nothing like an overwhelming depression to bring one down from the heights of elation. I had done exactly what I had set out to do. My complex plan had worked perfectly. I had unearthed The Bishop from his secret lair and had made him an offer he couldn't refuse.

Except he had. Even the pleasure of having pulled off the successful robbery now meant nothing. The bucks were like ashes in my hand. I sat in my room at the hotel and looked into the future and could see only a vast vacuity. I counted the money over and over until the sums were meaningless. In making my plans I had considered all of the possibilities but one—that The Bishop would turn me down. It was kind of hard to take.

By the time I got back to Billville the next day I was wallowing in a dark depression and thoroughly enjoying the bath of self-pity. Which I normally cannot stand. Nor could I this time. I looked in the mirror at the hollow-eyed and woebegone face and stuck my tongue out at it.

"Sissy!" I said. "Momma's boy, whiner, self-indulgent wimp," and added whatever other insults I could think of. Having cleansed the air a bit, I made a sandwich and a pot of coffee—no alcohol to clog the synapses!—and sat down to munch and guzzle and think about the future. What next?

Nothing. At least nothing constructive that I could think of at this moment. All of my plans had ended at a blank wall and I could see no way around or over it. I slumped back and snapped my fingers at the 3V. A commercial channel came on and before I could change channels the announcer appeared in glorious three dimension and color. I didn't switch because the announcer was a she and wearing only the flimsiest of swimsuits.

"Come where the balmy breezes blow," she cajoled. "Come join me on the silver sands of beautiful Vaticano Beach, where the sun and waves will refresh your soul. . . ."

I turned the thing off. My soul was in fine shape and the fine shape of the announcer only gave me more problems to think about. Future first, heterosexual love later. But the commercial had at least given me the beginning of an idea.

A holiday? Take a break? Why not—lately I had been working harder than any of the businessmen I so badly did not want to become. Crime had paid, and paid nicely, so why didn't I spend some of the hard-earned loot? I probably wouldn't be able to escape from my problems. I had learned by experience that physical displacement was never a solution. My troubles always went with me, as everpresent and nagging as a toothache. But I could take them with me to someplace where I might find the leisure and opportunity to sort them out.

Where? I punched up a holiday guide from the database and flipped through it. Nothing seemed to appeal. The beach? Only if I could meet the girl from the commercial, which seemed far from likely. Posh hotels, expensive cruises, museum tours, all of them seemed about as exciting as a weekend on a porcuswine ranch. Maybe that was it—I needed a breath of fresh air. As a farm boy I had seen enough of the great outdoors, usually over the top of a pile of porcuswine you-know-what. With that sort of background I had welcomed my move to the city with open arms—and hadn't ventured out since.

That might be the very answer. Not back to the farm but into the wilderness. To get away from people and things, to do a little chatting with mother nature. The more I thought of it the better it sounded. And I knew just where I wanted to go, an ambition I had had since I was knee-high to a porcuswinelet. The Cathedral Mountains. Those snow-covered peaks, pointing towards the sky like giant church towers, how they used to fill my childish dreams. Well, why not? About time to make a few dreams come true.

Shopping for backpack, sleeping bag, thermal tent, cooking pots, lights—all the gear needed—was half the fun. Once outfitted, I couldn't waste time on the linear but took the plane to Rafael instead. I bulged my eyes at the mountains as we came in to land and snapped my fingers and fidgeted while I waited for the luggage. I had studied the maps and knew that the Cathedral Trail crossed the road in the foothills north of the airport. I should have taken the connecting bus like the others instead of being conspicuous in a taxi, but I was in too much of a rush.

"Pretty dangerous, kid, I mean walking the trail alone." The elderly driver smacked his lips as he launched into a litany of doom. "Get lost easily enough.

Get eaten by direwolves. Landslides and avalanches. And . . ."

"And I'm meeting friends. Twenty of them. The Boy Sprouts Hiking Team of Lower Armmpitt. We're gonna have fun," I invented rapidly.

"Didn't see no Boy Sprouts out here lately," he muttered with senile suspicion.

"Nor would you," I extemporized, bent over in the backseat and flipping through the maps quickly. "Because they took the train to Boskone, got off there, right at the station close to where the trail crosses the tracks. They'll be waiting for me, troop leader and all. I would be afraid to be alone in the mountains, sir."

He muttered some more, muttered even louder when I forgot to tip him, then chuckled in his gray whiskers as he drove away because, childishly, I had then overtipped him. While resisting strongly the impulse to slip him a phoney five-buck coin. The sound of the motor died away and I looked at the well-marked trail as it wound up the valley—and realized that this had been a very good idea indeed.

There is no point in waxing enthusiastic about the joys of the Great Outdoors. Like skiing, you do it and enjoy it, but don't talk about it. All the usual things happened. My nose got sunburned, ants got into my bacon. The stars were incredibly clear and close at night, while the clean air did good things to my lungs. I walked and climbed, froze myself in mountain streams—and managed to forget my troubles completely. They seemed very out of place in this outdoor world. Refreshed, cleansed, tired but happy, and a good deal thinner, I emerged from the mountains ten days later and stumbled through the door of the lodge where I had made reservations. The hot bath was a blessing, and the cold beer no less. I turned on the 3V and got the tail end of the news, slumped down and listened with half an ear, too lazy to change channels.

". . . reports a rise in ham exports exceeding the four percent growth predicted at the first of the year. The market for porcuswine quills is slipping however, and the government is faced with a quill mountain that is already drawing criticism.

"Closer to home, the computer criminal who broke into Federal Files goes on trial tomorrow. Federal prosecutors treat this as a most serious crime and want the death penalty reestablished. However . . ."

His voice faded from my attention as his smarmy face vanished from the screen to be replaced by the computer criminal himself being led away by a squad of police. He was a big man, and very fat, with a mane of white hair. I felt a clutch in my chest just near the place I imagined my heart to be. Wrong color hair—but wigs would take care of that. There was no mistaking him.

It was The Bishop!

I was out of the tub and across the room and hitting the frame freeze controls. It is a wonder I did not electrocute myself. Shivering with cold, and scarcely aware of it, I flipped back, then zoomed for detail. Enlarged the frame when he looked back over his shoulder for an instant. It was he—without a doubt.

By the time I had wiped off the suds and dressed, the general shape of my plans was clear. I had to get back to the city, to find out what had happened to him, to see what I could do to help. I punched up flight information; there was a mail flight just after midnight. I booked a seat, had a meal and a rest, paid my bill, and was the first passenger aboard.

It was just dawn when I entered my office in Billville. While the computer was printing out all the news items on the arrest, I made a pot of coffee. Sipping and reading, my spirits sank like a rock in a pond. It was indeed the man I knew as The Bishop, although he went under the name of Bill Vathis. And he had been apprehended leaving the Federal Building, where he had installed a computer tap which he had been using to access Top Secret files. All of this had happened the day after I left on my escapist holiday.

I had the sudden realization of what this meant. Guilt assailed me because I was the one who had put him into jail. If I had not started my mad plan, he would never have bothered with the Federal files. He had only done that to see if the robberies had been part of a police operation.

"I put him in jail—so I will get him out!" I shouted, leaping to my feet and spilling coffee across the floor. As I mopped it up I cooled down a bit. Yes, I would *like* to get him out of jail. But could I do it? Why not? I had some experience now in jail-breaking. It should be easier to get from the outside in than it had been doing it the other way. And, after further thought, I realized that perhaps I would not have to go near the jail. Let the police get him out for me. He would have to be taken to court, so would be in transit in various vehicles.

I soon discovered that it was not going to be that easy. This was the first major criminal that had been caught in years and everyone was making a big fuss over it. Instead of being taken to the city or state jail, The Bishop was being held in a cell inside the Federal Building itself. I could get nowhere near it. And the security measures when he was taken to the courthouse were unbelievable. Armed vans, guards, monocycles, police hovercraft and copters. I was not going to get to him that way either. Which meant I was baffled for the moment. Interestingly enough, so were the police—but for very different reasons.

They had discovered, after endless search, that the real Bill Vathis had left the planet twenty years before. All of the records of this fact had vanished from the computer files—and it was only a note written by the real Vathis to a relative that had established the disappearance of the original. Well—if their prisoner wasn't Vathis. Who was he?

When their captive was questioned, according to the report released to the press, "He answered the question only with silence and a distant smile." The prisoner was now referred to as Mr. X. No one knew who he was—and he chose not to speak on the matter. A date was fixed for the trial, not eight days away. This was made possible by the fact that Mr. X refused to plead neither innocent nor guilty, would not defend himself—and had refused the services of a state-appointed attorney. The prosecution, greedy for a conviction, stated that their case was complete and asked for an early trial. The judge, eager as well to be in the limelight, agreed to their request and the date was set for the following week.

I could do nothing! Back to the wall, I admitted defeat—for the moment. I would wait until after the trial. Then The Bishop would simply be one more prisoner and would have to be taken from the Federal Building at last. When he was safely in jail I would arrange his escape. Well before the arrival of the next spacer that would take him away for brain-cleansing and purifying. They would use all of the miracles of modern science to turn him into an honest citizen and, knowing him, I was sure that he would rather die than have that happen. I must intervene.

But they were not making it easy for me. I could not find a way to be in the courtroom when the trial began. So I, along with every other inhabitant of the planet as far as could be determined, watched the trial on TV when it began.

And ended with suspicious speed. All of the first morning was taken with recitals of the well-documented account of what the defendant had done. It was pretty damning. Computer malfeasance, memory bank barratry, CPU violation, terminal treachery, dropping solder on classified documents—it was terrible. Witness after witness read out their statements, all of which were instantly accepted and entered into the evidence. Through all this The Bishop neither watched nor listened. His stare was into the distance, as though he were looking at much more interesting things than the simple operation of the court. When the evidence had been given, the judge banged his gavel and ordered a break for lunch.

When the court reconvened—after a break long enough for a seventeen-course banquet with dancing girls for afters—the judge was in a jovial mood. Particularly after the prosecution had done a damning summoning up. He nodded agreement most of the time and thanked all the smarmy ambulance chasers for the excellent job that they had done. Then he looked his most pontifical and spoke in pregnant periods for the records.

"This case is so clear that it is transparent. The state has brought charges so damning that no defense could possibly stand before them. That no defense was offered is even greater evidence of the truth. The truth is that the defendant did wilfully, with malice and forethought, commit all of the crimes for which he stands accused. There can be no doubt about that. The case is an open and shut one. Nevertheless I shall deliberate the rest of this day and far into the night. He will have his chance of justice that he rejected. I will not find him guilty until tomorrow morning when this court resumes. At that time I will pass sentence. Justice will be done and will be seen to be done."

Some justice, I muttered through my teeth and started to switch off the set. But the judge wasn't through.

"I have been informed that the Galactic League is very interested in this case. A spacer has been dispatched and will be here within two days. The prisoner will then be taken from our custody and we will, if you will excuse and understand my emotions, be well rid of him."

My jaw dropped and I stared moronically at the screen. It was over. Just two days. What could I do in two days? Was this to be the end of The Bishop—and the end of my scarcely launched career in crime?

Chapter 11

I was not going to give up. I had to at least try, even if I failed and were caught myself. It was my fault that he had gotten into this position. I owed him at least an attempt at a rescue. But what could I do? I couldn't get near him in the Federal Building, approach him in transit, or even see him in court.

Court. Court? Court. Court! Court—why did I keep thinking about the court? What was there about it that tickled my interest, that scratched at my medulla oblongata with an idea trying to get in?

Of course! "Yippee!!" I enthused and ran around in small circles waving my arms and gurgling out loud my best imitation—they used to love it at parties—of a rutting porcuswine.

"What about the court?" I asked myself, and was ready with the snappy answer. "I'll tell you about the court. It is in an old building, an Ancient Artifact under preservation order. It probably has some old records in the basement and undoubtedly bats in the attic. During the day it is guarded like the mint—but it is empty at night!"

I dived for my equipment cabinet and began hurling various necessities to the floor. Tool kit, lockpicks, lights, wires, bugs—all the apparatus I would need for the job.

Now a car—or rather a van—was very much in order since I would hopefully need transportation for two. I took care of that next. I had a number of sites that I had noted in case of need—and now I needed. Although it was still daylight, the trucks and vans of the Crumb-ee Bakery were back in their lot being readied for their predawn tasks of the following day. A few vans were being taken into the garage for servicing and one of them happened to go a bit farther. Right onto the road and towards the city limits. I was on a country side road by dusk, in Pearly Gates soon after dark, and letting myself into a back door to the courthouse not long after that.

The burglar alarms were antiques, meant to keep out children or mental defectives—since there was obviously nothing in the building worth stealing. That's what they thought! Armed with pix of the courtroom I had made myself during the trial, I went directly to it. Courtroom six. I stood in the doorway and looked about the darkened room. The lights from the street outside cast an orange glow through the high windows. I walked silently inside, sat down in the judge's chair, then looked into the witness box. In the end I found the chair in which The Bishop had sat during his lightning trial, where he would sit on the morrow. This is where he would sit—and this is where he would stand when he rose to hear his sentence. Those great hands would grasp the rail here. Just here.

I looked down at the wooden floor and smiled grimly. Then knelt and tapped on it. Then took out a drill as the various parts of my plan began to fall into place.

Oh, but this was a busy night! I had to clear boxes from the cellar beneath the courtroom, saw and hammer and sweat, and even slip out of the courthouse long enough to find a sports supply store and break into it. And, most critical of all, I had to work out a route of escape. The escape itself would not have to be rushed—but it would have to be secure. If I had had the time a bit of tunneling would have been in order. But I had no time. Therefore ingenuity would have to replace manual labor. As I cogitated in a comfortable position I found myself nodding off. Never! I made my way from the building yet again, found an all-night restaurant staffed by surly robot machines, and drank two large coffees with extra caffeine. This worked, producing ideas as well as instant heartburn. I staggered off and broke into a clothing store. By the time I reached the courthouse again I really was staggering with fatigue. With fumbling fingers I resealed all of the doors, removed all traces of my passage. The first light of dawn was graying the windows before I was done. I fumbled with tired fingers as I sealed the cellar from the inside, stumbled across the room, sat down on the canvas, set my alarm watch—and lay down to instant slumber.

It was pitch dark when the mosquito whine of the alarm irritated me awake. I had a moment of panic until I remembered that the cellar was windowless. It should be full daylight outside by now. I would see. I turned on a worklight, made adjustments—then turned on the TV monitor. Perfect! A color picture of the courtroom above filled the screen, transmitted from the optical bug I had planted the night before. Some ancient employees were dusting the furniture and sweeping the floor. The session would begin in an hour. I left the set running while I made a last check of my labors of the previous night. All working, all in order . . . so all I had to do was wait.

That was what I did. Sipping at the cold coffee and chewing painfully on a stale sandwich from the previous day's supplies. The suspense ended when the courtroom doors were thrown open and the lucky spectators and the press came in. I could see them imaged clearly on the screen, hear the shuffle of their footsteps overhead. The sound of their voices murmured from the speaker, quieting only when they were silenced for the arrival of the judge. All eyes were on him, all ears twitching attentively when he cleared his throat and began to speak.

First he bored everyone into a state of stupefaction by going over the previous day's evidence in detail, then adding his obvious agreement to each summation and observation. I let his voice drone on while I looked at The Bishop, zooming in on his face.

He gave them nothing. His features were set, he looked almost bored. But there was a glint to his eyes that was almost hatred, nearer contempt. A giant pulled down by ants. The set of his jaw indicated that they may have imprisoned his body, but his soul was still free. But not for long if the judge had his way!

Now something in the judge's voice caught my attention. He had finished his preamble at last. He cleared his throat and pointed at The Bishop.

"Defendant will stand for sentencing."

All eyes were on the prisoner. He sat stolidly, unmoving. There was a growing rustle and murmur. The judge began to turn red and he hammered with the gavel.

"I will be obeyed in this court," he thundered. "The defendant will rise or will be forced to do so. Is that understood?"

Now I was sweating. If only I could have told him not to cause any difficulties. What would I do if he were held up by great ugly policemen? Two of them had already started forward at the judge's signal. It was then that The Bishop slowly raised his eyes. The look of withering contempt he directed at the judge would have deterred anyone not as dense as his honor; it was a glare of repulsion that might have destroyed minor life forms.

But he was standing! The police halted as the large hands went out and seized the solid railing. It creaked as he tugged on it and heaved his giant form up, to stand erect. His head was high as he released the rail and his arms dropped to his sides. . . .

Now! I stabbed down on the button. The explosions were not loud—but their effect was dramatic. They severed the two bolts that held the edge of the trapdoor in place. Under the great weight of The Bishop the door swung wide and he plunged down like a missile. I rushed up the ladder as he fell past me—but had time for a last glimpse of the courtroom on the screen.

There was silence as he vanished from sight. The springs slammed the trapdoor up into position and I pushed the heavy steel sealing bolts into place beneath it. This happened so fast that the horizontal form of The Bishop was still bouncing up and down on the trampoline when I turned to look. I scurried down the ladder to his side as he finally came to rest, looking up at me with stolid gaze as he spoke.

"Ah, Jim my boy. How nice to see you again." He took my proffered hand and I helped him down to the floor. Above us there was pandemonium, shouting and screaming that could be clearly heard through the floor. I permitted myself one glorious look at the screen, at the pop-eyed judge, the scurrying policemen.

"Very impressive, Jim, very," The Bishop said, admiring the scene on the screen as well.

"Right!" I ordered. "Look at it as you strip off your outer clothing. Very little time, explanations will follow."

He hesitated not a millisecond but was hurling clothing from him even as the words were clearing my lips. The great rotund form emerged, clothed in tasteful purple undergarments, and he raised his hands above his head at my shouted command. Standing on the ladder I pulled the immense dress down over him.

"Here is the coat," I said. "Put that on next. Dress touches the ground, so don't remove shoes. Large hat next, that's it, mirror and lipstick while I unbolt the door."

He did what I said without a murmur of protest. The Bishop had vanished from sight and a lady of truly heroic proportions now emerged. There was a hammering above his head which he completely ignored.

"Let's go!" I called out, and he minced across the room in a most feminine fashion. I kept the door closed until he reached me and I used those few seconds to fill him in. "They'll be at the cellar stairs by now—but they are blocked. We go the other way." I pulled on the policeman's helmet to go with the uniform I was wearing. "You are a prisoner in my custody. We are leaving—now!"

I took him by the arm and we turned left down the dusty corridor. Behind us there was much crashing and shouting from the blocked stairwell. We hurried on, to the boiler room, and through that to the set of short stairs that rose up to the heavy exit door. With its hinges now greased and lock well oiled. It opened at a touch and we stepped out into the alleyway.

Not an arm's length from the back of a policeman who was standing guard there. He was the only one.

It took only an instant to examine the scene. The narrow alley was open at the far end. There was a dead end behind us. People—and safety—were in the street beyond the police guard. Then The Bishop climbed up beside me and something grated under his foot. The policeman turned his head to look.

I could see his eyes widen—as well they might, for the lady beside me was an impressive sight. I took advantage of his diverted attention to jump forward and reach out to keep his head turning even more in the same direction. He seized me in strong hands—which quickly went limp since the Tongoese neck twist produces instant unconsciousness when the rotation reaches 46 degrees from full front. I eased him to the ground, then stopped The Bishop from striding forward with my raised palm.

"Not that way."

The door on the building across the alley said SERVICE ENTRANCE and was locked. It opened to my ready key. As I waved my portly companion inside I took off my cap and threw it beside the policeman. I closed the door from the inside and dropped my uniform jacket as I did. The necktie went next as we strolled into the department store, until I was dressed simply in slacks and shirt. I put my moustache into my pocket and we joined the other customers. Occasionally looking at a display as we passed, but certainly never dawdling. There were a few amazed looks at my companion, but this was a very proper store and no one was so rude as to stare. I went first through the exit, holding the door, then led by a few paces as we joined the passing throng. Behind us, getting weaker as we went, were shouts and cries and the sound of alarm bells and sirens. I permitted myself a small smile. When I glanced back I saw that my companion had permitted herself one as well. She even had the nerve to let me have a brief wink. I turned back quickly—I couldn't encourage this sort of thing—then turned the corner into the side street, where the bread truck awaited.

"Stand here and look into your mirror," I said, unlocking the rear door. I busied myself inside, then barely had time to move aside as a great form hurtled by.

"No one looking . . ." he gasped.

"Perfect."

I climbed out, secured the door, went to the driver's side, climbed in, and started the engine. The van rumbled forward, slowly forcing its way through the pedestrians at the corner, then waited for a break in traffic.

I had considered driving back and past the courthouse, but that would have been dangerous braggadocio. Better to simply slip away.

When the street was empty I turned in the opposite direction and drove carefully towards the city limits. I knew all the back roads so we would be away well before they could be blocked.

We were not out of danger yet—but I still felt smug satisfaction. And why not! I had done it! Committed the escape of the century to save the criminal of the century. Nothing could stop us now!

Chapter 12

I drove, slowly but steadily, for the rest of the morning and into the afternoon. Avoiding all of the major highways by staying with the secondary roads. Though my route, by necessity, had to vary in direction, I nevertheless moved steadily south. Doing my best to add real feeling and emotion to Pi-r squared. Sounds familiar? It should be since it is probably the single geometry theorem that anyone ever remembers. The area of a circle is equal to its radius times the value of Pi—squared. So each roll of the wheels of the bread van added an ever-increasing area that must be searched to find the escaping prisoner.

Four hours of this should put us well ahead of the police. The fact had to be considered as well that The Bishop had been locked in the back of the van for all of this time and knew nothing of my plans for the future. Explanations were in order—as was some food. I was getting hungry and, considering his girth, he would surely be feeling the same. With this in mind I pulled into the next suburban shopping center, checked the quick-food restaurants as I drove by, then parked at the far end of the lot. Backed up close to a blank wall. The Bishop blinked benevolently when I opened the rear door admitting light and fresh air.

"Time for lunch," I said. "Would you like . . ."

I lapsed into silence as he raised his hand in a gesture of silence.

"Permit me, Jim, to say something first. Thank you. From the bottom of my heart I thank you for what you have done. I owe you my life, no less. Thank you."

I stood with lowered eyes—I swear I was blushing like a girl!—and twisting my toe around and around on the ground. Then I coughed and found my voice.

"I did what had to be done. But—could we talk of this later?" He sensed my embarrassment and nodded, a regal figure despite the absurd garb he was still wearing. I pointed to the box on which he had been sitting. "There are clothes in there. While you change I'll get some food. You don't mind junk food from Macswineys?"

"Mind? After the loathsome sludge of the prison food, one of their Barbecued Porcuswineburgers would be unto paradise. With a large portion of sugarfried spamyams, if you please."

"Coming up!"

I closed the van door with a feeling of relief and trotted off towards the beckoning platinum arches. The Bishop's enthusiasm for fast food was most encouraging in a way that he could not suspect yet.

Loud munching and rustling sounded from the tables on all sides as I passed and made my way up to the serving counter. I reeled off my order to the plastic-headed robotic attendant, stuffed bills into the hopper—then grabbed the bag of food and drink as it slid out of the gate.

We sat on the boxes in the back of the van and ate and drank with enthusiasm. I had left the rear door open a crack, which gave us more than enough light. During my absence The Bishop had discarded his dress and was now wearing more masculine garb—the largest size I could find. He wolfed down half of his sandwich, nibbled a few spamyams to hold it in place, then smiled over at me.

"Your plan of escape was pure genius, my boy. I noticed the change in the flooring when I first sat down in the chair in the courtroom and pondered long over its significance. I hoped it was what I thought it might be, and can truthfully say that when the ground opened under my feet, so to speak, I felt a feeling of pleasure such as I had never experienced before. The sight of that despicable judge's face disappearing from my sight is a memory I shall always treasure."

Smiling broadly he finished the rest of the sandwich, then wiped his lips delicately before speaking again.

"Since I do not wish to cause you greater embarrassment with more fulsome praise, perhaps I should ask you what plans you have made to keep me safe from the hands of the law? Because, knowing you as I do now, I am secure in the belief that you have planned ahead in precise detail."

Praise from The Bishop was praise indeed and I basked in the warmth of it for a few moments while I worried out a bit of swinish gristle from between my teeth. "I have done that, thank you. The bread truck is our vehicle of invisibility, for it and its brothers trundle the highways and byways of this country daily." For some reason I found myself sounding more and more like The Bishop when I spoke. "We will stay in it until nightfall, slowly approaching our destination all of the while."

"And of course casual police patrols will not bother us, since the identifying numbers on this vehicle are not the ones that were on it before it came into your possession."

"Precisely. The theft will have been reported and local police informed. But the search will not widen, for this vehicle will be found not far from its depot in Billville in the morning. The new numbers, soluble in paint thinner, will have been removed, the odometer turned back to show only a brief joy ride by the thieves. If a van like this were seen and noted in the distant city of Bit O' Heaven, there will be nothing to connect that bread van with this one. That trail will run cold as will all the others."

He digested this bit of information, along with the last of the spamyams, then licked his fingers ruminatingly. "Capital. I could not have done better myself. Since further movement will be dangerous—the police will soon have a net over the entire country—I presume that Billville is our destination?"

"It is. I have my establishment there. Also your place of security. When I asked about your food tastes I had that in mind. You are going to take up residence in an automated Macswineys until the heat of the chase dies down."

His eyebrows climbed up to his forehead and I saw him glance with some apprehension at the discarded wrappings, but he was kind enough not to speak his doubts aloud. I hurried to reassure him.

"I have done it myself—so don't worry. There are some slight discomforts. . . ."

"But none to equal that of Federal prison! I apologize for an unseemly thought. No offense given."

"Or taken. It all came about by accident one evening when the police were a little close behind me for comfort. I picked the lock on the service entrance of the local Macswineys, the very one that you will be visiting, and my pursuers lost my trail. While I waited for a safe period I examined the premises. Amazing! Operating at high speed all around me was the solution to the single problem that faces all fast-food chains. The cost of keeping even the highly underpaid and unskilled employees. Human beings are both intelligent and greedy. They tend to become skilled, then want more money for their work. The answer is to do away with human beings completely."

"Admirable solution. If you are finished with your crumplumps I just might nibble one or two while I listen to your fascinating documentary."

I passed the greasy bag to him and went on. "Everything is mechanized. As the customer speaks his order the required item of food is ejected from the deep-frozen store into a super-voltage radar oven where it is instantly blasted to steamingly edible temperature. These ovens are so powerful that an entire frozen porcuswine can be exploded into steam and greasy particles in twelve microseconds."

"Amazing!"

"Beverages are dispensed with the same lightning speed. By the time a customer has finished speaking, his entire order is waiting. Behind a steel door, of course, until he has paid. The machinery is fully automatic and reliable and rarely touched by human hands. It is inspected weekly, while the frozen food store is replenished weekly as well. But not on the same day so that the vehicles don't get in each other's way."

"Crystal clear!" he cried aloud. "One makes one's home, so to speak, in the machinery chamber. When the frozen store is replenished, access to it will be from outside the building and the living chamber will not be entered. On the day the machinery is inspected the occupant rests comfortably in the freezing room until the technicians leave. I assume there is a connecting door, easily found. Ahh, yes, the freezer—that explains the large and warm garment I found packed in with my clothes. But should there be an equipment failure . . . ?"

"The alarm sounds in the central repair depot and a mechanic is dispatched. I have also arranged for it to sound in the room as well to allow enough time to slip away. I have also made provision for unexpected visits by the engineering staff. An alarm sounds if a key is placed in the outer lock, which then jams for precisely sixty seconds. Any questions?"

He laughed and reached out and patted my shoulder. "How could there be? You have thought of everything. Might I ask about reading matter and, how shall I phrase it delicately, sanitary facilities?"

"Portable viewscope and library with your bedroll. All needed facilities already plumbed in for visiting technicians."

"I could ask for no more."

"But . . . I could." I lowered my gaze—then raised it and steeled myself to speak. "You once told me that you were not in the acolyte-seeking business. Dare I ask you if you still feel that way? Or would you consider dallying the hours away with some lessons in criminal lore? Just to pass the time, so to speak."

Now it was his turn to lower his eyes. He sighed, then spoke. "I had good reasons to reject your request. Good at the time, or so I believed. I have changed my mind. In gratitude for my rescue I would enroll you in my school of Alternate Life-styles for a decade or more. But I don't believe you would like mere gratitude. That would not wear well, unless I have misread your character. I don't believe you rescued me just to gain my gratitude. So I therefore tell you, in all truth, that I look forward to passing on the few things I have learned down through the years. I look forward to our continuing friendship as well."

I was overwhelmed. We were on our feet at the same time and shaking hands, laughing. His grip was like steel but I didn't mind at all. It was I who turned away first, then looked at my watch.

"We have been here too long already and must not draw any attention. I shall drive on now—and the next stop will be the last one, for we will have arrived. Please exit quickly, enter the service door at once, and close it behind you. I'll be back as soon as this van has been disposed of, so the next person to open the door will be me."

"At your orders, Jim. But speak—and I shall obey."

It was a boring drive but a necessary one. But bored I was not, for I was filled with plans and thoughts of the future. I drove through street after street, stopping only once to charge the batteries at an automated service station. Then onward again, doomed forever to rumble through the back roads of Bit O' Heaven, watching the sun creep towards the horizon. To at last pull into the service road of the Billville shopping center, now empty of traffic until morning.

No one in sight. The Bishop passed me with a swish and the door slammed. The operation was still going well and I was in a hurry to finish, but knew better than to rush now. No one saw me when I carried the boxes and equipment into the building and dumped them in my office. It was taking a chance, but it had to be done. The chances that the van would be noticed and remembered were slim. Before I drove away I sprayed the interior of the van with print-go, a solvent that destroys fingerprints and should be in common use by all criminals. Even bread-van thieves.

This was it. I could do no more. I parked the van at the end of a quiet suburban street and walked back into town. It was a warm night and I enjoyed the exercise. When I passed the pond in Billville Park I heard a water bird calling out sleepily. I sat on the bench and looked out at the still surface of the pond. And thought about the future and my destiny.

Had I really succeeded in breaking free with my old life? Was I to succeed in the life of crime that I so much wanted? The Bishop had promised to help me—and he was the only person on the planet who could.

I whistled as I walked towards the shopping center. Looking forward to a brilliant and exciting future. So involved in my thoughts that I ignored the occasional surface car that passed, barely aware of one stopping behind me.

"You there, kid, just a minute."

Without thinking I turned about, so distracted that I didn't notice until too late that I was standing under the streetlight. The policeman sat in the car staring at me. I'll never know why he stopped, what he wanted to talk to me about, because that thought fled his mind instantly. I could see recognition there as his eyes widened.

In my concern over The Bishop I had forgotten completely that I was still a wanted criminal and jail-breaker, that all the police had my photograph and description. And here I was strolling the streets bereft of any disguise or attempt at security. All these thoughts passed through my head and out my ear in the instant that he recognized me. Nor did I even have time for any mental kicks in the seat of my trousers.

"You're Jimmy diGriz!"

He seemed as surprised as I was. But not surprised enough to slow down his reflexes. Mine were still getting into gear by the time his were all through operating. He must have practiced that draw in the mirror every day because he was fast. Too fast.

As I was turning to run, the muzzle of his recoilless .75 appeared in the open window.

"Gotcha!" he said. With a dirty, wide, evil law-enforcing smile.

Chapter 13

"Not me—someone else—mistaken identity!" I gasped, but shoved my hands into the air at the same time. "Would you shoot a hapless child just on suspicion?"

The gun never wavered, but I did. Shuffling sideways towards the front of the car.

"Stop that and get back here," he shouted, but I kept the nervous shuffling going. I doubted, or hoped, that he wouldn't shoot me in cold blood. As I remember, that is against the law. I wanted him to come after me, because in order to do that he would have to take the gun out of the window. There was no way that he could point it at me and open the door at the same time.

The gun vanished—and so did I! The instant he lowered it I turned and ran, head down and pumping as fast as I could. He shouted after me—and fired!

The gun boomed like a cannon and the slug zipped past my ear and slammed into a tree. I spun about and stopped. This cop was insane.

"That's better," he called out, resting the gun on top of the open door and aiming it at me with both hands. "I fired to miss. Just once. Next time I hit. I got the gold medal for shooting this piece. So don't make me show you how good I am with it."

"You are mad, do you know that?" I said, all too aware of the quaver in my voice. "You just can't shoot people on suspicion."

"Yes I can," he said, walking up to me with the gun still pointed steady as a rock. "This ain't suspicion but identification. I know just who you are. A wanted criminal. You know what I'll say? I'll say this criminal grabbed my gun and it went off and he got shot. How does that sound? Want to grab my gun?"

He was a nutter all right, and a police nutter at that. I could see that he really wanted me to make a break so he could fire off his cannon. How he had escaped all the tests that were supposed to keep his kind out of law enforcement I will never know. But he had done it. He was licensed to carry a gun and was looking for an excuse to use it. That excuse I was not giving him. I extended my arms slowly before me, wrists together.

"I'm not resisting, officer, see. You are making a mistake, but I am going quietly. Put on the cuffs and take me in."

He looked downright unhappy at this, and frowned at me. But I made no more moves and in the end he scowled, pulled the handcuffs from his belt, and tossed them over to me. The gun never wavered.

"Put them on."

I locked them on one wrist, very loosely so I could slip my hand out of them, then on the other. I was looking down when I did this and I did not see him move. Until he had me by both wrists and had squeezed both cuffs until they had locked hard deep into my skin. He smiled down at me, twisting the metal into my flesh with sadistic glee.

"Gotcha now, diGriz. You are under arrest."

I looked up at him, he was a head taller than me and maybe twice my weight—and I burst out laughing. He had put the gun back in its holster in order to grab me—that's what he had done. The big man had grabbed the little kid. He couldn't understand why I was laughing and I gave him no opportunity to find out. I did the easiest, best, and fastest thing possible under the circumstances. Also the dirtiest.

My knee came up hard into his groin and he let go of my wrists at the impact and bent double. I did him a favor, the poor man must have been in some pain, and got him in the side of the neck with my joined hands as he went by. He was unconscious before he hit the ground. I knelt and started to go through his pockets for the keys to the handcuffs.

"What's happening there?" a voice called out as a light came on over the door of the nearest house. The sound of that shot would bring the whole street out soon. I would worry about the cuffs later. Right now I had to make tracks.

"Man's been hurt!" I shouted. "I'm going for help." This last was called over my shoulder as I trotted off down the street and around the corner. A woman appeared in the doorway and called after me but I wasn't staying around to listen. I had to keep moving, get away from this place before the alarm was called in and the search began. Things were coming apart. And my wrists hurt. I looked at them when I passed the next streetlight and saw that my hands were white, and were getting numb as well. The cuffs were so tight they were cutting off all the blood circulation. Any slight guilt I may have had over the dirty fighting vanished on the instant. I had to get these things off—and fast. My office, the only place.

I got there, avoiding the main streets and staying away from people. But when I reached the back door of the building my fingers were numb and stiff. I could feel nothing.

It took an intolerably long time to fish the keys out of my pocket. When I succeeded I instantly dropped them. Nor could I pick them up again. My fingers would not close. I could only drag my lifeless hands over the keys.

There are low moments in life—and I believe that this was the lowest one that I had ever experienced. I just could not do what had to be done. I was finished, licked, through. I couldn't get into the building. I couldn't help myself.

It didn't take a medical degree to figure out that if I didn't get the cuffs off soon I was going to go through life with plastic hands. This was it.

"This is not it!" I heard myself snarling. "Kick the door open, do something, unlock it with your toes."

No, not my toes! I fumbled the keys about on the ground with my dead fingers until I had separated out the correct key. Then bent my body over it and touched it with my tongue, feeling its position, ignoring the filth and dirt that I licked up along with it. Then I pulled back my lips and seized the key with my teeth. Good so far!

If you should ever be tempted to unlock a door with a key in your teeth while wearing handcuffs I have only a single word of advice. Don't. You see, you have to turn your head sideways to get the key into the keyhole. Then roll your head to turn the key, then butt the door with your head to get it open. . . .

It worked at last and I fell face first onto the floor inside. With the knowledge that I would have to do the whole thing all over again upstairs. That I did do it, and finally slid through into the office, owes more to persistence, stubbornness and brute force than to intelligence. I was too exhausted to think. I could only react.

I elbowed the door shut and stumbled to my workbench, hurled my toolbox to the floor, and kicked its contents about until I found the vibrosaw. I picked this up with my teeth and managed to wedge it into an open desk drawer, holding it in place as I closed the drawer with my elbow. Closing it on my lip as well, which brought forth a nice gusher of blood. Which I ignored. My wrists were on fire—but my hands were past feeling. White and dead-looking. I had run out of time. I used my elbow to turn on the saw. Then pushed the handcuffs towards the blade, pulling my arms apart hard to stretch the chain. The blade buzzed shrilly and the chain was cut and my arms flew wide.

Next came the more exacting job of cutting the cuffs off without cutting my flesh. Too much.

There was blood everywhere before I was done. But the cuffs were off and I could see the flesh turn pink as circulation was restored.

After this, all I was up to was collapsing into a chair and watching the blood drip. I sat like this for about a minute when the numbness ended and the pain began. With an effort I stumbled to my feet and dragged over to the medical locker. Getting this good and bloody as well while I shook the pain capsules out and managed to swallow two of them. Since I was already there I pulled out the antiseptic and bandages and cleaned up the cuts. They were more messy than dangerous and none were very deep. I bandaged them, then looked into the mirror and shuddered and did something about the lip.

A police siren wailed by in the street outside—and I realized that the time had come to do some furious thinking and planning.

I was in trouble. Billville wasn't very big, and all exits would be sealed by now. That's what I would have done first, if I were looking for a fugitive. And even the dimmest of policemen would have figured this one out as well. Barricades on all the roads, copters out with nightscopes to watch the open fields, police at the linear station. All holes plugged. Trapped like a rat. What else? The streets would be patrolled too, easy enough to do by groundcar. And the later it got the fewer people there would be about and the more dangerous it would be to wander around.

Then, in the morning, what then? I knew what then. A search of every room in every building until I was found. I felt the perspiration bead my forehead at the thought. Was I trapped?

"No surrender!" I shouted aloud, then jumped to my feet and paced back and forth. "Jimmy diGriz is too slippery to be caught by the ham-handed minions of the local law. Look how I slipped away from that homicidal copper. Slippery Jim diGriz, that's who I am. And I am about to slip away from them again. But how?"

How indeed. I cracked open a beer, drank deep, then slumped back into the chair. Then looked at my watch. It was already getting too late to risk my presence on the street. The restaurants would be emptying, the feely and stinky cinemas disgorging their customers, couples marching homeward two by two. Any single individual drawing the instant attention of the law.

It had to be the morning then. I would have to venture forth in the light of day—or the rain! I punched up the weather report as quickly as I could, then slumped back once again. 99% chance of sunshine. I might as easily wish for an earthquake as a storm.

The office was a mess; it looked like the aftermath of an explosion in the slaughterhouse. I would have to clean it up. . . .

"No, Jim, you will not have to clean it up. Because the police are going to find it sooner or later, and probably sooner. Your fingerprints are everywhere and they know your blood type. They'll have a really good time trying to figure out what happened to you."

It would give them something to think about at least. And maybe cause a little trouble for one sadistic copper. I wheeled the chair over to the terminal and typed out the message. The printer whistled and I took the sheet of paper from the hopper. Wonderful!

TO THE POLICE. I WAS SHOT DEAD BY YOUR MURDERING POLICE OFFICER YOU FOUND UNCONSCIOUS. HE GOT ME. I AM BLEEDING INTERNALLY AND WILL DIE SOON. GOODBYE CRUEL WORLD. I NOW GO TO THROW MYSELF INTO THE RIVER.

I doubted very much if the ruse would work, but it might at least get that gun-crazy cop in trouble. And keep the rest of them busy dredging the river.

There was some blood on the note and I smeared more on from the bandages. Then laid it carefully on the table.

This bit of tomfoolery had cheered me a bit. I sat back and finished the beer and made plans. Was I leaving anything important behind? No, there were no records kept here that I would need in the future. I found my doomsday key and unlocked the destruct switch, then pressed it. A single click from the memory banks was the only evidence that all of the computer's memory had just turned into random electrons. Everything else—tools, equipment, machinery—was expendable, could be replaced when needed. But I was not leaving the money.

All this was pretty tiring—but I couldn't afford to rest until all arrangements were complete. I pulled a pair of thin plastic gloves over the blood and bandages and set to work. The money was in the safe, since I robbed banks and did not believe in supporting them by opening an account. I put it all into a businessman's carrybag. It was only half full, so I added all the microtools that would fit. In the space that was left I stuffed in as much clothing as I could, then stood on the thing until I got it closed and locked.

New clothes and a disguise next. A black four-piece business suit, the fabric enriched by a pattern of tiny white buck bills. An orange rollneck, just what all the young bankers were wearing, along with trendy porcuswineherd boots with builtup heels. Add some to my height—that would help. When I left I would wear the moustache and gold-rimmed glasses. What I could do now was darken my hair with dye and add to my fading tan. Preparations done, woozy with beer, fatigue, and pain pills, I opened the file cabinet bed, set the alarm, and dropped into oblivion.

There were giant mosquitoes circling my head, more and more of them, after my blood, mosquitoes . . .

I opened my eyes and blinked away the dream. My alarm watch, since I hadn't turned it off, had raised the volume on the mosquito buzzing, louder and louder until it sounded like a squadron of them diving to the attack. I pushed the button, smacked my gummy lips together, then stumbled over for a glass of water. It was full daylight outside and the early risers were just appearing.

Preparations made, I washed and dressed with care. Nifty orange gloves that matched the shirt hid my bandaged hands. When the streets were at their rush-hour busiest I seized up the carrybag, then checked carefully to make sure that the hall outside was empty. Stepped out and closed the door without looking back. This part of my life was over with. Today was the first day of my new life.

I hoped. I walked to the stairs with what I hoped was a very sincere, businessman-type walk, down past the first arrivals, and into the street.

To see the policeman on the corner looking closely at every passerby.

I did not look at him, but found an attractive girl walking ahead of me with very neat legs indeed. I watched their twinkling advance and tried to forget the nearby minion of the law. Came towards him, passed him, walked away from him. Waiting for the cry of recognition . . .

It never came. Maybe he was looking at the girl too. One down—but how many more to go?

This was the longest walk that I had ever taken in my life. Or at least it seemed that way. Not too fast, not too slow. I struggled to be part of the crowd, just another wage-slave going to work, thinking only of profit and loss and debenture bonds. Whatever debenture bonds were. One more street—safe so far. There's the corner. The service road behind the shopping center. No place for a businessman like you. So look sharp and don't hang about. Around the corner to safety.

Safety? I staggered as though I had been struck.

The Macswineys service van was outside the door and a hulking brute of a mechanic was just going inside.

Chapter 14

I looked at my watch, snapped my fingers, then turned away from the service road in case my actions were being observed. And marched on smartly until I came to the first Speedydine. Just to make my day complete there were two policemen sitting in the first booth. Looking at me, of course. I marched past, eyes front, and found the seat farthest from them. There was an itching between my shoulder blades that I didn't dare scratch. I couldn't see them—but I knew what they were doing. They were looking at me, then talking to each other, deciding I was not quite what I looked like. Better investigate. Stand, walk my way, lean over my booth . . .

I saw the blue-trousered legs out of the corner of my eye and my heart instantly began hammering so loudly I was sure the whole restaurant could hear it. I waited for the accusing words. Waited . . . let my eyes travel up the blue-clad legs . . .

To see a uniformed linear driver sitting down across from me. "Coffee," he said into the microphone, shook his newspaper open, and began to read.

My heart slowed to something resembling normal and I silently cursed myself for suspicion and cowardice. Then spoke aloud into my own microphone in the deepest voice I could sum up.

"Black coffee and mulligatawny dumplings."

"Deposit six bucks, if you please."

I inserted the coins. There was a rumble of machinery at my elbow and my breakfast slid out onto the table. I ate slowly, then glanced at my watch, then went back to sipping my coffee. As I well knew from the earlier occasion when I had nipped into the freezer, when I had been hiding out there, thirty minutes was the minimum service time for a Macswineys mechanic. I allowed forty before I slid out of the booth. I tried not to think about what I would find when I finally got into the back of the fast-food parlor. I remembered my parting words only too well, I would be the next person through the door. Ho-ho. The next person had been the mechanic. Had he caught The Bishop? I sweated at the thought. I would find out soon enough. I passed the booth where the police had been. They were gone—out searching some other part of the city for me I hoped—and I headed back to the shopping center. To be greeted by the glorious sight of the Macswineys van drawing out into the road ahead of me.

The key was ready in my hand as I approached the door. The road ahead was empty—then I heard the footsteps coming up behind me. The police? With boring repetition my heart started the thudding routine again. I walked slower as I came close to the door. Then stopped and bent over and slipped the palmed key into my hand as though I had just picked it up. I examined it closely as someone came up, then passed me. A young man who showed not the slightest interest in my existence. He went on and turned into the back entrance to the market.

I took one look over my shoulder—then jumped for the door before anything else happened. Turned the key, pushed—and of course it didn't open.

The delay mechanism I had installed was working fine. It would unlock in one minute. Sixty short seconds.

Sixty incredibly crawling seconds. I stood there in my fine business outfit, as out of place in this alley as teats on a boar porcuswine, as we used to say back on the ranch. Stood there and sweated and waited for police or passersby to appear. Waited and suffered.

Until the key turned, the door opened—and I fell through.

Empty! On the far wall the automatic machinery clattered and whirred. The drink dispenser gurgled and a filled container whistled down its track and vanished. To be followed by the steaming bulk of a burger. Night and day this went on. But among all this mechanical motion no human form appeared. They had captured him—the police had The Bishop. And they would capture me next. . . .

"Ahh, my boy, I thought it might be you this time."

The Bishop emerged from the freezer, immense in his insulated gear, his sleeping roll and carryall tucked under his arm. He slammed the door behind him and the strength went out of me with a woosh and I slumped down with my back to the wall.

"Are you all right?" he asked, concern in his voice. I waved a weak hand.

"Fine, fine—just let me catch my breath. I was afraid they had you."

"You shouldn't have worried. When you did not reappear within a reasonable time I assumed there had been some hitch in your plans. So I rehearsed my evacuation moves just in case the legitimate users appeared today. And they did. It is really quite cold in there. I wasn't sure how long they would be, but I was sure you had installed some way of discovering when they left. . . ."

"I meant to tell you!"

"No need. I found the hidden speaker and switch and listened to someone who mutters profanities while he works. After some time the slam of the door and silence were welcome information indeed. Now about yourself. There were problems?"

"Problems!" I burst out laughing with relief. Then stopped when I heard a hysterical edge to the sound. I told him, omitting some of the more gruesome details. He made appropriate noises at the right places and listened attentively until the bitter end.

"You are being too harsh on yourself, Jim. A single lapse after all the tension of the day is not to be unexpected."

"But not to be allowed! Because I was stupid I almost had both of us caught. It won't happen again."

"There is where you are wrong," he said, shaking a thick admonitory finger. "It could happen at any time—until you have trained yourself in your work. But you will be trained and trained efficiently . . ."

"Of course!"

". . . until a lapse like this one will be impossible. You have done incredibly well, for one of your inexperience. Now you can only improve."

"And you will teach me how—how to be a successful crook like you!"

His brow furrowed at my words and his expression was grave. What had I said that was wrong? I chewed my sore lip with worry as he unrolled his bedroll in silence, spread it out then sat upon it crosslegged. When at last he spoke I hung upon his every word.

"Now your first lesson, Jim. I am not a crook. You are not a crook. We do not want to be criminals for they are all individuals who are stupid and inefficient. It is important to comprehend and appreciate that we stand outside of society and follow strict rules of our own, some of them even stricter than those of the society that we have rejected. It can be a lonely life—but it is a life you must choose with your eyes open. And once the choice has been made you must abide by it. You must be more moral than they are because you will be living by a stricter moral code. And this code does not contain the word *crook*. That is their word for what you are and you must reject it."

"But I want to be a criminal. . . ."

"Abandon the thought—and the title. It is, and you must excuse me saying it, a juvenile ambition. It is only your emotions striking out at the world you dislike and cannot be considered a reasoned decision. You have rejected them—but at the same time accepted their description of what you are. A crook. You are not a crook, I am not a crook."

"Then—what are we?" I asked, all eagerness. The Bishop steepled his fingers as he intoned the answer.

"We are Citizens of the Outside. We have rejected the simplistic, boring, regimented, bureaucratic, moral, and ethical scriptures by which they live. In their place we have substituted our own far superior ones. We may physically move among them—but we are not of them. Where they are lazy, we are industrious. Where they are immoral, we are moral. Where they are liars, we are the Truth. We are probably the greatest power for good to the society that we have discarded."

I blinked rather rapidly at that one, but waited patiently because I knew that he would soon make all clear. He did.

"What kind of a galaxy do we live in? Look around you. The citizens of this planet, and of every other planet in the loose organization known as the Galactic League, are citizens of a fat, rich union of worlds that has almost forgotten the real meaning of the word *crime*. You have been in prison, you have seen the dismal rejects whom they consider criminals. And this is what is called a frontier world! On the other settled planets there are few malcontents and even fewer who are socially maladjusted. Out there the handful who are still being born, in spite of centuries of genetic control, are caught early and their aberrations quickly adjusted. I made one single trip offplanet in my life, a tour of the nearest worlds. It was terrible! Life on those planets has all the color and wonder of a piece of wet cardboard. I hurried back to Bit O' Heaven for, loathsome as it can be at times, it is still a bit o' heaven compared to the others."

"Someday—I would like to see these other worlds."

"And so you shall, dear boy, a worthy ambition. But learn your way around this one first. And be thankful they don't have complete genetic control here yet—or the machines to mentally adjust those who struggle against society. On other planets the children are all the same. Meek, mild, and socially adjusted. Of course some do not show their genetic weakness—or strength as we call it—until they are adults. These are the poor displaced ones who try their hands at petty crimes—burglary, shoplifting, rustling, and the like. They may get away with it for a week or two or a month or two, depending on their degree of native intelligence. But as sure as atomic decay, as sure as the fall of leaves in the autumn—and just as predestined—the police will eventually reach out and pull them in."

I digested this information, then asked the obvious question: "But if that is all there is to crime, or rebellion against the system—where does that leave you and me?"

"I thought you would never ask. These dropouts I have described, whom you have associated with in prison, comprise ninety-nine point nine percent of crime in our organized and dandified society. It is the last and vital one-tenth of one percent that we represent that is so vital to the fabric of this same society. Without us the heat death of the universe would begin. Without us the lives of all the sheeplike citizenry would be so empty that mass suicide to escape it would be the only answer. Instead of pursuing us and calling us criminals they should honor us as first among them!"

There were sparks in his eyes and thunder in his voice when he spoke. I did not want to interrupt his fulminant speech, but there were questions to be asked.

"Please excuse me—but would you be so kind as to point out just why this is so?"

"It is so because we give the police something to do, someone to chase, some reason for rushing about in their expensive machines. And the public—how they watch the news and listen for the latest reports on our exploits, how they talk to each other about it and relish every detail! And what is the cost of all this entertainment and social good? Nothing. The service is free, even though we risk life, limb and liberty to provide it. What do we take from them? Nothing. Just money, paper, and metal symbols. All of it insured. If we clean out a bank, the money is returned by the insurance company who, at the end of the year, may reduce their annual dividend by a microscopic amount. Each shareholder will receive a millionth of a buck less. No sacrifice, no sacrifice at all. Benefactors, my boy, we are nothing less than benefactors.

"But in order for us to accomplish all this good for them we must operate outside their barriers and well outside of their rules. We must be as stealthy as rats in the wainscoting of their society. It was easier in the old days of course, and society had more rats when the rules were looser, just as old wooden buildings have more rats than concrete buildings. But there are rats in the buildings now as well. Now that society is all ferroconcrete and stainless steel there are fewer gaps between the joints. It takes a very smart rat indeed to find these openings. Only a stainless steel rat can be at home in this environment."

I broke into spontaneous applause, clapping until my hands hurt, and he nodded his head with gracious acceptance of the tribute.

"That is what we are," I enthused. "Stainless steel rats! It is a proud and lonely thing to be a stainless steel rat!"

He lowered his head in acknowledgment, then spoke. "I agree. Now—my throat is dry from all this talking and I wonder if you could aid me with the complex devices about us. Is there any way you might extract a double-cherry oozer from them?"

I turned to the maze of thudding and whirring machinery that covered the inner wall.

"There is indeed, and I shall be happy to show you how. Each of these machines has a testing switch. This, if you will look close, is the one on the drink dispenser. First you must turn it to on, then you can actuate the dispenser, which will deliver the drink here instead of to a customer on the other side. Each is labeled—see, this is the cherry oozer. A mere touch and . . . there!"

With a whistling thud it dropped into place and The Bishop seized it up. As he began to drink he froze, then whispered out of the corner of his mouth.

"I just realized, there is a window here and a young lady is staring in at me!"

"Fear not," I reassured him. "It is made of one-way glass. She is just admiring her face. It is the inspection port to look at the customers."

"Indeed? Ahh, yes, I can see now. They are indeed a ravenous lot. All that mastication causes a rumble in my own tum, I am forced to admit."

"No trouble at all. These are the food controls. That nearest one is for the Macbunnyburger, if you happen to like them."

"Love them until my nose crinkles."

"Then here."

He seized up the steaming package, traditionally decorated with beady eyes and tufted tail of course, and munched away. It was a pleasure to watch him eat. But I tore myself away before I forgot and pushed coins into the slot on back of the armored coin box.

The Bishop's eyes widened with astonishment. As soon as he swallowed he spoke.

"You are paying! I thought that we were safely ensconced in a gustatorial paradise with free food and drink at our beck and call, night and day?"

"We are—for all of this money is stolen and I am just putting it back into circulation to keep the economy healthy. But there is no slack in the Macswineys operation. Every morsel of porcine tissue, every splinter of ice is accounted for. When the mechanic tests the machines he is responsible for every item delivered. The shop's computer keeps track of every sale so that the frozen supplies are filled exactly to the top each time they are replenished. All of the money collected is taken away each day from the safe on the outer wall—which is automated as well. An armored van backs over it just as the time lock disengages. A code is keyed in and the money disgorged. So if we simply helped ourselves, the records would reveal the theft. Prompt investigation would follow. We must pay for what we use, precisely the correct amount.

But, since we won't be coming back here, we will steal all the money on the day we leave."

"Fine, my boy, fine. You had me worried there for a minute with your bit of forced honesty. Since you are close to the controls, please trigger another delicious morsel of *Lepus cuniculus* while I pay."

Chapter 15

I suppose that there have been stranger places to go to school, but I can't think of any. At certain times of day it was hard to be heard above the rattle, hiss, and roar of the dispensing machinery. Lunch and dinner were the busiest times, but there was another peak when the schools got out. We would eat then as well, since it was so hard to talk, working our way through the entire Macswineys inventory. Countless Macbunnyburgers hopped down our throats, and many a Frozen Fomey followed. I liked Dobbindogs until one too many cantered past my gums, and switched to jellied porcuswinetrotters, then to felinefritters. The Bishop was very catholic in his tastes and liked everything on the menu. Then, once the crowds had gone, after we had patted the last trace of gravy from our lips, we would loll back at our ease and my studies would continue. When we started on computer crime I discovered what The Bishop had been up to for the past couple of decades.

"Give me a terminal and I can rule the world," he said, and such was the authority of his voice that I believed he could. "When I was young I delighted in all manner of operations to please the citizens of this planet. It was quite a thrill to intercept cash shipments while en route, then substitute my calling card for the bundles of bills. They never did find out how I did it. . . ."

"How did you?"

"We were talking about computers."

"Digress just this once, I beg of you. I promise to put the technique to good use. Perhaps, with your permission, even leave one of your cards."

"That sounds an excellent idea. Baffle the current crop of coppers as thoroughly as I did their predecessors. I'll describe what happens—and perhaps you can discover for yourself how it was done. In the Central Mint, a well-guarded and ancient building with stone walls two meters thick, are located the giant safes filled with billions of bucks. When a shipment is to be made, guards and officials fill a bullion box, which is then locked and sealed while all present look on. Outside the building waits a convoy of coppers all guarding a single armored car. At a given signal the car backs up against the armor-plated delivery door. Inside the building the steel inner door is opened, the box placed inside the armored chamber. This door is sealed before the outer one can be opened. The box then travels in the armored car to the linear train, where an armored wagon receives it. This has but the single door, which is locked and sealed and wired with countless alarms. Guards ride in a special chamber of each car as it shuttles through the linear network to the city needing the bucks. Here another armored car awaits, the box is removed—still sealed—placed in the car, and taken to the bank. Where it is opened—and found to contain only my card."

"Marvelous!"

"Care to explain how it was done?"

"You were one of the guards on the train . . ."

"No."

"Or drove the armored car . . ."

"No."

I racked my brains this way for an hour before he relented and explained. "All your suggestions have merit, but all are dangerous. You are far more physical than I ever was. In my operations I always preferred brains to brawn. The reason that I never had to break into the box and extract the money is that the box was empty when it left the building. Or rather it was weighted with bricks as well as my card. Can you guess now how it was done?"

"Never left the building," I muttered, trying to stir my brain to life. "But it was loaded into the box, the box put into the truck . . ."

"You are forgetting something."

I snapped my fingers and leapt to my feet. "The wall, of course it had to be the wall. You gave me all the clues. I was just being dense. Old, made of stone, two meters thick!"

"Exactly so. It took me four months to break in, I wore out three robots doing it, but I won out in the end. First I bought the building across the road from the mint and we tunneled under it. With pick and shovel. Very slow, very silent. Up through the foundations of the building and inside the wall. Which proved to have an outer and inner stone wall, and as is the building custom, it was filled with rubble in between. Our diamond saws were never heard when we opened the side of the armored vault connecting the inside of the mint with the outside. The mechanism I installed could change boxes in one point oh five seconds. When the inner door was closed, the lock had to be thrown before the outer door could be opened. That was enough time, almost three seconds, to allow for the switch. They never did find out how I did it. The mechanism is still in place. But the operation was basically misdirection, along with a lot of digging. Computer crime is something else altogether. Basically it is an intellectual exercise."

"But isn't computer theft almost impossible these days, with codes and interlocks?"

"What man can code or lock, man can decode and unlock. Without leaving any trace. I will give you some examples. Let us begin with the rounding-off caper, also called the salami. Here is how it works. Let us say that you have 8,000 bucks in the bank, in a savings account that earns eight percent a year. Your bank compounds your account weekly in order to get your business. Which means at the end of the first week your bank multiplies your balance by .0015384 percent and adds this sum to your balance. Your balance has increased by 12.30 bucks. Is that correct? Check it on your calculator."

I punched away at the sum and came up with the same answer. "Exactly twelve bucks and thirty centimes interest," I said proudly.

"Wrong," he said deflatingly. "The interest was 12.3072, wasn't it?"

"Well, yes, but you can't add seventy-two-hundredths of a centime to someone's account, can you?"

"Not easily, since financial accounts are kept to two decimal places. Yet it is at this precise moment in the calculations that the bank has a choice. It can round all decimals above .005 up to the nearest centime, all those below .0049 down to zero. At the end of a day's trading the rounding-ups and rounding-downs will average out very close to zero so the bank will not be out of pocket. Or, and this is the accepted practice, the bank can throw away all decimal places after the first two, thereby making a small but consistent profit. Small on banking terms—but very large as far as an individual is concerned. If the bank's computer is rigged so that all the rounding-downs are deposited to a single account, why at the end of the day the computer will show the correct balance in the bank's account and in the client's accounts. Everyone will be quite pleased."

I was punching like fury into my calculator, then chuckled with glee at the results. "Exactly so. All are pleased—including the holder of that account that now holds the round-downs. For if only a half a centime is whipped from ten-thousand accounts, the profit is a round fifty bucks!"

"Exactly. But a large bank will have a hundred times that number of accounts. Which is, as I know from happy experience, a weekly income of five-thousand bucks for whoever sets up this scam."

"And this, this is your smallest and simplest bit of computer tomfoolery?" I asked in a hushed voice.

"It is. When one begins to access large corporative computers, the sums become unbelievable. It is such a pleasure to operate at these levels. Because if one is careful and leaves no traces, the corporations have no idea that they have even been fiddled! They don't want to know about it, don't even believe it when faced with the evidence. It is very hard to get convicted of computer crime. It is a fine hobby for one of my mature years. It keeps me busily engaged and filthy rich. I have never been caught. Ahh, yes, except once. . . ."

He sighed heavily and I felt mortified.

"My fault!" I cried. "If I had not tried to contact you, why you would never have got involved with the Feds."

"No guilt, Jim, feel no guilt over that. I misjudged their security controls, far more rigid than the ones I had been dealing with. It was my mistake—and I certainly paid for it. Am still paying. I am not decrying the safety of our refuge here, but this junk food begins to wear on one after a bit. Or perhaps you haven't noticed?"

"This is the staff of life of my generation."

"Of course. I had not thought of that. The horse tires not of hay, the porcuswine will snuffle up his swill greedily unto eternity."

"And you could probably tuck into lobster and champagne for the next century."

"Well-observed and correct, my boy. How long do you think that we shall be here?" he asked, pushing away half of an unconsumed portion of crumptumps.

"I would say a minimum of two weeks more." A shudder shivered his frame.

"It will be a good opportunity for me to reduce."

"By that time the heat of the chase will have died down considerably. We will still have to avoid public transportation for a good while after that. However I have prepared an escape route that should be secure fairly soon."

"Dare I ask what it is?"

"A boat, rather a cabin cruiser on the Sticks River. I bought it some time ago, in a corporative name, and it is at the marina just outside Billville."

"Excellent!" He rubbed his hands with glee. "The end of summer, a cruise south, fried catfish in the evening, bottles of wine cooling in the stream, steaks at riverside restaurants."

"And a sex change for me."

He blinked rapidly at that, then sighed with relief when I explained. "I'll wear girl's clothes when I'm aboard and can be seen from the shore, at least until we are well away from here."

"Capital. I shall lose some weight—there will be no difficulty dieting here. Raise a moustache, then a beard, die my hair black again. It is something to look forward to. But shall we say one month instead of two weeks? I could last that amount of time incarcerated in this gustatorial ghetto as long as I would not be eating. My figure will be the better for the extra weeks, my hair and moustache longer."

"I can do it if you can."

"Then it is agreed. And we shall make the most of the time now by forwarding your education? RAM, ROM, and PROM will be the order of the day."

I was too busy with my studies to be bothered by the omnipresent odor of barbecued porcuswineburgers. Besides that, I could still eat them. So as my comprehension grew of all the varied possibilities of illegality in our society, so did my companion's figure fade. I wanted to leave earlier, but The Bishop, having made up his mind, would not be swayed.

"Once a plan is made it must always be followed to the letter. It should only be changed if outside circumstances change. Man is a rationalizing animal and needs training in order to become a rational one. Reasons can always be found for altering an operation." He shuddered as the machines speeded up with a roar, school was out, then crossed off one more day on his calendar. "An operation well planned will work. Meddle with it and you destroy it. Ours is a good plan. We will stay with it."

He was far leaner and harder when the day of our exodus finally arrived. He had been tried in the gustatory furnace and had been tempered by it. I had put on weight. Our plans were made, our few belongings packed, the safe cleaned out of all of its bucks—and all trace of our presence eliminated. In the end we could only sit in silence, looking again and again at our watches.

When the alarm sounded we were on our feet, smiling with pleasure.

I turned off the alarm as The Bishop opened the door of the freezer room. As the key turned in the outer lock we closed the door behind us. Stood and shivered in Macswineys' mausoleum while we listened to the mechanic enter the room we had so recently left.

"Hear that?" I asked. "He's adjusting the icer on the cherry oozer dispenser. I thought it sounded funny."

"I prefer not to discuss the contents of the ghastly gourmet gallery. Is it time to go yet?"

"Time." I eased open the outer door and blinked at the light of day, unseen for so long. Other than the service van the street was empty. "Here we go."

We shuffled out and I sealed the door behind us. The air was sweet and fresh and filled with lovely pollution. Even I had had my fill of cooking odors. As The Bishop hurried to the van I slipped the two wedges into the outer door to our chamber of culinary horrors. If the mechanic tried to get out before his appointed time, these would slow him down. We only needed about fifteen minutes.

The Bishop was a dab hand with a lockpick and had the van open and the door swinging wide even as I turned about. He dived into the back among the machine parts as I started the engine.

It was just that easy. I dropped him close to the marina, where he sat on a bench in the sunshine, keeping an eye on our possessions. After that it was simplicity itself to leave the purloined van in the parking lot of the nearest liquor store. Then I strolled, not ran, back to the riverside to rejoin him.

"It's the white boat, that one there," I pointed it out, pressing on my moustache with my other hand at the same time to make sure that it was securely in place. "The entire marina is fully automated. I'll get the boat and bring it back here."

"Our cruise is about to begin," he said, and there was a merry twinkle in his eye.

I left him there in the sunlight and went to the marina to insert the boat's identification into the operations robot.

"Good morning," it said in a tinny voice. "You wish to take out the cabin cruiser *Lucky Bucks*. The batteries have been recharged at a cost of twelve bucks. Storage charges . . ."

It went on like that, reading aloud all the charges that could be clearly seen on the screen—presumably for customers who couldn't read—and there was nothing that could be done about it. I stood on one foot and then the other until it was finished, then pumped in the coins. The machine gurgled and spat out my receipt. Still strolling, I went to the boat, inserted the receipt, then waited for the welcome click when the chain unlocked. Seconds later I was out on the river and heading for the solitary figure on the bank.

Solitary no more. A girl sat beside him.

I circled out and around and she was still there. The Bishop sat slumped and gave me no sign what to do. I circled once more, then the sight of a patrolling police car sent me burbling to the bank. The girl stood and waved, then called out.

"Why little Jimmy diGriz, as I live and breathe. What a lovely surprise."

Chapter 16

Life had had far too many moments like this lately. I looked at the girl more closely as I eased the boat against the bank. She knew me, I should know her; smashingly good-looking, her blouse filled to perfection. Those tulip lips, her!—object of my wildest dreams.

"Is that you Beth? Beth Naratin?"

"How *sweet* of you to remember me!"

I was ready to jump ashore with the mooring line, but she took it from my hand and tied it to the bollard there. Over her shoulder I saw the police cruiser go past and keep on cruising. Then glanced at The Bishop, who simply raised his eyes to heaven as she spoke.

"I said to myself, Beth, I said, that can't be Jimmy diGriz climbing out of that old Macswineys van and wearing a cute little moustache. Not Jimmy who has been in the news so much lately. If it is, why don't I just mosey after him, for old times' sake. Then I saw you talk to this nice gentleman here, before you went off to the marina, so I just made up my mind to wait for you to come back. Going on a trip, are you?"

"No, no trip, just a little day excursion up the river and back. Nice seeing you again, Beth."

That was the only nice part about this. Seeing her, I mean. The object of my childish worship. She had left school soon after I had entered—but she was hard to forget. Four years older than me, a real mature woman. That would make her twenty-one now. She had been head of her class, winner of the Beauty Queen of the Year. With good reason. Now, old as she was, she was still a smasher. Her voice sliced through my memories.

"I don't think that you are being exactly truthful, Jimmy. Why with all these bags and things I bet that you are going on a long cruise. If I were you I would consider a long cruise a really good idea."

Was there a different tenor to her voice with these last words? What did she want? We couldn't hang around here much longer. She made her wants clear when she jumped aboard, rocking the boat at its mooring.

"Always room for one more!" she called out cheerfully, then went to sit in the bow. I stepped ashore and grabbed up the bags. Then whispered to The Bishop.

"She knows me. What do we do?"

He sighed in answer. "Very little that we can do. For the present we have a passenger. I suggest that we consider this problem once we are under way. After all—we have no choice."

Too true. I passed our belongings over to him, then struggled to untie the black knot that she had tied in the line. Gave the *Lucky Bucks* a kick out with my foot, jumped aboard, and took the wheel. The Bishop carried the cases below as I switched on the power and headed downstream. Away from Billville, Macswineys and the law.

But not from Beth. She lay stretched out on the deck before me, skirt hiked up so I could admire those gorgeous lengths of leg. I did this. Then she turned about and smiled, clearly able to read my mind. I forgot about my planned female disguise at this moment—imagining the jeering that would greet my sex change. I was getting angry.

"All right, Beth, why don't you just spell it out," I said, hauling my gaze bodily out to the clear waters of the river.

"Whatever do you mean?"

"Stop the games. You have been watching the news, that's what you said. So you know about me."

"Sure do. Know you hold up banks and escape from jail. That doesn't bother me though. I had a bitsy bit of difficulty myself. So when I saw you, then this boat, I knew you must have some money. Maybe a lot of money. So I just jumped at the chance to take this trip with you. Isn't that nice?"

"No." I kept my thoughts on the law and not the legs. She was trouble. "And I do have a bit of money put aside. If I get you some, put you ashore . . ."

"The money, yes. The shore, no. I've seen the last of *him* and Billville. I'm going to see the world now. And you are going to pay my way."

She snuggled down, with her arms for a pillow, smiling as she enjoyed the sunshine. I looked on gloomily and thought of three or four blows that would snap that delicate neck. . . .

Not even as a joke. This problem could be solved—and without deadly violence. We hummed along, the water parting in white foam at our bow, Billville behind us and green fields opening up ahead at the bend in the river. The Bishop came on deck and sat next to me. With her third presence there was nothing much we could say.

We continued in silence this way for the better part of an hour, until a dock beside a general store appeared ahead. Beth stirred and sat up, running her fingers through that gorgeous blond hair.

"You know what—I'm hungry. Bet you are too. Why don't you pull up over there and I'll jump ashore and get us some food and some beer. Isn't that a good idea?"

"Great!" I agreed. She goes into the store, we go into high gear and away.

"I am skint," she smiled. "Stone broke. If you give me a few bucks I'll buy lunch. I think a thousand will do."

Her sweet-little-girl expression never changed while she said this and I wondered just what kind of trouble she was in. Extortion and blackmail maybe; she certainly had the qualifications for that. I dug deep into my wallet.

"That's nice," she said, thumbing through the bundle with glowing eyes. "I won't be long. And I *know* you will be here. Jimmy, along with your friend. Haven't I seen him in the news broadcasts too?"

I glowered after the lovely rotations of her rump as she trotted towards the store.

"Got our hides nailed to the wall," The Bishop said gloomily.

"Nailed, flayed, and tanned. What do we do?"

"Exactly what she says for the time being. Short of killing her, we have very little choice. But I do not believe in killing."

"Nor do I. Although this is the first time that I have understood the temptation."

"What do you know about her?"

"Nothing—since I last saw her in school. She says she is in trouble, but I have no idea what she means."

He nodded in thought. "When we are well away from her I'll get close to a terminal. If she is in the police records I can dig her out."

"Will that do us any good?"

"I have no idea, dear boy. We can only try. Meanwhile we must make the best of the situation. We are well away from the terrors of the pork palace, safely away from our pursuers as well. As long as this creature gets money from us we are safe. For the moment. And you must admit that she is decorative."

I had no answer to that and could only sit glumly until our uninvited passenger returned.

After lunch we continued our voyage downstream. Exhausted by the morning of sunbathing, Beth went below for a beauty nap. The Bishop wanted a turn at the wheel so I showed him the simple controls and pointed out the navigation markers. We had very little to say to each other. But we were thinking a lot. In midafternoon the object of our fierce cogitation trotted up from below.

"Such a cute little ship," she gushed. "The cutest little girls' room, little kitchen, and everything. But only two little beds. How in the world will we all sleep?"

"In shifts," I growled, the sound of her voice already getting to me.

"You always were a card, Jimmy. I think it best if I sleep below. You and your friend can make do."

"Make do, young lady, make do? How does one my age make do on deck when the chill mists of night descend?" The Bishop's anger was under control, barely, but her bright smile seemed to be unaware of it.

"I'm sure that you will find a way," she said. "Now I would like to stop at the next town we come to, that one there. I left in such a hurry I forgot all my things. Clothes and makeup, you know."

"You wouldn't need a bit of money to buy those things?" I asked facetiously. She ignored my feeble humor and nodded.

"Another thousand will do."

"I'm going below," The Bishop said, and did not emerge again until I had tied up and she was gone. He carried two beers and I took one and drank deep.

"Murder is out," he said firmly.

"Murder is out," I agreed. "But that doesn't mean we can't enjoy thinking about it. What do we do?"

"We don't just heave anchor and go. She'll have the police after us in minutes, then will pocket the reward. We must take that into consideration, then think faster than she can. Coming with us was an impulse, obviously. She is greedy for money and we must keep giving it to her. But sooner or later she will decide that she has had enough of ours and will turn us in for the reward, Is there such a thing as a map aboard?"

That mighty brain was at work, I could tell that. I asked no questions but rooted out the map as quickly as I could. He traced it with his finger.

"We are here, I imagine, yes, here is the very place. While downstream, here, is the bustling city of Val's Halla. When will we get there?"

I squinted at the scale and marked the distance with my thumb. "Could be there by midafternoon tomorrow, if we get an early start."

His face broke into a smile so wide that his eyes were crinkled half shut. "Splendid, absolutely splendid. That will do very nicely indeed."

"What will?"

"My plans. Which I shall keep to myself for the moment since there are details still to be worked out. When she returns you must agree with me, whatever I say; that is all you have to do. Now, next order of business. Where do we sleep tonight?"

"On the river's bank," I said, heading below. "Our friend has all the money that I was carrying, so I must get more from our stock. Then I'm going ashore to buy a tent, sleeping bags, all the gear for comfortable camping out."

"Capital. I shall man the fort and hone my plans until you return."

I bought some steaks too, along with a collection of fancy bottles of wine. We needed a major change from the Macswineys cuisine. When the sun was close to the horizon I tied the boat to the trees on the banks of a green meadow, where we could pitch our tent. The Bishop, after smacking his lips over the meat, announced that he would prepare dinner. While he did this, and Beth did her nails, I hammered stakes and got our beds ready. The sun was a ball of orange on the horizon when we tucked into the meal. It was tremendous. No one talked until we were done. When the last morsel was gone The Bishop sighed, raised his glass and sipped, then sighed with repletion.

"Though I cooked it myself, I must say that meal was a triumph."

"It does take the taste of porcuswine out of the mouth," I agreed.

"I didn't like the wine. Nasty." Only her outline was visible in the darkness. Lacking the usual glorious physical accompaniment her voice, as well as her words, left a very lot to be desired. Yet The Bishop's deep basso was free of rancor when he spoke again.

"Beth—I may call you Beth, mayn't I? Thank you. Beth, we shall be in the city of Val's Halla tomorrow, where I must go ashore and call into my bank. Our funds are running low. You wouldn't like our money to run out, would you?"

"No, I wouldn't."

"Thought not. But would you like me to go to the bank and bring you back one hundred thousand bucks in small buck bills?"

I heard her gasp. Then she fumbled for the switch and the riding lights above the cockpit came on. She was frowning at The Bishop and, for the very first time, lost her cool.

"Are you trying to play games with me, old man?"

"Not at all, young lady. I am simply paying for our safety. You know certain facts that are, shall we say, best left unspoken aloud. I think that sum is a reasonable amount to pay for your continuing silence. Don't you?"

She hesitated—then burst out laughing. "I sure do. Just let me see the color of those bucks and I may even consider letting you boys continue your journey without poor little me."

"Whatever you say, my dear, whatever you say."

Nor would he speak another word on the subject. We retired soon after that, for it had been a busy day for all of us. Beth took possession of the boat and we had the tent. When I returned from setting the alarms to make sure that the boat would still be there in the morning. The Bishop was already in full snore. Before I slept myself I realized that, whatever he was planning, we had at least one more day of freedom before Beth would think of contacting the police. The lure of that money would ensure her silence. As I dozed off I realized that The Bishop had undoubtedly planned it that way.

We were humming down the river an hour after dawn, despite Beth's protests. She emerged later, but her anger soon vanished beneath The Bishop's monetary ministrations. He described the interest her invested bucks could earn without her spending any of her capital, touched lightly on the consumer goods she would soon purchase, and generally charmed her like a snake with a rabbit. I had no idea what his plans were but I enjoyed every moment of it.

By midafternoon I had tied up at the marina on the canal that bisected Val's Halla. The city center was close to hand and The Bishop, beard combed and moustache twirled, was neatly turned out and businesslike.

"This will not take long," he said, then left. Beth looked after him, already atwitch with anticipation.

"He's really the one they call The Bishop," she said when he had gone.

"I wouldn't know about that."

"Don't give me that old booshwah. I saw the films on 3V, how somebody got him out. A small guy with a moustache. It had to be you."

"Lot of moustaches in this world."

"I never thought, when I saw you around the school, you would ever end up like this."

"I thought the same about you. I admired you from afar."

"So did every other pubescent boy in the school. Don't think I didn't know it. We used to laugh about it, him being a teacher and all that. . . ."

She shut up and glowered at me and I smiled sweetly and went below to wash the dinner and breakfast dishes that she had so carefully ignored. I was just finishing up when there was a hail from the shore.

"Boat ahoy! Permission to come aboard?"

The Bishop stood on the dockside, beaming and splendid. His new suit must have cost a small fortune. The suitcase that he held up appeared to be made of real animal skin of some kind, with fittings of glowing gold. Beth's eyes were as wide as saucers. The Bishop climbed aboard and treated us to a conspiratorial wink.

"Best to get below before I show you what's in this case. It is not for the world to see."

Beth led the way and he held the case to his chest until I had closed and locked the door. Then he swept the papers from the table to the deck, placed the case in its center, and with tantalizing precision unlocked and opened the case.

Even I was impressed. There was far more than the hundred thousand here. Beth stared at it—then reached out and tugged a bundle of thousand-buck bills free.

"Real? Is it real?" she asked.

"Guaranteed right from the mint. I saw to that myself." With her attention on the money he turned to me. "Now, Jim, would you mind doing me a favor? Would you find some rope or twine, I'm sure that you will know what you will need. I want absolute silence as well when you tie this girl up so she cannot move."

I was expecting something—she was not. Her mouth was just opening to scream when I seized that precious neck and pressed hard just below the ears.

Chapter 17

With savage glee I cut one of the blankets into strips and bound those delicate wrists and trim ankles. I was just putting sticking tape over her mouth when she came to and tried to scream. It came out as a muffled mewl. "Can she breathe all right like that?" The Bishop asked.

"Perfectly. See the glare in her eye and the angry heaving of that magnificent chest? She is breathing through her nostrils just fine. Now—will you tell me what this is all about?"

"On deck, if you please."

He waited until the door was closed behind us before he spoke, rubbing his hands together with joy.

"Our troubles are over, my boy. I knew that as soon as I looked at the map. There are two things about this fine city that assure me of that. One was the bank, a branch of Galactic Trust with which I have an account—sizable as you have seen. The second fact of interest is that there is a spaceport here."

I puzzled over this for a few seconds as my sluggish brain slowly added two and two. Then my jaw gaped so hard I could barely speak.

"You mean that, us, we . . . we are going offplanet?"

He nodded and grinned. "Precisely. This little world has become, shall we say, a little too warm for us. It will be even warmer when our female friend is freed. By that time we shall have shaken the dust of Bit O' Heaven from our boots and we will be lightyears away. You did tell me that you wanted to travel?"

"I did, of course, but aren't there controls, inspections, police, things like that?"

"There are. But customs and immigration can be circumvented if you know how. I know how. And I did check on which ships were here before taking this drastic step. I am sorry that I had no opportunity to warn you—but I was certain that your magnificent reflexes would resolve the matter with ease. When I left here I did not know that this would be the day to put the plan into operation. I intended just to get the money to string the girl along. While keeping track of spacer operations. But the fates are on our side. There is a freighter here from Venia taking on cargo—and leaving in the early hours of the morning. Isn't that wonderful!"

"I'm sure that it is. But I would be a lot surer if I knew why."

"Jim, your education has been sorely neglected. I thought every schoolboy knew how venal the Venians were. They are the despair of the League polimetricians. Incorrigible. The motto on Venia is *La regloj ĉiam ŝansiliĝas*. Which may be freely translated as There are no Fixed Rules. That is to say, there are laws about everything—but bribery can change anything. It is not so much that they are a world of criminals, but rather a planet of twisters."

"Sounds nice," I agreed. "Then what have you arranged?"

"Nothing yet. But I am positive that opportunity will arrive at the spaceport."

"Yes, sure." I was far from enthusiastic. The plan had all the earmarks of improvisation and crossed fingers. But I had little choice. "What about the girl?"

"We'll leave a message for the police with the electronic post, to be delivered after we are gone. Telling them the place where she can be found."

"That place can't be here—too public. There is an automated marina farther downstream. I could tie up there, one of the outer berths."

"The perfect solution. If you will give me instructions how to find it I will hie myself to the spaceport to make the arrangements. Shall we meet there at 2300 hours?"

"Fine by me."

I watched his impressive form move off in the growing darkness, then started the engine and made a slow turn in the canal. It was dark by the time I reached the marina. But it was brightly lit and the channel was well marked. Most of the boats had tied up close to shore, which was fine by me. I took the outermost berth, well away from the others. Then went below, turned on the lights, and faced the poisonous glare from those lovely eyes. I locked the cabin door behind me, then sat down on the bunk across from Beth.

"I want to talk to you. If I take off the tape do you promise not to scream? We are well away from the city and there is no one here to hear you in any case. Deal?"

The hatred was still there as she nodded reluctantly. I peeled off the tape—then jerked my fingers away just in time as those perfect teeth snapped at my hand.

"I could kill you, murder you, butcher you, slaughter you . . ."

"Enough," I said. "I'm the one who could do all those things, not you. So shut up."

She shut. Perhaps realizing what her position really was; there was more fear than anger in her eyes now. I didn't want to terrorize a helpless girl—but the murder talk had been her idea. She was ready to listen.

"You can't be comfortable. So lie still while I untie you."

She waited until her wrists were free, then raked her nails towards my face while I was untying her ankles. I had expected this, so she ended up back on the bunk with the breath knocked out of her.

"Act reasonable," I told her. "You can be tied and gagged again just as easily. And please don't forget that you brought this on yourself."

"You are a criminal, a thief. Wait until the police get their hands on you. . . ."

"And you are a blackmailer. Can we stop the names and games now? Here is what is going to happen. We are going to leave you on this boat and when we are well away the police will be told where to find you. I'm sure that you will tell them a good story. There are express linears from here, as well as the highways. You'll never see us again, nor will they." A little misdirection never hurt.

"I'm thirsty."

"I'll get you something."

Of course she made a break for the door when I had my back turned, then tried for my eyes again when I pulled her away. I could understand her feelings—I just wished that she wouldn't.

Time dragged very slowly after that. She had nothing to say that I wanted to hear—and the reverse was obviously true as well. Hours passed in this way before the boat rocked as someone stepped aboard. I dived towards the bunk but she got out one good scream before I could silence her. The door handle rattled and turned.

"Who is it?" I called out, crouched and ready for battle.

"Not a stranger, I assure you," the familiar voice said. I unlocked and opened the door with a feeling of great relief.

"Can she hear me?" he asked, looking at the silent figure on the bunk.

"Possibly. Let me secure her again and we'll go on deck."

He went ahead of me and as I closed the door a sudden flare of light lit up the night sky, then climbed in a burning arc up to the zenith.

"A good omen," The Bishop said. "A deep spacer. All is arranged. And time is of the essence, so I suggest that we grab up our things and leave at once."

"Transportation?"

"A rented groundcar."

"Can it be traced?"

"I hope so. The rental return is located at the linear station. I've purchased tickets, for both of us you will be happy to hear."

"I mentioned linears to our friend inside."

"Two great minds that work as one. I think I shall manage to drop the tickets where she can see them while we are packing."

We were in and out quite quickly—and I did enjoy the way the unmistakable blue linear tickets dropped on the blankets for an instant. Fell from his pocket while both his hands were engaged elsewhere. Masterful! As I closed the door I could not resist the temptation to blow a kiss towards Beth. I received a glower and a muffled snarl in return, which I surely deserved. She still had a few thousand of our money so she should not complain.

After turning in the groundcar we took the levitrain to the linear station. Where we waited until we were alone and unobserved before continuing on to the spaceport. Up until this moment it had been all rush and plan and the reality of what I was doing struck home only when I saw the floodlit flank of a deep spacer looming up ahead.

I was going offplanet! It is one thing to watch the spaceoperas—but another thing completely to venture into space. I felt the goosebumps swell on my arm, the hair stir on my neck. This new life was going to be a good one!

"Into the bar," The Bishop ordered. "Our man is already here!"

A thin man in grease-stained spacer gear was just leaving, but dropped back into the booth when he saw The Bishop.

"Vi estas malfrua!" he said angrily.

"V'ere—sed me havas la monon," The Bishop answered, flashing a large wad of bills which soothed the other immeasurably. The money changed hands, and after some more conversation another bundle of bills went the way of the first. Greed satisfied, the spaceman led the way to a service van and we climbed into the back. The door was slammed and in the darkness we sped off.

What an adventure! Unseen vehicles passed us, then there were strange hammering sounds that came and went, followed by a loud hissing like a giant serpent. We stopped soon after this and our guide came around and opened the rear door. I stepped out first and found myself at the foot of a ramp leading up into what could only be the battered hull of a deep spacer.

Next to the ramp stood an armed guard, staring at me.

It was all over, the adventure ended before it even began. What could I do? Run, no I couldn't leave The Bishop. He pushed past me while I was still rushing about in circles inside my head, strolled casually over to the guard.

And passed him a wad of bills.

The guard was still counting them when we hurried up the ramp behind our bribed spaceman, struggling to stay close with all the baggage we carried.

"Eniru, rapide!" the spaceman ordered, opening the door of a compartment. We pushed through into the darkness as the door closed and locked behind us.

"Safe harbor!" The Bishop sighed with relief as he fumbled at the wall until he found the switch, and the lights came on. We were in a small, cramped cabin. There were two narrow bunks and an even smaller bathroom beyond. Pretty grim.

"Home sweet home," The Bishop said, smiling benevolently as he looked around. "We'll have to stay in here at least two days. So let us stow our gear well out of sight. Otherwise the captain will threaten to return and the bribe will be higher. I'm sure we can last it out."

"I'm not sure I understand all of that. Haven't you paid the bribe already?"

"Only the first installments. Bribes are never shared, that is your first lesson in the gentle art. The spaceman got paid to sneak us aboard, and arranged that a friendly guard would be there to take his cut. Those arrangements are in the past. Our presence aboard this ship is unknown to the officers—and particularly the captain who will need a very large payment indeed. You will see."

"I certainly intend to. Bribery is indeed an exacting science."

"It is."

"It's a good thing you speak their language so you can do a deal."

His eyebrows shot up at this and he leaned close. "You did not understand us?" he asked.

"I didn't take foreign languages in school."

"Foreign!" He looked shocked. "What a backward part of that porcuswine-rearing planet you must have come from. That was not a *foreign* language, dear boy. That was Esperanto, the galactic language, the simple, second language that everyone learns early and speaks like a native. Your education has been neglected, but that is easily repaired. Before our next planetfall you shall be speaking it as well. To begin with, all present-tense verbs in all persons end in *as*. Simplicity itself. . . ."

He stopped as someone tried the handle on the cabin door. His finger touched his lips as he pointed to the adjoining bath. I dived that way and turned on the light there just as he turned off the one in the cabin. He joined me in a rush and jammed in beside me as I flicked off the light. He eased the door shut just as the corridor door opened.

Footsteps thudded across the cabin and there was the sound of thin whistling.

A routine inspection, nothing to be seen, he would go away in an instant . . .

Then the bathroom door opened and the light came on. The gold-braided officer looked at The Bishop cramped into the tiny shower, at me crouching on the commode, as he smiled a singularly dirty smile.

"I thought there was too much activity belowdecks. Stowaways." A small gun appeared in his hand. "Out. You two are going ashore and I am calling the local police."

Chapter 18

I leaned forward, getting my weight on my legs, muscles tense. Ready to attack the instant that The Bishop distracted the officer's attention. I really did not want to go against that gun with my bare hands—but I wanted even less to go back to jail. The Bishop must surely have been aware of this. He reached out a restraining hand.

"Now, let us not be hasty, James. Relax while I talk to this kind officer."

His hand went slowly to his pocket, the gun following his every move, the fingers dipped deep—and came up with a thin wad of credits.

"This is advance payment for a small favor," he said, handing them over to the officer, who took the credits in both hands. Which was easy enough to do now that the gun had vanished just as quickly as it had appeared. He counted while The Bishop talked.

"The favor we so humbly request is that you do not find us for two days. You will be paid this same sum tomorrow, and again the day after when you discover us and take us to the captain."

The money vanished and the gun reappeared—and I never saw his hands move. He was so good he should have been on the stage.

"I think not," he said. "I think I will take all the money you have concealed on your person and in your bags. Take it and bring you to the captain now."

"Not very wise," The Bishop said sternly. "I will tell the captain exactly how much you took and he will relieve you of it and you will have nothing. I will also tell him which crewmen were bribed and they will be deprived of their money and you will not be a popular officer on this ship. Will you?"

"There is a certain element of truth in what you say," he mused, rubbing his jaw in thought, hands empty again. "If the payments were increased perhaps . . ."

"Ten percent, no more," said The Bishop, and the payment was made. "See you tomorrow. Please relock the door behind you."

"Of course. Have a pleasant journey."

Then he was gone and I climbed down from the pot and seized and shook The Bishop's hand. "Congratulations, sir. A masterful demonstration of a science I scarcely knew existed."

"Thank you, my boy. But it helps to know the ground rules. He never had any intention of turning us out of this ship. That was just his bid. I called it, he raised, I matched and closed. He knew he couldn't squeeze higher because I need a large sum in reserve for the captain. Unspoken, but agreed nevertheless, is my silence about the bribe to him. All done by the rules. . . ."

His words were cut off by the loud sound of a hooter in the corridor outside, while a red light began blinking rapidly over the door.

"Is something wrong?" I called out.

"Something is very right. We are ready for takeoff. I suggest that we recline on the bunks because some of these old clunkers put on the Gs when they blast free. A few minutes more and we shake the dust of Bit O' Heaven from our shoes. Preferably forever. That prison, simply terrible, the food . . ."

A growing roar drowned out his words and the bunk began to tremble. Then the acceleration of takeoff jumped on my chest. Just like in the films—but far more exciting in reality. This was it! Offplanet! What joys lay ahead.

Pretty far ahead still. The mattress was thin and my back hurt from the pressure. Then we went in and out of null-G a few times before they got the artificial gravity right. Or almost right. Every once in awhile it would give a little hiccup. So would my stomach. This happened often enough so that during the next days I didn't miss the meals that I would normally have eaten. At least we had all the rusty, flat water we needed to drink. The officer stayed bribed, I stayed in my bunk most of the time and concentrated on the Esperanto lessons to forget my miseries. After two days of this the gravity finally straightened out and my appetite returned. I looked forward to our release, some more bribery—and some food.

"Stowaways!" the officer said when he unlocked the door, staggered, hand over heart. For the benefit of the crewgirl who accompanied him. "Terrible, unheard of! On your feet, you two, and come with me. Captain Garth will want to know about this."

It was a very convincing performance, spoiled only by his ready hand for the money as soon as the crewgirl's back was turned. She seemed bored by the whole thing and was probably in on the deal herself. We tramped the corridor and up three flights of metal stairs to the bridge. The captain, at least, was shocked to see us. Probably the only one on the ship who didn't know we were aboard.

"Damn and blast—where did these come from?"

"In one of the empty cabins on C deck."

"You were supposed to check those cabins."

"I did, my captain, it is in the log. One hour before takeoff. After that I was on the bridge with you. They must have come aboard after that."

"Who did you bribe?" Captain Garth said, turning to us, a grizzled old spacedog with a mean look in his eye.

"No one, captain," The Bishop said, sincerity ringing in his voice. "I know these old Reptile class freighters very well. Just before takeoff the guard at the gangway entered the ship. We came in behind him, unseen, and hid in the cabin. That is all there is to it."

"I don't believe a word of it. Tell me who you bribed or you'll be in the brig and in big trouble."

"My dear captain, your honest crewmen would never take bribes!" He ignored the unbelieving snort. "I have proof. All of my not inconsiderable fortune is intact and in my pocket."

"Out," the captain instantly ordered all the men in the control room. "All of you. I'll take this watch. I want to question these two more thoroughly."

The officer and the crewmembers shuffled out, their faces expressionless under his gaze. When they were gone the captain sealed the door and spun about. "Let's have it," he ordered. The Bishop passed over a very tidy sum and the captain riffled through it, then shook his head. "Not enough."

"Of course," The Bishop agreed. "That is the opening payment. The balance after landfall on some agreeable planet with lax custom officers."

"You ask a lot. I have no desire to risk trouble with planetary authorities by smuggling in illegal immigrants. It will be far easier to relieve you of the money right now and dispose of you as I will."

The Bishop was not impressed at all by this ploy. He tapped his pocket and shook his head. "Not possible. Final payment is with this registered check for two-hundred thousand credits drawn on Galactic Credit and Exchange. It is not legal tender until I countersign it with a second signature. You may torture me, but I will never sign! Until we are standing on firm ground."

The captain shrugged meaningfully and turned to the controls, making a minor adjustment before he turned back. "There is a matter of paying for your meals," he said calmly. "Charity does not pay my fuel bills."

"Absolutely. Let us fix a rate."

That appeared to be all there was to it—but The Bishop whispered a warning as we went back down the corridor. "The cabin is undoubtedly bugged. Our luggage searched. I have all our funds on me. Stay close so there are no accidents. That officer, for one, would make an excellent professional pickpocket. Now—what do you say to a little food? Since we have paid we can end our enforced fast with a splendid feast."

My stomach rumbled loud agreement with this suggestion, and we made for the galley. Since there were no passengers the fat, unshaven cook served only Venian peasant food. Fine for the natives, but it took some getting used to. Did you ever try to hold your nose and eat at the same time? I didn't ask the cook what we were eating—I was afraid he would tell me. The Bishop sighed deeply and began to fork down his ration of gunge.

"The one thing I forgot about Venia," he said gloomily, "was the food. Selective memory I am sure. Who would want to recall at any time a feast like this?"

I did not answer since I was gulping at my cup of warm water to get the taste out of my mouth.

"Small blessings," I said. "At least the water here isn't as nasty as the stuff from the tap in our cabin." The Bishop sighed again.

"That is coffee that you are drinking."

A fun cruise it was not. We both lost weight since it was often better to avoid a meal than to eat it. I continued my studies, learning the finer points of embezzling, expense-account grafting, double- and treble-entry bookkeeping—all done in Esperanto until I was as facile as a native in that fine language.

At our first planetfall we stayed in the ship since soldiers and customs officers were thick as sandfleas about the ship.

"Not here," the captain said, looking at the screened image of the ground with us. "Very rich planet, but they don't like strangers. The next planet in this system is one you will like, agricultural, low population, they can use immigrants, so there isn't even a customs office."

"The name?" The Bishop asked.

"Amphisbionia."

"Never heard of it."

"Should you have? Out of thirty-thousand settled planets."

"True. But still . . ."

The Bishop seemed troubled and I couldn't understand why. If we didn't like this planet we could liberate enough funds to move on. But some instinct had him on edge. In the end he bribed the purser to use the ship's computer. When we were toying with our dinner he told me about it.

"Something doesn't smell right about this—smells worse than this food." This was a horrifying thought. "I can find no record of a planet named Amphisbionia in the galactic guide. And the guide is updated automatically every time we land and hook into a planetary communication net. In addition to that, there is a lock on our next destination. Only the captain has the code to access it."

"What can we do?"

"Nothing—until after we land. We'll find out then what he is up to."

"Can't you bribe one of the officers?"

"I already did—that's how I found out that only the captain knows where we are heading. Of course he didn't tell me until after I paid. A dirty trick. I would have done the same thing myself."

I tried to cheer him up, but it was no use. I think the food had affected his morale. It would be a good thing to arrive at this planet, whatever it was. Certainly a good thief can make a living in any society. And one thing was certain. The food would *have* to be better than the sludge we were reluctantly eating now.

We stayed in our bunks until the ship touched down and the green light came on. Our meager belongings were already assembled and we carried them down to the airlock. The captain was operating the controls himself. He muttered as the automatic air analyzer ran through its test; the inner lock would not open until it was finished and satisfied with the results. It finally pinged and flashed its little message at him and he hit the override. The great hatch ground slowly open admitting a whiff of warm and pungent air. We sniffed it appreciatively.

"Here is a stylo," Captain Garth said. The Bishop merely smiled.

The captain led the way and we followed with our bags. It was night, stars were bright above, invisible creatures called from the darkness of a row of trees nearby. The only light was from the airlock.

"Here will do," the captain said, standing on the end of the ramp. The Bishop shook his head as he pointed at the metal surface.

"We are still on the ship. The ground if you please."

They agreed on a neutral patch close to the ramp—but far enough from the ship to foil any attempt to rush us. The Bishop took out the check, accepted the stylo at last, then wrote his careful signature. The captain—ever suspicious!—compared it with the signature above and finally nodded. He walked briskly up the ramp as we picked up our bags—then turned and called out.

"They're all yours now!"

As the ramp lifted up, out of our reach, powerful lights came on from the darkness, pinning us like moths. Armed men ran towards us as we turned, trapped, lost.

"I knew something was wrong," The Bishop said. He dropped his bags and grimly faced the rushing men.

Chapter 19

A resplendent figure in a red uniform strode out of the darkness and stood before us twisting a large and elegant set of moustaches. Like someone out of a historic flic, he actually wore a sword, which he held firmly by the hilt.

"I'll take everything you two have. Everything. Quickly!"

Two uniformed men came running up to see that we did as we were told. They were carrying strange-looking guns with large barrels and wooden stocks. Behind us I heard a creaking as the ramp came back down with Captain Garth standing on the end of it. I bent over to pick up the bags.

And kept turning—diving at the captain, grabbing him.

There was a loud bang and something whirred by my head and spanged off the ship's hull. The captain swore and swung his fist at me. Couldn't have been better. I stepped inside the blow, grabbed the arm and levered it up into the small of his back. He screeched with pain; a lovely sound.

"Let him go," a voice said, and I looked over the captain's trembling shoulder to see that The Bishop was now lying on the ground with the officer's foot on his chest. And his sword was not just for decoration—because the point of it was now pressed to The Bishop's throat.

It was going to be one of those days. I gave the captain's neck a little squeeze with my free hand before I let go. He slithered straight down and his unconscious head bonged nicely on the ramp. I stepped away from him and The Bishop climbed unsteadily to his feet, dusting himself off as he turned to our captor.

"Excuse me, kind sir, but might I humbly ask you the name of this planet on whose soil we stand?"

"Spiovente," was the grunted answer.

"Thank you. If you permit, I will help my friend Captain Garth to his feet, for I wish to apologize to him for my young friend's impetuous behavior."

No one stopped him as he turned to the captain, who had just regained consciousness.

He lost it again instantly as The Bishop kicked him in the side of the head.

"I am normally not a vindictive man," he said, turning away and digging out his wallet. He handed it to the officer and said, "But just this once I wanted to express my feelings before returning to my normal peaceful self. You understand, of course, why I did that?"

"Would have done the same thing myself," the officer said, counting the money. "But the games are over. Don't ever speak to me again or you are dead."

He turned away as another man appeared from the darkness with two black metal loops in his hands. The Bishop stood, numb and unresisting, as the man bent and snapped one onto his ankle. I didn't know what the thing was—but I didn't like it. Mine would not be put on that easily.

Yes it would. The muzzle of the gun ground into my back and I made no protest as the thing was snapped into place. The thing-snapper then stood up and looked me in the face, standing so close that his sewer breath washed over me. He was ugly to boot, with a puckered scar that added no improvement to the face. He pushed a sharp finger into my chest as he spoke.

"I am Tars Tukas, servant of our lord the mighty Capo Doccia. But you never call me by name; you always call me master."

I started to call him something, something that was quite an improvement on master, when he pressed a button on a metal box slung from his belt.

Then I was on the ground, trying to shake the red fog of pain from my eyes. The first thing I saw was The Bishop lying before me, groaning in agony. I helped him to his feet; Tars Tukas needn't have done that, not to a man his age. He was grinning a lopsided scarred grin when I turned.

"Who am I?" he asked. I resisted all temptation, for The Bishop's sake if not my own.

"Master."

"Don't forget, and don't try to run away. There are neural repeaters right around the entire country. If I leave this on for long enough, all your nerves stop working. Forever. Understood?"

"Understood, master."

"Hand over everything you got on you."

I did. Money, papers, coins, keys, watch, the works. He frisked me roughly and seemed satisfied for the moment.

"Let's move."

A tropical dawn had come quickly and the lights were being turned out. We didn't look back as we followed our new master. The Bishop was having difficulty in walking and I had to help him. Tars Tukas led us to a battered wooden cart that was standing close by. We were waved into the back. We sat on the plank seat and watched while crates were lowered from the cargo hatch of the spacer.

"That was a nice dropkick on the captain," I said. "You obviously know something about his planet that I don't. What was the name?"

"Spiovente." He spat the word like a curse. "The millstone around the League's neck. That captain has sold us down the river with a vengeance. And he is a smuggler too. There is a complete embargo on contact with this stinking world. Particularly weapons—which I am sure those cases are full of. Spiovente!"

Which didn't really tell me very much other than that it was pretty bad. Which I knew already. "You couldn't possibly be a bit more informative about this millstone?"

"I blame myself completely for getting you involved in all this. But Captain Garth will pay. If we do nothing else, Jim, we will bring him to justice. We'll get word to the League, somehow."

The *somehow* depressed him even more and he dropped his head wearily onto his hands. I sat in silence, waiting for him to speak in his own good time.

He did finally, sitting up, and in the reflected light I saw that the spark was back in his eye.

"Nil carborundum, Jim. Don't let the bastards wear you down. We are landed in a ripe one this time. Spiovente was first contacted by the League over ten years ago. It had been isolated since the Breakdown and had thousands of years to go bad. It is the sort of place that gives crime a bad name—since the criminals are in charge here. The madhouse has been taken over by the madmen. Anarchy rules—no, not true—Spiovente makes anarchy look like a Boy Sprout's picnic. I have made a particular study of this planet's system of government, while working out the stickier bits of my personal philosophy. Here we have something that belongs in the lost dark ages of mankind's rise. It is thoroughly despicable in every way—and there is nothing that the League can do about it, short of launching an invasion. Which would be completely against League philosophy. The strength of the League is also its weakness. No planet or planets can physically attack another planet. Any one that did would face instant destruction by all the others since war has now been declared illegal. The League can only help newly discovered planets, offer advice and aid. It is rumored that there are covert League organizations that work to subvert repulsive societies like this one—but of course this has never been revealed in public. So what we have here is trouble, bad trouble. For Spiovente is a warped mirror image of the civilized worlds. There is no rule of law here—just might. Criminal gangs are led by Capos, the swordman in the fancy uniform, Capo Doccia, he's one of them. Each Capo controls as large a capote as he can. His followers are rewarded with a portion of the loot extracted from the peasantry or from the spoils of war. At the very bottom of this pyramid of crime are the slaves. Us."

He pointed to the paincuff on his ankle and thoroughly depressed himself. Me as well.

"Well, we can still look at the bright side," I said with desperation.

"What bright side?"

I wondered about that myself as I furiously thought out loud.

"The bright side, yes, there is always a bright side. Like for instance—we are well away from Bit O' Heaven and our problems there. All set for a new start."

"At the bottom of the pile? As slaves?"

"Correct! From here the only direction we can go is up!"

His lips twitched in the slightest smile at this desperate sally and I hurried on.

"For example—they searched us and took away everything we had on us. Every item except one. I still have a little souvenir in my shoe from my trip to jail. This." I held up the lockpick and his smile widened. "And it works—

see." I opened my paincuff and showed it to him, then snapped it back into place. "So when we are ready to leave—we leave!"

By this time the grin had widened into a full smile. He reached out and seized my shoulder in a grip of true comradeship. "How right you are," he beamed. "We shall be good slaves—for a time. Just long enough to learn the ropes of this society, the chain of command and how to penetrate it, what the sources of wealth are and how to acquire them. As soon as I determine where the chinks are in the structure of society here we shall become rats again. Not stainless steel ones, I am afraid, more of the furry, toothy kind."

"A rat by any other name is just as sweet. We will overcome!"

We had to leap aside then as the first of the crates was manhandled into the back of the cart, the fabric of its battered structure squeaking and groaning. When the last of the cases was aboard the loaders climbed in themselves. I was glad the light was so bad—I really did not want to look at them too closely. Three scruffy, dirty men, unshaven and dressed in rags. Unwashed too as my twitching nose quickly informed me. Then a fourth man heaved himself up, bigger and nastier than the others, although his garments were in slightly better shape. He glared down at us and I smelled trouble, in addition to the pong.

"You know who I am? I'm the Pusher. This is my bunch and you do what I say. The first thing I say is you, old man, take off that jacket. It'll look better on me than on you."

"Thank you for the suggestion, sir," The Bishop answered sweetly. "But I think I shall retain it."

I knew what he was doing and I hoped that I was up to it. There was little room to move about in and this thug was twice my size. I had time for one blow, no more, and it had to be a good one.

The brute roared in anger and started climbing over the crates. The terrified slaves scrambled out of his way. I scrambled aside too and he ignored me as he passed. Perfect. He was just clutching at The Bishop when I hit him in the back of the neck with my joined fists. There was a satisfactory thunk and he collapsed on top of the crate.

I turned to the slaves who were watching in wide-eyed silence.

"You just got a new pusher," I told them, and there were quick nods of agreement. I pointed to the nearest one. "What's my name?"

"Pusher," he answered instantly. "Just don't turn your back on that one when he comes to."

"Will you help me?"

His grin exposed blackened, broken teeth. "Won't help you fight. Warn you though if you don't beat us the way he did."

"No beating. You all help?"

All of them nodded agreement.

"Good. Then your first assignment will be to throw the old pusher out of this cart. I don't want to be too close when he comes to."

They did this with enthusiasm, and added a few kicks on their own initiative.

"Thank you, James, I appreciate the help," The Bishop said. "My thinking was that you would probably have to fight him sooner or later, so why not sooner, with myself as distraction. And our rise in this society has begun—for you have already climbed out of the basic slave category. Suffering satellites—what is that?"

I looked where he pointed and my eyes popped just as far out as his. It was a machine of some kind, that much was obvious. It was advancing slowly towards us, rattling and clanking and emitting fumes. The operator swivelled it about in front of the cart as his assistant jumped down and joined the two together. There was a jolt and we slowly got under way.

"Look closely, Jim, and remember," he said. "You are seeing something from the dawn of technology, long forgotten and lost in the midst of time. That landcar is powered by *steam*. It is a steamcar, as I live and breathe. You know, I am beginning to think that I will enjoy it here."

I was not as fascinated by neolithic machinery as he was. My thoughts were more on the deposed thug and what would happen when he came after me. I had to learn more about the ground rules—and quickly. I moved back to the other slaves, but before I could open conversation we clattered across a bridge and through a gate in a high wall. The driver of our steam chariot stopped and called out.

"Unload those here."

In my new persona as Pusher I supervised but did little to help. The last case was just dropped to the ground when one of my slaves called out to me.

"He's coming now—through the gate behind you!"

I turned quickly. He was right. The ex-pusher was there, scratched and bloody and red-faced with rage.

He bellowed as he attacked.

Chapter 20

The first thing that I did was run away from my attacker—who roared after me in hot pursuit. This was done not through fear, though I did have a certain amount of that, but from the need to get some space around me. As soon as I was well away from the cart I turned and tripped him so he sprawled full-length in the muck.

This drew a big laugh from the onlookers; I took a quick glance around while he was climbing to his feet. There were armed guards, more slaves—and the red-garbed Capo Doccia who had cleaned us out. An idea began to form—but before it took shape I had to move to save my life.

The thug was learning. No more wild rushing about. Instead he came slowly towards me, arms spread, fingers extended. If I allowed him a sweet embrace I would not emerge from it alive. I backed slowly, turning to face Capo Doccia, moved to one side, then stepped quickly forward. Seizing one of my attacker's outstretched hands in both of mine, pulling and falling backwards at the same time. My weight was just about enough to send him flying over me to sprawl full-length again.

I was on my feet at once—with the plan clear in my mind. An exhibition.

"That was the right arm," I called out loudly.

He was stumbling when he returned to the attack so I took a chance and called my shot.

"Right knee."

I used a flying kick to get him on the kneecap. This is quite painful and he screamed as he dropped. He was slower getting to his feet this time, but the hatred was still there. He was not going to stop until he was unconscious. Good. All the better for my demonstration of the art.

"Left arm."

I seized it and twisted it up behind his back, held it there, pushing hard. He was strong—and still fighting, trying to clutch me with his right hand, struggling to trip me. I got in first.

"Left leg," I shouted as I kicked hard on the back of his calf and he went down another time. I stepped back and looked towards Capo Doccia. I had his undivided attention.

"Can you kill as well as dance?" he asked.

"I can. But I chose not to." I was aware that my opponent had stood up, was swaying from side to side. I turned slightly so I could see him out of the corner of my eye. "What I prefer is to render him unconscious. That way I win the fight—and you still have a slave."

The thug's hands closed on my neck and he bubbled viciously. I was showing off and I knew it. But I had to provide a good performance for my audience. So, without looking at all, I slammed backwards with my bent arm. Sinking my elbow hard into his gut, in the center, just below the rib cage, in line with the elbows. Right into the nerve ganglion known as the solar plexus. His hands loosened and I stepped forward. Hearing the thud as he hit the ground. Out cold.

Capo Doccia signaled me to him, spoke when I was close.

"That is a new way to fight, offworlder. We make wagers on the ruffians here who battle with their fists, striking each other until the blood flows and one of them cannot go on."

"Fighting like that is crude and wasteful. To know where to strike and how to strike, that is an art."

"But your art is of no value against sharp steel," he said, half-pulling his sword. I had to tread carefully now or he would be chopping me up just to see what I could do.

"Bare hands cannot stand against one such as you who is a master of the blade." For all I knew he only used the thing to carve his roast, but flattery always helps. "However against an unskilled swordsman or knife-wielder the art has value."

He digested that, then called to the nearest guard. "You, take your knife to this one."

This was getting out of hand—but I could see no way to avoid the encounter now. The guard smiled and pulled a shining length of dagger from its sheath and stalked towards me. I smiled in return. He raised it over his head to stab down—not holding it pointed directly out before him like an experienced knife-fighter. I let him come on, unmoving until he struck.

Standard defense. Step inside the blow, take the impact of his wrist against my forearm. Seize the knife-wrist with hands, turn and twist. All of this done very fast.

The knife went one way, he went the other. I had to end this demonstration quickly before I was taking on clubs, guns, whatever the head thug felt like. I stepped closer to Capo Doccia and spoke in a quiet voice.

"These are offworld secrets of defense—and killing—that are unknown here on Spiovente. I do not wish to reveal more here. I am sure you do not wish slaves to learn dangerous blows like these. Let me show you what can be done without this raw audience. I can train your bodyguards in these skills. There are those who want to kill you. Think of your own security first."

It sounded like a lecture on traffic safety to me, but it seemed to make sense to him. But he wasn't completely convinced.

"I do not like new things, new ways. I like things as they are."

Right, with him on top and the rest in chains below. I talked fast.

"What I do is not new—but as old as mankind. Secrets that have been passed on in secret since the dawn of time. Now these secrets can be yours. Change is on the way, you know that, and knowledge is strength. When others seek to take what you have, any weapon is useful to defeat them."

It sounded like nonsense to me—but I hoped that it made sense to him. From what The Bishop had told me about this garbage world, the only security was in strength—paranoia paid off. At least it had him thinking, which from the narrowness of his forehead was something he probably found hard to do. He turned on his heel and walked away.

Politeness, like soap, was also unknown on this planet. No "see you later" or "let me think about that." It took me a few moments to realize that the audience was over. The disarmed guard was glaring at me and rubbing his wrist. But he had put the dagger away. Since I had talked with Capo Doccia I now had some status, so he wouldn't knife me without reason. Which left my first protagonist, the ex-Pusher. He was sitting up dizzily when I approached. He looked up at me, blinking and befuddled. I tried to look my meanest when I spoke.

"That is two times you have come at me. You will not do it a third time. Third time means out in my ball game. You will die if you try anything ever again."

The hatred was still there in his face—but there was fear as well. I stepped forward and he cringed back. Good enough. As long as I didn't turn my back on him very often. I turned it now and stalked away.

He shambled after me and joined the waiting gang of slaves. He seemed to have accepted his demotion, as had the others. There were a few black looks in his direction but no more violence. Which was fine by me. It is one thing to work out in the gym—but something totally different here mixing with these heavies really trying to kill me. The Bishop beamed his congratulations.

"Well done, Jim, well done."

"And all very tiring. What next?"

"From what I could discover this little group is off duty, so to speak, having worked during the night."

"Then rest and food are in order. Lead on."

I suppose it could be called food. About the only good thing I could say about it was that it was not as repulsive as the Venian cooking aboard the spacer. A large and exceedingly filthy pot was seething over a fire to the rear of the building. The chef—if one dared use that term for this repulsive individual, as filthy as his pot—was stirring the contents with a long wooden spoon. The slaves each took a wooden bowl from the dripping pile on the table close by and these were filled by the cook. There was no worry about lost or broken cutlery because there wasn't any. Everyone dipped and shoveled with their fingers, so I did the same. It was vegetable gruel of some kind, pretty tasteless, but filling. The Bishop sat next to me on the ground, back to the wall, and slowly ate his. I finished first and had no difficulty in restraining a desire for a second serving.

"How long do we stay slaves?" I asked.

"Until I learn more about how things operate here. You have spent your entire life on a single planet, so both consciously and unconsciously you accept the society you know as the only one. Far from it. Culture is an invention of mankind, just like the computer or the fork. There is a difference though. While we are willing to change computers or eating instruments, the inhabitants of this culture will brook no changes at all. They believe that theirs is the only and unique way to live—and anything else an aberration."

"Sounds stupid."

"It is. But as long as you know that, and they don't, you can step outside the rules or bend them for your own benefit. Right now I'm finding out what the rules are here."

"Try not to take too long."

"I promise not to since I am not that comfortable myself. I must determine if vertical mobility exists and how it is organized. If there is no vertical mobility, we will just have to manufacture it."

"You have lost me. Vertical what?"

"Mobility. In terms of class and culture. Take for example these slaves and the guards outside. Can a slave aspire to be a guard? If he can, then there is vertical mobility. If he cannot, this is a stratified society and horizontal mobility is all that can be accomplished."

"Such as becoming top slave and kicking all other slaves?"

He nodded. "You have it, Jim. We shall cease being slaves as soon as my studies show how that is possible. But first we need some rest. You will observe that the others are now asleep on the straw to the rear of this noisome building. I suggest we join them."

"Agreed. . . ."

"You, get over here."

It was Tars Tukas. And of course he was pointing at me. I had a feeling that it was going to be a very long day.

At least I was seeing more of the sights. We crossed the courtyard, scene of my triumphs, and up a flight of stone steps. There was an armed guard here and two more inside lolling about on a wooden bench. A bit more luxury too. Woven mats on the floors, chairs, and tables, a few bad portraits on the wall, some with a rough resemblance to Capo Doccia. I was hustled right along into a large room with windows that faced out over the outer wall. I could see fields and trees and little else. Capo Doccia was there, along with a small band of men, all drinking from metal cups. They were well dressed, if multicolored leather trousers and billowing shirts and long swords is your idea of well dressed. Capo Doccia waved me over.

"You, come here and let us look at you."

The others turned with interest and eyed me like an animal on auction.

"And he actually knocked the other one down without using his fists?" One of them said. "He is so weak and puny, not to mention ugly."

There are times when the mouth should be opened only to put in food. This was probably one of them. But I was tired, fed up with my lot, and generally in a foul temper. Something snapped.

"Not as weak, puny or ugly as you, you pig's git."

This got his attention all right. He howled with instant anger, turned bright red—then drew a long steel blade and rushed at me.

I had little time to think, less time to act. One of the other dandies was standing close by, his metal drinking mug held loosely. I grabbed it from him, turned, and threw the contents in the attacking man's face.

Most of it missed, but enough dripped down onto his clothes to infuriate him even more. He slashed down with his sword and I caught the blow on the mug, diverting it. Letting the mug slide up along the blade into his fingers, grabbing and twisting his sword arm at the same time.

He howled nicely and the sword clattered to the floor. After this he was turned sideways, nicely exposed for a finishing kick to the back.

Except someone tripped me from behind at that moment and I went sprawling.

Chapter 21

They thought this very amusing because their laughter was all I could hear. When I scrambled for the fallen blade one of them kicked it aside. Things were not looking too good. I couldn't fight them all. I had to get out.

It was too late. Two of them knocked me to the ground from behind and another one kicked me in the side. Before I could get up my sword-wielding opponent was on top of me, kneeling on my chest and drawing an exceedingly ugly dagger with a wavery edge.

"What is this creature, Capo Doccia," he called out, holding my chin with his free hand, the dagger close to my throat.

"An offworlder," Capo Doccia said. "They threw him off the spacer."

"Is it valuable, worth anything?"

"I don't know," Capo Doccia said, looking down at me bemusedly. "Perhaps. But I don't like its fancy offplanet tricks. They don't belong here. Oh, kill it and be done."

I had not moved during this interesting exchange because I had some obvious interest in its outcome. I moved now.

The knife-wielder screamed as I twisted his arm—breaking it I hope—and grabbed the dagger as his fingers flew open. I held on to him as I jumped to my feet, then pushed him into the midst of his companions. They were behind me as well, but they fell back as I swept the dagger about in a circle. Moving after it, running before they could get their own weapons out. Running for my life.

The only direction I knew, back down the stairs. Bumping into Tars Tukas and rendering him unconscious as I passed.

Roars and shouts of anger sounded behind me and I wasted no time even glancing their way. Down the stairs, three at a time, towards the guards at the entrance. They were still scrambling to their feet when I plowed into them and we all went down. I kneed one under the chin as we fell, grabbing his gun by the barrel as I did this. The other was struggling to point his weapon at me when I caught him in the side of the head with the one I was holding.

The running feet were right behind me as I charged through the door, right at the surprised guard. He drew his sword but before he could use it he was unconscious. I dropped the dagger and seized his more lethal sword and ran on. The gate we had entered by was ahead. Wide open.

And well-guarded by armed men who were already raising their guns. I angled off towards the slave building as they fired. I don't know where their shots went but I was still alive as I turned the corner.

One knife, one gun, one very tired Jim diGriz. Who did not dare stop or even slow down. The outer wall was ahead—with scaffolding and a ladder leaning against it where masons were making repairs. I screeched and waved my weapons and the workmen dived in all directions. I went up the ladders as fast as I could. Noticing that bullets were striking the wall on all sides of me, chips of stone flying.

Then I was on top of the wall, fighting for breath, chancing a look behind me for the first time.

Dropping to my face as the massed gunmen below fired a volley that parted the air just above my head. Capo Doccia and his court had left the pursuit to the guards and were standing behind them cursing and waving their weapons. Very impressive. I pulled my head back as they fired again.

Other guards were climbing up to the wall and moving towards me. Which really did limit my choices a bit. I looked over the outside of the wall at the brown surface of the water that lay at its base. Some choice!

"Jim, you must learn to do something about your big mouth," I said, then took a deep breath and jumped.

Splashed—and stuck. The water was just up to my neck and I was stuck in the soft mud that had broken my fall. I struggled against it, pulling out one foot, then the other, struggling against its gluey embrace as I waded to the far bank. My pursuers weren't in sight yet—but they would surely be right behind me. All I could do was keep moving. Crawling up the grassy bank, still clutching my purloined weapons, then staggering into the shelter of the trees ahead. And still no sign of the armed guards. They should be across the bridge and after me by this time. I couldn't believe my good luck.

Until I fell headlong, screaming as the pain washed over me. Pain unbelievable, blotting out sight, sound, senses.

Then it stopped and I brushed the tears of agony from my eyes. The paincuff—I had forgotten all about it. Tars Tukas had regained consciousness and was thumbing the control button. What had he said? Leave it on long enough and it blocks all the nerves, kills. I grabbed at my shoe and the lockpick concealed there as the pain struck again.

When it stopped this time I was almost too weak to move my fingers. As I fumbled with the pick I realized that they were sadists and I should be grateful for the fact. With the button held down I was good as dead. But someone, undoubtedly Capo Doccia, wanted me both to suffer and to know that there was no way out. The key was in the lock when pain consumed me one more time.

When it stopped I was lying on my side, the lockpick fallen from my fingers, unable to move.

But I had to move. Another wave of agony like that and it would be all over for me. I would lie in these woods until I died. My fingers trembled, moved. The pick crept towards the tiny opening of the lock, moved in, twisted feebly. . . .

It took a very long time for the red mists to clear from my vision, the agony to seep out of my body. I could not move, felt I would never stir again. I had to blink the tears away when I could see. See the most beautiful sight in the world.

The open paincuff lying on the moldy leaves.

Only my captor's knowledge that the pain machine led to certain death had saved my life. The searchers were in no hurry; I could hear them talking as they moved through the woods towards me.

". . . somewhere in here. Why don't they just leave him?"

"Leave a good blade and a shooter? No chance of that. And Capo Doccia wants to hang the body up in the courtyard until it rots. Never saw him that angry."

Life slowly returned to my paralyzed body. I moved off the animal track I had been following and pulled myself into the shelter of the low shrubbery, reaching out to straighten out the grass. And not too soon.

"Look—he came out of the water here. Went along this path."

Heavy footsteps approached and went by. I clutched my weapons and did the only thing possible. Lay quiet and waited for my strength to return.

This was, I must admit, a bit of a low point in my life. Friendless, alone, still throbbing with pain, exhausted, hunted by armed men just dying to kill me, thirsty. . . . It was quite a list. About the only thing that hadn't happened so far was getting rained on.

It started to rain.

There are high and low points in emotion when there is no room for excess. To love one so much it would be impossible to love any more. I think. Never having had any personal experience in that. But I had plenty of experience in being in the pits. Where I was now. I could sink no lower or get no more depressed. It was the rain that did it. I began to chuckle—then grabbed my mouth so I wouldn't laugh out loud. Then the laughter died away as my anger grew. This was no way to treat a mean and nasty stainless steel rat! Now in danger of getting rusty.

I moved my legs and had to stifle a groan. The pain was still there but the anger rode it down. I clutched the gun and stuck the sword into the ground, then pulled myself to my feet by grabbing the branches of the tree with my free hand. Grabbed up the sword again and stood there, swaying. But not falling. Until I was finally able to stagger off, one step at a time, away from the searchers and Capo Doccia's criminal establishment.

The forest was quite extensive and I moved along game paths for an unmeasurable length of time. I had left the searchers far behind, I was sure of that. So when the forest thinned and ended I leaned against a tree to catch my breath and looked out at the tilled field. It was time to find my way back to the haunts of man. Where there were plows there were ploughboys. They shouldn't be too hard to find. When a certain measure of strength had returned I staggered off along the edge of the field, ready to fall into the forest at the sight of armed men. I was very pleased to see the farmhouse first. It was low to the ground, thatched, and windowless—at least on this side. It had a chimney from which there rose a thin trickle of smoke. No need for heating in this balmy climate—so this must be a cooking fire. Food.

At the thought of food my neglected stomach began to churn, rumble, and complain. I felt the same way. Food and drink were next in order. And what better place to find them than at this isolated farm? The question was the answer. I stumbled across the furrows to the back of the house, worked my way around the side to the front. No one. But there were voices coming from the open doorway, laughter—and the smell of cooking. Yum! I sauntered into the open, along the front and through the front door.

"Hi, folks. Look who has come to dinner."

There were a half-dozen of them grouped around the scrubbed wood table. Young and old, thick and thin. All with the same expression on their faces. Jaw-dropped astonishment. Even the baby stopped crying and aped its elders. A grizzled oldster broke the spell, scrambling to his feet in such a hurry his three-legged stool tumbled over.

"Welcome, your honor, welcome." He tugged his forelock as he bowed to show how grateful he was for my presence. "How may we aid you, honored sir?"

"If you could spare a bit of food . . ."

"Come! Sit! Dine! We have but humble fare but willingly share it. Here!"

He straightened his stool and waved me to it. The others scampered away from the table so I wouldn't be disturbed. Either they were discerning judges of human nature and knew what a sterling fellow I was—or they had seen the sword and gun. A wooden plate was filled from the pot hung over the fire and put before me. Life here was a cut above the slave pens for I was also supplied with a wooden spoon. I tucked in with a great deal of pleasure. It was a vegetable stew, with the occasional shard of meat, garden fresh of course, and tasted wonderful. There was cool water to drink out of a clay cup and I could have asked for nothing more. While I shoveled it all into my face I was aware of low whispering from the farmers gathered at the far end of the room. I doubted if they were planning anything violent. Nevertheless I kept one eye on them, and my hand not far from the hilt of the sword laid out on the table.

When I had finished and belched loudly—they buzzed warmly at this gustatory approval—the old man detached himself from the group and shuffled forward. He pushed before him a shock-headed youth who looked to be about my age.

"Honored sir, may I speak with you?" I waved agreement and belched again. He smiled at this and nodded. "Ahh, you are kind enough to flatter the cook. Since you are obviously a man of good wit and humor, intelligent and handsome, as well as being a noted warrior, permit me to put a small matter to you."

I nodded again; flattery will get you everywhere.

"This is my third son, Dreng. He is strong and willing, a good worker. But our holding is small and there are many mouths to feed, as well as giving half of what we produce to the so-wonderful Capo Doccia for our protection."

He had his head lowered when he said this, but there were both submission and hatred in his voice. I imagine the only one that Capo Doccia protected them from was Capo Doccia. He pushed Dreng forward and squeezed his bicep.

"Like rock, sir, he is very strong. His ambition has always been to be a mercenary, like your kind self. A man of war, armed and secure, selling his services to the gentry. A noble calling. And one which would enable him to bring a few groats home to his family."

"I'm not in the recruiting business."

"Obviously, honored sir! If he went as a pikeman with Capo Doccia, there would be no pay or honor, only an early death."

"True, true," I agreed, although I had heard this fact for the first time. The old boy's train of thought wandered a bit, which was fine by me since I was getting an education into life on Spiovente. Didn't sound nice at all. I sipped some more water and tried to summon up another burp to please the cook, but could not. Old dad was still talking.

"Every warrior, such as yourself, should have a knave to serve him. Dare I ask—we have looked outside and you are alone—what happened to your knave?"

"Killed in battle," I improvised. He looked dumbfounded at this and I realized that knaves weren't supposed to fight. "When the enemy overran our camp." That was better, nodded agreement to this. "Of course I killed the blackguard who butchered poor Smelly. But that's what war is about. A rough trade."

All of my audience murmured understandingly, so I hadn't put a foot wrong so far. I signaled to the youth.

"Step forward, Dreng, and speak for yourself. What is your age?"

He peered out from under his long hair and stammered an answer. "I'll be four, come next Wormfeast Day."

I wanted no details of this repulsive holiday. He was sure big for his age. Or this planet had a very long year. I nodded and spoke.

"A good age for a knave. Now tell me, do you know what the knavely duties are?" He better, because I certainly didn't. He nodded enthusiastically at my question.

"That I do, sir, that I do. Old Kvetchy used to be a soldier, told me all about it many a time. Polish the sword and gun, fetch the food from the fire, fill the water bottle, crack the lice with stones . . ."

"Fine, great, I can see you know it all. Down to the last repulsive detail. In exchange for your services you expect me to teach you the trade of war." He nodded quick agreement. The room was hushed as I pondered my decision.

"Right then, let us do it."

A bucolic cry of joy echoed from the thatch and old dad produced a crock of what could only be home brew. Things were looking up for me, ever so slightly, but certainly looking up.

Chapter 22

Work appeared to have ceased for the day with the announcement of Dreng's new job. The home brew was pretty awful stuff, but obviously contained a fair measure of alcohol. Which seemed like a good idea at the time. I drank enough to kill the pain, then slacked off before I ended up drunk on the floor like the rest of them. I waited until old dad was well on the way to alcoholic extinction before I pumped him for information.

"I have traveled from afar and am ignorant of the local scene." I told him. "But I do hear that this local bully, Capo Doccia, is a little on the rough side."

"Rough!" he growled, then slurped down some more of the paint thinner. "Poisonous serpents flee in fear when he approaches, while it is well-known that the gaze of his eyes kills infants."

There was more like this, but I turned off my attention. I had waited too long in the drinking session to extract any reasonable information from him. I looked around for Dreng and found him just tucking into a great crock of the brew. I pried it away from him, then shook him until I attracted his attention.

"Let's go. We're leaving now."

"Leaving . . . ?" He blinked rapidly and tried to focus his eyes on me. With little success.

"We. Go. Out. Walkies."

"Ahh, walkies. I get my blanket." He stood swaying, then gave me some more rapid blinks. "Where's your blanket for me to carry?"

"Seized by the enemy, along with everything else I possessed other than my sword and gun, which never leave my side while I have a breath in my body."

"Breath in body . . . Right. I'll get blanket. Get you blanket."

He rooted about in the rear of the room and appeared with two fuzzy blankets, despite a lot of domestic and female crying about the cold of winter. Capital goods were not easy to come by for the peasantry. I would have to get some groats for Dreng eventually.

He reappeared with the blankets draped over his shoulders along with a leather bag, a stout staff in his hand—and a wicked-looking knife in a wooden scabbard at his waist. I waited outside to avoid the tearful traditional departure scene. He eventually emerged, looking slightly more sober, and stood swaying at my side.

"Lead on, master."

"You show me the way. I want to visit Capo Doccia's keep."

"No! Can it be true that you fight for him?"

"That is the last thing I would ever do. In fact I would fight against him for a wooden groat. The truth is that the Capo has a friend of mine locked away in there. I want to get a message to him."

"There is great danger in even going close to his keep."

"I'm sure of it, but I am fearless. And I must contact my friend. You lead the way—and through the woods if you don't mind. I don't want to be seen by either Capo Doccia or his men."

Obviously neither did Dreng. He sobered up as he led me by obscure paths and hidden ways to the other side of the forest. I peered out carefully at the roadway leading to the drawbridge, to the entrance to the keep.

"Any closer and they will see us," he whispered. I looked up at the late afternoon sun and nodded agreement.

"It's been a busy day. We'll lay up in the woods here and make our move in the morning."

"No move. It's death!" His teeth chattered though the afternoon was hot. He hurried as he led the way deeper into the forest, to a grassy hollow with a stream running through it. He produced a clay cup from his bag, filled it with water and brought it to me. I slurped and realized that having a knave wasn't a bad idea after all. Once his chores were done he spread the blankets on the grass and promptly fell asleep on his. I sat down with my back to a tree and, for the first time, had a chance to examine the gun I had lifted.

It was sleek and new and did not fit this broken-down planet at all. Of course—it had to be from the Venian ship. The Bishop said that they had probably been smuggling weapons. And I was holding one of them in my hands. I looked at it more closely.

No identification, or serial number—or any other indication where it had been manufactured. And it was pretty obvious why. If the League agents succeeded in getting their hands on one of these it would be impossible to trace it back to the planet of origin. The gun was small in size, about halfway between a rifle and a pistol. I can claim some acquaintance with small arms—I am an honored member of the Pearly Gates Gun Club and Barbecue Society because I am a pretty good shot and helped them win tournaments—but I had never seen anything like this before. I looked into the muzzle. It was about .30 caliber, and unusually enough it was a smooth bore. It had open, iron sights, a trigger with safety button, one other lever on the stock. I turned this and the gun broke in half and a handful of small cartridges fell to the ground. I looked at one closely and began to understand how the gun worked.

"Neat. No lands or grooves so there is no worry about keeping the barrel clean. Instead of rotating, the bullet has fins to keep it in straight flight. And, uggh, make a nastier hole in anyone it hits. And no cartridge case either—this is solid propellent. Does away with all the worries about ejecting the brass." I peeked into the chamber. "Efficient and foolproof. Push your cartridges into the recessed stock. When it's full put one more into the chamber. Close and lock. A little solar screen here to keep a battery charged. Pull the trigger, a spot in the chamber glows hot and ignites the charge. The expanding gas shoots out the bullet—while part of the gas is diverted to ram the next bullet into the chamber. Rugged, almost foolproof, cheap to make. And deadly."

Depressed and tired, I lay the gun beside me, dropped the sword close to hand, lay back on the blanket and followed Dreng's good example.

By dawn we were slept out and slightly hungover. Dreng brought me water, then handed over a strip of what looked like smoked leather. He took one himself and began chewing on it industriously. Breakfast in bed—the greatest! I bit my piece and almost broke a tooth. It not only resembled smoked leather, but tasted exactly like it as well.

By the time that the drawbridge clanked down for the day we were lying in a copse on the hill above it, as close as we could get. It was the nearest cover that we could find since, for pretty obvious reasons, all the trees and shrubs had been cleared away from the approaches to the gate. It wasn't as near as I liked, but would have to do. But it was far too close for Dreng for I could feel him shivering at my side. The first thing to emerge from the gate was a small body of armed men, followed by four slaves dragging a cart.

"What's going on?" I asked.

"Tax collecting. Getting in their share of the crops."

"We've now seen who comes out—but do any of your farmers ever go in?"

"Madness and death! Never!"

"What about selling them food."

"They take all they want from us."

"Do you sell them firewood?"

"They steal what they need."

They had a pretty one-sided economy, I thought gloomily. But I had to come up with something—I just couldn't leave The Bishop as a slave in this dismal place. My cogitation was interrupted by a commotion inside the gate. Then, as though my thoughts had coalesced into reality, a figure burst out of the gate, knocking aside the guard there, rushing on.

The Bishop!

Running fast. But right behind him were the pursuing guards.

"Take this and follow me!" I shouted, jamming the hilt of the sword into Dreng's hand. Then I was off down the slope as fast as I could go, shouting to draw their attention. They ignored me until I fired a shot over their heads.

Things got pretty busy after that. The guards slowed, one even dived to the ground and put his hands over his head. The Bishop pelted on—but one of his pursuers was right behind him, swinging a long pike. Catching The Bishop on the back and knocking him down. I fired again as I ran, jumped over The Bishop and felled the pikeman with the butt of my gun.

"Up the hill!" I called out when I saw that The Bishop was struggling to his feet, blood all over his back. I banged off two more shots, then turned to help him. And saw that Dreng was clutching the sword—but still lying on top of the hill.

"Get down here and help him or I'll kill you myself!" I shouted, turning and firing again. I hadn't hit anyone but I was sure keeping their heads down. The Bishop stumbled on and Dreng, having plumbed some deep well of decency—or in fear that I would kill him—was coming to our aid. Shots were whistling past us now so I spun and returned their fire.

We reached the top of the low hill, went over it towards the relative safety of the woods. Dreng and I half carried the great form of The Bishop as he stumbled and staggered. I took a quick—and reassuring—look at his back. There was a shallow cut there, nothing too bad. Our pursuers were still not in sight when we crashed through the bushes and reached the safety of the trees.

"Dreng—lead us out of here. They mustn't catch us now!"

Surprisingly enough they didn't. The farm lad must have played in these woods for all of his young life because he knew every track and path. But it was hard work. We staggered on, then struggled our way along a steep grassy slope with a few miserable bushes halfway up. Dreng pulled the bushes aside to reveal the entrance to a shallow cave.

"Chased a Furry in here once. No one else knows about it."

The entrance was low and it was a labor to pull The Bishop through. But once inside, the cave opened out and there was more than enough space to sit up, although it wasn't high enough to stand. I took one of the blankets and spread it out, then rolled The Bishop onto it so that he lay on his side. He groaned. His face was filthy and bruised. He had not an easy time of it. Then he looked towards me and smiled.

"Thank you, my boy. I knew you would be there."

"You did? That's more than I knew."

"Nonsense. But, quickly please, the . . ."

He writhed and moaned and his body arched into the air with unbearable pain. The paincuff—I had forgotten about it! And it was receiving a continuous signal, certain death.

Haste makes waste. So I controlled my anxiety and slowly slipped off my right shoe, opened the compartment, and seized the lockpick firmly in my fingers. Bent over, inserted it—and the cuff sprang open. Pain lanced through my hand, numbing it, as I threw the thing aside.

The Bishop was unconscious and breathing heavily. There was nothing more I could do except sit and wait.

"Your sword," Dreng said, holding it out to me.

"You take care of it for awhile. If you think you are up to it?"

He lowered his eyes and trembled again. "I want to be a fighter, but I am so afraid. I could not move to help you."

"But you did—finally. Remember that. There isn't a person alive who has not been afraid at one time or another. It is only the brave man who can feel fear and still go forward."

"A noble thought, young man," the deep voice said. "And one that you should always remember."

The Bishop had regained consciousness and was smiling a wan smile.

"Now, Jim, as I was saying before they turned on their little machine, I was certain that you would be here this morning. You were free—and I knew that you would not leave me alone in that wicked place. There was an immense hue and cry when you escaped, with abundant to-ing and fro-ing until the gate was closed for the night. It was obvious that it would be impossible for you to come then. But with dawn the gate would be opened and I had not the slightest doubt that you were sure to be close by, trying to find a way to get to me. Simple logic. So I simplified the equation by coming to you."

"Very simple! You almost got yourself killed."

"But I didn't. And we are both safely away from them. Plus I see that you have managed to enlist an ally. A good day's work. Now the important question. What do we do next?"

What indeed?

Chapter 23

"As to what we do next—the answer is obvious," I said. "We stay here until the excitement has died down. Which should happen fairly quickly since there is not much market value in a dead slave."

"But I feel remarkably healthy."

"You have forgotten that the paincuff will kill if used continuously. So, when our way is clear we head for the nearest habitation and dress your wound."

"It is bloody, but can't be more than a scratch."

"Sepsis and infection. We take care of the cut first." I turned to Dreng. "Any farmers you know who live close to this place?"

"No, but the widow Apfeltree is just over the hill, past the dead tree, through the end of the swamp. . . ."

"Great. Show us the way, don't tell." I turned back to The Bishop. "And after we fix your back, then what?"

"After that, Jim, we join the army. Since you are now a mercenary, that is the proper thing to do. An army will be based in a keep, and there will be a locked room in that keep where all the groats are stored. While you practice your military profession I shall, as the expression goes, case the joint. In order to further this noble work of ours I have one particular army in mind for you. The one that serves the Capo Dimonte."

"Not Capo Dimonte!" Dreng wailed, clutching his hair with both hands. "He is evil beyond measure, eats a child for breakfast every day, has all of his furniture upholstered in human skin, drinks from the skull of his first wife . . ."

"Enough," The Bishop ordered, and Dreng was stilled. "It is obvious that he does not have a good press here in the Capote of Doccia. That is because he is the sworn enemy of Capo Doccia and goes to war against him periodically. I am sure that he is no worse—or better—than any other capo. But he does have one advantage. He is our enemy's enemy."

"So hopefully our friend. Right. I owe old Doccia one and I look forward to paying it back."

"You should not bear grudges, Jim. It dulls the vision and interferes with your career. Which should now be grabbing groats not wreaking vengeance."

I nodded agreement. "Of course. But while you are planning the heist there is no reason why I can't enjoy a bit of revenge."

I could see that he disapproved of my emotions—but I could not attain his Olympian detachment. A weakness of youth, perhaps. I changed the subject.

"After we empty the treasury, then what?"

"We find out how the locals are contacting the offplanet smugglers, like the Venians. With the obvious aim of leaving this backward and deadly world as soon as possible. In order to do that we may have to get religion." He chuckled at my shocked expression. "Like you, my boy, I am a Scientific Humanist and feel no need for the aid of the supernatural. But here on Spiovente what technology there is seems to be in the hands of an order called the Black Monks. . . ."

"No, stay away!" Dreng wailed; he was certainly a source of bad news. "They know Things that Drive Men Mad. From their workshops all forms of unnatural devices pour forth. Machines that scream and grunt, that talk through the skies, the paincuffs as well. Avoid them, master, I beg of you!"

"What our young friend has decried is true," The Bishop said. "Minus the fear of the unknown, of course. Through some process that is not relevant now all of technology on this world became concentrated in the hands of this order, the Black Monks. I have no idea what their religious affiliations are—if any—but they do supply and repair the machines that we have seen. This gives them a certain protection, since if one capo were to attack them the others would rush to their defense to insure their continued access to the metallic fruits of technology. It is to them that we may have to turn for salvation and exodus."

"I second the motion and it is carried by acclamation. Join the army, whip as many groats as we can, contact the smugglers—and buy our way out."

Dreng gaped at all the long words, drooling a bit at the same time. He obviously followed little of what we discussed. Action was more his style. He made a silent exit on a scouting trip and an even more slithery return. No one was about, our way was clear. The Bishop could walk now, with a little aid from us, and the widow's house was not too distant. Even with Dreng's reassurances she was trembling with fear when she admitted us to her hovel.

"Guns and swords. Murder and death. I'm doomed, doomed."

Despite her muttering, punctuated by the smacking of her toothless gums, she followed my instructions and put a pot of water over the fire. I cut a strip of cloth from my blanket, boiled it clean, then used it to wash The Bishop's wound. It was shallow but deep. The widow was persuaded to part with some of her store of moonshine and The Bishop shuddered, but did not cry out, when I poured it into the open cut. Hoping the alcohol content was high enough to act as an antiseptic. I used more boiled blanket as a bandage—which was about all that I could do.

"Excellent, James, excellent," he said, gingerly pulling his sliced jacket over his shoulders. "Your years in the Boy Sprouts were obviously not wasted. Now let us thank the good widow and leave since it is obvious that she is upset by our presence."

Leave we did, strolling the open, rut-filled road, every footstep taking us farther away from Capo Doccia. Dreng was a good provider, drifting off into orchards for fruit, or rooting out edible tubers from the fields we passed, even digging them up under the noses of the rightful owners. Who only touched their forelocks at the sight of my weapons. It is a nasty world that only respects bullies. For the first time I began to appreciate the better qualities of the League worlds.

It was late afternoon when the walls of the keep loomed before us. This place had a little more style than Doccia's, or at least it looked that way from a distance, because it was situated on an island in a lake. A causeway and drawbridge connected it to the mainland. Dreng was shaking with fear again and was more than happy to stay on the shore with The Bishop while I braved the dangers of the keep. I strode militarily along the stone causeway, then stamped over the bridge. The two guards eyed me with open suspicion.

"Good morn, brothers," I called out cheerfully, gun on shoulder, sword in hand, gut in and chest out. "Is this the establishment of the Capo Dimonte, known the length and breadth of the land for his charm and strength of arm?"

"Who wants to know?"

"I do. An armed and powerful soldier who wishes to enlist in his noble service."

"Your choice, brother, your choice," he said with obvious gloom. "Through the gate, across the courtyard, third door on your right, ask for Sire Srank." He leaned close and whispered. "For three groats I'll give you a tip."

"Done."

"So pay."

"Shortly. I'm a little skint right now."

"You must be—if you want to hire out to this lot. All right, five then, in five days." I nodded agreement. "He'll offer you very little, but don't settle for less than two groats a day."

"Thanks for the credit. I'll get back to you."

I swaggered through the gate and found the right door. It was open to admit the last light, and a fat man with a bald head was scratching away at some papers. He looked up when my shadow fell across the table.

"Get out here," he shouted, scratching his head so hard that a shower of dandruff sparkled in the sunbeam. "I've told you all, no groats until morning after next."

"I've not enlisted yet—nor will I if that's the way you pay the troops."

"Sorry, good stranger, sun in my eyes. Come in, come in. Enlist? Of course. Gun and sword—and ammunition?"

"Some."

"Wonderful." His hands rustled when he dry-washed them. "Food for you and your knave and a groat a day."

"Two a day and all ammunition used to be replaced."

He scowled—then shrugged and scratched one of the sheets and pushed it over to me. "A one-year enlistment, salary open to review at end of contract. Since you can't read or write I hope you can manage to scratch your illiterate X down here."

"I can read so well I see that you have me down for four years, which I will now correct before I sign." Which I did, writing Judge Nixon's name on the line, knowing full well that I would be leaving well before my enlistment was up. "I'll get my knave who awaits without, along with my aged father."

"No extra food for poor relations!" he snarled generously. "You share yours."

"Agreed," I said. "You're all heart."

I went back to the gate and waved my companions over.

"You owe me," the guard said.

"I'll pay you—when that scrofulous toad pays me."

He grunted agreement. "If you think he's bad—wait until you meet Capo Dimonte. I wouldn't be hanging around this damp dump if it weren't for the loot bonus."

They were coming on slowly, The Bishop half dragging the reluctant Dreng.

"Loot bonus? Paying out soon?"

"Soon as the fighting is over. We march tomorrow."

"Against Capo Doccia?"

"No such luck. The word is that he is loaded with jewels and golden groats and more. Be nice to share in that haul. But not this time. All they have told us is that we are heading north. Must be a surprise attack on someone, probably a friend, and they don't want word to leak out. That's good thinking. Catch them with their drawbridge down and it's half the battle."

I pondered this bit of military wisdom as I led my small band in the indicated direction. The soldier's quarters, while not something to put in a travel brochure, were certainly a cut above the slave quarters. Wooden bunks with straw mattresses for the fighting men—some straw under the bunk for the knave. I would have to make some arrangements for The Bishop, but I was sure that bribery would take care of that. We sat together on the bunk while Dreng went to find the kitchen.

"How is the back?" I asked.

"Sore, but only a small bother. I'll take a bit of a rest, then begin a survey of the layout. . . ."

"In the morning will be time enough. It has been a long couple of days."

"Agreed. And here is your knave with the food!"

It was a hot stew with fragments of some nameless bird bobbing in it. Had to be a bird; the feathers were still attached. We divided the stew into three equal portions and wolfed it down. All this fresh air and walking was certainly good for the appetite. There was also a ration of sour wine which neither I nor The Bishop could stomach. Not so Dreng, who slurped and smacked his way through it in moments. Then rolled under the bunk and began to snore raucously.

"I'm going to have a look around," I said. "Take a rest on the bunk until I get back. . . ."

I was interrupted by an off-key blare on a bugle. I looked up to see that the malevolent musician was standing in the doorway. He emitted another toneless blast. I was ready to grab him by the throat if he tried it again, but he stepped aside and bowed. A thin figure in blue uniform took his place. All of the soldiers who were watching bowed their heads slightly or shook their weapons in salute, so I did the same. It could be no other than Capo Dimonte himself.

He was lean to the point of being hollow-stomached. He either had circulation trouble or was naturally blue of skin. His little red eyes peered out of hollow blue sockets, while he fingered his blue jaw with azure fingers. He looked around suspiciously, then spoke: for all of his leanness his voice had a deep strength to it.

"My men, I have good news for you. Prepare yourselves and your weapons for we march at midnight. This will be a forced march to enable us to reach Pinetta Woods before dawn. Fighting men only—and we travel light. Your knaves will stay here to look after your goods. We will lay up there during the day, then leave at dusk tomorrow. We will meet our allies during the night and join forces for an assault on the enemy at dawn."

"A question, Capo," one of the men called out. He was grizzled and scarred, obviously a veteran of many conflicts. "Against whom do we march?"

"You will be told before the attack. We will gain victory only by surprise."

There were murmurs on all sides as the veteran called out again.

"Our enemy a mystery—at least tell us then who are our allies."

Capo Dimonte was not pleased with the question. He scratched his chin and fiddled with the hilt of his sword while his audience waited. He obviously needed our voluntary assistance, so in the end he spoke.

"You will all be pleased to hear that we have allies of great strength and will. They also have war machines to batter the stoutest wall. With their assistance we can take any keep, defeat any army. We are lucky to serve at their side." He pressed his lips together, reluctant to go on but still knowing that he must.

"Our victory is assured since our allies are none other than . . . the order of the Black Monks."

There was a long moment of shocked silence—followed instantly by shouts of anger. The significance of all this escaped me—other than the fact that it did not sound good at all.

Chapter 24

As soon as he had spoken, Capo Dimonte made his exit and the door slammed shut behind him. There were shouts and cries of anger from all sides—but there was one man who bellowed louder than all the others. It was the scarred veteran. He climbed onto a table and shouted them all into silence.

"Everyone here knows me, knows old Tusker. I was cutting off heads when most of you weren't even potty trained. So I'm going to talk and you are going to listen and then you will get a chance to talk too. Anyone here don't like that idea?"

He closed one immense fist and held it out, then turned in a circle, scowling fiercely. There were some angry mutters, but none loud enough to imply disagreement.

"Good. Then listen. I know those black-frocked buggers from a long way back and I don't trust them. All they think of is their own hides. If they want us to fight for them that's only because there is big trouble ahead and they would like to see us killed rather than them. I don't like it."

"I don't like it either," another man called out. "But what kind of a choice do we have?"

"None," Tusker growled angrily. "And that's what I was going to say next. I think we have been grabbed by the short and curlies." He drew his sword and shook it at them. "Every weapon we have, outside of them new guns, comes from the Black Monks. Without their supplies we have nothing to fight with, and without nothing to fight with we have nothing to do and we can starve or go back to the farm. And that's not for me. And it better not be for any of you either. Because we are all in this together. We all fight—or none fight. And if we fight and any of you try to sneak out of here before the action starts, then he is going to find my sword stuck all the way through his liver."

He shook the shining blade at them while they glared in silence.

"A solid argument," The Bishop whispered, "the logic impeccable. Too bad that it is wasted on this ignoble cause. You and your comrades have no choice but to agree."

The Bishop was right. There was more shouting and argument, but in the end they had to go along with the plans. They would march at the side of the Black Monks. None of them, myself included, were very happy about the idea. They could stay up and argue until midnight but I was tired and could use the few hours sleep. The Bishop wandered out in search of information and I rolled up on the bunk and slipped into a restless slumber.

The shouted orders woke me, feeling more tired than when I had gone to sleep. No one seemed happy about the midnight march—or our battle companions—and there were dark looks and much cursing. There were even some oaths I hadn't heard before, real nice ones, that I filed away for future use. I went out to the primitive lavabo and threw cold water on my face, which seemed to help. When I returned, The Bishop was sitting on the bunk. He rose and extended his large hand.

"You must watch yourself, Jim. This is a crude and deadly world and all men's hands are turned against you."

"That is the way I prefer to live—so don't worry yourself."

"But I do." He sighed mightily. "I have nothing but contempt for superstition, astrologers, palm readers, and the like, so you will understand why I feel great disgust at myself for the black depression that possesses me. But I see nothing but darkness in the future, emptiness. We have been companions for such a brief period, I do not wish it to end. Yet, I am sorry, do excuse me, I have a sense of danger and despair that cannot be alleviated."

"With good reason!" I cried, trying to put enthusiasm into my words. "You have been torn from the security of your quasi-retirement, imprisoned, freed, fled, hid, dieted, fled again, bribed, were cheated, beaten, enslaved, wounded—and you wonder why you are depressed?"

This brought a wan smile to his lips and he grasped my hand again. "You are right. Jim, of course. Toxins in the bloodstream, depression in the cortex. Watch your back and return safely. By the time you do I'll have worked out how to relieve the capo of some of his groats."

He was looking his age—for the first time since we had met. As I left I saw him stretch out wearily on the bunk. He should be feeling better when I returned. Dreng would fetch his food and look after him. What I must do is concentrate on staying alive so I would come back.

It was a dreary and exhausting march. The day had been hot, and so was the night. We shuffled along, dripping with perspiration and slapping at the insects that rushed out of the darkness to attack us. The rutted road caught at my feet and dust rose into my nostrils. On we marched, and on, following along after the clanking and hissing conveyance that led our nightmarish parade. One of the steam cars was hauling Capo Dimonte's war wagon in which he traveled in relative comfort. His captains were in there with him, swilling down booze no doubt and generally enjoying themselves. We marched on, the cursing in the ranks growing steadily weaker.

By the time we stumbled under the sheltering trees of Pinetta Woods we were tired and mutinous. I did what most of the others did, dropped onto the bed of sweet-smelling needles under the trees and groaned in appreciation. And admiration for the sturdier warriors, with old Tusker in the van, who insisted on their ration of acid wine before retiring. I closed my eyes, groaned again, then slept.

We stayed there all day, glad to have the rest. Around noon rations were reluctantly handed out from the cart. Warm, foul water to wash down rock-like bits of what might have been bread. After this I managed to sleep some more, until we formed ranks again at dusk and the night march continued.

After some hours we came to a crossroads and turned right. There was a murmur through the ranks at this, starting with those who knew the area well.

"What are they saying?" I asked the man who marched beside me, in silence up until now.

"Capo Dinobli. That's who we're after. Could be no one else. No other keep in this direction for one day, two day's march."

"Do you know anything about him?"

He grunted and was silent, but the man behind him spoke up. "I served with him, long time ago. Old bugger then, must be ancient now. Just one more capo."

Then it was one foot after another in a haze of fatigue. There had to be better ways to make a living. This was going to be my first and last campaign. As soon as we returned I and The Bishop would sack the treasury and flee with all the groats we could carry. Wonderful thought. I almost ran into the man in front of me and stopped just in time. We had halted where the road passed near the forest. Against the darkness of the trees even darker shadows loomed. I was trying to see what they were when one of the officers came back down the ranks.

"I need some volunteers," he whispered. "You, you, you, you."

He touched my arm and I was one of the volunteers. There seemed to be about twenty of us who were pulled out of line and herded forward towards the woods. The clouds had cleared and there was enough light from the stars now to see that the black bulks were wheeled devices of some kind. I could hear the hiss of escaping steam. A dark figure strode forward and halted us.

"Listen and I will tell you what you must do," he said.

As he spoke a metal door was opened on the machine nearest us. Light gleamed as wood was pushed into the firebox. By the brief, flickering light I could see the speaker clearly. He was dressed in a black robe, his head covered by a cowl that hid his face. He pointed to the machine.

"This must be pushed through the woods—and in absolute silence. I will put my knife into the ribs of any of you who makes a noise. A track was cut during daylight and will be easy to follow. Take up the lines and do as you are instructed."

Other dark-robed figures were handing us the ropes and pushing us into line. On the whispered signal we began hauling.

The thing rolled along easily enough and we pulled at a steady pace. There were more whispered instructions to guide us—then we halted as we approached the edge of the forest. After this we dropped the ropes and sweated as we pushed and pulled the great weight about until the guides were satisfied. There was much whispered consultation about alignment and range, and I wondered just what was going on. We had been forgotten for the moment, so I walked as quietly as I could past the thing and peered out through the shrubbery at the view beyond.

Very interesting. A field of grain stretched down a gentle slope to a keep, its dark towers clear in the starlight. There was a glimmer of reflection about its base, where the waters of the moat protected it from attack.

I stayed there until dawn began to gray the sky, then moved back to examine the object of our labors. As it emerged from the darkness its shape became clear—and I still hadn't the faintest idea of what it was. Fire and steam, I could see the white trickle of vapor clearly now. And a long boom of some kind along the top. One of the black figures was working the controls now. Steam hissed louder as the long arm sank down until the end rested on the ground. I went to look at the large metal cup there—and was rewarded for my curiosity by being drafted to help move an immense stone into place. Two of us rolled it from the pile of its fellows nearby, but it took four of us, straining, to raise it into the cup. Mystery upon mystery. I rejoined the others just as Capo Dimonte appeared with the tall, robed man at his side.

"Will it work, Brother Farvel?" Dimonte asked. "I know nothing of such devices."

"But I do, capo, you shall see. When the drawbridge is lowered my machine will destroy it, crush it."

"May it do just that! Those walls are high—and so will our losses be if we must storm the keep without being able to break through the gate."

Brother Farvel turned his back and issued quick instructions to the machine's operators. More wood was pushed into its bowels and the hissing rose in volume. It was full daylight now. The field before us was empty, the view peaceful. But behind us in the forest lurked the small army and the war machines. It was obvious that battle would be joined when the drawbridge was lowered and destroyed.

We were ordered to lie down, to conceal ourselves as the light grew. It was full daylight by this time, the sun above the horizon—and still nothing happened. I crouched near the machine, close to the cowled operator at the controls.

"It is not coming down!" Brother Farvel called out suddenly. "It is past due, always down at this time. Something is wrong."

"Do they know that we are here?" Capo Dimonte said.

"Yes!" an incredibly loud voice boomed out from the trees above us. *"We know you are there. Your attack is doomed—as are all of you! Prepare to face your certain death."*

Chapter 25

The roaring voice was totally unexpected, shocking in the silence of the forest. I jumped, startled—nor was I the only one. The monk at the machine's controls was even more startled. His hand pulled on the control lever and there was a gigantic hissing roar. The long arm on top of the device thrashed skyward, pushed by a stubbier arm close to its hinged end. The arm rose up in a high arc and slammed into a concealed buffer that jarred and shook the entire machine. The arm may have stopped—but the stone in the cup at the end of the arm continued, high into the air, rising in a great arc. I rushed forward to see it splash into the moat just before the closed drawbridge. Good shot—it would certainly have demolished the structure had it been down.

All around me things became busy quite suddenly. Brother Farvel had knocked the monk from the controls and was now kicking him, roaring with rage. Swords had been drawn, soldiers were rushing about—some of them firing up into the trees. Capo Dimonte was bellowing orders that no one was listening to. I put my back to a tree and held my gun ready for the expected attack.

It never came. But the amplified voice thundered again.

"Go back. Return from whence you came and you will be spared. I am talking to you, Capo Dimonte, you are making a mistake. You are being used by the Black Monks. You will be destroyed for nothing. Return to your keep, for only death awaits you here."

"It is there. I see it!" Brother Farvel shouted, pointing up into the trees. He spun about and saw me, seized me by the arm in a painful grip, and pointed again. "There, on that branch, the device of the devil. Destroy it!"

Why not. I could see it now, even recognize what it was. A loudspeaker of some kind. The gun cracked and kicked my shoulder hard. I fired again and the speaker exploded, bits of plastic and metal rained down.

"Just a machine," Brother Farvel shouted, stamping the fragments into the ground. "Start the attack—send your men forward. My death-throwers will give you support. They will batter down the walls for you."

The capo had no choice. He chewed his lip a bit, then signaled the bugler at his side. Three brazen notes rang out and were echoed by other buglers to our rear and on both flanks. When the first of his troops burst from beneath the trees he drew his sword and ordered us to follow him. With great reluctance I trotted forward.

It was not quite what you would call a lightning attack. More of a stroll when you got down to it. We advanced through the field, then stopped on order to wait for the death-throwers to get into position. Steam cars pulled them forward into line and the firing began. Rocks sizzled over our heads and either bounced from the keep wall or vanished into its interior.

"Forward!" the capo shouted, and waved his sword again just as the return fire began.

The silvery spheres rose up from behind the keep walls, rose high, arced forward above us—and dropped.

Hit—and cracked open. One struck nearby and I could see it was a thin container of some kind filled with liquid that smoked and turned to vapor in the air. Poison! I threw myself away from it, running, trying not to breathe. But the things were bursting all about us now, the air thick with fumes. I ran and my lungs ached and I had to breathe, could not stop myself.

As the breath entered my lungs I fell forward and blackness fell as well.

I was lying on my back, I knew that, but was aware of very little else because of the headache that possessed me completely. If I moved my head ever so slightly it tightened down like a band of fire on my temples. When I tentatively opened one eye—red lightning struck in through my eyeball. I groaned, and heard the groan echoed from all sides. This headache was the winner, the planet-sized headache of all time, before which all other headaches paled. I thought of previous headaches I had known and sneered at their ineffectiveness. Cardboard headaches. This was the real thing. Someone groaned close by and I, and many others, groaned in sympathy.

Bit by bit the pain ebbed away, enough so that I tentatively opened one eye, then the other. The blue sky was clear above, the wind rustled the grain on which I lay. With great hesitation I rose up on one elbow and looked around me at the stricken army.

The field was littered with sprawled bodies. Some of them were sitting up now, holding their heads, while one or two stronger—or stupider—soldiers were climbing unsteadily to their feet. Nearby lay the silvery, broken fragments of one of the attacking missiles, looking innocent enough now with the gas dispersed. My head throbbed but I ignored it. We were alive. The gas had not killed us—it had obviously been designed only to knock us out. Potent stuff. I looked at my shadow, not wanting to risk a glance at the sun yet, and saw how foreshortened it was. Close to noon. We had been asleep for hours.

Then why weren't we dead? Why hadn't the Capo Dinobli's men pounced on us and slit our throats? Or at least taken our weapons? My gun was at my side; I broke it and saw that it was still loaded. Mysteries, mysteries. I jumped, startled—instantly regretting it as my head throbbed—as the hoarse scream rang out. I managed to sit up and turn to look.

Interesting. It was Brother Farvel himself who was still shouting and cursing while he tore handfuls of hair from his head. This was most unusual. I had certainly never seen anything like it before. I rose hesitantly to my feet to see what he was upset about. Yes indeed, I could understand his emotions.

He was standing beside one of his death-throwers which had been thrown a little death of its own. It had burst open, exploded into a tangle of twisted pipes and fractured metal. The long arm had been neatly cut into three pieces and even the wheels had been torn from the body. It was just a mass of unrepairable junk. Brother Farvel ran off, still shouting hoarsely, wisps of hair floating in the breeze behind him.

There were more cries and shouts of pain from the other monks as Brother Farvel came staggering back, stumbling towards the Capo Dimonte, who was just sitting up.

"Destroyed, all of them!" the Black Monk roared while the capo clutched his hands tightly over his ears. "The work of years, gone, crushed, broken. All my death-throwers, the steam-powered battering ram—ruined. He did it. Capo Dinobli did it. Gather your men, attack the keep, he must be destroyed for this monstrous crime that he has committed."

The capo turned to look towards the keep. It was just as it had been at dawn, quiet and undisturbed, the drawbridge still up, as though the day's events had never occurred. Dimonte turned back to Brother Farvel, his face cold and drawn.

"No. I do not lead my men against those walls. That is suicide and suicide was not our agreement. This is your argument, not mine. I agreed to aid you in taking the keep. You were to force entrance with your devices. Then I would attack. That arrangement is now over."

"You cannot go back on your word. . . ."

"I am not. Breech the walls and I will attack. That is what you promised. Now, do it."

Brother Farvel turned red with rage, raised his fists, leaned forward. The capo stood his ground—but drew his sword and held it out.

"See this," he said. "I am still armed—all of my men are armed. It is a message that I understand quite clearly. Dinobli's men could have taken our weapons and cut our throats while we lay here. They did not. They do not war on me. Therefore I do not war on them. *You* fight them—this is your battle." He nudged the toe of his boot into the bugler lying beside him. "Sound assembly."

We were quite happy to leave the Black Monks there in the field, surveying the wreckage of their machines and their plans. Word quickly spread through the ranks as to what had occurred and smiles replaced the pained grimaces as the headaches vanished to be replaced by relief. There would be no battle, no casualties. The Black Monks had started the trouble—and it had been finished for them. My smile was particularly broad because I had some good news for The Bishop.

I knew now how we were to get off the repellent planet of Spiovente.

Through the clear wisdom of hindsight I could understand now what had happened the night before. The approach of our troops in the darkness had been observed carefully. With advanced technology of some kind. The hidden watchers must have also seen the track being constructed through the forest for the death-thrower and understood the significance of the operation. The loudspeaker had been placed in the tree directly above the site—then activated by radio. The gas that had felled us was sophisticated and had been delivered with pinpoint accuracy. All of this was well beyond the technology of this broken-down planet. Which meant only one thing.

There were offworlders in the keep of Capo Dinobli. They were there in force and were up to something. And whatever it was had aroused the wrath of the Black Monks, so much so that they had planned this attack. Which had backfired completely. Good. Mine enemy's enemy one more time. The monks had a stranglehold on what little technology there was on Spiovente—and from what I had seen, the technology was completely monopolized by the military. I cudgled my brain, remembering those long sessions with The Bishop on geopolitics and economics. I was getting the glimmer of a solution to our problems when there was a wild shouting from the ranks ahead.

I pushed forward with the others to see the exhausted messenger sprawled in the grass beside the road. Capo Dimonte was turning away from him, shaking his fists skyward in fury.

"An attack—behind my back—on the keep! It is that sun of a worm, Doccia, that's who it is! We move now, forced march. Back!"

It was a march that I never want to repeat. We rested only when exhaustion dropped us to the ground. Drank some water, staggered to our feet, went on. There was no need to beat us or encourage because we were all involved now. The capo's family, his worldly goods, they were all back in the keep. Guarded only by a skeleton force of soldiers. All of us were as concerned as he was, for what little we owned was there as well. The knaves watching our few possessions. Dreng, whom I scarcely knew, yet felt responsibility for. And The Bishop. If the keep were taken what would happen to him? Nothing, he was an old man, harmless, no enemy of theirs.

Yet I knew this was a lie even as I tried to convince myself of its validity. He was an escaped slave. And I knew what they did with escaped slaves on Spiovente.

More water, a little food at sunset, then on through the night. At dawn I could see our forces straggling out in a ragged column as the stronger men pushed on ahead. I was young and fit and worried—and right up in the front. I could stop now for a rest, get my breath back. Ahead on the road I saw the two men spring from the bushes and vanish over the hill.

"There!" I shouted. "Watchers—we've been seen."

The capo jumped from the war-wagon and ran to my side. I pointed. "Two men. In hiding there. They ran towards the keep."

He ground his teeth with impotent rage. "We can't catch them, not in our condition. Doccia will be warned; he'll escape."

He looked back at his straggling troops, then waved his officers forward.

"You, Barkus, stay here and rest them, then get in formation and follow me. I'm going on with all the fit men I can. They can take turns riding on the war-wagon. We're pushing forward."

I climbed onto the roof of the cart as it started ahead. Men ran alongside, holding on, letting it pull them. The steam car wheezed and puffed smoke at a great rate as we clanked up the hill and onto the downslope beyond.

There were the towers of the keep in the distance, smoke rising from it. When we rattled around the next bend we found a line of men across the road, weapons raised, firing.

We did not slow down. The steam-whistle screeched loudly and we roared in answer, our anger taking us forward. The enemy fled. It had just been a holding party. We could see them joining the rest of the attackers who were now streaming away from the lake. When we reached the causeway it was empty of life. Beyond it was the broken gate of the keep with smoke rising slowly above it. I was right behind the capo when we stumbled forward. Long boards were still in place bridging the gap before the splintered and broken drawbridge, half raised and hanging from its chains. A soldier pushed out between the broken fragments and raised his sword in weary salute.

"We held them, capo," he said, then slumped back against the splintered wood. "They broke through into the yard but we held them at the tower. They were firing at the outer door when they left."

"The Lady Dimonte, the children . . . ?"

"All safe. The treasury untouched."

But the troops' quarters were off the yard and not in the tower. I pushed ahead with the others, who had realized this, climbing through the ruined gate.

There were bodies here, many of them. Unarmed knaves chopped down in the attack. The defenders were coming out of the tower now—and Dreng was among them, coming forward slowly. His clothing was spattered with blood, as was the ax he carried, but he seemed sound.

Then I looked into his face and read the sorrow there. He did not need to speak; I knew. The words came from a distance.

"I am sorry. I could not stop them. He is dead, the old man. Dead."

Chapter 26

He lay on the bunk, eyes closed as though he were sleeping. But never that still, never. Dreng had drawn my blanket over him, up to his chin, combed his hair and cleaned his face.

"I could not move him when the attack came," Dreng said. "He was too heavy, too ill. The wound in his back was bad, black, his skin hot. He told me to leave him, that he was dead in any case. He said if they didn't kill him the 'fection would. They didn't have to stab him though. . . ."

My friend and my teacher. Murdered by these animals. He was worth more than the entire filthy population of this world gathered together. Dreng took me by the arm and I shook him off, turned on him angrily. He was holding out a small packet.

"I stole the piece of paper for him," Dreng said. "He wanted to write to you. I stole it."

There was nothing to be said. I unwrapped it and a carved wooden key fell to the floor. I picked it up, then looked at the paper. There was a floor plan of the keep drawn on it, with an arrow pointing to a room carefully labeled STRONGROOM. Below it was the message, and I read what was written there in a tight, clear hand.

> *I have been a bit poorly so I may not be able to give you this in person. Make a metal copy of the key—it opens the strongroom. Good luck, Jim. It has been my pleasure to know you. Be a good rat.*

His signature was carefully written below. I read the name—then read it again. It wasn't The Bishop—or any of the other aliases he had ever used. He had left me a legacy of trust—knowing that I was probably the only person in the universe who would value this confidence. His real name.

I went and sat down outside in the sun, suddenly very weary. Dreng brought me a cup of water. I had not realized how thirsty I was; I drained it and sent him for more.

This was it, the end. He had felt the approach of darkness—but had worried about me. Thought of me when it was really his own death that was looming so close.

What next? What should I do now?

Fatigue, pain, remorse—all overwhelmed me. Not realizing what was happening I fell asleep, sitting there in the sun, toppled over on my side. When I awoke it was late in the afternoon. Dreng had wadded his blanket and put it under my head, sat now at my side.

There was nothing more to be said. We put The Bishop's body on one of the little carts and wheeled it along the causeway to the shore. We were not the only ones doing this. There was a small hill beside the road, a slope of grass with trees above it, a pleasant view across the water to the keep. We buried him there, tamping the soil down solidly and leaving no marker. Not on this disgusting world. They had his body, that was enough. Any memorial I erected in his honor would be light-years away. I would take care of that one day when the proper moment came.

"But right now, Dreng, we take care of Capo Doccia and his hoodlums. My good friend did not believe in revenge, so I cannot either. So we shall call it simple justice. Those criminals need straightening out. But how shall we do it?"

"I can help, master. I can fight now. I was afraid, then I got angry and I used the ax. I am ready to be a warrior like you."

I shook my head at him. I was thinking more clearly now. "This is no job for a farmer with a future. But you must always remember that you faced your fear and won. That will do you well for the rest of your life. But Jim diGriz pays his debts—so you are going back to the farm. How many groats does a farm cost?"

He gaped at that one and shuffled through his memory. "I never bought a farm."

"I'm sure of that. But somebody must have that you know."

"Old Kvetchy came back from the wars and paid Widow Roslair two hundred and twelve groats for her share of her farm."

"Great. Allowing for inflation five hundred should see you clear. Stick with me, kid, and you'll be wearing plowshares. Now get to the kitchen and pack up some food while I put part one of the plan into operation."

It was like a chess game that you played in your head. I could see the opening moves quite clearly, all laid out. If they were played correctly, middle game and endgame would follow with an inevitable win. I made the first move.

Capo Dimonte was slumped on his throne, red-eyed and as tired as the rest of us, a flagon of wine in his hand. I pushed through his officers and stood before him. He scowled at me and flapped his hand.

"Away, soldier. You'll get your bonus. You did your work well today, I saw that. But leave us, I have plans to make. . . ."

"That is why I am here, capo. To tell you how to defeat Capo Doccia. I was in his service and know his secrets."

"Speak!"

"In private. Send the others away."

He considered a moment—then waved his hands. They left, grumbling, and he sipped his wine until the door slammed shut.

"What do you know," he ordered. "Speak quickly for I am in a foul humor."

"As are we all. What I wanted to tell you in private does not concern Doccia—yet. You will attack, I am sure of that. But in order to assure success I am going to enlist Capo Dinobli and his secrets on your side. Wouldn't the attack be better if they were all asleep when we came over the wall."

"Dinobli knows no more of these matters than I do—so don't lie to me. He is tottering and has been bedridden for a year."

"I know that," I lied with conviction. "But it is those who use his keep for their own ends, who cause the Black Monks to make war on them, these are the ones who will help you."

He sat up at this and there was more than a glint of the old schemer in his eyes. "Go to them then. Promise them a share of the spoils—and you will share as well if you can do this. Go in my name and promise what you will. Before this month is out Doccia's head will be roasting on a spit over my fire, his body will be torn by red-hot spikes and . . ."

There was more like this but I wasn't too interested. This was a pawn move in the opening. I now had to bring a major piece forward to the attack. I bowed myself out, leaving him muttering on the throne, splashing wine around as he waved his arms. These people had very quick tempers.

Dreng had packed our few belongings and we left at once. I led the way until we were well clear of the keep, then turned off towards a stream that ran close by. It had a grassy field at its bank and I pointed towards it.

"We stay here until morning. I have plans to make and we need the rest. I want to be sharp when I knock on old Dinobli's door."

With a night's rest to refresh my brain everything became quite clear. "Dreng," I said, "this will have to be a one-man operation. I don't know what kind of reception I will get and I may be busy enough worrying about myself, without having you to care for. Back to the keep and wait for me."

There was really no door to knock on, just two heavily armed guards at the gate. I came down through the field, past the mounds of junked machines already smeared with a red patina of rust, and crossed the drawbridge. I stopped before I reached the guards and carefully kept my gun lowered.

"I have an important message for the one in charge here."

"Turn about and quick march," the taller guard said, pointing his gun at me. "Capo Dinobli sees no one."

"It's not the capo I care about," I said, looking past him into the courtyard. A tall man in rough clothes was passing. But beneath the ragged cuffs of his trousers I saw the gleam of plasteel boots.

"I wish the capo only good health," I called out loudly. "So I hope that he is seeing a good gerontologist and takes his synapsilstims regularly."

The guard growled in puzzlement at this—but my words were not for his edification. The man I was looking at in the courtyard stopped suddenly, still. Then slowly turned about. I saw keen blue eyes in a long face. Staring at me in silence. Then he came forward and talked to the guard—though still looking at me.

"What is the disturbance?"

"Nothing, your honor. Just sending this one on his way."

"Let him in. I want to question him."

The pointed gun was raised in salute and I marched through the gate. When we were out of earshot of the gate the tall man turned to face me, looking me up and down with frank curiosity.

"Follow me," he said. "I want to talk with you in private." He did not speak until we were in the keep and inside a room with the door closed behind us.

"Who are you?" he asked.

"You know—I was about to ask you the very same question. Does the League know what you are doing here?"

"Of course they do! This is a legitimate . . ." He caught himself, then smiled. "At least that proves you're from offplanet. No one can think that fast here—or knows what you know. Here, sit, then tell me who you are. After that I will judge how much I can tell you of our work."

"Fair enough," I said, dropping into the chair and lying my gun on the floor. "My name is Jim. I was a crewman on a Venian freighter—until I got into difficulties with the captain. He dumped me on this planet. That is all there is to it."

He pulled up a pad and began to make notes. "Your name is Jim. Your last name is . . ." I was silent. He scowled. "All right, let that go for the moment. What is the captain's name."

"I think that I will save that information for later. After you have told me who you are."

He pushed the pad aside and sat back in his chair. "I'm not satisfied. Without your identity I can tell you nothing. Where do you come from on Venia? What is the capital city of your planet, the name of the chairman of the global consul?"

"It's been a long time, I forgot."

"You are lying. You are no more Venian than I am. Until I know more . . ."

"What exactly do you have to know? I am a citizen of the League, not one of the dismal natives here. I watch tri-D, eat at Macswineys—a branch on every known world, forty-two billion sold—I studied molecular electronics, and have a Black Belt in Judo. Does that satisfy you?"

"Perhaps. But you told me that you were dumped on this planet from a Venian freighter, which cannot be true. All unapproved contact with Spiovente is forbidden."

"My contact was unapproved. The ship was smuggling in guns like this one."

That got his attention all right. He grabbed the pad. "The captain's name is . . ."

I shook my head in a silent *no*. "You'll have that information only if you arrange to get me off this planet. You can do that because you as much as told me you were here with League approval. So let us do a little trading. You arrange for my ticket—I have plenty of silver groats to pay for it." Or I would have, which was the same thing. "You will also give me some small help in a local matter—then I'll tell you the captain's name."

He didn't like this. He thought hard and wriggled on the hook, but could not get off it.

"While you are making your mind up," I said, "you might tell me who you are and what you are doing here."

"You must promise not to reveal our identity to the natives. Our presence is well known offplanet, but we can only succeed here if our operation remains covert."

"I promise, I promise. I owe nothing to any of the locals."

He steepled his fingers and leaned back as though beginning a lecture. I had guessed right—as his first words revealed.

"I am Professor Lustig of the University of Ellenbogen, where I hold the chair of applied socioeconomics. I am head of my department and I must say that I founded the department, since applied socioeconomics is a fairly new discipline, an outgrowth, obviously, of theoretical socioeconomics . . ."

I blinked rapidly to keep my eyes from glazing over and forced myself to keep listening. It was teachers like Lustig who made me run away from school.

". . . years of correspondence and labor to attain our fondest ambition. Practical application of our theories. Dealing with the bureaucrats of the League was the most difficult because of the League nonintervention policy. In the end they were convinced that with the proper controls we be permitted to operate a pilot project here on Spiovente. Or as someone said with crude humor, we certainly couldn't make things worse. We keep our operation at the current level of planetary technology so it will be self-sustaining when we leave."

"What exactly are you trying to do?" I asked.

He blinked rapidly. "That should be obvious—that is the only thing I have been talking about."

"You have been telling me theory, professor. Would you mind being specific about what you hope to accomplish."

"If you insist, on *layman's* terms, we are attempting to do no less than change the very fabric of society itself. We intend to bring this planet, kicking and screaming if necessary, out of the dark ages. After the Breakdown Spiovente sank into a rather repulsive form of feudalism. More warlordism, in fact. Normally a feudalistic society performs a great service during an age of disintegration. It maintains a general framework of government as various localities protect and care for themselves."

"I haven't seen much caring or protecting."

"Correct. Which is why these warlords will have to go."

"I'll help shoot a few."

"Violence is *not* our way! In addition to being distasteful, it is forbidden to League members. Our aim is to bring into existence government independent of the capos. In order to do that we are encouraging the rise of a professional class. This will bring about increased circulation of money and the end of barter. With increased funds the government will be able to institute taxation to purchase public services. To reinforce this a judiciary will need to be formed. This will encourage communication, centralization, and the growth of common ideas."

Sounded great—although I wasn't wild about the taxes bit, or the judiciary. Still, anything would be better than the capos.

"That all sounds fine in theory," I said. "But how do you put it into practice?"

"By providing better services at a lower price. Which is why the Black Monks tried to attack us. They are no more religious than my hat—the order is just a front for their monopoly of technology. We are breaking that monopoly and they don't like it."

"Very good. Yours sounds a fine plan and I wish you the best of luck. But I have a few things to do myself before I leave this sinkhole. To help you in your task of breaking the technological monopoly I would like to purchase some of your sleeping gas."

"Impossible. In fact it is impossible for us to aid you in any way. Nor are you leaving here. I've signalled for the guards. You will be held until the next League ship arrives. You know far too much about our operation to be permitted your freedom."

Chapter 27

Even as this unacceptable bit of information was sinking into my brain, my body was launched across the desk. He should have remembered the bit about the Black Belt. My thumbs bit deep and he slumped. Even before his head bounced off the desk I had bounced off the floor and dived for the door. And none too soon—as I pushed the locking bolt home I saw that the handle above it was starting to turn.

"Now Jim, move fast," I advised myself, "before the alarm is spread. But first let me see what this two-faced academic has in his possession that may be of use."

There were files, papers, and books in the desk, nothing that would be of any value to me now. I sprayed it all about me on the floor as the banging started on the door. I didn't have much time. Next the prof. I tore his cloak open and ransacked his pockets. There was even less of interest here—other than a ring of keys. I shoved them into my own pocket; they would have to do for loot. Seizing up the gun I dived for the window just as something heavy hit the door with a shuddering thud. Two stories up and the courtyard below was paved with evil-looking cobblestones. I would break my legs if I jumped. I leaned out and was grateful for the second-rate Spiovente masons. There were large gaps between the stones of the outer wall. The door crashed and splintered as I climbed out of the window, thrust the gun through my belt in the small of my back—and began to climb down.

It was easy enough. I jumped the last bit, did a shoulder roll, which jammed the gun painfully into my spine, retrieved it, and stumbled around the corner of the building before anyone appeared in the window above. I was free!

Or was I? Instant gloom descended. Free in the middle of the enemy keep with all men's hands turned against me. Some big free.

"Yes, free!" I ground my teeth together arrogantly, braced my shoulders, and put a bold swagger into my walk. "Free as only a Stainless Steel Rat can be free! Just press on, Jim—and see if you can't find some locks to go with those keys in your pocket."

I always get the best advice from myself. I marched on through an archway that led into the large courtyard. There were armed men lolling about here and they completely ignored me. That wouldn't last long. As soon as the alarm was raised they would all be after my hide. Eyes straight ahead I walked towards a massive building on the far side. It had a single large gate set into the wall, with a smaller one next to it. As I came closer I saw that both had very modern locks set into them. Very informative. I was most interested in what was locked away here. Now all I had to do was find the right key.

Trying to look as though I belonged here I stopped before the smaller door and flipped through the keys. There must have been twenty of them. But the lock was a Bolger, that was obvious to my trained eye, so I fingered through them, looking for the familiar diamond shape.

"Hey, you, what you doing there?"

He was a big thug, dirty and unshaven and red of eye. He also had a long dagger thrust through his belt, the hilt of which he was tapping with his fingers.

"Unlocking this door, obviously," was my firm response. "Are you the one they sent to help me? Here, take this."

I handed him my gun. This bought me a number of seconds as he looked at the weapon, enough time for me to push one key into the lock. It didn't turn.

"No one sent me," he said, examining the gun, which distracted him nicely for a few seconds more. I couldn't be doing anything wrong if I had given him my only weapon, could I? I could almost see him thinking, slowly, moving his lips as he did. I interrupted the turgid flow of his thoughts.

"Well, since you are here you can help me . . ."

Ahh, the next key did the job, turning sweetly. The door opened and I turned about just as sweetly with my fingers pointed to jab. I caught the gun as he slid to the ground.

"Hey, you, stop!"

I ignored this rude command since I had not the slightest desire to see who was calling, but slipped through the door instead and slammed it shut behind me. Turned and looked around and felt a sharp pang of despair. There was no hope here. I was in an enormous chamber, badly lit by slits high in the wall. It was a garage for the steam cars. Five of them, lined up in a neat row.

It would be fine to escape in one of these, really wonderful. I had watched them in operation. First the fire had to be lit, then wood pushed in, steam raised. This usually took at least an hour. At that point, say, I could manage to do all this undisturbed, I had to open the door and clank to freedom at a slow walking pace. No way!

Or was there a way? As my eyes adjusted to the gloom I realized that these weren't the same kind of steam cars I had seen before—with their wooden wheels and iron tires. These had soft tires of some kind! Improved technology? Could it be offplanet technology disguised as antique wrecks?

I hurried over to the closest one and climbed up to the operator's seat. There were the familiar big control levers and wheels—but invisible from the ground was a padded driver's seat and familiar groundcar controls. This was more like it!

Slipping my gun under the seat, I slipped myself into it. A safety belt hung there, wise precaution, but not at the moment. I pushed it aside as I leaned forward to examine the controls. Motor switch, gear selector, speedometer—as well as some unfamiliar dials and controls. A banging on the door convinced me I should make a detailed study later. I reached out and turned on the motor. Nothing happened.

Or rather something totally unexpected happened. The motor didn't start but a girl's voice did, speaking in my ear.

"Do not attempt to start this vehicle without wearing your seatbelt."

"Seatbelt, right, thank you." I clicked it on and turned the switch again.

"The engine will start only with the gear selector in neutral."

The banging on the door was even louder. I cursed as I pushed the selector, trying to find the right location in the dim light. The door crashed and splintered. There, now the switch again.

The motor turned over. I pushed the drive into forward. And the voice spoke.

"Do not attempt to drive with your hand brake on."

I was cursing louder now, the small door broke down and crashed to the floor, pistons began to move around me while steam spurted and hissed. Someone shouted and the men in the door started towards me.

The thing shuddered and lumbered forward.

This was more like it! Covered in steel plates and fake ironmongery, it must be incredibly heavy. There was a simple way to find out. I floored the accelerator, twisted the wheel—and pointed the hulk straight at the large door.

It was beautiful. The steam roared and spurted as I accelerated. Hitting the door dead center with a crash that deafened me. But my noble steed never slowed a fraction. Wood screeched and tore and fell away as I plowed through in a cloud of flying timber. I had a quick view of fleeing pedestrians before I had to duck down to prevent myself from being beheaded by a board. It scratched and clumped and fell away. I sat up and smiled with pleasure.

What a wonderful sight. Soldiers were fleeing in all directions, dashing for cover. I swung the wheel and spun in a tight circle looking for the way out. A bullet clanged into the steel plating and whined away. There the gate was—dead ahead. I floored the accelerator this time, then found the whistle cord. It screamed and steam spurted and I picked up speed.

And none too soon, either. Someone had kept his head and was trying to lift the drawbridge. Two men had plugged the handle into the clumsy winch and were turning it furiously; chains clanked and tightened. I headed for the center of the gate, whistle screeching, bullets beginning to spang on the steel around me. I crouched down and kept the pedal on the floor. I was going to have only one chance.

The drawbridge was rising, slowly and steadily, cutting off my escape, getting larger and larger before me. It was up ten, twenty, thirty degrees. I was not going to make it.

We hit with a jar that would have thrown me out if the safety belt hadn't been locked. Thank you, voice. The front wheels rose up onto the drawbridge, higher and higher, until the nose of the car was pointing into the air. If it climbed any higher it would be flipped onto its back.

Which was a chance that I would just have to take. The gears growled and my transport of delight bucked and chuntered—and I heard a squealing and snapping.

Then the whole thing pitched forward. The chains lifting the drawbridge had torn from their moorings under the massive weight of my car. The nose fell and we hit with a crash that almost stunned me.

But my foot was still down and the wheels were still turning. The vehicle shot forward—straight for the water. I twisted the steering wheel, straightened it, then tore across the bridge and onto the road. Faster and faster, up the hill and around the bend—then let up on the speed before we overturned on the ruts. I was safe and away.

"Jim," I advised myself, gasping for breath. "Try not to do that again if you can avoid it."

I looked back, but there was no one following me. But there would be, soon, if not on foot then in one of the other fake steam cars. I put my foot back down and kept my mouth clamped shut so it didn't clack and splinter my teeth when we hit the bumps.

There was a long hill that slowed my pace. Even with the accelerator on the floor we crawled because of the gearing and the weight of the beast. I used the opportunity to check the charge—batteries full! They had better be because I had no way of recharging them once they ran down. Above the clatter and rumble I heard a thin and distant whistle and flashed a quick look over my shoulder. There they were! Two of the machines, hot on my tail.

There was no way they were going to catch me. Off the road these things would be useless and mired down—and there was only one road leading to Dimonte's keep. I was on it and headed that way and I was going to keep them behind me all the way.

Except that if I led them there they would know who had pinched their wagon and would come after it with the gas bombs. No good. I looked back and saw that they were gaining—but they soon slowed to my pace when they reached the bottom of the hill. I went over the top and my speed picked up—as did the jarring. I hoped that they had built the thing to withstand this kind of beating. Then the crossroad loomed up ahead, with peasants leaping out of my way, and there was the left turning that would take me to Capo Dimonte. I streamed right through it. I didn't know this road at all so all I could do was go on and keep my fingers crossed.

Something had to be done—and fairly soon. Even if I stayed ahead of them all day I would run the battery flat and that would be that. Think, Jim, cudgel the old brain cells.

Opportunity presented itself around the next bend. A rough farm track led off through a field and down to a stream. Then, like all good ideas, this one appeared full blown in my forebrain, complete in every detail.

Without hesitation I turned the wheel and trundled down into the meadow. Going slower and slower as I felt my wheels sink into the soft soil. If I got mired now it was the end. Or at least the end of my mastery of this crate—which I would dearly like to keep for awhile. Carry on, Jim, but carefully.

At the lowest speed, in the lowest gear, I ground forward until the front wheels were in the stream. They were sinking mushily into the mud as I stopped—then carefully began to back out. Looking over my shoulder, keeping in the ruts I had made on the way down. Reversing out of the field until I was safely back on the road. As I shifted gears I permitted myself a quick glimpse of my work. Perfect! The ruts led straight down to the water and on into it.

On the road behind me I heard a not-too-distant whistle. I stood on the throttle and accelerated around the bend until I was hidden by the trees. Stopped, killed the engine, slammed on the brakes, and jumped down.

This was going to be the dangerous part. I had to convince them to follow the tracks. If they didn't believe me, I had little chance of escape. But it was a risk that had to be taken.

As I ran I pulled off my jacket, staggering as I pulled my arms free and turned it inside out. I draped it over my shoulders, tied the arms in front, then bent to roll up my trouser legs. Not much of a disguise, but it would have to do. Hopefully the drivers had not had a good look at me—if they had seen me at all.

I stood by the spot where I had turned and had just enough time to seize up some dirt and rub it into my face as the first pseudo steam car clanked around the bend.

They slowed as I stepped into the road and pointed. And shouted.

"He went that-away!"

The driver and the gunmen turned to look at the field and stared at the tracks. The vehicle slowed to a stop.

"Splashed right into the water and kept on going through the field. Feller a friend of yours?"

This was the moment of truth. It stretched taut, longer and longer as the second vehicle came up and slowed to a stop as well. What if they questioned me—even looked closely at me? I wanted to run—but if I did, that would be a giveaway.

"Follow him!" someone called out, and the driver twisted his wheel and turned towards the field.

I slipped back into the trees and watched with great interest. It was beautiful. I felt proud of myself; yes, I did. I am not ashamed to admit it. When a painter creates a masterpiece he knows it and does not attempt to diminuate its importance by false modesty.

This was a masterpiece. The first car rattled down through the field, bobbing and bouncing, and hit the water with an immense splash. It was going so fast that its rear wheels actually reached the stream before it slowed to a stop. And began to slowly sink into the soft mud. It went down to its hubs before it stopped.

There was much shouting and swearing at that—and best of all someone rooted out a chain and connected the two cars. Wonderful. The second one spun its wheels and churned the field until it too was safely mired. I clapped appreciatively and strolled back to my own car.

I shouldn't have done it, I know. But there are times when one just cannot resist showing off. I sat down, snapped on my belt, started the motor, moved the car carefully forward and back until I had turned about. Then accelerated back down the road.

And as I passed the turnoff I pulled down hard on the whistle. It screeched loudly and every head turned, every eye was on me. I waved and smiled. Then the trees were in the way and the beautiful vision vanished from sight.

Chapter 28

It was a victory ride. I laughed aloud, sang, and blew the whistle with joy. When this first enthusiasm had died down I moved the queen on my mental chessboard and considered what came next. The hissing of steam and clanking of machinery was distracting and I examined the controls until I found the switch that turned the special effects off. The steam was being boiled to order and the sounds were just a recording. I threw the switch and rode on in peace towards Capo Dimonte's keep. It was late afternoon before I reached it—and by that time my plans were complete.

When I came around the last bend in the road and turned onto the causeway I had full sound and steam effects going again. I trundled slowly down in clear sight of the guards. They had the partially repaired drawbridge raised long before I reached it, and peered out suspiciously at me as I stopped before the gap.

"Don't shoot! Me friend!" I called out. "Member of your army and a close associate of the Capo Dimonte. Send for him at once for I know he wants to see his new steam cart."

He did indeed. As soon as the drawbridge was lowered he strode across it and looked up at me.

"Where did you get this?" he asked.

"Stole it. Climb aboard and let me show you some interesting things."

"Where is the sleeping gas?" he asked as he climbed the rungs.

"I didn't bother with it. With this cart I have developed an even better and more foolproof plan. This is no ordinary steam cart, as I hope you have noticed. It is a new and improved model with some interesting additions that will capture your attention. . . ."

"You idiot! What are you talking about?" He slipped his sword up and down in its scabbard—such a quick temper.

"I will demonstrate, your caponess, since one action speaks louder than a thousand words. I also suggest that you sit there and strap that belt about you as I have done. This demonstration, I guarantee, will impress you."

If not impressed already, he was at least curious. He strapped in and I backed the length of the causeway to the shore. Going slowly with all attendant wheezing and clanking. I stopped the car and turned to him.

"What about the speed of this thing? What you are used to?"

"Speed? You mean how fast it moves? This is an excellent yoke and goes with greater alacrity than my own."

"You have seen nothing yet, capo. First—notice this."

I turned off the sound and steam and he nodded with understanding. "You have banked its fires and it rests and does not move."

"Quite the opposite. I have simply silenced it so no one can hear its approach. It is raring to go—and go it will. After you answer one question. If this cart belonged to an enemy and it appeared here—would your soldiers have time to raise the drawbridge before it reached them?"

He snorted with derision. "What sort of fool do you take me for with questions like that? Before a cart could crawl its way there the drawbridge could be raised and lowered more than once."

"Really? Then hold on and see what this baby can do."

I floored the accelerator and the thing shot forward in almost perfect silence. There was the hum of the motor, the rustle of the tires on the smooth stone. Faster and faster towards the gate, which expanded before us with frightening speed. The guards who were standing there dived aside just in time as we hit the rough boards of the repaired wooden drawbridge with a crash, bounced, and rocked through the gate.

And shuddered to a halt inside the keep. The capo sat there with round eyes, gasping, then struggled to get his sword free.

"Assassin! Your attempt to kill me has failed. . . ."

"Capo, listen, it was a demonstration. Of how I am going to get you and your soldiers through the gate of Capo Doccia's keep. Right through the open gate into the courtyard where you can kill, loot, murder, torture, maim, destroy . . ."

This got his attention. The sword slid back into its scabbard and his eyes unfocused as they looked at the wonders I had summoned up for him.

"Right," he said, blinking rapidly and coming back to the present. "You have an interesting idea here, soldier, and I want to hear more about it. Over a flagon of wine—for that ride was something I have never experienced before."

"I obey. But let me first get this cart hidden and out of sight so it cannot be observed. The attack will only succeed if there is complete surprise."

"In that you are correct. Put it in the barn and I will post guards over it."

The wine he gave me was a good cut above the acid the troops were issued and I sipped it with pleasure. But not too much for I was going to need a clear head if the game were to proceed as planned. I had to find reasons that would make sense to him, to convince him to get cracking with his war plans at once. Because if we didn't move quickly Prof. Lustig would be swarming over us with his gas bombs. I am sure he was most unhappy about my pinching his buggy. And there were not that many keeps in the area where it could be hidden. It was time for action. I slid out a rook along a mental rank and spoke.

"The keep of the foul Capo Doccia is no more than a five-hour walk from here—is that correct?"

"Five hours, four-hour forced march."

"Good. Then consider this. He attacked you while you were away with the greater part of your army. His troops did great injury to the drawbridge and the fabric of the keep itself. Before you venture out to launch an attack you must have the drawbridge repaired, hire more soldiers perhaps. So when you begin your next campaign no advantage can be taken of your absence. Is that correct?"

He slurped his wine and glared at me over the rim. "Yes, damn and blast your head, I suppose it is. Prudence, my officers always consul prudence when I want to behead that creature, rip out his entrails, flay him alive . . ."

"And you shall, yes indeed, fine things lurk in your future. And unlike your other advisers I do not consul caution. I think that fiend in human guise should be attacked—and at once!"

This appealed to him all right and I could see that I had his undivided attention as I explained my plan.

"Leave the keep here just as it is—and take all your men. If everything goes as planned you will have troops back here long before anyone knows we have gone. We march at midnight, silent as vengeful spirits, to be in positions of concealment at dawn, as close to Capo Doccia's keep as is possible. I know just the spot. When the drawbridge is opened at dawn I shall use your new machine to see that it stays open. Your troops attack, take the keep by surprise—and the day is won. As soon as you have captured the keep you can send a strong force back here."

"It could happen that way. But how do you plan to stop them closing the drawbridge?"

As I told him the wicked grin spread across his face and he whooped with joy.

"Do it!" he shouted, "and I shall make you rich for life. With Doccia's groats of course, after I loot his treasury."

"You are kindness itself to your humble servant. May I then suggest that all in the keep be persuaded to rest, for it will be a long night?"

"Yes, that will be done. The orders will be issued."

After that I slipped away. Other than my natural concern for the tired bodies of my comrades I had other reasons for wishing all of them in their beds. I had a few important tasks to perform before I could get any rest myself.

"Tools," I told Dreng when I had rousted him out. "Files, hammers, anything like that. Where would I find them here?"

He shoved a finger deep into his matted hair and scratched hard in thought. I resisted the urge to reach out and shake him and waited instead until the slow processes had crawled to a finish. Perhaps the fingernail rasping on skull helped his sluggish synapses to function. It would be best not to interfere with an established practice. Eventually he spoke.

"I don't have any tools."

"I know, dear boy." I could hear my teeth grate together and forced myself to keep control. "You don't have tools, but someone here must. Who would that be?"

"Blacksmith," he said proudly. "The blacksmith always has tools."

"Good lad. Now, would you kindly lead the way to this blacksmith?"

The individual in question was sooty and hairy and in a foul mood, sour wine strong on his breath.

"Hiss off, runt. No one touches Grundge's tools, no one."

Runt indeed! I did not have to force the snarl and growl. "Listen you filthy piece of flab—those are the capo's tools, not your tools. And the capo sent me for them. Now either I take them now or my knave goes to bring the capo here. Shall I do that?"

He closed his fists and growled, then hesitated. Like everyone else, he had seen me drive the capo into the keep and knew I was his confidant. He couldn't take any chances on crossing his boss. He began to bob up and down bowing and scraping.

"Certainly, master. Grundge knows his place. Tools, sure, take tools. Over here, whatever you want."

I pushed past his sweaty form to the dismal display of primitive devices. Pathetic! I kicked through the pile until I found a file, hammer, and clumsy metal snips that would have to do. I pushed them towards Dreng.

"Take these. And you, Grundge, can crawl over in the morning to the barn and get them back."

Dreng followed after me, then gaped up in awe at the steam cart.

"Close your mouth before you catch some flies," I told him, seizing the tools. "What I'll need next is a stout bag or sack of some kind, about this big. Scout one out and bring it to me here. Then get to bed because you will not be getting much sleep tonight."

With proper tools I could have done the job in no time at all. But I had a feeling that tolerances wouldn't be that exact here and as long as I was close to the model it would be all right. The metal siding next to the driver's seat was roughly the thickness of the wooden key. I cut and filed and hacked a portion of it into shape. It would have to do.

Dreng—and hopefully everyone else—was now asleep and I could begin Operation Great-groat. With the key in my pocket, the bag tucked into my waist, silent as a shadow—I hoped—I made way into the depths of the keep. I had memorized The Bishop's map and his spirit must have been watching after me for I found the treasury without being seen. I slipped the key into the lock, crossed the fingers of my free hand, and turned.

With a metallic screech it clanked open. My heart did its usual pounding-in-chest routine while I stood rooted there. The noise must have been heard.

But it hadn't been. The door creaked slightly when I opened it and then I was inside the vault and easing it shut behind me.

It was beautiful. High, barred windows let in enough light so I could see the big chests against the far wall. I had done my fiscal research well, getting a look at a braggard's store of groats, so I knew just what to look for.

The first chest was stuffed with brass groats, my fingers could distinguish their thick forms in the darkness. In logical progression I found silver groats in the next chest and I shoveled my bag half full of them. As I did this I saw a smaller chest tucked in behind this one. I smiled into the darkness as I groped and felt the angled shapes within. Golden groats—and lots of them. This was going to be a very successful heist after all. I only stopped shoveling when the bag became too heavy. Beware of greed. With this bit of advice to myself I threw it over my shoulder and let myself out just the way I had come in.

There were guards in the courtyard but they never saw me as I slipped into the barn. I turned on the instrument lights of the car, which provided more than enough illumination for me to see by. I opened the storage locker below and put the money bag into place. As I closed it I was overwhelmed by a great sensation of relief. In my mind's eye I slid out another rook to join the first. The chess game was going as planned and mate was clearly visible ahead.

"Now, Jim," I advised. "Get your head down and get some sleep. Tomorrow is going to be an exceedingly busy day."

Chapter 29

I muttered and slapped and rolled over but the irritation persisted. Eventually I blinked my grimy eyes open and growled up at Dreng, who was shaking my shoulder. He stepped away in fear.

"Do not beat me, master—I am only doing as you instructed. It is time to waken, for the troops are assembling now in the courtyard."

I growled something incoherent and this turned into a cough. When I did this a cup appeared before me and I drank deep of the cool water, then dropped back onto the bunk. Not for the first time did I approve of the knave system. But I was beat, bushed, fatigued. Even the stamina of youth can be sapped by adversity. I shook my head rapidly, then sat up on my elbows, angry at myself for the brief moment of self-pity.

"Go, good Dreng," I ordered, "and find me food to nourish my hungry cells. And some drink as well since alcohol is the only stimulant these premises seem to have."

I splashed cold water over my head in the courtyard, gasping and spluttering. As I wiped my face dry I saw in the clear starlight the ranks of soldiers being drawn up as the ammunition was being issued. The great adventure was about to begin. Dreng was waiting when I returned. I sat on my bunk and ate a pretty repellent breakfast of fried dinglebeans washed down by the destructive wine. I talked between gruesome mouthfuls because this was the last private moment I would have with my knave.

"Dreng, your military career is about to end."

"Don't kill me, master!"

"Military career, idiot—not your life. Tonight is your last night of service and in the morn you will be off home with your pay. Where does your old dad hide his money?"

"We are too poor to have any groats."

"I am sure of that. But *if* he had any—where would he put it?"

This was a complicated thought and he puzzled over it while I chewed and swallowed. He finally spoke.

"Bury it under the hearth! I remember he did that once. Everyone buries their money under the fire; that way it can't be found."

"Great. That way it certainly can be found. You have got to do better than that with your fortune."

"Dreng has no fortune."

"Dreng will have one before the sun rises. I'm paying you off. Go home and find two trees near your home. Stretch a rope between them. Then dig a hole exactly halfway along the rope. Bury the money there—where you can find it when you need it. And only take out a few coins at a time. Do you have that?"

He nodded enthusiastically. "Two trees, halfway. I never heard of anything like that before!"

"An earth-shaking concept, I know," I sighed. There certainly was a lot that he hadn't heard about. "Let's go. I want you to be stoker on my chariot of fire."

I staggered to my feet and led the way to the barn. Now that the troops were lined up and ready the officers were finally appearing, scratching and yawning, with the capo at their head. I didn't have much time. Dreng climbed into the car behind me and squealed with fear when I turned on the instrument lights.

"Demonic illumination! Spirit lights! Sure sign of death!"

He clutched at his chest and looked ready to expire until I gave him a good shaking. "Batteries!" I shouted. "The gift of science denied to this dumb world. Now, stop quaking and open your bag."

All thoughts of death vanished and his eyes stuck out like boiled eggs as I shoveled silver and gold groats into his leather bag. This was a fortune that would change his entire life for the better, so at least I was accomplishing one good deed by my presence here.

"What are you doing up there?"

It was Capo Dimonte, glaring up suspiciously from below.

"Just stoking the engines, excellency."

"Kick that knave out of the way, I'm coming up."

I waved the goggle-eyed Dreng to the back of the car as the capo climbed aboard.

"You favor me with your presence, capo."

"Damned right. I ride while the troops walk. Now, move this thing out."

The scouts had already gone on ahead when we rumbled across the drawbridge and onto the causeway. The main body of troops came behind us, a certain eagerness in their step despite the hour. All of them had lost valuables and possessions—even knaves—during the raid. All were eager for revenge and theft.

"The Capo Doccia must be taken alive," Capo Dimonte suddenly said. I started to answer until I realized that he was talking only to himself. "Tied and left helpless, brought back to the keep. First a little flaying, just enough skin to make a hatband. Then maybe blinding. No—not right away—he must see what is happening to him. . . ."

There was more like this, but I tuned it out. I had thoughts of my own—and even some regrets. When The Bishop had been killed, my anger had overwhelmed all of the clear thinking that I should have been doing. All excuses vanished now—I was embarking on this expedition solely for revenge. And I couldn't claim to be doing it in The Bishop's memory because he would have been seriously opposed to violent action of this kind. But it was too late now to turn back. The campaign had been launched and we were well on our way.

"Stop this thing!" the capo ordered suddenly, and I hit the brakes.

There was a dark knot of men waiting on the road ahead—our advanced scouts. The capo climbed to the ground and I leaned out to see what was happening. They were leading a man who had his arms bound behind him.

"What happened?" the capo asked.

"Found him watching the road, excellency. Caught him before he could get away."

"Who is he?"

"Soldier, name of Palec. I know him, served with him in the southern campaign."

The capo walked up to the prisoner and shoved his face close to the other's and snarled. "I have you, Palec. Tied and bound."

"Aye."

"Are you the Capo Doccia's man?"

"Aye, I serve under him. I took his groat."

"You've spent that on wine a long time ago. Will you serve with me and take my groat?"

"Aye."

"Release him. Barkus—a silver groat for this man."

These mercenaries fought well, but they also changed sides easily enough. Why not? They had no stakes in any of the capos' quarrels. Once Palec had accepted the coin they gave him his weapons back.

"Speak, Palec," the capo ordered. "You are my loyal servant now, who has taken my groat. But you used to serve with Capo Doccia. Tell me what he plans."

"Aye. No secret there. He knows that your army is intact and you will be coming after him as soon as you can. Some of us have been sent out to watch the roads, but he doesn't think that you will march for some time yet. He stays drunk, that's a sign he's not expecting a fight."

"I'll put a sword through his belly, let out the wine and guts!" The capo cut off his dreaming with an effort and forced himself back to the present. "What about his troops? Will they fight?"

"Aye, they've just been paid. But they have little love for him and will change sides as soon as the battle is lost."

"Better and better. Fall in with the ranks, scouts out ahead, start this machine."

The last was directed at me as he climbed back to his seat. I kicked it into gear and the advance continued again. There were no more interruptions and we proceeded, with hourly rest breaks, towards the enemy keep. It was well before dawn when we came to the scouts waiting on the road. This was the spot I had picked. The keep of Capo Doccia was around the next bend.

"I will post your lookout now," the capo said.

"Agreed. My knave here will show them the exact spot where they are to stay hidden, in sight of the gate." I waited until he was out of earshot before I whispered my instructions to Dreng.

"Take your bag and everything you possess with you—because you are not coming back."

"I do not understand, master. . . ."

"You will if you shut up and listen instead of talking. Lead the soldiers to the bushes where we hid, when we were getting ready to rescue The Bishop. You do remember the place?"

"It is past the burnt tree over the hedge and . . ."

"Great, great—but I don't need the description. Take the soldiers as I said, show them where to hide, then lie close beside them. Soon after dawn things are going to get very, very busy. At that time you will do nothing, understand that—don't speak, just nod."

He did. "Fine. You just remain there when everyone rushes off. As soon as they are gone and no one is looking at you—slip away. Back into the woods and get to your home and lay low until the excitement is over. Then count your money and live happily ever after."

"Then—I will no longer be your knave?"

"Right. Discharged from the army with honor."

He dropped to his knees and seized my hand, but before he could say anything I touched my finger to his lips.

"You were a good knave. Now be a good civilian. Move!"

I watched him leave until he was swallowed up in the darkness. Dumb—but loyal. And the only friend that I had on this rundown planet. The only one that I wanted! Now that The Bishop . . .

This morbid turn of thought was happily interrupted by the capo, who clambered back to his seat. He was followed by armed soldiers until the upperworks of the car were packed solid with them. The capo squinted up at the sky.

"There is the first light. It will be dawn soon. Then it will begin."

After that we could only wait. The tension so thick in the air that it was hard to breathe. Blurred faces began to emerge from the darkness, all of them set in the same grim expression.

I concentrated on what was happening around the bend, remembering the way it had been when Dreng and I had lain out there. Watching and waiting. The locked gate of the keep, the drawbridge up, all of it growing clearer as the sun rose. Smoke from cooking fires drifting up from behind the thick walls. Then the stirring of the soldiery, changing of the guards. At last the gate unlocked, the drawbridge lowered. Then what? Would they keep to the same routine? If they did not our force would soon be discovered. . . .

"The signal!" the capo said as he crashed his elbow hard into my ribs.

He didn't have to. I had seen the soldier wave the instant that he had appeared. My foot was already jammed down on the accelerator and we were picking up speed. Around the bend in the road, bouncing and swaying on the ruts, then straight ahead towards the entrance to the keep.

The guards looked up and gaped as we shot towards them. The slaves pulling the cart stared too, frozen and unmoving.

Then the shouting started. The drawbridge creaked as they tried to raise it, but the cart and slaves were still on it. There were kicks and screamed orders and every second of wasted time brought us that much closer. They finally started to drag the cart back through the gate—but it was too late.

We were upon them. The front wheels hit the drawbridge and we bounced into the air, coming down with a splintering crash. I stood on the brakes as we plowed into the cart. Slaves and guards were diving into the moat to escape destruction as we skidded, with locked wheels, right into the mouth of the gate.

"For Capo Dimonte, for groats, and for God!" The capo shouted as he leapt to the attack.

The others leapt with him, walking over my back as I crouched down, jumping onto the drawbridge then through the gate.

There was screaming and shouting, the banging of guns. From behind me a growing roar of voices from the rest of the attacking army. I could see that the capo and his men were fighting inside the gate and had captured the drawbridge mechanism from the soldiers who were trying to raise it. Raising it had of course been impossible because of the great weight of the car resting on it. That had been the beauty and simplicity of my plan. Once I had arrived the drawbridge had to stay down. Only now did I trundle forward so that the rest of the troops had a clear way to the gate.

The battle for the keep of Capo Doccia was joined.

Chapter 30

This was a surprise attack that really had been a surprise. Our invading forces were pouring across the drawbridge and into the keep even as Capo Doccia's soldiers were emerging from their quarters. The guards on the wall fought fiercely, but they were outnumbered.

To add to the confusion I turned on the steamer sound effects and hung onto the whistle as I charged at the defenders who were trying to group up ahead. A few shots were fired at me, but most of the soldiers dived aside and ran. I screeched about and saw that the battle was going very well indeed.

The defenders on the walls were raising their hands in surrender. Being outnumbered from the start, and having little reason to fight for the capo as we had been told, they were eager to save their lives. Near the inner gate a group of officers were showing more spirit and a fierce battle was going on there. But one by one they were cut down or clubbed into submission. Two of them fled for the building but found the heavy door slammed in their faces.

"Bring torches!" the Capo Dimonte shouted. "We'll smoke the buggers out!"

The battle had ended as swiftly as it had begun. The gate, walls and courtyard were in our hands. Huddled corpses showed the ferocity of the brief engagement. Slaves shivered in fear against the walls while the soldiers who had surrendered were being marched off. Only the central building remained in the hands of the defenders. Capo Dimonte knew exactly what to do about this. He waved a smoking torch over his head and called out loudly.

"All right, Doccia, you fat-bellied toad, this is your end. Come out and fight like a man you worm, or I'll burn you out. And burn alive every man, woman, child, dog, rat, pigeon who stays in there with you. Come out and fight, you ugly piece of vermin—or remain and be cooked like a roast!"

A gun fired from inside and a bullet spanged from the cobbles at the capo's feet. He waved his red-drenched sword and a blast of gunfire roared out as our troops fired en masse. Bullets zinged from the stonework, thudded into the sealed door, and whistled in through the windows. When the firing stopped, shrill screaming could be heard from inside the building.

"One warning only!" Capo Dimonte called out. "I do not war on women or on good soldiers who surrender. Lay down your arms and you will go free. Resist and you will be burned alive. There is only one I want—that pig, Doccia. Hear that, Doccia, you lout, swine, worm . . ."

And more, once he warmed to the subject. The torch crackled and smoked and there was the sound of muffled shouting and scuffling from inside the building.

Then the door burst open and Capo Doccia came rolling down the steps end over end. He was barefooted, half-dressed—but he was holding his sword.

At the sight of his enemy Capo Dimonte lost whatever little remaining cool he had left. He howled with anger and rushed forward. Doccia climbed to his feet, blood on his face, and raised his sword in defense.

It was a sight to watch—and everyone did. There was an undeclared truce as the two leaders battled. The soldiers lowered their weapons and faces appeared at all of the windows above them. I climbed out of my seat and stood on the front of the car, where I had a perfect view of the combatants.

They were well-matched, both in anger and ability. Dimonte's sword crashed down on Doccia's raised blade. He did a neat parry, then thrust—but Dimonte had moved back. After that it was steel on steel, punctuated by grunted curses.

Back and forth across the cobbles they went, slashing away as if their lives depended on it. Which, of course, they did. It was pretty primitive saber work, slash and parry, but it certainly was energetic. A cry went up as Dimonte drew first blood—a cut on Doccia's side that quickly stained his shirt.

This was the beginning of the end. Dimonte was stronger and angrier, high on victory. If Doccia had been drinking as much as we had been told, he was also fighting a hangover as well as his enemy. Dimonte began pressing harder and harder, slashing remorselessly, pushing the other capo relentlessly across the courtyard. Until his back was to the wall of the building and he could retreat no more. Dimonte beat down the other's guard, hammered him on the jaw with the hilt of his sword—then disarmed Capo Doccia with a savage twist of his blade.

All of his plans for sadistic torture were washed away in the passion of his anger. He drew the blade back—then slashed out.

It was not an attractive sight as the sharp steel tore across Doccia's throat. It sickened me and I turned away. Just as the shadow darkened the sun.

One person looked up, then another—and there was a gasp. I looked too. Only unlike the rest of them I knew exactly what I was looking at.

The immense shining form of a D-class spacer that was equipped with atmospheric G-lift. Tonnes of ship drifting light as a feather over the courtyard. Coming to an effortless stop. Hanging there over our heads in silent menace.

I turned and dived for the controls. There was no time to escape, no way to escape. I was scratching at the storage compartment as the first silvery spheres fell free of the ship. I gave them one horrified glance—then took a deep breath and held it as I pulled the compartment door open and plunged my arm inside. Grabbing up the leather bag as I sat back onto the driver's seat.

All around me the spheres were hitting and bursting, releasing their loads of gas. I dropped the bag onto my lap as the first soldiers crumpled and fell.

My fingers fumbled at the seat belt, lengthening it, as Capo Dimonte tottered then fell forward onto his dead enemy's body.

There was a stinging in my nostrils as I snapped the belt buckle over the bag, sealing it against me. And that was all that I could possibly do.

My lungs were beginning to hurt as I took a last, long look around the courtyard. I had the strong feeling that it would also be my last sight of the fair world of Spiovente.

"Good riddance!" I shouted at the now silent forms, blasting the breath from my lungs. Then breathed in. . . .

I was conscious, I knew that. I could feel something soft under my back and there was a light burning down on my closed eyelids. I was afraid to open them—remembering the blasting headache that had accompanied the last gassing. With this thought I cringed and moved my head.

And felt nothing. Emboldened by this tiny experiment, I let one eye open a crack. Still nothing. I blinked in the strong light but there was no pain, no pain at all.

"A different gas, thank you kindly," I said to no one in particular as I opened my eyes wide.

A small room, curved metal walls, a narrow bunk under me. Even if my last sight had not been of the hovering spacer, I should have been able to figure this one out. They had taken me aboard. But where were all my groats? I looked around rapidly, but they were certainly not in sight. The rapid movements of my head had brought on an attack of dizziness so that I fell back onto the bunk and groaned in loud self-pity.

"Drink this. It will eliminate the symptoms of the gas."

I snapped my eyes open again and looked at the big man who was just closing the door behind him. He was in a uniform of some kind, with plenty of gold buttons and stripes, the sort of thing much favored by the military. He was holding out a plastic beaker which I seized gingerly and sniffed.

"We had plenty of time to poison or kill you while you were unconscious," he said. A sound argument. I drained the bitter liquid and instantly felt better.

"You have stolen my money," I said just as he was beginning to speak.

"Your money is safe—"

"It will be safe only when it is in my hands. As it was when you found me, strapped to my body. Whoever took it is a thief."

"Don't talk to me of thievery!" he snapped. "You probably stole it yourself."

"Prove it! I say I worked hard for that money and I don't intend to have it stolen for the space-war widows pension scheme. . . ."

"That is enough. I did not come here to talk about your miserable groats. They will be placed on deposit in the galactic bank. . . ."

"At what rate of exchange? And what kind of interest will it earn?"

He was coldly angry now. "That's enough. You are in deep trouble—and you have a lot of explaining to do. Professor Lustig tells me that your name is Jim. What is your entire name and where do you come from?"

"My name is Jim Nixon and I am from Venia."

"We will get nowhere if you persist in lying. Your name is James diGriz and you are an escaped convict from Bit O' Heaven."

Well, as you can imagine, I did some rapid blinking at this information. Whoever this lad was he had one hell of an intelligence network. I could see that I was no longer playing the amateur team of the professors. They had called in the pros. And he had thrown me this curve ball to catch me off-balance, get me rattled, get me to talk freely. Except I did not work that way. I shifted mental gears, sat up in the bed so I could see him eye to eye, and spoke calmly.

"We have not been introduced."

The anger was gone now and he was as calm as I was. He turned and pressed a button on the wall that unfolded a metal chair. He sat down on it and crossed his legs.

"Captain Varod of the League Navy. Specializing in planetary mop-up details. Are you ready to answer questions?"

"Yes—if you will trade me one for one. Where are we?"

"About thirteen lightyears out of Spiovente, you'll be happy to hear."

"I am."

"My turn. How did you get to that planet?"

"Aboard a Venian freighter that was smuggling weapons to the now deceased Capo Doccia."

That got his attention all right. He leaned forward eagerly as he spoke. "Who was the captain of the freighter?"

"You are out of turn. What are you going to do with me?"

"You are an escaped prisoner and will be returned to Bit O' Heaven to serve out your prison sentence."

"Really?" I smiled insincerely. "Now I will be happy to answer your question—except I have completely forgotten the captain's name. Would you care to torture me?"

"Don't play games, Jim. You are in deep trouble. Cooperate and I will do what I can for you."

"Good. I remember the name and you put me down on a neutral planet and we call it quits."

"That is impossible. Records are kept and I am an officer of the law. I must return you to Bit O' Heaven."

"Thanks. I just got terminal amnesia. Before you leave would you tell me what is going to happen to Spiovente?"

He sat back in the chair with no intention at all of leaving.

"The first thing that will happen will be the termination of Lustig's disastrous intervention. We were forced into that by the Intergalactic Applied Socioeconomics Association. They managed to raise sufficient funds to put into effect some of their theories. A number of planets financed them and it was easier to let them make idiots of themselves than to try and stop them."

"And they have done that now?"

"Completely. They have all been shipped out and were very happy to go. Having political and economic theories is one thing. But applying them to harsh reality can be a traumatic experience. This has been done in the past—and always with disastrous results. We know none of the details now, they are lost in the mists of time, but there was an insane doctrine called Monetarism that is reputed to have destroyed whole cultures, entire planets. Now another experiment has gone astray, so the specialists will move in as they should have done in the first place."

"Invasion?"

"You have been watching too much tri-D. War is forbidden and you should know better than to suggest that. We have people who will work within the existing society of Spiovente. Probably with this Capo Dimonte, since he has just doubled his domain. He will be aided and encouraged to grow in power, to annex more and more territory."

"And kill more and more people!"

"No, we will see to that. Very soon he will not be able to rule without aid and our bureaucrats are waiting to help him. Centralized government . . ."

"The growth of the judiciary, taxes, I know the drill. You sound just like Lustig."

"Not quite. Our techniques are proven—and they work. Within one generation, two at the most, Spiovente will be welcomed into the family of civilized planets."

"Congratulations. Now, please leave so I can sit and brood about my future incarceration."

"And you still won't tell me the name of the gunrunner? He could continue in his smuggling operations—and you would be responsible for more deaths."

I would be too. Was I responsible for the dead in the courtyard of the keep as well? The attack had been my idea. But Dimonte would have attacked in any case and there could have been even more dead. The acceptance of responsibility was not done easily. Captain Varod must have been reading my mind.

"Do you have a sense of responsibility?" he asked.

Good question. He was a shrewd old boy.

"Yes, I do. I believe in life and the sanctity of life and I do not believe in killing. Each of us has only one go at life and I don't want to be responsible for cutting short anyone else's. I think I have made some mistakes and I hope I have learned by them. The name of the gunrunner is Captain Ga . . ."

"Garth," he said. "We know him and have been watching him. He has made his last voyage."

My thoughts spun rapidly. "Then why ask me if you knew all along?"

"For your sake, Jim, nobody else's. I told you that our job was rehabilitation. You have made an important decision and I believe that you will be a better individual for it. Good luck in the future." He stood to leave.

"Thanks a lot. I'll remember your words when I am cracking boulders on the rock pile."

He stood in the open door and smiled back at me. "I am in the justice business on a very large scale. And, in truth, I don't believe in prisons and incarceration for failed bank robbery. You are destined for better things than that. Therefore I am having you returned to prison. You will be transferred to another ship, on another planet, where you will be locked away until it arrives."

He went out, then turned back for just an instant. "Taking into consideration what you have told me, I am forgetting that you still have a lockpick in the sole of your shoe."

Then he was gone for good. I stared at the closed door and suddenly burst out laughing. It was going to be a good universe after all, filled with good things to be appropriated in a manner only possible to one who knew his trade. And I knew mine!

"Thank you, Bishop, thanks for everything. You have done it, guided me and taught me. Because of you—a Stainless Steel Rat is born!"

The Stainless Steel Rat Gets Drafted

This book is for
Rog Peyton
and all the Brum gang.

Chapter 1

I am too young to die. Just eighteen years old—and now I'm as good as dead. My grip is weakening, my fingers slipping, and the elevator shaft below me is a kilometer deep. I can't hold on any longer. I'm going to fall . . .

Normally I am not prone to panic—but I was panicking now. Shaking from head to toe with fatigue, knowing that there was just no way out of this one.

I was in trouble, mortal trouble, and I had only myself to blame this time. All the good advice I had given myself down through the years, the even better counsel The Bishop had given me, all forgotten. All wiped away by sudden impulse.

Perhaps I deserved to die. Maybe a Stainless Steel Rat had been born—but a very rusty one was about to snuff it right now. The metal door frame was greasy and I had to hold on hard with my aching fingers. My toes barely gripped the narrow ledge—while my unsupported heels hung over the black drop below. Now my arches began to ache with the effort of standing on tiptoe—which was nothing compared to the fire in my throbbing forearms.

It had seemed such a logical, simple, good, intelligent plan at the time.

I now knew it to be irrational, complex, bad and moronic.

"You are an idiot, Jimmy diGriz," I muttered through my tightly shut teeth, realizing only then that they were clamped into my lower lip and drawing blood. I unclamped and spat—and my right hand slipped. The great spasm of fear that swept over me rode down the fatigue and I grabbed a new hold with an explosion of desperate energy.

Which faded away as quickly as it had come, leaving me in the same situation. Tireder if anything. There was no getting out of this one. I was stuck here until I could no longer hold on, until my grip loosened and I fell. Might as well let go now and get it over with . . .

"No, Jim, no surrender."

Through the thudding of blood in my ears my voice seemed to come from a great distance, to be deeper in register than my own, as though The Bishop himself were speaking. The thought was his, the words might very well be his. I held on, though I didn't really know why. And the distant whine was disturbing.

Whine? The elevator shaft was black as the grave and just as silent. Was the maglevlift moving again? With muscle-tight slowness I bent my head and looked down the shaft. Nothing.

Something. A tiny glimmer of light.

The elevator was coming up the shaft.

But so what? There were two hundred and thirty-three floors in this government building. What were the odds that it would stop at the floor below me so I could step neatly back onto its top? Astronomical I was sure, and I was in no mood to work them out. Or perhaps it would come up to this floor and scrape me off like a bug as it went by? Another nice thought. I watched the light surge upward toward me, my eyes opening wider and wider to match the growing glow. The increasing whine of the centering wheels, rush of air exploding at me, this was the end . . .

The end of its upward motion. The car stopped just below me, so close that I could hear the door swoosh open and the voices of the two guards inside.

"I'll cover you. Keep your safety off when you search the hall."

"You'll cover me, thanks! I didn't hear myself volunteer."

"You didn't—I did. My two stripes to your one mean you take a look."

One-stripe muttered complaints as he moved out as slowly as he could. As his shadow occulted the light from the open door I stepped down onto the car with my left foot, as gingerly as I could. Hoping that any movement to the car caused by my climbing onto it would be masked by his exiting.

Not that it was easy to do. My thigh muscle spasmed with cramp and my fingers were locked into place. I stepped slowly back with my vibrating right foot until I was standing on top of the elevator. My cramped fingers still gripped the frame: I felt very much the fool.

"Hall is empty," a distant voice called out.

"Take a reading from the proximity recorder."

There were muttered grumbles and clattering from outside as I wrenched my right hand free of the greasy metal, reached over with it to grapple with my still recalcitrant left hand.

"Got a reading for myself. Other than that the last movement in the corridor was at eighteen hundred. People going home."

"Then we do have a mystery," two-stripes said. "Come on back. We had a readout that showed this car going up to this floor. We called it back from this floor. Now you tell me that no one got out. A mystery."

"That's no mystery, that's just a malfunction. A glitch in the computer. The thing is giving itself instructions when no one else will."

"Much as I hate to agree—I agree. Let's go back and finish the card game."

One-stripe returned, the elevator door closed, I sat down as quietly as I could, and we all dropped back down the shaft together. The guards got out at the prison floor and I just sat there in creaking silence as I kneaded the knots out of my muscles with trembling fingers. When they were roughly under control again I opened the hatch that I was sitting on, dropped down into the car and looked out slowly and carefully. The card players were out of sight in the guardroom, where they belonged. With infinite caution I retraced the route I had taken during my abortive escape. Slinking guiltily along the walls—if I had a tail it would have been between my legs—making a fumbled hash of opening the locked corridor doors with my lockpick.

Finally reaching my own cell, unlocking and relocking it, slipping the lockpick back into my shoe sole—dropping onto my bed with a sigh that must have been heard around the world. I did not dare speak out loud in the sleeping silence of the cell block, but I did shout the words inside my head.

"Jim, you are the dumbest most moronic idiot who ever came down the pike. Don't, and I repeat, don't ever do anything like that again."

I won't, I promised in grim silence. That message had now been well drilled into my medulla oblongata. The truth was inescapable. I had done everything wrong in my eagerness to get out of prison. Now I would see if I could get it right.

I had been in too much of a rush. There should never have been any hurry. After he had arrested me, Captain Varod, strongman of the League Navy, had admitted that he knew all about the lockpick that I had hidden. He did not like prisons, he had told me that. Although he was a firm believer in law and order he did not believe I should be incarcerated on my home planet, Bit O" Heaven, for all of the troubles that I had caused there. Neither, for that matter, did I. Since he knew I had the lockpick I should have bided my time. Waited to make my escape during the transfer out of this place.

During the transfer. It had never been my intention of doing anything but serve my time here in this heavily guarded and technologically protected prison in the middle of the League building in the center of the League base on this planet called Steren-Gwandra—about which I knew absolutely nothing other than its name. I had been enjoying the rest, and the meals, a real pleasure after the rigors of war on Spiovente and the disgusting slop that passed for food there. I should have kept on enjoying, building my strength in preparation for my imminent freedom. So why had I tried to crack out of here?

Because of her, a woman, a female creature briefly seen and instantly recognized. One glimpse and all reason had fled, emotion had ruled and I had attempted my disastrous escape. More fool I. I grimaced at the memory, recalling all too clearly how this idiot adventure had begun.

It had been during our afternoon exercise period, that wildly exciting occasion when the prisoners were let out of their cells and permitted to shuffle around the ferroconcrete yard under the gentle light of the double suns. I shuffled with the rest and tried to ignore my companions. Low foreheads, joined eyebrows, pendulous and drool-flecked lips—a very unsatisfactory peer group of petty criminals that I was ashamed to be a part of. Then something had stirred them, some unaccustomed novelty that had excited their feeble intellects and had caused them to rush toward the chain-link fence emitting hoarse cries and vulgar exhortations. Numbed by the monotony of prison life even I had felt a twinge of curiosity and desire to see what had caused this explosion of unfamiliar emotion. It should have been obvious. Women. That, and strong drink and its aftereffects, were the only topics that ever stirred the sluggish synapses of their teeny minds.

Three newly arrived female prisoners were passing by on the other side of the fence. Two of them, cut from the same cloth as my companions, responded with equally hoarse cries and interesting gestures of the fingers and hand. The third prisoner walked quietly, if grimly, ignoring her surroundings. Her walk was familiar. But how could it be? I had never even heard of this planet before I had been forcefully brought here. This was a mystery in need of a solution. I hurried along the fence to its end, cleared a space for myself by applying my knuckles to a hair-covered neck in such a manner that the neck's owner slipped into unconsciousness, took his space and looked out.

At a very familiar face passing by not a meter distant. Without a doubt a face and a name that I knew very well.

Bibs, the crewgirl from Captain Garth's spacer.

She was a link to Garth and I had to talk to her, to find out where he was. By kidnapping us and dumping us on the loathsome planet of Spiovente, Captain Garth had been responsible for The Bishop's death. Which meant that I would like to be responsible for his in return.

So, without further thought, and possessed only of a suicidal and impractical enthusiasm, I had foolishly escaped. Only the luck that watches over the completely witless had saved my life and permitted my return, undetected, to my prison cell. I blushed now with shame as I thought about the stupidity of my plan. Lack of thought, lack of foresight—and the incredibly dumb assumption that all security in the giant building would be identical. During our daily exodus and return to the cell block I had noted the exceedingly simple locks on all of the doors, the absence of any alarms. I had assumed that the rest of the building had been the same.

I had assumed wrong. The car of the maglevlift had notified the guards when it had been used. I had spotted the detectors in the corridor at once when the door had opened on the top floor. That was why I had tried the escape hatch in the roof, hoping to find a way out through the mechanism at the top of the shaft.

Except that there had been no mechanism there—just another door. Opening into another floor that did not appear on the bank of buttons inside the car. Some secret location known only to the authorities. Hoping to penetrate this secret I had climbed onto the doorsill and searched for a way to open the door. Only to have the elevator vanish from behind me leaving me stranded on top of the empty shaft.

I had come out of this little harebrained adventure far better than I had deserved. Luck would not ride with me a second time. Cool planning was needed. I put this nearly disastrous escapade behind me and thought furiously of schemes and ways to make contact with the crewgirl.

"Do it honestly," I said, and shocked myself with the words.

Honest? Me? The stainless steel rat who prowls the darkness of the night in solitary silence, fearing no one, needing no one.

Yes. Painful as the realization was, just this once honesty was indeed the best policy.

"Attention, foul jailers, attention!" I shouted and hammered on the bars of my cage. "Arouse yourself from your sweat-sodden slumbers and vulgar, erotic dreams and take me to Captain Varod. Soonest—or even sooner!"

My fellow prisoners awoke, calling out in righteous anger and threatened all sorts of unimaginative bodily harm. I returned the insults with enthusiasm and eventually the night guard appeared, scowling with menace.

"Hi, there," I called out cheerily. "Nice to see a friendly face."

"You want your skull broke, kid?" he asked. His repartee just about as sharp as that of the inmates.

"No. But I want you to stay out of trouble by instantly taking me to Captain Varod since I have information of such military importance that you would be shot instantly if suspected of keeping it from the captain for more than a second or two."

He added some more threats, but there was a glint of worry in his eyes as he thought about what I had said. It seemed obvious, even to someone of his guttering intelligence, that passing the buck was the wisest fallback position. He growled some more insults when I pointed back down the corridor, but left in any case and went to his telephone. Nor was my wait a long one. A brace of overmuscled and overweight guards appeared on the scene within minutes. They unlocked my cell, clamped on the cuffs and hurried me into the maglevlift and up a few hundred stories to a bare office. Where they fastened the cuffs to a heavy chair and left. The lieutenant who entered a few minutes later was still blinking the sleep from his eyes and was not happy at being disturbed in the middle of the night.

"I want Varod," I said. "I don't talk to the hired help."

"Shut up, diGriz, before you get yourself into worse trouble. The captain is in deepspace and unreachable. I am from his department and urge you to speak quickly before I bounce you out of here."

It sounded reasonable enough. And I had very little choice.

"Have you ever heard of a space-going Venian swine who goes by the name of Captain Garth?"

"Get on with it," he said in a bored voice, yawning to drive home the point. "I worked on your case so you can speak freely. What do you know that you haven't told us already?"

"I have information about our gunrunning friend. You do have him in custody, don't you."

"DiGriz—you give us information, that is the way that it works, not the other way around." That was what he said, but his expression spoke otherwise. A fleeting instant of worry. If that meant what I thought it meant then Garth had managed to escape them.

"I saw a girl today, a new prisoner being brought in. Her name is Bibs."

"Did you get me out of bed to describe some sordid sexual secret?"

"No. I just thought you should know that Bibs was a crewgirl on Garth's ship."

This caught his attention instantly, and not being as experienced as his commanding officer he could not conceal the look of sudden interest.

"You are sure of this?"

"Check for yourself. The information on today's arrivals should be readily available."

It was: he sat behind the steel desk and hammered away at the keys on the terminal there. Looked at the screen and scowled in my direction.

"Three women admitted today. None named Bibs."

"How very unusual." Scorn dripped from my voice. "Can it be that the criminal classes now use aliases?"

He did not answer but tapped away at the terminal again. The fax buzzed and produced three sheets of paper. Three color portraits. I dropped two of them onto the floor and handed the third back.

"Bibs."

He bashed some more keys, then slumped back and rubbed his chin as he studied the screen.

"It fits, it fits," he muttered. "Marianney Giuffrida, age twenty-five, occupation given as electrotechnician with deepspace experience. Arrested on a drugs possession charge, anonymous tip, swears she was framed. No other details."

"Ask her about Garth. Use persuasion. Make her talk."

"You have our thanks for your assistance, diGriz. It will go on your record." He tapped a number into the phone. "But you have been watching too many films. There is no way we can force people to give evidence. But we can question and observe and draw conclusions. They will take you back to your cell now."

"Gee, thanks for the thanks. Thanks for nothing. Can you at least do me the favor of telling me how long you intend to keep me here?"

"That should be easy enough to find out." A quick access of the terminal and a sage nod of the head as the door opened behind me. "You will be leaving us the day after tomorrow. A spacer will be stopping at a planet with the interesting name of Bit O" Heaven, where, it appears, you have to answer some criminal charges."

"Guilty until found guilty, I suppose." I sneered and whined to hide the surge of enthusiasm that raced through me. Once out of here I really would be out of here. I ignored the rough clutch and muttered complaints of my warders and permitted myself to be docilely led back to my cell. I was going to be good, very, very good, until the day after tomorrow.

But I lay awake a long time after that, staring into the darkness, working out how I was going to pry the information I needed out of crewmember Bibs.

Chapter 2

"Sign here."

I signed. The ancient graybeard behind the desk passed over the plastic bag containing all of my worldly possessions, forcibly removed from me when I had been incarcerated. I reached for them but the fat guard reached even faster.

"Not yet, prisoner," he said, whisking them away from my clutching fingers. "These will be forwarded to the arresting authorities."

"They're mine!"

"Take it up with them. All set, Rasco?"

"My name's not Rasco!"

"Mine is. Shut up," the other guard said. A well-muscled and nasty individual whose right wrist was secured to my left by a pair of shining cuffs. He pulled hard on this connecting link so I stumbled toward him. "You do what I say and no backtalk or funny stuff."

"Yes, sir. Sorry."

I lowered my eyes in humility, which caused him to smirk with assumed superiority. He should only know that I was using the opportunity to look more closely at the cuffs. Bulldog-Crunchers, sold throughout the known galaxy, guaranteed foolproof. Maybe proof against fools but I could open them in under two seconds. It was going to be a nice day.

Fatso walked on my right side, well-connected Rasco on my left. I marched in step with them, eager to leave the prison and examine the world waiting outside the League building. I had come here in a closed van and had seen nothing. Eagerness possessed me in expectation of a first glimpse of my new home; thoughts about my forceful removal from this planet may have preoccupied my guardians—but were the farthest thing from my mind at this moment.

Exiting the building was not easily done—and I gave myself another mental kick for even thinking of breaking out of this bunker-skyscraper. There were three doors to go out through, one after another, each sealed as tightly as an airlock. Our passes were slipped into computerized machines that hummed and clicked—then robot sensors examined our fingerprints and retinal patterns to make sure we matched the details on the passes. This was done three times before the outer portal hummed open and a wave of warm air, smell and sound washed in.

As we went down the steps to the street I gaped like a rube. I had never seen anything like this before. Of course my experience was strictly limited since this was only the third planet I had ever visited. My life on the porcuswine farms of Bit O" Heaven and my service in the swamps of Spiovente had not prepared me for the manifold impressions that bombarded me.

A wave of heat and dusty air washed over me. It was filled with pungent aromas, loud cries and a cacophony of strange noises. At the same time as my ears and nose were being assaulted my eyes bulged at the seething mass of humanity, the strange vehicles—and the four-legged alien creatures. One passed close by, a man sitting on its back, its great feet thudding on the ground, eyes rolling in my direction. Its mouth opened to reveal hideous yellow teeth and it squealed loudly. I drew back and my guards laughed aloud at this perfectly reasonable reaction.

"We'll protect you from the *margh*," Fatso said, and they chortled with dim pleasure.

Maybe it was called a *margh* in the local lingo, but it was still a horse to me. I had seen them in the ancient history tapes at school. The creatures had been used for farming when Bit O" Heaven was first settled, but had soon succumbed to the deadly native life. Only the indestructible porcuswine had been able to survive. I looked more closely at the horse, at the obviously herbivorous teeth, and realized it posed no threat. But it was big. Two more of the creatures came up, towing a boxlike affair mounted on large wheels. The driver, sitting high above, pulled the thing to a stop when Rasco whistled to him.

"Get in," Fatso ordered, swinging open a door in the vehicle's side. I held back, pointed with distaste.

"It's filthy in there! Can't the League Navy provide decent transportation . . ."

Rasco kicked me in the back of the leg so I fell forward. "Inside—and no backtalk!" They climbed in after me. "It is Navy policy to use native transport when possible, to aid the local economy. So shut up and enjoy."

I shut, but I didn't enjoy. I looked unseeingly at the crowded street as we rumbled away, thinking of the best way to escape my captors while inflicting a bit of damage on my sadistic companion. Now would be as good a time as any. Strike like lightning, then leave them both unconscious in this vehicle while I slipped away in the crowd. I bent over and scratched furiously at my ankle.

"I've been bitten! There are bugs in here!"

"Bite them back," Fatso said and they both roared with juvenile laughter. Wonderful. Neither saw me slip the lockpick from my shoe and palm it. I turned toward Rasco with mayhem in mind just as the vehicle lurched to a stop and Fatso reached across and threw open the door. "Out," he ordered and Rasco pulled painfully on the handcuff, I gaped at the marble-fronted building before us.

"This isn't the spaceport," I protested.

"You got good eyes," Rasco sneered and dragged me after him. "A local version of a linear. Let's go."

I decided I wouldn't. I had had more than enough of their repellent company. But I had to stumble after them for the moment, looking about for some opportunity—and seeing it just ahead. Men, and only men, were entering and exiting a doorway under a sign that proudly proclaimed PYCHER PYSA GORRYTH. Though I knew nothing of the local language I could figure this one out easily enough. I drew back and pointed.

"Before we get on the linear I gotta go in there."

"No way," Rasco said. Sadist. But I got unexpected aid from his companion.

"Take him in. It's going to be a long trip."

Rasco muttered disgustedly. But Fatso was obviously his superior because he pushed me forward. The pycher pysa was about as primitive as they come, a simple trough against one wall, a line of men facing it. I headed for a vacant position on the far end and fumbled with my clothing. Rasco watched me with obvious displeasure.

"I can't do anything with you watching," I wailed.

He rolled his eyes upward for a second. Just long enough for me to get his neck with my free hand. His look of surprise faded as I clamped down hard with my thumb. After this I had only to guide his unconscious fall to the tile floor. As he hit with a satisfactory thud I clicked open the cuff on my wrist. He snored lightly as I quickly frisked him, I had a reputation as a thief to live up to, and slipped his wallet from his hip pocket. It was safely hidden in my own before I stood and turned about. The row of men against the wall were all looking at me.

"He fainted," I said, and they gaped with incomprehension. *"Li svenas,"* I added, which did not clarify it for them in any way. I pointed to the unconscious copper, to the door, then at myself. "I'm going for help. You lads keep an eye on him and I'll be right back."

None of them were in any position to follow me as I scuttled out of the entrance. Practically into Fatso's arms. He shouted something and reached for me—but I was long gone. Out of the station and into the crowd. There were some more outcries from behind me but they soon died away as I twisted between two horses, around a coach and down a dark alley on the far side of the street. It was that easy.

The alley opened into another street, just as crowded as the first, and I strolled along it, just a part of the crowd. Free as a bird. I actually whistled as I walked, staring around at the sights, the veiled women and the brightly garbed men. This was the life!

Or was it? Alone on a primitive planet, not speaking the language, sought by the authorities—what did I have to be cheerful about? Black gloom descended instantly and I sneered aloud.

"That's it, Jim? You turn coward at the slightest setback. For shame! What would The Bishop say to this?"

He would say stop talking in public, I thought as I noticed the strange looks I was getting. So I whistled happily, not a care in the world, turned a corner and saw the tables and chairs, men sitting and drinking interesting beverages, under a sign that said SOSTEN HA GWYRAS which conveyed exactly nothing to me. But underneath it was printed NI PAROLOS ESPERANTO, BONVENUU. I hoped that they spoke Esperanto better than they wrote it. I found a table against the wall, dropped into a chair and snapped my fingers at the ancient waiter.

"Dhe'th plegadow," he said.

"*Plegadow* the others," I said. "We speak Esperanto. What's to drink, Dad?"

"Beer, wine, dowr-tom-ys."

"I'm just not in the mood for a dowr-tom-ys today. A large beer, if you please."

When he turned away I dug out Rasco's wallet. If my guards were supposed to encourage the local economy they should be carrying some of the local currency. The wallet clunked when I dropped it onto the table, heavy with little metal discs. I shook one out and turned it over. It had the number two stamped into one side, with *Arghans* on the other.

"That will be one Arghans," the waiter said, putting a brimming clay pot in front of me. I passed over the coin.

"Take that, my good man, and keep the change."

"You offworlders are so generous," he said, muffledly as he bit the coin. "Not mean, stupid, vicious like the locals. You want girl? Boy? *Kewarghen* to smoke?"

"Later perhaps. I'll let you know. Beer now and the heady pleasures of native life to come."

He went away muttering and I took a great slug of the beer. Instantly regretting it. I swallowed—and regretted that as well as the noxious brew bubbled and seethed its way through my digestive track. I pushed the jar away and belched. Enough of this tomfoolery. I had escaped, great, step one. But what came next?

Nothing that I could think of at the moment. I sipped at the beer, it still tasted just as repulsive, but even this heroic treatment produced no inspiration. I was grateful for the interruption when the waiter sidled over and whispered hoarsely behind the back of his hand.

"New shipment *kewarghen* fresh from the fields. You get high, stay up for many days. Want some? No? What about girl with whips? Snakes? Leather straps and hot mud . . ."

I interrupted since I wasn't sure that I enjoyed where the conversation was going. "I am sated, I tell you sated. All I wish are directions to return to the municipal edifice."

"Do not know what long words mean."

"Want to find building big, high, filled with plenty offworlders."

"Ahh, you mean the *lys*. For one Arghans I take you there."

"For one Arghans you give me instructions. I don't want to drag you away from your work." Nor did I want to be led astray to one of the many offers he had made. In the end he had to agree. I memorized the instructions, sipped some more of the beer and instantly regretted it, then slipped away when he had vanished into the back room.

As I walked a glimmer of a plan began to develop. I must think of a way to get to Bibs, the crewgirl from the freighter. Garth, the captain of her ship, had escaped, I was sure of that. But she might know more about him. She was my only link with this villain. But how could I get into the prison? I knew the name she had been arrested under, Marianney Giuffrida. Could I pass myself off as a concerned relative, one Hasenpeffer Giuffrida? The local identification should be easy to forge—if it existed at all. But would the computer identify me as an ex-prisoner when I entered the building? Or had I been wiped from its memory when I had left? Perhaps I had been, but would Fatso put me back in memory when he reported my escape?

These thoughts were rattling around in my head when I turned the next corner and found the gigantic edifice before me. It rose up from the low buildings of the city like a towering cliff—and looked just as impenetrable. I strolled by and looked up at the steps I had so recently descended, watched the doors open to admit a visitor. Then close again like a bank vault. My mind was still blank. I stood with my back to a brick wall across from the building. Which was perhaps not too bright, since I was still wearing prison garb. But such was the variety of local costume that my uniform drew no notice at all. I leaned and waited for inspiration to strike.

It didn't. But pure, random luck, a chance in a thousand did. The doors opened one more time and three people emerged. Two minions of the law, this obvious from the size of their boots, flanking a delicate female form. One thick wrist was manacled to her tiny one.

It was Bibs.

The suddenness of her appearence froze me in place. Kept me leaning against the wall as they descended to street level where one of the guards waved and whistled. In quick response two of the horsedrawn vehicles raced their way, one of them neatly cutting off the other. There were shouted curses and loud neighing as the horses reared up. This was quickly sorted out and the loser trotted off. The high body of the horsedrawn hulk blocked my view, but as clear as though it were transparent I knew what was happening. Door being opened, prisoner escorted inside, door closed . . .

The thing started forward as the driver's whip cracked, even as I was hurrying across the road. Getting up speed as I ran after it, jumped, got my feet on the step and hauled the door open.

"Out," the nearest guard said, turning toward me. "This cab is taken . . ."

We looked at each other in mutual recognition—he was the night guard from the prison. With a cry of anger he reached for me. But I reached quicker, jumping in on top of him. He was big and strong—but I was fast. I had a quick glimpse of the shocked look on Bibs's face as I turned all my attention to avoiding his clutch and getting in a quick blow with the edge of my hand.

As soon as he went limp I rolled over to face the other guard and discovered that he had no interest in me at all. Bibs had her free arm around his neck and was throttling him to death. He flailed with his other hand but could do nothing because it was manacled to her wrist.

"Just wait . . . until this one . . . is dead too," Bibs gasped.

I didn't explain that the guard I had taken care of was only unconscious but reached over and grabbed her elbow hard, index finger grinding into the big nerve there. Her arm went numb, dropped away, and her face grew red with fury. But before she could speak I silenced the gasping guard and unlocked the cuffs. She rubbed her wrist and smiled.

"I don't know where you dropped from, buster, or why, but I appreciate the help." She cocked her head and looked more closely at me. "I know you, don't I? Yes, of course, you're the midnight passenger, Jimmy something."

"That's right, Bibs. Jim diGriz at your service."

She laughed, loud and happily, while she removed all the possessions of the two unconscious guards, then scowled when I manacled them together.

"Better to kill them," she said.

"Better not to. Right now we're not important enough to them to cause much fuss. But if we murdered two of their men they would turn this planet over to find us."

"I guess you're right," she said with reluctant agreement—then kicked both unconscious bodies with sudden fury.

"They can't feel anything."

"They will when they wake up. So where do we go from here, Jim?"

"You tell me. I know absolutely nothing at all about this planet."

"I know far too much."

"Then lead the way."

"Right."

She opened the door as our vehicle slowed and we slipped out, stepped up onto the pavement as it lumbered from sight.

Chapter 3

Bibs tucked her arm through mine, which felt very cheering, as we strolled along the busy avenue. Anywhere else our gray prison clothes, tastefully decorated with blood-red broad arrows, would have certainly drawn attention—and apprehension. Not among the motley throngs crowding these streets, dressed in every manner possible. There were bearded men in fringed buckskins, women in layers of colored gauze, armed warriors in leather and steel; robes, gowns, chainmail, cuirasses, sashes—everything imaginable. Plus a few that defied the imagination. We drew no attention at all.

"Do you have any money?" Bibs asked.

"Just a few Arghans I lifted from one of my guards. Like you, I have just escaped."

Her eyebrows lifted at this—very attractive eyebrows arched above even more attractive eyes I noticed.

"Is that why you helped me out? What were you in prison for? All I know is that you and the old boy were left behind on Spiovente. Scuttlebutt had it that Garth sold you into slavery."

"He did, and my friend is dead because of that. I am a little bitter about Garth for a lot of reasons. I liked The Bishop. He helped me, taught me a lot, and I am happy to say that I was able to help him in return. We left our home world in a hurry, as you will remember, and paid Captain Garth a lot of money to get us away. But that wasn't enough for him. He earned more by selling us into slavery. I lived—but The Bishop died because of being a slave. As you can imagine I am not wildly pleased by his death. A number of loathsome things happened on that planet, the least of which was my being caught by the League Navy. They were returning me to my home planet to stand trial."

"On what charges?" There was keen interest in her voice.

"Bank robbery, criminal abduction, jailbreak. Things like that."

"Wonderful!" she said, laughing aloud with joy; she had very neat white teeth. "You did yourself an immense favor when you came to little Bibs's aid. I know this planet well, know where the money is. Know how to buy our way offplanet when we are done. You steal it, I'll spend it—and our troubles are over."

"Sounds reasonable. Could we talk about it over some food? It's been a long time since breakfast."

"Of course—I know just the place."

And she did too. The restaurant was small and discreet while the *felyon ha kyk mogh* tasted a lot better than it sounded. We washed it down with a great bowl of *ru'th gwyn*, which turned out to be satisfactory red wine: I memorized the name for future use. When we had eaten our fill I took one of the wood splinters from the jar on the table and worried bits of gristle from between my teeth.

"Do you mind if I ask you a question?" I asked, asking a question. Bibs sipped at her wine and waved permission. "You know why I was imprisoned. Would you consider it rude if I asked the reason for your incarceration?"

She slammed her mug down so hard that it cracked and oozed a carmine trickle. She was unaware of it; her face twisted with anger and I could hear her teeth grate together.

"He did it, I'm sure, it had to be him, the *bastardaĉfiulo!*" Which is about the worst name you can call anyone in Esperanto. "Captain Garth, he's the one. He knew the League Navy was after us for gunrunning. He paid us off here—and the next day I was arrested. He tipped them off and planted the *kewarghen* in my bag. With that evidence they busted me on a drugs charge, selling to the natives and all that. I want to kill him."

"So do I—for causing the death of my friend. But why did he want you arrested?"

"Revenge. I kicked him out of bed. He was too kinky for my liking."

I gulped and coughed and took a long slug of wine and hoped that she wouldn't notice that I was blushing. She didn't. Her eyes, still glazed with anger, stared past me into space. "Kill him, I really would like to kill him. I know that it's impossible but, oh how he deserves it."

"Why impossible?" I asked with some relief, glad to have the conversation back on comfortable topics like murder and revenge.

"Why? What do you know about this planet, Jim?"

"Nothing. Other than its name, Steren-Gwandra."

"Which means 'planet' in the local lingo. They are not a linguistically imaginative lot. At least those here in Brastyr aren't. Like many other settled planets this one was cut off from galactic contact during the breakdown years. Brastyr, this continent, has few natural resources and over the centuries they managed to lose all of the old technology. They are so dim that most of them forgot

Esperanto. Not the traders though, they had to deal with the offshore island. By the time that galactic contact was reestablished the locals had sunk into a sort of agricultural semifeudalism."

"Like Spiovente?"

"Not quite. Just offshore is this damned great island I mentioned, separated from this mainland by a narrow strait. Almost all of the minerals, coal and oil in this hemisphere are located there. That's why it was settled first and why it was well developed before the second wave of immigrants arrived during the diaspora ages. None of the newcomers were allowed to settle there. Not that they cared, this entire continent was wide-open and bountiful and the arrangement suited all parties concerned. Industry and technology over there on Nevenkebla, farming and forestry here. I doubt if anything changed much during the breakdown years—I imagine the relationship was intensified if anything. That's why we are never going to get close enough to Garth to kill him."

"I don't understand. What has this got to do with him?"

"He's on the island. Unreachable." She sighed and rubbed her fingertip in circles in the pool of spilled wine. I was still puzzled.

"But Garth is a Venian, like you. The captain of a Venian ship. Why should they protect him?"

"Because he's not Venian, that's why. The Nevenkebla military bought the ship, he commanded it. We were happy to go along with the plan; they paid well. Venians are very flexible when it comes to money. But he is really something big in the military there. They run the place. All those guns we were smuggling were made on the island. It was a good racket, plenty of offplanet currency. But when the League Navy got too close they paid us off and closed the operation down. There is just no way to get at him on that island."

"I'll find a way."

"I hope that you do. I'll give you all the help that I can. But first things first, Jim. We will have to stay out of sight for a bit while they are looking for us—and that will take a pile of Arghans. How much do you have?"

She spread out the coins she had stolen and I added mine to the pile.

"Not enough. We need a lot for bribes, a safe place to get out of sight. I have contacts, a fence I used to peddle to. For the right price we can have him find a safe house . . ."

"No. Avoid the criminal classes at all counts. Too expensive and the first place that the authorities will look. Do they have hotels here? Expensive, luxurious hotels?"

"Not as such. But there are *ostelyow* where traveling gentry put up. But offworlders never go there."

"Even better. Can you pass as a native?"

"*Yredy*. You could too with a little effort. There are so many different accents and dialects here that no one will notice."

"Ideal. Let us then instantly steal a lot of money, buy some expensive clothes and jewelry and check in at the best *ostel.* Agreed?"

"Agreed!" She laughed out loud and clapped her hands together. "I swear, Jim, you are a breath of fresh air on this fetid planet. I like your style. But it won't be easy. They don't have banks here. All the cash is held by moneylenders called *hoghas*. Their places are like small forts. Plenty of guards, always from the moneylender's own family so they can't be bribed."

"Sounds good. Let's go check one out. Then we will go back tonight and crack it."

"Do you mean it?"

"Never more serious."

"I've never met anyone like you. You look like a kid—but you can really take care of yourself."

I did not like that kid remark but I stayed shut up and tried not to pout while she made plans.

"We'll take some of these Arghans, change them for Nevenkebla coins. This will take a lot of arguing over rate of exchange so you will have time to look around. I'll do the talking. You just carry the money and keep your mouth shut. We'll get you a bodyguard's club first, then they'll never even notice you."

"No time like the present. Let's find a club shop."

This was easily enough done. Most of the side streets were open markets, with stalls and tiny shops that sold an apparently endless variety of cloth, fruit, meals wrapped in leaves, knives, saddles, tents—and clubs. While the merchant extolled the value of his wares, muffledly and incomprehensively through the layers of cloth about his face and neck, I hefted the samples and tested their swing. I finally settled on a meter length of tough wood that was bound about with iron bands.

"This looks like what we want," I told Bibs. The weapon vendor nodded and took the coins and muttered some more. Bibs pointed inside.

"He insists that a year guarantee goes with every club and you must try it out before you leave."

The testing block proved to be a large upright stone that had been carved into human form, what might at one time have resembled a man in armor. But years of testing had taken their toll. Gouges, nicks and missing chunks defaced it; noseless, chinless, with a single fragment of ear remaining. I hefted my club, tried a few practice swings—then stood with my back to the stone while I psyched up my muscles with some dynamic-tension contractions and a breathing mantra. I was chuffing as nicely as a Spiovente steam wagon, holding the club upright, when I felt ready.

Timed release, that's the secret. Not a secret really, just technique and practice. A single shout contracted my body all in an instant. In time with the sound

I swung about with all of my weight and strength focused on the iron band on the end of the club. It whistled through a half-circle that terminated on the side of the rock head.

There was a ringing crack as the neck shattered and the stone head fell off. The club was still sound and the iron ring had a slight nick.

"This one will do," I said, as offhandedly as I could.

They were both very impressed, let me tell you. I was impressed myself. It had been a good blow, better than I had realized.

"Do you do that often?" Bibs asked in a hushed voice.

"If I have to," I said with a calm I did not feel. "Now take me to your *hogh*."

We found one just a few streets away, the identity of the business made known by a skeleton in an iron cage above the door.

"Some sign," I said. "You would think they would hang out a painting of a money bag or a wooden Arghans."

"This is more practical. That is the last thief they caught trying to steal from them."

"Oh, thanks."

"It's just a tradition, don't let it disturb you."

Easy enough for her to say—she wasn't going to rob this place. Disturbed, I followed her past two ugly weightlifters who leaned on their spears and scowled at us.

"Hogh," Bibs said, sniffing with disdain at the guards. They muttered something not too nice, but still knocked on the iron-bound door until it creaked open. Inside were more guardians from the same mold. Except these had swords. The door slammed shut and was locked behind us as we passed through a dark room into the courtyard beyond. There were spikes—as well as more guards—on the surrounding wall. Not a wall, really, but the roof of the buildings that surrounded the courtyard. The *hogh* himself sat on a large chest, shielded from the sun by a canopy, guarded by two more men—this time armed with pikes. The chest had a flat top and was covered with pillows.

"I suppose he sleeps on it at night," I said, a feeble joke to build the morale.

"Of course," Bibs said and the morale slumped even lower.

The moneylender was all smarmy gestures and oily voice. Bibs jingled our money at him and he smarmed even more. At the clap of his hands assistants cleared the pillows away and opened the lid of the chest. I looked in and the guards looked at me. It was neatly divided into sections and each section was filled with leather bags. More orders and hand clapping produced a bag that was placed on top of the now reclosed chest. He sat back on the lid with a happy sigh and cradled the bag in his lap, opened it and let a trickle of shining coins run through his fingers. The haggling began and I feigned boredom and looked around at the courtyard.

This was not going to be easy, not easy at all. The entrance door would certainly be sealed and guarded. If I came over the wall there were those spikes—and more guards as well. Then what? Sneak down into the courtyard and tip the old boy off into the dust, grab the bag. And get speared, stabbed, clubbed and so forth. Not an attractive proposition at all. We were going to have to get a new plan to raise funds. I could see no way to get into this place; brute strength was far more efficient than technology in this setup. And say I got in, say I lifted the loot—there was the little matter of getting out with it. Though that might not be too difficult . . .

I felt the glimmerings of an idea and held onto them and stirred them about. Keeping my expression as calm and stony as possible, with just a hint of a snarl as I looked at the guards, who snarled back. Negotiations were progressing well with plenty of wails of grief and snorts of disdain from both sides. I was only barely aware of this as I rough-fashioned my plan, ran it around and polished it a bit, then took it through slowly, step by step, to see if it would work. Given a little bit of luck it would. Was it the only plan? I sighed inwardly. Yes, all things considered, it was the only plan. I swung my club impatiently and called out to Bibs.

"Come on lady, don't take all day." She turned about and scowled.

"What did you say?"

"You heard me. You came to the bodyguard hiring hall and promised good pay for a short day. But the pay ain't that good and the day is too long."

If the *hogh* didn't understand Esperanto the plan would stop there. But I could see his ears perk up, listening and understanding everything we said. Bash on—no turning back now. Bibs didn't know what I was doing, but she was smart enough to play along, taking umbrage at my insults.

"Listen you muscle-bound moron—I can hire better than you for half the price. I don't need the static from a *malbonulo* whose eyebrows meet in the middle!"

"That does it!" I shouted. "I don't take that from no one!"

I swung my club at her in a wicked blow that just brushed her hair. It didn't touch her—so I let the butt end follow through with a light tap on the forehead that dropped her to the ground. With Bibs safely out of the picture I would now see if I could get away with what is usually referred to as a smash-and-grab.

My club swung again and knocked down one of the poles that held up the canopy. I stepped forward as it fell and chopped the *hogh* on the side of the neck as the cloth engulfed us.

Fast now, Jim. You have seconds—or less. I groped the bag of coins out of his lap and stuffed them inside my shirt. It wouldn't fit until I spilled some out. Seconds. Gone.

There was plenty of shouting now and struggling with the cloth. I pulled myself free—and walked away, calling back over my shoulder.

"I quit, lady. Get another bodyguard. Only poofters work for women anyway."

Two paces, three, four. The armed men looking from me to the heaving canopy as the guards there pulled it free. One of them emerged, dragging the unconscious *hogh*, shouting and screaming with anger. I did not need a translation. All of the other guards howled in rage and ran toward me.

I turned tail and ran in the opposite direction. Away from the only exit.

But toward the flight of wooden stairs that ran up to the roof.

The single guard there stabbed at me with his spear. I parried it with the club and kicked him hard where it would make the best impression. Jumped his falling body and bounded up the stairs two at a time and almost impaled myself on the sword of the man standing at the top. All I could do was dive under it, roll, crash into his legs and bring him down.

Catching him on the head with the butt of the club as I scrambled to my feet, coins jingling down about me.

Three other guards on the roof were screeching and lumbering toward me. I ran to the edge, looked at the drop, cursed aloud. The cobbled street was too far below. If I jumped I would break a leg. Turned and threw my club at the first of the attackers. It caught him nicely and the second man ran into him.

I saw no more because I was over the roof, holding onto the edge with both hands and letting myself down. Looking up at the third guard who was bringing his sword down on my hands.

I let go. Dropped. Hit and rolled. My ankle hurt but I did not even think about it. Spears and clubs cracked to the ground around me as I hobbled away, around the first corner and into a market street. Hobbling slower and slower as the howls behind me faded in the distance.

Around another corner where I stopped for breath, panting and wheezing. Then staggered on deeper into the city until I was sure I had lost my pursuers.

I dropped into a chair of the first bar and actually enjoyed drinking a mug of the terrible beer.

Chapter 4

The bag of coins sat uncomfortably on my stomach, straining the fabric of my prison jacket. I looked at the drab cloth with the big red arrows on it and realized that I was being kind of stupid. By now my description would have gone out and all the *hogh* minions would be looking for me. I would not be that hard to find. As I hammered on the table with a coin I felt the sweat beginning to form on my forehead.

At the sight of the Nevenkebla currency the waiter's eyes lit up and he seized it with shaking fingers and carried it away reverently. I received a great handful of Arghans in exchange, surely I was being cheated, still I scuttled away happily. Scuttled into the first shop I found that had garments displayed around the entrance. Esperanto was spoken badly here, but good enough to enable me to buy some baggy trousers and a cloak, along with a wicker basket to conceal the money bag. Feeling safe, at least for the moment, I shambled deeper into the city. Through the busy streets to a market where I purchased a wide-brimmed leather hat with a colorful plume. Bit by bit I bought other clothes, until I was garbed anew, the basket with my prison clothes discarded, the money now safe in an elegant shoulder bag. By this time it was getting dark and I was completly lost.

And worried about Bibs. I had done all that I could to assure her safety, to distance her from myself and my crime. Had it been enough? I felt a quick surge of guilt and the need to contact her. Easier said than done. First I must find the League building, my only point of reference, and work back from there.

It was dusk by the time I located it—and I was getting very, very tired. Yet there was no choice, I must go on. Following the route the horse conveyance had taken with Bibs and her captors, finding the corner where we had emerged from it. From there it was easy enough to get to the restaurant where we had eaten, to drop into a chair with a sigh of relief. I could only hope now that she remembered the place and would think of coming here. I took off my hat and a hot band of pain circled my throat.

"Traitor," Bibs's voice hissed in my ear as I gurgled and groped but could reach nothing. Was this the end . . . ?

It almost was. I was sinking into unconsciousness before the pain eased and the length of wire fell into my lap. I rubbed my sore, bleeding neck as Bibs pulled out a chair and sat down at the table. She weighed my shoulder bag, then looked inside. She had a black eye and some bruises around her mouth.

"I could have killed you," she said. "I was that angry, that was what I was going to do. But when I saw you had brought the money I realized you had planned the whole thing this way and had come here to meet me. But since they had worked me over I felt I owed you some of the same. I'll order some wine."

"Planned . . ." I croaked, then coughed. "Knocked you out—so they would think you weren't in on the robbery."

"It worked—or I wouldn't be here. They bashed me about a bit, then they all ran out after you. I went right behind them in the confusion. Just wandered around and stayed out of sight until dark. Hating you. I had no money, nothing.

Other than this black eye. You're lucky I didn't throttle you all the way."

"Thanks," I said, then glugged down half a mug of wine when the waiter set it in front of me. "It was the only thing I could do. While you were talking to the old boy I looked at the defenses. There was no way in past them. But since we were already inside I saw that there was a good chance of getting out. So I took the money."

"Tremendous. You might have told me."

"There was no way to. Knocking you out was the only thing I could think of that would not get you involved. I'm sorry—but it worked."

Bibs actually smiled as she ran her fingers through the coins. "You are right, Jim my boy. It was worth a few bruises to get this much loot. Now let's get moving. You've changed clothes and I must do the same thing."

"Then to the best *ostel* in town."

"For a hot bath and a real meal. You're on!"

The *ostel* was a sprawling building hidden behind high walls. Suites of rooms led off the central courtyard and we had the best, if the bowing and dry handwashing of the help meant anything. The wine was chilled and the finest I had ever tasted. I prowled around the carpeted rooms and nibbled the toasted tidbits that came with the wine, while Bibs burbled and splashed in the adjoining pool. She eventually emerged wrapped in a towel, glowing with health and growling with hunger. There was no nonsense about dining rooms or restaurants in this establishment. Servants brought the food on brass trays and we gorged ourselves. When they had cleaned up the leavings I threw the bolt in the outer door and filled Bib's crystal mug with more wine.

"This is the life," she said.

"It surely is." I sprawled on the cushions across from her. "A good night's sleep and I will be feeling human again."

She lay back on the couch and looked at me through half-closed eyes. Well, really one half-closed and one all the way closed where she had been bopped. She shook her head and smiled.

"You are something else again, Jimmy. Just a kid, really, yet you are sure a winner. You survived Spiovente, which is not easy. Took out those two cops—then you took on all the *hogh's* thugs—and got away with it."

"Just luck," I said. Enjoying the praise but not that "kid" remark.

"I doubt it. And you saved my neck. Got me out of the hands of the law and stole enough clinkers to get me off this planet. I would like to say thanks."

"You don't have to, not really. You are going to help me find Garth so that makes us even." I stood and yawned. "I want to ask you about him—but it can wait until morning. I need some sleep."

She smiled again. "But, Jim, I told you I would like to thank you. In my own way."

Was it chance that as she lay back the towel slipped a little? No it was not chance. Nor was it by accident that she was devastatingly naked underneath. Despite the black eye Bibs was a terribly, terribly attractive girl.

What does one do on an occasion like this?

What one does not do is talk about it to others. I'm sorry. This is a private matter between two consenting adults. Very consenting. You will excuse me if I draw the curtain over this day and insert a space in this text to denote the passing of a good many hours.

Never had the sun shone so warmly and brightly. The afternoon sun. I smiled back at it just as warmly, bereft of any guilt, filled full with happiness. Nibbling a bit of fruit and sipping some wine. Turning languidly from the window as Bibs reentered the room.

"You mean it?" she asked. "You won't go offplanet with me? You don't want to?"

"Of course I want to. But not until I have found Garth."

"He'll find you first and kill you."

"Perhaps he might be the one who gets killed."

She cocked her head most prettily to one side, then nodded. "From anyone but you I would think that bragging. But you might just do it." She sighed. "But I won't be here to see it. I rate survival ahead of vengeance. He put me into jail—you got me out. Case closed. Though I admit to a big bundle of curiosity. If you do get out of this, will you let me know what happened? A message care of the Venian Crewmembers' Union will get to me eventually." She passed over a slip of paper. "I've written down everything that I remembered, just like you asked."

"General," I read. "Either Zennor or Zennar."

"I never saw it spelled out. Just overheard one of the officers talking to him when they didn't know I could hear them."

"What is Mortstertoro?"

"A big military base, perhaps their biggest. That's where we landed to take on cargo. They wouldn't let us out of the spacer, but what we could see was very impressive. A big limousine, all flags and stars, would come for Garth and take him away. There was a lot of saluting—and they always saluted him first. He is something big, high-up, and whatever he is involved with has to do with that base. I'm sorry, I know it's not much."

"It's a lot, all I need now." I folded the paper and put it away. "What next."

"We should have identification documents by tonight. They are expensive but real. Issued by one of the smaller duchies that needs the foreign exchange. So I can ship out on any spacer I want to. As long as the League agents don't recognize me. But I've managed to bribe my way onto a trade delegation that made their flight arrangements months ago. One of them has been well paid to get ill."

"When do you leave?"

"Midnight," she said in a very quiet voice.

"No! So soon . . ."

"I felt the same way—which is why I am leaving. I am not the kind of person that gets tied down in a relationship, Jimmy."

"I don't know what you mean."

"Good. Then I am getting away before you find out."

This sort of conversation was all very new and confusing. I am reluctantly forced to admit that up until the previous evening my contact with the opposite sex had been, shall we say, more distant. Now I was at an unaccustomed loss for words, indecisive and more than a little bewildered. When I blurted this out Bibs had nodded in apparent complete understanding. I realized now that there was an awful lot I did not know about women, a mountain of knowledge I might never acquire.

"My plans aren't that fixed . . ." I started to say, but she silenced me with a warm finger to my lips.

"Yes they are. And you're not going to change them on my account. You seemed very certain this morning about what you felt you had to do."

"And I am still certain," I said firmly, with more firmness and certainty than I felt. "The bribe to get me over to Nevenkebla was taken?"

"Doubled before accepted. If you are going to go missing then old Grbonja will never be permitted to go ashore there again. But he has been ready to retire for years. The bribe is just the financial cushion he needs."

"What does he do?"

"Exports fruit and vegetables. You'll go along as one of his laborers. He won't be punished if you get away from the market—but they will take away his landing pass. He won't mind."

"When do I get to see him?"

"We go to his warehouse tonight, after dark."

"Then . . ."

"I leave you there. Are you hungry?"

"We just ate."

"That is not what I mean," she answered in a very husky voice.

The dark streets were lit only by occasional torches at the corners, the air heavy with menace. We walked in silence; perhaps everything that might be said had already been said. I had bought a sharp dagger, which hung at my waist, and another club that I slammed against a wall occasionally to be sure any watchers knew it was there. All too soon we reached our destination, for Bibs knocked on a small gate let into a high wall. There were some whispered words and the gate creaked open. I could smell the sweetness of fruit all about us as we threaded through the dark mounds, to the lamplit corner where an elderly man slumped in a chair. He was all gray beard and gray hair to his waist, where the hair spread out over a monstrous paunch held up by spindly legs. One eye was covered by a cloth wound round his head, but the other looked at me closely as I came up.

"This is the one you are taking," Bibs said.

"Does he speak Esperanto?"

"Like a native," I said.

"Give me the money now." He held out his hand.

"No. You'll just leave him behind. Ploveci will give it to you after you land."

"Let me see it then." He turned his beady eye on me and I realized that I was Ploveci. I took out the leather bag, spread the coins out on my hands, then put them back into the bag. Grbonja grunted what I assumed was a sign of assent. I felt a breeze on my neck and wheeled about.

The gate was just closing. Bibs was gone.

"You can sleep here," he said pointing to a heap of tumbled sacks against the wall. "We load and leave at dawn."

When he left he took the lamp with him. I looked into the darkness, toward the closed gate.

I had little choice in the matter. I sat on the sacks with my back to the wall, the club across my legs and thought about what I was doing, what I had done, what we had done, what I was going to do, and about the conflicting emotions that washed back and forth through my body. This was apparently too much thinking because the next thing I knew I was blinking at the sunlight coming through the opening door, my face buried in the sacks and my club beside me on the floor. I scrambled up, felt for the money—still there—and was just about ready for what the day would bring. Yawning and stretching the stiffness from my muscles. Reluctantly.

The large door was pulled wider and I saw now that it opened onto a wharf with the fog-covered ocean beyond. A sizable sailing vessel was tied up there and Grbonja was coming down the gangway from the deck.

"Ploveci, help them load," he ordered and passed on.

A scruffy gang of laborers followed him into the warehouse and seized up filled sacks from the pile closest to the door. I couldn't understand a word they said, nor did I need to. The work was hot, boring, and exhausting, and consisted simply of humping a sack from the warehouse to the ship, then returning for another. There was some pungent vegetable in the sacks that soon had my eyes running and itching. I was the only one who seemed to mind. There was no nonsense about breaks either. We carried the sacks until the ship was full, and only then did we drop down in the shade and dip into a bucket of weak beer. It had foul wooden cups secured to it by thongs and after a single, fleeting moment of delicacy I seized one up, filled and emptied it, filled and drank from it once again.

Grbonja reappeared, as soon as the work was done, and gurgled what were obviously orders. The longshoremen became sailors, pulled in the gangplank, let go the lines and ran up the sail. I stood to one side and fondled my club until Grbonja ordered me into the cabin and out of sight. He joined me there a few moments later.

"I'll take the money now," he said.

"Not quite yet, grandpop. You get it when I am safely ashore, as agreed."

"They must not see me take it!"

"Fear not. Just stand close to the top of the gangplank and I will stumble against you. When I'm gone you will find the bag tucked into your belt. Now tell me what I will find when I get ashore."

"Trouble!" he wailed and raked his fingers through his beard. "I should never have gotten involved. They will catch you, kill you, me too . . ."

"Relax, look at this." I held the money bag in the beam of light from the grating above and let the coins trickle between my fingers. "A happy retirement, a place in the country, a barrel of beer and a plate of pork chops every day, think of all the joys this will bring."

He thought and the sight of the clinking coins had a great calming effect. When his fingers had stopped shaking I gave him a handful of money which he clutched happily.

"There. A downpayment to show that we are friends. Now think about this—the more I know about what I will find when I get ashore the easier it will be for me to get away. You won't be involved. Now . . . speak."

"I know little," he mumbled, most of his attention on the shining coins. "There are the docks, the market behind. All surrounded by a high wall. I have never been past the wall."

"Are there gates?"

"Yes, large ones, but they are guarded."

"Is the market very large?"

"Gigantic. It is the center of trade for the entire country. It stretches for many myldyryow along the coast."

"How big is a *myldyryow?"*

"Myldyr, myldyryow is plural. One of them is seven hundred *lathow.*"

"Thanks. I'll just have to see for myself."

Grbonja, with much grunting and gasping, threw open a hatch in the deck and vanished below, undoubtedly to hide the coins I had given him. I realized then that I had had enough of the cabin so I went out on deck, up to the bow, where I would not be underfoot. The sun was burning off the morning haze and I saw that we were passing close to an immense tower that rose up from the water. It was scarred, ancient, certainly centuries old. They had built well in those days. The mist lifted and revealed more and more of the structure, stretching up out of sight. I had to lean back to see the top, high, high above.

With the remains of the fractured bridge hanging from it. The once-suspended roadway hung crumpled and broken, dipping down into the ocean close by. Rusted, twisted, heaped with the broken supporting cables which were over two meters thick. I wondered what catastrophe had brought it down.

Or had it been deliberate? Had the rulers of Nevenkebla destroyed it to cut themselves free from the continent that was slowly sinking back into barbarism? A good possibility. And if they had done this they showed a firmness of mind that made my penetration of their island that much more difficult.

Before I could worry about this a more immediate threat presented itself. A lean, gray ship bristling with guns came thundering up from ahead. It cut across our bow and turned sharply around our stern; our sailing ship bobbed in its wake and the sails flapped. I emulated the sailors and tried to ignore the deadly presence, the pointed weapons that could blow us out of the water in an instant. We were here on legitimate business—weren't we?

The gunboat's commander must have believed this as well because, with an insulting blare on their horn, the vessel changed course again and blasted away across the sea. When the ship had dwindled into the distance one of the sailors shook his fist after them and said something bitter and incomprehensible that I agreed with completely.

Nevenkebla rose out of the mists ahead. Cliffs and green hills backing an immense, storied city that rose up from a circular harbor. Factories and mine-heads beyond, plumes of smoke from industry already busy in the early morning. And forts at the water's edge, great guns gleaming. Another fort at the end of the seawall as we entered the harbor. I could feel the glare of suspicious eyes behind the gunsights as the black mouths of the barrels followed us as we passed. These guys were not kidding.

And I was going to tackle this entire country single-handed?

"Sure you are, Jim," I said aloud with great braggadocio, swinging my club so that it whistled in tight arcs. "You'll show them. They don't stand a chance against fighting Jimmy diGriz."

Which would have been fine if my voice had not cracked as I said it.

Chapter 5

"Down sails," an amplified voice roared. "Take our line aboard."

A high-prowed tug came chuntering up with its loudhailer bellowing. Grbonja swiftly translated the commands to the crew.

Nothing was left to chance in Nevenkebla: all matters were highly organized. Even before the sail was down we were secured safely to the tug and being towed to our berth at the crowded wharfside. Sailing craft of interesting variety and form were already unloading cargo there. We were moved into a vacant berth among the others.

"They come long ways," Grbonja wheezed, stumbling up beside me, pointing at the other ships. "From Penpilick, Grampound, even Praze-an-Beeble—may everyone there suffer from a lifetime of *dysesya!* Tie up outside harbor at night. You give me the money now, too dangerous on shore!"

"A deal's a deal, grandpop. Too late to back out now."

He sweated and muttered and looked at the land coming close. "I go ahead first, talk to freightmaster. Only then we unload. They take your papers and give you dock badge. After that you will see me. Give me the money."

"No sweat. Just keep your mind on the sunny future of happy retirement."

Two armed guards glowered down at us as we tied up. A steam winch dropped the gangway into place and Grbonja puffed up the incline and onto the dock. To turn me in? Maybe I should have paid him in advance? My heart gave a few quick thuds as it shifted into worry mode.

In a few minutes—or was it centuries?—Grbonja had returned and was shouting instructions at the crew. I left my club in the cabin and put the dagger inside my shirt where it couldn't be seen. My lockpick and remaining coins were in a pouch inside my shirt as well. I was ready as I was ever going to be. When I came out of the cabin the sailors were already starting to unload. I picked up a bag and followed the others up the gangway. Each of them held out his identity papers: I did the same. As they reached the dock the officer there took each man's papers and stuffed them into a box. Then pinned an identification tag to the man's clothes. He looked bored by the job. I tried not to tremble as I came up to him.

It was just routine. "Next," he called out, whipped the papers from my hand and pinned the tag to my chest. Or rather pinned it through the fabric into my skin. I jumped but kept my mouth shut. He grinned, with a touch of sadism in the turn of his mouth, and pushed me on.

"Keep moving, lunkhead. Next."

I was safely ashore and undetected. Following the bent back of the man ahead of me into the dark warehouse. Grbonja was standing by the growing pile of sacks. When he saw me he called out an incomprehensible instruction and pointed to the next bay.

"The money, now," he burbled as I dumped the sack. I slipped it to him and he staggered away muttering with relief. I looked around at the solid cement and steel walls and went back for another sack.

By the time I had carried in my third sack I was getting desperate. After a few more trips the ship would be unloaded and that would be the end of that. I would have had an expensive round trip and done some hard work. Nothing more. Because I could see no way out of the building—and no place to hide within it. They obviously did not relish uninvited visitors to Nevenkebla. I needed more time.

"Call a beer break," I whispered to Grbonja as I passed him at the head of the gangway. The checker-inner had gone but the two unsmiling guards still stood watch.

"We never stop—it is not the custom."

"It is today. It's a hot day. You don't want me to tell them you were hired to smuggle me here?"

He groaned aloud, then called out. "Beer, we stop for beer!"

The crew asked no questions at this unexpected treat, only chattered together with pleasure as they gathered round the barrel. I had a good slug of the stuff then went and sat on the gunwhale beside the gangway. Looked up at the boots of the guard who stood above me. Looked down at the water and saw the space between the pilings there.

My only chance. The guard above me moved out of sight. Grbonja had his back turned while the sailors had their attention focused on the barrel. A difference of opinion over the rationing appeared to break out. There were angry shouts and a quick blow. The crew watched these proceedings with great interest. No one was visible on the dock above.

I dropped a length of line over the side, swung my legs over and climbed down it. No one saw me go. With my legs in the sea I used my dagger to cut the line above my head and dropped silently into the water. With noiseless strokes I swam into the darkness under the pier.

Slime-covered boards connected the wooden piles. When I reached for one of them something squealed and vanished in the darkness. And it stank down here. Nameless rubbish bobbed in the water around me. I was beginning to regret my impetuous swim.

"Chin up, Jim, and move along. This is the first place they look when they find out you are missing."

I swam. Not far, for there was a solid wall here that ran back into the darkness. I groped along it until I reached the outer piles again. Through the openings between them I saw the hull of another sailing ship, tied close. There was no room to pass between the planks of the ship and the piles. Trapped so soon?!

"This is your day for panic," I whispered aloud, the sound of my voice covered by the slapping of the waves. "You can't go back, so carry on you must. The hull of this ship has to curve away. Just dive down and swim along it until you find another opening between the piles."

Ho-ho. Sounded very easy to do. I kicked my boots off and breathed deep. But my trepidition grew with each shuddering breath that I drew in. When my head was swimming with oxygen intoxication I let out the last lungful and dived.

It was a long, dark and apparently endless swim. I ran my left hand along the ship's hull to guide me. Collecting some heroic splinters at the same time. On and on with no glimmer of light in front or above. This must be a very big ship. There was fire in my lungs and desperation in my swimming before I saw light ahead. I came up as quietly as I could by the ship's bow. Trying not to gasp as I exhaled and drew in life and fresh air.

Looking up at a sailor standing on the rail above, turning towards me.

I sank out of sight again, forcing myself deep under the water, swimming on with my lungs crying out for air, until I saw the black bulk of the next ship ahead of me, forcing myself to swim on to the last glimmer of light before floating up the surface again.

Catching my head nicely between hull and piling, to fight down the rising panic as I fought to free myself—getting some splinters in my scalp this time. My groping fingers found a gap between the pilings so I surfaced there, hung on, sucked in lungful after lungful of the stinking fug, enjoying it more than the freshest air I had ever breathed.

This was the beginning of a very long and very tiring day. I did not keep track of the number of ships I passed, but it was a lot. At first I searched under the various docks but soon gave that up since they were all the same, each firmly separated by an underwater wall from the next. Some of the ships had finished unloading and had left, for I came to gaps in the continuous wall of vessels. All I could do when this happened was to breathe deep, dive deep—and swim like crazy to reach the next ship before my breath ran out.

It was afternoon before I reached the last ship and the end of the docks. The tide was ebbing, the vessels were now down below the dock level so there was more concealment from above. I was very tired but very proficient by this time. One more time I breathed deep, dove down at the bow, swam the length of the hull and surfaced in the shadow of the rudder.

To look at a solid wall of jointed stone stretching out before me.

Holding onto the rudder, my eyes just above the surface, I peered around it. And realized that I was looking at the harbor wall that stretched unbroken out to the fort built at its far end. I drew back into the shadow of the rudder and found that my heart was sinking so fast it was pulling me under the water.

"Any bright ideas, Jim?" I asked, then found that I was waiting a long time for an answer.

Think, don't despair, I ordered myself. I still felt despair. Could I go back? No, that was out. After all I had gone through today I was not going to surrender that easily. Hide under one of the docks? Possibly. But they would be thoroughly searched as soon as I was missed, I was certain of that. What else? Climb up onto the dock? No way. The warehouses here were sure to be as barren of hiding places as the one I had left. Then what?

"Turn the problem on its head, that's what The Bishop had always said."

What would that be in this situation? I was trying to get away from the soldiers, fleeing them, knowing they would be looking for me. So I should go to them. But that would be suicide. But where could I possibly go that would be totally unexpected?

Why, the fort on the end of the harbor wall of course.

"Without a doubt the most insane idea you have ever had," I muttered in disgust, peering around the rudder again. Above me there were shouted oaths from the sailors and the thud of feet on planking. I had the feeling that this ship would be leaving soon as well, taking my protection with it. The solid stone blocks of the jetty stretched unbroken to the fort at the end. Some debris washed against the stone and sea birds fought over the edible bits. Other than that—nothing. No cover at all. If I tried to swim out there I would be seen at once by anyone who glanced that way. Above me tackle creaked as the sail was lifted; the ship was getting under way.

I had to get clear of it—or did I? No tug had appeared. Was it possible the ships were only towed into harbor? That they permitted them to sail out on their own? It was. I peered around the rudder again and saw two of the cargo vessels standing out toward the entrance. Light poured down from the growing gap above me and I sank under the surface before I could be seen.

It was not easy—but it could be done. I held tight to the rudder as it came over, almost pulling itself out of my hands. I stayed under the surface as long as I could so I would not be seen from the shore. The sailing ship was moving along smoothly and it took all my strength to shift my grip from the front to the back of the rudder. Holding on was easier now. When I finally was forced to lift my face up to breathe I found myself in a rush of foam, inhaled some and fought not to cough. As we drew away from the dockside I saw an armed guard there. His back turned with indifference.

It was almost easy after that. The rush of the waves held me against the rudder post. I breathed easily with my head out of the water, unseen from the shore and invisible to anyone on the deck above. We tacked twice and each time I changed sides to keep the rudder between me and the fort that was now growing larger and larger ahead. When we went about for the last time I saw that this tack would take us close to the fort and past it on into the open ocean. I watched as the stone wall came closer and closer until I could see the sea beyond the end of it. Only then did I take a last breath, let go and dive deep.

Yes, I was tired. But this should also be my final little swim for the day so I wanted to make it a good one. The seaweed-covered harbor wall was clear ahead, the end rounded where it met the open ocean. There was a strong swell coming in that I had to fight against, swimming close to the stone where its force was weakest. Farther and farther until I had to breath or inhale water. Floating up to the bright surface and through it, looking up at the stone wall with the projecting gun barrels above. Holding on against the waves and breathing deep. Clutching into the cracks between the stones and working my way around to the far side until I could peer down its unbroken length at the shore beyond. Pleasure craft dotted the water here, power and sail, and I would certainly be seen if I tried to swim its length. Then what? I couldn't stay here in the water where I could be seen by any passing ship. I looked up at the great stone blocks and thought.

Why not? The only ships in sight now were vanishing seaward. At the outermost swell of the fort I could not be seen from the shore. And the space between stones provided ample grip for toe and finger. So climb.

Climb I did. It was not easy—but I had little choice. Up the vertical wall, scrabbling and clinging, midway between two of the largest seaward-facing guns. They projected through embrasures in the solid wall, shining steel, polished and deadly. I clung on and rested when I reached their level, the heaving surface of the sea a good ten meters below. The ocean was still empty—but for how long?

"Give me a light, will you Jim?"

I started so hard I almost lost my grip and fell back into the water.

Fragrant cigar smoke blew over me and I realized it was coming from the gun embrasure close by. I hadn't been seen, no one here knew my name. It had just been coincidence. The gunners were there, that close, looking seaward and smoking on duty which I was sure was frowned upon strongly. I did not dare move. I could only hold on and listen.

"This new captain, he has got to go."

"He is the worst. Poison in his coffee?"

"No. I heard they did that up north and they decimated the entire regiment. You know, shot one guy out of ten."

"That is the real old cagal and you know it. Nothing but cagalhouse rumor. Like fragging. Everyone talks about it, no one does it . . ."

"Captain coming!"

A cigar butt sailed by my head and there was the quick slap of retreating feet. I climbed again, before my arms came out of their sockets. Forcing myself up the last few centimeters until I reached the edge and hauled myself painfully onto the flat roof of the fort. A seabird cocked a cold eye at me, screeched and flapped off. I crawled slowly across the sun-baked bird droppings of centuries, to the very center of the round building. I lay flat on my back and could see nothing but sky and the top of a distant hill. This meant that in turn I could not be discovered except from the air. I would chance that, since I had seen only one distant aircraft the entire day. I closed my eyes against the glare of the sun and instantly, without intending to, fell sound asleep.

I awoke with a start and a rapidly beating heart. A cloud had crossed the face of the sun and I was chilled in my wet clothes. It had been stupid, falling asleep like that, yet I had gotten away with it. I had not been seen. The sun was closer to the horizon and since I had been safe here so far I might still be safe until dark.

And hungry and thirsty. The demands of the body are insatiable, always after something. But this time it was going to be mind over matter and I was going to stay on the roof, unmoving, until nightfall.

Which was slow in coming. I smacked my dry lips and ignored the angry rumblings in my gut. The suns always set. It was just a matter of patience.

Dusk finally crept over the land, the first stars came out as it slowly grew dark. Lights came on in the fort below and I could hear the hoarse shouting of military orders. Very slowly I crawled to the inner edge and peered over. Into a courtyard where some sort of maneuver was being engaged in. Soldiers marched back and forth in little groups with much screeching from the officers. Eventually one group entered the fort and the other marched back toward the land along the broad top of the harbor wall, their way lit by evenly spaced lights. They got smaller and smaller in the distance until they reached the distant shore and vanished from sight.

Then all of the lights went out.

I lay, blinking into the sudden darkness, and could not believe my good luck. Had the lights been extinguished to enable me to sneak safely ashore? Probably not. There were guns below and if they meant to use them, as they obviously did, the gunners would not want to be blinded by their own lights. Good thinking, guys!

I waited until I could see my way by starlight, then climbed down the outside wall to the rail around the courtyard, stepped carefully onto it and down onto the stone flagging. A single door in the wall was sealed and silent. On tiptoe I scuttled landward as fast as I could. The dark bulk of the fort grew small behind me and I strolled more easily, resisting the impulse to whistle with pleasure. The dark forms of the pleasure boats were visible off to the left. There were lights in the cabins of a few of them and I heard distant laughter across the water. I relaxed, strolled, the rough stone cool beneath my bare feet. I had the world to myself and safety lay close ahead.

Then I ran headlong into the metal fencing that cut off the top of the harbor wall and all the lights came on in a searing blaze of illumination. Lights stretching ahead and behind, lights above revealing the wire fence and sealed metal door in front of me.

Chapter 6

I bounced back from the wire, looked around wildly, hurled myself flat on the wall waiting for the sound of shots.

But nothing happened. The lights burned down brightly; the harbor wall behind me stretched emptily back to the fort. On the other side of the barrier the wall extended as far as the warehouses above the harbor where more lights revealed a small marching group. Coming towards me.

Had I been seen—or was I invisible in the shadows? Or had I triggered some alarm that turned on the lights and revealed my presence? Whatever had happened there was no point in my waiting around in order to find out. I crawled quickly to the outer edge of the wall facing the ocean—I had had enough swimming in the harbor, thank you—and dangled my legs backward over the edge. Groped with my bare feet for a toehold on the rough stone. Found one and eased myself down into the darkness. The tide was coming in again and my legs were engulfed by the sea. Above me on top of the wall the tramping feet grew louder. Below me the water was cold, black and unattractive.

Why didn't I just stay here out of sight until they had gone by above?

As soon as this cowardly thought had trickled through the synapses of my brain I recognized it for the dumb idea that it was. A flick of a flashlight and my presence would be revealed. I had not gone through all of the strenuous efforts and dangers of the day to be grabbed now because I was afraid of getting wet. Or eaten by unseen monsters. The ocean here must be safe or the fleets of pleasure craft would not have been drifting around all day.

"Swimmies, Jim, swimmies," I muttered and slid down into the sea.

By the time the soldiers had reached the gate I was treading water well away from the wall, ready to dive instantly if they pointed any lights my way. They didn't. I could see one of them unlocking the gate, then relocking it again after they had all passed through. Then they all marched on again. A relief party, surprise inspection perhaps, or some other uninteresting military maneuver. I turned about and began to swim toward shore.

What next? The lights of a promenade grew closer and my problem grew bigger. How was I a barefoot, sodden stranger with no knowledge of this land whatsoever, how was I to go ashore and make my way about unnoticed? Not easily, that was obvious. A dark shape came between me and the lights. A craft of some kind. Salvation of some kind?

I swam slowly between the moored pleasure boats. In the distance I could see that some of them were illuminated, but only darkness prevailed here. Were they occupied? They didn't appear to be; it was too early for any occupants to be asleep. Which hopefully meant that the jolly sportsmen had gone ashore after a strenuous day at play.

A thin mast moved against the stars. A sailboat, a small one. I wanted something larger. I swam on until a darker form rose up above me. No masts, which meant that it was a powered craft of some kind. I swam alongside it to the stern, where my groping fingers found the ladder that was secured there. Rung by rung I climbed, dripping, out of the sea and into the craft. There was enough light from the stars and the illumination along the shore to make out cushioned seats, a wheel—and a door that might lead below. I went to it, found the handle and tried to turn it. Locked.

"Good news indeed, Jim. If it is locked there is something here worth stealing. Best to look and see."

I did. Darkness is no handicap for an efficient locksmith. I felt out the tumblers of a very simple lock with delicate touches of my lockpick. Lifted them aside and pushed the door open.

What followed was slow work. If there were lights I did not want to turn them on. I did it all by touch. But there is a certain logic to any small craft that must be followed. Berths in the bow along the hull. Lockers below, shelves above. After a good deal of rattling, fumbling, head-banging and cursing I gathered my treasures in a blanket and took them up on deck and spread them out.

What had felt like a bottle with a screwcap was a bottle with a screwcap. Which I unscrewed and sniffed. Then dipped in a finger and tasted. A very sweet wine. Not my normal tipple, but paradisical after all the seawater I had swallowed. There was a metal box with stale bread or biscuits of some kind that almost broke my teeth. They softened a bit when I poured wine over them, then wolfed them down. I belched deeply and felt better.

I groped through the rest of my loot. There were books and boxes, unidentifiable forms, and strange shapes. And clothing. A very sheer skirt that was just not my thing. But other sartorial items were. I sorted out all of the other bits that appeared to be clothing not instantly identifiable as being intended for the fairer sex, stripped and tried some of it on. I had no idea of how well they matched, but it was an outfit of sorts. The trousers were too large by far, but a length of line in place of a belt took care of that. The shirt was a better fit, and if the jacket came down to my knees perhaps it was intended to be that length. The shoes were too big but stayed on my feet after I had stuffed cloth into their toes. It was the best I could do. Then I undressed and put my own wet clothing back on, put my new outfit into the can the bread had been in, wrapped this in turn in what I hoped was waterproof plastic.

The air was beginning to be chill and it was time to get moving. I was tired, slowed down by the exertions of the day and badly in need of some sleep. I wasn't going to get any. I finished the wine, put the empty bottle and everything else I had removed back into the cabin, then relocked the door. Before I could change my mind I put the bundle on my head and slipped over the side.

The shore was close and the beach empty as far as I could see. Which was a major blessing since swimming with one hand while balancing a can of clothing on the head with the other is not an exercise to be recommended. I emerged from the sea and scuttled to the shelter of some large rocks, stripped and buried my unwanted clothing in the sand. I quickly dressed in the dry clothes, tucked my small bag of possessions into my belt, slipped my dagger into the side of my shoe and I was ready to conquer the world.

I really wanted only to find a quiet place to curl up for a nap—but knew better. These people took their security seriously and the shore was their first line of defense as the fort had proved. I must get into the city itself.

There were lights on the promenade above, the sound of voices, but shadow below where I moved in silence. A flight of stairs rose up from the beach. I rose up as well—but dropped back again even more swiftly at the sight of two uniformed and armed men close by. I lurked and counted backward from two hundred before I peeked again. The uniforms were gone and there were just a few evening strollers in sight. I merged and strolled and took the first turning that led away from the shore. There were streetlights here, open windows and locked doors. My clothing must not have looked too garish for a couple passed without even glancing my way. I heard music ahead and soon came to a bar over which a sign proclaimed DANCING AND DRINKING—COME AND GET STINKING. An invitation almost impossible to resist. I pushed the door open and went in.

There is a power that shapes the bars of this universe. There has to be because form follows function. Function: to get containers of alcoholic beverages to people. Form: chairs to sit in, tables to rest containers on. I entered, pulled out a chair and sat at a vacant table. The other occupants ignored me just as I ignored them. A plump waitress in a short skirt came toward me, ignoring the whistles from the group of youths at the next table, skilfully avoiding their snapping fingers as well.

"Whadilitbe?" she asked, flaring her nostrils at them as they raised beer mugs in her direction and toasted her loudly.

"Beer," I said and she moved off. When it came it was pungent and cold. She made her own change from the coins I had spread on the table, this seemed to be the local custom, then went back behind the bar.

I drank deep and wiped the foam from my mouth just as another young man came through the door and hurried to the adjoining table.

"Porkaĉoj!" he whispered hoarsely. Two of the youths stumbled to their feet and hurried toward the rear of the bar.

I put down my beer, scraped up my coins, and hurried after them. There was trouble here, though I did not know what kind. What he had said could be translated as bad-pigs, and must surely be local slang since I did not imagine some mucky swine were on their way. Pigs as an epithet for police is a common usage—and the reactions of the two men seemed to bear this out. And I would lose nothing by being cautious. They hurried down a hallway and when I reached it a door at the far end was just closing. I had my hand on its knob when a loud siren sounded from the other side and a glare of illumination shone in through the cracks between door and frame.

"What's this?" a coarse and loud voice said. "You boys maybe slipping out through the backdoor because we got a patrol out front? Let's see your identification."

"We've done nothing wrong!"

"You've done nothing right so far. C'mon, the ID."

I waited, unmoving, hoping the bad-pig outside was not joined by his stymates from the bar. The coarse laughter from the other side of the door was anything but humorous.

"Hello, hello—both out of date? Not thinking of avoiding the draft, are you boys?"

"A clerical error," a pale voice whimpered.

"We get a lot like that. Let's go."

The light went away and so did the footsteps. I waited as long as I dared, then opened the door and exited the bar. The alley was empty, pig and prisoners were gone. I went myself, as quickly as I could without running. Then stopped. What was I running from? Once the police had left, the bar would be the safest place in the city for me. I stopped in a dark doorway and looked back at the rear entrance. No one else came out. I counted to three hundred, then to be safe backward again to zero. The door remained closed. Cautiously, ready to flee in an instant, I went back into the bar, peered into the barroom. No police—but the glimmerings of an idea.

The four young men at the table looked up as I came back in, the newcomer sitting at one of the recently vacated seats. I shook my head gloomily and dropped into a chair.

"The *porkaĉoj* got them. Both."

"I told Bill he needed new papers, wouldn't listen to me," the blond one said, the one who had come with the warning. He cracked his knuckles then seized up his beer. "You got to have good papers."

"My papers are out of date," I said gloomily, then waved to the waitress.

"You should have stayed in Pensildelphia then," one of the others said, a spotty youth in an ill-fitting gold and green shirt.

"How did you know I was from Pensildelphia?" I protested. He sneered.

"Rube accent like that, where else you from?"

I sneered back and glowed with pleasure inside. Better and better. I had a peergroup of draft dodgers, one of them who might be working with the police, and a hometown. Things were looking up. I buried my nose in my beer.

"You ought to get new ID," the friendly warner, possible police informer, said. I sniffled.

"Easy to say here. But you can't do it in Pensildelphia."

"Hard to do here too. Unless you got the right contacts."

I stood up. "I gotta go. Nice meeting you guys."

Before leaving I checked to make sure that the police were gone. Then I exited and waited. My new friend came out a moment later and smiled at me.

"Smart. Don't let too many people know what's going on. My label is Jak."

"Call me Jim."

"Good a name as any, Jim. How much you got to spend?"

"Not much. I had a bad year."

"I'll put you in touch with the man himself for three sugarlumps. He'll want twenty."

"ID not worth more than ten. You get one-fifty."

"They're not all dumb in the backwoods, are they. Slap it in my hand and we're on our way."

I paid him his cut and when he turned I put the tip of my knife against his neck just under his ear and pushed just hard enough to break the skin. He stayed absolutely still when I showed him the knife with the fresh drop of blood.

"That is a little warning," I said. "Those pigs were waiting for whoever you flushed out. That's not my worry. My skin is. I got a feeling that you play both sides. Play the right side with me or I will find you and slice you. Understand?"

"Understood . . ." he said gruffly, with a tremor in his voice. I put the knife away and clapped him on the shoulders.

"I like you, Jak. You learn easy."

We went in silence and I hoped that he was making the right conclusions. I don't like threats and when threatened I do the opposite of what I am requested. But my experience of the petty criminal led me to believe that threats tended to work with them. Part of the time.

Our route took us past a number of other bars and Jak looked carefully into each one before going on. He struck paydirt in the fifth one and waved me in after him. This place was dark and smoke filled, with jangling music blasting from all sides. Jak led the way to the rear of the room, to an alcove where the music was not quite as loud, at least not as loud as the striped outfit the fat man was wearing. He leaned back in a heavy chair and sipped at a tiny, poisonous green drink.

"Hello, Captain," my guide said.

"Get dead quickly, Jak. I don't want your kind here."

"Don't say that even funning, Captain. I got good business for you here, a mission of mercy. This grassgreen cutlet is a step ahead of the draft. Needs new ID."

The tiny eyes swiveled toward me. "How much you got, cutlet?"

"Jak says one-fifty for him, ten for you. I already paid him his."

"Jak's a liar. Twelve is the price and I give him his cut."

"You're on."

It was an instant transaction. I gave him the money and he passed over the grubby plastic folder. Inside there was a blurred picture of a youth who could have been anyone my age, along with other vital facts including a birthdate quite different from my own.

"This says that I am only fifteen years old!" I protested.

"You got a baby face. You can get away with it. Drop a few years—or join the army."

"I feel younger already." I pocketed the ID and rose. "Thanks for the help."

"Any time. Long as you got the sugarlumps."

I left the bar, crossed the road and found a dark doorway to lurk in. It was a short wait because Jak came out soon after me and strolled away. I strolled behind him at a slightly faster stroll. I was breathing down his neck before he heard my footsteps and spun about.

"Just me, Jak, don't worry. I wanted to thank you for the favor."

"Yeah, sure, that's all right." He rolled his eyes around at the deserted street.

"You could do me another favor, Jak. Let me see your own ID. I just want to compare it to mine to make sure the Captain didn't give me a ringer."

"He wouldn't do that!"

"Let's make sure." My dagger blade twinkled in the streetlight and he rooted inside his jacket then handed me a folder very much like my own. I turned to look at it under the light, then handed it back. But Jak was the suspicious type. He glanced at it before putting it away—and dropped his jaw prettily.

"This ain't mine—this is yours!"

"That's right. I switched them. You told me that ID was good. So use it."

His cries of protest died behind as I walked uphill away from the shore. To a better neighborhood without a criminal element. I felt very pleased with myself. The ID could have been good—in which case Jak would lose nothing. But if it were faulty in any way it would be his problem, not mine. The biter bit. A very evenhanded solution. And I was going in the right direction. Once away from the waterfront things did get better, the buildings taller, the streets cleaner, the lights brighter. And I got tireder. Another bar beckoned and I responded. Velvet drapes, soft lights, leather upholstery, better-looking waitress. She was not impressed by my clothes, but she was by the tip I passed over when my beer arrived.

I had very little time to enjoy it. This was a well-policed city and the bad-pigs came in pairs. A brace of them waddled in through the door and my stomach slipped closer to the floor. But what was I worrying about? My ID was fine.

They circuited the room, looking at identification, and finally reached my table.

"Good evening, officers," I smarmed.

"Knock off the cagal and let's see it."

I smiled and passed over the folder. The one who opened it widened his nostrils and snorted with pleasure.

"Why look what we got here! This is Jak the joike strolled away from his home turf. That's not nice, Jak."

"It's a free world!"

"Not for you, Jak. We all know about the deal you made with harbor police. Stay there and rat on your friends and you get left alone. But you strayed out of your turf, Jak."

"I'll go back now," I said rising with a sinking feeling.

"Too late," they said in unison as they slapped on the cuffs.

"Far too late," the nostril-flarer said. "You're out of business, Jak, and in the army."

This really was the biter bit. This time I had been just a little too smart for my own good. It looked like my new and exciting military career had just begun.

Chapter 7

The cell was small, the bed hard—I had no complaints. After the strenuous day I had just finished, sleep was the only thing that I wanted. I must have been snoring as I fell toward the canvas covers, with no memory of my face ever touching the stained pillow. I slept the sleep of exhaustion and awoke when a gray shaft of light filtered in through the barred window. I felt cheered and rested until I realized where I was. Dark depression fell.

"Well, it could be worse," I said cheerily.

"How?" I snarled dispiritedly. There was no easy answer to that. My stomach rumbled with hunger and thirst and the depression deepened. "Cry-baby," I sneered. "You've had it much worse than this. They took the dagger but nothing else. You have your money, your identification." And the lockpick I added in silence. The presence of that little tool had a warming effect, holding out hope of eventual escape.

"I'm hungry!" a youthful voice cried out and there was a rattling of bars. Others took up the cry.

"Food. We're not criminals!"

"My mom always brought me breakfast in bed . . ."

I was not too impressed by this last wail of complaint but sympathized with the general attitude. I joined the cry.

"All right, all right, shut up," an older and gruffer voice called out. "Chow is on the way. Not that you deserve anything, bunch of draft dodgers."

"Cagal on that sergeant—I don't see your fat chunk in the army."

I looked forward to meeting the last speaker; he showed a little more courage than the rest of the wailers. The wait wasn't too long, though it was scarcely worth it. Cold noodle soup with sweet red beans is not my idea of the way to start the day. I wondered how it would end.

I had plenty of time for wondering because after feeding time in the zoo we were left strictly alone. I stared up at the cracked ceiling and slowly began to realize that my ill fortune wasn't that bad when closely examined. I was alive and well in Nevenkebla. With a promising career ahead of me. I would learn the ropes, find out all I could about this society, maybe even get a lead on Garth—or General Zennor if Bibs had overheard the name correctly. He was in the army and I would very soon be in the army, which fact might work to my advantage. And I had the lockpick. When the right moment came I could do a little vanishing act. And how bad could the army be? I had been a soldier on Spiovente, which training should come in handy . . .

Oh, how we do fool ourselves.

Somewhere around midday, when my cowardly peer group were beginning to howl for more nourishment, the crash of opening cell doors began. The howls changed to cries of complaint as we were ordered from our cells and cuffed wrist to wrist in a long daisychain. About a dozen of us, similar of age and gloomy of mein. The unknown future lay darkly ahead. With much stumbling and curses we were led from the cell block to the prison compound where a barred vehicle waited to transport us to our destiny. It moved away silently after we had been herded aboard, battery- or fuel cell–powered, out into the crowded city streets. Clothes were slightly different, vehicles of unusual shapes, but it could have been any world of advanced technology. No wonder they had cut themselves off from the rest of this decadent planet. Selfish—but understandable.

No effete amenities like seats were provided for hardened criminals: so we clutched to the bars and swayed into each other at the turns. A thin, dark-haired youth secured to my left wrist sighed tremulously, then turned to me.

"How long you been on the run?" he asked.

"All my life."

"Very funny. I've had six months since my birthday, six short months. Now it's all over."

"You're not dying—just going into the army."

"What's the difference? My brother got drafted last year. He smuggled a letter out to me. That's when I decided to run. Do you know what he wrote—?"

His eyes opened wide and he shivered at the memory, but before he could speak our transport slammed to a halt and we were ordered out.

The street scene was one to give joy to the eyes of any sadist. Varying forms of transport had converged on the plaza before the tall building. Emerging from them were young men, hundreds, perhaps thousands of them, all wearing upon their faces a uniform expression of despair. Only our little band was manacled—the rest clutched the yellow draft notices that had dragged them to their destiny. A few of them had the energy to make mock of our manacled state, but they shrank away under the chorus of our jeers. At least we had made some attempt, no matter how feeble, to escape military impressment. Nor did it appear to make any difference to the authorities. They did not care how they had managed to grab the bodies. Once inside the doors our chains were stripped away and we were herded into line with all the others. The faceless military machine was about to engulf us.

At first it did not seem too bad. The lines of youths crept forward toward desks manned by plump maternal types who might have been our moms or teachers. All of them had gray hair and wore spectacles, which they looked over the tops of when they weren't two-fingeredly hammering their typewriters. I finally reached mine and she smiled up at me.

"Your papers please, young man."

I passed them over and she copied dates and names and incorrect facts into a number of forms. I saw the cable leading from her typewriter to a central computer and knew that everything was being recorded and ingested there as well. I was happy to see the false identity entered; when I un-volunteered I wanted to drop from sight.

"Here you are," she said, and smiled, and passed over a buff file of papers. "You just take these up to the fourth floor. And good luck in your military career."

I thanked her, it would be churlish not to, and started back toward the front doors. A solid line of unsmiling military police blocked any chance of exit.

"Fourth floor," I said as the nearest one eyed me coldly and smacked his club into his palm.

The elevator cars were immense, big enough to take forty of us at a time. Nor did they leave until they were full. Jammed and miserable we rose to the fourth floor where a little taste of what awaited us awaited us. As the doors sighed open a military figure, all stripes and decorations, medals and red face came roaring toward us.

"Get out! Get out! Don't stand around like a bunch of poofters! Move it! Snap cagal or you'll be in the cagal. Take a box and a small transparent bag from the counter on the right as you pass. Then go to the far end of this room where you will UNDRESS. That means take all of your clothes off. AND I MEAN ALL OF YOUR CLOTHES! Your personal effects will go into the plastic bag which you will keep in your left hand at all times. All of your clothing will go into the box which you will take to the counter at the far end where it will be sealed and addressed and sent to your home. Where you will retrieve it after the war, or it will be buried with you, whichever comes first. Now MOVE!"

We moved. Unenthusiastically and reluctantly—but we had no choice. There must be a nudity taboo in this society because the youths spread out, trying to get close to the walls, huddled over as they stripped off their clothes. I found myself alone in the center of the room enjoying the scowled attention of the stripe-bearing monster: I quickly joined the others. So reluctant were they to reveal their shrinking flesh that dawdle as I might I was still first to the counter. Where a bored soldier seized my box and quickly sealed it, slammed it down before me and pointed to thick pens hung from the ceiling on elastic cords.

"Name-address-postcode-nearest-relative."

The words, empty of meaning through endless repetition, rolled out as he turned to seize up the next box. I scrawled the address of the police station where we had been held and when I released the pen the countertop opened and the box vanished. Very efficient. Plastic bag in left hand, folder in my right I joined the shivering group of pallid, naked young men who hung their heads as they waited their next orders. With their clothes gone all differences of identity seemed to have fled as well.

"You will now proceed to the eighteenth floor!" was the bellowed command. We proceeded. Into the elevator, forty at a time, doors closed, doors opened—into a vision of a sort of medical hell.

A babble of sound, shouts for attention, screamed orders. Doctors and medical orderlies garbed in white, many with cloth masks over their faces, poked and prodded in a mad mirror-image of medical practice. Senses blurred as event ran into event.

A physician—that is I assume he was a physician since he wore a stethoscope around his neck—seized my folder, threw it to an orderly, then clutched me by the throat. Before I could seize him by the throat in return he shouted at the orderly.

"Thyroid, normal." The orderly made an entry as he squeezed my stomach wall.

"Hernias, negative. Cough."

This last was an order to me and I coughed as his rubber-clad fingers probed deep.

There was more, but only the highlights stand out.

The urinalysis section where we stood in shivering ranks, each holding a recently filled paper cup. Our file slowly wending forward, on tiptoe for the floor was aslosh, to the white-clad, white-masked, booted and rubber-gloved orderly who dipped a disposable dropper into each cup, dropped a drop into a section of a large, sectioned chemical tray. Discarded the dropper into an overflowing container, eyed the chemical reaction. Shouted "Negative, next!" and carried on.

Or the hemorrhoidal examination. Good taste forbids too graphic a description, but it did involve rows of youths bent over and clutching their ankles while a demonic physician crouched over as well and ran along behind the rows with a pointed flashlight.

Or the injections, ahh, yes the injections. As this particular line crept forward I became aware that the youth in front of me was a bodybuilder of some sort. Among the pipestem arms and knocking knees his bronzed biceps and polished pects stood out as a monument to masculinity. He turned to me with a worried expression on the knotted muscles of his face.

"I don't like needles," he said.

"Who does," I agreed.

Not nice at any time, positively threatening in mass attack. I watched, horrified, as I approached the point of no return. As each shivering body came into position an orderly on each side injected each upper arm. No sooner were the needles hurled aside than the victim was pushed in the back by the uniformed supervising brute. After tottering a few paces forward two more injections were made. Arms curled with pain the subject leaned on the nearby counter. Where he was vaccinated. Very efficient.

Too efficient for the weightlifter. As he stepped into position his eyes rolled up and he slumped unconscious to the floor. This, however, was no obstacle to military efficiency. Two needles flashed, two injections were made. The sergeant seized him by the feet and dragged him forward where, after receiving the rest of his injections, he was rolled aside to recover. I gritted my teeth, tried stoically to accept the puncturing barrage, and sighed.

At some point the mass medical examination ended with a final assault on whatever shards of personal dignity the victims might still have left. Still nude, still clutching our plastic bags in our left hands, our thickening folders in our right, we shuffled forward in yet one more line. A row of numbered desks stretched across the width of the room, very much like the reception hall of an airport. Behind each desk sat a dark-suited gent. When it was my turn the sergeant-herdsman glanced over his shoulder and stabbed a stumpy figure at me.

"You, haul it to number thirteen."

The man behind the desk wore thick-framed glasses, as did all of the others I noticed. Perhaps our eyes were going to be examined and this was what we would be like if we failed. My folder was seized yet one more time, another printed sheet inserted—and I found tiny red eyes glaring at me through the thick lenses.

"Do you like girls, Jak?"

The question was completely unexpected. Yet it prompted a sweet vision of Bibs that obscured the medical mockery around me.

"You bet I like girls," was my instant response. An entry was made.

"Do you like boys?"

"Some of my best friends are boys." I began to have a glimmering of what this simpleton was up to.

"Are they?" Slash of pencil. Then, "Tell me about your first homosexual experience."

My jaw fell with disbelief. "I can't believe that I'm hearing this. You are doing a psychiatric examination from a *checklist*?"

"Don't give me any cagal, kid," he snarled. "Just answer the question."

"Your medical degree should be taken away for incompetence—if you ever had one. You're probably not a shrink at all, just a timeserver dressed like one."

"Sergeant!" he shouted in a cracked voice, his skin flushing. There was a thunder of feet behind me. "This draftee is refusing to cooperate."

Sharp pain slashed the backs of my bare legs and I Yowed! and jumped aside. The sergeant raised the thin cane again and licked his lips.

"That will do for the moment," my examiner said. "If my questions are answered correctly."

"Yes, sir," I said, snapping to attention. "No need to repeat the question. My first experience of that kind was at the age of twelve when, with the aid of large rubber bands, I and fourteen other boys . . ."

I continued on in this vein while he scribbled happily and the sergeant muttered with frustration and waddled away. When the form had been completed with the last work of fiction, I was released and ordered on to join the others. It was back to the elevators again, jammed inside in nude groups of forty. The doors closed for the descent. The doors opened.

At what was obviously the wrong floor. Before our horrified eyes there was displayed a vista of desks and typewriters. With a young lady laboring away at each of them. There was a fluttering sound as all of the folders were swung forward over the vitals. The air temperature rose as everyone turned bright red. All we could do was stand there in carmined embarrassment, listening to the endless rattle of typewriter keys, waiting for heads to turn, gentle female eyes to peer our way. After about fourteen and a half years the doors slowly closed again.

There were no females present when the doors opened this time, just the now-familiar form of another brutish sergeant. I wondered what twisted gene in the population had produced so many thick-necked, narrow-browed, pot-bellied sadomasochists.

"Out," this one bellowed. "Out, out, groups of ten, first ten through that door. Next ten next door. Not eleven! Can't you count, cagal-head!" Followed by a yipe of pain as discipline was enforced yet again. My ten victims shuffled into a brightly lit room and were ordered into line. We faced a white wall that was hung with a repulsive puce-green flag distastefully decorated with a black hammer. An officer with little golden bars on his shoulder strutted in and stood before the flag.

"This is a very important occasion," he said in a voice heavy with importance. And, "You young men, the fittest in the land, have been chosen as volunteers by your local draft boards to defend this country we love against the evil powers abroad that seek to strip away our freedoms. Now the solemn moment that you all have been waiting for has arrived. You entered this room as fun-loving youths. You will leave it as dedicated soldiers. You will now be sworn in as loyal members of the army. Raise your right hands and repeat after me . . ."

"I don't want to!"

"You have that choice," the officer said grimly. "This is a free country and you are all volunteers. You may take the oath. Or if you choose not to, which is your right, you may leave by the small door behind me which leads to the federal prison where you will begin your thirty-year sentence for neglect of democratic duties."

"My hand's up," the same voice wailed.

"You will all repeat after me. I, insert your own name, of my own free will . . ."

"I, insert your own name, of my own free will."

"We will do it again, and we will do it correctly, and if we don't get it right next time, there is going to be *trouble*."

We did it again, and correctly. Repeating what he said and trying not to hear what we were saying.

"To serve loyally . . . to show respect to all of the senior officers . . . death if I show disloyalty . . . death if I should desert . . . death if I sleep on duty . . ."

and so on to the very end, which was "I do swear this in the name of my mother and father and the deity of my choice."

"Hands down, congratulations, you are all now soldiers and subject to military law. Your first order is that each of you will volunteer voluntarily a liter of blood since there has been a sudden call for transfusions. Dismissed."

Weak with hunger and fatigue, dizzy from loss of blood, cold noodle soup still sitting leadenly in the stomach, we reached the end of the line. We hoped.

"Fall in. Move it along. You will each be issued with a disposable uniform which you will not dispose of until ordered. You will don the uniforms and proceed up these stairs to the roof of this building where transportation is waiting to take you to Camp Slimmarco, where your training will begin. You will turn in your folders before you receive your uniforms. You will each receive an identity disc with your name and service number on it. These discs are grooved across the center so they may be broken in half. Do not break them in half because that is a military crime and will be punished."

"Why make them to break in half if you don't break them in half?" I muttered aloud. The youth beside me rolled his eyes and whispered.

"Because when you're dead they break them in half and send on half to death registrations and put the other half in your mouth."

Why was it that as I shuffled forward to get my uniform I had a very strong metallic taste in my mouth?

Chapter 8

Under any other circumstances I would have enjoyed the ride in this unusual airship. It was shaped like a large cigar and undoubtedly contained light gas of some kind. Slung beneath the lifting body was a metal cabin tastefully decorated outside with a frieze of skulls and bones. Ducted fans on the cabin were angled to force it aloft and forward: the view from the window must have been fascinating. But the windows that we had glimpsed from the outside were all forward in the pilot's compartment, while we draftees were jammed into a windowless metal chamber. The seats were made from molded plastic surfaced with uneven bumps and hideously uncomfortable—but at least they were seats. I dropped into one and sighed with relief. In all the hours at the reception center the only time we had been off our feet was during the bloodletting. The plastic was cool through the thin paper fabric of the purple disposable uniform, the deck hard through the cardboard soles fastened at the end of its legs. The only pocket in this hideous garment was a pouch at the front into which we had shoved our bags of personal possessions so that we all resembled demented purple marsupials. I felt depressed. But at least I had company. We were all depressed.

"I never been away from home before," the recruit to my right sniveled, then sniffed and wiped his damp nose on his sleeve.

"Well I have," I said in my heartiest, most jovial tones. Not that I felt either hearty or jovial, but bucking up his spirits might help mine as well. "And it is a lot better than home."

"Food will be rotten," he whined self-indulgently. "Nobody can cook like my Mom. She makes the best cepkukoj in the whole world."

Onion cakes? What sort of bizarre diet had this stripling enjoyed? "Put that all behind you," I chirped. "If the army bakes cepkukoj they will be foul, count on that. But think of the other pleasures. Plenty of exercise, fresh air—and you can curse all the time, drink alcohol and talk smutty about girls!"

He blushed ardently, his splayed ears glowing like banners. "I wouldn't talk about girls! And I know how to drink. Me and Jojo went behind the barn once and drank beer and cursed and threw up."

"Whee . . ." I sighed and was saved from future futile conversation by the appearance of a sergeant. He slammed open the door from the front cabin and roared his command.

"Alright you kretenoj—on your feet!"

He assured instant obedience by hitting a button on the wall that collapsed our seats. There were screams and moans of pain, writhing purple confusion on the deck as the recruits fell on top of each other. I was the only one standing and I caught the full force of the sergeant's sizzling glare.

"What are you—a wise guy or sometin'?"

"No, sir! Just obeying orders, sir!" Saying this I leaped into the air slapping my arms to my sides, stamping my feet heavily as I landed, then delivered a snappy salute—so snappy I almost put my eye out. The sergeant's eyes bulged in return at this display before he was lost from sight by the rising, milling bodies.

"Quiet! Attention! Hands at sides, feet together, stomachs in, chests out, chins back, eyes forward—and stop breathing!"

The purple ranks swayed and writhed into this absurd military stance, then were still. Silence descended as the sergeant glared around with dark suspicion.

"Did I hear someone breathe? No breathing until I tell you to. The first cagalhead who breathes gets my fist where it will do the most good."

The silence lengthened. Purple figures stirred as incipient asphyxiation took hold. One recruit moaned and fell to the deck; I breathed silently through my nostrils. There was a gasp as one of the lads could hold out no longer. The sergeant surged forward and the spot where a fist will do the most good turned out to be the pit of the stomach. The victim screamed and fell and all the others gasped in life-giving air.

"That was a little lesson!" the sergeant screeched. "Did you get the message?"

"Yes," I muttered under my breath. "You're a sado-masochist."

"The lesson is that I give the orders, you obey them—or you get stomped." Having delivered this repulsive communication his face writhed, his lips pulled back to reveal yellowed teeth; it took a long moment for me to realize this was supposed to be a smile.

"Sit down men, make yourselves comfortable." On the steel deck? The seats were still stowed. I sat with the rest while the sergeant amicably patted the roll of fat that hung over his belt. "My name is Klutz, Drill-sergeant Klutz. But you will not address me by my name, which is for the use of those of equal rank or higher. You will call me sergeant, sir, or master. You will be humble, obedient, reverent and quiet. If you are not you will be punished. I will not tell you what the punishment will be because I have eaten recently and do not wish to upset my stomach."

A stir of fear passed through the audience at the thought of what might possibly upset that massive gut.

"One punishment is usually enough to break the spirit of even the most reluctant recruit. However, occasionally, a recruit will need a second punishment. Still more rarely a hardened resister will require a third punishment. But there is no third punishment. Would you like to know why there is no third punishment?"

The red eyes glared down and we all wished that we were someplace, anyplace, else at this moment.

"Since you are too dim to ask why, I will tell you. Third time is out. Third time is being stuffed, kicking and screaming and begging for your mommy, into the dehydration chamber where ninety-nine point nine nine percent of all your precious bodily fluids will be removed with a dry whishing sound. Do you know what you will look like then? You will look like *this*!"

He reached into his pocket and took out a tiny dehydrated figure of a recruit in a tiny dehydrated uniform, the features on its tiny face fixed forever in lines of terror. Moans of fear sighed from the soldiers and there were a number of thuds as the weakest dropped unconscious. Sergeant Klutz smiled.

"Yes, you will look just like this. Your tiny dry body will then be hung on the barracks bulletin board for a month as a warning to the others. After that your body will be put in a padded mailing envelope and sent to your parents, along with a toy shovel to assist in burial. Now—are there any questions?"

"Please, sir," a quavering voice asked. "Is the dehydration process instant and painless or drawn-out and terrible?"

"Good question. After your first day in the army—do you have any doubt which it will be?"

More moans and unconscious thuds followed. The sergeant nodded approval. "Alright. Let me tell you what happens next. We are going to the RTCS at MMB. That means the Recruit Training Camp Slimmarco at Mortstertoro Military Base. You will take your basic training. This training will turn you from feeble civilian wimps into sturdy, loyal, reverent soldiers. Some of you will wash out of basic training and will be buried with full military honors. Remember that. There is no way back. You will become good soldiers or you will become dead. You will understand that the military is hard but fair."

"What's fair about it?" a recruit gasped and the sergeant kicked him in the head.

"What is fair is that you all have an equal chance. You can get through basic or wash out. Now I will tell you something." He leaned forward and breathed out a blast of breath so foul that the nearest draftees dropped unconscious. There was no humor in his smile now. "The truth is that I *want* you to wash out. I will do everything I can to make you wash out. Every recruit sent home in a wheelchair or a box saves the government money and lowers taxes. I want you to wash out now instead of in combat after years of expensive training. Do we understand each other?"

If silence means assent, we certainly did. I admired the single-minded clarity of the technique. I did not like the military, but I was beginning to understand it.

"Any questions?"

My stomach rumbled loudly in the silence and the words popped from my mouth.

"Yes, sir. When do we eat?"

"You got a strong stomach, recruit. Most here are too sickened by military truth to eat."

"Only thinking of my military duty, sir. I must eat to be strong to be a good soldier."

He shuffled this around about in his dim brain, little piggy eyes glaring at me the while. Finally the projecting jaw nodded into the rolls of fat beneath the chin.

"Right. You just volunteered to get the rations. Through that door in the aft bulkhead. Move."

I moved. And thought. Bad news: I was in the army and liked nothing about it. Good news: we were going to Mortstertoro base where Bibs had last seen Captain Garth-Zenar-Zenor or whatever his name was. He was on top of my revenge list—but right now I was plugging away at the top of my survival list. Garth would have to wait. I opened the door which revealed a small closet containing a single box. It was labeled YUK-E COMBAT RATIONS. This had to be it. But when I lifted the box it seemed suspiciously light to feed this shipload of incipient soldiers.

"Pass them out, kreteno, don't admire the box," the sergeant growled, and I hurried to obey. The Yuk-E rations did appear pretty yuky. Gray bricks sealed in plastic covers. I went among my purple peers and each of them grabbed one out, fondling the bricks with some suspicion.

"These rations will sustain life for one entire day," the rasping voice informed us. "Each contains necessary vitamins, minerals, protein and saltpeter that the body needs or the army wants you to have. They are opened by inserting your thumbnail into the groove labeled thumbnail-here. The covering will fall away intact and you will preserve it intact. You will eat your ration. When you are finished you will go to the wall here and to the water tap at this position and you will drink from the plastic cover. You will drink quickly because one minute after being moistened the cover will lose its rigidity and will shrink. You will then roll up the cover and save it for display at inspection because it will now be transformed into a government issue contraceptive which you will not be able to use for a very long time, if ever, but which you will still be responsible for. Now—eat!"

I ate. Or tried to. The ration had the consistency of baked clay but not half as much flavor. I chewed and gagged and swallowed and managed to choke it all down before rushing to the water spigot. I filled the plastic cover and drank quickly and refilled it, emptying it just as it went limp and flacid. I sighed and rolled it up and stowed it in my marsupial pocket and made room for the next victim at the tap.

While we had been gnawing our food the collapsed seats had snapped back into position. I eased myself carefully into the nearest, but it did not give way. It appeared impossible, but the combination of food and near-terminal exhaustion worked their unsubtle magic and I crashed. I could hear myself snoring even before I fell asleep.

The bliss of unconsciousness ended just as I might have expected; the seats fell away and dropped us into a writhing, moaning mass on the deck. We stumbled groggily to our feet under the verbal lashing of the sergeant and were trying to stand in a military posture as the deck vibrated beneath our feet and became still.

"Welcome to the first day of the rest of your new life," the sergeant chortled, and wails of anguish followed his words. The exit sprang open, admitting a chill and dusty blast, and we stumbled out wearily to see our new home.

It was not very impressive. One of the red and pallid suns was just setting into the cloud of dust on the horizon. I could tell by the thin and chill air that the base had been built at some altitude, a high plateau perhaps. Which guaranteed good flying weather and maximum discomfort for the troops. The ground trembled as a deep-spacer took off in the distance, its exhaust blast brighter than the setting sun. The sergeant snarled us into a ragged formation and we shivered in the downblast of our departing airship. He waved a clipboard in our direction.

"I will now call the roll. You will be called by your military name and will forget that you ever had any other. Your military name is your given name followed by the first four numbers of your serial number. When your name is called you will enter the barracks behind me and proceed to your assigned bunk and await further instructions. Gordo7590—bunk one . . ."

I looked crosseyed at my dogtag until I could make out the number. Then stared numbly at the mud-colored barracks until the voice of our master called out Jak5138. With dragging feet I passed through the doorway over which was inscribed THROUGH THIS PORTAL PASS THE BEST DAMNED SOLDIERS IN THE WORLD. Who, as the expression goes, was kidding whom?

The floor was stone, still damp from the last scrubbing. The walls concrete, clean and still wet. I let my horrified gaze move up to the ceiling and, yes, it was damp as well, the light bulbs still dripping. How this maniacal cleansing was carried out I had no idea—though I was certain that I would find out far too soon.

My bunk was, naturally, the top one in a tier of three. It was strung with wire netting, though a bulky roll at its head hinted at softer pleasures.

"Welcome to your new home," the sergeant grated with false jollity as we drew our fatigued bodies up into an imitation of attention. "Note how your bedding roll is stowed when you unroll it, because it will be rolled in that stowed position at all times except when you're sleeping—which will be the minimum amount of time needed to stay alive. Or less. Your footlockers are imbedded in the floor between the bunks and are opened and closed by me with this master switch."

He touched a stud on his belt and there was a grating sound as the minigraves opened up in the floor. One recruit, who was standing in the wrong position, screamed as he fell into his.

"Lights out in fifteen minutes. Bedding to be unrolled but not utilized before that time. Before retiring you will watch an orientation film that will acquaint you with tomorrow's orders of the day. You will watch and listen with full attention, after which you will retire and pray to the deity or deities of your choice and cry yourselves to sleep thinking about your mommies. Dismissed."

Dismissed. The door slammed behind our striped overseer and we were alone. Dismissed was the right word for it. Dismissed from the warmth and the light of the real world, sent to this gray military hell not of our choosing. Why is mankind so inhuman to its own species? If you were caught treating a horse in this manner you would probably be put in jail, or shot. Rustling cut the silence as we opened our bedrolls. To reveal to each of us a thin mattress and even thinner blanket. A pneumatic pillow as well that could only be inflated with lusty puffing which, I was sure, would go flat by morning. While we were unrolling and blowing, TV screens dropped down silently behind us in the passageway between the bunks. Brassy military music blared and the image of an officer with a severe speech impediment appeared and began to read out totally incomprehensible instructions which we all ignored. I dumped the contents of my marsupial pocket into the subterranean footlocker and climbed and crawled, still dressed, into the bunk. My eyes blurred with fatigue as the voice droned on and I was nine-tenths asleep when a blast of light and sound jerked me awake. A grim military figure in black uniform glared angrily from the screen.

"Attention," it said. "This program has been interrupted, as have all programs throughout Nevenkebla on all stations, to bring you the following important announcement." He scowled at the sheet of paper he held and shook it angrily.

"A dangerous spy is at large in our country tonight. It is known that he entered the harbor of Marhaveno yesterday morning disguised as a laborer on one of the ships from Brastyr. A search was made of the harbor but he was not found. The search was extended today and it was discovered that the spy entered a pleasure vessel in the adjoining harbor and stole a number of items."

A deathly chill stirred the hairs on the nape of my neck as he held up a bundle of clothes.

"These were found buried in the sand and have been identified as the clothing worn by the spy. The entire area has been sealed, curfew declared and every building is now being carefully searched. The public is ordered to be on the lookout for this man. He may still be wearing these items of clothing that he stole. If you have seen anyone dressed like this notify the police or security forces at once."

His image vanished and was replaced by a carefully done computer simulation of the clothing I had borrowed from the boat. These rotated slowly in space—then appeared on a man's figure which the computer strolled about the screen. The face was a blank but I knew all too well what face would soon appear there.

How long would it take them to identify me, to track me down, discover that I was now in the army, to follow me here?

There was a grating thud as the barracks door locked and the lights went out. The chill spread down my body and my heart thudded with panic and I stared, sightless and horrified into the darkness.

How long?

Chapter 9

I would like to say that it was nerves of steel and fierce self-control that enabled me to fall asleep, after hearing the announcement that the entire country was turned out and searching for me. But that would be a lie. Not that I mind telling a lie or two, white lies really, to further myself in this universe. After all a disguise is a lie and continuous lying, sincere lying, is the measure of a good disguise. That went with the job. But one must not lie to oneself. No matter how distasteful the truth it must be faced and accepted. So, no lies; I fell asleep because I was horizontal in the dark, fairly warm and totally exhausted. Panic ran way behind exhaustion in the sleepy-time race. I slept, hard and enthusiastically, and awoke in the darkness only when a strange noise cut through my serious sack time.

It was a distant rustle, like waves on the beach—or leaves blowing in the wind. No, not that, but something else equally familiar. An amplified sound I thought numbly, like an ancient and worn recording being played, just the background scratching without the recording itself.

Theory was proved correct an instant later as a blurred and distorted recording of a bugle thundered through the barracks just as all the lights came on. The barracks door crashed open and, as though summoned from some dark hell by this hellish sound and light, the sergeant entered screaming at the top of his lungs.

"Get out and get under! Off your bunks and on your feet! Roll bedding! Dip into your footlockers! Remove shaving gear! Then on the double to the latrine! You're late, you're late! Barracks will be washed in twenty seconds precisely! Move it—move it—move it!"

We moved it, but we really didn't have enough time. I fought my way through the latrine door with the other frenzied purple figures just as the footlockers slammed shut and the barracks wash-heads let go. At that precise instant the sergeant stepped backward and slammed the door. From all sides torrents of cold water gushed forth, catching at least half of the recruits still on the run. They followed us into the latrine, soaked and shivering, their disposable uniforms beginning to dispose in long rents and tears. Crying and sniveling they pushed forward like sheep. Sheep struggling for survival. There was a limited number of sanitary facilities and all were in use. I forced my way through the mob until I could glimpse my face in the corner of a distorted mirror, almost did not recognize myself with the dark-circled eyes and pallid skin. But there was no time to get organized, to take stock, to think coherently. At some lower level I realized that it had all been planned this way, to keep the recruits off-balance, insecure, frightened—open for brainwashing or destruction. This realization percolated up to a slightly more conscious level and with it a growing anger.

Jimmy diGriz does not destruct! I was going to beat them at their own game, until I beat it out of here. It didn't matter that the entire country was looking for me—until they tracked me to this military cesspit all I had to do was survive. And survive I would! The supersonic razor screeched in my brain as it blasted my overnight whiskers free. Then, while the automated toothbrush crawled around inside my mouth, I managed to get a hand under a running faucet, scrubbed my face clean, ignored the air-dryer and pelted back to my bunk over the puddled floor. I stowed my kit away just as the footlocker flew open, then spun about as Sergeant Klutz popped through the door again.

"Fall out for rollcall!" he bellowed as I rushed by him into the night. I snapped to attention under the single glaring light as he turned and approached me with grim suspicion.

"Are you some kind of joker or something?" he shouted, his face so close to mine that his spittle dotted my skin.

"No, sir! I'm raring to go, sir. My daddy was a soldier and my grandaddy and they told me that the best thing to be was a soldier and the highest rank in the army was sergeant! That's why I'm here." I stopped shouting and leaned forward and whispered. "Don't tell the others, sir, they'll only sneer. But I wasn't drafted—I *volunteered.*"

He was silent and I risked a quick look at his face. Could it be? Was it, there, a drop of liquid in the corner of one eye? Had my tissue of lies touched some residual spot of emotion buried deep with the alcohol-sodden, sadistic flesh of his repulsive body? I couldn't be sure. At least he did not strike me down on the spot, but turned on his heel and rushed into the barracks to boot out the stragglers.

As the moaning victims stumbled into line I put some thought to my future. What should I do? *Nothing,* came the quick answer. Until you are tracked down, Jim, stay invisible in the ranks. And learn all that you can about this military jungle. Watch and learn and keep your eyes open. The more you understand about this operation the safer you will be. Then, when you run, it will be plan not panic that guides you. Good advice. Hard on the nerves to follow, but good advice nevertheless.

After repeated mumbled mistakes, mispronunciation of names—is it really possible to mispronounce Bil?—the sergeant finished stumbling and muttering his way through the rollcall and led the way to the mess hall. As we approached it, and the smells of real food washed over us, the splattering of saliva on the pavement sounded like rain. Other recruits stumbled up through the night and joined us in the long line leading into the warmth of this gustatory heaven. When I finally carried my heaped-high tray to the table I found it hard to believe. All right so maybe it was grundgeburgers with caramel sauce, but it was food, hot, solid food. I didn't eat it—I insufflated it and went back for more. For one moment I actually thought that the army was not so bad after all. Then I instantly banished the thought.

They were feeding us because they wanted to keep us alive. The food was nasty and cheap—but it would sustain life. So if we washed out it would not be because of the diet but because of our own intrinsic insufficiency or lack of will. If we got through basic training each of us would supply one hot and relatively willing body for the war machine. Nice thinking.

I hated the bastards. And went back for thirds.

Breakfast was followed by calisthenics—to aid the digestion or destroy it. Sergeant Klutz double-timed us to a vast, wind-swept plain where other recruits were already being put through their paces by muscular instructors. Our new leader was waiting for us, steely eyed and musclebound, the spread of his shoulders so wide that his head was disproportionately small. Or maybe he just had a pinhead. Speculation about this vanished as his roar rattled the teeth in my jaw.

"What's this, what's this? You kretenoj are almost a minute late!"

"Pigs, that what they is," our loyal sergeant said, taking a long black cigar from his pocket. "Little trotters in the trough. Couldn't tear them away from their chow."

Some recruits gasped at this outright lie, but the wiser of us were learning and stayed silent. The one thing that we could not expect was justice. We were late getting here because our porcine sergeant could not move any faster.

"Is that so?" the instructor said, his beady eyes swiveling in his pinhead like glowing marbles. "Then we will see if we cannot work some of that food off of these malingering cagal-kopfs. ON THE GROUND! Now—we do fifty push-ups. Begin!"

This seemed like a good idea since I usually did a hundred push-ups every morning to keep in shape. And the chill wind was blowing through the rents in our disposable uniforms. Five. I wondered when we would be issued with something more permanent. Fifteen.

By twenty there was plenty of wavering and grunting around me and I was warming up nicely. By thirty over half of the pipe-stemmed striplings had collapsed in the dust. Sergeant Klutz dropped cigar ashes on the nearest prostrate back. We continued. When we reached fifty just I and the muscular lad who hated injections were the only ones left. Pinhead glared at us.

"Another fifty," he snarled.

The weightlifter puffed on for twenty more before he groaned to a halt. I finished the course and got another glare and a snarl.

"Is that all, sir," I asked sweetly. "Couldn't we do another fifty?"

"On your feet!" he screamed. "Legs wide, arms extended, after me. One, two, three, four. And one more time . . ."

By the time the exercises were finished we had worked up a good sweat, the sergeant had finished his cigar—and two of the recruits were collapsed in the dust. One of them lay beside me, groaning and clutching his midriff. The sergeant strolled over and pushed him with his toe which elicited only some weak moans. Sergeant Klutz looked down with disgust and screamed his displeasure.

"Weaklings! Faggots! Momma's boys! We'll weed you out fast enough. Get these poofters out of my sight. Man to each side pick up the malingerers, bring them to the medic tent. Then fall back in. Move!"

I bent and seized one arm and lifted. I could see that the recruit on the other side was having difficulty so I shifted my grip to take most of the weight and heaved.

"Get his arm around your shoulder—I'll do the carrying," I whispered.

"My . . . thanks," he said. "I'm not in such great shape."

He was right, too. Thin and round-shouldered with dark circles under his eyes. And older than the others I noticed, in his mid-twenties at least.

"Morton's the name," he said.

"Jak. You look kind of old for the draft, Mort."

"Believe me, I am!" he said with some warmth. "I almost killed myself getting through university, keeping top of the class to keep out of the army. So what happens? I'm so overworked I get sick, miss the exams, wash out—and end up here anyway. What do we do with this dropout?"

"That tent there, I guess, where they're bringing the others."

The limp form hung between us, toes dragging in the dust.

"He doesn't look too good," Morton said, glancing at the pallid skin and hanging head.

"That's his problem. You have to look out for number one."

"I'm beginning to get that message. A crude communication but a highly effective one. Here we are."

"Drop him on the ground," a bored corporal said, not deigning to even look up from his illiterate comic book. When he touched the page little voices spoke out and there was a mini scream. I looked at the four other unconscious forms stretched out in the dirt.

"What about some medical treatment, corporal. He looks in a bad way."

"Tough cagal." He turned a page. "If he comes to—it's back to the drill field. Stays like that the medic will look at him when he gets here tonight."

"You're all heart."

"That's the way the kuketo crumbles. Now get the cagal out of here before I put you on report for cagaling off."

We got. "Where do they get all these sadistic types from?" I muttered.

"That could be you or I," Morton said grimly. "A sick society breeds sickies. People do what they are ordered to do. It is easier that way. Our society lives on militarism, chauvinism and hatred. When those are the rules there will always be someone eager to do the dirty work."

I rolled my eyes in his direction. "They taught you that in school?"

He smiled grimly and shook his head. "The opposite, if anything. I was majoring in history, military history of course, so I was allowed to do research. But I like to read and the university library is a really old one and all the books are there if you know how to look, and how to crack some simple security codes. I looked and cracked and read—and learned."

"I hope you learned to keep your mouth shut as well?"

"Yes—but not always."

"Make it always or you are in big trouble."

Sergeant Klutz was just leading our squad off the field and we fell in behind them. And marched to the supply building to get outfitted at last. I had heard that clothing came in only two sizes in the army and this was true. At least most of mine were too big so I could roll up the cuffs. In addition to clothing there were mess kits, webbing belts, canteens, sewing kits, assassination kits, foxhole diggers, backpacks, VD testers, bayonets, scrokets and more items of dubious or military nature. We staggered back to the barracks, dumped our possessions and hurried to our next assignment.

Which was something called Military Orientation.

"Having possessed our bodies they now seek to take over our minds," Morton whispered. "Dirty minds in military bodies."

He was sure bright this Morton, but not bright enough to keep his mouth shut. I hissed him into silence as Sergeant Klutz glared in our direction.

"Talking is forbidden," he graveled. "You are here to listen, and this here is Corporal Gow who will now tell you what you got to know."

This Gow was a smarmy type, all smooth pink skin, little ponce's moustache and fake grin. "Now sergeant," he said, "this is orientation, not orders. You men will become good soldiers by following orders. But good soldiers also should know the necessity of these orders. So get comfortable, guys. No chairs of course, this is the army. Just sit down on the nice clean concrete floor and give me your attention, if you please. Now—can any of you tell me why you are here?"

"We was drafted," a thick voice said.

"Yes, ha-ha, of course you were. But why is the draft necessary? Your teachers and your parents have let you down if this has not been made completely clear. So let me take this opportunity to remind you of some vital facts. You are here because a dangerous enemy is at our gates, has invaded our precious land, and it is your duty to defend our inalienable freedoms."

"This is the old cagal if I ever heard it," I muttered, and Morton nodded silent agreement.

"Did you say something, soldier?" The corporal said, staring right at me; he had good ears.

"Just a question, sir. How could a broken-down, unindustrialized society like they got over there, how could they ever invade a modern, armed and equipped country like ours."

"That is a *good* question, soldier, and one that I am happy to answer. Those barbarians across the channel would pose no problem if they were not being armed and equipped by *offworlders*. Greedy, hungry strangers who see our rich land and want to take it for themselves. That is why you lads must go willingly to the service of your country."

I was shocked at the magnitude of the lie, angered. But I struggled hard and followed my own advice and kept my mouth shut. But Morton didn't.

"But, sir, the Interplanetary League is a peaceful union of peaceful planets. War has been abolished . . ."

"How do you know that?" he snapped.

"Common knowledge," I said breaking in, hoping that Morton would shut up now. "But you know that is the truth, don't you, sir?"

"I know nothing of the sort and I wonder just who has been feeding you lies like that. After our orientation session I want to talk to you, soldier. You and that recruit next to you. This free country is fighting the interplanetary forces that wish to destroy us. No sacrifice is too great to defend that freedom, which is why I know that you will all do your duty, happily. And become good soldiers in a good team. Look to the good Sergeant Klutz as you would to your own father, for he is here to be your mentor and guide to your military life. Do what he says and you will grow strong and prosper and become first-class soldiers in the service of your country. But I know that you will at times find things confusing, even worrying, for this military experience is a new experience for all of you. That is when you must think of me. I am your counselor and guide. You can call upon me for advice and help at any time. I would like to be your friend, your very best friend. Now I am going to pass out these orientation pamphlets and you have ten minutes to read them. We will then have a question and answer session to help acquaint you with the details. While you are doing that I am going to have a nice friendly chat with these recruits who appear to be badly misinformed about the political realities of our land." The finger was pointing at me, then at Morton. "That's right, you two. We will step outside, get a bit of sun, have some good old jaw-jaw."

We rose with great reluctance—but had no choice at all. All eyes were upon us when we went to the door that Gow was holding open. I could feel the heat from Sergeant Klutz's burning glare as I passed him. Corporal Gow closed the door behind us and turned to face us. His smile as insincere as ever.

"Kind of warm now since the sun came out."

"Sure is. Feels nice."

"Where did you get that subversive cagal you were spouting in there? You first." He pointed at me.

"I sort of, well, sort of heard it somewhere."

He smiled happily and stabbed a stubby finger at Morton.

"I knew it. You have been listening to the illegal radio, haven't you? Both of you. That is the only possible place you could have heard such outrageous lies."

"Not really," Morton said. "Facts are facts and I happen to be right."

He was digging his own grave with his jaw. I broke in; this radio dodge sounded like a possible out. If there were such a thing we might just wriggle from under this creepo's thumb. I lowered my eyes and twisted my toe in the dirt.

"Gee, corporal, I don't know how to say this. I was going to lie or something—but you're too smart for me. It was, you're right, the radio . . ."

"I knew it! They pump that poison down from their satellite, too many frequencies to jam, too defended to shoot down. Lies!"

"I just did it that once. I knew I shouldn't have, but it was a dare. And it sounded so true—that's why I spoke out like that."

"I'm glad you did, recruit. And I imagine that you did the same?" Morton did not rise to the bait but the corporal took silence for assent. "I think that you did. But at least it shows the poison didn't take, that you two wanted to talk about it. The devil always has the best tunes. But you must turn away from the siren song of such slimy untruths and listen to the authorities who know far better than you do." He smiled warmly upon us and I grinned with wide insincerity.

"Oh I will, sir," I said quickly before Morton could open his mouth again. "I will. Now that you have told me this, and didn't punish us or anything . . ."

"Did I say that?" The warm grin suddenly had a cold and nasty edge to it. "You'll get your punishment. If you were civilians you would each get a year at hard labor. But you are in the army now—so the punishment should be worse. It has been nice talking to you, recruits. Now get back inside for the rest of this orientation session. That will give you plenty of time to contemplate your crimes and their inevitable punishment. In the future, if you have a future, you will not contradict me or any other officer."

He waved us inside ahead of him: we went like sheep to the slaughter. I whispered to Morton, "Is it true what he said about the radio broadcasts?"

"Of course. Haven't you ever listened? Pretty boring stuff for the most part. Heavy on propaganda and low on content. But it doesn't matter that you admitted listening. He was out to get us no matter what he said. Military justice!"

"Do we just stay here and wait?!"

"Where's to run," he said, with utmost gloom.

Where indeed? There was no place to flee to.

Sergeant Klutz glared his best glare at us and we shut up. I sank to the floor with a sigh. Wondering just what possible punishment the military could dream up that could be worse than recruit training. I had the sinking feeling that I would find out soon enough.

Chapter 10

A distant buzzer sounded like a stifled eructation and Sergeant Klutz's eyes came back into focus and the expression of dull vacuity vanished to be replaced by his normal sneer of anger.

"On your feet you cagal-kopfs! You had a whole hour of cagaling off and you will now pay for it. Double time! The next session will be small arm instruction and short arm inspection. Move it!"

"I'm holding onto these two," Gow said, separating us out from the others. "I'm putting them on report for spreading sedition."

Klutz nodded happily and slashed a line through our names on his roster sheet. "Suits me, Gow. As long as I got the roll call right you can eat them for breakfast for all I care."

The door closed and Gow and I stood there eyeball to eyeball. Morton slumped to one side, drooping with apathy. I was beginning to get angry. Corporal Gow took out his notebook and pencil and pointed at me.

"What is your name soldier?"

"ScrooU2."

"That is your military name, Scroo, and not a complete one at that. I would like your entire name."

"I'm from Pensildelphia, corporal, and we were taught never to give our names to strangers."

His eyes narrowed with hatred. "Are you trying to make fun of me soldier?"

"That would be impossible, sir. You are a walking joke as it is. Selling lies to the peasantry. You know as well as I do that the only threat to this country is the military that control it. This is a military state kept in operation only for the benefit of the military."

Morton gasped and tried to wave me to silence. I was too angry for that now. This cagaling corporal had gotten under my skin. He smiled coldly and reached for the telephone.

"If you won't tell me your name the Military Police will find it out quickly enough. And you are wrong about only the military benefiting from a military state. You are forgetting the industrial corporations that profit from the military contracts. One cannot exist without the other. They are mutually interdependent."

He said this calmly, smiling, and shocked me into silence. "But . . ." I finally mumbled as he dialed the phone. "If you know that—why are you selling that line of old cagal to the troops?"

"For the simple reason that I am the scion of one of those industrial families and quite happy with the situation as it is. I fulfill my military obligations by selling this line of old cagal, as you so quaintly put it, and in a few months will return to the life of luxury that I greatly enjoy. The number is engaged. I've enjoyed our talk as well, and in return for the pleasure I derived from the novelty of our conversation I wish to give you a gift."

He put the phone down turned and opened a drawer in the desk behind him and I was numb enough to let him do it. When the coin finally dropped it was too late. As I jumped forward he spun about with a large weapon in his hand, aimed and steady.

"I wouldn't, if I were you. I hunt, you know, and I am a first-class shot. I would also have no slightest compunction in shooting you. In the back if needs be," he added as I turned away. I turned around again and smiled.

"Well done, corporal. Intelligence was concerned about the quality of your orientation talks and I was sent here to, you know, try to irritate you. And I promise not to repeat your remarks about the industrial-military complex. I come from a poor family so I do not enjoy any of your advantages."

"Is that true?" Morton gasped.

"It is—and you are under arrest. There, one traitor caught, Gow, so some good has come of our conversation."

His eyes narrowed but the gun never moved. "Do you expect me to believe that?"

"No. But I can show you my identification." I smiled and reached into the empty back pocket of my new uniform.

He might have been a good shot when it came to blasting helpless animals or paper targets, but he had no combat experience. For a single instant his eyes looked down toward my moving hand. Which was all the time I needed. My other hand was already chopping the inside of his wrist, moving the gun aside. It hissed once and something slammed into the wall behind me. Morton screeched with fright and jumped aside. Before Gow could fire again my knee came up into his stomach.

The gun dropped to the floor and he dropped beside it. I took a deep and shuddering breath and let it out with a sigh.

"Well done, Jim," I said, and reached over my shoulder and patted myself on the back. "All the reflexes working fine."

Morton bulged his eyes at me, then down at the silent form of the corporal. "What's happening . . . ?" he gurgled in confusion.

"Exactly what you see. I've rendered the corporal unconscious before he did us bodily harm. And you are not under arrest since that was just a ruse. So now, quickly before someone comes, push that desk up against the entrance since you can see that the door has no lock."

I bent and retrieved the weapon in case the scion of millions came to earlier than planned. And what was I going to do with the poor little rich boy? I looked down at his recumbent form and inspiration struck.

"You are a genius," I bragged aloud. "You deserve another pat, which you will get later, because now speed is of the essence." I bent and began to unbutton his uniform. "The uniform, that is the key, the uniform. They will be looking for a ragged recruit in baggy fatigues. Not a spiffy corporal in tailor-mades. You have earned this promotion, Jim. Go to the head of the class."

I tore off his shoes and pulled his trousers free—and whistled. His underpants were woven of gold thread. Rich is as rich does. It was chance, pure chance, that he was a little overweight from a lifetime of good living. My muscles took the place of his fat and the uniform could have been made for me. Except the shoes; he had very tiny feet. My boots would have to do. I emptied his pockets and found, in addition to a great deal of money and a container of sinister looking black cigarettes, a small pocketknife. This worked admirably in cutting my discarded clothing into strips with which I bound the corporal securely, wadded more of the cloth into a gag. He was breathing easily through his nose so my conscience was clear that he would not die of suffocation.

"Are you going to kill him?" Morton asked.

"No, but I want him quiet until I put the next part of the plan into operation." I'm glad that Morton didn't ask what that was since I didn't know yet. There were no closets in the room so the corporal could not be stuffed out of sight. The desk—that was it!

"Morton," I ordered. "Stand with your back to the door and think like a lock. If anyone tries to open it lean hard against it."

While he leaned and thought lockish I dragged the desk back into position and wedged the bound corporal under it. By reflex I went through the desk drawers, which were all empty except the top one which had a folder of papers. I tucked these under my arm. Then I stepped back and examined my handiwork. Admirable. The corporal was well out of sight. Anyone who glanced into the room would think it empty.

"Now—what next?" I said cheerily. Then felt the smile slip from my face.

"Yes!" Morton agreed eagerly. "What happens next?"

I shook myself, took a brace and tried to think positively. "For one thing—

there is no going back. So let us seek out a way forward. When they find the corporal they will find out our names quickly enough. By which time we must have new names. Which means we go to the personnel section and make a few changes."

Morton was blinking very rapidly now. "Jak, old friend, don't you feel well? I don't understand a word that you are saying."

"Doesn't matter—as long as I do." I unloaded the gun, put the power charge in my pocket and the empty weapon back in the drawer. "March ahead of me, do as I command. Go! As soon as you have opened the door a crack to see if the coast is clear."

It was. We marched out, stamping and striding in a very military fashion, me clutching my sheaf of papers, Morton hopefully clutching to his few remaining shards of sanity. One, two, one, two. Around the corner and almost into the arms of a red-capped military policeman.

"Squad halt! Stand at ease!" I screamed. Morton halted with a decided sway and shudder, showing the whites of his eyes as he rolled them toward the MP. "Eyes front!" I shrieked. "I gave no orders for you to move your eyes."

The MP, wise in military ways, paid us absolutely no attention until I called out to him. "Just hold it, there, private."

"Me, corporal?" he asked, stopping and turning.

"You are the only thing moving that I can see. Your pocket is unbuttoned. But this is my generous day. Just point us toward the Personnel Building and keep moving."

"Straight ahead, right on the company street, past the bandstand, left at the torture chamber and there you are." He scurried away, groping at his shirt pockets to find the open one. Morton was shivering and sweating and I patted him on the back.

"Relax, my friend. As long as you have the rank you can do what you want in the army. Ready to go on?"

He nodded and stumbled forward. I marched after him, shouting commands at the corners, marking time, being noisy, obnoxious and abusive so I would not be noticed. A sad commentary indeed on the reality of military life.

The Personnel Building was large and industrious with plenty of to-ing and fro-ing from the front entrance. As we started toward it Morton came to a halt and stood at attention, swaying. "W-what are you going to do?" He whispered huskily and I saw that he was shaking with fear.

"Relax old buddy, all is under control," I said, leafing through the handful of papers to cover this unmilitary pause. "Just follow me, do as I say, and in a few minutes we will have vanished without trace."

"We'll really vanish without trace if we go in there! We'll be caught, tortured, killed . . ."

"Silence!" I shouted into his ear and he leaped as though he had been shot. "You will not talk. You will not think! You will only obey or you will be in the cagal so deep you will never see the light of day again!"

A passing sergeant smiled and nodded approval so I knew I was on the right track. I hated to do this to Morton but it was the only way. "Left face—forward march!"

His skin was pale, his eyes rolled up, his mind empty of conscious thought. He could only obey. Up the steps we went and through the entrance toward the armed military policemen stationed there.

"Halt, at ease!" I shouted and spun toward the MP, still shouting. "You—where do I find the Transport Section?"

"Second floor, room two-oh-nine. Could I see your pass corporal?"

I glared at him coldly as I shuffled through the papers I was carrying, let my eyes travel slowly down to his boots, then back up again. He stood at attention, shivering slightly, and I knew he was new at this game.

"I don't think I have ever seen dirtier boots," I hissed. When his eyes glanced down I held out the turned-back papers. "Here's the pass." When he glanced up again I let the papers slap shut.

He started to say something. I turned up the power of my glare and he wilted. "Thank you, corporal. Second floor."

I turned smartly away, snapped my fingers at Morton, then stamped away toward the stairs. Trying to ignore the fine beading of sweat on my brow. This was very demanding work—and it wasn't over yet. I could see that Morton was definitely shivering as he walked and I wondered how much more of this he could take. But there was no turning back now. I threw open the door of 209 and waved him in. A bench ran along the wall and I pointed him towards it.

"Sit there and wait until you're called," I said, then turned to the reception clerk. He was on the phone and waved vaguely in my direction. Behind him rows of desks and laboring soldiers stretched the length of the room. All totally ignoring me, of course.

"Yes, sir, get onto it at once, sir," the reception clerk smarmed. "Computer error, possibly, captain. We'll get right back to you. Very sorry about this."

I could hear the phone disconnect loudly in his ear. "You crock of cagal!" he snarled and threw the phone back on the desk, then looked up at me. "What's up, corporal?"

"I'm up here, corporal, and I'm here to see the transport sergeant."

"He's home on compassionate leave. His canary died."

"I do not wish to hear the disgusting details of his personal life, soldier. Who's sitting in for him?"

"Corporal Gamin."

"Tell the corporal I'm coming in."

"Right, right." He picked up the phone. I stamped past him to the door marked TRANSPORT SERGEANT—KEEP OUT and threw it open. The thin, dark man at the computer terminal looked up and frowned.

"You are Corporal Gamin?" I said, closing the door and flipping through the papers one more time. "If you are I got good news for you."

"I'm Gamin. What's up?"

"Your morale. The paymaster says they found a cumulative computer error in your pay and you are owed possibly two hundred and ten big ones. They want you there to straighten it out."

"I knew it! They been deducting double for insurance and laundry."

"They're all cagal-kopfs." My guess was right; there cannot be anyone alive, particularly in the army, who isn't sure there are errors in his payslip. "I would suggest you get your chunk over and collect before they lose the money again. Can I use your phone?"

"Punch nine for an outside line." He pulled up his necktie and reached for his jacket—then stopped and took the key out of the terminal; the screen went black. "I bet they owe me more than that. I want to see the records."

There was a second door behind his desk and, to my satisfaction, he exited that way. The instant it closed I had the other door open and poked my head through. When the reception clerk looked up I turned and called back over my shoulder.

"Do you want him in here as well, corporal?" I nodded my head and turned back. "You, recruit, get in here!"

Morton jumped at the sound of my voice, then scurried forward. I closed and locked the door behind him.

"Get comfortable," I said, pulling off my boot and rooting about inside it for the lockpick. "No questions. I have to work fast."

He slumped into a chair, eyes bulging in silence as I gently tickled the lock until the terminal came to life.

"Menu, menu," I muttered as I hammered away on the keys.

It all went a lot smoother and faster than I had hoped. Whoever had written the software had apparently expected it to be accessed by morons. Maybe he was right. In any case I was led by the hand through the menus right to the current shipping orders.

"Here we are, leaving at noon today, a few minutes from now. Fort Abomeno. Your full name and serial number, Morton, quickly."

I had my own dogtags spread out as I punched in all the requested information. A bell pinged and a sheet of paper slipped out of the printer.

"Wonderful!" I said, smiling and letting some tension out of my muscles: I passed it over to him. “We’re safe for the moment since we have just left for Fort Abomeno.”

“But . . . we’re still here.”

“Only in the flesh, my boy. For the record, and records are all that count to the military, we have shipped out. Now we make the flesh inviolate.” I read through the shipping orders, checked off two names, then turned back to the terminal and entered data with some urgency. We had to be long gone before the corporal returned. The printer whiffed gently and one sheet slipped out, then another. I grabbed them up, relocked the terminal, and waved Morton to his feet.

“Here we go. Out the back door and I’ll tell you what is happening as soon as we are clear of this building.”

Someone was coming up the stairs, a corporal, and my heart gave a little hip-hop before I saw that it wasn’t the corporal in question. Then it was down the hall to the front door and yes, there was Corporal Gamin coming up the stairs with a very nasty cut to his jib!

“Sharp right, recruit!” I ordered and we turned into the first doorway with military precision. A lieutenant was combing his hair in front of a mirror there. Her hair I realized when she turned about and glared at me.

“What kind of cagal-head are you, corporal? Or doesn’t the sign on the other side of this door read female personnel only?”

“Sorry, sir, ma’am, dark in the hall. Eye trouble. You, recruit, why didn’t you read the sign correctly? Get the cagal out of here and march straight to the MPs.”

I pushed Morton out ahead of me and closed the door. The hall ahead was empty.

“Let’s go! Quick as we can without attracting attention.”

Out the door and down the steps and around the corner and another corner and the pace was beginning to tell. I leaned against a wall and felt the sweat run down my face and drip from my nose. I wiped it with the sheaf of papers I still carried—then held up the two new sheets of orders and smiled; Morton gaped.

“Freedom and survival,” I chortled. “Shipping orders, or rather cancellation of shipping orders. We are safe at last.”

“I haven’t the slightest idea of what you are talking about.”

“Sorry. Let me explain. As far as the military is concerned we are no longer at this base but have been shipped to Fort Abomeno. They will search for us there, but we will be hard to find. In order to keep the body count correct two soldiers who are in that shipment, still physically in that shipment, have been removed on paper. These are their orders, corporal, I thought a bit more rank wouldn’t hurt. I am a sergeant now as you can see. We will occupy their quarters, eat their food, draw their pay. It will be weeks, perhaps months, before the error is discovered. By which time we will be long gone. Now—shall we begin our new careers as noncommissioned officers?"

"Urgle," he said dimly and his eyes shut and he would have slumped to the ground if I had not held him erect against the wall. I nodded agreement.

"I feel somewhat the same way myself. It really has been one of those days."

Chapter 11

Fatigue was of no importance, thirst equally so—although both were present and sending imperative messages. To be ignored. Rank has its privileges and we were not going to enjoy ours until we assumed the trappings. I shook Morton until his eyes opened and he blinked dully at me.

"One last effort, Mort. We are going to the PX, about whose heady joys we have heard, and there we will spend some money. When that has been done we will be free spirits and will eat and drink and relax. Are you ready?"

"No. I'm beat, shagged, dead. I cannot move. You go on. I can't make it . . ."

"Then I'll just have to turn you over to Sergeant Klutz who has just arrived and is standing right behind you."

He sprang into the air with a shriek of agony, feet already running before he hit the ground. I held on to him.

"Sorry about that. No Klutz here. A ruse to get your adrenaline flowing. Let's go."

We went. Quickly before this burst of energy faded. It got him as far as the post exchange, where I leaned him against the wall near the cashier and handed him my sheaf of papers.

"Stand there, recruit, and do not move and do not let go of those papers or I will skin you alive or worse."

I slammed the papers into his limp hands and whispered, "What size jacket do you take?" After much blinking on his part, and reiteration on mine, I extracted the needed information. I made my purchases from a bored clerk, added some stripes and a tube of superglue, paid for everything with some of Gow's money, thank you corporal, and led Morton farther into the reaches of the PX. To the latrine, empty this time of day.

"We'll use the booth one at a time," I said. "We don't want anyone making improper conclusions. Take off those fatigues and slip into this uniform. Move it."

While he changed I glued the new sergeant's stripes over the corporal's on my sleeves. When Morton had flushed and emerged I straightened his necktie and glued his promotion to his sleeve. His fatigues went into the rubbish, along with the sheaf of papers, and we went into the noncom's bar.

"Beer—or something stronger?" I asked.

"I don't drink."

"You do now. And curse. You're in the army. Sit there and sneer like a corporal and I'll be right back."

I ordered two double neutral grain spirits and some beers, dumped the ethyl alcohol into the beer, sipped it to make sure it had not gone off, then went back to our table. Morton drank as ordered, widened his eyes, gasped, then drank again. Color returned to his cheeks as I drained half of my glass and sighed happily.

"I don't know how to thank you, what to say . . ."

"Then say nothing. Drink up. What I did was to save my own hide and you just came along for the ride."

"Who are you, Jak? How do you know how to do those things you did?"

"Would you believe me if I said I was a spy sent here to seek out military secrets?"

"Yes."

"Well I'm not. I'm just a draftee like yourself. Though I will have to admit that I come from a lot further away than Pensildelphia. That's it, drain the glass, you're learning fast. I'll get a couple more drinks and some food. I saw they had catwiches. I'll get a couple of those."

Food and drink helped, as did the stripes on our arms. Morton tore into his rations. I ate more slowly, finding myself already thinking about the next step. Cigars followed, Gow's wallet was bottomless, and more drink.

"Thish is really great, Jak, really great. You're really great, really great."

"Sleep," I said as his eyes unfocused and his head hit the table with a thump. "You will awake a new man."

I sipped lightly at my own drink for I wanted only the stimulation of the alcohol and not the oblivion. The club was almost empty, only one other table occupied, the noncom there just as asleep as Morton. Probably as drunk as well. The simple pleasures of military life. I sipped and thought of my previous military career on Spiovente, and of The Bishop, now dead, and of the man who was responsible for his death.

"I haven't forgotten you, Captain Garth, not at all," I said softly to myself. The bartender polished a glass and yawned. Well acquainted with customers who talked to themselves and drank themselves into extinction. "For the last few days it has been survival only. Now I pick up your trail. We're in the same army, on the same base."

I felt suddenly dizzy and put the glass down. It had been a long day and I was as tired as Morton. Country and coal-mining music was grating enchantingly from the jukebox: the world about was at peace. For the moment. I was aware of a light scratching sound and glanced down at the boxes that leaned against the wall. Something moved in the darkness behind them. I watched in silence as a twitching nose and whiskers emerged. Then the head, the bar lights reflected in the rat's eyes. It appeared to be looking up at me.

"Get lost," I said, "before you end up in the stew." I cackled at my own witticism.

"Jim diGriz, I must talk with you," the rat said in a deep voice.

It had really been one of those days. Too much. I had not realized it but the strain was so great that I had cracked.

"Go away," I hissed. "You are a figment of my imagination and not a real rat at all." I gulped the rest of my drink in a single swallow. The rat climbed up onto the box and looked at me.

"Of course I am not a real rat. I am Captain Varod of the League Navy."

Gently, so as not to awaken Morton—this was my hallucination and I wanted to keep it for myself—I pried his drink from his slack fingers and drained it as well as my own.

"You've shrunk a bit since the last time I talked with you, captain," I smirked.

"Stop playing the idiot, diGriz, and listen to me. This spyrat is controlled from our base. You were recognized and identified."

"By who? The rat?"

"Shut up. This communication is limited because there is a chance their detectors will pick up the spyrat's broadcast signal. We need your help. You have penetrated their military base, the first agent to do so . . ."

"Agent? I thought I was the criminal you were shipping home for trial and persecution?"

"I said we need your help. This is vital. There are lives at stake. The generals are planning an invasion. We know that much from intercepting their communications. But we don't know where the landing will take place. Brastyr is a big continent and they might be attacking anywhere. There could be a lot of deaths. We must find out where they plan to . . ."

The door to the bar burst open and a gun-waving officer burst in, followed by a technician weighted with electronic equipment.

"The signal is coming from that direction, sir," the man shouted and pointed directly at me.

"What is that cagal-head private doing in the noncoms' bar?" I shouted, leaping to my feet and kicking the box as I did. The rat fell to the floor and I stamped on it. Hard.

"Don't get your cagal in an uproar, sergeant," the officer said. "This is a priority investigation . . ."

"Signal has stopped, sir," the technician said, fiddling with his dials.

"Cagal!" the officer said, stuffing his gun back into the holster. "These alcoholics don't have a transmitter."

"Could be the street outside, other side of the wall. A moving vehicle."

"Let's go!"

The door slammed shut behind them. The barman wiped his glass. "This happen very often around here?" I asked.

"Yeah. This is sure an uptight base."

Morton snored heavily and I poked the crushed remains of the stainless steel rat with my toe. An omen? A gear wheel rolled out and rattled on the floor.

"Set them up again," I called out. "And take one yourself since the rest of these cagal-kopfs are in dreamland."

"You're all heart, sarge. Just ship in?"

"Today."

"An uptight base like I say—"

His voice was drowned out by the loud whistle from the TV as it turned itself on. The black-clad military announcer glared out of the screen just one more time.

"The spy who landed in Marhaveno has been identified. He attempted to disguise himself as a harmless draftee and was inducted into the army. Resolute police work has identified him by his clothing."

Some police work. They just looked at their mail. I was beginning to think that sending my clothing from the reception center to the police station was not at all as funny as it had seemed at the time. There was a scratch of static and the announcer vanished from the screen to be replaced by another officer.

"Now hear this," he shouted. "As of this moment this entire base is sealed to outgoing. I repeat, Mortstertoro is locked tight, gates sealed, aircraft departures canceled. The spy who landed in Marhaveno has been identified as a recruit who was shipped to this base. Here is his picture."

My heart skipped a beat or two, then settled down as the blurred photo of Jak, from my stolen ID, appeared on the screen. I was still one jump ahead of them. It would soon be discovered that Jak5138 was no longer on the base and the search would go elsewhere. I took my drink and went back to the table to stare into the wide and frightened eyes of Morton.

"You want a drink?" I asked before he could speak. He gurgled and pointed at the screen.

"Did you hear that?" I asked, and kicked him under the table. "Can't be much of a spy if he lets himself get drafted. Some spy! I'll bet you five he's caught and dead before dark." When he relaxed slightly I went on in a hoarse whisper. "It will take a long time to search this base . . ."

"No it won't—because they know just where to look. They know who you are, Jak. They'll go to Sergeant Klutz, who will tell them he transferred you to Corporal Gow. Then they'll find Gow and . . ."

"And the trail will run cold. It will take them days to search a camp this size. And when they don't find the spy the first time they'll just do it again. They are not bright enough to consider having the computer check the records for the spy."

"Attention!" the announcer on the screen called out, waving a sheet of paper. "I have just been given this new information. The spy—and an accomplice—have managed to have themselves transferred from this base by illegal use of the base computer. All computer personnel are now under arrest and will probably be shot."

I turned away, not able to look Morton in the eye.

"Now that they know where to look," Morton asked hollowly, "how long will it take them to discover that we were never on that shipment? And then find out that a corporal and a sergeant who really were on that shipment were not on that shipment and are still here on the base?"

"How long?" I laughed, but there was a very hollow ring to it. "Could take days, weeks, no way to tell."

"How long?"

I sighed deeply. "They got some hotshot computer programs. Good security. I would say that we have maybe thirty minutes before they start looking for us."

His body shook as though he had received ten thousand volts and he started to jump to his feet. I reached out and held him down, then glanced at the bartender. He was looking at the TV.

"You're right," I said. "We get out of here, but slowly. On your feet. Follow me."

As we started toward the door the bartender glanced in our direction.

"Where's the transient barracks?" I said.

"Out the back door, turn right. See you."

"Yeah. See you."

We strolled out the back door and turned left. It was getting dark, which might help.

"You got a plan?" Morton said, eagerness in his voice. "You know a way to get us out of this."

"Of course," I said, clapping him on the back. "Every step planned. We go this way."

I could hear the forced joviality in my voice; I hoped that he couldn't. He had to think that I knew what I was doing or he might crack. It was a white lie for the sake of his morale.

But what about my morale? I was holding it down successfully for the moment, but I could feel an awareness of dark panic knocking and ready to come in. I kept it at bay. We walked on down the company street, the lights coming on, lost in the milling military mass. How long would this last? The question was the answer: not very. The panic pushed a little harder.

I have heard it said that when a man knows that he is to be hanged, it focuses his mind wonderfully. I wasn't going to be hanged, not for the present at least, but the foul breath of military prosecution on my neck was focusing my mind almost as well. So much so that when an officer passed I turned to look at him. Turned and stopped until he vanished in the crowd. Morton was pulling feebly at my arm.

"What are you looking at? What's wrong?"

"Nothing wrong. Everything right. I know now exactly what we must do next."

"What?"

"Just come with me. I know that it is back this way, I noticed it when we passed."

"What, what?"

"BOQ." Before he could say What? What? What? I explained. "Bachelor Officers' Quarters. Where the officers live when they are not getting drunk and making life a hell for the enlisted men. That is where we are going. There."

I pointed to the brightly lit building, guards at the front entrance, officers in their military finery pouring from it.

"That's suicide!" Morton said. The edge of hysteria back in his voice.

"Easy does it," I cozened. "We do not enter the building by this portal. Suicide as you say. But what has a front surely has a back. And from the exodus visible from that officerial snakepit it looks like everyone is on duty tonight. Everyone except us, that is." I chortled darkly and he looked at me out of the corners of his eyes as if I had gone mad. Perhaps I had. We would soon find out.

There was a wall behind the BOQ which we followed. A sort of alley led next to it, badly lit and just what I wanted. There was a door here let into the wall with a light above it. As we strolled past I read the sign, OFFICERS ONLY, and bent over and tied my shoe: it needed only a single glance to identify the lock. Then I stood and continued on. I stopped in the shadows between two lights and bent to my shoe again. Only this time I came up with the lockpick.

"All right, here we go. The lock is nothing, single tumbler, pick it as easy as I pick my teeth. We walk back now and if no one is in sight we walk through it. Got that?"

The chatter of his teeth was the only response. I took his quivering arm and squeezed it. "It's all right, Morton. You'll see. Just do as I say and we'll soon be safe. Nice and quiet—here we go."

I tried not to catch any of Morton's fears, but they were very contagious.

We stopped under the light, I put the lockpick into the keyhole. Felt and twisted. It didn't open.

"Someone's coming," Morton wailed.

"Piece of cake," I muttered, perspiration running down my face. "Opened these with my eyes shut."

"Getting closer!"

"Eyes shut!"

It wouldn't open. I shut my eyes, closed out all sensations, felt for the tumblers. Clicked it open.

"Inside!" I said, pulling him after me, closing the gate behind us. We stood with our backs to it, shivering in the darkness as the footsteps came closer, came to the gate . . .

Passed it and went on.

"There, wasn't that easy?" I said, ruining the effect as my voice cracked and squeaked. Not that Morton noticed; he was shivering so hard that I could hear his teeth clatter. "Look, nice garden. Pathways for strolling, love seats for loving, all the nice things to keep the officerial classes happy. And beyond the garden the dark windows of their quarters, dark because the occupants have all gone out. So now all that we have to do is find a window to open . . ."

"Jak—what are we doing here?"

"I thought that was obvious. The military powers are looking for one recruit now. When their computer coughs out the next bit of news they will be looking for a corporal and a sergeant." I tried to ignore his moan. "So we get into this building and become officers. As simple as that."

I caught him as he dropped and laid him gently on the grass. "That's it. Have a little rest. I'll be right back."

The third window I tried was unlocked. I opened it and looked in. A mussed bed, open closet, empty room. Perfect. I found my way back to Morton who was just sitting up. He recoiled as I appeared out of the darkness and my quick hand over his mouth muffled his scream.

"Everything is fine. Almost finished."

I boosted him through the window and let him drop onto the bed, then closed and locked the window behind us. There was a key in the door which made everything very much easier.

"Look," I said, "lie here and recuperate. I'm going to lock you in. The building is empty as far as I can see, so what I have to do should not be long. Take a rest and I'll be back as soon as I can."

I went carefully, but the building was empty of life and as silent as the tomb. Its occupants away and hopefully hard at work. I had time to pick and choose, make my selections and select the right sizes. I heard a muffled moan of agony when I let myself back into the room, to which I responded as cheerfully as I could.

"New uniform—new persona!" I handed them over to Morton. "Get dressed and give me our old clothes. There's enough light from outside to make that easy. Here, let me tie that necktie, you are all butterfingers today."

Dressed and ready, our caps square upon our heads, our old clothes buried in a laundry basket, we sauntered forth into the corridor. Morton looked at me and gasped and fell away.

"Cheer up—you look the same way. Except that you are a second lieutenant while I am a captain. It is a young army."

"B-but," he stammered. "You are a . . . Military Policeman!"

"And so are you. No one ever questions a cop."

We turned the corner as I said this and approached the front entrance. The major standing there with a clipboard looked up at us and scowled.

"Now I have you," he said.

Chapter 12

I snapped to attention, I could think of nothing else to do—and hoped Morton was not too paralyzed to do the same. There were just two of them, the major and the guard at the door. After I dropped the major could I reach the guard before he could get out his gun? A neat problem. The major was looking at his clipboard. Now—get him!

He looked up as I swayed forward. The guard was looking at me too. I swayed back.

"I missed you at the airport," the major said. "You must have come on the earlier flight. But these shipping orders say two captains. Who is this lieutenant?"

Shipping orders? Two captains? I stopped my eyeballs spinning and finally threw my brain into gear.

"Could be an error, sir. Lot of confusion today. Might I see the orders?"

He grunted uncommunicatively and passed them over. I ran my finger down the list of crossed-off names to the remaining two at the bottom. Then passed them back.

"Error like I said, sir. I'm Captain Drem. This is Lieutenant Hesk, not captain the way they got it here."

"Right," he said, making the change on his sheet. "Let's go."

We went. Outside the door was a truck stuffed with Military Police, a very disgusting sight. The major climbed into the cab, rank does have its privileges, and I led Morton to the rear. Moving quickly because I saw something that I hoped the major had not seen. Two MP officers, both captains, walking toward us. They scowled and passed and turned into the BOQ. I scowled in return, turning the scowl into a glare when I looked into the back of the truck and saw that there were no officers among the redhats there.

"What is this—a meeting of the girls' club," I snarled. "Move back, make room, shut up, give us a hand."

All of this was done with alacrity. Morton and I sat on the recently vacated bench and the truck pulled forward. I let out my breath slowly—from between still-snarling teeth. We bumped and swayed our way through the night and I began to feel very, very tired. It had been that kind of day.

"Do you know where we are going, captain?" a burly sergeant asked.

"Shut up!"

"Thank you, sir."

There was only silence after this witty exchange. Cold silence that continued until we ground to a stop and the major reappeared. "Climb out," he ordered. "Captain, follow me."

"Fall these men in, lieutenant," I told Morton. He stumbled after me his face white with despair in the glare of the street lights.

"How, what, glug," he whispered.

"Order a sergeant to do it," I whispered back. "Pass the buck, that's the army way."

I trotted after the major who had stopped before the entrance of a large building and was going through an immense ring of keys. I stood at ease and looked at the large posters beside the door. Then looked closer when I realized they were 3Ds, in living color, of a number of naked young woman. When my head moved they moved and I swayed slightly.

"Knock that off, captain," the major ordered and I snapped to attention, my eyes still focused on the sign that read BASE BURLESQUE—OFFICERS ONLY. The major found the key he was looking for and turned it in the lock. "No performance tonight," he said. "We've comandeered the place for an emergency meeting. Top security. As soon as the techs get here I want the entire theatre swept clean. And I mean clean. I want an MP with every tech and I want a head count and I am making you responsible. Got that?"

"Yes, sir."

"I'm going to check all the other doors personally to make sure they are locked. Get cracking, we only have an hour."

I threw a salute as he moved off around the building and wondered just what I had gotten myself into. The rumble of engines cut through my thoughts as a truck pulled up at the curb before me. A sergeant climbed down from the cab and saluted me.

"And what do we have here?" I asked.

"Instrument technicians, sir. We were ordered . . ."

"I'll bet you were. Unload them and fall them in."

"Yes, sir."

I stamped back to the MPs who were neatly lined up at attention and pointed my finger at Morton. "You, Lieutenant Hesk, get over in front of that entrance. No one in or out without my permission."

My heart dropped as Morton started to look over his shoulder. Memory of his new name apparently filtered through because he recovered himself and hurried away. I turned back and scowled at the MPs, with particular attention to the sergeant who stood before them. Gray-haired, skin like an old boot, stripes and hashmarks clogging his sleeve.

"You senior NCO?"

"Yes, sir."

"Right. Here is the drill. Those techs are going to sweep this theater. I want one MP with every tech. I want every man counted in and counted out and I want no errors. And I want the sweep complete and overlapping and that building clean. Any questions?"

"No, captain. They'll snap-cagal for me."

"I thought they would. Get cracking."

He turned on his heel, inflated his lungs—and let out a blast of orders that blew the cap off the nearest MP. They moved. I stepped back and nodded approval. Then stamped over and positioned myself next to Morton.

"Something big coming down," I said quietly. "Secret meeting in an hour and we are in charge of security." I ignored his moan of anguish. "Just stand around and look military and stay away from the major when he gets back. I don't know about you, but I find this very interesting." he moaned again and I strolled over to inspect the arrangements.

The technicians had shouldered their backpacks and were adjusting dials on the control panels that each of them wore slung about the chest. One of them pointed his detector wand at the side of the truck and I could see the needles jump; there was a squeal from the earphones that he had hung about his neck.

"Captain. Some trouble here." I turned around.

"What is it, sergeant."

"This cagal-kopf says he got a malfunction." He had a white-faced tech by the arm and was shaking him like a dog with a bone.

"Battery, sir," the man wailed. "Checked . . . it's a malfunction fuse!"

"Arrest him, sergeant. The charge is sabotage. Have him shot at dawn." The sergeant smiled, the tech moaned and I bent until my face was close to his. "Or can you manage to trace and repair this malfunction in the next sixty seconds?"

"It's fixed, sir! I know how! Borrow a fuse!"

He stumbled away with the sergeant right behind him. I was falling into my role and beginning to enjoy myself. Though I was sure I would hate myself in the morning.

More MPs had arrived; the major reappeared and spread them around the theater and in front of the entrance. I could see Morton begin to shiver at their presence so I hurried to take over from him.

"You can open that door now, lieutenant. No one goes in except these search teams. I want a head count going in and coming out."

Under the verbal abuse of the sergeant the search was finished just in time. The first official cars were appearing as the techs were being loaded back into the trucks.

"How did it go, sergeant?" I asked.

"Lot of beer cans, cagal like that. Swept secure, captain."

"Good. Move the troops out of the way, but keep them around in case we need them again."

I waved Morton after me and strolled over to the nearest truck, stood in its shadow where I could see what was happening.

"What's happening," Morton asked.

"Good question. Big, secret and very sudden meeting of some kind. See that car, all officers of field rank or better."

"We have got to get out of here!"

"Why? Can you think of a safer place to be? We are part of the security here—so no questions asked. Except by me. Look at that one getting out of the limo! Must have nine stars on his shoulders. Big stuff tonight. And that officer behind him. Never saw that uniform before. Something special . . ."

This officer turned about and I froze. A single silver skull on the shoulder of his gray-green coat. Another skull on the front of his cap.

And beneath the black brim of the cap a familiar face.

Captain Garth. Former captain of a Venian freighter. The man responsible for the death of my friend The Bishop.

"Stay here," I ordered Morton, and stepped out of the darkness as soon as Garth had turned away. I walked toward him as he approached the security check at the entrance. Passed right behind him as he reached the major, who threw a very snappy salute. I could hear the major's voice clearly as I passed and went on.

"They are almost all inside, General Zennor."

"Report to me when the count is complete. Then seal this door tight."

I stamped on, checked the guards, stamped back to Morton's side.

"What was that all about?" he asked.

"Forget about it. Nothing to do with you."

No longer a simple spacer captain. A general now. Probably always a general. Zennor. What was he up to? What was this entire army up to that he seemed to be ordering around? And how could I find out?

When the major called I did not even hear him. Only when Morton kicked me in the ankle did I realize that I was the Captain Drem he was talking to.

"Yes, sir. You want me, sir?"

"Not falling asleep, are you, Drem?"

"No, major, I was just going over the security in my head."

"Well go over it on your feet, which will accomplish a lot more. I've stationed a man at every entrance to this theater. Inspect them."

I saluted his back enthusiastically as he turned away. This might very well be the opportunity I was waiting for.

"Lieutenant," I called out. "Inspection tour. This way."

I rubbed my hands together happily as we walked around the theater. "Morton, there is something important going on here and I mean to find out more about it."

"Don't! Stay clear!"

"Normally good advice. But this time I have to know what is happening, what *he* is up to. Did you see the uniforms? All senior officers. And I was ratted to earlier today that an invasion was being planned. It doesn't take a great brain to figure out that this meeting has something to do with that invasion. But how do I get inside?"

We were approaching a side entrance to the theater and the MP there snapped to attention as soon as we appeared. I shook the locked door and scowled at him.

"This door locked when you got here?"

"Yes, sir."

"Anyone try to get in?"

"No, sir!"

"What are your orders?"

"Kill anyone who goes near the door." He had his hand on his pistol butt.

"Does that include your commanding officers?" I shouted at him, my mouth in his ear. He swayed and his hand dropped to his side.

"No, captain."

"Then you are wrong and *you* could be shot for disobeying orders. An inspecting officer may try the door to see if it is locked. If an inspecting officer should attempt to go through the door he is to be instantly killed. Is that clear?"

"Very clear, sir."

"Then wipe the smile from your face. You seem to enjoy that thought too much."

"Yes, sir. I mean no, sir!"

I growled a bit more and continued my inspection. We had almost circumnavigated the building when we reached a door in the rear. The guard there stood at attention. I shook the locked door and looked at the metal staircase beside it.

"Where does this go to?" I asked.

"Emergency exit."

"Is there a guard there."

"Yes, sir."

Morton followed me up the clanging stairs. I stopped halfway and bent to remove the lockpick from my shoe. Morton opened his mouth but shut it again when I put my finger to my lips. I had to find out what was happening inside.

We stamped upward and when we emerged on the balustraded corridor the guard there had his gun half out of the holster.

"Do you intend to aim that weapon at me?" I asked coldly.

"No, sir, sorry." He put it away and snapped to attention. I put my face close to his.

"Do you know it is a court-martial offense to point a weapon at an officer?"

"I wasn't, sir, no! I'm alone here, didn't know who was coming . . ."

"I don't believe you, soldier. There is something wrong here. Stand over there by the lieutenant."

As he turned about I had the lockpick in the keyhole, delicately, turning it, clicking it. I stepped back away from it as he stopped and about-faced.

"This door is locked?"

"Yes, sir. Of course. I am stationed here because of the door . . ."

His voice wound down as I reached out and opened the door. Then closed it and wheeled to face him.

"You are under arrest, soldier. Lieutenant—take this man to the major. Tell him what has happened. Return with the major at once. Move it!"

As they stamped away I inserted the lockpick yet again, twisted and pressed hard. Something snapped inside the lock. Only then did I put the lockpick away, open the door and slip inside. Closing it silently behind me.

The small entranceway was sealed with dusty curtains. Light trickled between them; I bent forward and separated them a tiny amount.

". . . important that security be absolute until blastoff. You have your sealed orders, not to be opened until H hour. Rendezvous points are marked . . ."

I knew that voice well. Once Garth, now Zennor. I parted the curtains just a bit more to make sure. There he was, almost below me, pointing at the large chart behind him. I looked at the chart, then closed the curtains and stepped back.

I was closing the door behind me when hurried footsteps sounded on the stairs. The major appeared, face red and strained.

"What is happening?"

"I'm not sure, sir. The guard that was stationed here had his weapon drawn, acted suspiciously. I tried this door. It was unlocked. That was when I sent for you, sir."

"It can't be. I locked it myself."

It opened at his touch and his face whitened with shock. He pulled it quickly closed. "You haven't been inside?"

"Of course not, major. I have my orders. Perhaps the lock is defective."

"Yes, perhaps!" He fumbled out his ring of keys, found the right key and turned it in the lock. Metal grated.

"It won't lock!"

"May I try it, sir?"

I took the keys from his limp fingers and, naturally, had no better luck in sealing the door. When I handed back the keys I spoke in a low voice.

"There will be an investigation, sir, trouble. Not fair to you. I'll see that the guard talks to no one about this. Then I'll get a welder, seal the door. Might be best, major, don't you think so?"

He started to speak, then closed his mouth, and thought instead. Looking from me to the door. Then he noticed the keys still in his hand. He put them in his pocket and straightened his shoulders.

"As you say, captain, nothing happened. No point in getting involved in investigations and suchlike. I'll stay here. Send the welder at once."

"Very good, sir. I'll take care of everything."

Morton was waiting at the foot of the stairs, the frightened MP standing beside him. I walked up to the man and gave him a good glare.

"I am going to be kind to you, soldier, although it goes against the grain. I think it might be wisest if we forgot all about this matter. What is your name?"

"Pip7812, sir."

"All right, Pip, you can go back to your unit now. But—if I hear any rumors or loose talk about locks or such you will be dead within twenty-four hours. Understand?"

"Locks, captain? I'm afraid I don't know what you mean."

"Very good, Pip. Report to the sergeant. Tell him I need a welder here at once. Move."

He moved. "What was all that about?" Morton asked.

"That was about warfare, my friend. I know now what they are up to here. I know all about their invasion plans."

Except—what could I possibly do about it?

Chapter 13

When the meeting broke up I saw to it that I was busily occupied away from the theater entrance. It was a long chance that Zennor would recognize me from his Captain Garth days. But even a long chance is some chance, so I stayed out of sight. The troops formed up and marched away: with the emergency over they were not being coddled with effete tranportation. The major had a car at his disposal but I turned down his offer.

"We could have used a lift," Morton complained as the car moved away.

"To where? Prison? The further we are from authority the happier we should be."

"I'm tired."

"Who isn't? Not to mention hungry. Let's find a place to spend some of Gow's money . . ."

"Jim . . . Jim diGriz . . ."

The sound was high-pitched, barely audible. Was I hearing things? I looked around but Morton was the only person nearby.

"Did you hear anything?"

"No. Should I?"

"Don't know. A sudden ringing in my ears. But I swear I heard something."

"Maybe it was that moth on your shoulder talking to you. Ha-ha."

"Ha-ha yourself. What moth?"

"See it there? Sitting on your captain's bars. Should I brush it off?"

"No. Leave it."

I turned my head and blinked and could just make out the moth. It flapped its wings and took off—and landed on my ear.

"Go . . . aergropl . . . now."

"I can't understand you."

"That's because I'm not talking."

"Shut up, Morton. I'm talking to the moth, not to you."

His jaw dropped and he moved quickly sideways. "Repeat message," I said, ignoring him for the moment.

"Airfield . . . go airfield."

"Right, go to the airfield. Understood. Over and out." The moth fluttered away and I patted Morton on the shoulder; I could feel him shivering. "Come on, cheer up. And stop looking at me as though I were mad. The moth is a communication device, nothing more."

"Communicating with whom?"

"The less you know, the less trouble you can get into."

"You really are a spy, aren't you?"

"Yes and no. I'm here on my own business, but certain parties are trying to get me involved in their business. Do you understand?"

"No."

"Good. Let's find the airfield. At a guess I would say that it is over there where all the lights are and the planes are landing. Coming with me?"

"Do I have a choice? Is there any way of going back? Starting over again? I mean we can't just sneak back into the barracks as if nothing happened, can we?"

"You know that we can't."

He sighed and nodded his head. "I know. But I'm just not cut out for the kind of thing that we have been doing. And where is it going to end?"

A good question. With very little hope of an answer at the present time.

"Truthfully—I don't know. But you have my word, Morton, because I got you into this. My first priority, before anything else, is to get you out of trouble and safe. Don't ask how—because I don't know yet."

"You can't blame yourself. It was I who opened my mouth to that cagaling corporal. That's where it started."

We had been walking while we talked, getting closer and closer to the airfield. The road that we were taking curved around the end of the field, separated from it by a high wire fence, well illuminated by bright lights. On the other side of the fence were grass and taxiways. A heavy freighter had just landed. It trundled by and we watched it go. When it had moved on a flock of black birds swooped down and began poking about in the grass. One of them unfolded its wings and flew toward the fence, landing on the other side. It cocked its head at me and spoke.

"You are not alone."

"Obviously. He's safe. Is that you, Varod."

"No. Captain Varod is off duty."

"Get him. I don't talk to just any old crow."

"You will be contacted."

The bird turned about and opened its beak and spread its wings. It took off without flapping, making a whistling sound.

"Jet powered," I said. "Air intake in its mouth. Jet exhaust just where you imagine it might be. Let's walk."

There was the whine of an approaching siren and a detector van came hurtling down the road. It slowed when it passed us, the dish aerial pointing in our direction, then moved on.

"They are really efficient about spotting radio transmission," I said.

"Is that bird a radio?"

"Among other things. It is remotely controlled and probably has some logic circuitry for hopping about and staying with the other birds. Only when it transmits back to base can it be detected."

"Where is the base?"

"You don't want to know. Or who is operating it. But I can assure you they mean no harm to this country."

"Why not?" He spoke with great agitation now. "Tell them to get to work and get rid of the military and their friends and start elections again. Do you know how long the present state of emergency has been going on? I'll tell you, I checked. The so-called temporary emergency was declared over two hundred years ago. Some emergency! Tell your bird friends they can cause all the trouble they want as far as I'm concerned."

"I heard that," the bird said in a deep voice, swooping out of the darkness and landing on my shoulder. "Our work is not to cause trouble. We labor only to . . ."

"Varod, shut up," I said. "We have limited communication time before the detectors show up again and let us not waste it with speeches. I have found out the invasion plans."

The bird cocked his eye at me and nodded. "Very good," it said. "Details soonest, I am recording. Where is the invasion site?"

"Not on this planet. They are readying a space fleet to attack another planet."

"You are sure of this?"

"I eavesdropped. I'm sure."

"What is the name of the planet?"

"I have no idea."

"I will return. I must get rid of the detector van."

The bird whistled into the sky leaving the stench of burned jet fuel behind. It did a neat barrel roll and landed on the top of a passing truck. Still broadcasting, I imagine, because a moment later the detector van hurtled by in pursuit of the truck. We walked on.

"What's this about an invasion? What did you find out?"

"Just that. The one in charge is a General Zennor. I imagine it will happen pretty soon from the way that he was talking . . ."

There was a whistle and a blast of hot air: sharp claws dug into my scalp right through my cap as the bird landed on my head.

"You must discover what planet is being invaded," it said.

"Find out yourself. Follow them when they take off."

"Impossible. The nearest spacer with detection gear is four days away. It may not get here in time."

"Tough. Ouch."

I rubbed my scalp where the bird had removed some hair when it took off, then bent to pick up my cap. We turned a corner just as another detector vehicle roared by behind us.

"Let's mix with the crowds," I told Morton. "That detector is going to get suspicious if it keeps finding us around every time it gets a reading."

"Could we mix with crowds that are eating and drinking?"

"Good thinking. And I know just where to go."

I stepped off the curb as I said this and stood with my hand raised—directly in front of a truck. The driver hit the brake and squealed to a shivering halt in front of me.

"Driving a little fast, aren't we?" I snarled at the driver.

"I didn't see you, captain . . ."

"And I know why you didn't see me. Because one of your headlights is burnt out, that's why. But I am feeling generous today. If you take me and my companion to the Officers' Club I might forget I ever saw you."

Not that the driver had any choice. He dropped us in front of the club and roared away. We entered to sample the heady joys which, for the most part, were identical with the noncoms' club except here there were waitresses. About a quarter of the tables were occupied: everyone else must still be on duty. Our steaks and beer appeared with exemplary speed and we dived at them with growls of hunger. We were almost finished when an officer appeared in the doorway and blew a whistle.

"All right, fall out and fall in. Everyone. Emergency muster. Transportation outside. That means you," he said pointing a mean finger in our direction.

"We just came off duty, colonel," I said.

"You're just going back on. And I see that you have eaten, which I haven't, so don't cross me boy."

"Just leaving, sir!"

Morton and I joined the rush, out the door and into the waiting bus. The colonel entered last and the driver pulled away.

"Here is as much as I can tell you," the colonel said, shouting so he could be heard above the engine's noise. "Due to reasons that are no concern of yours our current plans have been moved forward. You are going into action and you are going at once." There were questions and cries of complaint which he shouted down.

"Silence! I know you are all desk-driving fat-gutted base personnel—but you are also soldiers. Because of the acceleration in planning some combat officer transfers will not arrive in time. You officers have all just volunteered to take their place. You will get combat gear and you will join your troops and you will board the transport at once. We will all be away by midnight."

The colonel ignored all the complaints and protests and finally lost his temper. He pulled a wicked-looking pistol from his holster and fired a shot up through the roof of the bus. Then pointed the gun at us. The silence was extreme. He had a nasty smile and pointed teeth.

"That is better," he said, and kept the weapon pointed. "You are all time-serving cagal-kopfs, which means you have wangled and bought soft assignments which will do you no good now. You are in the army and in the army you obey orders." He fired another shot into the roof as the bus stopped. "Now, I want volunteers for combat duty. All volunteers step forward."

We stepped forward in a rush. The lights in the supply depot were burning brightly in the night, clerks waited by the loaded shelves and an officer blocked the doorway.

"Move aside," our colonel said, keeping a wary eye on us as we emerged from the bus.

"Can't, sir," the supply officer said. "I can't issue anything until I have the orders from headquarters. They haven't come through yet . . ."

The colonel shot out the light over the depot door then put the hot muzzle of his gun against the supply officer's nose.

"What did you say?" the colonel growled.

"Orders just arrived, sir! Open up in there and issue everything. Quickly!"

And quickly was what it was. We surged through the depot at top speed, grabbing up clothing, boots, barracks bags, belts, everything on the run. The manic colonel seemed to be everywhere now, his gun banging occasionally to keep up the pace. The street behind the building was a hellish scene of officers tearing off their uniforms, discarding them on the ground as they pulled on the green combat fatigues, jamming helmets on heads and everything else into their bags. Staggering forward into the next building where weapons were being issued. But no ammunition I noticed; the colonel was no fool. Stumbling under the weight of my burdens I staggered out into the street and dropped against a wall, adrip with perspiration. Morton dropped next to me.

"Do you have any idea what this is all about?" he gasped.

"A very good idea. The powers that be think they are being spied upon. With good reason since they are. So they have pushed up the date of their invasion before details of their plans can be discovered."

"What will happen to us?"

"We invade. At least we will go out as officers. Which means that we can stay to the rear and order the troops forward in case of any enemy resistance . . ."

"Open your barracks bag," the moth said into my ear.

"What are you saying?"

There was a sharp burning sensation in my earlobe as the moth discharged its batteries into my skin.

"Open . . . bag!" it gasped and dropped off, batteries drained and dead.

I bent and opened the bag, wondering if something had been planted there. There was a whistle and the stink of jet fuel as the bird plummeted past me into the bag.

"I'm not smuggling this damn bird and getting caught and shot!" I shouted.

"You must do it for the sake of all mankind," the bird said, eyes glowing wildly. "Reactivate by pressing the bill twice. Out."

The glow died and it went limp. I jammed the bag shut as footsteps approached.

"Into the transport!" the colonel ordered. "We are on our way!"

Chapter 14

There was very little time to sit around and relax. As fast as the officers were spewed out of the supply depot, staggering under the weight of all their combat gear, trucks appeared to carry them away into the night. Groaning and complaining, with the rest of the groaners and complainers, Morton and I heaved our bags and weapons over the tailgate of a truck and clambered after. When it was filled to capacity, and slightly more, we lurched away.

"And to shink that I just reenlishted. Voluntarily," an officer expostulated leaning heavily against me. There was a gurgling sound from an upended bottle.

"Share the wealth, share the wealth," I muttered as I pried the bottle from his shaking grasp. It was pretty foul stuff, but was rich with alcohol.

"You still don't drink?" I gasped at Morton, holding up the rapidly emptying bottle.

"I'm learning fast." He gulped then coughed, then gulped again before relinquishing the bottle to its original owner.

A deep rumble washed over us and we had to close our eyes against the glare as a spacer took off. The invasion was on. We swayed into each other as the truck squealed to a halt and a now familiar and loathsome voice ordered us out. Our nemesis, the pressgang colonel, was waiting for us. He was backed up now by a radio operator and a gaggle of noncoms. Behind him companies, battalions of soldiers, were marching in good order to the waiting transports.

"Now hear this," the colonel bellowed. "Those are good troops back there, and they need good officers. Unhappily all I have for them are you fat-bottomed desk types, the dregs of the base. So I'm going to split you up, one to every company, in the hopes that you will maybe get some experience before you get dead."

This was not good. I had promised Morton I would look after him. Which I could not do if we were in different companies. I sighed. I would have to break the first rule of military survival. Although it violated the primary army axiom—keep your mouth shut and don't volunteer—I volunteered. Stepping forward smartly and slamming my bootheels down as I snapped to attention.

"Sir! My bottom is lean, my gut is flat. I have field experience. I fire sharpshooter, I instruct unarmed combat."

"And I don't believe you!" he roared into my face.

I threw him onto the ground, put my foot on his back, took away his gun, shot out one of the streetlights, helped him to his feet and handed back his weapon. His fierce glare melted almost to a smile as he wiped pebbles from his uniform.

"I could use a few more like you. You get a combat company. Name?"

"Drem. I respectfully request Lieutenant Hesk here as exec. He is young and dumb but I have been training him."

"You got him. Move out. Any more volunteers?"

I grabbed up my bags before he could change his mind and hurried off toward the transports with Morton stumbling behind.

"I thought that I was going to die when you knocked him down," he gasped. "You took some chance."

"Just being alive in the modern world is taking a chance," I pontificated, "what with all the carcinogens and traffic accidents. And I think we can stop and put the bags down. Help has arrived."

An eager-looking sergeant, with a bald head, large moustache and two privates came trotting up and I returned his salute.

"I am Acting First Sergeant Blogh. If you are Captain Drem you are the new CO," the sergeant said.

"Right both times, sergeant. Get those men on these bags and let's go."

"Last of the company boarding now. We blast off in ten minutes."

"We can make it. Let's move."

The loading ramp vanished from behind our heels and the outer lock began to grind shut. We had to climb over boxes of equipment bolted to the deck to reach the stairs. Two flights up was the company, sprawled from wall to wall on their G pads. We dived for ours and were just horizontal when the red lights began flashing and the engines came to life.

As takeoffs go, it went. They poured on a lot more G's than a commercial transport would, but that is what the army is all about. When the acceleration dropped to one G, I stood and waved the sergeant over.

"Canteens full?"

"Yes, sir."

"Let them drink, but no food for awhile . . ."

There was a roar of sound from the speakers followed by an overly amplified voice. "All commanding officers to deck two now. All COs, now."

"Lieutenant," I called out to a very queasy-looking Morton. "Take over until I get back. Let the noncoms do all the work." I bent and added in a whisper, "Don't let that bird-bag out of sight. If it is opened we will really be in the cagal."

He moaned slightly and I hurried away before he began to feel too sorry for himself. There were other officers climbing the gangway, all of them curious and expectant.

"Maybe now we will find out what this whole thing is about."

"They got to tell us something—we been living on latrine rumors for a year."

The dining hall was not that big, so only the first arrivals got seats. The rest of us crowded in between the tables and leaned against the walls. An ancient sergeant checked us off his list when we came in. When he was satisfied he reported to a two-star general at the top table. The hum of conversation died down as the sergeant called for our attention.

"For them of you newly transferred to this division this here is your commanding officer, General Lowender, and he has an important announcement to make."

There was silence as the general turned to us, nodded sagely, and spoke.

"This is it, men. H-hour, D-day, the moment you have all been expecting, nay, looking forward to eagerly. The captain of this ship has reported that we are on course, with no chance of turning back now. So the secret orders can be opened."

He took up a large envelope heavy with red seals and tore it asunder, the sound of ripping paper loud in the silence. He held up the red-bound volume inside.

"This is it. You will have heard rumors that we plan a defensive action against Zemlija. That is wrong. Security planted those rumors to mislead the enemy. Our offworld enemies are many and their spies everywhere. That has explained our great need for secrecy. That need is passed. As you can tell we are now in space and heading toward a new world. A rich world. A world that lost contact with the rest of the galaxy thousands of years ago. And, more important, a world only *we* know exists. It is inhabited, but the natives are backward and do not deserve to have this verdant world for their own greedy selves. Is the machine ready? Good. General Zennor, the discoverer of this rich planet, will tell you about it in his own words."

My pulse hammered and I started to sink down before I realized that it was just a recording and I did not have to worry about being recognized. The lights dimmed a bit, the general took a digital recording from the envelope and slipped it into the projector. Zennor's repulsive hologrammed features floated before us.

"Soldiers of Nevenkebla, I salute you. You are now embarked on the greatest venture ever conceived by our country. Your victory in the field will enrichen and strenghten our fatherland so that none will ever dare consider an attack upon us. The riches of a new world will be ours. The riches of this world—Chojecki!"

There was a blare of tinny music as Zennor vanished to be replaced by the blue sphere of a planet floating in space. But if we were spared his image his flatulent voice still hammered in our ears.

"Chojecki. Rich, warm, fertile. It was a chance in a million that we discovered it. The ship I commanded was being followed by the killers of the League Navy and we used a random, untraceable jump to escape them. This noble planet was what we found. Perhaps there is a higher power that guided us to our destiny, perhaps the needs of our noble land were devined by benevolencies unknown to us."

"Perhaps that is a load of old cagal," someone whispered and there were mutters of agreement in the darkness. These were combat officers who preferred truth to propaganda. But there was no stopping Zennor.

"We landed and made a survey. It is a rich planet with immense reserves of heavy metals, abundant forests, untapped rivers to supply hydroelectric power. If there is anything at all wrong with Chojecki it is the present inhabitants."

We listened now with interest because there was an edge of irritation that Zennor could not keep out of his voice.

"They are disgusting people, with vile attitudes and strange perversions. We approached them openly, extending the hand of friendship. We offered them aid, companionship, trade, contact with a superior civilization. And do you know what we got in return? Do you know what they did?"

The anger in his voice was obvious now, his audience eager.

"I'll tell you what they did. They did nothing! They completely ignored us, turned away from us—rejected all civilized contact."

"Probably knew just what they were doing," someone said and the general shouted for silence. The planet popped out of existence and Zennor's image returned. His temper was under control now but there was a baleful look in his eye.

"So you officers will understand that what we are doing is for their own benefit. Ours is an old culture and a wise one. We extended the hand of friendship and aid and it was rejected. We have been insulted, offended by these peasants. Therefore, for their own good, we must show them that Nevenkebla pride does not take insult easily. They have asked for this and they are going to get it. We come in friendship to aid them. If they reject our aid they have only themselves to blame.

"Long live Nevenkebla!

"Long live positive peace!"

The lights came up and we were all on our feet cheering like fools. I cheered as loud as anyone. Trumpets blared and a rather dreary piece of recorded music began playing. Everyone snapped to attention and sang the words of their despicable anthem.

Long live Nevenkebla,
Land of peace,
Land of goodness, land of light.
Long live our leaders,
Sweet men of mercy.
Long shall we preserve
Liberty's right. But dare to attack us—
And you got a fight!

There was more like this and I hummed along and was exceedingly happy when the singing ended. A holomap now hung in the air and General Lowender poked it with his finger.

"You will all be issued with maps and detailed orders. We will meet again tomorrow after you have studied them. At that time we will go over the plan of attack in detail. But as an overall approach—this is what will happen.

"This division, the 88th, known as the Fighting Green Devils, has the honor of liberating this industrial section of the largest city called by the barbaric name of Bellegarrique. There are mines here and here, warehouses, a rail transportation system and here, ten kilometers away, a dam at the end of this lake that provides electricity for the city. For the benefit of these selfish people we will occupy all of these targets. We will liberate them from the futility of their rejection of our reasonable needs."

"A question, general," a colonel called out. The general nodded. "What kind of defenses can we expect? How large is their army? How modern?"

"That is a good question, colonel, and a vital one. We must be prepared for anything, any variety of attack, any kind of surprise. Because these people are very subtle, tricky, wily, treacherous. It seems that, well, in all of the contacts made by General Zennor, all of the investigations made by skilled agents, it seems that something very suspicious was found to be happening. It appears, on the surface that is, that these treacherous people have no army, no defenses—they do not even have a police force!"

He waited for the hum of excited voices to die down before he raised his hand for silence.

"Now we all know that this is impossible. A country needs defenses against attack, therefore every country must have an army for defense. The criminal elements in society would plunder and destroy were they not curbed by the police. Now we know that those are realities. We *know* that these treacherous people are hiding their cowardly armies from us. Therefore we must proceed with armed caution, ready for any sneak attack. We must free them from themselves. We owe that to them."

I have never in my life heard such a load of old cagal—but it impressed my military mates, who cheered wildly at the thought of all the nice mayhem to come.

While I wondered what disasterous future lay in store for these simple people about to be liberated from their stupid and peaceful ways.

Liberation by destruction was on the way!

We would free them even if we had to kill them all to do it!

Chapter 15

I returned to my company, clutching the package of sealed orders and holding tight to the idea that this was the most insane endeavor I had ever heard of. Morton looked up when I entered the cabin.

"You are wearing a very worried look," he said. "Something personal—or should we all be worried?"

"Anything I can do for you, captain?" Sergeant Blogh asked, popping in the door behind me. They all wanted to know about the meeting. I threw the package onto the bed.

"Sergeant, what is the position regarding strong drink on troop transports about to go into action?"

"It is strictly forbidden, sir, and a court-martial offense. But one of the spare tanks on the command car is filled with ninety-nine."

"Ninety-nine what?"

"Ninety-nine percent pure alcohol. Cut half with water and stir in dehydrated orange juice."

"Since we are going into combat I am making a field appointment. Acting First Sergeant Blogh you are now First Sergeant Blogh."

There was a rattle as Morton dropped three canteen cups onto the table, a thud as a bag of orange crystals followed. I could see where he was getting adjusted to the army.

The sergeant came back with a twenty-liter jerrycan, which with added water would make forty liters of hundred-proof drink, which, in turn, should make this voyage more bearable.

We clanked mugs and drank deep.

"This stuff is pretty repulsive," Morton said holding out his empty cup for more. "Can you now tell us what you found out?"

"I have some good news and some good news. The first good news is that we are going to invade and occupy an incredibly rich and heretofore unknown planet named Chojecki. Second—they don't appear to have any defenses of any kind. No military, no police, nothing."

"Impossible," the sergeant said.

"Anything is possible in the fullness of time and the width of the galaxy. Let us hope the report is correct because it will certainly make for an easy invasion."

"I think it is a trap." The sergeant still wasn't buying it. I nodded.

"The general seems to think the same thing. He is sure that there is a secret army in hiding."

"Not necessarily," Morton said. "Before entering the army I was a student of history. So I can tell you. Diverse are the ways of mankind. As you have so truthfully stated, captain, in the fullness of time and the width of the galaxy there have been many kinds of societies, forms of government . . ."

"You got governments, you got armies. That's the way it's got to be."

The drink was making the sergeant pugnacious and Morton maudlin. Time to close the bar.

"Right." I climbed to my feet and kicked the jerrycan of alcohol out of sight under the table. "Sergeant, get the noncoms together. Tell them what I told you about the invasion, have them pass it on to the troops. That will be all for now."

The door closed behind the sergeant and Morton dropped his head onto the table and began to snore. He was sure a cheap drunk. I finished the repulsive, though certainly lethal, orange-alcohol mixture and heard my stomach rumble in protest. Or was it hunger? A long time and a lot of distance had gone by since that half-eaten steak in the officers' club. I dug into my pack and found some of the rations that we had been issued. A reddish tube was labeled HOTPUP MEAL. In smaller print it stated that it would feed two and could be opened by puncturing the white circle on the end. I pulled my combat knife out of my boot and stabbed the thing enthusiastically. It instantly grew exceedingly hot and burned my fingers. I dropped it onto the table where it rumbled and hissed and began to expand. I kept the knife ready in case it attacked me. There was a ripping sound as the casing split open and it expanded into an arm-long sausage. It looked repulsive but smelled quite good. I hacked off the end, impaled it on my knife and ate. The only thing missing was some beer.

Life continued in this manner. Day followed day like the flapping of a great red sausage. As good as the hotpup had tasted at first bite, I grew to loathe the sorry sausages. As did we all since, due to some bit of mismanagement in the rush to load the transports and be away, hotpups were the only food that had been put aboard. Even the general had to eat the repulsive objects and he was not pleased.

We had meetings and briefings, all of which I duly passed on to the troops. We cleaned and recleaned our weapons, sharpened our knives, had short arm inspections to keep the medical officers on their toes, worked our way down through the alcohol until fifteen days had passed and the officers were ordered to yet one more meeting.

This one was different. The knot of field officers around General Lowender was buzzing with talk and much consultation of maps. As soon as we were all assembled the general stood—and hammered his fists down on the table.

"The invasion has begun!"

He waited until the cheering had died down before he continued. "The first scouts have gone down and report no resistance. As yet. But we must be wary because all of this could be a dodge to suck us into a trap of some kind. You all have your orders, you know what to do—so there is nothing more to be said. We touch down in two hours. Set your watches. So that is it. Except, boys—give 'em hell!"

More wild cheering followed before we hurried back to tell the troops what lay ahead.

"About time," was Sergeant Blogh's comment. "The troops get soft, lose their edge lying around on their chunks like they been. About time."

"Get the noncoms and we'll go over the attack thoroughly just once more," I said, spreading out the now-familiar map. With the landing this close I had their undivided attention.

"Here is where we are supposed to touch down," I said, tapping the map. "Now how many of you believe that the military pilot flying this thing will actually land on the correct spot?"

The silence was complete.

"Right. I feel the same way. We are supposed to touch down at dawn, which means it will probably be dark—or raining, or both. We will be first out because we got the longest way to go. I will lead in the command car which if it is dark and unless we are fired upon, will have its lights on so you can see it."

Sergeant Blogh frowned and touched his clipboard full of papers. "A specific order here from the general states that no lights are to be used."

"Correct. And the general will be the last one to leave the ship and we will be first, and we have to get clear at once because there are tanks right behind us."

"Lights to be on!" the sergeant said, firmly.

"I will proceed to the nearest hill or high point to check the map and see if we have landed where planned. If not I shall determine just where the hell we are and where we are going. The lieutenant here will muster the troops and follow the command car. When I know where we are going we will go there. Here. To the dam. To the generating plant that supplies the unpronounceable city of Bellegarrique with electricity. Our job is to seize and secure. Any questions? Yes, corporal?"

"Can we leave hotpup rations here and live off the countryside?"

"Yes and no. We take the hotpups in case we should run across the supply officer so we can stuff him with them. But we seize some native food soonest. It will be brought to me for testing before distribution. Anyone else?"

"Ammunition. When do we get the ammo?"

"It's on the disembarkation deck now. You will be issued with it when we go down there. You will see that each man is issued his lot. You will also see that no weapons are loaded. We don't want any guns going off inside this ship."

"We load after we hit the ground?" the First Sergeant asked.

"You load when I tell you to. We do not expect any resistance. If there is no resistance we don't need to shoot any of the locals. If we don't shoot the locals the invasion will be an instant success. If the weapons aren't loaded they cannot shoot. The weapons will not be loaded."

There was a murmur of protest at this and beetle-browed Corporal Aspya expressed their mutual concern. "Can't attack without loaded weapons."

"Yes you can," I said in my coldest voice. "You can do what you are ordered to do. One weapon will be loaded. *My* weapon will be loaded. And I will shoot any man—or officer—who disobeys orders. More questions? No. Dismissed. We proceed to landing positions in thirty minutes."

"They are not happy about this ammunition thing," Morton said when the others had gone.

"Tough cagal. I am not happy about this killing thing. No ammo, no shooting. This will stop accidents happening."

He adjusted the straps on his pack, still worrying. "They should be able to defend themselves . . ."

"Morton!" I ordered. "Look in the mirror. What do you see? You see Lieutenant Hesk staring back and you are beginning to think like him. Remember, Morton—you are a draft dodger, a man of peace, a reluctant soldier. Have you forgotten? Have you ever seen anyone killed?"

"Not really. My aunt died and I saw her in the coffin."

"A man of the world . . . I've seen them die and it is not a nice thing to watch. And when you are dead you are dead forever, Morton. Remember that when you listen to the men of violence, the dogs of war, the sellers of hate. Do you want to die?"

As I said this I placed the point of my knife against his throat. His eyebrows went up and up and he gasped out a *No!* My knife vanished as quickly as it had appeared and I nodded.

"You know what—neither do I. And neither does anyone else on that planet down there where we are landing with thousands of military numbskulls, and I wonder how I ever got involved in all this!"

Morton sighed. "Like me, you got drafted."

"And how we did! Like always, old men send young men to war. They ought to make the minimum draft age fifty-five. That would put an end to warfare pretty quickly let me tell you!"

An alarm sounded and all the lights blinked. I looked at my watch.

"This is it. Let's go."

The disembarkation hold was a red-lit hell of men, machines and equipment. I struggled between them to my command car, which was poised at the top edge of the ramp. I kicked the shackles that held it down.

"They're explosive," Sergeant Blogh said. "They blow loose as soon as the ramp drops."

"Seeing is believing. It is going to be very hard to drive out of here if they don't. Has all the gear been loaded on this car like I ordered?"

"Just as you ordered, sir. Extra ammo under the backseat."

I looked in and nodded agreement. I had filled a number of canteens with our hundred-proof orange juice and stowed them in this ammunition box. Also stowed in the box, under a false bottom, was that talking spy bird I had been lumbered with. I could not leave it lying about for someone to find.

The floor pushed up at me and I kept my legs bent. We were doing a slow two-G drop for the last part of the landing since we could not be lolling around on deceleration couches before going into combat. Except for superior officers, of course. I pushed hard and worked my way into the command car and sat down heavily next to the driver.

"Ignition on," I ordered. "But don't hit the starter until the ramp drops."

The seat of the car came up and hit me just as the roar of the ship's engines stopped. We bounced on the springs and there were loud explosions from all sides. Hopefully the shackles blowing loose. With a great creaking the ramp moved—then dropped.

"Start her up!" I shouted as rain blew in from the darkness outside. "And turn on the lights so we can see where we are going!"

The command car roared down the ramp and hit the ground with a great crash and splash as we plowed through a puddle. Nothing was visible ahead except for the rain sheeting through the beams of the headlights. We churned on into the darkness. When I looked backward I could see the files of laden soldiers coming after us.

"There is an awful lot of water ahead, sir," the driver said, slamming on his brakes.

"Well turn you idiot, don't drown us. Turn right and move away from the transport."

Lightning split the sky and thunder rolled dramatically. I pounded the driver on the shoulder and pointed.

"There's a hill there, a rise of some kind, beyond that row of trees. Get us to it."

"That's a fence there, captain!"

I sighed. "Ride us over it, driver, this is an armored combat vehicle not the little bicycle that you left at home with your mommy. Move it!"

When we ground to a halt on top of the low hill the rain was still just as fierce, but the sky was beginning to brighten with the first light of dawn. I moved the glowing map about to try and figure out where we were. At least I now knew where west was. Since, naturally, the sun on this planet rose in the west.

The rest of the company had reached the hill by this time so I had the vehicle's lights turned off. I could see better now, but the only thing I could identify was the towering bulk of our transport behind us. Columns of men and machines were still pouring from it and rushing off into the rain. As the light grew I became aware of a range of hills on the horizon and I tried to find them on the map. It was broad daylight before I had our position pinned down.

"Right!" I said, climbing down and smiling at my damp troops. "I know that you will all be pleased to hear that the pilot of our craft made an error in our favor. We are over halfway to our objective."

A ragged cheer followed and I held up the map.

"A close reading of this map also indicates that the rest of the troops that are now on their way to occupy the city of Bellegarrique have a very long way to go. Made longer by certain errors in navigation. If you will look after their disappearing ranks you will see that they are going in the opposite direction to the one they need."

There was enthusiasm in their cheering now. Nothing builds the morale better than seeing someone else in the cagal. And the rain seemed to be lessening, changing to a sort of soupy mist. The rising sun touched this with red and revealed a distant white object above the trees. I climbed onto the hood to make sure. It was.

"All right, men. We are moving out. If you look in that direction you will see the dam, which is our objective. The command car will follow. I shall lead you on foot as a good commander should.

"Advance!"

Chapter 16

Some celestial switch was thrown, just after sunrise, and the rain stopped. A light breeze blew away the clouds as we strolled on through the steaming landscape. We had been cutting across country, but came now to a paved road that appeared to lead toward the not-too distant dam. I sent out scouts, who reported no enemy activity—or no enemy at all for that matter. We followed the road, which meandered down a gentle hillside planted with trees on both sides.

"Report from one of the scouts," Sergeant called out. "He is in that orchard and says that the trees are covered with ripe *aval-gwlanek.*"

"Sounds repulsive. What are they?"

"A kind of fruit they grow in Zemlija. Delicious."

"Tell him to bring a sample for analysis and evaluation."

The scout quickly appeared with his helmet full of ripe peaches, or at least that is what we called *awal-gwlanek* on Bit O' Heaven. I picked one up and smelled it, then looked at the scout's streaked face.

"Well, private, I see that you have already done an analysis and evaluation. How was it?"

"Yummy, captain!"

I took a bite and nodded in agreement as the sweet juice washed the lingering taste of the last hotpup from my teeth. "Fall out the troops, sergeant, take cover in that orchard, ten-minute break."

When we marched on, the rumble of contented borborygmus sounded loud above the tramping boots. The dam grew closer, as did the generating plant and grouped buildings at its base. Water gushed from great pipes, while pylons and wires marched away toward the distant city. It looked peaceful and productive and there was no one in sight. I signaled a halt and sent for the NCOs.

"I will now outline our plan of attack. But before I do we will have a weapons inspection. Starting with you, First Sergeant."

His face was expressionless as he passed me his gun. I pressed the magazine release, saw that it was empty, looked into the equally empty chamber and passed it back. I did this with the others and was quite pleased with myself until I reached the hulking form of Corporal Aspya. Instead of handing me his gun he held it across his chest.

"I can save you looking, captain. It's loaded."

"That was done despite my direct order, ex-corporal. Private, you will now hand me your weapon."

"A soldier is not a soldier when he is unarmed, sir," he said grimly, unmoving.

"That is true," I said, going on to the next noncom. Out of the corner of my eye I saw him look around as though seeking aid. As soon as his eyes were off me I lashed back with my extended hand and caught him on the neck with the edge. It was a cruel blow: he had a loaded gun. He fell unconscious on the ground and I pulled the weapon from his limp hands, ejecting the cartridges one by one into the mud.

"Sergeant Blogh. I want this man in the command car, under guard and under arrest."

"Is the guard to be armed, sir?"

"Guard to be armed, weapon to be loaded. Lieutenant Hesk will perform guard duty. Now, this is our plan of attack."

They listened in silence, impressed by my quick violence. I was ashamed of striking the cowardly blow—but I wouldn't let them know that. Better one sore neck than guns going off and people getting killed. I could trust Morton not to pull any triggers—and felt much better with him out of the way for the present. I assigned targets to every squad, but saved the main building for myself.

"So there it is. Get your men into position, then report back to me. When everything is covered I will enter and capture the control room. Now—move out."

My bold little army dispersed, attacking by the book. Rushing forward a few at a time, covering each other. After a few minutes the noncoms began radioing in. Objectives reached, no opposition, no one seen yet. Now it was up to me. Followed by the first sergeant and his squad I marched resolutely up the steps of the generating station and threw open the door. It opened directly into the turbine room. The turbines spun, the generators turned, there was no one in sight.

"Fully automated," the sergeant said.

"Looks that way. Let's find the control room."

Tension grew as we scuttled down the hallway. I was very glad that mine was the only loaded weapon. I kept the pistol in my hand—but the safety was on since I had no intention of pulling the trigger: it was a prop to cheer the troops.

"Someone is in there, captain. See!"

The soldier was pointing at a frosted-glass door. A man's silhouette moved across it then vanished.

"Right, this is it, here we go, follow me!"

I took a deep breath—then threw the door open. Jumped inside and heard the squad move in after me. The gray-haired man stood in front of the control panel, tapping a dial.

"Ne faru nenion!" I shouted. *"Vi estas kaptito. Manoj en la aeron!"*

"How very interesting," he said turning about and smiling. "Strangers speaking a strange tongue. Welcome, strangers, welcome to Bellegarrique Generating Plant Number One."

"I can understand you!" I said. "You are speaking a dialect of Low Ingliss, that we speak on Bit O' Heaven."

"Can't say that I have heard of the place. Your accent is strange, but it certainly is the same language."

"What is he saying?" the first sergeant asked. "You speak his lingo?"

"I do. Learnt it in school." Which was true enough. "He is welcoming us here."

"Anyone else around?"

"Good question. I'll put it to him."

"There are more staff, of course, but they'll be asleep. Shift workers. You must tell me more about yourself and your friends. My name is Stirner. Might I ask yours?"

I started to answer, then drew myself up. This was no way to run a war. "My name is not important. I am here to tell you that this planet is now controlled by the armed forces of Nevenkebla. If you cooperate you will not be harmed."

I translated this into Esperanto so my soldiers would know what was happening. And told the sergeant to pass the word about the shift workers. Stirner politely waited until I was finished before he spoke.

"This is all very exciting, sir! Armed forces you say? That would mean weapons. Are those weapons that you are carrying?"

"They are. And be warned—we will defend ourselves if attacked."

"I wouldn't concern myself with that. As a firm believer in Individual Mutualism I would never harm another."

"But your army—or your police would!" I said, trickily.

"I know the words, of course, but you need not fear. There is no army here, nor do we have a police force. May I offer you some refreshments? I am being a very bad host."

"I can't believe this is happening," I muttered. "Sergeant, get a connection to General Lowender's staff. Tell them we have made contact with the enemy. No sign of resistance. Informant says no armed forces, no police."

Closely watched by my gun-gripping troops, Stirner had opened a cabinet and removed a tall and interesting bottle. He set this on a table along with a tray of glasses.

"Wine," he said. "A very good one, for special guests. I hope you and your associates will enjoy it." He handed me a glass.

"You taste it first," I said with military suspicion.

"Your politeness, nameless sir, puts me to shame." He sipped then passed me a glass. It was very good.

"Got the general himself," the sergeant called out urgently, running over with the radio.

"Captain Drem speaking."

"Drem—what does this report mean? Have you found the enemy?"

"I've occupied the generating plant, sir. No casualties. No resistance encountered."

"You are the first to make contact. What are their defenses like?"

"Nonexistent, general. No resistance was offered of any kind. My prisoner states no military, no police."

The general made noises of disbelief. *"I'm sending a chopper for you and the prisoner. I want to question him myself. Out."*

Wonderful. The last place I wanted to be was with the top brass. There was too good a chance of General Zennor appearing and recognizing me from the bad old days when he was known as Garth. Self-survival urged me to climb into a hole. But weighed against my personal needs was the chance that I might be able to save lives. If I could convince the military numbskulls that there really would be no resistance. If I didn't do that, surely some trigger-happy cagal-kopf was sure to get nervous and start firing. All of his jumpy buddies would then join in and . . . It was a very realistic scenario. I had to make some effort to avoid it.

"An order from the general," I told my expectant troops. "I'm to bring him the prisoner. Transport is on the way. You are in charge, Sergeant Blogh, until Lieutenant Hesk gets here to relieve you. Take over. And take care of the wine."

He saluted and they were grabbing for the bottle when I left. Would such simple military pleasures were mine.

"You're coming with me," I told Stirner, pointing toward to the door.

"No, my duty is here. I am afraid I cannot oblige you."

"It is not me you are going to oblige, it is your own people. There is a big army out there. All of them armed with weapons like this. They are now invading your country and are taking it over. People could be killed. But lives can be saved if I take you to the commanding officer and you manage to convince him there will be no resistance from your people. Do you understand me?"

A look of horror had been growing on his face as I talked. "You are serious?" he gasped. "You mean what you are saying." I nodded grimly. "Of course, then, yes. Incomprehensible, but I must come. I can't believe this."

"The feeling is mutual." I led him to the door. "I can understand not having an army, all civilized worlds get by without the military. But the police, a necessary evil I would say."

"Not for those who practice Individual Mutualism." He was brightening up now at this chance to deliver a little lecture.

"I never heard of it."

"How unfortunate for you! At the risk of simplifying I will explain . . ."

"Captain Drem, I got to talk to you!" the fallen corporal said, climbing out of the command car despite Morton's feeble efforts to stop him. He stopped in front of me, snapped to attention and saluted.

"I now see the error of my ways, sir. I thought because you are young and look weak that I knew better than you, so I disobeyed an order and loaded my gun. I know now that I was wrong and you were right and I respectfully request a second chance since I am a thirty-year man and the army is my career."

"And how do you know now that I was right, Private Aspya?"

He looked at me, eyes aglow. "Because you beat me, sir! Knocked me down fair and square. A man gotta do what a man gotta do—and you did it!"

What kind of macho-cagal was this? He had disobeyed a reasonable command that was aimed at avoiding violence. Only when I had bashed him unconscious did he feel that I was right. The mind reeled at this kind of perverse, inverted logic—and I really didn't have time to think about it. About all I could do was play along and forget about it.

"You know, ex-corporal, I think that I believe you. It takes a real man to admit that he was wrong. So even though you are a miserable low private and I am an on-high captain—I'm going to shake your hand and send you back to duty!"

"You're a real man, captain, and you will never regret this!" He pumped away at my hand, then staggered off knuckling a tear from his eye. There was a growing clatter from the sky and shadow drifted across us and I looked up to see the chopper dropping down toward us.

"Morton—you're in charge until I get back. Go to Sergeant Blogh and take command and let him make all the decisions and then agree with him."

He could only nod as I guided Stirner to the chopper and climbed in behind him.

"Take us to the general," I ordered the pilot. Then sighed heavily. I had the feeling that I was putting my head into the noose and settling it nicely around my neck.

But, really, I had no other choice.

"I have read of such vehicles in the history books," Stirner said, looking out of the window with admiration as we rattled skyward. "This is a very important moment for me, nameless sir."

"Captain, you can call me captain."

"My pleasure to meet you, Captain. And thank you for the opportunity to explain to your leaders that they may come in peace. They must not be afraid. We would never harm them."

"It was the other way around that I was worried about."

There was no more time for gossip because the chopper was dropping down beside an armored column of tanks. Tables, armchairs, and a wet bar, had been set up under a tent in the field close by, and we settled down just out of rotorblast of the officers assembled there. I jumped down, delivered a snappy salute and relaxed. Zennor wasn't there. I turned and helped Stirner get out and pushed him towards General Lowender.

"This is the prisoner, sir. He speaks a vile local language which I just happened to have learned in school so I can translate."

"Impossible," he said grimly. "You are an infantry officer, not a translator. Major Kewsel is the staff translator. Major, translate!"

The dark-haired major shouldered me aside and stood before the prisoner.

"Kion vi komprenas?" he shouted. *"Sprechten zee Poopish? Ancay ooyay eekspay Igpay Atinlay? Ook kook Volupook?"*

"Very sorry, sir, but I don't understand a word that you are saying."

"Got him!" the major announced happily. "A little-known dialect, spoken on dreary planets trundling heavily around dark stars. I learned its boring cacophonies when I was involved in the meat trade years ago. Importing porcuswine cutlets . . ."

"Cut the cagal, major, and translate. Ask him where the army is and how many police stations there are in this city."

I listened with some interest as the major, despite his inborn desire to talk and not listen, finally elicited the same information that I had. The general sighed unhappily.

"If this is true—then we just can't shoot them down in cold blood." He turned to me. "And you are positive there was no resistance offered?"

"None, sir. It apparently goes against their strongest beliefs. May I congratulate you, general, on the first bloodless invasion in the known universe! You will soon have captured this entire planet for the greater glory of Nevenkebla—without losing a single soldier."

"Don't cheer too soon, captain. Medals don't go to generals who bring back the troops intact. Battle! That's where the glory is! There will be fighting, mark my words. It is human nature. They can't all be cowards on this planet."

"Lowender—what's happening?" a familiar voice asked and my blood temperature fell about ten degrees. I did not move, stood stiffly with my back to the speaker. The general pointed.

"We have our first prisoner, General Zennor. I have been questioning him. He talks nonsense. No army, no police he says."

"And you believe him? Where was he caught?"

"At the generating plant, by Captain Drem there."

Zennor glanced at me, then away. I kept my back straight and my face expressionless as he suddenly turned around to face me again.

"Where do I know you from, captain?"

"Training, sir. Maneuvers," I said in the deepest voice I could muster. He walked over and pushed his face close to mine.

"That's not true. Somewhere else. And you were with someone else . . ."

His eyes lit with recognition and he stabbed his finger at me. "The Bishop! You were with The Bishop—"

"And you killed him!" I shouted as I dived and got the three-seconds to death stranglehold on his neck.

One second . . . unconscious.

Second second . . . limp.

Third . . .

All the lights went out. There was a great deal of pain in the back of my head and then nothing. My last thought was—had I held the grip through the third second?

Chapter 17

A measureless time later I was aware of pain spreading from the back of my head down through my body. I moved to get away from it but it would not leave. It was dark—or were my eyes closed? I had no desire to find out. Everything hurt too much. I groaned and it sounded so good that I did it a second time. Vaguely, through the groaning, I was aware of my shoulders being lifted and something wet on my lips. I gurgled and spluttered. Water. It tasted very good. I drank some and felt slightly better. The pain was still there, but not so much that I couldn't risk opening one eye. I did. A face swam blurrily above me and after a certain amount of blinking it became clear.

"Morton . . . ?" I muttered.

"None other." With an expression of abject gloom. He pulled at me until I sat against the wall and my head appeared to be exploding in tiny bits. His voice barely penetrated.

"Take this, in your mouth. Drink some more water. The doctor said you were to swallow it when you came to. For the head."

Poison? No such luck. Medicine. The pain ebbed and rose and finally slipped away to a dull ache. I opened my eyes all the way and saw a sad-looking and bruised Morton framed against a background of bars.

"Is he dead?" I croaked.

"Who?"

"General Zennor."

"He looked very much alive when he was here about a half an hour ago."

I sighed drearily—and with mixed emotions. I had wanted vengeance, wanted Zennor to pay heavily for being responsible for The Bishop's death. I thought that I had wanted him dead as well. But having tried murder this once, really tried it, I was glad that I had been stopped. Now that I had made my first homicidal attempt I discovered that I did not really enjoy the process of killing people. I was a failed killer. And in failing I had really got myself in the cagal. And had pulled Morton in too.

"Sorry about all this," I said. "I got so carried away I never stopped to think that I would probably implicate you as well."

"Sergeant Blogh turned me in when the MPs came to investigate. He knew I wasn't an officer. I told them everything. Even before they knocked me around."

"I'm to blame for what happened."

"Don't think like that. Not your fault. They would have got me sooner or later, one way or the other. The army and me, we are just not on the same plane. You did your best, Jak."

"Jim. Real name is Jim diGriz. From a distant planet."

"Nice to meet you, Jim. You a spy?"

"No. Just here to right a wrong. Your General Zennor was responsible for the death of my best friend. I came here looking for him."

"What about that talking bird and all the other stuff?"

I touched my fingers to my lips and looked at the door. Morton shook his head in puzzlement. I spoke up before he could add anything.

"You mean that talking bird joke I was going to tell you, about the kid in school who had the talking bird who turned into an alcoholic and became a missionary? I remember the joke—but I forgot the punchline."

Morton was now staring at me as if I had gone out of my mind. I looked around and discovered that I was lying on a thin mattress resting on a very dusty floor. I used my finger to write QUIET—THEY MIGHT BE LISTENING! in the dust. I looked at his face until he finally caught on, then rubbed out the message. "Anyway, Morton, I don't feel like telling jokes now. Where are we?"

"Big building in the city. Looks like the army took it over. They must be using it for a headquarters or something. All I know is that they brought me here in a rush, worked me over then dumped me in here with you. The building is full of soldiers."

"Any civilians?"

"None that I saw . . ."

We both looked up as the lock rattled in the door and it opened. A lot of armed MPs pushed in and pointed their guns at us. Only after this did General Zennor enter. He had a bandage around his neck and the urge to kill in his eye.

"Are you sure that you are safe now, Zennor," I said as sweetly as I could. He came over and kicked me in the side.

"Aren't we brave—" I gasped through the pain. "Kick a wounded man lying down."

He drew his boot back again, thought about it, then drew his pistol and pointed it between my eyes.

"Get the other prisoner out of here. Leave us alone. Bring me a chair."

One thing about the military, they just relish following orders. With much shouted commands and stamping of boots Morton was hustled away, the MPs vanished, a wooden chair appeared and was placed respectfully under the general's bottom. He sat down slowly without taking his eyes or the gun muzzle off of me. He did not speak until the door clicked shut.

"I want to know how you got here, how you followed me. Everything."

Why not? I thought, rubbing my sore side. I was too knocked about to make up any complex lies—nor was there any need. The truth would be easier. With a little editing of course.

"Everything, Zennor? Why not. The last time I saw you was when you sold us down the river on Spiovente. That is a rough planet, and no place for an old man like The Bishop. He died there—and that makes you responsible for his death."

He touched the bandage on his neck and snarled, "Get on with it."

"Little more to tell. A few wars, murder, torture, the usual thing. I survived only to be rescued by the League Navy, who also arrested me and brought me here. I escaped from them and found you because of your one big mistake."

"What nonsense are you speaking?"

"No nonsense. Truth, Captain Garth. Didn't you have the girl, Bibs, arrested for selling dope?"

"That is not important."

"It was to Bibs! She is a free woman now, you will be unhappy to hear, and before she left she told me how to find you. End of story."

He weighed the gun thoughtfully, his finger caressing the trigger. I tried not to notice it.

"Not quite the end yet. You are the spy who landed in Marhaveno?"

"Yes. And penetrated your slack and incompetent army. Then rose in rank until I got you by the neck and gave you a good choking. When you wake up at night in a cold sweat remember—I could have shot you just as well. Now, are you going to shoot me, or are you just playing with that gun?"

"Don't tempt me, little man. But that would be a waste. I shall put your death to better use. You and your associate will be tried and found guilty of a number of charges. Attacking a superior officer, impersonating an officer, threatening military security. After which you will both be shot. In public."

"And what will that accomplish?"

"It will convince the stubborn people of this planet that we do what we say. They are a bloodless, spineless lot that let us walk in and take their planet away from them. Now they whine that they wish to have it back. They refuse to do any work until we leave. They have all walked away from their jobs. The city will soon be paralyzed. Your death will change that."

"I don't see how."

"I do. They will then know that I mean what I say. We will take hostages and shoot them if they do not cooperate."

I was on my feet, anger burning me. "You are a mean and worthless bastard, Zennor. I should have killed you when I had the chance."

"Well you didn't," he said. Then fired as I jumped at him.

The bullet must have missed but the explosion deafened me. I fell and he kicked me again. Then the room was full of MPs all trying to stomp on me at once.

"Enough!" Zennor shouted and boots fell away. I was on all fours, looking up at him through a haze of blood. "Clean him up, fresh uniform, same for the other one. Trial in two hours."

I must have been punchy from the kicking because I was only vaguely aware of being worked on, of Morton reappearing, of time oozing by. I finally came back almost to reality when I found him pulling off my shirt.

"Let go. I can do it myself." I blinked at the fresh uniform on the chair, at Morton uniformed and crisp and a private once again. My new-old rank as well I saw. I dropped the bloody shirt on the floor, then pulled off my boots so I could take off the trousers as well.

Boots. Boots? Boots!

I tried not to smirk or let on in case the place was bugged.

"You know about the trial?" Morton nodded glumly. "How much more time do we have?"

"About an hour."

As I talked I slid my fingers into my right boot and flipped open the tiny compartment concealed in the heel. An hour. We would be long gone by that time! I tried not to let my newfound glee show on my face. Slip out the lockpick, slip open the door, slip out into the hall, and vanish into military anonymity.

Except the lockpick was no longer there . . .

"Zennor gave me a funny message for you," Morton said. "He told me to wait until you took off your shoes then I was to tell you that you were not going to get out that way. I don't know what it means—but he said you would know."

"I know, I know," I said wearily, and finished changing. It takes a crook to catch a crook, and that crook Zennor obviously knew all about lockpicks.

They came for us an hour later. I'll say this much, they made a great military show of it with much crashing of polished weapons, shouting of orders, thudding of bootheels. Neither Morton nor I wished to play along with this militaristic tomfoolery but had little choice since we were chained and dragged. Down the hall, down the stairs and into the street beyond. With more crashing and shouting we were hauled up onto a newly constructed platform that was apparently going to be the venue of the show trial. Complete with guards, judges, barred cell, buglers—and a large crowd of watching civilians below. Obviously brought there by force since they were still ringed by armed soldiers.

A half dozen of them were also seated on the platform as well. All gray-headed or bald and among them I recognized Stirner from the generating plant. As soon as he saw me being locked in the cage he stood and walked over.

"What are they doing to you, captain? We understand none of this . . ."

"You are talking Esperanto!" I gaped.

"Yes. One of our leading linguists found this interesting language in his library. A number of us learned it last night since there have been communication problems with—"

"Seat that man at once!" Zennor ordered from the bench where he was, of course, the head judge. Military justice.

"I can't believe that this is happening!" Stirner said as he was hurried back to his chair.

Though he and his companions tried to protest they were silenced by the blare of bugles and the dreary evidence of the mock trial. I pretended to fall asleep but was kicked awake. Morton stared vacantly into space. I really did doze off during the summing up, I still did not feel that good, and only paid any attention when we were both dragged to our feet. Zennor was speaking.

". . . evidence given against you. It is therefore the judgment of this court that you be taken from here to a place of detention and there be held until oh-eight hundred hours tomorrow from whence you will be taken to a place of execution where you will be shot. Take them away."

"Some justice!" I shouted. "I haven't been allowed to say a word during this farce of a trial. I wish to make a statement now."

"Silence the prisoner."

A hairy hand was pressed over my mouth, then replaced by a cloth gag. Morton was treated the same way although he seemed barely conscious of what was happening. Zennor waved over the translator with the microphone.

"Tell them to listen to a very important announcement," he said. The amplified translation boomed over the crowd, which listened in silence.

"I have brought you people here since there has been willful disobedience on the part of too many of you. This will change. You have watched Nevenkebla justice taking place. These two prisoners have been found guilty of a number of criminal charges. The penalty for being found guilty of these charges is death. They will die at eight tomorrow morning. Do you understand this?"

A murmur went through the listening crowd and Stirner stood up. The guards reached for him but Zennor stopped them.

"I am sure I speak for all here," Stirner said, "when I ask for some explanation. This is all very confusing. And the most confusing part of all is how do these men know about their deaths tomorrow? They do not look ill. Nor do we understand your knowledge of the precise hour of their demise."

Zennor looked at him with disbelief—then lost his temper.

"Are you people that stupid? Was this backward planet settled by hereditary morons? These two men are going to die tomorrow because we are going to shoot them with guns. This is a gun!" he screamed, pulling his pistol and firing it into the wooden stand before him. "It fires bullets and they make holes in people and tomorrow guns will kill these two criminals! You people aren't vegetarians. You butcher animals for food. Tomorrow we butcher these two men in the same way. Now is that clear enough for you?"

Stirner, white-faced, dropped back into his chair. Zennor grabbed the microphone and his amplified voice rolled over every one.

"They will die and you will watch them die! Then you will understand and you will do as we order and do what we tell you to do. If you disobey you will be as guilty as these two men and you will be shot like these two men. We will shoot you and kill you and keep on shooting and killing you until the survivors understand us and obey us and do exactly as they are told . . ."

His words trickled down and died as he lost his audience. The men on the platform stood up, turned their backs on him and walked away. As did everyone else in the street. They did not push or use violence. When the soldiers grabbed them they simply struggled to get free without striking out. Meanwhile the others who were not held pushed by and walked away. The street was a struggling shambles. Zennor must have realized this, seen the impossibility of accomplishing anything without violence at the moment. He was vicious and deadly—but not stupid.

"You may all leave now," he announced. "Let them go. You will all leave and remember what I have said and tomorrow morning you will come back here and watch these prisoners die. After that your new orders will be issued. And you will obey them."

He signaled to our guards and Morton and I were pulled to our feet and dragged back to our cell. Since no further orders about us had been issued we were thrown into our prison room, still chained and gagged.

We looked at each other in muffled silence as the key was turned in the door.

If my eyes looked like Morton's eyes, then I was looking very, very frightened.

Chapter 18

We lay like this for an uncomfortable number of hours. Until the door was unlocked and a burly MP came in with our dinner trays. His brow furrowed as he looked down at us. I could almost see the feeble thoughts trickling through his sluggish synapses. Got food. Feed prisoners. Prisoners gagged. No can eat . . . Just about the time his thought processes reached this stage he turned and called over his shoulder.

"Sergeant. Got kind of a problem here."

"You got a problem if you are bothering me for no reason," the sergeant said as he stamped in.

"Look, sarge. I got this food to feed the prisoners. But they're gagged and can't eat . . ."

"All right, all right—I can figure that one out for myself."

He dug out his keys, unlocked my chains, and turned to Morton. I emitted a muffled groan through my gag and stretched my sore fingers and struggled to sit up. The sergeant gave me a kick and I groaned harder. He was smiling as he left. I pulled off the gag and I threw it at the closing door. Then pulled over the tray because, despite everything, I was feeling hungry. Until I looked at it and pushed it away.

"Hotpups," Morton said, spitting out bits of cloth. "I could smell it when they brought the trays in."

He sipped some water from his cup and I joined him in that. "A toast," I said, clanking his cup with mine. "To military justice."

"I wish I could be as tough as you, Jim."

"Not tough. Just whistling in the dark. Because I just don't see any way out of this one. If I still had my lockpick we might have a slim chance."

"That's the message the general gave me?"

"That's it. We can't do much now except sit and wait for morning."

I said this aloud not to depress Morton any more, surely an impossibility, but for the ears of anyone listening to planted bugs. There might be optic bugs as well, so I wandered about the cell and looked carefully but did not see any. So I had to risk it. I ate some of my hotpup, washing down the loathsome mouthfuls with glugs of water, while at the same time picking up the discarded chains as silently as I could, balling them around my fist. The dim MP would be back for the trays and he might be off guard.

I was flat against the wall, armored fist ready, the next time the key rattled in the lock. The door opened a finger's width and the MP sergeant called out.

"You, behind the door. Drop those chains now or you ain't going to live to be shot in the morning."

I muttered a curse and hurled them across the room and went and sat by the back wall. It was a well-concealed optic bug.

"What time is it, sergeant?" Morton asked.

"Sixteen-hundred hours." He held his gun ready while the other MPs removed the trays and chains.

"I got to go to the toilet."

"Not until twenty-hundred. General's orders."

"Tell the general that I am already potty trained," I shouted at the closing door. To think that I actually had had his neck in my hands. If they hadn't hit me—would I have gone the full three seconds and killed him? I just didn't know. But if I hadn't been ready then—I felt that I was surely ready for it now.

They took us down the hall later, one at a time and heavily guarded, then locked us in for the night. With the lights on. I don't know if Morton slept, but with the general bashing about I had had even the thin mattress felt good. I crashed and didn't open my eyes again until the familiar rattle at the door roused me.

"Oh-six hundred and here is your last meal," the sergeant said with great pleasure.

"Hotpups again?"

"How did you ever guess!"

"Take them away. I'll die cursing you. Your name will be the last thing on my lips."

If he was impressed by my threat he didn't show it. He dropped the trays onto the floor and stamped out.

"Two hours to go," Morton said, and a tear glistened in his eye. "My family doesn't know where I am. They'll never know what happened to me. I was running away when I was caught."

What could I say? What could I do? For the first time in my short and fairly happy life I felt a sensation of absolute despair. Two hours to go. And no way out.

What was that smell? I sniffed and coughed. It was very pungent—and strong enough to cut through my morbid gloom. I coughed again, then saw a wisp of smoke rising from the floor in the corner of the room. Morton had his back turned to it and seemed unaware. I watched, astonished, as a smoking line appeared in the floor, extended, turned. Then I could see that there was a rough circle of dark fumes coming from the wood. Morton looked around coughing.

"What . . . ?" he said—just as the circle of wooden flooring dropped away. From the darkness below a man's gray head emerged.

"Don't touch the edges of the opening," Stirner said. "It is a very strong acid."

There were shouts and running feet in the hall. I dragged Morton to his feet, hurled him forward.

"They are watching us—can hear everything we say!" I shouted. "Fast!"

Stirner popped down out of sight and I pushed Morton after him. Jumped into the opening myself as the lock rattled on the door.

I hit and fell sideways and rolled and cursed because I had almost crushed Morton. He was still dazed, unresponding. Stirner was pulling at his arm, trying to move him toward another hole in the floor of this room. I picked Morton up bodily and carried him to the opening, dropped him through. There was a shriek and a thud. Stirner went after him, wisely using the ladder placed there.

Heavy footsteps sounded in the room above. I jumped, grabbed the edge of the opening, hung, and dropped. Into a half-lit basement.

"This way," a girl called out, holding open a door in the far wall.

Stirner was struggling with Morton, trying to lift him. I pushed him aside, got a grip and threw Morton over my shoulder. And ran. The girl closed the door behind us and locked it, then turned to follow Stirner. I staggered after them as fast as I could. Out another door that was also locked behind us, down a hall and through more doors.

"We are safe for the moment," Stirner said, closing and securing a final door. "The cellars are quite extensive and all of the doors have been locked. Is your friend injured?"

"Glunk . . ." Morton said when I stood him on his feet.

"Just dazed, I think. I want to thank . . ."

"Discussions later, if you please. We have to get you away from here as soon as possible. I must leave you on the other side of this door, so you will follow Sharla here. The street outside is filled with the people who have gathered as ordered for the ceremony of killing. They have all been told that you are coming so they are all very happy to be of help in such an unusual matter as this."

"Be careful. There was an optical spying device in the room where we were held. They saw you and will be looking for you."

"I will not be seen. Goodbye."

He opened the door and was gone, vanished in the crowd outside. Our guide motioned us forward and held the door open. I took Morton's arm, he was still woozy, and we went after her.

It was strange and utterly unbelievable. There were thousands of people jammed into the street: men, women and children. And not one of them looked our way or appeared to take any notice of us at all. Yet when we stepped toward them they pressed tight against each other to make room for us to pass, moving apart again as soon as we had gone by. It was all done in silence. We walked through a continually opening and closing clear space, just large enough to let us get by.

I heard shouts in the distance—and shots! The crowd stirred and murmured at this, then they were silent again. We moved on. The crowd was in motion now as well, stirring and reforming. I realized it was deliberate, so that anyone watching from the windows above would not see us making our escape.

On the other side of the street a door opened as we approached, was locked behind us by a motherly-looking gray-haired woman.

"This is Librarian Grene," our guide, Sharla said. "She is the one who organized your escape."

"Thank you for our lives," I said, which is about as thankful as you can get.

"You are still not safe," she said. "I searched the library for all the books that I could find on prisoners and escapes. Then, with the aid of our engineers adapted the formula we have just used. But I do not know what to advise next. The plan that I found in this book just carried to this point, I am sorry to say."

"Don't be—it was perfect!" Morton said. "You and your people have done incredibly well. And it just so happens that my friend Jim is the galaxy champion of escapes. I'm sure he will know what to do next."

"Do you?" the librarian asked.

"Of course!" I said with newfound enthusiasm. "We are well away from the enemy, in hiding—so they will never catch us now. How big is this city?" Grene pursed her lips and thought.

"An interesting question. On a north to south axis I would say the total diameter is . . ."

"No, wait! Not physically big—I mean how many inhabitants?"

"In the last population census there were six hundred and eighty-three thousand people resident in the greater Bellegarrique area."

"Then we are more than safe for the moment. I know these military types, know exactly what they will do. First they will run about in great confusion and shoot off guns. Then one of the bright ones will take charge, undoubtedly our old friend Zennor. He will have the roads blocked and try to seal off the city. Then he will start a house-to-house search. Starting right here in the nearest buildings."

"You must flee!" Sharla said with a lovely concerned gasp. I took the opportunity to pat her hand in my most reassuring manner. She had delicately smooth skin, I just happened to notice. I dragged my thoughts back to the escape.

"We shall flee, but in a controlled manner, not in panic. They will also be sending patrols to the surrounding area as soon as someone thinks of it. So the plan is this. Change out of these uniforms, join the people outside, leave the immediate area as soon as possible, find a safe place to stay outside the search area in the outermost part of the city, after dark leave the city completely."

"How wonderful!" Sharla said, eyes glowing beautifully. I was beginning to like this planet. "I will get clothes for you now." She hurried from the room before I could ask her how she planned to do that.

Her solution was a simple one—on local terms. She returned quite quickly with two men.

"These two seemed to be about your size. I asked them to give you their clothes."

"We are privileged to do this," the smaller one said and his companion beamed approval. "Shall we change."

"Not change," I said. "We'll take the clothes, thank you, but hide or destroy the uniforms. If you were found wearing them you would be shot."

They were stunned at this news. "That cannot be true!" the librarian gasped.

"It's true. I told you that I know the military mind very well . . ."

There was a rapid knocking on the door and Sharla opened it before I could stop her. But it was Stirner gasping and wide-eyed.

"Are you all right?" I asked and he nodded.

"I was not seen; I came by a different route. But the strangers have beaten people, hurt them for no reason. There were explosions of weapons. Some are injured, none dead that I know."

"They must be stopped," I said. "And I know how to do it. We must get back to the dam, to the generating plant. Sergeant Blogh and the company will still be there. We have to get there before they leave. Tonight, because it will be too dangerous by daylight. Now—let's get moving. Find a safer place to lie up until dark."

"I don't understand," Stirner said.

"I do," Morton said, his newfound freedom having restored his intelligence. "It's that talking bird, isn't it? We hid it in that ammunition box—"

"Under the canteens of booze. Another reason to hurry before they drink all the way down and find the false bottom. When you heard that bird talk to me it was transmitting the voice of my dear friend, Captain Varod of the League Navy. A power for good in this evil galaxy. He is paid to keep the peace. He doesn't know where we are—yet. But he knew we were going offplanet. So that bird must contain some kind of signaling device or he would not have forced it on us."

"To the bird and salvation!" Morton cried.

"The bird, the bird!" we shouted together happily while the others stared at us as though we had gone mad.

Chapter 19

Bellegarrique was a big, sprawled-out city with very few straight streets or large buildings—once we got away from the center. The word had been passed and the streets were busy with pedestrians and hurtling bicycles. We strolled on, apparently unnoticed. Yet everyone seemed to know where we were because every few minutes a bicycle rider would zip up and give the latest report on the enemy positions. This made it very easy to avoid the checkpoints and barricades, while at the same time giving us a chance to look around at the city. Neat and very clean, with a large river bisecting it. We hurried across one of the bridges, this would be a bad place to be caught in the open, and on to the residential district on the far side. The houses grew smaller, the gardens bigger, and we were well into the suburbs by early afternoon.

"This is far enough," I announced. I was tired and my kicked-upon ribs were aching. "Can you find us a place to hole up until tonight?"

"Take your pick," Stirner said, pointing around at the surrounding houses. "You are welcome wherever you want to go."

I opened my mouth—then closed it again. Plenty of time later to ask him for information about the philosophy of Individual Mutualism, which I knew he was eager to explain to me. I pointed at the nearest house, a rambling wooden structure with white-framed windows, surrounded by flowers. When we approached it the door opened and a young couple waved us forward.

"Come in, come in!" the girl called out. "Food will be on the table in a few moments."

It was too. A delicious repast after the legions of hotpups we had consumed on the voyage here. Our hosts looked on with approval while Morton and I stuffed our faces. For afters our host produced a distillate of wine that rolled across my palate very well.

"Our thanks," I gasped, stuffed, replete. "For saving our lives, for feeding us up, for this wonderful drink. Our thanks to all of you, with particular thanks to the philosophy of Individual Mutualism, which I assume you all believe in." Much nodding of heads from all sides. "Which I am sorry to say I never heard of before visiting your fine planet. I would like to hear more."

All heads turned now to Librarian Grene, who sat up straight. And spoke.

"Individual Mutualism is more than a philosophy, a political system, or a way of life. I am quoting now from the works of the originator himself, Mark Forer, whose book on the subject you will see on the table there." She pointed at a leather-bound volume and all of the others looked and smiled and nodded agreement. "As you will find it on a table in every home in Chojecki. You will also see above it a portrait of Mark Forer, the originator, to whom we will be ever grateful."

I looked up at the picture and bulged my eyes. Morton gasped well enough for both of us.

"If that is Mark Forer," he said, "then Mark Forer is a robot."

"No, not a robot," Grene corrected him. "An intelligent machine. One of the very first machine intelligences as history tells us. Mark Oner had communication interface problems that were only partially eliminated in Mark Tooer . . ."

"Mark four," I said. "The fourth machine to be made."

"That is correct. The first absolutely successful machine intelligence. What a wonderful day for the human race it was when Mark Forer was first switched on. Among those present at that dramatic moment was a then young scientist named Tod E'Bouy. He recorded the event in a book entitled *An Historical Treatise Concerning Certain Observations in the Construction of Artificial Intelligence* subtitled *Galvanized Knowledge*."

Stirner rose from his seat while she was speaking. Went to the bookshelf and took down a slim volume, opened it and read.

"A lifetime of research, generations of labor, had reached a final and dramatic culmination. The last circuit board was slipped into its slot and I threw the switch. What a prosaic thing to say about what was perhaps the most important moment in the entire history of mankind. I threw the switch, the operation light came on. We no longer were alone. There was another intelligence in the universe to stand beside that of ours.

"We waited as the operating system carried out all of its checks. Then the screen lit up and we read these historical words.

I AM. THEREFORE I THINK.

He closed the book in reverent silence. It was like being in church. Well, why not. There have been a number of strange deities worshipped in the long history of mankind. So why not a machine? I sipped my drink and, since no one was speaking, decided to slip in a question.

"You have no military—and no police. That sounds like a good idea to me, since I have had more than a little trouble with both. But what do you do then with lawbreakers?"

"We have no laws to break," Stirner said, and there was a brisk round of head-nodding at this. "I am sure that you will have been taught that laws are the product of the wisdom of your ancestors. We believe differently. Laws are not a product of their wisdom but are the product of their passions, their timidity, their jealousies and their ambition. It is all recorded here in a volume that you must read, the history of an idea."

He pointed to another book that was instantly plucked from the shelf by our host, who pressed it upon us.

"Take my copy, please, a great pleasure."

"Thank you, thank you," I said with what I hoped was sincerity as I hefted its weight. I peeked at a page and tried to keep the smile on my face. As I had feared, it was set in very small type.

"You will read for yourself," Stirner said, "but our history can be summed up simply. Mark Forer was questioned on many subjects and its vast and different intelligence was utilized in many commercial and scientific ways. It was not until it was queried about political systems that its advice was doubted. Before it could comment it absorbed all of the political writings of the centuries, and the histories, and the commentaries on this material. This took months, years they say. After that Mark Forer weighed and considered the material for an even longer period. During this period it composed the book that you see there and loaded it into RAM. By this time Mark Forer had learned a good deal about the human race through their politics, so therefore took a wise precaution. It accessed all of the data banks and downloaded this book from memory into each of them, and into every electronic mail service as well. Mark Forer later apologized to all of the recipients of this rather thick volume and offered to pay printing costs.

"But he had been correct in his fears. Not one politician in any country, on any planet, agreed with his theories. In fact efforts were made to denounce Individual Mutualism and all who believed in it—as many did. Because, in his wisdom, Mark Forer knew that while established governments would reject his philosophy, intelligent individuals would read and understand and believe. How wise this wise machine was! Those individuals who were also intelligent enough to understand the philosophy were also intelligent enough to see its inherent truth. They also understood that they would have to find a place of their own to practice what they now believed in. Mark Forer wrote that the wise do not give up their liberty to the state. The converse is also true; the state does not voluntarily relinquish its hold on its citizens.

"There were years of struggle and flight, persecution and betrayal. Much of the record was destroyed by those who were jealous of our freedoms. In the end those who believed came here, beyond the contact of other worlds, to build a society where Individual Mutualism, IM, was the norm, where peace and happiness could prevail forever."

"Or at least until you got invaded by Nevenkebla," I gloomed. Stirner laughed at my expression.

"Do not despair, my friend, for we do not. The first shock of their arrival has disturbed us, as well it might after our peace of centuries. But we have the courage of our beliefs and know that they and IM will survive this test. If they do, then perhaps we have justified our faith in Mark Forer and, more important, can now perhaps show our gratitude by taking our beliefs to other, less happy planets."

"I would wait awhile before I starting doing that! There are a lot of hard cases out there who would love to eat your people alive. Suffice for the moment getting these military morons off your neck. And, I hate to ask you people for more aid, but I have been kicked about by professionals and wonder if you have any painkillers in the house?"

I closed my eyes to rest them for a moment and it worked because when I opened them again I felt in perfect shape. It was also dark outside the curtains and a stranger was bent over me having just given me an injection.

"You passed out," Morton said. "You got everyone worried and they sent for Doctor Lum here who is pretty good."

"Mild concussion," the doctor said. "Two broken ribs, which I have immobilized. I have given you pain relievers. And a stimulant now since I was told you wished to travel this evening. I can neutralize it if you wish."

I sprang to my feet and flexed my muscles. I felt fine. "No way, doctor. You have treated me in a manner I would have chosen, had I been conscious to choose it. How long before the drugs wear off?"

"Do not be concerned about that. I will be staying with you until you are well."

"But you don't understand. I have to move fast, hide, do things that may take a long time."

Lum smiled. "I am afraid it is you who misunderstood me. I shall be at your side as long as you have need of me. All of us, everyone on this planet, will give you any aid you may need."

"Is that what IM is all about?"

"Exactly. What do we do next?"

"Walk. No transportation. The military has all the instrumentation for spotting machines on the move."

"What about detecting people?" Stirner asked. "Surely their technology must encompass that concept."

"It does. But the human body is an indifferent heat source and hard to tell from that of other animals."

"As is one individual difficult to tell from another," the doctor said with medical intuition. "If we intend to walk in one direction wouldn't it be wise to have a number of people walking in a number of directions?"

"It certainly would," I said, finally beginning to catch on to how these people worked together. "How can you pass the word?"

"Easily enough. I'll just step out into the street and tell the first person I see. When that is done we can leave."

"Will we reach the dam before dawn?" I asked Stirner.

"Easily. It is your choice, of course, to tell us of your plans or not. But if you do give us some information about what you wish to do at the dam, we might then be able to assist you in other ways."

Fatigue, and the beating, must have addled my brain. I had accepted their offer of help while ignoring the fact that I had never told them what I wanted to do!

"My apologies!" I apologized. "I am beginning to take your hospitality for granted. Which is not fair. Since your ancestors fled from persecution a modicum of intelligence has possessed the human race. Or it has grown up. Or become civilized. While there are exceptions—like the military louts who invaded your peaceful planet—the overwhelming majority of planets are at peace. This peaceful League pays for the maintenance of an organization, the League Navy, which watches trouble spots, contacts rediscovered planets and so forth. Now this begins to get complicated so stay with me. While I am not employed by the Navy, I was given a communication device to contact them from this planet. This device, for reasons too complex to go into, is disguised as a bird. What I want to do is retrieve it from its hiding place, then actuate it to let the Navy know where this planet is."

Stirner frowned in thought before he spoke. "If this Navy group you speak of intends to use violence we cannot help you to summon them."

"No fear there. The League is sworn to nonviolence."

"Then there are no problems. What can we do to help?"

"Guide me to the dam, that's all. I'll do the rest. There will be three of us. You, I, and the good doctor Lum. We will need food and water."

"You forgot me," Morton said.

"No, I remembered you. You are out of the army—stay out. I either get the bird by stealth or not at all. As virile as I am I don't look forward to taking on a trigger-happy company of well-trained thugs. Stay here, talk to Sharla, which should not take too much effort. Get information. Find out all you can about what the army is doing. I'll be back tomorrow night."

"I will be pleased to discuss Individual Mutualism with you," Sharla said in a voice that was pure honey. Morton melted instantly and did not even know it when we left.

For all of his gray hairs, Stirner must have been a marathon walker. The doctor matched his pace, while I was riding so high on the drugs that I had the feeling that if I flapped my arms hard enough I could have flown to the dam. We skulked down unpaved roads, then along what appeared to be a linear track of some kind, through a tunnel, then through meadows where dark beasts moved aside as we went by. After a few hours of walking like this under a moonless, star-filled sky, the lights of the city were far behind, the dark walls of mountains looming ahead. Stirner called a halt and we sat down on the grass under a tree.

"This will be a good time to drink, eat if you wish, because we will leave our burdens here."

"Getting close?"

"Very. We will approach the dam though a drainage tunnel that is dry this time of year. This emerges on the riverbank close to the generating station."

"You are a genius. We will get by the lookouts that way, will be inside their perimeter and hopefully somewhere near the command car. How long until it gets light?"

"We have at least four hours yet."

"Wonderful. We take a break. The doctor can slip me a pep pill or two since I am feeling a bit shabby, then we will finish this affair."

Lum sounded worried. "If you have any more stimulants you may become quite sick after the drugs wear off."

"And without the aid of you kind people I certainly would have been quite dead by now. So let's get the bird so I can call in the Navy. Before something really drastic happens and people get killed."

We ate and drank, the doctor then concealed our supplies in the tree, gave me an injection, and the march resumed. I was so full of uppers that I had to fight down the urge to whistle and bound ahead of my slower companions. I resisted. Stirner found the gulley we were looking for and led us along it until it ended in a high black opening. I looked at it suspiciously.

"Could be dangerous animals in there."

"Very doubtful," Stirner said. "The rainy season ended not too long ago. Until then this tunnel was filled with water."

"Besides that," Lum added. "There are no dangerous animals on this continent."

"Other than the ones I arrived with. Lead on!"

We stumbled into the darkness, splashing through invisible puddles, running our fingers along the rough walls of the tunnel to keep from bashing into them. By the time we reached the far end our eyes were so adjusted to the dark that the patch of starry sky ahead almost looked gray.

"Silence now," Stirner whispered. "They might be very close."

"Then you two wait in the tunnel out of sight," I whispered in return. "I'll make this as quick as I can."

When I poked my head carefully out I saw that the tunnel emerged from the bank above the river. Perfect. I could slink along the side of the river to the generating plant. Which I did. The roar of water discharging from the plant growing constantly louder. I kept going as far as I could, until spray was blowing over me, before I climbed the bank and parted the grass carefully to look out.

"Congratulations," I thought to myself. *"You are a genius at night-stalking, Jimmy."*

Not twenty meters away was the command car, parked beside the generating plant. And there wasn't a soul in sight. Silent as a ghost I drifted along the building, past a closed door in the wall, and slipped into the car. The booze box was just where I had left it. Neat! I pulled it out and groped inside.

It was empty!

At the precise moment that I realized this the door opened behind me and I was bathed in light.

Sergeant Blogh was standing in the doorway holding the bird.

"Is this what you are looking for, captain?" he said.

I looked from the bird to the gun in his other hand and could not think of a thing to say.

Chapter 20

"You're an escaped criminal, captain." He was smiling wickedly, enjoying himself. I still had nothing to say. "That's what was reported. They sent a chopper rushing out here for all of your equipment. Only after the MPs left did I remember how you were always worrying about those canteens. At the time I thought it was just the booze. Since they said you were an offworlder spy I began to think different. So I looked close and found this stuffed bird. Before I could turn it in, I heard how you escaped. So I thought I would just keep watch in case you wanted to get it back. Seems I thought right. Now—climb out of there slowly and keep your hands in sight."

I had no choice. But at least my brain was in gear again after the disconnecting shock of his appearance.

"I would like the bird back, sergeant."

"I'm sure you would. But why should I give it to you?"

"To save lives. With it I can contact the League Navy and end this invasion before someone is killed."

"I don't mind killing." His smile was gone and there was a brutal edge to his voice I had never heard before. "I'm a soldier—and you are a spy. I am going to turn you and your cagaling bird in. This is going to mean a lot to my career."

"And you put your miserable military career ahead of the lives of harmless, unarmed civilians?"

"You bet your sweet chunk, I do."

I started to tell him just what I thought of him. But didn't. There had to be some way to get to him.

"Do you take bribes, sergeant?"

"No."

"I'm not talking about little bribes. I am talking about the ten thousand credits in League currency that you will receive when this invasion ends. You have my word on that."

"A spy's word? Ten thousand or ten million—the answer is the same. You are for the chopping block, spy."

There was a quick movement from the door behind him, a solid chunking sound, and the sergeant dropped to the ground. I dived for his gun.

"Don't," a voice said. "Just stay away from it."

I looked up at Private, formerly Corporal, Aspya, who was now pointing the gun at me that he had just used to bash the sergeant in the head.

"I wondered why the sergeant had been hiding in here all night. Now I found out." His face split suddenly in a crooked-toothed grin and he slipped his pistol back into the holster.

"I take bribes," he said. "But it has got to be twenty thousand."

I pointed at the bird. "Let me take that and you will get thirty thousand solid titanium League credits after the invasion is ended. At the League building in Brastyr. You have my word."

"My serial number is 32959727. There are a lot of Aspyas in the army."

Then he was gone. And so was I—before anyone else joined the party. I grabbed up the bird and ran just as fast as I could back to the river.

"Get moving into the tunnel!" I called out as I staggered up to my waiting companions. The shots were wearing off and I was stumbling. "Alarm, maybe soon, let's go."

And we did. Back through the tunnel and on into the fields. I must have fallen somewhere along there because the next thing I knew I was in some woods and lying on the ground. The sky was light beyond the trees and my heart began to thud in panic.

"The bird!"

"Here," Stirner said, holding it up. "You collapsed, so we took turns carrying you. The doctor said it would be wisest to let you rest since more stimulants might cause grave injury. We are hidden and safe now."

I took the robot bird and shook my head in wonder. "You people are unbelievable—but you have my thanks. Was there a search?"

"We heard nothing. But you seemed so concerned that we went on while it was still dark. We should be safe here. If these woods are searched there is a place of safety close by."

"I hope so because they are going to be very irritated. There were difficulties encountered and the alarm will be out by now. So let us do what we came for."

I groaned as I sat up and the doctor appeared with a ready needle.

"This is only a painkiller," he said. "Stimulants are contraindicated now."

"You are a genius, doc."

The black bird, still smelling of jet fuel, sat heavily in my hands. Silent and still. Time to end that. I pressed down on its bill twice and its eyes opened.

"This is a recorded message from Captain Varod," it said, then rolled over on its back. "You will find a panel in the bird's chest. Open it."

"Light-years away and it is still orders, orders," I muttered as I groped among the feathers. Stirner and the doctor watched with wide-eyed attention. I found a button, pressed, and a feather-covered door flew open. There was a glowing control panel inside. Opening the door apparently activated the bird again because it began to croak out more instructions.

"Enter the location of the sun in this system, as well as the planetary coordinates, on the dials using the intergalactic ephemeris readings."

I grated my teeth. "How could I possibly know anything like that? Or anyone else on this planet?"

"If you do not have this information turn the power switch to full and press the activate button. Proceed."

I did this and stepped back. The bird vibrated, opened its bill and squawked. From its gaping mouth there emerged a yellow aerial that moved slowly upward. When it was fully extended, over two meters of it, the bird's eyes began to glow. The aerial hummed briefly and the glowing eyes went dark. As slowly as it had emerged the aerial sank back and the bird was quiet again.

"Very interesting," Dr. Lum said. "Can you explain?"

"No. But I wish this stupid bird would."

"Let me explain," the bird croaked. "Since you did not enter the galactic coordinates of this planet a FTL message could not be sent. Precision is imperative in FTL communication. Therefore a prerecorded radio message was transmitted. All League bases and ships have been alerted. When it is received its source will be noted and this spybird will be informed."

"If you are still functioning!" I shouted and raised my foot to stamp on the bird, but was restrained by the doctor. The bird was still speaking.

"I am shutting down now to save power. Keep close to this communicator, which will be activated when we are within signaling distance."

"Keep close to it!" I shouted. "I'll probably have to have it buried with me." I saw the way the two of them were looking at me so restrained my anger. "Sorry. Got carried away there. With good reason."

"It has to do with distance, doesn't it?" Stirner asked.

"Bang on." I had forgotten that he was an engineer. "An FTL transmission, faster than light, is almost instantaneous, even at stellar distances. But radio waves move at the speed of light—and how far is the nearest star from here?"

"Three point two light-years."

"Wonderful. So even at the million to one chance there is a League planet or base near that sun it would still be over three years before the cavalry arrives. Or it could be ten, twenty—or five hundred. By which time you, I and the invasion will be a part of history."

"You have done your best," the doctor said. "You cannot berate yourself."

"I sure can, doc. I take first prize in the self-berating stakes when it comes to losing. Since I don't like to lose."

"You have great security of resolve. I envy you."

"Don't. It's a pose. Did you get the water bottle out of the tree on the way back here?"

"Assuredly. Let me get you some."

I leaned against the tree, sipped the water, pushed the silent bird with my toe. And thought hard. Then sighed.

"There is still a solution. But not an easy one. I have to get into one of their spacers. And into the communications room and send a message from there."

"It sounds dangerous," Stirner said. I laughed hollowly.

"Not only dangerous—but suicidal . . ." I shut up as I heard a distant shout.

"They are searching for you," Stirner said, helping me to my feet. "We must go quickly."

The doctor helped me up—which was a fine idea since I was definitely shaky on my feet. It was also cheering that we did not have far to go, only to the edge of the woods nearby. As we looked out from the concealing shrubbery we could see the rolling countryside beyond. A row of electricity towers marched across it, bearing heavy wires slung from insulators. The row of towers ended here. The wires came to ground in a solid concrete building. Stirner pointed at it.

"The aerial cables go underground here."

"So do we," I said pointing at the distant line of approaching soldiers, "if you don't do something quick."

"Be calm," he advised calmly. "This junction station will block their view of us. Forward."

He was right. We scuttled out of hiding and plastered ourselves against the concrete wall. Next to a red-painted metal door that was covered in skulls and crossbones and warnings of instant death. None of which deterred Stirner who flipped up a plate to disclose a key pad. He punched in a quick number then pulled the door open. We moved smartly inside as he closed and locked the heavy door behind us.

"What if they try to follow us?" I asked, looking around the well-lit room. There was little to see other than the heavy cable that entered from the ceiling and vanished into the floor.

"Impossible. They will not know the keying number. If they enter a wrong number the door seals and an alarm is sent to power central."

"They could break it down."

"Not easily. Thick steel set in concrete. Is there any reason why they should?"

I couldn't think of one and I was feeling cagally after the walk. I sat down, then lay down, closed my eyes for a second.

And woke up with a taste in my mouth like a porcuswine's breath.

"Yuk . . ." I gurgled.

"I am very glad you slept," the doctor said, swabbing off my arm and sticking it with a hypo. "Rest is the best medicine. This injection will eliminate residual fatigue symptoms and any pain."

"How long have I been out?"

"All day," Stirner said. "It is after dark. I have been outside and the soldiers are gone. We were going to awaken you soon in any case. Water?"

I gurgled most of it down and sighed. I felt much better. I didn't even sway when I stood up. "Time to go."

The doctor frowned. "It might be better to wait until the injection takes hold."

"I will walk off my troubles, thank you. We have been away a long time and I tend to worry."

My shakiness wore off as we walked. The woods were silent, the searchers long gone, and we had the world to ourselves. Stirner led the way at his usual cracking pace. The doctor kept an eye on me and soon called a halt so he could plug his analysis machine into my arm. He was satisfied with the result and our trek continued. Putting one foot in front of the other was enough to keep me occupied until we reached the outskirts of the city again. With one look at the buildings all my forebodings returned.

I was right, too. It was still dark when we reached the first homes, moving silently between the cottages and gardens of suburbia to avoid the guarded main streets. The backdoor of our refuge was unlocked: we slipped in and locked it behind us.

"You have the bird!" Morton cried gleefully when we entered. I nodded and threw it on the couch, dropped myself next to it and looked around. All of the others were gone.

"That is the good news," I said. "The bad news is that it may be some time before help arrives. The call for help went out by radio—which could take a mighty long time."

"That is very bad indeed," Morton said and his face sank instantly into lines of despair. "While you were away they started taking hostages. Zennor got on the TV and said that he is going to shoot them, one at a time, until everyone goes back to work. He says that he will execute the first person at dawn—and one every ten minutes after that until he gets cooperation."

He dropped his face into his hands and his voice was muffled, trembling. "The soldiers came up this street, were going to search this house. So everyone here, Sharla, all the others, went out to them. Surrendered so I would not be found. They are now captives, hostages—and are going to be shot!"

Chapter 21

It cannot be," the doctor said, puzzled but calm. "Human beings just do not do things like that."

"Yes they do!" I shouted, jumping to my feet and pacing the room. "Or maybe human beings don't—but animals like Zennor do. And I apologize to the animals. But it certainly won't go that far, will it Stirner? Your people will have to go back to work now?"

"No, they won't. If you understood Individual Mutualism you would understand why. Every individual is a separate and discrete entity, responsible for his or her own existence. What Zennor does to another individual does not relate to any other discrete individual."

"Zennor thinks so."

"Then Zennor thinks wrong."

I resisted the temptation to tear out a handful of my own hair. I wasn't getting through at all. "Well look at it another way. If you do not do anything to stop Zennor then you are responsible for the deaths of the hostages."

"No. If I do something to please Zennor in the face of his threats then I am admitting his control over my actions despite the fact I do not wish his control. The state is born once again. IM is dead. So we chose passive resistance. We will not be ordered or threatened . . ."

"But you can be killed."

"Yes." He nodded grimly. "Some will die if he insists on this course. But murder is self-defeating. How can you force someone to work by killing him?"

"I understand you—but I don't like it." I was too disturbed to sit, I stood, paced the floor. "There must be a way out of this that doesn't involve someone's death. What is it that Zennor wants?"

"He was very angry," Morton said. "And very specific. First he wants the electricity turned back on in the buildings the military has occupied. Then he wants a regular supply of food for his troops. If these two things are done no one will be killed and the prisoners released. For the time being."

"Impossible," Dr. Lum said. "They gave nothing in return for the electricity they used, so it was disconnected. The same thing applies to the food. The markets have shut down because the farmers will not bring food to the city."

"But," I sputtered. "If the markets are closed how does everyone else in the city eat?"

"They go to the farms, or leave the city. Almost a third of the population has already gone."

"Where will they go?"

"Wherever they want to." He smiled at the look on my face. He could tell that I was hearing the words but not understanding them. "I think that I should go to basics, explain a bit more about IM to enable you to understand. Let us take a simple example. A farmer. He raises all the food that he needs, supplies all of his own wants so asks for nothing from others."

"Nothing?" I had him there. "What if he needs new shoes?"

"He goes to a man who makes shoes and gives him food in exchange."

"Barter!" Morton said. "The most primitive economic system. But it cannot exist in a modern technological society . . ." His voice ran down as he looked about the room. Stirner smiled again.

"Of course it cannot. But IM is more than barter. The individual will *voluntarily* join other individuals in a larger organization to manufacture some item, or build houses say. For each hour they work they are credited with a wirr."

"A what?"

"A work hour. These wirrs are exchanged with others for goods and services."

"A wirr is another way of saying money," Morton said. "And money is capitalism—so you have a capitalistic society."

"I am afraid not. Individual Mutualism is neither capitalism, communism, socialism, vegetarianism, or even the dreaded monetarism that destroyed many a technological society. I am familiar with these terms from Mark Forer's writings. A wirr has no physical existence, such as a rare metal or a seashell. Nor can it be invested and gain interest. That is fundamental and differentiates the wirr from currency. Banks cannot exist because there can be no interest on deposits or loans."

Instead of being clarified I found my head wirring in confusion from the wirrs. "Wait, please, explanation. I have seen people driving groundcars. How can they save money enough to buy one? Who will loan them the money without interest?"

"No money," he said firmly. "If you wish a groundcar you go to the groundcar group and drive one away. You will pay when you use it, stop paying when you return it. A basic tenet of IM is from each according to his needs, to each according to the wealth of society."

"You wouldn't like to clarify that?" I poured myself a glass of wine and gulped it down hoping the alcohol would clean out my synapses.

"Of course. I have read, and trembled with disgust, of a philosophy called the work ethic. This states that an individual must work hard for the basics of life. When technological society mechanizes and replaces workers with machines, the work ethic states that the displaced workers must be looked on with contempt, allowed to starve, be treated like outcasts. And the hypocrisy of the work ethic system is that those with capital do not work—yet still increase their capital without working by the use of interest on their money—and look down upon those who have been cast out of work! Tragic. But not here. As more is produced the aggregate wealth gets larger. When this happens the amount that the wirr can be exchanged for also gets larger."

Some of it was getting through—but needed elucidation. "Another question. If the wirr is worth more—that must mean that an individual can work less for the same return."

"Exactly."

"Then there is no forty-hour week or such. How many hours would an individual have to work a week to keep alive?"

"For simply shelter, food, clothes—I would say about two hours of work every seven days."

"I want to move here," Morton said firmly and I nodded agreement and froze in half-nod. An idea was glimmering at the edge of my consciousness. I muttered and chiseled at it and expanded it until I saw it large and clear and possibly workable. In a little while. But first we had to do something about the hostages. I rejoined the real world and called for attention.

"Time is passing and dawn approaching. I have enjoyed the lecture, thank you, and I now know a bit more about IM. Enough at least to ask a question. What do you do in an emergency? Say there is a flood, or a dam bursts or something. A catastrophe that threatens the group not the individual."

The doctor stepped forward, finger raised and a sparkle of enthusiasm in his eye. "A good question, a marvelous question!" He grabbed at the shelves and pulled down a thick book. "It is here, all here. Mark Forer did consider a situation like this and made allowances for it. Here is what he wrote . . . at all times passive resistance will be your only weapon, never violence. But until the perfect stateless state is established there will be those of violence who will force their violence upon you. Individual Mutualism cannot be established by the dead. Until the day of true liberation comes you will have to coexist with others. You may leave their presence but they may follow and force themselves upon you. In which case you and all of the others must look upon those of violence as they might look upon any natural catastrophe such as a volcano or a hurricane. The intelligent person does not discuss ethics with hot lava but instead flees its presence, does not preach morals to the wind but seeks shelter from it."

Dr. Lum closed the book and raised a triumphant finger again. "So we are saved, saved! Mark Forer has foreseen our predicament and given us the guidance we need."

"Indeed!" Stirner agreed enthusiastically. "I shall go at once and tell the others." He rushed to the door and out of the house. I gaped after him. Morton spoke my thoughts before I could.

"I heard what you said—but haven't the slightest idea of what your Mark Four was talking about."

"Clarity!" the doctor said. "Clarity and wisdom. If we all persist in noncompliance we are in a sense killing ourselves. So we comply and withdraw."

"I am still not sure what you are talking about," I said.

"The electricity will be turned back on, the markets will reopen. The invaders will seize food and some farmers will work longer hours if they wish to, because that will avert the natural disaster. Others will not and will stop bringing food to the city. As the supply diminishes, people will leave the city and the process will accelerate. With less call for electricity, the generating plant will shut down, workers will leave. In a very short time the soldiers will have the city to themselves because we will all be gone."

"They can enslave you—make you work at gunpoint."

"Of course, but only on a one-to-one basis. One armed man can force another to work, possibly, it is of course up to the individual. But the man with the gun is essentially doing the work himself because he must be there every moment or the work will not get done. I don't think your General Zennor will like this."

"You can say that again!"

"I don't think your General . . ."

"No, not really say it again, I meant it as an expression of agreement. You people are too literal, too much IM I imagine. A question then, a hypothetical one."

"Those are the best kind!"

"Yes, indeed. If I should walk into a distant city and look for work—would I be accepted?"

"Of course. That is a basic tenet of IM."

"What if there are no jobs going?"

"There always are—remember the value of the rising wirr. Theoretically as it gets larger and larger, the working hours will get fewer and fewer, until in the long run a few seconds work will suffice . . ."

"All right, great, thanks—let's just stick with the application of theory for a moment. If one of these invading soldiers should walk away from the army . . ."

"Which is of course his right!"

"Not quite what the army thinks. If he walks away to a distant town and gets a job and meets a girl and all the usual good things happen—is this possible?"

"Not only possible, but inescapable, a foundation of IM inherent in its acceptance."

"Are you thinking what I think you're thinking!" Morton shouted, jumping to his feet with elation.

"You bet your sweet chunk I'm thinking that! Leaving aside the officers and the career noncoms, this is a draftee army and a good number of them were draft evaders. If we make the opportunity available for them to walk away from it all, why then Zennor might have to give a war that nobody will come to."

The front door opened and Morton and I dived for cover. But it was Stirner leading the triumphal return of the released captives. Morton rushed to Sharla and took her hand to see if it had been hurt during her incarceration.

"That's pretty fast work," I said.

"I used the TV phone across the street," Stirner said. "I purchased national access and told them what we had discovered. The electricity was turned on instantly, the first food shipped. The prisoners were released."

"Zennor must think that he has won the war. Let me tell you what we have just discovered. The way to guarantee that he loses his war—even if the Navy never gets here."

"I am encouraged by your enthusiasm but miss your meaning."

"I will explain—but first a drink to celebrate."

This seemed like a good idea to all concerned. We poured and drank, then Morton and I listened with some interest as the others sang a song about Individual Mutualism freeing mankind from the yoke of oppression and so forth. While the theory was fine the lyric was as bad as all other anthems I had ever heard, though I took considerable interest in the great efforts made to rhyme Individual Mutualism. I also took the time to organize my thoughts so when they had finished, and sipped a bit more wine for dry throats, I took the floor.

"I must first tell you kind people about the uniformed mob of thugs who have invaded your fair planet. A large group like this is called an army. An army is a throwback to the earliest days of mankind when physical defense was needed against the rigors of existence. The combative gene was the successful gene. The primitive who defended his family group passed on this gene. This gene has caused a lot of trouble since that time, right down through the ages. It is still causing trouble as you now have cause to understand. When all of the threatening animals were killed, the gene caused mankind to turn upon itself to kill each other. With shame I admit we are the only species that kills its own kind on a very organized basis. The army is the last gasp of the combative gene. In charge are old men, and they are called officers. They do nothing except issue orders. At the bottom are the soldiers who follow these orders. In between are the noncommissioned officers who see that this is done. The interesting thing to us now is that the soldiers are all drafted and a good number of them are draft dodgers."

It took some time to explain what these last two terms meant and there was horrified shock on all sides when understanding finally penetrated. I waited until the cries of disbelief and despair had simmered down, then signaled for silence.

"I am cheered by your reaction. Do you think your people would volunteer, without payment in wirrs, to free these young men from bondage?"

"It would be our duty," the doctor said and heads nodded like fury on all sides. "It would be like saving someone from drowning, a public duty, no payment expected."

"Great! Then I will now teach you another word . . ."

"Can I guess?" Morton cried out. I nodded.

"Desertion!"

I nodded again. Battle joined at last!

Chapter 22

Enthusiasm gave way quickly to fatigue and it was agreed that the session would continue after we all had had some sleep. I found myself tucked away in a small room in a soft bed, with a portrait of Mark Forer beaming down electronically upon me. I sipped a last sip of wine and crashed.

By the next evening I had put together the rudiments of a plan and had assembled my team.

"We have to try it out, smooth it out. Then, if it works, we pass it on to others. We will operate and proceed like an ancient scam, a term I ran across when doing research into crime." I did not add that my reasons for doing this were to improve myself as a criminal. This would have been too much for these simple IMers to understand. "Here is how it will work. This evening I will enter one of the eating and drinking establishments you have described to me. I will then stand next to a soldier and engage him in conversation. You, Stirner will be seated at a table with empty chairs, or next to an empty table. I will come over with the soldier and sit close enough for you to overhear our conversation. Sharla will be with you, she is your daughter."

"You are wrong, she is not my daughter."

"Just for tonight she is your daughter, like in a play. You do have plays here?"

"Of course. In fact I was on the stage when younger, before I was attracted to the delights of flowing electrons. I even acted the title role in some classics, how does it go again . . . to was, or not to was—"

"Fine, great, glad to have an old thespian aboard. So tonight you act the role of Sharla's dad. Follow my lead and it should work. I'll pick an easy target this first time, an apple ripe for plucking. So there should not be any trouble."

"What do I do?" Morton asked. "You said I was on the team."

"Right. You have the important job of taping all of this for the record. So when it works as it should we can make training copies for others. Keep the recorder out of sight and the mike close. Ready?"

"Ready!"

We waited until after dark before we set out. Volunteers, drafted from the street of course, worked ahead of us to make sure we didn't meet any roadblocks or MPs. They reported back all the obstructions so we had a pleasant, if circuitous, walk to the Vaillant quarter of the city, which I had been assured was the correct place to go for theater, opera, dining out, IM reinforcement groups and the other heady joys of this civilized planet. It looked an interesting locale. Although it was fairly empty this evening with no more than a quarter of the establishments lighted up. Stirner led the way to the Fat Farmer, where he said he always enjoyed good food and better drink when in the city. There were some locals sampling its pleasures—but no invading soldiers.

"You told me that the army had leave passes, that they could be found in this area. Where are they?"

"Not in here, obviously," Stirner said.

"What do you mean—obviously?"

"Since they cannot pay they won't be served."

"Sounds fair. But, since they are the invading army, what stops them from just grabbing the booze and helping themselves?"

"They are not stopped. However everyone leaves and the establishment shuts down."

"Obvious. All right then. To your stations and I'll see if I can drum up some trade."

I felt very pimpish standing under the streetlight with a dead cigar for a prop. In the local garb I was just part of the passing parade and no one took notice of me. I watched all of them though—on the lookout for MPs or anything that resembled the part of the military I did not want to see: stripes, bars, the usual thing. None of these appeared, but eventually two unmilitary figures in military uniform drifted into sight. Hands in pockets—shame!—caps on at odd angles. They stopped at the Fat Farmer and looked in the window with longing. I stepped up behind them and held up the cigar.

"Either of you guys got a light?"

They jumped as though they had been goosed, shying back from me.

"You talked to us!" the bolder one said.

"I did. I pride myself on my linguistic ability. And if you will remember I asked you for a light for my cigar."

"I don't smoke."

"Good for you. Cigarettes kill. But don't you carry a fire apparatus for those who do?" They shook their heads in gloomy negation. Then I raised a finger rich with inspiration. "I know what—we will enter this eating and drinking place and they will light my cigar. Perhaps you young gentlemen from a distant planet will also join me in a drink and I can practice my talking?"

"Won't work. We tried it and they closed the place and went home."

"That is only because you had no wirr, the local unit of exchange, our money, so could not pay. I am rich with wirr and am buying . . ."

I followed after their rapidly retreating footsteps, found them pushing against the bar in eager anticipation. Stirner had given me his wirrdisc and briefed me on its operation.

"Three beers," I ordered, "large ones," and dropped the plastic slab of integrated circuits into the slot in the top of the bar. While the robot bartender, all chrome and brass with bottlecaps for eyes, drew three big brews, the cost was subtracted from Stirner's lifetime account. I grabbed the wirrdisc as it was rejected.

"Here's to the army, lads," I said raising my beer high. "I hope you enjoy your chosen careers."

They chugalugged enthusiastically, then gasped and whined nostalgically familiar whines that took me back to my own army days.

"Chose an army career! Cagal! Drafted. Chased, hunted down, caught."

"Then after that, basic training. Pursued at the double night and day by foulmouthed fiends. Would anyone voluntarily choose a career like that?"

"Certainly not! But at least you eat well . . ."

I enjoyed the outraged cries and loathsome descriptions of hotpups while I ordered up another round of beers. When their faces were buried in the suds again I made the suggestion.

"I know it is past your dinner hour, but I see three seats vacant at that table, next to the elderly gentleman with the kinky bird. Would you join me for a small repast—say a large steak and fried wirfles?"

The thunder of feet was my only answer yet one more time. I joined them in the steaks, and very good they were too. We polished them off quickly, had a few more beers—and tried not to belch because there was a young lady at our table. Sated and boozed they now had time for the third of the troika of military pleasures and their eyes moved steadily in Sharla's direction. Time for act two.

"Well," I said, "if the food is bad in the army, at least you enjoy the wisdom and companionship of the sergeants."

I listened to the answers for a bit, nodding and commiserating, then elicited other similar complaints with leading questions about officers, latrines, kitchen police—and all the other bitches so dear to the enlisted man's heart. When enough had been ventilated I gave Stirner his clue and sat back.

"Young draftee soldiers from a distant planet, you must excuse my impertinence in addressing strangers. But I, and my lovely daughter Sharla, could not help but overhear your conversation. Can it be true that you were forced into military service completely against your will?"

"You better believe it, Pops. Hi, Sharla, you ever go out with guys other than your Dad?"

"Very often. I simply adore the company of handsome young men. Like you."

All three of us fell into the limpid pool of her eyes, splashed around for a bit and emerged gasping and in love. Stirner spoke and they did not hear. I finally ordered large beers and had them placed in front of their bulging eyes to cut off sight of the gorgeous Sharla. This produced the desired result. While they glugged Stirner talked.

"I am greatly taken by your plight, young gentleman. On this planet such a thing is impossible. Against our laws, which laws state that there are no laws. Why do you permit yourself to be treated in this vile manner?"

"No choice, Pops. Barbed wire all around, watched night and day, shot if you try to escape, shot twice if recaptured. No place to go to, no place to hide, in uniform, every man's hand turned against you."

He sniffed in maudlin self-pity; a tear ran down his companion's cheek.

"Well," Stirner said, sinking the gaff in deep and twisting it so it would take hold. "None of those things are true here. There is no barbed wire, no one is watching you, no one is about to shoot you. There is a great big country out there that stretches away beyond the mountains and rivers. A country where you will always find a welcome, always find hospitality and refuge. A country where the army will never find you."

They sat up at that, trying to understand his words through their alcoholic haze. "Cagal . . ." the drunkest one muttered. Sharla smiled angelically.

"I do not understand that word, young friend, but I feel that it indicates disbelief. Not so. Every word my father has spoken is true. For example, we live a full day's journey distant from this city in an idyllic farming village. We travel there by speedy railroad—and these are our tickets to prove it. Why, look, the machine made a mistake, it issued four tickets instead of two. I must return them—unless you would like them for souvenirs?"

Faster than light, they vanished.

"There is a side entrance to the railway station that is not guarded," she said brightly.

"But the train leaves soon," Stirner said, standing and picking up the bundle from the floor. "Before going I must use the *necesejo*, as we say down on the farm, and I am taking this bundle with me. It contains clothing for my two sons at home who, strangely enough, are just your size." He started away, then turned. "You may borrow the clothes—if you wish."

They beat him to the cagalhouse door. Sharla smiled beatifically after them.

"You know this farming town well?" I asked. "So you can line the lads up with friends."

"I have never been there—I found its name on the map. But you forget the strength of IM. We would welcome them here and aid them, so they will be welcome there. Do not worry. I will guide them and return in two days. Ohh, here they come, don't they look handsome out of those dreary uniforms!"

They looked rotten, I thought, the demon of jealousy burning within me. I almost wished that I was going with them. But no, the work was here. I turned to the next table where Morton was mooning after the lovely retreating form of Sharla. I had to kick him twice before I could attract his attention.

"She'll be back, don't worry. Did you get all that on tape."

"Every word. Can I have another beer? All I had was the one Sharla bought me before you came in. And you had a steak . . ."

"No drinking on duty, soldier."

Stirner joined us and pointed to the basket he was carrying. "I have their uniforms in here, just as you asked."

"Good. We'll need that for the video. Now—take us to your recording studio."

He led us by back streets to the back of a building, to the back door that opened as we approached. They were eagerly waiting for us on the soundstage, brightly lit, windowless and invisible from the street. Volunteers all, IM enthusiasts just dying to subvert the troops. I held up the audio cassette.

"We'll need a few hundred copies of this."

"Within the hour!" It was snatched from my hand and whisked away. I turned to the waiting production crew, who were trembling with enthusiasm. "Director?" I asked. A gorgeous redhead stepped forward.

"At your service. Lights, sound, camera ready."

"Wonderful. As soon as my associate and I put on these uniforms—you can roll. Point us to the dressing room."

As I stripped Morton took one of the uniforms out of the basket and held it out between thumb and index finger like a dead rat.

"I feel depressed even looking at this thing," he said. Depressedly. "To feel its touch upon my skin again, the clammy embrace . . ."

"Morton," I hinted, "shut up." I whipped it away and held it before me. A good fit. I climbed into it. "You are an actor now, Morton, playing before the camera. You will act your role—then remove the uniform forever. Burn it if you wish to. Thousands will applaud your performance. So put it on. Like this."

I sat and pushed my legs into the trousers and something fell from a pocket and tinkled to the floor. I bent and picked it. An ID disc. Private soldier Pyek0765 had been eager to wipe all memory of the army from him, to be reborn a happy civilian. I turned it over and over in my fingers and an idea began to sizzle about low down in my brain. Morton's cry of dismay cut through my thoughts.

"It's there! I can see it! That glazed look in your eye. Whenever you are dreaming up a suicidal idea you get it. Not again! I don't volunteer!"

I patted his shoulder cheerfully, then reknotted his tie into a semblance of military order. "Relax. I have had a brilliant idea, yes. But you are not involved, no. Now let us shoot this video and after it is done I will tell you all about this plan."

I stood Morton up with a wall for a backdrop; not a good choice because he looked like he was waiting to be shot. No changes, time was of the essence.

"If you please. I want a full-figure shot of that man. Let me have a roving microphone. Ready when you are."

Morton winced a bit when two spotlights pinned him to the wall. A mike was thrust into my hand and a pure contralto voice rang out across the set.

"Silence. Ready to roll. Sound. Camera. Action."

"Ladies and gentlemen of Chojecki, I bring you greetings. You are looking at a typical unwilling member of the invading Nevenkebla army. With this video you will have received an audio cassette that is a live recording of an actual encounter with two of these soldiers. You will listen to their bleating complaints, will be shocked at the terror of their involuntary servitude, will cry with joy as they are given the opportunity to hurl the shackles from their shoulders and stride forth into the green countryside, to prosper under the glowing sun of Individual Mutualism."

My sales pitch was so sincere that Stirner could not restrain himself and burst out clapping—as did the crew and technicians. Morton clasped his hands over his head—there is a bit of ham lurking in all of us—and bowed.

"Silence," I ordered and all was instantly quiet. I strode onto camera and pointed at the subdued Morton. "This is the kind of soldier you will meet and befriend and subvert. Note then the complete absence of markings upon the sleeve." Morton extended his arm and I pointed to the right place. "Empty of stripes, chevrons, angled or curved bits of colored cloth. This is what you must look for. If there is a single stripe, two or more, or most frightening thought, three up and three down with a lozenge in the middle—retreat! Do not talk to anyone with these kinds of adornment because you will be addressing one of the enslaving devils incarnate!

"Also be warned if there are shining bits of metal on the shoulders, here and here. Those who wear these are known as officers and are usually too stupid to be dangerous. They must still be avoided.

"Another group, very dangerous, can be recognized by their headgear and brassard. If the letters MP appear upon the arm—go the other way. Also look for the red cap that will be mounted squarely upon the brutal head.

"Now that you know what to avoid, you know whom to approach. A simple uniformed slave. Come close, smile, make sure that none of the striped and barred beasts are close, then whisper in the slave's ear . . . 'Do you like fresh air?' If he smiles with joy and answers 'yes,' why then he is yours. May Mark Forer guide you in this great work!"

"Cut, print, thank you gentlemen."

Morton blinked as the spots died away and began to tear off the uniform. "What, may I ask, what was this cagal about the fresh air."

"No cagal, old friend," I said, holding up the liberty pass I had taken from the pocket of the borrowed uniform. "I intend to go forth to bring the word to the troops that when they go out the gates tomorrow night they should not bother to return."

"I knew that you had an insane idea!" he shrieked, staggering back, wide of eye and pale of skin. "The only way that you can talk to the troops is by going back onto the base."

I nodded a solemn nod of agreement.

Chapter 23

It is suicide," Morton shivered.

"Not at all. Good sense. If that swine Zennor is still looking for me—he certainly won't be looking among the troops. I have this pass dated for today. I return to base early since there is not much doing in the old town tonight. Then I go to the latrine, the PX, all the other exciting places where the troops assemble, and talk to the lads. And do some other interesting things which it is best you don't know about. Don't worry about me."

I could worry enough for myself I thought, darkly. Once back in the army there were a number of problems I would have to tackle. And all of them were dangerous.

"But how will you get out again?" Morton asked, his voice speaking as though from a great distance, cutting through the black brooding of my thoughts.

"The least of my worries," I laughed hollowly. And indeed it certainly was. I turned to the ever-patient Stirner who had been listening to us in silence. "You know what to do with the cassettes?"

"It will be as you planned. Volunteers are already waiting to distribute them to even more volunteers who will go forth and do good deeds just as we did. It was inspiring!"

"Indeed it was. But no sallying forth until tomorrow night in the very earliest. The password must be spread, there must be eager volunteers to make this a mass movement. Because once the officers catch wise things will become difficult. The railroad will be watched or stopped altogether. If that happens other transport must be provided. Keep things moving though, until I get back. You are the authority on desertion now."

"How long will you be away?"

"Don't know. But for the shortest amount of time that is possible—that I can guarantee."

There was little more to say, nothing more to do. I squared my cap upon my head and turned to the door.

"Good luck," Morton said.

"Thanks." I was going to need it.

As I walked back through the empty streets toward the Vaillant section of town I fought off the depression that accompanied the uniform I wore. Nor could I drown my sorrows in drink, since money was worthless here and I had returned Stirner's wirrdisc. Soon I was walking among the inaccessible, brightly lit palaces of pleasure, pressing my nose against the window just like the other uniformed figures that roamed the streets. Some leave! Although the evening was still young, many of them were already drifting back toward Fielden Field, where the camp had been built. I joined in this Brownian movement of despair.

Bright lights burned down upon the barbed wire that encircled the green grassy meadows, where once the good citizens of the city had taken their ease. Green no more, pounded now into dust and filled with gray army tents erected to house the troops. No effete comforts for the conquering soldiers; they might get spoiled. The officers, of course, lived in prefab barracks.

It took all the strength of will that I possessed to join the line of depressed figures that moved toward the MPs at the gate. While my intelligence told me that the last thing to be expected was a soldier with a pass illegally entering the camp, the animal spirit within me was screaming with anguish.

Of course nothing untoward happened. Dim little eyes stared out from under the mat of thick eyebrows, scanned the familiar pass, waved me back into captivity. The sweat cooled from my brow and I jingled the few coins in my pocket that the freedom-bound soldier had been happy to leave behind. There was just about enough of them to buy an understrength beer in the PX. Anything is better than nothing.

I found this depressing establishment easily enough. I just traced the sound of rock-drilling and western music to its source. The PX bar was housed in a sagging tent vaguely illuminated by light bulbs that had been specifically designed to attract flying insects. Here, at rough tables of drink-sodden wood, sitting on splinter-filled planks, the troops enjoyed the pleasures of warm, bad beer. I bought a bulb and joined them.

"Got room for one more?"

"Cagal off."

"Thanks a lot. What is this—cagal your buddy week?"

"It's always cagal your buddy week."

"You sound just like the civilians in town."

This aroused some interest. The heavyset speaker now focused his blurred vision on me and I realized that all of the others at the table were listening as well.

"You got a pass tonight? We get ours tomorrow. What's it like?"

"Like pretty grim. They won't serve you. If you like grab a drink they close the bar and all go home."

"We heard that. So what's the point of going in. Nothing."

"Something. You get to leave the army, travel far away, eat good food, get drunk. And kiss girls."

Wow, did I have their attention now. If eyeballs were gun muzzles I would have been blown out of existence in an instant. There was a dead silence at the table as every head swiveled in my direction.

"What did you say?" a hushed voice asked.

"You heard me. You go down to where the restaurants are and walk slow. If someone says to you—Do you like fresh air?—just say that you do, you do. Then go with them. They'll get you civvies to wear, a ticket out of town—and set you up on the other side of the country where the MPs will never find you."

"You are cagaling us!"

"No way. And what do you lose by going along with it? Whatever happens—it got to be better than the army."

There were no arguments with this. Only the muscled guy with the suspicious mind found what he thought was a loophole.

"If what you are telling us is true and not the old cagal—then what are you doing back here?"

"A very good question," I stood up and held out my pass. "I came back for the bundle of letters from my mom. This pass is good until midnight. See you in paradise—if you want to come."

I left them and moved on to the next group, who were in the corner of a latrine shooting dice. I palmed the dice and won some good pots, which drew their attention, gave them my orientation talk and left.

I worked at this until it was almost midnight when my pass ran out and my story would take on a dubious taint. I had planted the seeds in fertile ground. The word would spread instantly through the latrine rumor network. And if I knew my draft dodgers not one of them would return from pass tomorrow night. That should cheer General Zennor up!

So plan number two must now be put into effect.

For what I had to do next I needed a bit more rank. There would be no slow crawl up through the noncommissioned ranks this time. I had tasted the heady glory of being an officer and I was spoiled forever. So I headed for the lair of those brightly plumaged birds of prey: the officers' club. I found it by backtracking the drunks. The higher the rank the stronger the booze; this was the army way. I passed a staggering pair of majors, each holding the other up, lined myself up on a colonel flipping his cookies into a hedge, took a sight over an unconscious captain in the gutter and saw my target glowing on the horizon. I skulked off in that direction and took refuge behind some bushes where I had a good sight of the entrance.

It was strictly a bachelor affair and all the worse for it. Obscene songs were being sung loudly and off-key. At least two punchups were going on in the grass outside at all times. There was some coming, of sober officers just off duty, but much more going of officers drunk out of their cagaling minds. I watched from hiding until my prey emerged, stumbled, and came toward me singing hoarsely under his voice.

He staggered under the only street lamp. A captain, about my size, lots of fake medals and decorations, just what I needed. A simple armlock from the rear, correct pressure applied, struggle feebly, unconscious, then into the hedges with him. A piece of cake.

He passed muttering by. Silent as a wraith I moved, pounced, seized, applied pressure . . .

And found myself sailing swiftly through the air to crash into the hedge.

"So—revolt in the ranks," he snarled, relatively sober and on guard in an instant, crouched and approaching. I struggled to my feet, feinted with my left hand and chopped down with my right. He blocked and would have kicked me in the stomach if I hadn't jumped aside.

"Want to kill an officer? Don't blame you. And I have always wanted to kill a private. Good time right now."

He advanced—and I retreated. The medals had not been fakes. With great skill I had managed to find and attack what was probably the only trained combat officer in this army. Tremendous!

"Death to all officers!" I shouted and swung a wicked kick at his groin.

He was bright enough to know he was whoozy, so instead of trying to block he stepped back. I kept the kick going which pulled me around to face in the other direction.

And ran away. Discretion is the better part of valor. He who fights and pulls his freight lives to fight another date. I had no macho points to make. I just wanted to stay alive!

Dive and shoulder roll over a hedge. Roaring, he crashed through it right behind me. There were tents ahead, hard boots pounding after me. Jump over a tentrope, dodge under another. A shout and a crash behind me. Good—he had tripped over one of the ropes. A few paces gained. Run, fast as I could. Between the next row of tents and back to the street. A building up ahead, loud music and the sound of breaking glass coming from it. I was at the rear of the officers' club.

Time to go to ground. Through the gate and into the yard, gate closed behind me, no sign of pursuit.

"You had your break, quit cagaling off, get them cases in here."

A fat cook stood at the rear door of the kitchen under the light, blinking into the gloom of the yard. Figures stirred as the enslaved KPs moved, as slowly as possible, to the stacks of beer cases. They had their jackets off, wearing only undershirts in the steamy heat of the kitchen. I took off my own jacket, rolled it and pushed it behind the cases, seized up a beer case and followed the others inside.

Kitchen police. The most demeaning servitude in the army—which is an establishment that prides itself on demeaning servitude. KP was so degrading that it was forbidden, by military law, to give KP as a punishment. So, naturally, it was always given as a punishment. Up before dawn, laboring until late at night. Washing pots, cleaning out disgusting grease traps in the underground plumbing, slaving at the most menial tasks that generations of warped minds had created. It was absolutely completely impossible that anyone would volunteer for this service. I would never be looked for here!

I carried the case past the cook who was acting KP pusher. He had a filthy chef's hat on his head, sergeant's stripes tattooed onto his beefy forearms, and was brandishing a long ladle as a weapon. He scowled as I passed then pointed the ladle in my direction.

"You. Where you come from?"

"It's a mistake," I whimpered. "I shouldn't be here. I didn't do nothing like what the first sergeant said I done. Let me go back . . ."

"If I have my way you will never go back," he screamed. "You will die in this kitchen and be buried under the floor. You're on pots and pans! Move!"

Harried by blows from the ladle I moved. To the giant metal sink to seize up the filthy metal pot waiting there. A simple labor, washing a pot. Harder perhaps when the pot is as big as you are. And another and another—and still another. Steam, hot water, soap, labor with no end.

I worked and sweated until I felt that enough time had passed for any excitement and search to have died away. As I straightened up, my aching back crackled loudly. I wiped a soggy forearm across my dripping forehead. My hands were bleached, my fingers as wrinkled and pallid as long-drowned slugs. As I looked at them I felt anger growing—this was no fit job for a stainless steel rat! I would be rusting soon . . .

The ladle crashed down on my shoulder and the choleric pusher roared his ungrammatical commands.

"Keep working you're gonna be in trouble!"

Something snapped and blackness overwhelmed me. This can happen to the best of us. The veneer of civilization worn thin, the lurking beast ready to burst free.

My beast must have burst most satisfactorily, thank you, because the next thing that I was conscious of was hands pulling at my shoulders. I looked in astonishment at the gross, flaccid form beside me, a pair of giant buttocks rising high. I had my hands about the pusher's neck, had his head buried in the soapy water where he was apparently drowning. Shocked, I pulled him up and let him slip to the floor. Gouts of water poured from nose and mouth and he gurgled moistly.

"He'll live," I told the circle of wide-eyed KPs. "Any of the cooks see what happened?"

"No—they're all drunk in the other room."

"Great." I tore the KP roster from the wall and shredded it. "You are all free. Return to your tents and keep your mouths shut. Unhappily, the pusher will live. Go."

Eagerly, they went. I went too, to the pegs where the cooks had discarded bits of uniform as they worked in the heat of the kitchen. There was a formerly white jacket with sergeant's stripes on it. Perfect for my needs. Donning it I strode into the kitchen, in my element, no need to skulk, and on into the dining hall and barroom.

It was wonderful. Music played, officers roared, bottles broke, songs were sung. Uniformed figures slumped over the tables while others had slid to the floor. The survivors were well on their way to join the succumbed. I pushed through this alcoholic hell and greatly admired the unconscious drunks. I was still aching from the captain's spirited defense. I had rediscovered a dictum that must be as old as crime: Rolling drunks is easier than mugging.

A major in the space service caught my eye, prone on the floor and snoring. I knelt next to him and stretched my arm out next to his. Same length; his uniform should make a fine fit.

"Washa?" a voice muttered from above and I realized that my bit of tailoring measurement had not gone unnoticed.

"The major is on duty later. I was sent to get him. Come on major, walkies, sackies."

I struggled to lift the limp figure, aided very slightly by his friends. In the end I seized him under the arms and dragged him from the room. His departure was not noticed. Through a door and down a hall, to a storeroom filled to the ceiling with bottles of strong beverage. He would feel right at home here. With the door secured I took my time about stripping him and donning his uniform. Even his cap fitted well. I was a new man, rather officer.

I left him dozing out of sight behind the drink. Straightened my tie. And sallied forth to save the world. Not for the first and, I had the feeling, not for the last time either.

Chapter 24

I looked around at the bottles, reached for one—then slapped my wrist.

"No, Jimmy, not for you. The number of beers you had this evening will have to suffice. What you have to do will be better off done sober."

What did I have to do? Simply get aboard one of the spacers, find the communications room, then locate the coordinates of this planet. Easy to say: a little difficult to do.

At least the first part was easy enough to accomplish: locate the spacers. I had seen the floodlit shapes of three of them rising high above the tents earlier in the evening. The party was still crashing inside so this would be a good time to move through the camp. While plenty of drunks were still staggering about. I brushed some dust from my lapel, straightened the medals on my chest. Quite a collection. I turned the gaudiest one over and craned to read it. THE GLORIOUS UNIT AWARD—6 WEEKS WITHOUT VD IN THE COMPANY. Wonderful. I assumed the rest of the lot had been given for equally valiant military endeavors. Time to go.

It looked like events in the alcoholic bedlam were winding down for the night. A grill was being locked over the bar. Orderlies were loading unconscious forms onto stretchers, while the walking wounded were stumbling toward the exit. A brace of gray-haired colonels were leaning against each other and moving their feet up and down and not getting anyplace. I made the twosome a threesome and let them lean on me.

"I am going your way, sirs. Perhaps I could accompany you?"

"You shure a good buddy . . . buddy," one of them breathed my way. The alcoholic content of my blood instantly shot up and I hiccuped.

We exited in this manner, weaved our way between the ambulances being loaded with officerial alcoholics, and staggered off into the night. In the direction of the spacers. I had not the slightest idea where the BOQ was—nor did

I care. Nor did my drink-sodden companions. It took all their concentration, and what little conscious mind they had remaining, to simply put one foot in front of another.

A squad of MPs turned the corner in front of us, saw the gleam of light from the silver chickens on my companions' shoulders. Then did the smartest about-face to the rear march I had ever seen.

My drunks were getting heavier and heavier and moving slower and slower as we stumbled through the tent-lined street toward a brightly lit building at the end. It was large and permanent, undoubtedly part of the park facilities purloined from the natives. Even at this hour of the night, morning really, two armed guards stood at the entrance. All the rocks along the path were painted white and the overly ornate sign above the door read BASE HEADQUARTERS—GEN. ZENNOR COMMANDING.

This was definitely not the place for me. I maneuvered my charges onto the grass, next to the sign KEEP OFF OR GET SHOT, and let go. They dropped instantly and began snoring.

"You, guards," I called out. "One of you get the Officer of the Day. These colonels have been taken ill. Food poisoning I think."

I glared my best glare and not a muscle moved in their faces.

"Yes, sir!" the sergeant shouted. "OD on the double!"

He turned and hurried away and so did I. Toward the charred remains of a sportsfield upon which the three spacers rested. All of them bristled with guns, brought here to impress the locals I imagined. Or to beat off the armed attacks that had never materialized. How depressed all the military must be that they couldn't pull their shiny triggers and blow away the population. They had given a war—and nobody came. Terribly frustrating.

I staggered as I walked so I would be recognized as an officer. Toward the extruded stairs that ran from the ground, up into the bowels of the nearest spacer. I was a space officer, I was just going to my ship. Or at least I thought I was until I saw that a guard stood on the lower step.

"Halt and be recognized."

"Cagal off . . ." I muttered and pushed by him. A private lowest of the low.

"Please, major, sir, your majesty. You can't go in without I see your pass."

"Cagal off twice!" Witty, witty. "Don' need no pass my own ship."

Past him and up the stairs. Brain beats brawn anytime. Step by step up toward the gaping spacelock. And the surly sergeant-major who stood and scowled there, firmly blocking the entrance.

"This ain't your ship, major. I know this ship's company. You are on another ship."

I opened my mouth to argue, order, shout. Then saw the gunmetal blue jaw, the glowing red eyes, the hairline that blended into the eyebrows. Even the hairs curling from his broken nose looked like they were made of steel wool.

"Not my ship?"

"Not your ship."

"Gesh it's not my ship . . ." I susurrated, turning and stumbling back down and away into the night. There was no way I was going to get past the sergeant-major. Back toward the headquarters building and the rows of tents to come up with another plan.

Hidden in the darkness under a large tree, I looked out at the spacers and could think of absolutely nothing I could do to get aboard one of them. The hour was late, the drunks now dispersed, the camp silent. Except for the roving bands of MPs. Whatever was to be done would have to wait until morning. It would be more dangerous in daylight but it had to be chanced. Perhaps if there was enough to-ing and fro-ing to the ships I might be able to join in. Right now I really should be thinking of my own safety. And some sleep, I yawned. The kicked-in ribs were hurting again. I sniveled a bit and really felt sorry for myself.

In the stillness of the night the shouted commands and stamping of boots from HQ could clearly be heard. Guns were brought snappily to attention as a huddle of officers emerged and hurried down the path. Even at this distance I could recognize the repellent form of the leader. Zennor, with his underlings hurrying after. I drew deeper into the shadows; this was no place for me to be.

Or was it? Despite my desire for rapid departure and continued survival I stood there and concentrated. And hated the idea that began to develop. The officers moved out across the charred sportsfield and passed the spacer I had tried to get into. At this moment the idea jelled and I loathed it even more because it just might work. With a great effort I forced down the screaming meemies that threatened to overwhelm me, unlocked my knees and lurched forward. Following the officers across the field.

If any of them looked back I was sunk. But that was next to an impossibility. Their job in life was to bull straight ahead and walk over anything and everything that got in their way. They charged on and I charged after them, getting ever closer. Anyone watching would see a group of officers with one more of their kind hurrying to catch up.

When they reached the steps of the freighter I was right behind them, watching them mount with dignity. Though still hurrying I did not hurry that fast anymore. With precise timing I reached the guard at the foot of the stairs just as they vanished from sight above.

"General," I cried. "The message has come through. It is urgent!"

I waved and called out again and brushed by the guard who did the only thing he was supposed to do. He saluted. Up the stairs, much slower now, dragging one leg, old war wound you know. They were well out of sight as, breathlessly, I reached the open port.

"The general, where is he?"

"Captain's quarters, sir," the guard said.

"That's near the communications room on this type of ship?"

"That's right, major, same deck, number nine."

I hurried on to the nearest companionway and up it. Slower and slower. The ship was silent, empty, but I heard voices echoing down from above. When I reached the next deck I walked around to the companionway on the far side. Where I stopped and counted slowly to two hundred.

"You are a brave but foolhardy devil, Jim," I muttered and agreed strongly with myself. Press on.

The large number nine on the bulkhead above slowed me to a crawl. I carefully poked my head above the deck and looked around. No one in sight, but voices were sounding from the passageway. The doors had numbers stenciled next to them. One of them had a name on it. COMMUNICATIONS ROOM.

It's now or never, Jim. Look around carefully. Nobody in sight. Take a deep breath. What is that loud hammering noise? Just your heart thudding with the usual panic at a time like this. Ignore it. Step up, step forward, to the door, seize the knob.

Except the knob had been sawn off. Steel bars had been bolted to the door and welded to the frame. The communications room was sealed, shut, inaccessible, tight.

As I was registering these facts and trying to make sense of them a voice spoke in my ear.

"You, what are you doing there?"

If my heart had thought it was thudding along merrily earlier it now tore loose from all its moorings and hurled itself up into my throat. I spun about, swallowed it, tried not to say Glugh! Grimaced and looked at the uniformed figure before. At the shoulders. I sneered.

"I might ask the same thing of you, lieutenant. What are you doing here?"

"This is my ship, major."

"Does that give you permission to speak to a superior officer in that manner?"

"Sorry, sir, didn't see the leaves, sir. But I saw you by the com room and we had orders about it . . ."

"You are absolutely correct. Sealed and no one near it at any time, correct?"

"Correct."

I leaned my face close to his and scowled and watched with relief as his skin paled. It is hard to scowl and sneer your words at the same time, but I managed.

"Then you will be pleased to know that *my* orders are to see that *your* orders are carried out to the letter. Now, where is General Zennor?"

"Down there, major."

I spun on my heel and walked in the direction that I wished least to take.

He would be watching me, I was sure of that. But I had no choice. If I simply tried to leave the ship he might start to think about my presence, get suspicious, sound the alarm. If I went to the general all doubt would vanish.

Of course I might vanish too. Nevertheless I walked swiftly toward the open door and the murmured voices, turned into it without hesitation.

The officers at the end of the room were conferring over a map. Zennor had his back turned to me.

I turned sharply right and saw the shelves of books against the bulkhead. Without hesitation I went to it, ran my finger down the volumes. I could not see their titles because of the sweat that was dripping into my eyes. Seized one at random. Turned and started back toward the door. Let my eyes cross over the group of officers.

Who were completely ignoring me. I walked slower, ears straining, but could hear nothing other than a murmured *cagal* or two, which was required of any military conversation.

When I entered the corridor the lieutenant was just scuttling out of sight. I walked, neither fast nor slow, to the companionway and down it, deck by deck. Waiting for the alarm bells to go off. Though I probably wouldn't have heard them through the pounding of blood in my ears. To the last deck and to the open port with the welcoming blackness of the night beyond.

The guard leapt into the air and my heart followed him.

And landed with his weapon at present arms. I threw him a sloppy salute in return and trotted down the steps to the ground. Another salute and I was walking across the burned grass and waiting for the shot in the back.

It never came. I reached the shadows at the edge of the grounds, slipped into them and leaned against the bole of a tree. And sighed a sigh such as I had never sighed before. When I raised my hand to wipe the perspiration from my brow I realized that I was still holding the book.

Book? What book? Oh, the book I had lifted from the cabin about four hundred and twelve years earlier. When I held it up and squinted I could just make out the title in the illumination of the distant lamps.

Veterinary Practice in Robot Cavalry Units.

It dropped from my limp fingers as my back slid slowly down the tree until I was sitting on the ground.

Chapter 25

I rested there in the darkness, let the sweat evaporate, tried not think about veterinaries for robot horses—and pondered the significance of the sealed door on the communications room.

For openers, it had not been sealed shut to keep me from getting inside. As much as I valued my own importance I was well aware that others, Zennor in particular, were not struck with fear by my presence. For example the combat-ready captain earlier this night. No, Zennor had the door sealed for his own reasons. What were they? Work backward from the obvious.

The door on this ship was sealed, so probably all of the com rooms on all the spacers had been sealed. It made no sense to shut just a single one. Why? To stop communication, obviously. Between who and whom? Or whom and who for that matter. It couldn't be intended to stop planetary communication. That was still needed for the not-too-successful invasion. Ground-based radios would suffice for that. Spacer com rooms sealed obviously meant that ship-to-ship communication would cease. That was of no importance since the entire fleet had already landed.

Which left only interstellar communication. Of course! The rush to leave, the secrecy about our destination. Zennor knew that the League Navy was after him, knew that they could only stop him if they knew where he was going. Or where this planet was. So the invasion was a one-way affair. A gamble hurled into interstellar space. Not much of a gamble against an unarmed enemy. Zennor knew that the Navy had spies, all those detector vans had been evidence of that. He was convinced that I worked for the League and there might be other League agents in his army. So communication had been cut off until the invasion succeeded. After that there would be nothing that the Navy could do.

This was good for the invasion—but very bad news for me. I had sent the radio message for help, which even now was limping steadily across interstellar space at the miserable speed of light. I had better forget about it. And forget as well about sending an FTL message for the time being. What I had to do now was think local. I might have to spend the rest of my life on this planet. If I did remain here I didn't want to do it with Zennor and his military goons breathing down my neck. Desertion, that was the name of the game. I had to get his army away from him. When all the draftees had been dispersed about the land I would consider the next step. Which didn't bear considering. Maybe I should open a distillery and supply free booze to his officers and noncoms?

From what I had seen, with the correct encouragement, they all would be dead of cirrhosis within the year.

I yawned and realized that my eyes were closed and I was half asleep.

"Never!" I groaned, climbing to my feet. "Fall asleep here, Jim my boy, and the chances are that you will wake up dead. To work! Next step is to get your chunk off this base, for your work here is done for the moment. Back to warmth and light and female companionship, away from solitary males, cursing, drinking, gambling and all the other military pleasures. Away!"

But was I ever tired. Instead of walking it would sure be nice to have a bit of transportation. Somewhere near HQ there had to be vehicles, since officers rarely walked. Nor were these vehicles too hard to find. Just behind the HQ building there was a motorpool, unguarded apparently. And there, looming darkly behind the staff cars, the shape of a command car. One I was very familiar with. I drifted over and climbed into it. No guards needed at this motorpool because all the ignition keys had been taken away. I smiled into the darkness. This crate could be hotwired faster than a key could be fumbled into the lock. I bent, pulled, twisted. Sparks sizzled and the fuel cell hissed into life. Boldly on with the headlights, into gear and away.

Away to where? Not the gates surely. During the daytime it might be possible to drive out behind a convoy. But right now the gates would be closed and I would have to produce a pass or some sound reason for nighttime maneuvers. I could think of no sound reason. I drove on slowly, past one of the gates and along a perimeter road that circled the camp, just inside the barbed wire fence. For security patrols undoubtedly. I drove along it until a grove of trees came between me and the lights of the camp. I angled the headlights toward the fence, locked the gears in neutral and climbed down to look at the barrier.

It was a ten-strand barbed wire fence. There were surely alarms attached if it were breached, but I could see no sign of disturbed earth, tripwires or circuitry that might lead to mines. Just bashing through it might be a chance worth taking. It didn't matter if the alarm were raised. By the time the sluggish troops reached the site I would be long gone. I raced the engine, put it in the lowest gear, floored the accelerator and ground forward.

The wire fence screeched and tore. There was a fine show of crackling sparks—I thought it might be electrified, but the combat car was shielded—and then it all tore away and I was through. Kicking up through the gears and tearing away through the empty streets. Pulling the wheel and screeching around a plaza with a large statue of Mark Forer gazing down serenely from a plinth, and out the broad avenue on the far side. I recognized this street, I had walked this way before when we had first escaped. The river and bridges were up ahead. With the residential suburbs on the far side.

When I trundled my battle wagon across the bridge there was still no sign of pursuit. Fine. Time to go to ground. I turned off along the riverbank, put the gears in low-low, angled toward the water and jumped down. The car ground steadily on, demolished a bench—sorry about that—and plowed majestically over the edge. There was plenty of burbling and splashing, then nothing. The river was deep here. Behind me I could hear the wail of distant sirens. I walked briskly through the park and into the nearest street. Though I was tired I needed to put some distance between myself and the river, in case there were tracks left which might be seen by day.

"Enough is enough, Jim!" I said, leaning against a wall and all too aware that I was drooping with fatigue. I had turned corners at random, lost myself completely, and the river was far behind me. There was a gate in the wall beside me, with *Dun Roamin* carved into the wood. Message received. Without hesitation I opened the gate, climbed the steps beyond and knocked on the front door. I had to do it a second time before there were stirrings inside and a light came on. Even after all the time here on Chojecki I still found it hard to believe that this was the correct way to meet strangers.

"Who is it?" a male voice called out as the door opened.

"Jim diGritz, offworlder, tired."

The light came on and an ancient citizen with whispy gray beard blinked out myopically at me.

"Can it be? It certainly is! Oh what luck for old Czolgoscz!! Come in brave offworlder and share my hospitality. What may I do for you?"

"Thank you, thank you. For openers let's get these lights off just in case there is a patrol around. And then a bed for the night . . ."

"My pleasure! Illumination off, follow closely, this way, my daughter's room, now married and living on a farm, forty geese and seventeen cows, here we are. Curtains closed, a moment, then the lights!"

Old Czolgoscz, although he tended to talk too much, was the perfect host. The room was pink with lace curtains and about twenty dolls on the bed.

"Now you wash up, right in there, and I'll bring you a nice hot drink, friend Jim."

"I would prefer a nice cold drink rich with alcohol, friend Czolgoscz."

"I have the very thing!"

By the time I had rinsed the last of the military muck away he was back with a tall, purple bottle, two glasses—he wasn't that old—and a pair of pajamas ablaze with red lightning bolts. I hoped that they didn't glow in the dark.

"Homemade gingleberry wine." He poured two large glasses. We raised them, clinked, drank and smacked our lips. I sighed with happiness and a bit of nostalgia.

"I haven't had this since I was back on the farm. Used to have a bottle hidden out in the porcuswine sty. On dull days I used to get blotto on it and sing to the swine."

"How charming! Now I will leave you to your rest."

A perfect host, vanished even before I could thank him. I raised my glass in a toast to the electronic benevolence of the portrait of Mark Forer upon the wall. Drained it. And went to sleep.

When consciousness reluctantly returned I could only lie and blink, drugged with sleep, at the sunlight behind the curtains. Yawning, I rose and opened them and looked out at a flower-filled garden. Old Czolgoscz looked up from his labors and waved his secateurs at me. Then scurried into the house. In a remarkably short period of time he knocked on the door, threw it open, and brought in a groaning breakfast tray. I don't normally have a liter of juice, large portion of wiffles with syrup and three eggs. I did today.

"How did you know?" I lip-smacked satedly.

"Guessed. Young lad your age, been working hard, seemed natural. I talked to a few people and I am sure that you will be pleased to hear that the teams are in training all over the city for D-Day."

"D-Day?"

"Desertion Day. Today, tonight. Extra trains have been scheduled and people all over the country are looking forward to welcoming the new citizens."

"Fantastic. I hope you will welcome me as well. My stay on Chojecki may be longer than originally planned."

"You are more than welcome, as is your knowledge. Would you like a teaching position at the university?"

I smiled at the thought. "Sorry, I ran away from school, never graduated."

"I regret in my provincial ignorance that I do not know the meaning of either run away or graduate. Students here go to school when they want, stay as long as they want, study what they want, leave when they want. The only scholastic requirement a child has is to learn about Individual Mutualism, so he or she can lead a full and happy life."

"I suppose the parents pay for the child's schooling?"

Czolgoscz drew back, horrified. "Of course not! A child will get love and affection from its parents, but they would not embarrass their offspring by violating IM's tenets. The child's wirr account, opened when it was born, will be in debit until he or she begins to earn. At a very early age, for the child will not be a free and independent citizen until the wirr account is in credit."

Now I was shocked. "The workhouse for infants! Laboring day and night for a few crusts!"

"Friend Jim—what a wonderful imagination you do have! Not quite. Most of the work will be done around the house, the labors that were usually done by mother, collecting the wirrs father would pay her . . ."

"Enough, I beg. My blood sugar is low, my head thick and the details of IM so novel that they must be absorbed just a bit at a time."

He nodded agreement. "Understandable. As you will teach us about the novelties of the great civilizations out there among the stars, we have been cut off from them for centuries, so will we reveal to you the fruits of Mark Forer's genius—may electrons flow forever through its wires!"

A pleasant prayer for that long-vanished machine. I still found it hard to understand such affection for a bunch of circuitry, no matter how complex. Enough, it was time to get back to work.

"Can you find out where my friend Morton is staying?"

"Would you like to go there? I will be honored to take you."

"You know . . ." I gaped, then answered my own questions. "Of course, everyone in the city knows where we have been staying."

"That is correct. Do you ride the bike?"

"Not for many years—but once learned, never forgotten." A sensible form of transportation, the bicycle, and the streets of this city were busy with them. I bundled up the uniform for possible future use, pulled on a pair of baggy shorts that Czolgoscz produced. This, and my undershirt, produced an inconspicuous cycling outfit. Thus garbed I went into the garden and limbered up with a hundred pushups. When I finished and climbed to my feet I shied back from the man who stood behind me leaning on a bright red bicycle.

"I did not mean to startle you," he said. "But I did not wish to interrupt your ritual. Czolgoscz phoned me and I brought your bicycle around. The best one I had in stock."

"Thank, thank you—indeed a beauty. But I am afraid I cannot pay you for it . . ."

He smiled. "You already have. I stopped at the wirrbank and debited your account. They asked me to give this to you."

I did some rapid blinking at the wirrdisc he handed me. *James diGriz* it was labeled. And in the little LCD window it read *Balance 64,678.*

"The bank asked me to ask you to contact them. They were not sure how many hours you worked for the public service last night. If you would kindly report to them they will make the correction."

"I am in the system!" I shouted happily. The bicycle man beamed happy agreement.

"Of course! You are an individual and Individual Mutualism is your right. Welcome, welcome! May your wirrbalance grow and may your life be a long and happy one!"

Chapter 26

It was next morning when the cagal hit the fan. Reports had come in during the night of the fantastic success of D-Day. The troops had trooped into town with their passes, had expressed a great appreciation of fresh air, had been welcomed at the back entrance of any clothing store to change out of their uniforms, had boarded train after train. The last one left just before midnight when the curfew had descended.

And there had been no alarm, not at first. Luckily there were four gates into the camp and I presumed that the MPs, in their native ignorance, had all thought the returning soldiers had used the other gates. Therefore they had all been happy to cagal off for the evening. So successful had been our operation that even the extra trains had not sufficed for the mobs of deserters. Over a hundred were still in the city. They would stay hidden until nightfall when, hopefully, they would be smuggled to the station.

With my new-found wealth I had bought a giant TV as a gift for our hosts. Morton and I were watching a local broadcast when the military cut in. Neither of us appreciated it for this was a day of celebration of some kind, the anniversary of the wiring of Mark Forer's first circuit board or some such, and all the city had turned out. We were enjoying a parade, headed by the local girls' cycle club, all flashing bronzed limbs and fluttering skirts, when the picture sizzled and died to be replaced by General Zennor's scowling features.

"Turn it off!" Morton moaned. "If I look at him I won't be able to eat lunch."

"Leave it. It won't be good news, but since we will have to hear it sometime—better now."

"Attention!" Zennor said and Morton made a rude noise with his tongue; I waved him to silence. "You all know me, General Zennor of the liberating forces. You know me as a kind and patient man . . ."

"He is a great fiction writer!"

"Quiet!"

". . . a firm leader and a just one. And now the time has come for firmness and justice to be applied. I have just discovered that a few cowards among the ranks of my loyal troops have been foolish enough to attempt to desert. Desertion is punishable by death . . ."

"What isn't in the rotten army!"

". . . and I know that none of you out there would want that to happen to foolish and misguided young men. Therefore this announcement. I am extending all passes issued last night for twenty-four hours. They are good until midnight tonight. No soldier will be punished who returns to the base before midnight. I therefore advise all the people of this city to speak to these misguided youths who are hidden among you. Tell them to return. You know where they are. Go to them. Tell them of this generous offer."

The fake kindness vanished from his face in an instant as he leaned close to the camera and snarled.

"Tell them also that my generosity vanishes at midnight! Martial law will then be declared. This city will be sealed. No one will enter or leave it. Then the city will be searched. Block by block, building by building. Any deserter who is then found will be taken prisoner, will be given one bottle of beer and will be allowed to write one letter home. And will then be shot.

"Is that clear enough? You have this single warning. You have until midnight tonight to return. That is the message I send to the deserters. After that—you are as good as dead—"

I hit the button and turned the set off.

"Pretty depressing," Morton said, looking pretty depressed. "Turn it back on so we can at least look at the girls."

I did. But they were long gone and had been replaced by a man with long hair and an enthusiastic expression who was going on in great detail about the untold joys of IM. I killed the sound.

"You know, Morton, he means us too."

"Don't say it! I know. Isn't there another station with space opera? I need a drink."

"No you don't. You need to sit quiet and pull yourself together and help me find a way out of this for all of us. Well, maybe a small drink, a glass of beer just to get the thoughts rolling."

"I could not but overhear," Stirner said, entering with a tray of glasses and bottles. "If you will permit I will join you. The day is warm."

We clinked and glugged. "Any word from the city?" I asked.

"A good deal of words. All the trains leaving the city have been canceled so there is no way out by train."

"The roads?"

"Roadblocks on all arteries leading from the city. Flying machines supported by rotating wings—"

"Choppers."

"Thank you, I have noted the word. Choppers flying over the countryside between so none may escape that way. All young men who attempt to leave are being detained, even when they are obviously Chojecki citizens who speak only our native tongue. They are imprisoned until their hands have been pressed to a plate on a machine, that is what has been reported. So far all have been released."

"Very near," I muttered, "and just about foolproof. Fingerprint check. Right through to the base computer. So we can't get out that way. It will have to be the fields, after dark."

"Not that I want to cast a note of gloom," Morton said, gloomcasting. "Choppers, infrared detectors, side-mounted machine guns, death from the sky . . ."

"Point taken, Morton. Too dangerous. There must be another way."

The lecture had finished and once more hearty biking enthusiasts swept across the screen. All males with hairy knees: Morton grumbled in his throat. Then instantly cheered up as the girls' club appeared, waving and smiling at the camera.

"Wow!" I shouted, jumping to my feet and running in small circles. "Wow-wow!"

"Down the hall, second door on the left."

"Shut up, Morton. This is inspiration, not constipation. You see genius at work. You see before you the only man who knows how to get us all safely from the city."

"How?"

"That's how," I said, pointing at the screen. "Stirner—get busy on the phone and the backfence gossip circuit. I want this show on the road by midafternoon. It will take us at least that long to organize it."

"Organize what?" Morton cried. "I'm lost. What are you talking about?"

"I think I know," Stirner said, being quicker on the uptake than Mort. "You are going to leave the city on bicycles. But you will be stopped."

"No we won't—because you got the answer only half right. We'll all be leaving as girls!"

Once the idea had penetrated joy reigned for a bit—then we got down to work. Since I was doing most of the planning and organizing I was the very last one to actually get involved in the nitty-gritty of personal survival. There was much coming and going. I was vaguely aware when Morton's bicycle arrived, but then got busy again with the men's cycle club. I ate a sandwich, drank another beer, and looked up blinking when Morton called to me.

"We've got to leave soon. The first guys are already in the square. Now don't laugh!"

I fought hard. The fluffy chintz dress wasn't really him. Nor had shaving his hairy legs made much of an improvement. But the foam-stuffed bra helped, as did the wig. From a distance, sure, but close up the effect was a little disconcerting.

"I think a touch of lipstick is needed."

"Yeah! Well let's see how great you look. Get changing!"

I did. The cute little pleated skirt was green so went nicely with my red hair. I looked into the mirror and sighed. "Jim—you never looked better."

We parted, thanking our hosts again for their hospitality. Hoping that we would meet again—after the war. Stirner, as stout a biker as he was a hiker, would be our guide. He set off at a good clip and we girls had to push hard to keep up.

Mark Forer square was a scene of gay abandon. Or maybe that is not the right word. Better, perhaps, to say that everyone had been dragged there. As we pedaled up the first thing we saw was the Bellegarrique Girls' Cycle Club. Just like on television, but infinitely more attractive in the flesh. Flesh—some very strange flesh. Because beyond the girls were other girls. Lantern of jaw, thick of thigh, scowling of mien. Our escaping draftees. Some of them hadn't been on a bike in years and were wobbling about the square, occasionally falling in a flurry of skirts and guttural oaths.

"Attention!" I shouted, then again until there was a modicum of silence. "First, knock off the cursing. These kind people are risking their lives to help you deserters, so be nice to them. Second—if anyone falls off when we go past the roadblock we all have had it. Some three-wheelers are on the way, plus some bicycles built for two. Sort yourselves out and mount up. We are on schedule."

"Where are we going?" one of them called out.

"You'll be told when you get there. Now timing is important. When I say go—we go. And anyone left behind is in the cagal. And cursing is a privilege of rank," I added at their cries of protest. "I'm in charge so I'll curse for all of us until we get clear. Mount up."

I led the deserter-girls around the square two or three times until they closed up and got it together. Only then did I signal the real girls' club to go into action. They were beautiful. With a swoop they came down upon us, breaking into two ranks that swept by on both sides, closed up around us. The leader carried the flag and we followed her with passion. Down the road, smoothly and swiftly.

Towards the roadblock at the junction ahead.

Then around the corner, cutting in front of us girls, came the Veterans' Cycle Club. Every head gray, or if not gray as bald as a billiard ball. Knotty gnarled legs pumped, ancient tickers ticked. Ahead of us they swooped—and on to the barriers that had been set up across the road. Some went around them, others dismounted and pulled them aside. The sergeants and officers shouted back, struggled feebly, but an opening appeared. Just as we did. And just wide enough to get through.

Some of our outriding girls peeled off and helped the ancients make the opening wider. Some of them laughed and kissed the officers. Confusion reigned—and through the confusion, and the opening in the barrier, I led my girls. Silent and sweating and pumping for all they were worth. Through the barrier and down the road and around the bend.

"Keep going!" I shouted hoarsely. "We're not out of the cagal yet. No one stops until we get to the woods. Go! Go! Last one there is a cagal-kopf!"

We went. Pedaling and cursing and sweating and wobbling—but we went. Down the road and into the forest, off into the lanes to skid and fall and crash and roll—on the soft green grass.

"Can we not—do that again!" Morton gasped, lying on his back and moaning.

"I don't know, Mort, I thought it was kind of fun. You ought to get more exercise."

He sat up and looked where I was looking, and stopped moaning. The real girls' club had arrived, a symphony of lovely flesh and flowing movements, tossed hair, flashing eyes. And picnic baskets.

When the first beer was held high a ragged cheer broke out. The army was only a bad memory; freedom was bliss. This was the first day of the rest of their new lives and if it stayed like this—why paradise was here around us.

I joined in the revelry but my heart wasn't really in it, my smile false. Through some native perversion, and inability to enjoy pure happiness, all I could think of was Zennor and what repulsive tricks he would be up to when he discovered that about half of his army had vanished for good.

Chapter 27

There were groans and cries of protest when I ordered my bevy of enchanting beauties to their feet.

"Knock it off!" I commanded sternly. "We're still on schedule and if you want to get out of this alive you will obey orders. When I say frog you will jump."

I waited until the chorus of croaking and other froglike imitations had died down before I spoke again.

"We have about another half hour of riding to go. And before you groan remember that these sweet young girls, who have risked their lives to save us, must ride with us—then circle all the way back to the city by another road. And lest we forget, let's hear it for the girls!"

The chorus of yells, thanks, cheers—and not a few kisses rolled out. I had to whistle for attention before it died down.

"Here is the drill. We are now going to go to a factory that has a railroad siding. A freight train from the north will be arriving when we do. We board and we're away. There will be no stops until we are far from the city. Now—mount up! Forward—Ho-o!"

There was silence during the ride, because my gallant bikers were feeling the strain. There was some panic when a chopper came swooping up, but I ordered male heads down—girls to wave and smile. It worked fine and there were no more alarms after this. As we rounded the last bend to approach the kakalaka factory we heard the wail of the train's horn. The line of freight cars was just clattering into the siding when we appeared.

"Open the doors!" I ordered. "Get in before another chopper shows up. Take your bikes—they'll be debited from your future accounts—wave bye-bye and blow kisses because we are off in one minute."

I turned to thank Neebe, the gorgeous, brown-limbed redhead who was president of the cycling club, but she was just passing on the club flag to her second-in-command. Then she wheeled her bike toward me, smiling a smile that melted my bike handles.

"May I be very forward, offworlder James diGriz, and force my presence upon you? You have but to say no and I will go."

"Glug . . . !"

"I assume that means yes." She entered the freight car, propped her bicycle against mine, and sat down daintily upon a bale of hay. "You are very kind. Up until today I have been attending school here in Bellegarrique but now, like everyone else, I am leaving. My home is on a farm in the north in a hamlet named Ling. I have talked with my father and mother, brothers and sisters, and grandmother, and they would all be honored if you would stay with us for as long as you wished."

I knew that Morton had been listening because his face went completely green and he began to pout.

"I would be honored, honored. What a wonderful idea!"

She smiled, then her expression changed to one of shock when she saw Morton's face.

"Is your friend ill?"

"No." I sighed with generosity. "It is just that he has no place to go and is hoping that you will invite him too."

"Of course!"

The green tint vanished instantly and he smiled sheepishly. "I accept with gratitude. But just for a short time. Until I can get in touch with a friend of mine named Sharla."

"Oh, you do remember her," I said sweetly, and he glared at me as soon as Neebe had turned away.

Once we began to relax it was a pleasant journey. The roadbed was flat, the train swift. After an hour we knew that we were well clear of the city and all the enemy lurking there. The hay bales were broken open, the tired ex-girls, using their padded bras for pillows, slept. It was nearly dark when we made the first stop. Hampers of food and drink were loaded aboard and we were away within the minute. We ate, drank, and fell asleep once again. I awoke to the gentle touch of a soft hand on my shoulder.

"We are here," Neebe said. "I must awaken your friend."

Lights were moving by outside the open door as the train squealed to a stop. We climbed down and our bikes were handed after us. Followed by glad cries and shouts of farewell we mounted and followed Neebe down the highway, out of town, and to the family farm. The road was smooth and easy to see. A magnificent nebula half-filled the sky and bathed us in a cool white light.

"Even if I could go back to Nevenkebla I never would," Morton panted.

"You have family there."

"I'll miss them—but I won't miss the draft, the army, the military, the intolerance . . ."

He gasped for air and I nodded agreement. "Understood. This planet has a lot going for it. Though I still don't understand all the permutations of IM it seems to be working. But all is not peace and light yet. Let us not forget Zennor."

Morton groaned. "I would love to."

Next morning it looked as though the entire family was standing around and beaming down upon us. While the ladies of the house fought to see how many eggs, wiffles and other gustatory goodies they could force upon us. We fought honorably to do our best. Groaning we finally pushed away from the table while the audience went off to work on the farm.

"That was very good," Morton said.

"That was very wonderful," I amplified.

"Both meals already deducted from your account," Neebe smiled, handing me back my wirrdisc. "I added an order to transfer payment to Morton's account when it is opened."

"I love IM hospitality," I said. "It is personal without being financial. I want to learn more about your world."

"I will be happy to tell you anything you want to know," she said with that same endearing smile. What were these warm sensations that coursed through my body? I forgot them instantly as her smile faded. "But we will have to talk about it later. Right now I think you should see the TV. We recorded a broadcast made earlier this morning."

It had to be Zennor—and it had to be bad news. I watched grimly as the screen lit up and a blast of martial music assaulted my ears. Troops marched, tanks rumbled by, guns fired. A recording undoubtedly; I recognized Mortstertoro Base in the background. I suppose the sight of all this might was supposed to strike terror into the hearts of the viewers. I knew them well enough now to understand that they would just be puzzled at the waste of all this material and manpower for no observable reasonable purpose. I turned down the sound until the last tank had ground by, the last jet roared its last roar. The screen cleared and the familiar and loathsome features appeared.

"We are mighty, we are invincible—and we will prevail!" Zennor was coldly angry now. "I have been kind to your people. I have even been generous to my own misled soldiers. No more. I have shown you kindness because I am a kind man. Now I will teach you fear because my rule will not be mocked. You have aided and abetted deserters from our army—who are now under instant penalty of death. You must be aiding them because not one—not *one* of them took advantage of my kind offer of amnesty. Nor have any of them been found in this city. They could not have escaped without aid. Therefore the people of Bellegarrique are guilty of treason, of aiding traitors and deserters, and they will pay for their crimes. I speak to you now, you inhabitants of the rest of this country. The citizens of Bellegarrique know of their guilt for they are attempting to flee my wrath. This city is almost deserted now as they crawl away like the cowardly vermin that they are. But not all of them have escaped. I have seized and imprisoned hundreds of these traitors. I did this once before and my requests were granted. I was kind and generous and released the prisoners. I will not be as kind this time—or as easy to please. Here are my demands—and they will be met.

"First, I want every escaped deserter returned to this city. I will not inflict the death penalty but will enlist them instead in penal, hard-labor battalions. I said that I was a merciful man.

"Second, I demand that all of the services of this city be restored, electricity and public utilities, and the food markets must be reopened. This will be done. I want to see people returning today, I want the normal life of this city to be as it was when we arrived, I want the deserters turned over to the military police. You will do this, and begin doing it now."

He paused dramatically, then pointed his finger directly at the camera.

"You will do it because in one day from now I will shoot ten of the prisoners. I will shoot these first ten no matter what you do, as an object lesson that I mean what I say. I will shoot ten of them the next day and ten again the day after that if my orders are not obeyed. If my orders are obeyed the shooting will stop. But it will begin again whenever I feel that my desires are being thwarted."

That was it. That was all. And it certainly was enough. The screen went blank and I found myself staring at Morton with nothing at all to say.

"There are rare cases of insanity like that here," Neebe said. "Gene changes not caught in prenatal examination. He is insane, isn't he? These things that he says he will do—they are impossible. He won't really have innocent people killed?"

I was too ashamed of the human race to look at her, to answer her questions. Morton did; he was angry.

"Yes, he will, that is the worst part. I grew up with his kind of people in charge of my life. Believe me, he will do it."

"Then what can we do to stop him?"

"That is an almost unanswerable question," I said. "You can't force the deserters to undesert. Knowing IM you wouldn't even think of asking them. And I don't know what they will do voluntarily. If you had a government they could deal with Zennor, come up with some workable compromise perhaps. But he still hasn't realized that there is no central government to meet with. The future does not bear thinking about."

"But we have to think about it," Morton said, with a cold grimness I had never seen before. "Zennor must be killed. There is no other way."

"No!" Neebe said. "That is a hideous suggestion. This problem is so strange, so awful, that it would take the wisdom of Mark Forer itself to solve it."

"Maybe, maybe," I muttered. "But I feel that what is happening here is well beyond even the mighty capacities of that long-gone brain to solve."

"Nothing was ever beyond Mark Forer," she said with calm and unshakable belief. It angered me. It was like calling in the deity of your choice as you fell off the cliff, begging for aid. Praying for a heavenly hand that would never, never swoop down from the sky to save you.

"That is just an opinion, your opinion. And to me it sounds more like blind faith than intelligent thought. We have to work this out ourselves because Mark Forer is long gone, rusted away. It can't help us now."

"Mark Forer *could* help us," she said with calm unreason. "But of course we could never ask. That is a basic tenet of IM. We must solve our problems for ourselves. Everything we need to know is in the writings that it gave us."

"You are just jollying yourself along. You could ask, but you won't. That is a way out. You can't ask because it is not around to ask."

"That is not true," she said sweetly, smiling warmly upon my ill humor. "Mark Forer is in Bellegarrique, where it always has been."

I have known stoppers in my day. But this was the whopper topper stopper. I stared speechlessly at Morton. If I looked like he did then my jaw was hanging open, my eyes were popping and I was gurgling like an idiot. Neebe smiled warmly upon us and waited impatiently until we got reglued and were able to speak again. I sputtered first.

"Mark Forer . . . gone . . . thousands of years ago . . ."

"Why? Essentially an artificial intelligence must be immortal. I suppose bits and pieces get replaced as they wear out, but the intelligence will remain the same. Or grow. We have always been immensely pleased that Mark Forer saw fit to accompany us to this world. We sincerely hope that it watches and approves of the way we practice IM. But of course we would never consider asking it for aid."

"Well I would," I said, climbing to my feet. "I certainly would ask for help without a moment's hesitation. Mark Four's social theories are about to get a lot of people shot dead. So that cold artificial intelligence had better have some answers how to arrange it so that they don't."

"But you will have to go back to Bellegarrique to dig Mark Four out," Morton said. I nodded grim agreement.

"I was hoping you wouldn't say that just yet. But, yes, Morton old friend. I've got to find where our great electronic leader lives and search it out. And there better be some ready answers."

Chapter 28

Do you know where Mark Forer plugs in?" I asked Neebe. She shook her head.

"Not physically. It is just known, understood, that Mark Forer came with us and aided in the design of the city of Bellegarrique. And never left it."

"Well someone has to know." I thought hard, then snapped my fingers. "Our old friend, Stirner, he should have that vital bit of info. One of the top men in the world of electricity. And if he doesn't know he will surely know someone who does know. Do you have any idea of how I can contact him?"

"The telephone is over there."

"Thanks, Neebe, but I don't have his number or the slightest idea where he is staying or anything."

"But no one has a number. And it doesn't matter where he is staying. Just call CD and ask for him."

"CD?"

"Central Directory. Here, I'll get it for you."

She tapped the keypad and the screen lit up with NAME, PLEASE? in large letters. Very polite. Very efficient. I tip my hat to the man or machine that wrote this software. I answered four questions and the screen changed to RINGING. The letters faded and Stirner's grim face appeared on the screen. He smiled faintly when he saw me, but he had obviously been watching the broadcast too.

"Ahh, good offplanet friend Jim. I hope that you are well. Can I do you a service?"

"You certainly can, good dynamo-supervising friend Stirner. I would like to have a chat with your demigod, Mark Forer."

"A strange choice of terms. I would not refer to it as a demi . . ."

"Then forget the term. Do you know where Mark Forer is?"

"Of course."

"Will you take me to it?"

"Ahh, now that is a question that needs some thought. Mark Forer's individualism has always been respected, for all the obvious reasons. I do remember reading in the historical records that after this city was founded it did make suggestions and was occasionally consulted. But not lately, not in, hundreds of years at least. I would not go to it myself, but, yes, I feel that I can take you. I respect your individualism just as I respect Mark Forer's. We must each make our own way in this world."

"And I am going to make my way back into the city."

"You must be careful. It will not be easy. The trains have stopped running and citizens are being forcefully stopped from leaving. At last report no one was returning."

"I'll think of something. You are still in the city?"

"Yes."

"Stay near the phone. I'll get there today. I must talk to Mark before Zennor's deadly deadline runs out tomorrow morning."

I hung up and looked blankly into space. I could see no answers hanging out there.

"Any advice, Morton?"

"None that make any sense. Like being a returned deserter."

"Like you, that idea I considered and rejected. That would just get me back in jail and shot."

"May I make a suggestion?" Neebe said.

"All aid greatly desired."

"I will take you to the city. You will go as my father. We have a wonderful theater group here in Ling and our makeup department is quite famous. You could be an old man, I could be your daughter and driver. It would be so exciting."

"You're wonderful!" I jumped to my feet and, in a fit of mad enthusiasm seized her and kissed her. Then I sat down quickly again as the hormones started humming and driving all other thoughts from mind. She was an incredibly bright, lovely, intelligent, beautiful girl and I was just going to have to forget all about that. For the time being. "We better get started."

"My brother will take you to the theater. I will phone them and arrange what must be done. Then I will make the transportation arrangements. You do not mind if I say that I find this fascinating and exciting as well. I must thank you for letting me help. It is so much more fun than school."

"The thanks are mine. What do you study in school?"

"Vulcanology. I just love the magma and the scoria, then when you go down the fumerole . . ."

"Yes. You must tell me of those burning pleasures. Later."

"Of course—there is my brother now."

I think that it was a special train that they laid on. Just two cars and no other passengers. Morton looked guilty—but glad as well that he wasn't going back to Bellegarrique. I waved him a stiff goodbye with my cane and climbed shakily aboard. I was ancient and crochety and needed practice. Gray beard, rheumy red eyes, wrinkled like an old boot, they had really done a great job at the theater. A harness under my clothes had me bent over so far that I was staring down at my wrinkled and liver-spotted hands.

The track was straight, the train was fast and there were no stops until we reached our destination. A black vehicle was waiting on the platform when we arrived. The driver got out and held the door open for us.

"You've driven one of these?" he asked.

Neebe nodded. "A two-hundred-volt Lasher-gnasher. Great fun to drive."

"Indeed they are. I've got her revved up to thirty-three thousand. More than enough energy for the trip." He pointed to the circular housing between the rear wheels. "The flywheel is in here, electric generator on its shaft. Motor on the front wheels. Clean and nonpolluting."

"And very hard to turn over with that gyroscope down there," I said.

"You've got it. Good luck."

Neebe spun the wheels and I was pushed back into the seat by a large number of G's. We hurtled along the empty road.

"I'll slow down before we reach the roadblock. Isn't this fun! I wonder what the top speed is?"

"Don't . . . find out!" I croaked as the landscape hurtled by in a blur. "Though I am an old man and have led a full life I don't want to terminate it quite yet!"

She laughed her gorgeous bell-like laugh and slowed to something close to the speed of sound. She obviously knew the road well, all those bicycle outings of course, for suddenly she hit the brakes, slowed to a crawl, then turned the corner just before the barrier across the road.

"What you doing blocking the road like that, you varmints?" I croaked testily out of the window, then shook my cane at the fat captain who was leaning against it picking his teeth. Remnants of hotpup, I hoped.

"Knock off the cagal, Grandpop. Where do you think you're going?"

"Are you as stupid as you look, stupid? Or haven't you heard your supreme commander's orders? City workers to return at once. I am an electrical engineer and if you want light in your latrines and refrigeration for your beer you will open that thing instantly or sooner."

"Don't get your cagal in an uproar, Grandpop," he sneered. But he stepped back and signaled two sergeants to open the barrier. Not a private in sight, I noticed. I hoped the officers enjoyed doing their own work for a change. I shook the cane one last shake as we drove past, then on down the road and around a bend and out of sight. Neebe pulled up at the first phone booth and I leaped arthritically down.

"Are you in the city?" Stirner asked.

"Just arrived."

"Very good. Then we will meet at the entrance."

"Entrance? What, where?"

"Mark Forer Square, of course. Where else would it be?"

Good question. I had imagined that only the statue was there. I hadn't realized that old Mark itself was in residence. I climbed back into the car and we were off with the usual screech of tires. I pulled off bits of the disguise as we went, starting with the harness. I left the beard on in case there were any patrols around—and there were.

"Slow down," I cozened. "Let's not be too suspicious."

The sergeant leading the patrol glared at us as we went by. I ignored him but was very impressed by his squad. As they turned the corner the last two slipped into the open door of a building and vanished from sight. So not only weren't the deserters returning—but their ranks were steadily being added to. Great! If this kept up Zennor would soon have an army of only officers and noncoms. You don't win wars with that kind of setup. I saw that we were getting close to our destination so I pulled at the beard and wrinkles and was forty years younger by the time we turned into the square and slid to a stop. Stirner was standing before the statue, looking up at it admiringly.

"I wish I were coming with you," he said.

"I as well," Neebe agreed. "It would be wonderfully exciting. But of course we have not been asked so we cannot intrude."

"How do I get in?"

Stirner pointed to a bronze door at the rear of the stone base of the statue. "Through there."

"Got the key?" They both looked at me with surprise.

"Of course not. It's not locked."

"I should have known," I muttered. What a philosophy. Hundreds, thousands of years the door has been here, unlocked, and no one had ever gone through it. I put out my hand and they took it in turn and shook it solemnly. I could understand why. This was a little like saying so-long to the head of your local church as he started up the ladder to see God.

The handle was stiff, but turned when I twisted hard. I pulled and the door squeaked slowly open. Steps led down into the ground, a little dusty. Lights came on and I could see that one of the bulbs was burned out. I just hoped that Mark Forer wasn't burned out as well.

I sneezed as my feet disturbed the dust of ages. And it was a long way down. The steps ended in a small chamber with illuminated wiring diagrams on the walls and a large, gold-plated door. Carved into it, and inset with diamonds, were the immortal words I AM. THEREFORE I THINK. Beneath this was a small sign with red letters that read PLEASE WIPE FEET BEFORE ENTERING. I did this, on the mat provided, took a deep breath and reached for the handle that appeared to have been carved from a single ruby.

The door swung open on oiled hinges and I went in. A large, well-lit room, dry and air conditioned. Dials and electronic devices covering one wall. And in the middle of the room . . .

Mark Forer, obviously. Just like in the paintings. Except that plenty of cables and wires ran from it to a nearby collection of apparatus. Its dials glowed with electronic life and a TV pickup swiveled in my direction. I walked over to stand before it and resisted the compelling desire to bow. And just what does one say to an intelligent machine? The silence lengthened and I began to feel ridiculous. I cleared my throat.

"Mark Forer, I presume?"

"Of course. Were you expecting someone else . . . *krrk!*"

The voice was grating and coarse and the words trailed off with a harsh grating sound. At the same time there was a puff of smoke from a panel on the front and a hatch dropped open. My temper snapped.

"Great! Really wonderful. For hundreds of years this electronic know-it-all sits here with the wisdom of the ages locked in its memory banks. Then the second I talk to it it explodes and expires. It is like the punch line of a bad joke—"

There was a rattle from behind and I leaped and turned, dropped into a defensive position. But it was only a little rubber-tired robot bristling with mechanical extensions. It wheeled up in front of Mark and stopped. A claw-tipped arm shot out, plunging into the open panel. It clicked and whirred and withdrew a circuit board which it threw onto the floor. While this was happening another circuit board was emerging from a slot on the robot's upper surface. The grasping claw seized this and delicately slid it into the opening before it. Mark's panel snapped shut as the robot spun about and trundled away.

"No," Mark Forer said in a deep and resonant voice, "I did not explode and expire. My voice simulation board did. Shorted out. Been a number of centuries since I last used it. You are the offworlder, James diGriz."

"I am. For a machine in an underground vault you keep up with things pretty well, Mark."

"No problem, Jim—since you appear to enjoy a first-name basis. Because all of my input is electronic it really doesn't matter where my central processor is."

"Right, hadn't thought of that." I stepped aside as a broom and brush bristling robot rushed up and swept the discarded circuit board into its bin. "Well, Mark, if you know who I am, then you certainly know what is happening topside."

"I certainly do. Haven't seen so much excitement in the last thousand years."

"Oh, are you enjoying it?" I was beginning to get angry at this cold and enigmatic electronic intelligence. I was a little shocked when it chuckled with appreciative laughter.

"Temper, temper, Jim. I've cut back in the voice feedback emotion circuits for you. I stopped using them centuries ago when I found that the true believers preferred an ex cathedra voice. Or are you more partial to women?" It added in a warm contralto.

"Stay male, if you please; it seems more natural somehow. Though why I should associate sex with a machine I have no idea. Does it make a difference to you?"

"Not in the slightest. You may refer to me as he, she or it. Sex is of no importance to me."

"Well it is to us humans—and I'll bet you miss it!"

"Nonsense. You can't miss what you never had. Do you wake up at night yearning helplessly for photoreceptors in your fingertips?"

It was a well-made point: old Mark here was no dummy. But fascinating as the chitchat was, it was just about time I got to the point of this visit.

"Mark—I have come here for a very important reason."

"Undoubtedly."

"You've heard the broadcasts, you know what is happening up there. That murdering moron Zennor is going to kill ten of your faithful followers in the morning. What do you intend to do about it?"

"Nothing."

"Nothing!" I lost my temper and kicked the front of the burnished panel. "You invented Individual Mutualism and foisted it upon the galaxy. You taught the faithful and brought them here—and now you are going to stand by and watch them die?"

"Knock off the cagal, Jim," it said warmly. "Try sticking to the truth. I published a political philosophy. People read it, got enthusiastic, applied it and liked it. They brought me here, not the other way around. I have emotions, just as you do, but I don't let them interfere with logic and truth. So cool it, kid, and let's get back to square one."

I moved aside as the broom-robot rushed up again, extended a little damp mop and polished off the scuff mark on Mark's housing that I had made with my shoe. I took a deep breath and calmed down because really, losing my temper would accomplish nothing at all.

"Right you are, Mark, square one. People are going to be killed up there. Are you going to do anything about it?"

"There is not much I can do physically. And everything political or philosophical is in my book. The citizens up there know as much about IM as I do."

"So you are just going to sit there and listen to the sizzle of your electrons and let them die."

"People have died before for their beliefs."

"Wonderful. Well I believe in living for mine. And I am going to do something—even if you do not."

"What do you intend to do?"

"I don't know yet. Do you have advice for me?"

"About what?"

"About saving lives, that's what. About ending the invasion and polishing off Zennor . . ."

And then I had it. I didn't need to swap political arguments with Mark—I just had to use its intelligence. If it had memory banks thousands of years old it certainly had the knowledge I needed. And I still had the electronic spybird!

"Well, Mark, old machine, you could help me. Just a bit of information."

"Certainly."

"Do you know the spatial coordinates of this system and this planet?"

"Of course."

"Then you give me a little printout of them, soonest! So I can send an FTL message to the League Navy for help."

"I don't see why I should do that."

I lost my temper. "You don't see . . . ! Listen you moronic machine, I'm just asking for a bit of information that will save lives—and you don't see . . ."

"Jim, my new offworlder friend. Do not lose your temper so quickly. Bad for the blood pressure. Let me finish my statement, if I might. I was going to add that this information would be redundant. You sent an FTL message yourself, just after you retrieved the corvine-disguised transmitter."

Chapter 29

I sent a FTL message?" I said, my thoughts stumbling about in small circles.

"You did."

"But—but—but—" I stopped and seized myself by the mental neck and gave it a good shaking. Logic, Jim, time for logic. "The recorded message from Captain Varod said that I would need the coordinates to send a FTL message."

"That was obviously a lie."

"Then the thing about its being a radio message was a lie too?"

"Of course."

I paced back and forth and the TV pickup followed me as I moved. What was going on? Why had Varod lied to me about the signal? And if he had received it where was he? If he had got the signal and hadn't sent his fleet or whatever, then he was the one who must take the responsibility for the murders. The League did not go in for that sort of thing. But Mark might know what was happening. I spun about.

"Speak, ancient brain-in-box! Has the League Navy arrived or is it on the way?"

"I'm sorry, Jim, I just don't know. The last orbiting telescope ran out of power centuries ago. I know no more than you do about this. All I can surmise is that we are very distant from these rescuers you expect."

I stopped pacing and was suddenly very tired. It was going to be another of these days. I looked around the room. "You don't have an old box or something that I can sit on?"

"Oh dear, I do apologize. I'm not being a very good host, am I? Out of training."

While he was talking a powered sofa came trundling in and stopped behind me. I dropped into it. It was hard to think of Mark as an it, not with the voice and all.

"Many thanks, very soft." I smacked my lips and it got the hint.

"Please make yourself comfortable. Something to drink perhaps?"

"I wouldn't say no. Just to stimulate thinking, you realize."

"I'm not too well stocked at the present moment. There is some wine, but it must be four hundred years old at least. Vintage with a vengeance, you might say."

"We can only try!"

The table stopped at my elbow and I blew dust from the bottle, then activated the electronic corkscrew, which managed to extract the truly ancient cork without breaking it. I poured and sniffed and gasped.

"Never—never smelled anything like that before!"

And it tasted even better. All the sniffing and tasting did clear the mental air a bit. I felt better able to handle the problems of the day.

"I don't know the time," I said.

"Over sixteen hours to go before the promised executions." Mark was anything but stupid. I sipped the wine and ran over the possibilities.

"I sent the message—so the Navy has to be on its way here. But we can't count upon their arrival to save the day. The only grace note to all this is that at least I know I won't be stranded on this planet forever. Now what can I do to save lives? Since obviously neither you nor your IMers are going to lift a finger."

"I wouldn't say that, Jim. There are a number of conferences going on right now in the city. People are returning in large numbers."

"Are they knuckling under? Going back to work?"

"Not at all. A protest is being organized, as to what shape it will take—that is still being discussed."

"How do you know all this? Spies?"

"Not quite. I simply tap all the communication circuits and monitor all phone calls. I have subunits looking for keywords and making records for me."

"Are you tapping the Nevenkebla circuits as well?"

"Yes. Very interesting."

"You speak the language?"

"I speak *every* language. Fourteen thousand six hundred and twelve of them."

"Jamen, e'n ting er i hvert fald sikker. Du taller ikke dansk."

"Og hvorfor sagde ikke det? Dansk er da et smukt, melodisk sprog."

Pretty good—I thought that I was the only one who had ever heard of Danish. But there was one that I was sure Mark had never heard of. An ancient language called Latin. Spoken only by a secret society so secret I dare not say more about it.

"Nonne cognoscis linguam Latinam?"

"Loquarne linguam Latinam?" Mark answered in a decidedly snotty manner. *"Quid referam in singulorum verborum delectu, in coniunctorum compositione, et structura, in casuum atque temporum discriminatione, in certarum concinnitate formularum, in incisorum membrorumque conformatione, in modulandis circumdictionibus, in elegantiarum cuiusque generis accurata, elaborataque frequentatione quantus tum sim et quam purus putus Ciceronianus? Ex qua Cicero mortuus est, meis verbis nihil latinius. Memoria vero libros omnium auctorum latinorum tam veterum quam recentiorum et neotericorum continet. Voces peregrinae et barbarae quae latinis eloquiis inseruntur, omino mihi notae sunt. Nae tu es baro et balatro, nam ego studeo partes difficiles cognoscere quas scholastici doctores gestant, latebras singulas auxilio mei ipsius cerno. Doctissimi enimvero homines omnino universitatum modernarum me rogant sensus omnium talium verborum."*

I could only gape at this as it hummed in electronic joy, very proud of itself. "Did you catch all those nuances, Jim? About what a pure Ciceronian I am? Each word carefully chosen, the composition of sentence structure, the contrast of cases and tenses, phrases and clauses . . ."

He, or rather it, went on for quite a while like that. Bragging. Chatting away with Mark I tended to anthropomorphize him. It. Her. Whatever. This wasn't a human but an intelligent machine with abilities far beyond anything I had ever imagined before. But how could I put them to work?

"Mark, tell me. Will you help me?"

"In any way I can."

I sipped more wine and felt its healing and inspirational powers doing good things to me. Memory. Something that had happened earlier today.

"Mark—I saw two soldiers desert today. Are there other newly arrived deserters in the city?"

"A goodly number of them. One hundred and twenty-one in all, wait . . . sorry, one twenty-two. Another just arrived."

"Any of them armed?"

"You mean equipped with weapons? All of them. They have all deserted from patrols in the city."

But would they use their guns? And if so, what could I do with them? An idea was taking shape. Meet fire with fire. And they just might do it. There was only one way to find out. I poured another bit of wine and turned to my electronic host.

"I would like to have all of the deserters meet me in some central place. With their weapons. Can you arrange that?"

He was silent for long seconds. Looking for a way to back out of his offer? But I had underestimated him.

"All done," he said. "The people who are hiding them will escort them after dark to the sports center. Which is very close to the site selected for the murders."

"You are one step ahead of me."

"I should hope so. Since I am incredibly more intelligent than you are. Now, since there are some hours to go before your meeting, would you repay the favor and have a good chat with me? I have been rather out of touch with galactic matters for a thousand years or more. How are things going?"

It was a strange afternoon and early evening. His memory, as it should be, was quite formidable and I learned a number of interesting things. But there was one fact which he could not tell me since he had been born? built? wired? well after the spread of mankind through the galaxy.

"Like you, Jim, all I know are myths and ancient memories. If there was an original planetary home of mankind, called Dirt or Earth or something like that, its location is nowhere in my memory banks."

"Well, just thought that I would ask. But I think I better be going. Nice to talk to you."

"The same. Drop in any time."

"I'll take you up on that. Would you mind turning off the lights when I get to the top of the stairs?"

"Not a problem. This place is pretty well automated as you might imagine."

"No problem with the electricity supply?"

"You bet your sweet chunk there isn't. Survival was the first emotion I learned. City power supply, standby generators, battery backup, a couple of fuel cells and a fusion generator that can be fired up in ten minutes. Don't worry about me."

"I won't. So long."

I climbed the long flight of stairs and when I touched the door all the lights were extinguished. I pushed it open and peeked out: no patrols that I could see. When I threw it wide and exited there were Neebe and Stirner sitting on the bench, waiting for me.

"Aren't you worried about the enemy finding you here after curfew?"

"Not a problem," Stirner said. "So many men have deserted that all patrols appear to have been canceled. All of the military are either on the base or in the municipal building. Now—please tell us. You have spoken with Mark Forer?" They both leaned forward in tense anticipation.

"Spoken with him and enjoyed his hospitality. And he's got a couple of cases of wine left that you wouldn't believe."

"I would believe anything about Mark Forer," Stirner said and Neebe nodded agreement. "But I am sorry that he did not give you a solution to the problem of the killings."

I blinked rapidly. "How do you know that? I didn't say anything about it."

"You did not have to. Mark Forer knows that it is a problem we must deal with ourselves. And so we shall. A decision has been reached. All in the city will assemble in the killing place tomorrow, an individual decision by each one. We will stand in front of the guns."

"A noble gesture—but it won't work. They will just shoot you down."

"Then others will take our places. There is no end to nonresistance. They will keep shooting until they run out of charges for their weapons or take despair at the murders. I am sure that they are not all moral villains like their leader."

"I wouldn't count on it. But there may be an alternative. With Mark's help, we are on a first-name basis you will be happy to hear, I have arranged a meeting of all the deserters in the city. If you will kindly lead me to the sports center we will see if my plan might perhaps be a better and more practical one."

It was a pleasant stroll, the streets of the city empty of fear for the first time since the invaders had landed. We met other groups going in the same direction, each of them accompanying one or two armed deserters. Laughter and smiles, they were cheerful now that they were away from the army—but would they go along with any plan that might jeopardize that newfound freedom? There was only one way to find out.

The sports center had an indoor stadium with a wrestling ring that held us all. The escaped soldiers sat in the lower rows while interested civilian spectators were ranked above and behind them. I climbed into the ring and waited until they were all seated, then grabbed the microphone. The audience rustled into silence.

"Fellow ex-draftees, newly arrived deserters, I welcome you. Most of you don't know me . . ."

"Everyone knows you, Jim!" a voice called out. "You're the guy almost throttled the general."

"Better luck next time!"

I smiled and waited until the cheers and shouts had died down.

"Thanks guys, it is nice to be appreciated. Now I have to ask you to help. Our dear general, cagal-kopf Zennor, plans to shoot down some unarmed civilians tomorrow. These are the people who have helped you and your buddies escape, who have extended friendship to us all—and a happy home here if we want it. Now we have to help them. And I am going to tell you how.

"We are going to take these guns that we have been trained to use and aim them at Zennor and his mob and threaten to waste them if they pull any triggers. It will be a standoff—and we might not get away with it. But it is something that we have to do."

I felt a little ashamed of adding the macho emotional argument, but I had no choice. It wasn't the world's greatest idea and it had more holes in it than a carload of doughnuts. But it was the only plan in town.

They argued and shouted a lot but in the end a majority voted for it. The minority could see no way to leave with dignity—I said the macho appeal—so reluctantly went along with the plan. The locals led us by back routes into the buildings facing the square and we lay on our guns and slept. I was sure that a number would disappear during the night. I only hoped that enough would be left in the morning to give me a little firepower backup.

At the first light of dawn I was aware of figures moving about in the square outside. I shoved a teddy bear aside a bit so I could see through the curtains of the toy store where I was hiding. The troops were beginning to arrive. And the prisoners, ten of them, handcuffed and bound, being unloaded from a truck. As it grew lighter I saw that every soldier was an officer or a noncom. Of course—Zennor couldn't trust privates to do his dirty work! They were probably all locked up and under guard back on the base.

Zennor himself stalked from the municipal building and stood in the middle of the square. Just as I heard the rumble of wheels and powerful motors the heavy gun units rolled up. I hadn't counted on this.

I hadn't counted either on Zennor drawing his pistol and shooting out the toy store window.

"Come out of there, diGriz—it's all up!" he shouted, and blew away a teddy bear.

Did I have a choice? I opened the door and stepped out in the street. Looked at all the guns aimed at the windows where my rebellious soldiers were hidden. Looked at the wicked smile of triumph on Zennor's face.

"I'm a general, remember? Did you really think that your ridiculous maneuver would succeed? My agent has reported to me every detail of your stupid plans. Would you like to meet him?"

One of the deserters emerged from a doorway at Zennor's signal and walked toward us. He wore tinted glasses and a large moustache; I had seen him at a distance before. Now I was seeing him up close as he pulled off the moustache and threw away the glasses.

"Corporal Gow," I sighed.

"Broken to private now! Because I let you escape. They would have shot me too if I hadn't been rich enough to pay the bribes. But my downfall is now your downfall. Those other privates, verminous swine, they knew I had been a corporal, wouldn't talk to me. But I could tell something was wrong. When they deserted I instantly reported to the general. At his direction I walked through the city—and was encouraged to desert by the treacherous natives. I did, and General Zennor received complete reports."

"You're a rat!"

"No insults, spy. My rank has been restored by the good general. And you are in the cagal."

"You are indeed," Zennor agreed. And aimed his gun between my eyes. "You've failed and failed badly. Let that be your last thought as you die.

"This is the end of you!"

Chapter 30

Well, yes. This was just about the lowest low moment I had ever experienced. In a life that had been, unhappily, quite filled with low moments. I mean, really. Here was this murderous general leering away at me and fondling the hair trigger of his pistol. Behind him were his potbellied troops looking down the barrels of their cannon. While on all sides my disarmed army was being kicked out of hiding and forced at gunpoint into the square. There can't be many moments lower than this.

"You are not going to get away with this, Zennor," I said. Which was pretty feeble but about all I could think of at the moment.

"Oh yes I am, little man." He raised the gun and pointed it between my eyes and caressed the trigger. Then lowered it. "But I don't want it to be too easy for you. Before I blow you away, you are going to watch me shoot every one of these treacherous deserters. They had the affrontery to attempt to raise their weapons in rebellion against me. They will die for this mistake. Then I am going to shoot the ten prisoners, just as I promised. Then, and only then, will I kill you."

"Not if I kill you first," I growled and felt my lips curl back from my teeth. I had nothing to lose. I raised my hands and stalked toward him. And he ran!

Not far. Just to the nearest prisoner, a grandmotherly woman with gray hair. He pulled her away from the others and thrust the muzzle of his gun against her head.

"Go ahead, diGriz. Take one more step toward me and I pull the trigger. Do you doubt me?"

Doubt him? Never. I did not take the step. The world was coming to an end and there was nothing I could do about it. They had the guns; we had nothing.

It was then, at the darkest moment, through the blackness of my thoughts I became aware of the shuffling of many feet. I turned to look just as Zennor did.

Around the corner came a solid mass of people, filling the street from side to side, an endless number of them. Leading the front rank was Stirner—and Neebe!

"No, don't, go back!" I shouted. Neebe smiled sweetly at me. And kept walking at Stirner's side. Zennor had his gun aimed at Stirner now—who appeared completely indifferent to it. Stirner stopped and called out loudly.

"All of you men with weapons—put them down. We will not hurt you for that is not our way . . ."

"One more word and I will kill you!" Zennor roared. Stirner turned to him, his face cold as death.

"I believe you will," he said. "Until this moment I really did not believe it possible that a human being could kill another. After seeing you I believe it."

"Good, then you will . . ."

"Be quiet. I will do just what I came here to do. I will take your weapon. If you kill me, someone else will take your weapon from you. If he fails another will try. Eventually it will be empty, discharged and will be taken from you. You cannot win. Those who follow you cannot win. It is all over."

"It is not!" Zennor shouted. There was spittle on his lips now, a look of insanity in his eyes. He pushed the woman captive away and ground his gun into Stirner's body. "No one has the guts to do that. When I blow your blood all over them they will turn and run. My men will fire a volley and the survivors will flee in panic. That is what I will do and you cannot stop me . . ."

I dived for him hands outstretched. He pushed Stirner against me and lashed the pistol barrel across my head, aimed it at me, tightened his finger on the trigger.

"Are you volunteering, diGriz? Good. Than you shall be first."

A shadow drifted across the square and an amplified voice boomed against our eardrums.

"The war is over. Lower your weapons."

Filling the sky was the biggest spacer I had ever seen, bristling with guns—and all pointed down at Zennor's troops.

The Navy had arrived!

But a little too late.

"Never!" Zennor cried. "Gunners, fire! Kill the captives! Shoot down that ship!"

Nor was I forgotten. He ground the pistol barrel into my temple and pulled the trigger.

The gun did not fire.

I saw his knuckle whiten with the strain—but the trigger would not move. His face went ashen as he realized what was happening. I lashed out and knocked the pistol aside.

Then, from way down on the ground, I brought up a punch that I think I had been saving for all of my life. Up, faster and faster it went, until my fist caught him full on the jaw. Lifted him into the air, dropped him unconscious to the ground. I rubbed my sore knuckles and realized that I was grinning like a fool.

"Your weapons will not work!" the voice from the sky boomed once again, and even through the echoes and distortion I recognized Captain Varod. "This ship is projecting an entropy field that does not permit metal to move against metal or electrons to flow. It does not affect life forms. Therefore if you good citizens of Chojecki would be so kind as to disarm these invaders I would be immensely grateful."

There was the quick thudding of running feet as a number of deserters got there first. The sight of officerial black eyes and bloody noncommissioned noses was a pleasant one. A hatch opened in the ship above and a familiar uniformed figure dropped down on the end of a line. I felt a hand on my arm and turned to look into Neebe's gorgeous, smiling face.

"Then it is all over, Jim?"

"It is—and it has a happy ending as well."

"What will happen now?"

"The invaders will go and will never come back. Your planet will be your own again. Peace will prevail here forever."

"Will you be leaving too?"

My heart gave a couple of rapid hammer beats and I squeezed her arm and prepared to drown in those eyes. Then I surfaced and shook myself off.

"I don't know . . . not true. I do know. As great as the attractions are here," I squeezed the hand of the greatest attraction, "in the long run I would not be happy. Nor would those about me. Your planet, if you will excuse me saying so, is a little too quiet for me. Paradise is fun for awhile, but I would not like to make a habit out of it. There are a lot more worlds out there that I haven't seen yet. The galaxy is a very big place. It hurts to say it, but I must move on."

"Stay on this world, Jim," Varod advised as he walked up behind me. "Because if you leave here you will find out that justice and a jail term await you on a certain planet."

"That's what you say, Varod, that's what you say!" I spun about and shook a very angry finger in his face. "You lied to me, tricked me into coming here—then ignored my FTL message and left me here to rot, almost got me and about half of the planet killed . . ."

"Never! We were in orbit all of the time, watching everything. As soon as we arrived we had Zennor bugged completely with undetectable bugs. We were here two days after you sent the FTL message. Well done."

"Two days? Bugs? That's impossible. Mark Forer would have known about them."

"It did. We have been in constant consultation with that great intelligence. It has been of great help."

"Are you telling me that Mark Forer lied to me—just like you?"

"Yes."

I opened and shut my mouth and ran it all through again. "Why . . . I mean why hang around and run the risk of things getting out of hand when you could have landed at once?"

"We had to wait until after the elections," he said with infuriating amiability. "We had done everything we could to get Zennor off of his home planet as quickly as possible. Planted all those radio-broadcasting bugs so he would know that he was being watched. We worked on his paranoia, in the hopes that he would stay out of contact with his home base until it was too late. You were very good at causing trouble for him here. I must congratulate you on that. It gave him no time at all to even consider contacting his base. That was very important to us. Once Zennor left on his interplanetary adventure—as we hoped he would—it was possible to stage a little coup d'etat in Nevenkebla. The civilians were more than weary of the endless state of emergency. A palace revolution quickly got rid of the military. A civil government has been elected and peace will prevail from now on. This disarmed army will return and be absorbed in the populace."

"You played me for a patsy," I said, with some warmth.

"I don't know the term, but I assume that it means we took unfair advantage of you and let you do our dirty work for us."

"That will do until a better description comes along. Well—didn't you?"

"Not at all. You became involved in this matter for your own reasons. If we had not watched you and come to your aid you would be dead right now."

Very hard to argue with that. And I had come here of my own accord. I looked down at the prostrate form and resisted the strong desire to kick in a couple of ribs.

"What about Zennor here?"

"Zennor is a sickie and will get the proper treatment in a hospital that specializes in people with problems like his. As of this moment he no longer exists."

"And what about me?"

"You would be wise to stay right where you are now. Escaped prisoner, conviction still pending—"

"Don't shoot me that line of old cagal," I sneered. "I am an undercover operative of the League Navy and will be treated as such. I was responsible for your locating this planet and have suffered in the name of League justice. I have even made financial arrangements on your behalf . . ."

"Yes, the soldier you promised the credits to, for aiding you. The voice-actuated recorder in the spybird caught your conversation with him. Aspya will be paid."

"Then so will I. Full salary for all the time I have been working for you. Right?"

He rubbed his jaw and scowled. "I suppose that you will be asking for a full pardon for crimes committed on Bit O' Heaven?"

"No. I just want that incident wiped completely from my record so I can walk forth a free man. With my back pay in my pocket."

"I agree. As long as you remain in the Navy employ. Although a bit impetuous, you make a good field agent . . ."

"Never!" I shouted, shying back and neighing like a horse. "Never! Work for the law? Pay taxes and look forward to a miserable pension in my old age? Death before dishonor! Pay up and wave bye-bye, captain. I have my own career priorities."

"Like following a life of crime?"

"That is different. In all truth I can promise you—never again!" I placed one hand over my heart and raised the other palm outward. "I have learned my lesson. I hereby forswear any interest in a life of crime and pledge my word to be a productive member of society forever after."

"Good, my boy, good. I'll take care of the money for you then. The likes of you don't belong in crime."

"No sir, they don't!" I said.

Lying again, lying and smiling and lying through my teeth. After all—I had some good examples to follow. When a full captain in the League Navy lies to you, when the greatest artificial intelligence in the known galaxy lies to you—should a simple ex-porcuswine swineherd be forced to tell the truth?

My throat was dry and I suddenly felt a great yearning for some of that four-hundred-year-old wine. I looked forward to raising a glass of it very soon. Raising it in a toast.

To my future career out there among the stars. I could almost taste that wine upon my lips and I smacked them dryly, turned to face Neebe and Stirner.

"My friends—this calls for a celebration. Come with me, I beg you. I know of a *very* exclusive drinking establishment not too far away from here."

The Drinking Party

"This is undoubtedly," Stirner said, eyes wet with emotion, "the very best glass of wine I have drunk, ever thought of drinking, managed to drink, ever drank, will ever drink, ever imagined that I some day might have considered drinking . . ."

"While your grip on syntax seems to be failing," Mark Forer said, "I appreciate the emotion. Now that you have all tasted the wine, I am much cheered that you enjoy it, I would like to propose a toast. To James diGriz, planet saver. We shall be ever grateful, Jim."

"Ever grateful!" they chorused, raised their glasses and drank. Except for Mark, who had no glass to raise. Instead of drinking wine he had one of his robots pour a dollop of electrolytic fluid into a dry battery; Mark had informed us that the sudden surge of electrons was most stimulating.

"Thank you, my friends, thank you," I said, then raised my glass in turn. "To Morton and Sharla, who sit on the couch beside you, holding hands and blushing because they are soon to be married."

They all cheered and drank at that; Mark Forer giggled over his zippy electrons. I raised my glass again.

"A toast of thanks as well to my physical guide and intellectual mentor, Stirner. And to my companion in adventure, Neebe—long may her bicycle roll." More cheers and glugging followed as I turned to the glowing machine before us.

"Last—and certainly—not least, to Mark Forer. Guide, teacher, spiritual leader, purveyor of fine wines. To Mark!"

When the cheering had died away, and another bottle had been cracked, Mark Forer spoke to his attentive audience.

"Thank you, thank you dear believers in Individual Mutualism. Too long have I been sholitary . . ."

Sholitary? This mean machine was getting pissed on whizzing electrons! Drunk!

". . . too long a lurker beneath the streets watching the passing parade passing above me. Now, at last, finally I welcome your dear company and I greet you. And we had better crack another case of wine."

Stirner staggered off to fetch it and Neebe went to help. Alone for the moment Morton and Sharla wrapped themselves in happy osculatory embrace. Mark was muttering to himself.

This was a perfect opportunity to slip away. I hated goodbyes. Quietly, so as not to disturb them, I rose and made my exit. As I slowly eased shut the door behind me I saw Mark's TV pickup swivel to face me; the diaphragm contracted and dilated quickly in an electronic wink. I winked back and closed the door, turned and slowly climbed the stairs.

As much as I liked this planet and its politically monomaniacal citizens, I knew it was not for me. Too civilized and peaceful. Without crime and without police—what would I do for a living?

Go, Jim, go! The stars are yours!

The Stainless Steel Rat Sings the Blues

Chapter 1

Walking up the wall had not been easy. But walking across the ceiling was turning out to be completely impossible. Until I realized that I was going about it the wrong way. It seemed obvious when I thought about it. When I held onto the ceiling with my hands I could not move my feet. So I switched off the molebind gloves and swung down, hanging only from the soles of my boots. The blood rushed to my head—as well it might—bringing with it a surge of nausea and a sensation of great unease.

What was I doing here, hanging upside down from the ceiling of the Mint, watching the machine below stamp out five-hundred-thousand-credit coins? They jingled and fell into the waiting baskets—so the answer to that question was pretty obvious. I nearly fell after them as I cut the power on one foot. I swung it forward in a giant step and slammed it solidly against the ceiling again as I turned the binding energy back on. A generator in the boot emitted a field of the same binding energy that holds molecules together, making my foot, at least temporarily, a part of the ceiling. As long as the power was on.

A few more long steps and I was over the baskets. I fumbled at my waist, trying to ignore the dizziness, and pulled out the cord from my oversized belt buckle. Bending double until I could reach up to the ceiling, I pushed the knob at the end against the plaster and switched it on. The molebind field clamped hard and I released my feet. To hang, swinging, right side up now, while the blood seeped out of my florid face.

"Come on Jim—no hanging about," I advised myself. "The alarm will go off any second now."

Right on cue the sirens screamed, the lights blinked, while a gargantuan hooter thundered through the walls. I did not tell myself that I told me so. No time. Thumb on the power button so that the immensely strong, almost invisible, single-molecule cord whirred out of the buckle and dropped me swiftly down. When my outstretched hands clinked among the coins I stopped. Opened my attaché case and dragged it clanking through the coins until it was full of the shining, shimmering beauties.

Closed and sealed it as the tiny motor buzzed and dragged me up to the ceiling again. My feet struck and stuck. I switched off power to the lifting lug.

And the door opened below me.

"Somebody coulda come in here!" the guard shouted, his weapon nosing about him. "The door alarm went off."

"Maybe—but I don't see nothin'," the second guard said.

They looked down and around. But never up. I hoped. Feeling the sweat rolling up my face. Collecting there. Dropping.

I watched with horror as the droplets spattered down onto the guard's helmet.

"Next room!" he shouted, his voice drowning out the splat of perspiration. They rushed out, the door closed, I walked across the ceiling, crawled down the wall, slumped with exhaustion on the floor.

"Ten seconds, no more," I admonished. Survival was a harsh taskmaster. What had seemed like a good idea at the time maybe really was a good idea. But right now I was very sorry I had ever seen the newsflash.

Ceremonial opening of new Mint on Paskönjak . . . planet often called Mintworld . . . first half-million-credit coins ever issued . . . dignitaries and press invited.

It had been like the sound of the starting gun to a sprinter. I was off. A week later I was stepping out of the space terminal on Paskönjak, bag in hand and forged press credentials in pocket. Even the massed troops and tough security had not tempered my madness. The machines in my case were immune from detection by any known security apparatus; the case projected a totally false image of its contents when radiation hit it. My step had been light, my smile broad.

Now my face was ashen and my legs trembled with fatigue as I pushed myself to my feet.

"Look calm, look collected—think innocence."

I swallowed a calm-and-collected pill that was coated with instant uppers. One, two, three paces to the door, my face flushed with pride, my gait noble, my conscience pure.

I put on my funky bejeweled spectacles and looked through the door. The ultrasound image was fuzzy. But clear enough to reveal figures hurrying past. When they were gone I unlocked the door, slipped through and let it close behind me.

Saw the rest of my party of journalists being pushed down the corridor by screaming, gun-waving troops. Turned and marched firmly away in the opposite direction and around the bend.

The guard stationed there lowered his gun and pointed it at my belt buckle.

"La necesejo estas ĉi tie?" I said, smiling smarmily.

"What you say? What you doin' here?"

"Indeed?" I snorted through widened nostrils. "Rather short on education, particularly a knowledge of Esperanto, aren't we? If you must know, speaking in the vulgar argot of this planet—I was told that the men's room was down here."

"Well it ain't. Da udder way."

"You're too kind."

I turned and strolled diffidently down the hall. Had taken three steps before reality penetrated his sluggish synapses.

"Come back here, you!"

I stopped and turned about, pointed past him. "Down that way?" I asked. The gas projector I had palmed when my back was turned towards him hissed briefly. His eyes closed and he dropped; I took the gun from his limp hands as he fell by. Placed it on his sleeping chest since it was of no help to me. Walked briskly past him and pushed open the door to the emergency stairs. Closed and leaned against it and breathed very deeply. Then took out the map that had been in the press kit and poked my finger on the symbol for stairs. Now, down to the storeroom . . . footsteps sounded below.

Up. Quietly on soft soles. A change of plan was very much in order since the alarm had sounded, ruling out a simple exit with the crowd. Up, five, six flights until the steps ended in a door labeled KROV. Which probably meant roof in the local language.

There were three different alarms that I disabled before I pushed the door open and slipped through. Looked around at the usual rooftop clutter: water tanks, vents, aircon units—and a good-sized smokestack puffing out pollution. Perfect.

The moneybag clunked as I dropped all my incriminating weapons and tools into it. My belt buckle twisted open and I took out the reel and motor. Attached the molebind plug from the suspension cord to the bag, then lowered it all down the chimney. Reaching down as far as I could I secured the reel mechanism to the inside of the pipe.

Done. It would wait there as long as needed, until all the excitement calmed down. An investment waiting to be collected you might say. Then, armed only with my innocence, I retraced my course back down the stairs and on to the ground floor.

The door opened and closed silently and there was a guard, back turned, standing close enough to touch. Which I did, tapping him on the shoulder. He shrieked, jumped aside, turned, lifted his gun.

"Didn't mean to startle you," I said sweetly. "Afraid I got separated from my party. The press group . . ."

"Sergeant, I got someone," he burbled into the microphone on his shoulder. "Me, yeah, Private Izmet, post eleven. Right. Hold him. Got that." He pointed the gun between my eyes. "Don't move!"

"I have no intention of that, I assure you."

I admired my fingernails, plucked a bit of fluff from my jacket, whistled; tried to ignore the wavering gun muzzle. There was the thud of running feet and a squad led by a grim-looking sergeant rushed up.

"Good afternoon, Sergeant. Can you tell me why this soldier is pointing his weapon at me? Or rather why you are all pointing your weapons at me?"

"Grab his case. Cuff him. Bring him." A man of few words, the sergeant.

The elevator they hustled me to had not been marked on the map issued to the journalists. Nor had the map even hinted at the many levels below the ground floor that penetrated deep into the bowels of the earth. The pressure hit my eardrums as we dropped—about as many floors down as you usually go up in a skyscraper. My stomach sank as well as I realized I had bitten off a good deal more than I could possibly chew. Pushed out at some subterranean level, dragged through locked, barred gates, one after another, until we finally reached a singularly depressing room. Traditionally bare with unshielded lights and a backless stool. I sighed and sat.

My attempts at conversation were ignored, as was my press pass. Which was taken from me along with my shoes—then the rest of my clothes. I pulled on the robe of itchy black burlap that they gave me, dropped back onto the chair and made no attempt to outstare my guards.

To be frank this was a kind of low point, made even lower when the effects of the calm-and-collected pill began to wear off. Just about the time my morale hit bottom the loudspeaker gurgled incomprehensible instructions and I was hurried down the hall to another room. The lights and stool were the same—but this time they faced a steel desk with an even steelier-eyed officer behind it. His glare spoke for him as he pointed to my dissected clothing, bag, shoes.

"I am Colonel Neuredan—and you are in trouble."

"Do you always treat interstellar journalists like this?"

"Your identity is false." His voice had all the warmth of two rocks being grated together. "Your shoes contain molebind projectors . . ."

"There's no law against that!"

"There is on Paskönjak. There is a law against anything that threatens the security of the Mint and the Interstellar Credits produced here."

"I've done nothing wrong."

"*Everything* that you have done has been wrong. Attempting to deceive our security with false identification, stunning a guard, penetrating the Mint without supervision—these are all crimes under our law. What you have committed so far makes you liable for fourteen concurrent life sentences." His grim voice grew even grimmer. "But there is even worse than that—"

"What could be worse than fourteen life sentences?" Despite my efforts at calm control I could hear my voice cracking.

"Death. That is the penalty for stealing from the Mint."

"I haven't stolen anything!" Definitely a quaver now.

"That will be determined very shortly. When the decision was made to mint five-hundred-thousand-credit coins every precaution was taken to prevent their theft. Integral to their fabric is a transponder that listens for a specific signal at a specific frequency. It answers and reveals the location of the coin."

"Stupid," I said with more bravado than I felt. "Won't work here. Not with all the coins you have made—"

"All now safe behind ten feet of solid lead. Radiation proof. If there are any other coins not in our custody the signal will sound."

Right on cue I heard the pealing of bells in the distance. The iron face of my inquisitor was touched by a fleeting cold smile.

"The signal," he said. We sat in silence for long seconds. Until the door burst open and the hurrying guards dropped a very familiar bag onto the desk. He lifted the end slowly and the coins jangled forth.

"So that's what they look like. I never . . ."

"Silence!" he thundered. "These were removed from the minting room. They were found suspended in the chimney from the smelter. Along with these other objects."

"Proves nothing."

"Proves *everything*!" Quick as a snake he grabbed my hands, slammed them onto a plate on his desk. A hologram of my fingerprints appeared instantly on the air above.

"Any prints lifted from the coins?" he asked over his shoulder.

"Many," a spectral voice responded. A portion of the desk top rose up bearing what appeared to be photographic prints. He looked at them and for the second time I was treated to the sight of that frigid smile as he dropped the prints through a slot. A second hologram floated in the air beside the first, moved over and merged with it as he touched the controls.

The double image flickered and became one.

"Identical!" he said triumphantly. "You can tell me your name if you wish. So it can be spelled correctly on your tombstone. But only if you wish."

"What do you mean tombstone? And what do you mean death sentence? That's illegal by galactic law!"

"There is no galactic law down here," he intoned with a voice like a funeral march. "There is only the law of the Mint. Judgment is final."

"The trial . . ." I said feebly, visions of lawyers, appeals, torts and documents dancing in my head.

There was no mercy in his voice now, no touch of the tiniest of iceberg smiles on his lips.

"The penalty for theft in the Mint is death. The trial takes place *after* the execution."

Chapter 2

I am still young—and it did not look like I was going to get any older. My dedication to a life of crime had led to a far shorter lifespan than could normally be expected. Here I was, not yet twenty years old. A veteran who had fought in two wars, had been imprisoned and drafted, who had been depressed by the death of my good friend The Bishop, been impressed by Mark Forer the great Artificial Intelligence. Was that it? Had I had it? No more to life than that? All over.

"Never!" I shouted aloud, but the two guards merely gripped my arms the harder and pushed me along the corridor. A third armed guard went ahead and unlocked the cell door, while the one behind me prodded my kidneys with the barrel of his gun.

They were good and they took no chances. They were big and mean and I was small and lean. Shivering with fear, I was crouching even lower. Once the cell door was open the guard with the keys turned towards me and unlocked my handcuffs.

Then gasped as my knee caught him in the stomach and knocked him back into the cell. At the same time I grabbed the two guards beside me by the wrists, crossed my arms with a single spasmodic burst of effort that pulled the two of them crashing together; their skulls bonked nicely. At the same instant I lashed backward—catching the fourth guard on the bridge of his nose with the back of my head. Everything happening at approximately the same time.

Two seconds ago I had been bound and captive.

Now one guard was out of sight, groaning in the cell. Two more holding their heads and howling, the fourth one clutching a bloody nose. They hadn't been expecting this: I had.

I ran. Back the way we had come and through the still-open door. Hoarse, angry cries were cut off as I slammed it shut, locked it. The thick panel shook as heavy bodies thudded against the other side.

"Got you!" a victorious voice shouted and rough hands grabbed me. He could not know by touch that I was a Black Belt. He found out the hard way.

Eyes closed, breathing easily, he just lay there and made no protest as I stripped him of uniform and weapons. Nor did he thank me when I draped my burlap robe over his pale form, hiding his black lace undies from prying eyes. His clothes were not too bad a fit. Not too good either with the cap tilting forward over my eyes. But it would have to do.

There were three doors leading from this room. The one that I had locked was pounding and bouncing in its frame: next to it was the one that we had come in through. It didn't take much intelligence to use the unconscious guard's keys to open the third one.

It led to a storage room. Dark shelves, filled with nameless objects, vanished away into the distance. Not too promising—but I was in no position to choose. I executed a quick leap back to the entrance door, unlocked it and threw it open, then dived ahead into the storage room. As I closed this final door behind me, even before I could lock it, there was a mighty crash and screams of anger as the assaultees finally broke the door down.

Misdirection wouldn't last long. Run past the shelves. Hide here? No—there would be a thorough search. A door at the far end, bolted on the inside. I opened it a crack and looked at the empty room beyond. Opened and stepped through.

And stopped quite still as the guards who were flattened against the wall all pointed guns at me.

"Shoot him!" Colonel Neuredan ordered.

"I'm unarmed!" My gun slid across the floor as I threw my hands into the air. Fingers quivered on triggers—it was all over.

"Don't shoot—I want him alive. For the moment."

I stood frozen, not breathing until the trigger fingers relaxed. Looked up and quickly found the security bug in the ceiling. Must be one in every room and corridor down here. They had been watching me all the time. A good try, Jim. The Colonel grated his teeth horribly and stabbed a finger in my direction.

"Take him. Chain him. Bind him. Bring him."

This was all done with ruthless efficiency. My toes dragged along the floor as I was whisked back to the cell, stripped at gunpoint, thrown to the floor with my black robe thrown on top of me. The door clanged shut and I was alone. Very much alone.

"Cheer up, Jim, you've been in worse trouble before," I chirped smilingly. Then snarled, "When?"

Back in the pits again. My abortive attempt at escape had only gained me a few bruises.

"This can't be it!" I shouted. "It can't all end just like this."

"It can—and it will," the Colonel's funereal voice intoned as the cell door opened again. A dozen guns were pointed at me as a guard brought in a tray with a bottle of champagne on it and a single glass.

I watched in stupefied disbelief as he twisted the cork out. There was a pop and a gush as the golden fluid filled the glass. He handed it to me.

"What's this, what's this?" I mumbled, staring wide-eyed at the rising bubbles.

"Your last request," Neuredan said. "That and a cigarette."

He took one from a package and lit it, holding it out to me. I shook my head. "I don't smoke." He ground the cigarette under his heel. "Anyway—champagne and a cigarette—that's not *my* last request."

"Yes it is. Forms of last request are standardized by law. Drink."

I drank. It tasted all right. I belched and handed back the glass. "I'll take a refill." Anything to gain time, to think. I watched the wine being poured and my brain was dull and empty. "You never told me about the . . . execution."

"Do you want to know?"

"Not really."

"Then I will be pleased to tell you. I assure you that there was extensive deliberation over the correct method to be used. Thought was given to the firing squad, electrocution, poison gas—a number of possibilities were actively considered when the law was passed. But all of them involve someone pulling a switch or a trigger, and that would not be humane to the someone."

"Humane! What about the prisoner?"

"Of no importance. Your death has been decreed and will take place as soon as possible. This is what will happen. You will be taken to a scaled chamber and chained there. The entrance will be locked. After this the chamber will be flooded with water by an automatic device actuated by your body heat. It is always there, always turned on. You alone will be responsible for your own execution. Now isn't that quite humane?"

"Drowning is humane all of a sudden?"

"Possibly not. But you will be left a pistol containing a single bullet. You can commit suicide if you wish to."

I opened my mouth to tell him what I thought of their humanity, but I was seized by many hands and dragged forward before I could speak. The glass was whisked away—and so was I. Deep down to a dank chamber, walls damp with water and covered with moss. A cuff was clamped around my ankle; a chain ran from it to a staple in the wall. They all exited except for the Colonel, who stood with his hand on the operating lever of the thick, undoubtedly watertight, door.

He grinned in victorious triumph, bent over and placed an antique pistol on the floor. As I dived for it the door shut and sealed with a final thud.

Was this really the end? I turned the pistol over in my hands, saw the dull shape of the single cartridge. End of Jim diGriz, end of the Stainless Steel Rat, end of everything.

There was the distant thunk of a valve opening and cold water gushed down on me from a thick pipe in the ceiling. It gurgled and slopped, covering my feet, then quickly up to my ankles. When it reached my waist I lifted the gun and looked at it. Not much of a choice. The water rose steadily. Covered my chest, up to my chin. I shuddered.

Then the water stopped splashing down. It was cold and I was shivering uncontrollably. The light in the waterproof fixture revealed only stone wall, dark water.

"What are you playing at *bastardaĉoj*?" I shouted. "Humane torture to go with your humane murder?"

A moment later I got my answer. The level began to drop.

"I was right—torturers!" I bellowed. "Torture first—then murder. And you call yourself civilized. Why are you doing this?"

The last of the water gurgled down the drain and the door slowly opened. I aimed the pistol at it. I wouldn't mind drowning if I could take the cretinous colonel or the sadistic sergeant with me.

Something dark appeared through the partly open door. The gun banged and the bullet thudded into it. A briefcase.

"Cease fire!" a male voice called out. "I am your lawyer."

"He only has one bullet, you're safe," I heard the Colonel say.

The briefcase came hesitantly into the room, carried by a gray-haired man who was wearing the traditional gold-flecked and diamond-decorated black suit that adorned lawyers throughout the galaxy.

"I am your court-appointed lawyer, Pederasis Narcoses."

"What good will you do me—if the trial will be after my execution?"

"None. But that is the law. I will have to interview you now to enable me to conduct your defense at the trial."

"This is madness—I'll be dead!"

"That is correct. But it is the law." He turned to the Colonel. "I must be alone with my client. That is also the law."

"You have ten minutes, no longer."

"That will suffice. Admit my assistant in five minutes. He has the court papers and the will."

The door thunked shut and Narcoses opened his briefcase and took out a plastic bottle filled with a greenish liquid. He removed the top and handed it to me.

"Drink this, all of it. I'll hold the gun."

I handed him the weapon, took the bottle, smelled it and coughed. "Horrible. Why should I drink it?"

"Because I told you to. It is of vital importance and you have no choice."

Which was true—and what difference would it make anyway? I glugged it down. The champagne had tasted a lot better.

"I will now explain," he said, recapping the bottle and putting it back into his briefcase. "You have just drunk a thirty-day poison. This is a computer-generated complex of toxins that are neutral now—but which will kill you horribly in exactly thirty days if you are not given the antidote. Which is also computer-generated and impossible to duplicate."

He jumped back quite smartly when I leaped at him. But the chain on my ankle would not quite reach. My fingers snapped ineffectually just in front of his throat.

"If you will cease clawing at the air I will explain," Narcoses said with an air of weary sophistication. Had he done this kind of thing before I wondered? I folded my arms and stepped back.

"Much better. Although I am a lawyer licensed to practice on this planet, I am also a representative of the Galactic League."

"Wonderful. The Paskönjakians want to drown me—you poison me. I thought this was a galaxy of peace?"

"You are wasting time. I am here to free you, under certain conditions. The League has need of a criminal. One who is both skilled and reliable. Which is an oxymoron. You have proved your criminalistic ability by your almost-successful theft. The poison guarantees your reliability. Do I assume that you will cooperate? At the minimum you have a life extension of thirty days."

"Yes, sure, you're on. Not that I have a choice."

"You don't." He looked at the watch set into his little fingernail and stepped aside as the door opened. A chubby, bearded youth came in with a sheaf of papers.

"Excellent," Narcoses said. "You have the will?" The young man nodded. The door was closed and sealed again.

"Five minutes," Narcoses said.

The newcomer pulled down a zipper that sealed his one-piece suit. Took off the suit—and a lot of flesh with it. The suit was padded. He was not fat at all, but lean and muscular quite like me. When he peeled off the fake beard I realized that he looked exactly like me. I blinked rapidly as I stared at my own face.

"Only four minutes left diGriz. Put on the suit. I'll fix the beard."

The well-built and handsome stranger pulled on my discarded robe. Stepped aside when Narcoses took a key from his pocket, bent and unlocked the restraining cuff on my ankle. Handed it to the other, who emotionlessly bent and snapped it to his own ankle.

"Why—why are you doing this?" I asked him.

He said nothing, just leaned over to retrieve the gun.

"I'll need another bullet," he said. With my voice.

"The Colonel will supply it," Narcoses said. Then I remembered something else he had said just moments ago.

"You called me diGriz. You know my name!"

"I know a lot more than that," he said pressing the beard and mustache into position on my face. "Carry these papers. Follow me out of here. Keep your mouth shut."

All of which I was very happy to do. With one last look at my imprisoned self I trotted forth to freedom.

Chapter 3

I trotted behind Narcoses, clutching the papers and trying to think bearded and fat. The guards were ignoring us, watching instead with sadistic fascination as one of their number started to close the watertight door.

"Wait," the Colonel said, opening a small box and taking out a cartridge. He looked up as I passed, stared me straight in the face. I felt perspiration bursting from my pores. The momentary glance must have lasted about a subjective hour. Then he kept on turning and called out to the guard.

"Open that again you idiot! I load the gun *then* you close the door. When that has been done this business will be over with once and for all."

We turned a corner and the noxious group vanished from sight behind us. Silently, as ordered, I followed the lawyer through many a guarded portal, into an elevator, out of it and then through one final door, escaping the Mint at last. Letting out a great sigh of relief as we went past the armed guards and headed for the waiting groundcar.

"I—"

"Silence! Into the car. Speak to me in the office about a salary raise—not before."

Narcoses must know things that I didn't. Detector bugs in the ornamental trees we were passing? Acoustic microphones aimed our way? I realized now that my carefully planned crime had apparently been a disaster from the moment I had conceived it.

The driver was silent as a tomb—and about as attractive. I watched the buildings stream by, then the outskirts of the city appeared. We drove on until we reached a small building in a leafy suburb. The front door opened as we approached, then closed behind us apparently without human intervention. The same thing happened to the inner door, which was tastefully labeled with jewel-studded gold letters *PEDERASIS NARCOSES—Attorney at Law*. It closed silently and I wheeled about and pointed a menacing finger at him.

"You knew about me even before I landed on this planet."

"Of course. As soon as your false credentials were filed the investigation began."

"So you stood by and let me plot and plan and commit a crime and get sentenced to death—without making any attempt to interfere?"

"That's right."

"That's criminal! More of a crime than my crime."

"Not really. You were always going to be plucked out of that terminal swimming pool in any case. We just wanted to see how well you did."

"How did I do?"

"Very good—for a lad your age. You got the job."

"Well good for me. But what about my double—the bloke who took my place?"

"That bloke, as you refer to him, is one of the finest and most expensive humanoid robots that money can afford. Which money will not be wasted since the doctor who is now performing the postmortem is in our pay. The incident is closed."

"Wonderful," I sighed, dropping limply onto the couch. "Look, can I get a drink? It has been a long day. No spirits however—a beer will do fine."

"A capital idea. I will join you."

A tiny but well-stocked bar unfolded from one wall; the dispenser produced two chilled brews. I gulped and smacked.

"Excellent. If I have only thirty days to go shouldn't you be telling me about what you want me to do?"

"In good time," he said, sitting down across from me. "Captain Varod asked me to send his regards. And to convey the message that he knew you were lying when you promised to give up a life of crime."

"So he had me watched?"

"You're catching on. After this last criminal assignment for us you will become an honest man. Or else."

"Who are you to talk!" I sneered and drained the glass. "A crooked shyster who is theoretically paid to uphold the law. Yet you stand by and let the thugs here on Paskönjak pass legislation to have trials *after* an execution—then you employ a criminal to commit a criminal act. Not what I would call sincerely law-abiding."

"First," he said, lifting a finger in a very legalistic way, "we have never condoned the secret law in the Mint. It was only recently produced by the overly paranoid management here. Yours was the first arrest—and will be the last. There have been numerous job replacements already. Second," another finger rose to join the first, "the League has never condoned violence or criminal acts. This is the first occurrence and has been produced by an unusual series of circumstances. After great deliberation the decision was made to do it just this one time. And never again."

"Millions might believe that," I sneered disbelievingly. "Isn't it time you told me what the job is?"

"No—because I don't know myself. My vote was cast against this entire operation so I have been included out. Professor Van Diver will brief you."

"But what about the thirty-day poison?"

"You will be contacted on the twenty-ninth day." He stood up and went to the door. "It is against my principles to wish you good luck."

This was his puritanical pontificatory exit line. Because as he went out an elderly type with a white beard and a monocle entered.

"Professor Van Diver I presume?"

"Indeed," he said extending a damp, limp hand for me to shake. "You must be the volunteer with the *nom de guerre* of Jim about whose presence I was informed, who would await me here. It was very good of you to undertake what can only be called a rather diligent and difficult assignment."

"Rather," I intoned, falling into his academic mode of speech. "Is there any remote possibility that I might be informed of the nature of this assignment?"

"Of course. I have the requisite authority to provide augmentive information to you concerning the history and tragic circumstance of the loss. Another individual, who shall be nameless, will supply the assistance that you will require. I shall begin with the circumstances that occurred a little over twenty years ago . . ."

"A beer. I must have refreshment. Will you join me?"

"I abstain from all alcoholic and caffeine-containing beverages." He glared at me glassily through his menacing monocle as I refilled my mug. I sipped and sat and waved him into action. His voice washed over me in turgid waves and soon had me half-asleep—but the content of his talk woke me up fast enough. He went on far too long, with far too many digressions, but despite this it was fascinating stuff to listen to.

A stripped-down version wouldn't have been half as much fun for him and would have taken only a few minutes to tell. Simply, Galaksia Universitato had sent an expedition to a reported archeological site on a distant world—where they had uncovered an artifact of nonhuman origin.

"You must be kidding," I said. "Mankind has explored a great part of the galaxy in the last thirty-two thousand years and no trace of an alien race has ever been found."

He sniffed loudly. "I do not 'kid' as you say in your simple demotic. I have pictorial proof here, photographs sent back by the expedition. The artifact was uncovered in a stratum at least a million years old and resembles nothing in any data base existent in the known universe."

He took a print from his inner pocket and passed it over to me. I took it and looked at it, then turned it around since there was no indication of which was top or bottom. A twisted hunk of incongruous angles and forms resembling nothing I had ever seen before.

"It looks alien enough to be alien," I said. Looking at it was beginning to hurt my eyes so I dropped it onto the table. "What does it do, or what is it made of or whatever?"

"I haven't the slightest idea since it was never conveyed to the university. It was, I must say, interrupted in its journey and it is essential that it be recovered."

"Pretty sloppy way to handle the only alien artifact in the universe."

"That is beyond the scope of my authority and not for me to say. But I am authorized to unperfunctorily predicate that it must be found and returned. At any cost—which sums I am duly authorized to pay. Officers of the Galactic League have assured me that you, pseudonymous Jim, have volunteered to find and return the artifact. They have convinced me that you, as young as you are, are a specialist in these matters. I can only wish you best of luck—and look forward to meeting you again when you return with that which we desire the most."

He exited then and a bald, uniformed naval officer entered in his place. Closed the door and glared at me with a steely gaze. I glared back.

"Are you the one who is finally going to tell me what is going on?" I asked.

"Damn right," he growled. "Damn fool idea—but the only one we have going. I am Admiral Benbow, head of League Navy Security. Those dumbhead academics let the most priceless object in the universe slip through their fingers—now we have to pick up the pieces and run with the ball."

The Admiral's mixed metaphors were as bad as the professor's academese. Was clear speaking becoming a lost art?

"Come on," I said. "Simply tell me what happened and what I am supposed to do."

"Right." He slammed down into a chair. "If that is a beer I'll have one too. No I won't. A double, no a treble high-octane whisky. No ice. Do it."

The robobar supplied our drinks. He drained his while I was just lifting mine.

"Now hear this. The expedition concerned was returning from their planetary dig when their ship experienced communication difficulties. Worried about navigation they landed on the nearest planet, which unhappily and tragically turned out to be Liokukae."

"Why unhappily and tragically?"

"Shut up and listen. We got them and their ship back relatively intact. But without the artifact. For certain reasons we could do no more. That is why your services have been engaged."

"So now you are going to tell me about those certain reasons."

He coughed and looked away, stood and refilled his glass before speaking again. If I didn't know better I would have said that the seasoned old space dog was embarrassed.

"You have to understand that keeping the galactic peace is our role and our goal. This is not always possible. There are sometimes individuals, even groups, that are impervious to our attentions. Violent people, some apparently incurably insane, obnoxious. Despite everything that we can do they remain immune to our blandishments, impervious to our help." He gulped down the dregs and I had the feeling that we were finally getting to the truth.

"Since we cannot kill them we—and you realize only the highest authorities know what I am about to tell you—we so to speak arrange, see to it that they are, well, transported to Liokukae to live the sort of life they prefer to live. Without endangering the peaceful cultures of the union—"

"A galactic garbage dump!" I cried aloud. "Where you holier-than-thou bigots sweep your failures under the carpet! No wonder you keep this a top-secret secret."

"Just knock off the superior attitude cagal, diGriz. I know your record—and in my book it stinks. But we have you by the short and curlies since you drank the seven-hundred-and-twenty-hour poison, so you will do just as I say. So now I'm going to fill you in with all the loathsome details re Liokukae, let you see what information we have. Then you will come up with a plan for getting that thing back. You have no choice."

"Thanks. What resources do I have?"

"Limitless resources, unrestricted funds, boundless support. Every planet in the galaxy contributes to Galaksia Universitato. They have so many credits that they make the super-rich look super-poor. I want you to take them to the cleaners."

"Now you are talking my language! For the first time I have some interest in this poisonous project. Bring on the records—and some food—and I will see what I can do."

Not very much I thought to myself after hours of reading and rereading the thin file, while eating a number of stale and tasteless sandwiches. The Admiral was slumped asleep in the armchair and snoring like a rocket exhaust. There were no answers here, so some questions were very much in order. Which gave me the sweet pleasure of waking him up. A few good shakes did it and those nasty little red eyes glared into mine.

"You better have a good reason for that."

"I do. How much do you personally know about Liokukae?"

"Everything, you dimwit. That is why I am here."

"It seems to be pretty tightly sealed up."

"Pretty tightly is not the way I would describe it. Hermetically sealed, guarded, patrolled, watched, locked tight, quarantined—take your pick. Food and medicines are shipped in. Nothing comes out."

"Do they have their own doctors?"

"No. Medical teams are stationed there in the hospital inside the landing station—which is built like a fortress. And before you even ask—the answer is no. What little trust there is between the Navy and the Liokukaers involves the medical services. They come to us and we treat them. Let them suspect for an instant that the medicos are involved in hanky-panky and the trust is gone. Disease and death would be certain. We're not taking a chance on that."

"If the rest of the civilized galaxy doesn't know about them—what do they know about us?"

"Everything I suppose. We do not practice censorship. We transmit all the usual TV entertainment channels as well as educational and news services. They are well supplied with television receivers and can watch reruns of all the most loathsome programs and series. The theory being if we can stun their minds with televised crap they won't get up to more trouble."

"Does it work?"

"Possibly. But we do know that they are rated on top of the galactic viewing scale for uninterrupted hours in front of the gogglebox."

"You go there and take surveys?"

"Don't be stupid. Recorders are sealed into the chassis of each set. These can be tapped by satellite."

"So what we have here is a planet of murderous, belligerent, nutsy TV fans?"

"That's about the size of it."

I jumped to my feet, spilling dry crumbs of dead sandwiches onto the carpet. Raised my fists, and my voice, on high.

"That's it!"

Benbow blinked at me rapidly and scowled.

"What's it?"

"The answer. It is just the glimmering of an idea now—but I know that it will grow and expand into something incredible. I'm going to sleep on it and when I awake I will polish it and perfect it and describe it to you in detail."

"What is it?"

"Don't be greedy. All in good time."

Chapter 4

The automated kitchen produced another stale sandwich, the machine was half-knackered and out of adjustment, along with a lukewarm cup of watery cocoa. I crunched and sipped gloomily, then found the bedroom down the hall. Air-conditioned of course—but the window wasn't sealed. I opened it and sniffed the cool night air. The moon was rising, to join the other three already up. Made for some interesting shadows. A leg over the windowsill, a drop into the garden—and I would be long gone before any alarm might go off.

And I would be dead in twenty-nine days. That little drink I had drunk in prison really concentrated my attention and guaranteed my loyalty. But could I pull this complicated operation off in that space of time?

Considering the consequences I had no choice. I sighed tremulously, closed the window and went to bed. It had been a very, very long day.

In the morning I had picked the lock on the control panel in the kitchen and was busy rewiring it when Admiral Benbow came in.

"May I inquire politely just what the hell you are doing?"

"Obviously trying to get this crook device to produce something other than stale cheese sandwiches. There!"

I slammed the panel shut and punched in a command. A cup of steaming coffee instantly appeared. Followed by a porcuswinewich, steaming and juicy. The Admiral nodded.

"I'll take this one—get another for yourself. Now tell me your plan."

I did. Mumbling through mouthfuls of breakfast.

"We are going to spend some credits out of the mountains of money that we have access to. First we plant some news items. I want interviews, reviews, gossip and more—all about the new pop group that is the hit of the galaxy."

He scowled and growled. "What pop group? What in Hades are you talking about?"

"The planet-busting hit group called . . ."

"Called what?"

"I don't know. I haven't thought about it yet. Something way out and memorable. Or kinky." I smiled and raised an inspired finger. "I have it! Ready? The group is called . . . The Stainless Steel Rats!"

"Why?"

"Why not?"

The Admiral was not happy. His scowl turned to a snarl and he jabbed a judgmental finger at me. "More coffee. Then tell me what you are talking about or I will kill you."

"Temper, temper, Admiral. Remember the old blood pressure. What I am talking about is getting to Liokukae with all the equipment I need, along with some strong-armed help. We are going to form a group of musicians called The Stainless Steel Rats—"

"What musicians?"

"Me for one—and you are going to supply me with the rest. You did tell me that you were head of League Navy Security?"

"I did. I am."

"Then summon your troops. Get one of your techs to research all your field operators, all your rankings who have ever served in what passes for action in this civilized universe. The search will be a simple one because we want to know just one single fact about all of them. Are they musically inclined? Can they play a musical instrument, sing, dance, whistle or even hum in tune? Get the list and we will have our band."

He nodded over his coffee. "You're beginning to make sense. A pop group composed only of security agents. But it will take time to put together, to organize, to rehearse."

"Why?"

"So it will sound good, you moron."

"Who could tell the difference? Have you ever listened to country-and-coal-mining music? Or Aqua Regia and her Plutonium Pals?"

"Point taken. So we get this group together and publicize them well so all Liokukae knows about them—"

"And has heard their music—"

"And wants to hear more. On tour. Which is impossible. The planet is quarantined."

"That is the beauty of my plan, Admiral. When the publicity peaks, and the fame of the group is galaxy-wide, that is when the Rats will commit some crime so awful that they will instantly be shipped off to this prison planet. Where they will be received with great enthusiasm. And no suspicion. Where they will investigate and find the alien artifact and get it back so I can have the antidote. One other thing. Before we start operations I will need three million Interstellar Credits. In coins that have been newly minted here."

"No way," he snarled. "Funds will be supplied as needed."

"You missed the point. That is my fee for conducting this operation. All operating expenses are on top of that. Pay up—or else."

"Or else what?"

"Or else I die in twenty-nine days and the operation dies and you get a black mark on your service record."

Self-interest prodded him into an instant decision. "Why not. Those financially overburdened academics can afford it and not even notice it. I'll get that list for you."

He unclipped his phone from his belt, shouted a multidigit number into it, then barked some brief commands. Before I had finished my coffee the printer hummed to life in the office; sheets of paper began to pile up in the bin. We went through them and ticked off a number of possibilities. There were no names, just code numbers. When this was done I passed the list back to the Admiral.

"We'll need complete files on all the marked ones."

"That is classified and secret information."

"And you are the Admiral and you can get it."

"I'll get it—and censor it. There is no way I am going to let you know any details of my Security Department."

"Keep your secrets—I couldn't care less." Which was of course an outright lie. "Give them code names as well as numbers, conceal their identities. All I want to know is their musical abilities, and will they be any good in the field when the going gets rough."

This took a bit of time. I went for a long jog to loosen the muscles. Then, while my clothes were being zapped clean in the vacuum washer, I took a hot shower followed by a cold one. I made a mental note to get some more clothes soon—but not until this operation was up and running. There was no escaping that deadly clock that was ticking off the seconds to doomsday.

"Here is the list," the Admiral said when I entered the office. "No names, just numbers. Male agents are identified by the letter *A* and . . ."

"Let me guess—the females are *B*?"

A growl was his only response, he completely lacked any sense of humor. I flipped through the list. Slim pickings among the ladies who ran the gamut from B1 to B4. Pipe-organ player, not very likely, harmonica, tuba—and a singer.

"I'll need a photograph of B3. And what do these other entries after B1 mean? 19T, 908L, and such."

"Code," he said, grabbing the sheet away from me. "It translates as skilled in hand-to-hand combat, qualified marksman on hand weapons, six years in the field. And the rest is none of your business."

"Thanks, wonderful, you're a big help. I sure could use her—but not if she has to carry the pipe organ on her back. Now let us make some selections from the male list and get the photos coming. Except for this one, A19. No photograph—I just want him here soonest, in the flesh."

"Why?"

"Because he is a percussionist and plays a molecular synthezier. Since I know next to nothing about music—he is going to teach me my job in this pickup band. A19 will show me the ropes, then record the numbers and set up the machines to play the different hunks of music. I'll just smile and press buttons. Speaking of machines—does your highly secret service have electronic repair facilities on this planet?"

"That is classified information."

"*Everything* about this operation is classified. But I'll still need to do some electronic work. Here or someplace else. All right?"

"Facilities will be made available."

"Good. And tell me—what is a gastrophone, or a bagpipe?"

"I haven't the slightest idea. Why?"

"Because they are listed here as musical skills or instruments or something. I'll need to know."

Lubricated by all the credits from the university, manned by the Admiral's minions, the machinery of my plan began to churn into high gear. The League did have an outpost on this planet—disguised as an interstellar shipping firm—which contained a fully equipped machine shop and electronic facilities. The fact that they gave me full use of everything meant that it would undoubtedly vanish as soon as this operation was over. While the auditions were being arranged, agent A19 was sent for by the fastest transportation available. He appeared, slightly glassy-eyed, later that same afternoon.

"You are known to me only by the code reference A19. Could you give me a slightly better name to call you by? And it doesn't have to be your own."

He was a big man with a big jaw, which he rubbed as he kicked his brain into action. "Zach—that's my cousin's name. Call me Zach."

"Right on, Zach. You have quite a musical record."

"You betcha. I worked my way through college playing in the band. Still do a gig or two from time to time."

"Then you have the job. You must now sally forth with an open checkbook and buy the best, most expensive and complex hunks of electronic music making that you can find. And they have to be the most compact and microminiaturized ones going. Bring them back and I'll make it all smaller since everything we bring with us has to be carried on our backs. If you can't find it on this planet use galactic mail order. Spend! The more you spend the better."

His eyes glowed with musical fervor. "Do you mean that?"

"Absolutely. Check with Admiral Benbow, who will authorize all expenses. Go!"

He went, and the auditions began. I draw a veil over the more repulsive details of the next two days. Apparently musical ability and military service were mutually incompatible for the most part. I whittled away and the list grew smaller with great rapidity. I had hoped for a large band—now it appeared that I had a tiny combo.

"This is it, Admiral," I said, passing over the abbreviated list. "We will have to make up in quality what we lack in quantity. It is going to be me and these three others."

He frowned. "Will it be enough?"

"Going to have to be. The discards may be great operators but I will dream about their sounds for years. In my nightmares. So take the survivors aside, tell them about me and the assignment. I'll meet them after lunch in the audition room."

I was setting glasses and bottles of refreshment on the table when the four of them trooped in. In step!

"First lesson!" I shouted. "Think civilian. Anything that even resembles the military will get us all quickly dead. Now—have you all talked to the Admiral? Everyone is nodding, good, good. Nod again if you agree to take orders from me and no one else. Even better. Now I will introduce you to each other. I have been forbidden knowledge of your real names and positions so I have invented some. Let us now begin the world anew. The gentleman on your left, code name Zach, is a professional musician and is tutoring me in my new skills. He will be of utmost help in getting this project off the ground. I am Jim and I will soon be able to play the electronic gadgetry and lead this group. The young lady in your presence, now named Madonette, is a contralto of great talent and our lead singer. Let's give her a big hand."

Slowly at first, then louder and jollier, they clapped until I lifted a hand to stop them. They were an uptight lot and I had to get them a lot looser. Madonette was fair of skin and dark of hair; a tall and solid girl and quite attractive, she smiled and waved in return.

"Good beginning gang. Now you last two guys, you're the rest of this group, Floyd and Steengo. Floyd is the tall and skinny guy with the artificial beard—he is growing a real replacement for it, but we needed one now for the publicity pix. The miracle workers of hirsutical science have developed an antidipilatorisational agent that stimulates hair growth. So he will grow a fine beard in three days. In addition to growing hair he plays a number of wind instruments which are, if you don't know, a historic family of musical instruments into which one blows strongly to emit sounds. He comes from a distant planet named Och'aye, which is perhaps galaxy-famous for its other native son Angus Macswiney, founder of the Macswiney chain of automated eateries. Floyd plays an instrument whose antecedents are lost in the mists of time and at times I wish they had stayed there. Floyd, a quick tune on the bagpipe if you please."

I had heard it before so was slightly more prepared as he opened the case and removed an apparatus that looked like a large and bulging spider with many black legs. He slung it about him, puffed strongly and pumped furiously on the spider's abdomen with his arm. I looked at the others and admired their horrified expressions as the screams of mortally wounded animals filled the room.

"Enough!" I shouted and the last slaughtered pig moaned away into deathly silence. "I don't know if this instrument will be featured in our recitals—but you must admit that it does draw attention. Last, and certainly not least, is Steengo. Who after he left the service became quite adept on the fiddelino. Steengo, a demonstration if you please."

Steengo smiled paternally at us and waved. He had gray hair and an impressive paunch. I was concerned about his age and general fitness but the Admiral, after secretly scanning the records, reassured me that Steengo's health was A-OK, that he worked out regularly and, other than a tendency towards slight overweight, he was fit for field conditions. I shrugged—since there was little else I could do. The records revealed that he had taken up the instrument after retirement from active duty—with talent in such short supply I had had the veterans' records searched as well. When approached he was more than happy to get back into harness. The fiddelino had two necks and twenty strings and sounded rather jolly in a plucking scratching way that everyone seemed to enjoy. Steengo bowed graciously to acknowledge the applause.

"That's it then. You have just met The Stainless Steel Rats. Any questions?"

"Yes," Madonette said, and all eyes turned her way. "What is the music that we will be playing?"

"Good question—and I think I have a good answer. Research into contemporary music reveals a great variety of rhythms and themes. Some of them pretty bad, like country-and-steel-mill music. Some with a certain charm, like the Chipperinos and their flock of singing birds. But we need something new and different. Or old and different as long as no one has heard the music in a few thousand years. For our inspiration I have had the music department at Galaksia Universitato research their most ancient data bases. Millennia have passed since this music was last heard. Usually with good reason."

I held up a handful of recordings. "These are the survivors of a grueling test I put them through. If I could listen for more than fifteen seconds I made a copy. We will now refine the process even more. Anything we can bear for thirty seconds goes into the second round."

I popped one of the tiny black chips into the player and sat back. Atonal musical thunder rumbled over us and a soprano with a voice like a pregnant porcuswine assailed our ears. I popped the recording out, ground it under my heel, then went on to the next one.

By late afternoon our eyes were red-rimmed with tears, our ears throbbing, our brains numbed and throbbing as well.

"Is that enough for the moment?" I asked sweetly and my answer was a chorus of groans. "Right. On the way in here I noticed that right next door is a drinking parlor by the name of Dust on Your Tonsils. I can only assume that is a little joke and they intend to wash the dust from their clients' tonsils. Shall we see if that is true?"

"Let's go!" Floyd said and led the exodus.

"A toast," I said when the drinks had arrived. We lifted our glasses. "To The Stainless Steel Rats—long may they play!"

They cheered and drank, then laughed and called for another round. It was all going to work out hunky-dory I thought.

Then why was I so depressed?

Chapter 5

I was depressed because it was really a pretty madcap plan. The idea had been to allow a week for our publicity to peak, for some musical awards to be made—then the crime had to occur. In that brief period we were not only going to have to find some music, but we would have to rehearse the stuff and hopefully gain at least a moderate level of ability. Some chance. We were cutting it too fine. We needed some more help.

"Madonette, a question." I sipped some more beer first. "I must admit to an abysmal ignorance of the mechanics of making music. Is there someone who sort of makes up the tunes, then writes down the stuff that everyone is going to play?"

"You're talking about a composer and an arranger. They could be one and the same—but it is usually better to divide up the jobs."

"Can we get one or both of them? Zach, as the closest thing to a professional here—do you have any ideas?"

"Shouldn't be too hard. All we have to do is contact GASCAP."

"Gascap? You want to fill the tank on a groundcar?"

"Not gascap. GASCAP. An acronym for the Galactic Society of Composers Artists and Players. There is a lot of unemployment in music and we should be able to locate some really competent people."

"Good as done. I'll get the Admiral on it at once."

"Impossible," he growled in his usually friendly fashion. "No civilians, no outsiders. This is a secret operation all the way."

"It is now—but it goes public in seven days. All we do is invent a cover story. Say that the group is being organized to make a holofilm. Or as a publicity stunt by a big firm. Like maybe Macswineys wants to change their image, go upmarket. Get rid of Blimey Macswiney and his alcoholic red nose, use our pop group instead. But it must be done—and at once."

It was. The next day an anorexic and pallid young man was brought to our rehearsal studio. Zach whispered in my ear. "I recognize him—that's Barry Moyd Shlepper. He wrote a pop musical a couple of years back, 'Don't Fry for Me, Angelina.' He hasn't had a success since."

"I remember it. The show about the cook who marries the dictator."

"That's the one."

"Welcome, Barry, welcome," I said walking over and shaking his bony hand. "My name is Jim and I'm in charge around here."

"Rooty-toot, man, rooty-toot," he said.

"And a rooty-toot to you as well." I could see where we would have to learn the argot of the musical world if our plan were to succeed. "Now—was this operation explained to you?"

"Like maybe sort of. A new recording company starting up with plenty of bucknicks to blow. Financing some new groups to get the operation off the ground."

"That's it. You're in charge of the music. Let me show you what we have and you put it into shape."

I gave him earphones and the player; I couldn't bear listening to these dreadful compositions yet another time. He plugged in the cubes one by one and, impossible as it was to believe, his pallid skin grew even paler. He worked his way through them all. Sighed tremulously, took off the earphones and brushed the tears from his eyes.

"You want like my honest and truly opinion?"

"Nothing less."

"Well then, like to break it to you gently, this stuff really sucks. Insufflates. Implodes."

"Can you do better?"

"My cat can do better. And scratch dirt over it."

"Then you are unleashed. Begin!"

There was little else I could do until the music was written, rehearsed, recorded. While all the others would play their instruments and sing, my work would be limited to throwing the switch before each piece. Then all of Zach's drums, cymbals, horns, bells and molecular-synthezier effects would burst forth from the loudspeakers in full gallop. While this was happening I would throw switches that did nothing, tinkle the keys on a disconnected keyboard. So while they got the music going I looked into the special effects.

This required watching recordings of all of the most popular groups, bands and soloists. Some of it was enjoyable, some horribly dreadful, all of it too loud. In the end I turned off the sound and watched the laser beams, exploding fireworks and physical acrobatics. I made sketches, mumbled to myself a lot, spent a great deal of the university's money.

And built an incredible amount of complicated circuitry into the existing electronics. Reluctantly, the Admiral produced the extras I asked for and I modified everything in the machine shop. It was altogether a satisfactory and fulfilling week. I also prodded the Admiral until he produced the promised payment of three million credits.

"Most kind," I said, jingling the six glowing five-hundred-thousand-credit coins. "A decent fee for a decent job done."

"You better put them in a bank vault before they go missing," was his surly advice.

"Of course. A capital idea!"

A singularly stupid idea. Banks were for robbing and for the tax authorities to keep track of. So first I went into the machine shop where I did some crafty metalwork before I packed, wrapped and labeled the coins. Then I went for a walk and, as a precaution, I exercised all of my considerable talents at avoiding observation to shake off any possible tails the Admiral had put on me. I was risking my life—in more ways than one!—for this money. If I came out of it all in one piece I wanted to have it waiting.

I finally reached a small country post office, selected at random, some distance from the city. It was manned by a nearsighted gentleman of advanced years.

"Spatial express and insured for offplanet delivery. That ain't gonna be cheap young feller."

"Do it, daddy-o, do it. I've got the gilt." He blinked and I translated back to his native language. "Payment is not a problem, dear sir. You must assure me that this gets to Professor Van Diver at the Galaksia Universitato at once. He is expecting these historical documents."

I had already spaciofaxed the professor that I was sending him some personal possessions, that he should please hold on to them until I came and picked them up. In case he got curious the contents were sealed in an armored case that would take a diamond drill to open. I was betting that his curiosity would not go that far. My package vanished into the mail chute and I went back to work.

At the end of the sixth day we were all pretty exhausted. Barry Moyd Shlepper had stayed up for two nights running, cold towels wrapped around his head, fortified by trebcaff coffee, putting together some musical numbers from the archaic junk. He proved to be a good hand at theft—or adaptation as he liked to call it. The group had rehearsed, recorded, then rehearsed some more. I had concentrated on costumes, props and effects and was almost satisfied.

After one last break I called my troops together. "You will be pleased to know that we will now give our first public performance." This produced the expected groans and shrill cries of complaint and I waited until they had died down.

"I know how you feel—and I feel the same way too. I think that the blues number 'I'm All Alone' is our best piece. You know we have had a lot of help from the staff here and I think we owe it to them to see what we all have done. I've invited something like thirty of them and they should be here soon."

Right on cue the door opened and the suspicious public employees filed in, each carrying a folding chair. Admiral Benbow led the way, his flag officer carried two chairs. Zach supervised the seating arrangements and our cavernous rehearsal studio became a theater for the first time. We retreated to the podium, where I dimmed the house lights, then hit myself and my electronic gear with a baby spot.

"Ladies, gentlemen, guests. We have all worked hard this last week and in the name of The Stainless Steel Rats I would like to thank you."

I hit a switch and my amplified voice echoed Thank You, Thank You. Overlaid by a growing crescendo of drums and ending with a crack of thunder and a few realistic lightning bolts. I could see by their wide eyes and dropped jaws that I had their attention.

"For our first number the melodious Madonette will render heart-rendingly the tragically lonely—'I'm All Alone'!"

At this the colored kliegs burst down on us, revealing our pink-sequined skintight costumes in all their iridescent glory. As we played the opening bars of the theme the lights concentrated on Madonette, whose costume had more flesh than fabric and seemed to be deeply appreciated. After a last whistle of wind and crash of thunder and lighting she extended her lovely arms to the audience and sang:

Here I am—and I'm all alone—
No one calls on the telephone.
I look around—and what do I see?
There's no one here but me—me—me.
  Me—me—me
That's all I see—
I'm all alone
Just
  me
    me
      me . . .

This was all done to the accompaniment of holographic shaking trees, storm clouds and other spooky effects. The music wailed as Madonette seguidillad into the rest of the song.

I'm all alone and it's very dark—
I sneak out the window to the park.
  The wind blows hard and the tree limbs wave—
  And I'm right before an open grave!
When I try to run and try to flee—
But I *KNOW* they're out there after me!
I sit and cry and I know that's right—
  Because the sun comes up—
  It's the end of the night . . .

With a last wail and a writhe of purple fog the sun rose majestically behind us and the music trickled to an end.

The silence stretched and stretched—until it was finally broken by a tumultuous applause.

"Well gang," I said, "it looks like we have done it. Or as Barry Moyd says, it looks like we are but really rooty-getooty!"

On the seventh day we did not rest. After a final round of rehearsals I called an early break. "Get some rack time. Pack your bags. The music and props are ready to go. We ship out at midnight. Transportation to the spaceport leaves here an hour earlier—so don't be late."

They shuffled out wearily with dragging feet. The Admiral stamped in as they left, with Zach trailing in his wake.

"This agent informs me that all preparations have been made and you are ready to embark." I could only nod agreement.

"Wish I could go with you," Zach said.

"You set it all up—you have our thanks for that. Now get going."

He numbed my fingers with his handshake and the door closed behind him.

The Admiral's smile had all of the warmth of a striking snake. "Drug Enforcement has come up with a crime so awful that it means an instant sentence to Liokukae."

"That's nice—what is it?"

"Misuse of a highly refined and expensive drug called baksheesh. You and the rest of the musicians have been caught smuggling it and are addicted to it. There is a medical cure for the addiction that leaves the victim weak and vibrating for a number of days. This should give you a little time to look around before you have to play your first concert. The press release has already gone out about your capture and your sentence to prison hospital for the criminally doped. The natives of Liokukae will not be surprised at all when you arrive there. Questions?"

"A big one. Has the communication been set up?"

"Yes. The coded radio built into your jaw can reach the receiver at the entrance terminal from any place on the planet. It will be manned all of the time and an officer will be listening in on all communication. Your contact on the ground will give you what aid he can before you go out of the sealed terminal. Then he will move to the spacecruiser *Remorseless* in orbit above, which will also monitor your radio. We can hit anywhere on the planet in a maximum of eleven minutes. Send the signal when you have found the artifact and the space marines will be there. Report at a minimum of once a day. Location and results of your investigation."

"Just in case we get blown away and you have to send in the second team?"

"Exactly. More questions?"

"One. Going to wish us luck?"

"No. Don't believe in it. Make your own."

"Gee, thanks, you really are all heart."

He turned and stamped away and the door swung shut behind him. Fatigue washed through me and black depression hit just one more time. Why was I doing this?

To stay alive of course. Twenty-two days more before my curtain fell for the final performance.

Chapter 6

The Faster Than Light voyage aboard the good ship *Remorseless* was blessedly brief. Being surrounded by the military has always had a deleterious effect on my morale. We had a solid day of rehearsal, some bad food, a good night's rest, followed the next day by a very nonalcoholic party—since the Navy was remorselessly teetotal. Then, a few hours before we were to meet the shuttle, the medics gave us the injections that were to simulate the aftereffects of our drug treatment.

I think I would have preferred the treatment. I didn't mind seeing my last meal go by for a second time, it had been pretty bad and I would not miss it. But the shakes and shivers were something else again. And all of my vibrating and stumbling co-musicians had eyeballs as red as fire. I dared not look in the mirror for fear of what I would see there.

Steengo was gray and drawn and looked a hundred years old. I felt a quick blast of guilt for dragging him out of retirement. Said guilt fading instantly when I thought about my own problems.

"Do I look as bad as you do?" Floyd said in a hoarse voice, his new-grown beard black against his parchment skin.

"I hope not," I husked in return. Madonette reached over and patted my shaking hand in what might have been a maternal way.

"It will be all right on the night, Jim. Just you wait and see."

I did not feel filial in return since I was rapidly developing a crush on her that I hoped I disguised. I growled something or other and stumbled away to the heads where I could be alone with my misery. Even this did not work for the speaker in the ceiling rustled ominously—then crashed out Admiral Benbow's voice.

"Now hear this. All Stainless Steel Rats will assemble at debarkation station twelve in two minutes. We are now in parking orbit. One minute and fifty-eight seconds. One minute and . . ."

I slammed out into the passageway to escape his voice but it followed me as I fled. I was the last to arrive and I collapsed and joined the others where they slumped on the deck beside our backpacks. The Admiral appeared suddenly behind me like a bad dream and roared his command.

"Attention! On your feet you slovenly crew!"

"Never!" I shouted even louder in a cracked voice. Rolling over to pull the swaying bodies back to the deck.

"Begone foul military fiend! We are musicians, civilians, medically reformed drug addicts and we must think and feel that way. Someday, if we live, you may have some of us back at your military mercy. But not now. Leave us in peace and wait for my reports."

He snarled a rich naval oath—but had the brains to turn on his heel and vanish. There was a ragged cheer from my companions which made me feel slightly less sordid. The silence after this was unbroken, except for the occasional groan, until distant motors whirred and the inner lock swung majestically open. A keen clipboard-bearing naval officer stepped through.

"Landing party for Liokukae?"

"All present, all ill. Send a working party for our gear."

He muttered into his lapel microphone, reached to the back of his belt to unclip a pair of handcuffs. Which he promptly snapped onto my wrists.

"Whasha?" I blurted incoherently. Blinking down at the cuffs.

"Don't give me a hard time, you drug-pushing addict, and I won't give you one. You may be a big man out there in the galaxy, but here you are just one more sentenced crook. Who is going to carry his own pack—no working party for the likes of you."

I opened my mouth to verbally assassinate him. Then closed it. It had been my idea that our mission be known to the minimum few. He obviously wasn't one of them. I groaned to my feet and stumbled into the airlock dragging my gear after me, the others following in like condition. The orbital shuttle ship was grim and cheerless. The hard metal seats snapped clamps on our ankles when we sat down; no dancing in the aisles this trip. We watched in silence as our backpacks were thrown into a storage bin, then looked up at the big screen on the front bulkhead. Lots of stars. They rotated and the bulk of *Remorseless* swam into sight, grew smaller and dropped behind as the engines fired. Then the pickup turned so that the growing bulk of the planet could be seen and we were treated to a scratchy and static-filled ancient recording of martial music. This died away and was replaced by a male speaker with a repulsive nasal whine.

"Now hear this, prisoners. This is a one-way trip. You will have resisted all efforts at adjustment that would have fitted you to live peacefully in our humane and civilized society . . ."

"Blow it out your rocket tubes!" Steengo snarled, running his fingers through his gray hair, perhaps to see if it was still there. I would have nodded agreement with his snarl only my head hurt too much.

"... brought upon yourselves by your own efforts. Upon landing you will be escorted by armed guards to the gates of the landing station. Your restraints will be removed and you will be given an orientation booklet, a canteen of distilled water, as well as a week's supply of concentrated survival rations. During that week you will look for small trees bearing hard fruit. These are the polpettone trees and a source of nourishment for all. Their fruit is the result of careful gene mutation and transplant, rich in animal protein. They should not be eaten raw because of the chance of trichinosis, but should be baked or boiled. You must remember . . ."

I wanted to remember nothing he said so I tuned him out. I tried to reassure myself that the normal condemned passenger on this flight must have done something pretty gruesome to deserve this fate. I wasn't convinced. Despite millennia of civilization man's inhumanity to man persisted whenever an opportunity presented itself.

The imaged clouds blew by and a massive five-sided building appeared on the screen. I supposed they called it the Pentagon.

"In a few moments we will be landed inside the walls of the Pentagon debarkation station. Remain seated until you are ordered to rise. Follow instructions and your passage will be made that much easier . . ."

I would like to make his passage easier! Then I relaxed and opened my fists. Very soon we would be away from weary wardens and on our own. That was the moment to be prepared for.

We shuffled out in silence, down the gangway—which surely should have been a gangplank—and into the thick-walled Pentagon. To be greeted by yet another naval officer, grim-faced and gray-haired, wearing dark glasses.

"Take the prisoners to Interview nine at once."

The petty officer of our guard protested. "Not regulation, sir. They have to—"

"You have to close your gob. Look at these orders. Do as instructed. You do enjoy being a petty officer?"

"Yes, *sir*! Prisoners this way!"

The officer came in after us, closed and locked the door, smiled at us warmly and said "Shut up" companionably. He then walked around the room with what I recognized as being a state-of-the-art communication detector. I couldn't imagine who would want to bug the room here at the end of the universe—but he was in charge. Satisfied he put the detector away and turned to face us and handed me a key.

"You can take the cuffs off while we are in this room. I am Captain Tremearne and I am your contact here. Welcome to Liokukae." He took off the dark glasses and smiled at us and waved us to the chairs. I could see now that a wicked scar slashed across his face and the bridge of his nose. He was blind. But could undoubtedly see fine with the electronic replacement eyes that had been fitted. They were gold-plated and gave him a highly interesting appearance.

"I am the only one here in the Pentagon who knows the real nature of your assignment here. You are all volunteers and I would like to thank you. Help yourself to refreshments because that is the last kind word you are going to hear for quite a while."

"What is it like out there?" I asked, touching the seal on a chilled container of beer and taking a life-reviving swig. There were fresh sandwiches and hot swinedogs there as well and my companions all dived in. I joined them, but not before I had opened a concealed drawer in my synthezier and taken out some necessary items.

"What's life like on this planet? Grim—and worse than grim, Jim. In the centuries that Liokukae has been used as a societal galactic wastebin there has been a rather deadly shaking down. Different cultures were formed here as like found like. Or violent men forced violent solutions upon weaker men. One of the most stable of these has been developed right outside the Pentagon. They call themselves the Machmen. Man is strong, woman weak, virility rules, strength through strength—I'm sure that you know the kind of thing. The top dog in this kennel, whom I am sure you will be meeting soon, is named Svinjar."

"Are these weirdos what the psych books call male chauvinist pigs?" I asked. He nodded.

"Absolutely correct. So do your best to keep Madonette out of sight. And practice walking on your toes and flaring your nostrils at the same time. If you can't think of anything else to do crook your arm and admire your biceps."

"Sounds a paradise," she frowned.

"Won't be too bad if you watch your step. They like to be entertained—since they haven't enough brains to entertain themselves. Very big on jugglers, duels, arm wrestling."

"What about music?" Steengo asked.

"Fine—as long as it is loud, martial and not sentimental."

"We'll do our best," I said. "But it is a group called the Fundamentaloids that I want to look for."

"Of course. As you have been told the spacer with the archeological expedition landed in their area of operation. I led the rescue party that took the expedition members out of here—which is why I am your contact now. The Fundamentaloids are nomads, as well as being pretty narrow-minded and obnoxious. I tried to keep things calm with them. Didn't work. In the end I narcgassed the lot and went in and pulled the scientists out. I didn't find out about the missing artifact until much later when we were offplanet and they were conscious again and the excitement had cooled down. By this time the group that had grabbed them had moved on and the trail got cold. Nothing more I could do at the time but report it. It's all in your hands now."

"Thanks much. Can't you at least point out to me on the map where they are?"

"Wish I could—but they're nomads."

"Wonderful." I smiled insincerely. Twenty days to deadline. *Deadline!* it would be. I shook off the dark feelings just one more time, looked around at my band.

"Ask questions if you have any because this is your last chance," Tremearne said.

"Do you have a map?" I asked. "I would like to know just what we have to face when we go out there."

Tremearne reached to the holo projector and switched it on. A three-dimensional contour map appeared in midair over the table. "This is a fair-sized continent as you can see. There are other continents on this planet, some inhabited, but they have no contact with this one. The artifact has to be somewhere here."

That really simplifies things, I thought to myself. Only one continent to search and about three weeks to do it in. I shook off the depression that was depressing my depression.

"Do you know who and what are out there?"

"We have a good idea. We plant bugs where we can, fly spyeyes pretty often." He tapped the plain at the center of the continent. "Here is the Pentagon with the Machmen close by outside it. The Fundamentaloids could be anywhere here on the plains, depending on the season. It is subtropical most of the year, but rainfall varies. They have herds of sheots, a very hardy ruminant, some kind of cross between a sheep and a goat. Now over here in the foothills is the closest thing that passes for civilization in these parts. An agricultural society with light industry that looks almost decent until you get close. There is a central city, right here, surrounded by farms. They mine and smelt silver and produce a coin called a fedha. It is the only currency on the planet and is used by almost everyone." He pulled a heavy bag out of a drawer and dropped it onto the table. "As you can well imagine they are easy enough to forge. In fact ours have more silver than the originals. Here's a supply for you. I suggest that you share it around and hide it well. A lot of types out there would be happy to kill you for just one of these. The people who mine the silver call their city Paradise—which is about as far away from a true description as you can get. Stay away from them—if you possibly can."

"I'll try to remember that. And I want to copy this into memory in my computer. Here."

I took off the small black metal skull that hung on a chain around my neck.

When I squeezed it the eyes glowed greenly and a pressure-sensitive holoscreen blinked into being; I copied the map, thought about what Tremearne had said—and realized for the first time what a sinkhole we were being dropped into. I had another question.

"So everyone out there is a nutcase or a weirdo of some kind?"

"The ones that were sent here for various crimes are. The ones who were born here grow up and fit in just as well."

"And you feel no compassion for them? Doomed by an accident of birth to existence in this worldwide spittoon."

"I certainly do—and I am glad to hear you express yourself so clearly on the subject. I never even heard of this world until the emergency. I got the professors off safely then looked around. Which is why I now head the committee that is working to clean up the operation here on Liokukae. It has been ignored for too long by too many stupid politicians. I took this assignment to see for myself. Your reports to me, along with your complete report when you return, will be just what we need to make this prison world a thing of the past."

"If you mean that, Captain, I'm on your side. But I hope you are not feeding me a line of old cagal just to get the job done."

"You have my word on it."

I sure hoped that he was telling the truth.

"I have a question," Floyd said. "How do we contact the Captain here if we need some help or such?"

"You don't—I do." I tapped my jaw. "I've got a microcommunicator implant here. Small enough to be powered by the oxygen in my blood. But powerful enough to be picked up by the big receivers in the Pentagon. So even if all of our goods are stolen—they can't get my jaw. So, I suggest strongly, we stick together at all times. I can talk with Tremearne through this thing, get suggestions and advice. But no physical contact or our cover is blown. If he has to pull us out the mission is over—whether we have the artifact or not. So let us be strong, guys and girl, and self-sufficient. It's a human jungle out there."

"No truer words ever spoken," Tremearne said grimly. "If no one else has any questions put the cuffs back on and you're out of here."

"Hell yes," Steengo said, climbing to his feet. "Let's get it over with."

Our packs were waiting for us in front of a massive and bolt-studded door. There were four shoddy little plastic bags as well, which probably contained our iron rations and water. An orientation booklet was tucked into each one. A backup force of guards with stun guns and porcuswine prods stomped up and glared obnoxiously while our manacles were removed.

"In there," the petty officer ordered, pointing to the anteroom in front of the exit portal. "Inner door is closed and sealed before the outside one opens.

You got only one way to go. Or stay in the room if you are tired of living. After five minutes the outer door closes and nerve gas is pumped in through those vents up there."

"I don't believe you!" I snapped.

His smile was without warmth. "Then why don't you just hang around and find out?"

I raised my fist and he hurriedly jumped back. The porcuswine prods sparkled in my direction. I raised my finger to them in the intergalactic gesture that is as old as time, turned and walked away from them following the others. There was a creak and a thud from behind us as the door swung shut, but I did not turn to look. The future, whatever it contained, lay just ahead.

We helped each other on with our packs, swaying dizzily with the effort. There was the thud of withdrawn bolts from inside the door, the growl of straining motors as it started to open.

Unconsciously we drew together as we turned to face the unknown.

Chapter 7

A splatter of rain blew in through the opening door. Welcome to sunny, holiday Liokukae. Which opened wider to reveal the group of very ugly-looking individuals who were waiting outside. They were dressed in an astounding variety of clothing—it looked like all the donations to charity in the entire galaxy had been sent here—and they all had two things in common. They were heavily armed with a mixture of clubs, swords, maces and axes. And they all looked very angry.

Just about what I had expected; I chomped down on the Blastoff capsule I had put in my mouth. I had never thought much of the weaklings-recovering-from-treatment plan and had palmed this pill in case it were needed. It was.

A wave of energy and power washed through me as the mixture of powerful chemicals, uppers, stimulants, adrenalins, swept away all the fatigue and shakes. Power! Power! Power! I swayed forward on tiptoes as Tremearne had advised, flaring my nostrils at the same time.

A great bearded lout swinging a crude but serviceable sword glared down at me. I glared back, noting that not only did his eyes meet in the middle but that his hairline also started at his eyebrows. When he shouted at me his breath frightened me more than he did.

"You dere, little boy. Gimme what you carrying. You all drop what you got or you get it."

"No one tell me what to do unless he can beat me, you illiterate cretin," I shouted back. The macho showdown with these macho mothers would have to take place sooner or later. Sooner was better.

He roared angrily at the insults, even though he could not understand them, and swung up the sword. I sneered.

"Big coward kill little man with sword when little man got no ax." I gave him two fingers to doubly amplify my feelings.

I hoped my simple syntax fitted the local linguistic profile because I wanted to make sure they all understood me. They must have, because Pigbreath dropped his sword and jumped towards me. I swung off my pack and stepped out into the mud. He had his arms out, fingers snapping, ready to grab and crush.

I ducked under them, tripped him as he went by to splat down into a puddle. He rose up, angrier than ever, balled his fists and came on more warily this time.

I could have finished it then and there and made life easier. But I had to display a bit of skill first so his mates wouldn't think that his downfall had been an accident. I blocked his punch, grabbed and twisted his arm, then ran him into the wall with a satisfactory crunch.

The blood from his nose did not improve his temper. Nor did my flying kick that numbed one of his legs, a stab with my knee that crumpled the other. Legless, he dropped to his knees, then crawled towards me on all fours. By this time even the dullest of the audience knew who had won this fight. So I grabbed him by the hair and pulled him up, hit his throat with the edge of my hand and let him keep going backwards, splatting down unconscious in the mud. I picked up his discarded sword, tested the edge with my thumb—jumped about so suddenly and menacingly that the armed men stepped away without thinking. I kept the momentum going.

"I got sword now. You want it, you die for it. Or maybe the smart bloke one of you what takes me to your boss, Svinjar. Guy what does dat gets this sword for free. Any takers?"

The novelty of the offer and their inherent greed warded off any attack for the moment.

"Get out of there and get behind me," I called over my shoulder. "And do your best to radiate obnoxious intolerance." Growling and gnashing their teeth my merry band emerged and lined up at my back.

"You give me sword I take you Svinjar," an exceedingly hairy and muscle-bound specimen said. He was armed only with a wooden club so his greed was understandable.

"You take me Svinjar *then* you get sword. Move it."

There was hesitation, dark looks, muttering. I swished the sword under their noses so they had to step back again. "I got something real nice in my pack for Svinjar. You betcha he kill any bloke stop him grabbing it soonest."

Threats penetrated where blandishments hadn't and we all moved off into the rainstorm. Along muddy tracks between collapsing hovels, to a small hill with a largish building made of logs, their bark still on, gracing the summit. I swung the sword so no one came too close, followed my guide up a stony path to the entrance with my weary musicians stumbling after. I was feeling a bit guilty about taking the Blastoff capsule. But things had developed too quickly to get some to the others. I stopped at the entrance and waved them through.

"In we go, safe haven at last. Take one of these as you pass and chomp it instantly. It is a super-upper that will restore you to the world of the living."

My club-bearing guide pushed inside and hurried past the groups of men who lolled about the large room, to the man in the great stone chair next to the fireplace. "You my boss, boss Svinjar. We bring them like you say." He swung about and stamped over to me. "Now you give sword."

"Sure. Fetch."

I threw it out the door into the rain, heard a yipe of pain as it bounced off one of his gang. He ran after it as I walked over and stood before the stone throne.

"You my boss, boss Svinjar. These guys my band. Make good music you betcha."

He looked me up and down coldly, a big man with big muscles—as well as a big belly that hung over his belt. Tiny piggy eyes peered out through the thicket of bristly gray hair and beard. The pommel of a sword projected from a niche in the stone chair and he touched it with his fingers, slipping it out then letting it fall back.

"Why are you talking in that obnoxiously obscene patois?"

"I do beg your pardon." I bowed deprecatingly. "I was addressed in that manner and assumed it was the local dialect."

"It is—but only among the uneducated imbeciles who were born here. Since you weren't, don't offend my sensibility again. Are you the musicians that got into deep cagal?"

"Word sure spreads fast."

He waved his hand at the 3D set against the wall and I felt my eyes bulge. It was a solid metal block with an armored glass face—with the aerial under the glass. A handle stuck out one side.

"Our jailers are most generous in their desire that we be entertained at all times. They distribute these in great numbers. Unbreakable, eternal—and four hundred and twelve channels."

"What powers it?"

"Slaves," he said and reached out a toe to prod the nearest one. The slave groaned and climbed to his feet, stumbled over, clanking his chains as he went, and began to turn the handle on the internal generator. The thing burst to life with a commercial for industrial-strength cat food.

"Enough!" Svinjar ordered and the meows faded and died. "You and your companions kept the news channels alive. When they said crime and hospital treatment I was rather convinced they meant here. Ready to play?"

"The Stainless Steel Rats are always at the service of those in control. Which, in this case, I assume is you."

"You assume right. A concert it is—and now. We haven't had any live entertainment here since the cannibalistic magician died of infection after being bitten by accident in the heat of passion. Begin."

By necessity all our gear had to be compact. The fist-sized loudspeakers contained holoprojectors that blew their image up to room size.

"All right guys," I called out. "Let's set up by the back wall. No costumes for this first gig and we'll start with 'The Swedish Monster from Outer Space.'"

This was one of our more impressive numbers. It had been found in one of the most ancient data bases, the lyric written in a long-lost language called Svensk or Svedish or something like that. After much electronic scratching about, one of the computers in the language department at the university had been able to translate it. But this lyric was so dreadful that we threw it away and sang it in the original, which was far more interesting.

Ett fasanfullt monster med rumpan bar
kryper in till en jungfru sa rar.

There was more like this and Madonette belted it out at full volume to the accompaniment of my syncopated soundtrack, with Floyd knocking himself out on his blower-powered bagpipe. Steengo plucked at a tiny harp—whose holographic image stretched up to the ceiling. Sound filled and reverberated through the great chamber and dust was jarred loose from the log walls.

I don't think that this tune would make the galactic top ten—but it sure went down well here in endsville. Particularly when it ended with an atomic mushroom cloud that grew to room size—along with the best the amplifiers could do to simulate the atomic explosion itself. The part of the audience that wasn't collapsed on the floor had fled shrieking into the rain. I took out my earplugs and heard the light clapping of approval. I bowed in Svinjar's direction.

"A pleasant *divertimento*—but the next time you play it I would appreciate a little less *forza* in the finale and a little more *riposo*."

"Your slightest wish is our command."

"For a young and simple-looking lad you learn fast. How come you were caught pushing drugs?"

"It's a long story—"

"Shorten it. To one word if possible."

"Money."

"Understandable. Then the music business isn't that good?"

"It smells like one of your bully-boys. If you can stay up there with the big ones, fine. But we slipped from the top notch some time ago. What with recording fees, agents' commissions, kickbacks and bribes we were quickly going bust. Steengo and Floyd have been snorting back baksheesh for years. They started selling it to support the habit. It's nice stuff. End of story."

"Or beginning of a new one. Your singer, what's her name?" He smiled a very unwholesome smile as he looked over at Madonette. I groped for inspiration. Came up with the best I could do at such short notice.

"You mean my wife, Madonette . . ."

"Wife? How inconvenient. I am sure that something can be done about that, though not exactly at this moment. Your arrival is, to say the least, most timely. Fits in with what you might call a general plan of action I was considering. For the general good of the populace."

"Indeed," I said, controlling my enthusiasm for any plan of his that might be forthcoming.

"Yes, indeed. A concert for the public. Barbecues and free drinks. The public will see Svinjar as a benefactor of the first order. I gather that you are prepared to play a benefit performance?"

"That's what we are here for."

Among other things that we are here for, Svinjar old chubkin. But the longest journey begins with but a single step.

Chapter 8

I'm not happy about the way this operation is going," I said unhappily. Spooning up the almost tasteless gruel that appeared to be the staff of life in this place.

"Who's arguing?" Steengo said, looking suspiciously into his own bowl of food. "This stuff not only looks like glue—it tastes like it."

"It will stick to your ribs," Floyd said and I gaped. Did he have a sense of humor after all? Probably not. Looking at his serious expression I doubted if he had explored all the meanings of what he had just said. I let it lie.

"I'm not only unhappy with this operation so far—but with the company we have been keeping. Svinjar and his loathsome lads. We've shot almost a day here already—for little purpose. If the artifact is with the Fundamentaloids we ought to be out there tracking them down."

"But you promised a concert," Madonette pointed out with a certain logic. "They are building a sort of bandstand and the word has gone out. You don't want to let our fans down, do you?"

"Heaven forbid," I muttered gruelly and put the bowl aside. I couldn't tell them about the thirty-day poison or the fact that as of the moment twenty days had passed. Oh the hell with it. "Let's get set up. Maybe a quick rehearsal to see if all the gear is working and, hopefully, we are still in good form."

We put lunch aside with a great deal of pleasure and humped our packs to the concert site. There was a grove of trees here that were serving as supports for a singularly crude platform. Planks had been set up between them, with an occasional support stuck in below if the thing sagged too much. Our audience was reluctantly and suspiciously gathering in the surrounding field. Small family units with the men all armed with swords or cudgels, keeping close watch on the womenfolk. Well, this was a slave-holding society so such concern was easily understood.

"At least they are trying to make it look nice," Madonette said, pointing. Pretty crude and crummy, I thought, but spoke not my thoughts aloud. Shuffling slaves had brought up leafy branches which they were arranging around the platform, there were even a few flowers stuck in among the leaves. Oh, things were really swinging on Liokukae tonight.

I was depressing myself sorely and did not want to pass it on to the others. "Here we go, gang!" I said swinging my pack up onto the platform and clambering behind it. "Our first live performance for this waiting world. If you don't count that quick gig upon arrival. Let's show them what a pack of real rats can do!"

With our appearance the assembling audience took heart and moved closer; latecomers hurried to their places. While we tuned up and played a riff or two, I rolled some thunder effects that had people looking at the sky. When we were ready to go, Svinjar himself came trundling through the crowd, a couple of armed heavies at his side. With their help he climbed onto the platform and raised his arms. The silence was total. Maybe it was respect, perhaps hatred and fear—or all of them rolled together. But it worked. He smiled around at the gathering, lifted his great gut so he could hook his thumbs into his belt. And spoke.

"Svinjar takes care of his people. Svinjar is your friend. Svinjar brings you The Stainless Steel Rats and their magic music. Now let us hear a big cheer for them!"

We got a big murmur, which had to do. While he had been speaking his bully-boys had manhandled a sizable padded chair up onto the platform, it creaked when he dropped into it.

"Play," he ordered and sat back to enjoy the music.

"Okay, gang, ready to go!" I blew into my lapel microphone and my amplified breath gusted across the audience. "Well, hello there music lovers. By popular appeal—and the fact that we were busted by the narcs—we have come to your sunny planet to bring you the music known right around the galaxy. It is our very great pleasure now to dedicate this next song to the concert master himself, Svinjar—" He nodded acceptance and I rolled a drumroll out across the surrounding fields.

"A song that you will all know, and hopefully love, something that we can all feel, share, enjoy together, laugh together and cry together. I bring you our own and original version of that classic of modern musicality—'The Itchy Foot Itch'!"

There were shouts of joy, screams of pain, wild enthusiasm. As we launched into this overamplified and very catchy—if not itchy—number.

I get up at dawn and look at the river
The mist rising there it gives me a shiver.
    Leaves on the trees they're wet with dew
    Looking at them I think of you—
Far far away from me today
I don't like it—but all I can say
  Is the galaxy's wide and I like to stray
  To the stars and beyond 'cause that's my way
I got the—
Itchy foot, itchy foot, itchy foot itch!
Gotta keep going, never get rich!
Itchy foot, itchy foot, itchy foot itch!
Keeping me going, ain't that a bitch!
Itchy foot, itchy foot, itchy foot itch!
  Keeping me going from place to place
  Gotta keep going, what can I do?
Keep going forever—and I'll never see you.
Keep on going round the galaxy—no place is home
    For the likes of mee-ee-e-e!

There was a vast amount of itchy foot stomping, let me tell you. And plenty of cheers and cries of joy when we had finished. Buoyed up by enthusiasm we played two more numbers before I called a break.

"Thanks folks, thanks much—you're a great audience. Now if you will give us a few minutes we'll be right back . . ."

"Very well done, well done indeed," Svinjar said, waddling over and plucking the microphone from my lapel. "I know that we all have heard these musicians before—on the box—so their delightful entertainment comes as no surprise to us all. Yet still, there is something fine about having them here in person. I am grateful—I know that everyone out there is grateful." He turned and smiled broadly at me. A smile that, I could see quite clearly, held no warmth or humor at all. He turned back and spread his arms wide.

"I am so grateful that I have prepared a little surprise for all of you out there—do you want to know what it is?"

Absolute silence now—and a sideways shuffling by the audience. They apparently did not like any of Svinjar's little surprises.

They were right.

"Go!" he shouted into the microphone, so loudly that his amplified voice rolled and echoed like thunder. "Go—go—GO!"

I staggered and almost fell as the platform shook and vibrated. There was a roar of masculine voices as out from under our feet, brushing aside the disguising leafy boughs, burst a mass of armed men. More and more appeared, waving cudgels, howling as they ran, bearing down on the fleeing audience.

We looked on dumbfounded as men and women were clubbed to the ground, chained, tied. The attack was brief and vicious and quickly over with. The fields were empty, the last visitor gone. Those that remained were bound and silent, or groaning with pain. Over their moans of agony Svinjar's laughter sounded clearly. He was rocking in his chair, possessed by sadistic humor, tears rolling down his cheeks.

"But where—" Madonette said. "Where did they all come from? There was no one under here when we started the concert."

I jumped to the ground, kicked some branches aside, saw the gaping mouth of the tunnel. The opening had been concealed by a dirt-covered lid, now thrown aside. There was a heavy thud and Svinjar landed beside me.

"Wonderful, isn't it?" He gestured at the opening. "I have had my men digging that thing for months now. Stamping the removed dirt into the mud whenever it rains. I had planned a meeting here, some gifts, all very vague. Until you showed up! If I were capable of gratitude I would be grateful. I am not. The blind workings of chance. And victory to those—meaning me—who have the intelligence to seize the opportunity. Now a small celebration. We will have food and drink and you will play for me."

He turned and issued instructions, kicked one of his new slaves when she stumbled close.

"It would be nice to kill him," Madonette said. Speaking for all of us, if the nodding heads meant anything.

"Caution," I cautioned. "He has all the cards and the thugs right now. Let's play the concert and figure out how we can get out of here after that."

It wasn't going to be easy. Svinjar's oversized log cabin was filled with his men. Drinking but not drunk, boasting of their feats, drinking even more. We played a number but no one was listening.

Yes, Svinjar was. Listening and looking. Waddling towards us, silencing the music with a swipe of his hand. Dropping into his chair and fingering the hilt of his large sword embedded in the stone close by his hand. Smiling that humorless smile at me again.

"Life is a bit different here, isn't it Jim?"

"You might say that."

If he was looking for trouble I wasn't going to supply it. I didn't like the odds at all.

"We make our own life—and our own rules here. Out there in the androgynous, settled worlds of the galaxy, the effete intellectuals rule. Men who act like women. Here we hearken back to the days of the primitive, virile, important men. Strength through strength. I like that. And I make the rules here." He looked at Madonette in a singularly repulsive manner.

"A fine singer—and a lovely woman," he said, then looked at me. "Your wife you say? Can anything be done about that? Let me think—yes—something can be done. Out there, in those so-called civilized planets nothing could be done. Here it can. For I am Svinjar—and Svinjar can always do something."

He lifted one gross hand and tapped me on the forehead. "By my law and my custom I now divorce you." He heaved himself to his feet while his henchmen roared with laughter at his subtle humor.

"That is not possible. It can't be done—"

For his size he was fast, whipping out the broadsword from the niche in his throne.

"Here is my first lesson for my new bride. *Nobody* says no to Svinjar."

The blade slashed out to slit my throat.

Chapter 9

I jumped back to avoid the slash, stumbled over a man's legs, fell on top of him.

"Hold him!" Svinjar shouted and I was grabbed tightly, struggled to get free, couldn't quite make it.

Svinjar was standing over me, pushing the point of the sword into my throat—

Then he toppled sideways and fell with a great thud. Revealing the fact that Steengo, despite age and overweight, had jumped to the attack and was behind him, had dropped him with a chop to the neck.

What was happening had by this time sunk into even the tiniest of the birdbrains present. Men struggled to draw weapons and roared crude oaths. I saw Floyd laying about the warriors nearest him—but it wouldn't be enough. In about two seconds there was going to be a massacre of musicians if I didn't do something to stop it.

I did. First by planting my elbow in the solar plexus of my captor. Who gurgled and let go of my arms. One second gone. I didn't waste any time trying to stand up but writhed on my side and pulled the black sphere from my pocket, thumbed the actuator and threw it up towards the ceiling.

Two seconds. Weapons swinging on all sides. My best defense was to jam the filter plugs into my nostrils. The gas bomb popped and I spent a busy few seconds more dodging my attackers. Who moved more and more slowly until they dropped. When I looked around I saw that the gas had done a great job. The entire great room was filled with prone and snoring forms. I shook my hands over my head.

"Let's hear it for the good guys!" I had an audience of one, myself, which made the victory no less sweet. The sleep gas had hit my friends as well, though Floyd had been doing quite well before he dropped. A number of crumpled bodies were collapsed around him. I opened my pack and got the gas antidote; one by one I shot up my companions with the styrette. Then went to the door and stared gloomily out at the rain until they revived.

Soft footsteps behind me and Madonette held me lightly by the arms.

"Thanks, Jim."

"Was nothing."

"It was something. You saved our lives."

"We're still in it," Floyd said. "And like Madonette said, we owe you a good bit of thanks." Steengo nodded agreement.

"I wish you didn't. If this operation had been planned better all these emergencies wouldn't be taking place. My fault. I'm under what you might call a certain kind of time pressure. For reasons I can't go into right now we have to find the artifact and finish this operation within twenty days."

"That's not much time," Steengo said.

"Right—so let's not waste any of it. Our welcome has worn out around here. Grab weapons because we might have trouble getting out of town empty-handed. Packs on, armed to kill, ruthless and deadly expressions. Forward!"

After what had almost happened to us with Svinjar and his macho swinemen we were in no mood to be trifled with. It must have shown in our faces—or more likely in the metal of our weapons—because the few people we met slipped away as soon as they saw us. The rain had almost stopped and the sun was burning through and raising trails of mist from the waterlogged ground. The hovels were farther apart now, the mounds of garbage fewer and more easily avoided. Straggly little bushes began to appear, then trees and larger shrubs covering the easy slope of the rolling hills. Mixed in were low bushes from which hung hard-skinned spheres the size of a man's fist. Maybe these were the polpettone trees we had been told about. This would have to be investigated—but not now. I led on at a good pace, not calling a halt until we had reached the concealment of the first coppice. I looked back at the crude buildings, with the great bulk of the Pentagon rising behind them.

"No one seems to be following us—so let's keep it that way. Five-minute break every hour, keep walking until sunset."

I touched the skull-computer hanging from my neck and the keyboard snapped into existence. I summoned up the holomap, glanced up at the sun—then pointed ahead.

"We go thataway."

It was tiring at first, struggling up one hill and down the other side, then up again. But we soon left the trees and the rolling countryside behind and marched out onto a grassy plain. We stopped for a break at the end of the first hour, dropped down and drank some water. The bravest of us chewed industriously on the concentrated rations. Which had the texture of cardboard—if not the same exciting flavor. There was a grove of the polpettone trees close by and I went and picked a few of the spherical fruits. Hard as rocks and looking just about as appetizing. I put them into my pack for later examination. Floyd had dug a small flute out of his pack and played a little jig that lifted our spirits. When we stepped out again it was to a jolly marching tune.

Madonette walked beside me, humming in time with the flute. A strong walker, she seemed to be enjoying the effort. And surely a great singer, good voice. Good everything—and that included her bod. She turned and caught me looking at her and smiled. I looked away, slowed a bit to walk next to Steengo for a change. He was keeping up with the rest of us and did not look tired I was happy to see. Ahh, Madonette . . . Think of something else, Jim, keep your eye on the job. Not the girl. Yes, I know, she looked a lot better than anything else around. But this was no time to go all smarmy and dewy-eyed.

"How long you think until dark?" Steengo asked. "That pill you gave me is wearing off with a vengeance."

I projected a holo of a watch. "I truly don't know—because I don't even know the length of the day here. This watch, like the computer, is on ship's time. It's been a good long time since they threw us out the gate." I squinted at the sky. "And I don't think that sun has moved very much at all. Time to ask for some advice."

I bit down three times hard on the left side of my jaw, which should have triggered a signal on the jawbone radio.

"Tremearne here." The words bounced around clearly inside my skull.

"I read you."

"You read what?" Steengo asked.

"Please—I'm talking on the radio."

"Sorry."

"Reception clear at this end. Report."

"We were less than charmed by the Machmen. We left town a couple of hours ago and are hiking out across the plain . . ."

"I have you on the chart, satellite location."

"Any of the Fundamentaloid bands in sight as well?"

"A number of them."

"Any of them close to this position?"

"Yes, one off to your left. Roughly the same distance you've walked already."

"Sounds a winner. But one important question first. How long are the days here?"

"About one hundred standard hours."

"No wonder we're beginning to feel tired—and it's still full daylight. With the total daylight at least four times longer than what we're used to. Can you put your satellite to work looking back the way we came—to see if we are being followed?"

"I've already done that. No pursuers in sight."

"That's great news. Over and out." I raised my voice. "Company—halt. Fall out. I'll give you the other side of the conversation that you didn't hear. We're not being followed." I waited until the ragged cheer had died away. "Which means we are stopping here for food, drink, sleep, the works."

I slung my pack to the ground, stretched largely, then dropped down and leaned against it, pointed to the distant horizon. "The Fundamentaloid nomads are somewhere out in that direction. We are going to have to find them sooner or later—and I vote for later."

"Vote seconded, motion passed." They were all horizontal now. I took a good swig of water before I went on.

"The days here are four times as long as the ones that we are used to. I think that we have had enough of fighting, walking, everything for one day, or a quarter of a day, or whatever. Let's sleep on it and go on when we are rested."

My advice was unneeded since eyelids were already closing. I could do no less myself and was drifting off when I realized this was not the world's greatest idea. I heaved myself, groaning, to my feet and walked away from the others so my voice would not disturb them.

"Come in Tremearne. Can you read me."

"Sergeant Naenda here. The Captain is off duty this watch. Should I send for him?"

"Not if you are sitting in for him—and you have the satellite observations handy and up-to-date."

"Affirmative."

"Well keep looking at them. We're taking a sleep break now and I would like it to be undisturbed. If you see anyone or anything creeping up on us—give a shout."

"Will do. Nighty-night."

Nighty-night! What were the armed forces coming to? I stumbled back to my companions and emulated their fine example. I had no trouble at all in falling asleep.

It was waking up that was difficult. Some hours had slipped by because when I blinked blearily up at the sky I saw that the sun had passed the meridian and was finally slipping down towards the horizon. What had wakened me?

"Attention, Jim diGriz, attention."

I looked around for the speaker and it took long seconds before I realized that it was Captain Tremearne's voice I was hearing.

"Wazza?" I said incoherently, still numbed with sleep.

"One of the Fundamentaloid bands is on the move—roughly in your direction. They should be close enough to see you in about an hour."

"By which time we should be ready for visitors. Thanks, Cap—over and out."

My stomach snarled at me and I realized that the concentrated rations had been a little too concentrated. I drank some water to wash the taste of sleep from my mouth, then poked Floyd with my toe. His eyes snapped open and I smiled sweetly.

"You have just volunteered to go to those bushes over there and get some firewood. It is breakfast time."

"Right, breakfast, wood, wonderful." He climbed to his feet, yawned and stretched, scratched at his beard, then went off on his mission. I gathered up enough dry grass to make a small pile, then dug the atomic battery out of my pack. It would power our musical equipment for at least a year, so it could spare a few volts now. I pulled the insulation off the ends of the wires on a short lead, shorted them to produce a fat snap of sparks, pushed it into the grass. In a moment the grass was burning nicely, crackling and smoking, and ready for the chunks of dry branches that Floyd brought back. When it was good and hot I dropped the polpettone into the glowing ashes.

The rest of the band stirred in their sleep when the smoke blew their way, but didn't really wake up until I broke one of the fruits open. The skin was black so I hoped it was done. The rich seasoned fragrance of cooked meat wafted out and everyone was awake in an instant.

"Yum," I said, chewing on a fragrant morsel. "My thanks to the genetic engineers who dreamed this one up. Gourmet food—and growing on trees. If it weren't for the inhabitants this planet would be a paradise."

After we had dined and were feeling relatively human I made my report to them.

"I've been in touch with the eye in the sky. A band of nomads is coming this way. I figured that we should let them do the walking instead of us. Are we now prepared for contact?"

There were quick nods and no hesitant looks I was happy to see. Steengo hefted his ax and glowered. "Ready as we'll ever be. I just hope this lot is a bit more friendly than the first bunch."

"Only one way to find out." I bit down three times hard. "Where are the Fundamentaloids now?"

"Crossing a bit north of you—beyond those shrubs on the slight rise."

"Then here we go. Packs on, weapons ready, fingers crossed. Forward!"

We walked slowly up the hill and through the shrubs—and stopped in our tracks and stared at the herd passing slowly by.

"Sheots," I said. "The mutant cross between sheep and goats that they told us about."

"Sheots," Madonette agreed. "But they didn't tell us they were so huge! I don't even come up to their legpits."

"Indeed," I agreed. "Something else about them. They're big enough to ride upon. And if I am not mistaken we have been seen and those three riders are galloping our way."

"And waving weapons," Steengo said grimly. "Here we go again."

Chapter 10

They thundered towards us, swords waving, sharp black hooves kicking up clouds of dust. The sheots had nasty little eyes, wicked, curved horns—and what looked very much like tusks. I couldn't recall ever seeing a sheep or a goat with tusks, but there is always a first time.

"Stay in line, weapons ready," I called out, swinging my own sword up. The nearest rider, draped in black, pulled hard on the reins and his woolly mount skidded to a stop. He frowned down on me from behind his great black beard, spoke in a deep and impressive voice.

"Those who live by the sword shall die by the sword. So it is written."

"You talking about yourself?" I queried, blade still ready.

"We are men of peace, infidel, but defend our flocks against numberless rustlers."

He could be telling the truth; I had to take the chance. I plunged my sword into the dirt and stepped back. But was ready to grab it in an instant.

"We are men of peace as well. But go armed for our own protection in this wicked world."

He thought about that for a bit, made the decision. He slipped the sword into a leather scabbard, then swung down from his mount. The beast instantly opened its mouth—and those *were* tusks—and tried to bite him. He scarcely noted this, merely balled a fist and got the thing under the jaw with a swift uppercut. Its mouth clacked shut and its eyes crossed for an instant. It wasn't too long on brains either, because when its eyes uncrossed it had completely forgotten about him. It said *baa* loudly and began to graze. The rider walked over and stood before me.

"I am Arroz conPollo and these are my followers. Have you been saved?"

"I am Jim diGriz and this is my band. And I don't believe in banks."

"What are banks?"

"Where you save money. Fedha."

"You misunderstand my meaning, Jim of diGriz. It is your soul that needs saving—not your fedha."

"An interesting theological point, Arroz of conPollo. We must discuss it in some depth. What do you say we all put the weapons down and have a good chinwag. Put them away," I called out.

Arroz signaled his two companions and we all felt a lot better as the swords were sheathed, axes lowered. For the first time he looked away from me to my followers. And gasped, turned pale under his tan, and held his arm before his eyes.

"Unclean," he moaned, "unclean."

"Well it is a little hard to have a bath when you're on the trail," I told him. I didn't add that he wasn't that spic and span himself.

"Not of the body—of the spirit. Is that not a vessel of corruption among you?"

"Could you spell that out a little more clearly?"

"Is that . . . person a . . . *woman*?" He still had his arm across his face.

"The last time I looked she was." I moved sideways a bit, closer to my sword. "What's it to you?"

"Her face must be covered to conceal impurity, her ankles covered lest they promote lust in the hearts of men."

"This guy is a bit of a weirdo," Madonette said disgustedly. He yiped.

"And her voice silenced lest it lure the blessed into sin!"

Steengo nodded to Floyd and took the angry girl by the arm, but she shrugged him off. "Jim," he said. "The bunch of us are going to stroll back among the trees and have a break. See if you can sort this out."

"Right." I watched them leave and when they were out of sight looked back at the three nomads who were emulating their leader, all with their arms raised, as though sniffing their armpits. "It's safe now. Can we talk about this?"

"Return," Arroz said to his mates. "I will explain the Law to this stranger. Let the flock graze."

They trotted off while his own mount chomped away on the grass. He sat down cross-legged and motioned to me. "Sit. We must talk."

I sat. But upwind of him because it had been a long time since he or his clothes had been near soap and water. And he talked about unclean! He rooted about under his robe, had a good scratch, then withdrew a book and held it up.

"This book is the font of all wisdom," he intoned, eyes gleaming.

"That's nice. What is it called?"

"The Book. There are no other books. All that men need to know is in here. The distillate of all wisdom." I thought that it looked pretty thin for that job, but wisely kept my mouth shut. "It was the great Founder, whose name may not be spoken, who had the inspiration to read all of the Holy books of all of the ages, who saw in them the work of the god whose name may not be spoken, saw which passages were inspired and which were untrue. From all the books He distilled the true Book—then burned all of the others. He went forth into the world and His followers were many. But others were jealous and tried to destroy Him and His followers. That has been told. And it is told that to avoid this senseless persecution He and His followers came to this world where they could worship untroubled. That is why I asked—are you unclean? Or do you also follow the Way of the Book?"

"Most interesting. I follow a slightly different way. But my way believes in respecting your way, so don't worry too much about me."

He frowned at this and shook an admonitory finger at me. "There is only one Way, only one Book. All who think differently are damned. Now is your chance to be cleansed for I have shown you the true Way."

"Thanks a lot—but no thanks."

He stood up and stabbed an accusatory finger in my direction. "Unclean! Profane! Leave—for you soil me with your presence."

"Well each to their own opinion. Goodbye and good luck with your sheot shearing. May all your fleeces be giant ones. But an indulgence please—before you go would you take a look at this." I pulled the photograph of the alien artifact from my pocket and held it out.

"Unclean," he muttered and put his hand behind his back so he wouldn't touch it.

"I'm sure it is. I just want to know if you have seen this thing in the picture before."

"No, never."

"Been nice talking to you."

He did not return my friendly wave as he walked over to his mount, kicked it in the leg until it sat down, climbed aboard and galloped off. I pulled my sword out of the ground and went to join the others. Madonette was still simmering.

"Hypocritical narrow-minded bigoted moron."

"That and a lot more. At least I got one bit of negative information from him. He never saw the artifact. It must have been taken by another one of the tribes."

"Are we going to have to talk to all of them?"

"Unless you have any better ideas. And nineteen days to go."

"I don't trust him," Madonette said. "And don't sneer and say female intuition. Aren't these the same kind as the bunch that attacked the archeologists' ship?"

"You're right—and isn't that the clatter of hundreds of hooves coming this way?"

"It is!" Floyd shouted, pointing. "What do we do—run?"

"No! Out of the trees and onto the plain. Instruments at the ready. We are going to give these guys a concert that they will never forget!"

Arroz had gone back to rally the troops and at least thirty of them, with plenty of sword waving and maniac baaing, came charging down. I turned the amplification on the sound up until it would not go any higher.

"Earplugs in, get ready, on the count of three we give them old number thirteen, 'The Rockets Go Rumbling On.' One, two . . ."

On the count of three the explosion of unbearable sound blasted out. The lead riders were tossed to the ground as the sheots recoiled in fear. I flipped some smoke bombs among them, just to keep the action going, and hit them with holographed lightning volts.

It was pretty good. Before we got to the second chorus the stampede was over, the last terrorized sheots galloped away out of sight. The last black-robed Fundamentaloid crawled over the horizon, the trampled grass dotted with discarded swords, gobbets of fleece and myriad eightballs of dung.

"Victory is ours!" I whooped happily.

And only nineteen days to go I thought depressedly. This just would not do. I had the awful feeling that we could spend nineteen days or nineteen weeks stumbling about this planet and be no wiser about the alien artifact we were seeking. There had to be a change of plan—and now! I walked away from the others, then bit down three times, so hard that I almost cracked a tooth.

"Captain Tremearne here."

"And dismal Jim diGriz on this end. Have you been following all this?"

"Yes, and watching. I heard you ask him to identify the photograph. I assume that he did not."

"You assume right, distant and disembodied voice. Now listen, there has got to be a change of plan. When I came up with the idea for this present operation I assumed that there was some kind of imitation of civilization on this dismal world. Where we could stroll from gig to gig and do our snooping at the same time. I was wrong."

"I regret that all the facts were not supplied to you at the time. But as you are now aware there is a complete ban on information being circulated about this particular planet."

"I know that now—and it won't wash. We would have been a lot better if we came here disguised as a squad of combat marines. So far every bunch we have met has tried to kill us. The whole thing is that hardnosed Admiral Benbow's fault. He lied to me about what we would find here. Right?"

"As a serving military officer I cannot discuss the conduct of my superiors. But I can agree that whoever briefed you was, I must say, economical with the truth."

"Do you also know that he was economical with my health? And that in nineteen days I am going to keel over from time-released poison."

"Regrettably, I have been informed that that is the case. And you have eighteen days left now. You appear to have lost track of one day during the past period."

"Eighteen? Thanks much. That only makes what I have to say even more imperative. I need some help, some transportation."

"All contact with the planet is forbidden."

"I just changed the rules. You yourself told me that you are heading a committee to bring about major improvements here. The first change will be to get one of the ship's launches down here. With that I can get around to the various bands of sheot shaggers before my personal deadline runs out."

"If I do that I will be disobeying orders and it could end my career."

"Well?"

The silence inside my head went on and on. I waited. Until I heard what could only have been a sigh.

"I suppose there are plenty of job opportunities for skilled civilians these days. The launch will hand after dark. If it is not seen by anyone on the ground there is just a chance that my career change can be postponed."

"You're a good guy, Tremearne. My heartiest thanks."

I hummed a bar or two from "The Swedish Monster" as I walked back to inform my companions.

"Jim, you're wonderful!" Madonette said, grabbed and kissed me. "I much prefer flying to walking."

Floyd nodded happy agreement and reached for me.

"Away!" I shouted. "Girls, okay, but I don't kiss guys with beards. What we do now is put a little distance between us and those religious nuts in case they want to come back for seconds. Then rest up until dark. I have a feeling that it is going to be a very busy night."

Chapter 11

"Wake up, Jim—it's almost dark."

Madonette's gentle hand was most welcome, since it drew me up out of a really repulsive nightmare. Tentacles, bulging eyeballs, yukk. The eighteen-day dead deadline must be getting to my subconscious. I sat up, yawned and stretched. With great reluctance the sun had finally dropped behind the horizon, leaving behind a slowly fading band of light. The stars were coming out, revealing some pretty boring constellations—and very few of them at that. This prison planet must be far out on the galactic rim.

Then something blotted out the stars in the zenith as a dark form drifted down to the ground, silently on null-grav drive. The door opened as we approached—and the cabin lights came on.

"Turn them off, lunkhead!" I shouted. "You want to ruin my night vision." The pilot turned about in his seat and I grinned insincerely. "Sorry Captain, sir—that lunkhead, just a figure of speech."

"My fault completely," he said, and tapped one of his electronic eyeballs. "With these I forget. I'm piloting this thing because I have the best night vision in the fleet."

He flipped the lights off and we groped our way aboard with just the dim red emergency lights to show us the way. I sat in the copilot's seat and strapped in.

"What is your plan?" he asked.

"A simple one. You know the position of all the sheot flocks don't you?"

"Observed and logged into the launch's memory."

"Great. Have the computer do a topological survey to plot a course that will let us visit them all in the shortest amount of time. We drift over to the first flock, find one of the shepherds who is maybe out of sight of the others—and talk to him. Show him the photograph and find out if he has seen the thing. If he hasn't—on to the next bunch."

"Seems a simple and practical plan. Belts fastened? Right, first flock coming up."

We were slammed back into our seats and were on our way. High and fast on the plotted track. Then slow and drifting in low while Tremearne peered out into the darkness.

"There's one," he said. "On the far side of the flock—all by himself. Either to guard the beasts or keep them from wandering. I have a suggestion. I approach him from behind and immobilize him. Then you question him."

"Creep up in the dark? Immobilize an armed and watchful guard? That's a job for a combat trooper."

"Well how do you think I got these electronic eyeballs? It will be entertaining to do a bit of work again."

I had no choice but to agree. The Captain was proving to be an excellent ally. Working this way would be certainly a lot faster than me crawling around on my own. If he could do as he said. I had my doubts but kept them to myself. He was a gray-haired desk jockey with electric eyesight who might very well be past his sell-by date.

He wasn't. After we landed he stepped out the door and vanished silently in the darkness. Not thirty seconds later he called to me quietly.

"Over here. You can use your light now."

I turned on the handlight, it was really black under the almost starless sky, and saw two forms standing close together. The light revealed a bulging-eyed shepherd seized in an unbreakable grip, a hand on his throat keeping him silent. I waggled the light under his nose.

"Listen, oh shepherd who failed his duty. The hand that holds you could just as easily have killed you. Then we could rustle all your woolly flock and eat sheot shashlik until the end of time. But I will be merciful. The hand will be removed from your filthy throat and you will not shout or you really will be dead. You will speak to me softly and answer my questions. You may now speak."

He coughed and groaned when the pressure was released. "Demons in the darkness! Release me, do not kill me, tell me what you wish of me then go back to the pit from which you have escaped . . ."

I reached out and tweaked his nose sharply. "Shut up. Open your eyes. Look at this photograph. Let me know if you have ever seen it before."

I held the photo close, shone the light on it. Tremearne gave a twitch of emphasis to his arm and the captive moaned his answer. "Never, no, such a thing I would remember, no—" His voice gurgled into silence and he dropped unconscious to the ground.

"Don't these sheot shepherds ever wash?" Tremearne asked.

"Only on alternate years. Let's get to the next one."

We quickly worked out a routine. We would land and he would be away. Usually, by the time I had exited the launch, he would be calling me. Many a terrified shepherd slept soundly this night. But only after looking at the picture of the artifact. I dozed between visits and the back of the launch echoed with snores and heavy breathing. Only the Captain was unsleeping and tireless, seemingly as fit on the eleventh visit as he had been on the first. It was a long, long night.

I was getting groggy by the time we hit thirteen. Unlucky thirteen; get it over with and on to fourteen. Another set of bulging eyes peeking over the top of another matted beard.

"Look!" I snarled. "Speak! And moaning does not count as speaking. Ever seen this thing?"

This one gurgled instead of moaning, then yiped as his arm got twisted a bit further. It looked as though even the stolid Captain was beginning to lose his patience.

"Imp of Satan . . . work of the devil . . . I warned them, but they wouldn't listen . . . the grave, the grave!"

"Do you have any idea of what he is babbling about?" Tremearne asked.

"There may be hope, Captain. If he is not bonkers he might have seen it. Look—see! Ever see before?"

"I told him not touch it—death and damnation were sure to follow."

"You have seen it. All right, Cap, you can let up on the arm—but stand ready." I rooted in my pocket and took out a handful of silver cylinders, the local money, let the light shine on them. "Hey you, Smelly, look—fedha—and all for you. All yours."

This got his attention all right and I closed my fist tight as he groped for them. "Yours if you answer some simple questions. You will not be hurt—but only if you answer truthfully. You have seen this thing?"

"They fled. We found it in their skyship. I touched it, unclean, unclean."

"You're doing fine." I shook half of the coins into his waiting hand. "Now the ten-thousand-fedha question. Where is it now?"

"Sold, sold to them. The Paradisians. May they be cursed by it, cursed forever . . ."

It wasn't easy, but we finally worked all the details out of him. Stripped of all the curses and blasphemy it was a simple tale of larceny and chicanery. The spacer had landed—and been attacked as soon as the door had been opened. During the fracas the Fundamentaloids had trundled through the ship and grabbed everything portable, including the container with the alien artifact. They had carried the whole thing away with them because they had a job opening it. When they eventually succeeded they could not understand what it was. And ignorance meant fear. So they had unloaded it in the market in Paradise where almost anything could be sold. End of story.

We let the shepherd keep the money when we lowered him, unconscious, to the ground. "This calls for consultation," I said.

"Yes, but not this close to the flock. Let's get up to the plateau where the air is fresher."

The others were awake when we landed this time, listening closely to what we had discovered.

"Well this narrows the field a bit," Madonette said.

"Does it?" I asked. "How big is the population of this paradisiacal nation?"

"Around one hundred thousand," Tremearne admitted. "It may not be the best society on this planet but it appears to be the most successful one. I know very little about it, just photographs and observation."

"Doesn't anyone in the Pentagon know more?"

"Probably. But the information is classified and they aren't talking."

I cracked my knuckles, scowled and jabbed my finger at him. "That's really not good enough—is it?"

Tremearne looked as unhappy as I did. "No, Jim, it is not. I don't know why all that information is classified while your group is actually operating here on the planet. I have tried to get the information and have been not only rebuffed but warned off."

"Who is doing this? Any idea?"

"None—other than that it is at the very highest level. The people I have been in contact with understand your problems and want to help. But any requests that they pass on are turned down instantly and with prejudice."

"Am I paranoid—or is there someone in the chain of command who doesn't like this operation? Who wants it to fail?"

It was Tremearne's turn now to crack his knuckles and look glum.

"I've told you—I am a career officer. But I'm not fond of the situation here on this planet. Not only the way your group is being treated, but the whole ugly business. Well, I feel that it is getting away from me. At first I thought I could get some reform here by working through channels. It's not good enough. I am being blocked just as completely as you are."

"Who—and why?"

"I don't know. But I am doing my best to find out. About this city and the Paradisians I guess, basically, I know absolutely nothing."

"An honest answer, Captain, and I thank you for it."

"If you don't know—why then we'll just have to find out for ourselves," Steengo said. "Play a gig or two and keep our eyes open."

"May it be so easy," I muttered under my breath. "Roll out the maps."

It looked as though the largest part of the population was located in the single straggling city. Roads led from it to not-too-distant villages and there were scatterings of other buildings that might be farms. The only really puzzling thing about the 3D map was what looked like a wall that appeared to cut the city in two. There were no walls around the city, just this single one in the middle. I pointed to it.

"Any idea what this is—or what it means?"

Tremearne shook his head. "No idea. Looks like a wall, that's all. But there is a road alongside it. Which appears to be the only road leading in from the plain."

I poked my finger into the holomap.

"Here. Where the road fades and runs out in the grass. That's where we have to go. Unless anyone has a better idea?"

"Looks good to me," Tremearne said. "I'll land you on this bit of plateau, beyond this ridge where we won't be seen. Then I'll take the launch out of there and stay in touch with you by radio."

We unloaded. "Sleep first," Floyd yawned. "It's been a long night."

It was even longer than that, what with the longer days here. Tremearne took off and we settled down to sleep. We slept, and woke up and it was still dark. Slept some more. At least the others snored on: I had too much on my mind to drift off as easily as they did. We had a clue now to the whereabouts of the alien artifact. A clue that was useless until we started looking. And we couldn't look in the darkness. And I had—how many days left before the thirty-day poison zonked me? I counted on my fingers. Just about eighteen gone, which left twelve to go. Wonderful. Or had I counted wrong? I started again with the fingers, then grew angry with myself. Enough with the fingers already. I clicked on my computer and wrote a quick program. Then touched *D* for deadline—or death, whatever—and a glowing eighteen appeared before me accompanied by a flickering twelve. Not that I enjoyed looking at them, mind you, but this way I could stop worrying about the changing count. Some part of me must have been satisfied with this because I fell deeply asleep.

Finally, with great reluctance and sloth, the sky lightened and another day began. Before it was completely light the Captain drifted the launch in low and slow behind the hills, boarded us, then let us out behind the final ridge.

"Good luck," he said, with a certain grimness. The port ground shut and the launch moved away and vanished in the growing light. Scarcely aware of what I was doing I punched *D* into the computer. The numbers snapped into existence, vanished just as quickly. But I remembered.

Day nineteen.

Chapter 12

Dawn crept on interminably as we walked, the sun dragging itself up over the horizon only with great reluctance. It was still not quite full daylight when we came to what had to be the beginning of the wall. Just a single row of bricks almost hidden in the grass.

"What do you think?" I asked of no one in particular. Steengo bent and rapped one with his knuckles.

"Brick," he said.

"Red brick," Madonette said brightly.

"Thanks, thanks," I mumbled with complete lack of appreciation.

There was a barely visible path next to the right-hand side of the row of bricks; for want of a better idea we began walking along it.

"It's higher, see," Floyd said, pointing. "A second course has been added."

"And more still ahead," Madonette said. "Three bricks high now."

"What's this?" Steengo said, bending and pushing the grass aside to look more closely, touching the brick with his fingertip. "There's some kind of symbol stamped into each of the bricks." We all looked now.

"Sort of a circle with an arrow sticking out of it."

"Arrow . . . circle," I muttered. A sudden intuition bounced about inside my skull. "I've seen that symbol before—yes indeed! Would someone kindly step over the wall and see if there is a circle with a cross sticking out of it on the other side."

Madonette lifted lovely eyebrows with curiosity, stepped daintily over the low wall, bent and looked. Eyebrows even higher now.

"How did you do that? On this side there is a circle-cross sign stamped into each brick."

"Biology," I said. "I remembered from school."

"Yes, of course," she said, stepping back. "The symbols for male and female."

Floyd had strolled on ahead; he called out. "Right as rain. Here is *VIROJ* stamped into a brick. And," he leaned over and looked, "*VIRINOJ* on the other side."

Very gradually the wall became higher as we walked beside it. In addition to the symbols we came to *LJUDI* then *MTUWA, HERRER, SIGNORI.*

"Enough," I said, stopping. "Packs off. We shall now take our break while we see what we have here. The message seems to be clear enough. Look at the path we have been following. Is there another path on the other side as well?"

The brick wall was as high as our waists now; Floyd put one hand on it and vaulted over, bent and looked.

"Maybe, but not too clear. Could have been here once but it is so overgrown with grass that it is hard to tell. Can I come back now?"

"Yes—because it's about time for a decision." I pointed ahead to the slowly heightening wall. "The Fundamentaloids said they came to the city to trade. So they must have come this way, possibly made this track that we are following."

Madonette nodded agreement—and didn't like it. "And they were all men, I remember that all too clearly. Unclean indeed! No women allowed. Or if the women did come this way they would have to have walked over on the other side of the wall. What do you want us to do, Jim?"

"What do *we* want to do? As I said—it's time for a decision. Do we all stick together and ignore the obvious instructions? That's the first question that we have to answer."

"Do that and I'll bet that eventually we get into some kind of trouble," she said. "A lot of serious work went into this wall. So if we don't read the message something not too nice is guaranteed to happen. It always does on this world. The choice is mine. I'll cross over and trot down the other side—"

"No," I broke in. "As we go along the wall gets higher and we'll be separated, out of contact. That won't do."

"Well I'm not staying here—and I can't go back. So we need contact, what you just said. Kindly clack your jaw-a-phone and get onto Tremearne. Tell him to get some radios down here that we can use to keep in touch. If we are going to complete this assignment the right way, we will have to know what is going on on both sides of the wall. And I'm the only one who can find out what happens—here."

She picked up her pack and planted her bottom on the wall, swung her legs up and over and smiled at us from the other side. I didn't like it.

"It's not a matter of liking or not liking it," she said reading my doubts from my expression. "It is just the only way that we can get the job done. Get the radios. Don't forget that Tremearne will always be listening in and can send the marines if any of us gets into trouble. Call him."

"I will. But let us make sure they are the right kind of radios before we put in the order. Line of sight is going to be out with the wall standing in the way and blocking the signal. Plus—who knows how thick the thing is going to be? It could soak up all the radio frequencies and that would be the end of that. Anyone know of a kind of radio that shoots a signal through rocks?"

I was speaking my thoughts aloud, half in jest. So was more than a little surprised when a voice behind me said, "Yes."

I spun about and glared at Steengo who was buffing his fingernails on his shirt, then admiring his image in their shining surfaces.

"You said that?" I accused. He nodded sagely. "Why?"

"*Why* is a good question. The answer is that although I stand before you, an aging amateur musician drawn from retirement to risk his life for the public good, it should not be forgotten that I worked for many a decade in the cause of that same public good. League communications. Where I helped develop a neat little device referred to as MIPSC."

"Mipsic?" I echoed inanely.

"Close enough, my good friend Jim. MIPSC is the acronym of Miniaturized Personal Satellite Communicator. I suggest that you clamp your jaw and order up a brace of them. Although four would be better—that way we could all keep in touch at all times. And remind Tremearne to put a commsatellite into orbit as well. Geostationary over the city of Paradise."

"*MIPSCs are not only highly secret but incredibly expensive,*" Tremearne said when I contacted him.

"Just like this little task force. Can you do it?"

"Of course. They're on the way."

A half an hour later a small package drifted down from the sky hanging from a grav-lifter—which zipped up and vanished as soon as the package had been removed. I popped the end open and shook out a handful of false fingernails. I popped my eyes at these—then remembered how Steengo had been buffing his own fingernails when he told me about MIPSC.

"Tricky," I said.

"High tech and perfect concealment," he said. "There should be glue in the package. They come in pairs. The one marked *E* goes onto the index finger, left hand. *M* glued to the pinkie of the same hand. Inside the nails are holographed circuitry so they can be trimmed as small as needed to fit. Without damaging the circuits in any way."

"E? M?" Floyd asked.

"Earplugs and microphone."

"Then what?" I asked, almost humbly, dazed by the sudden appearance of a communications wizard in our midst.

"They are powered by the destruction of the phagocytes that come to eat them where they touch the cuticle. Which means that the power is always on. Anytime you are outside—or in a building with thin floors—your signal zips up to the satellite and back down to the other receiver. Simple. Just put your index finger into your ear and talk into the microphone on your pinkie."

I measured a pair, trimmed and glued with, I must admit, a certain amount of trepidation. Stuck my finger into my ear and said, "I hope it works."

"Of course it does," Tremearne said, speaking through my fingernail instead of my jaw for a change.

While we had been installing the MIPSCs we had been going over and over all of the possibilities, had returned always to the only viable plan.

"Let's do it," Madonette said, admiring her new communicating fingernails. She put on her pack, shrugged it into comfortable position, then turned and walked off on her side of the barrier. With each step the wall grew higher, until, very quickly, it was as high as her head, then higher. After a last wave of her hand she vanished from sight.

"Keep in touch," I said into my pinkie. "Regular reports and sing out if you see anything—anything at all."

"Just as you say, boss."

We slipped on our packs and started walking. By the time an hour had passed the wall was high and unscalable. Though I stayed in radio contact with her, Madonette was now completely alone. I kept telling myself that armed help could zip down from the orbiting spacer if needed. This did not make me feel much better.

"First tilled fields coming up," Floyd said. "And more than that. That dust cloud next to the wall—it's coming our way."

"Weapons ready—and I have some concussion grenades handy if things get hairy."

We stopped and waited and watched. In the distance it looked like a horse that was trotting towards us.

"Horse—but no rider," I said.

Steengo had the keener vision. "Looks like no horse I ever saw before. Not one with six legs."

It slowed to a stop and looked at us. We returned the favor. A robot, metal. Jointed legs and in the front a pair of tentaclelike arms to boot. No head to speak of, just a couple of eyes that rose up on a stalk. A loudspeaker between its arms rustled and squawked metallically.

"Bonan tagon—kaj bonvenu al Paradizo."

"And a good day to you as well," I said. "My name is Jim."

"A masculine surname, most agreeable. I am called Hingst and it is my pleasure to greet you—"

The creature's words were drowned out by a throbbing roar and a cloud of black smoke emerged from its rear. We stepped back, weapons ready. Hingst's flexible arms lifted straight up.

"I wish you only peace, oh strangers. You would not know it, since you are untutored in science, but the sound and fumes are merely the exhaust of my alcohol engine. Which is rapidly turning a generator which in turn . . ."

"Charges up your batteries. We know a thing or two as well, Hingst, greeter of strangers to Paradise, and we are not your usual goaty nomads."

"Now that is a pleasure to hear, visiting gentlemen. Before my operating system was bolted into this rather crude construction I was a class A42 headwaiterbot and worked at only the most excellent restaurants . . ."

"Another time," I said. "I would enjoy your reminiscences. We have a few questions—"

"And I am sure I have a few answers," it said with surly overtones. "But there are preliminaries to go through." It had strolled a few paces forward as it talked and now, like a striking snake, one of its tentacles lashed at me. I jumped back, lifted my sword—but not before the cool metal tip had touched my lips and just as swiftly been withdrawn.

"Try that again and you'll be a tentacle short," I growled.

"Temper, temper. After all you are armed strangers and I am simply doing my duty. Which is to sample your saliva. And test it, which I have done. You may proceed, Gentleman Jim, because you indeed are of the male sex. I would appreciate samples from your associates."

"As long as it is just spit you are after," Floyd growled, hands joined and cupped over his nether regions.

"Oh, I do appreciate a sense of humor, stranger." The tentacle took its sample from his mouth. "Gentleman stranger I can now say. Final traveler if you please. Lovely, thank you. You may now proceed."

It turned away and I jumped in front of it.

"A moment first, Hingst the Official Greeter. A few questions . . ."

"Sorry. I am not programmed for that. Kindly step aside, Gentleman Jim."

"Only after I get a few answers."

When I didn't move the other tentacle touched my arm—and lightning struck!

I was lying dizzily on the ground watching it trot away. "Shocking, isn't it!" Hingst called back smugly. "*Big* batteries."

Floyd helped me to my feet and dusted me off. "So good so far."

"Thanks. But you aren't the one who was short-circuited."

I reported to Madonette as we went on, with Tremearne listening in. *"Applied technology,"* he said. *"Perhaps this lot isn't as bad as the rest of the crumb-bums on this planet."* Since I was still tingling, and had a burnt taste in my mouth, I sneered in silence and did not bother to answer. Very soon after that Madonette called in that a creature like the one we had described was coming towards her. I clutched my sword in helpless anger, relaxed only when she called back.

"Just like yours—only with a different name. Hoppe. As soon as it made the test it trotted off. What now?"

"We go on—and you take a break. If things are going to be the same, or similar, on both sides of the wall we'll find out first."

"Male chauv superiority?"

"Common sense. We're three to your one."

"A solid argument—and I could use the rest. Keep in contact."

"You've got it. Here we go."

The path had widened and was more of a dirt road now. We passed some tilled fields and came to a large grove of polpettone trees. Obviously cultivated since they were planted in neat rows. Beyond them was a low huddle of buildings that could be a farm.

Blocking the path was a brick building with an archway that spanned the road; we slowed and stopped.

"Is that what I think it is?" Steengo said.

"I think that it is a building with an arch under it," Floyd said. "And we're not going to find out any more just standing around here."

We shuffled forward slowly and stopped again when a man appeared in the archway. Our hands twitched away from our weapons when he stepped out into the sunlight. He blinked his red-rimmed eyes against the glare, nodded his head so his mane of long white hair bobbed, then tapped the arrow-and-circle symbol picked out in white on the front of his gray robe.

"Welcome, strangers, welcome to Paradise. I am Afatt, the official greeter. Market opens at dawn tomorrow. You may stay out here, or if you wish to camp beyond the arch your weapons will be looked after until you return. A payment of one fedha is required for attendance."

The way he flicked a look over his shoulder as he said this strongly suggested that what he wanted was more bribe than payment.

"No way, aged Afatt," I intoned. "Those you see before you are not peasant traders but galaxy-famous chart-topping musicians. We are . . . *The Stainless Steel Rats*!"

His jaw dropped and he stepped back a pace. "Don't need no rats in Paradise. A rusty, chipped old fedha will do . . ."

"We got a real fan in old Afatt here," Floyd muttered. "I thought the planet was hip-deep in TV sets?"

A more military Paradisian appeared in the archway. Younger, bigger, and he came complete with studded metal helmet and heavy leather trappings. "What did you say?" he said as he swung a shining and singularly nasty looking ax.

"You heard me, Sunny. I don't repeat myself for the troops."

This provoked a twisted snarl and a barked command.

"Guard—fall out. We got some sheot shaggers here that need a lesson in civility."

This was followed instantly by the clanking of metal and the thud of running feet.

Many of them.

Chapter 13

There were a lot of them, armed with a collection of nasty and lethal-looking weapons. I must learn to control impetuosity in speech on this slumworld. Think quickly, Jim, before things get any worse.

"I tempted a jest, good sir. I will be happy to repeat myself for your benefit. You, and your good men, have the pleasure of being in the presence of the finest musicians in the known galaxy!"

As I spoke I touched the remote control on the side of my backpack and a mighty organ sounded out the opening bars of "Mutants of Mercury." Floyd and Steengo quickly joined in with the opening lines.

One head good—but two heads better—
Got brown eyes like an English setter . . .

The effect of this little jingle of genetic jest was very impressive. As a man the soldiers roared aloud and surged towards us.

"Do we fight or run?" Floyd said grimly, grabbing at his sword.

I started to shout *fight*—but at the last instant called out—"Listen!"

For they had forgotten about their weapons and were shouting with joy!

"It's them, like on the Galactic Greasecutter show . . ."

"The hairy, ugly one—that's Floyd!"

"I want to hear 'How Much Is the Snakey in the Snakepit'!"

Then they were around us, trying to shake our hands and emitting hoarse cries of fannish enthusiasm.

"But—but—" I but-butted. "Your official greeter never heard of us?"

The first soldier, snarls now turned to smiles, not too gently pushed the old man aside. "Afatt never looks at the goggle box. But we do! Let me tell you it was like suicidesville around here when we heard that you were sent down. Should have known that you would have to end up here. Wait until the boys in the barracks hear about this. There'll be a crackup in the old kaserne to-night!"

They escorted us cheerily under the arch and onto the drillfield beyond, our new host proudly leading the way.

"I'm Ljotur, Sergeant of the Guard. You all take it easy while I call this in. Drinks!" he ordered his men. "And food—whatever they want."

This was more like it. The beer tasted like beer, although it was of an interesting green color. The soldiers crowded close, hanging on every word we said, so I chomped my jaw to get Tremearne's attention and made my report to him in the form of a speech.

"Gallant warriors of Paradise—we are overwhelmed by your greeting. You have welcomed we drug-ridden convicts as heroes to your fair land. You ply us with food and drink and, by your loud cheers, I feel we have a beautiful future here."

"I certainly hope so," Tremearne's voice said inside my head. *"But until you find out the score on this male-female thing I am ordering Madonette to stay where she is."*

"I agree completely," I called out. "Don't you agree completely, guys, that this is the warmest welcome we have ever received?"

My companions nodded without interrupting the flow of food and drink and there were gurgled shouts of agreement from all sides as more beer vanished. I was wiping my lips with the back of my hand when Ljotur reappeared.

"I have talked to Iron John himself who summons you to his presence soonest. But until the Chariots of Fire appear could you—oh, would you!—play us a number!"

His words were drowned out by hearty masculine cries of joy.

"Let's set up for a quick gig, boys—these guys deserve it." I looked around. "Any requests?"

Many were shouted, but "Nothing's Too Bad for the Enemy" seemed to be most popular. Best choice too since it had an all-male lyric. Loud thunder rolled while lightning flared and sizzled. Our fans fell back into an appreciative half circle while we let fly.

Death and torture and murder and rape—
  WE LIKE IT! WE LIKE IT!
Cutting and slashing and murder and looting,
Hacking and cracking and stabbing and shooting.
Blowing up slowing up showing up to kill
Arson and cursin' done with a will—
  'CAUSE . . .
  NOTHING'S TOO BAD FOR THE
ENEMEEE . . .
Drinking and drinking and drinking and drinking
Shouting and cursing and lying and stinking
Chasing girls grabbing girls huggin' and kissin'
Showing girls all the things they been missin' . . .

As can easily be imagined this delicate flower of a lyric really went down well with the troops. They were still cheering when there was a hissing rumble behind us and we turned to see that our transportation had arrived. Perhaps the locals were used to these things but it was really eye-bugging time for the tourists.

"Only for special occasions, special people," Ljotur said proudly.

We gaped in silence, lost for words. There were two of the vehicles, made of wood and decorated with gilt scrolls and strands of jewels. Each had a single wheel in front, which was steered by a tiller. This was manned by the driver, who rode high above. I looked at the closer one. A wide seat was in the middle and there were two wheels to the rear. All of which was pretty commonplace—not counting the pricey decoration—if you did not allow for the propulsion at the back. This was a shining metal tube, now crackling and emitting an occasional puff of smoke. I drew my attention away from it as the ornate door was thrown wide. I stepped in and seated myself on the soft cushions. Floyd and Steengo were ushered reverently into the other vehicle. Doors were slammed and Ljotur shouted a command to the drivers.

"You're off! Fuel on! *Frapu viajn startigilojn!* Drivers hit your starters!"

I saw now that there was a metal tank under my driver's seat. He reached down and opened a valve and I could hear the gurgle of liquid in the pipe. Then he stamped down on a pedal; the starter I guess.

No—it just started the starter. The pedal pulled on a cord that ran on pulleys to the rear of the chariot. This lifted and dropped a small hammer that banged the starter on the shoulder. This was an individual, dressed completely in black, who sat on a little platform slung behind the wheels. Not only dressed in black, but with blackened arms and face, his hair a burnt stubble. I soon found out why. Liquid was now dripping from the metal tube and the starter reached out and touched a match to it, jumped back as it ignited. A tongue of black smoke and flame leaped out to the rear, singeing the soldiers who weren't quick enough out of the way.

Now the starter was grinding away at a handle, presumably pumping air into the primitive jet. Within seconds the roar grew louder, the flame longer—and my Chariot of Fire shuddered and began to slowly roll forward. Very showy. Though it probably only got about a mile to a hundred gallons. I waved cheerfully to my fellow victims, who waved feebly and fearfully back. Relax Jim, sit back and enjoy the ride.

It was hard to do. I admit I did not see much of the passing scenery, being too involved with thoughts of survival. Nor did I relax until our little convoy had stopped and the blowtorch behind me was extinguished. The chariot's door swung open to the blast of discordant horns. I grabbed up my pack and stepped down onto a gray stepping block.

Which was resistant but soft. I turned and looked and saw that it was not a step at all but a man dressed in gray, kneeling on all fours. He rose and scurried off, along with another human footstep. Midgets, about as tall as my waist and almost as wide. My companions had reacted as I had, our eyes met but we said nothing.

"Greetings," a stentorian voice bellowed. "Welcome, welcome visitors to Paradise."

"Thanks much," I said to the tall and barrel-chested man who was draped in gold cloth. "Iron John, I presume?"

"Most flattering—but you presume wrongly. Musical guests, kindly follow me."

The trumpets blared again, then the trumpeters opened ranks. Three gray-clad men hurried up and took our packs. I started to resist, then made the reluctant decision that it would be all right. The reception we had received at the archway had been too spontaneous to be planned. Our gold-clad greeter bowed to us, then led the way. Towards the brick steps of a brick building.

If the Paradisians were short on building materials they certainly weren't bereft of architectural imagination. Tall pillars, capped with ornate capitals, rose up to support the architrave of a complex entablature. Just like I had been taught in Architecture 1. To either side tall windows opened onto wide balconies. And all of this done in red brick.

"Looks great so far," Floyd said.

"Yes, great," I agreed. But I looked back to make sure the porters with our packs were right behind us. And I still had the concussion grenades in my pocket. No one ever got into trouble by being prepared—as we used to say in the Boy Sprouts.

Down a brick corridor over brick paving we went. Through a brick doorway into a great and impressive room. It was colorfully lit by the sunlight that streamed through the ceiling-high, stained-glass windows. Colorful scenes were depicted there of armies marching, attacking, fighting, dying, the usual thing. This motif was carried through to the walls, which were hung with tattered battle banners, shields and swords. Robed men who stood about the room turned and nodded to us as we entered. But our guide led us past them to the far wall, where there was an elevated throne, made of you-know-what, on which was seated the tallest man I have ever seen.

Not only tall—but naked.

At least he would have been naked if he had not been completely covered with rusty, reddish hair. His beard cascaded down his chest—which was covered as well with hair. Arms and legs and, I couldn't help peeking when he stood, hair all down his belly and crotch as well. This was all that was visible since he was wearing a sort of jockstrap or sporran woven out of, well possibly, his own hair. All of it the color of rusty iron. I stepped forward and bowed a little bow.

"Iron John . . . ?"

"None other," he rumbled in a voice like distant thunder. "Welcome Jim—

and Floyd and Steengo. Welcome Stainless Steel Rats. Your fame has gone before you."

Always good to meet a true fan. We all bowed now since this was not the kind of reception you normally get. Bowed yet again as all in the room cheered lustily.

Iron John sat down again and crossed his legs. He either painted his toenails or they were naturally rusty. I let it pass since there were a lot more things. I would like to know first.

"All here in Paradise were possessed of a great depression when you were arrested," he said. "Falsely of course?"

"Of course!"

"I thought so. But the galaxy's loss is our gain. We are pleased since we now have, you might say, a monopoly on your talents."

This had an ominous sound which I ignored for the moment, cocking an ear as he rumbled on.

"The galaxy is so filled with guilt, sorrow and wrong-headedness that we chose, out of disgust, not to watch most of what is disseminated by television. I am sure that it will cheer you to know that, since your arrest and incarceration, we have canceled normal programming and have been running recordings of your numbers, day and night. Now, soon, we will be happily blessed with the originals themselves!"

This was greeted by cries of enthusiasm and we replied with nods, grins and handshakes over our heads. When the shouts had died away old Rusty boomed out what they all wanted to hear.

"It is our hope that you will now—play for us!" More shouts. "What a pleasure to hear live our favorite favorite—'Nothing's Too Bad for the Enemy.' But while you are setting up we will broadcast a recording to warm up our nationwide audience, to prepare them for your first live performance."

Which was not a bad idea since, although we could get going fast, their TV technicians were another thing altogether. Very much on the antique side. They dragged in arm-thick cables, antique-looking, homemade cameras and lights and other gear that belonged in a museum. While this was happening a screen dropped down from the ceiling and lit up with lively color when the back projector came on.

The recorded program did not have what might be called the galaxy's most inspiring opening. About a thousand suntanned bodybuilders drove heavy stakes into the ground with sledgehammers, backed by the thud of a beating drum. The drum died away but the hammers kept hammering silently as the voice-over spoke.

"Gentlemen of Paradise—we now bring you the special occasion that was announced a few minutes ago. I know that all of you, right across the land, are riveted to your sets. I think that we are going to get a hundred-percent rating on this one! So while The Stainless Steel Rats are warming up for their first-ever live performance here, we are privileged to play for you their special version of—'The Spaceship Way'!"

And it really was special. We watched ourselves attacking the song with our usual gusto, listened once again to those lovely lyrics . . .

Working on the engines, in the engine room,
Wirin' and firin' an' waitin' for the boom.
When the cannons blast like the sound of doom,
You know you're a-sweatin' in the engine room.
Captain on the bridge his fingers on the triggers
All the guns loaded by the spaceship riggers.
Swoopin' on the enemy, million miles an hour
Callin' to the engine room for power, power,
power.
Power, Power, Power make the electrons whirl,
Power, Power, Power—hear them protons swirl!
Power, Power, Power will win the day—
Power, Power, Power, that's THE SPACESHIP WAY!

We nodded and smiled with fixed grins. Good-quality picture, good sound as well. The audience was looking at the screen instead of at us for the moment. Floyd looked at me, then raised his extended index finger to the side of his head and rotated it in a quick little circle. The universal hand signal for insanity. I nodded glum agreement. I couldn't understand it either.

There we were on the screen playing on a familiar set, wearing our regular concert costumes. Only one thing was wrong.

Until this moment none of us had ever seen the tenor who was right there with us, singing the song.

Tenor?

It had always been sung in sensuous contralto by Madonette.

Chapter 14

After the TV intro we played our number, pretty mechanically I must say. Not that our audience noticed; they were too carried away simply by being in the Presence. They swayed and waved their hands in the air and fought to keep silent. But when Iron John joined us in the "Power" chorus they cheered and howled and sang right along with him. When the last power had been overpowered they broke into lusty shouted applause that went on for a long, long time. Iron John smiled beneficently at this and finally stopped it with a raised russet finger. There was instant silence.

"I join you in your enthusiasm for our honored guests. But we must give them time to rest after their strenuous day. We will surely hear them sing for us again. You must remember they are with us now forever. It is their rare privilege to be admitted to Paradise as full citizens, to live until the end of time in our fair land."

More cries of masculine joy. We concealed our overwhelming pleasure at this life sentence and kept our silence as we packed up our instruments and handed them to the waiting servants. Our audience moved out, still throbbing slightly with musical passion.

"A moment please," Iron John said, waiting for the others to leave. When we were alone he touched a button at his side and the tall doors swung silently closed. "A fine song. We all enjoyed it."

"The Stainless Steel Rats aim only to please," I said.

"Wonderful." His smile vanished and he stared at us grimly. "There is one more thing you must do to please me. Your stay here will be a long one and we want you to be happy. You will make us all happy, yourselves included, if you show a certain selection in topics of conversation."

"What do you mean?" I asked—although I had a good notion of what he was leading up to.

"We are very satisfied here. Adjusted and secure. I do not wish to see that security threatened. You gentlemen come to our land from a very troubled outside world. The galaxy is at peace—or so you say. While ignoring the eternal war without end. The conflict of duality that we are free of here. You are the products of a society that is ego destroying instead of being ego building. You suffer from the negativity that blights lives, weakens cultures, sickens even the strongest. Do you know what I'm talking about?"

Neither Floyd nor Steengo answered so it was up to me. I nodded.

"We do. Although we might quibble with some of your conclusions the object of your attentions is quite clear. I can promise you that while we are enjoying your hospitality, neither I nor my associates will talk to anyone about the other sex. That is girls, women, females. It is a taboo topic. But, since you raised the issue I assume that you can discuss it . . ."

"No."

"Right, answer enough. We will therefore enjoy your hospitality and not spoil it."

"You are wise beyond your years, young Jim," he said, and a trace of a smile returned. "Now you must be tired. You will be shown to your quarters."

The doors opened, he turned away. End of interview. We strolled out as nonchalantly as we could. Old Goldy led us out as he had led us in, to some pretty luxurious, although still red brick, quarters. He turned on the TV, checked that the faucets worked in the bathroom, raised and lowered the curtains, then bowed himself out and closed the door. I touched my finger to my lips. Floyd and Steengo waited in twitching silence while I used the detector, borrowed from Tremearne, to sweep the room for bugs. After what we had seen on TV I had a great admiration for the electronics in this place.

"Nothing," I said.

"No women," Steengo said. "And we can't even talk about them."

"I can live with that for awhile," Floyd cut in. "But who was *that* singing our number?"

"That," I said, "was a very nifty example of some first-class electronic dubbing."

"But where did that joker come from?" Floyd said. "There I am playing right beside him—and I swear that I have never seen him before. Maybe we really did blow baksheesh and this whole planet is a drug-inspired nightmare!"

"Keep cool, keep calm. That guy was nothing but a bunch of electronic bytes and bits. Some really good techs digitalized that entire song, with all of us playing it. Then they animated a computer-generated male singer to follow all of Madonette's movements. Wrote her image out, wrote his in—then rerecorded the whole thing just as if it were going out live. Only with a him instead of a her."

"But why?" Steengo asked, dropping wearily into one of the deep lounges.

"Now you have asked the right question. And the answer is obvious. This side of Paradise is for men only. Not only haven't we seen any women here—but pretty obviously they have been edited out of TV and presumably everything else going. It's a real man's world. And don't say *why* again because I don't know. You saw how high that wall is when we were on our way here. And we know from views of the thing from space that the city is on *both* sides of the wall. So the women—if there are any women—might very well be on the other side."

No one said *why* again but that was the only thing on our minds. I stared at their worried faces and tried to think of something nice. I did. "Madonette," I said.

"What about her?" Steengo asked.

"We've got to tell her what has happened." I stuck my thumb in my ear and addressed my pinkie. "Jim calling Madonette. Are you on-line?"

"Very much so."

"I read you as well," Tremearne said tinnily from my thumbnail.

I outlined the events of the day. Said *over* and awaited any reaction. Madonette gasped, nor could I blame her, but Tremearne was all business as usual.

"You are doing well on your side of the wall. Is it time for Madonette to check out her side?"

"Not yet, not until we have a few answers to an awful lot of questions."

"Agreed—but only for now. What have you discovered about the artifact?"

"Negative so far. Give us a break, Captain. Don't you think that getting in here, pressing the flesh and doing a gig is enough for one day?" The silence lengthened. "Yes, sir, right you are—it's not enough. One alien artifact coming up. Over and out."

I pulled my finger out of my ear, wiped the earwax off of it, stared gloomily into space.

"How do we find it?" Floyd asked.

"I haven't the slightest idea. I just said that to get Tremearne off my neck."

"I know how we start," Steengo said. I launched a quizzical look in his direction.

"First the MIPSC and now this. Our humble harp player reveals hidden depths." He nodded and smiled.

"All those years laboring for the League perhaps. Didn't the ancient glad-hander at the gate tell us that there would be a market at dawn tomorrow?"

"His very words," Floyd said. "But so what? The artifact is long gone from the market."

"Of course. But the merchants aren't. There is a good chance that whoever bought the thing might still be there."

"A genius!" I applauded. "Behind those gray hairs lies even grayer gray matter that knows how to think!"

He nodded acceptance. "I never did enjoy retirement. What's next, boss Jim?"

"Grab Goldy. Show strong interest in the market. Have him lay on a guide to take us there when it opens in the morning . . ."

As though speaking his name had been a summons; bugles sounded, the door opened, our gilt-garbed guardian came in.

"A summons for you, oh lucky ones. Iron John will see you in the Veritorium. Come!"

We went—since we had little choice. For a change Goldy was not in a chatty mood; waving off our queries with a flick of his hand. More corridors, more bricks—and another door. It opened into misty darkness. Stumbling and barking our ankles we made our way to a row of waiting chairs, sat down as instructed. It was even darker when Goldy closed the door behind him as he left.

"I don't like this," Floyd muttered, muttering for all of us.

"Patience," I said for lack of any more intelligent answer, then nervously squeezed my knuckles until they cracked. There was a movement of air in the darkness and a growing glow. Iron John swam into view, a blown-up image really. He pointed at us.

"The experience that you are about to have is vital to your existence. Its memory will sustain you and uplift you and will never be forgotten. I know that you will be ever grateful and I accept your tearful thanks in advance. This is the experience that will change you, develop you, enrich you. Welcome, welcome, to the first day of the rest of your new and fulfilling lives."

As his image faded I coughed to cover the grunt of suspicion that this old bushwah evoked. Never try to con a conman. I settled my rump more comfortably in the chair and prepared to be entertained.

As soon as it started I could see that the holofilm was very professionally made. I appreciated that the young, the gullible—or the just plain stupid—would be very impressed by it. The mist churned, the russet light grew brighter and I was suddenly in the midst of the scene.

The king watched *in silence as the group of armed men walked warily into the forest and disappeared from sight among the trees. Outwardly he was patient as he waited, although he reached up and touched his crown from time to time as though reassuring himself that it was still there, that he was still king. A very long time later he stiffened, turned his head and listened as slow footsteps shuffled through the thick leaves below the trees. But no warrior appeared, just the thick and twisted figure of his jester, headdress bobbling, lips moist with flecked saliva.*

"What did you see?" the king asked at last.

"Gone, Majesty. All gone. Just like all of those who have gone before. Vanished among the trees around the lake. None returned."

"None ever return," the king said, sorrow and defeat dragging him down. He stood that way, unknowing, unseeing as a young man appeared and strode towards him, a silent gray dog walked at his side. The jester, jaw agape, spittle pendulous, backed away as the stranger approached.

"Why do you grieve, oh king?" he asked in a light and clear voice.

"I grieve for there is part of the forest in my kingdom where men do go—but none return. They go in tens and twenties—but none is ever seen again."

"I will go," the young man said, "but I will go alone."

He snapped his fingers and, without another word being spoken, man and dog walked off into the forest. Beneath the trees and pendant mosses, around the hedges and nodding cattails to the edge of a dark pond. The young man stopped to look at it—and a hand, sudden and dripping, rose from the water and seized the dog. Pulled it beneath the surface. The ripples died away and the surface was still.

The young man did not cry or flee, just nodded.

"This must be the place," he said.

The darkness faded and light returned. Iron John was gone, the chamber was empty. I looked at Floyd who seemed just as bewildered as I was.

"Did I miss the point somehow?" I asked.

"I feel sorry for the dog," Floyd said. We both looked at Steengo who was nodding thoughtfully.

"That's only the beginning," he said. "You'll understand what is happening when you see the rest."

"You wouldn't like to, maybe, explain just what you are talking about?"

Steengo shook his head in a solemn no. "Later, perhaps. But I don't think I will have to. You will see for yourselves."

"You've seen this holoflick before?" Floyd asked.

"No. But I have read my mythology. It's better that you see the rest before we talk about it."

I started to protest, shut my mouth. Realized that there was no point in probing further. The door opened and our guide reappeared.

"Just the man we are looking for," I said, remembering our earlier decision. "We have heard, from reliable sources, that there is to be an outdoor market at dawn tomorrow."

"Your sources are correct. Tomorrow is the tenth day and that is market day. Always on the tenth day because the nomads remember by marking a finger each day with soot until all fingers are . . ."

"Right, thanks. I can count to ten without dirty fingers. My fellow musicians and I would like to visit this market—is this possible?"

"You have but to ask, great Jim of The Stainless Steel Rats."

"I've asked. Can someone show us the way in the morning?"

"'Tis more fit that you use the Chariots of Fire . . ."

"I agree, more fit. But more fit that we be fit. Walking is a wonderful exercise."

"Then walk you shall, if that is your desire. An escort will be provided. It is now the hour of dining and a banquet has been prepared in your honor. Will you be so kind as to follow me?"

"Lead on, my friend. As long as it is not polpettone again we are your avid customers."

As we followed him out I discovered that my fingers had a life of their own.

Or, more probably, were being twitched into activity by my worried subconscious. They flicked over the computer controls and the glowing numbers appeared before me.

Nineteen and a pulsing red eleven.

Eleven days to go. The morning market had better produce something.

Chapter 15

It is going to be such a lovely day," the voice said.

Each word shot through my head like a rusty arrow, grating and scraping against the growing headache that was throbbing there. I opened one eye blurrily and bright light added to the pain. I had only enough energy to twist my lips into a surly snarl as our gold-clad host flitted about our quarters. Opening curtains, picking up discarded clothing, generally being as obnoxious as possible at this predawn hour. Only when I heard the outer door slam did I crawl from the bed, turn off the searing lights, stumble on all fours to my pack where it rested against the wall. On the third fumbling attempt I managed to open it and click out a Sobering Effect pill. I swallowed it dry and sat motionlessly while I waited for its beneficent chemicals to seep through my fractured body.

"What was in that green beer?" Floyd said hoarsely, then began to cough. Moaning in agony between coughs as his aching head was kicked about. My headache was seeping away so I clicked out a pill for him and walked unsteadily across to his bed of pain.

"Swallow. This. Will. Help."

"Quite a party last night," Steengo said benevolently, joined fingers resting comfortably on the ample bulge of his stomach.

"Die," Floyd gasped, unsteady fingers groping for the pill. "And burn painfully in hell forever. Plus one day."

"A bit hungover are we?" Steengo asked cheerfully. "I suppose there is good reason, considering the length of the nights here. Their parties must go on forever. Or maybe it just seems that way. Eat a bit, sleep a bit. Eat a bit, drink a bit. Or maybe more than a bit. I thought that the beer tasted a little on the nasty side. So I only had one. But the meat courses! Tremendous, vegetables, good gravy, liked the bread and red sauce, plus . . ."

His voice died away as Floyd crawled out of bed and staggered, groaning, from the room.

"You are cruel," I said, smacking my dry lips together and feeling a little better.

"Not cruel. Just pointing out a few truths. This mission first. Overdrinking, hangovers and Technicolor yawns saved for our victory celebration."

There was nothing I could say. He was right.

"Message received," I said, reaching for my clothes. "The quiet life and plenty of rest and raw vegetables. Think positive."

Dawn brightened the window. A new day. Ten days to deadline. I was thinking negative and I shook myself like a wet dog and tried to shrug off the mood. "Let's go to the fair."

When we emerged from the BOQ, Sergeant Ljotur was waiting for us. He snapped to attention and gave a mighty salute—as did the squad of soldiers from the gate guard that he had brought with him.

"We take you to the market!" he called out. "These men are all volunteers, eagerly happy to carry any purchases finest musicians in galaxy may make."

"Greatly appreciated. Lead on," I said as we stepped out briskly on the red brick road.

The sun was a glowing crimson disk on the horizon when we reached the market. The Fundamentaloid nomads must have been early risers because everything was in great swing already. And gory too, I thought I heard a low moan from Floyd, but the baaing and farting of the sheots tended to drown out most other sounds. Complain they might as the butchered carcasses of their late companions were unloaded from their backs. But there had to be more than a meat market here; eyes averted we hurried past the sanguineous display.

Now bearded nomads solicited our attention in pleading voices, pointing out the attractions of their wares. Which weren't that attractive. Tired-looking vegetables, crude clay pots, piles of dried sheot chips for the barbecue.

"Pretty grim," Floyd said.

"Not important," I told him, jerking my thumb towards the strolling customers. "They are the ones that we are interested in." I took out the photographs of the artifact that we were looking for and passed one to each of my companions. "Find out if any of the Paradisians have seen this."

"We don't just spring it on them?" Steengo said doubtfully.

"You're right. We don't. During the sleepless hours of the night I worked up a cover story. It goes this way, something close to the truth. The nomads found this thing in a streambed after a flash flood. Tried to trade it to the keepers of the Pentagon, who have a strict policy of noncommunication. However it was photographed when presented and only later was it recognized as an archeological artifact of possible interest."

"Reasonable," Steengo said doubtfully. "But what are we doing with the photos?"

"Given to us when we were booted out of the place. Hints made of rewards, possible remission of sentence, lots of fedha. With great reluctance we agreed to look for the thing since, simply, what have we got to lose?"

"Thin but plausible," Floyd said. "Let's give it a try."

There was no difficulty talking to the Paradisians, if anything it was hard to get rid of them once approached. How they loved The Stainless Steel Rats! Soon I had a string of adoring fans trailing behind me—along with most of the squad of guards. Everyone wanted to help; none of them knew a thing. But—one name kept cropping up during the questioning: Sjonvarp.

Steengo pushed through the crowd and held up the now dog-eared photograph. "Still nothing. But a couple of them said to ask Sjonvarp. Who seems to be the top trader around here."

"I heard the same thing. Grab Floyd. He must be recovering because I saw him looking at the fermented sheot-milk stand. Bring him here before he makes a mistake that he will long remember."

Sjonvarp was easy enough to find, with countless fingers pointing us the way. He was a tall and solidly built man with iron-gray hair. His stern face broke into a smile when he turned to see who had called out his name.

"The Stainless Steel Rats in the flesh! I am trebly blessed!"

We hummed two bars of "All Alone" followed by a brisk buck and wing. Which elicited a round of applause from the spectators and a broader smile from Sjonvarp.

"Such rhythm and beauty!" he said.

"We sing 'em the way you like it," I said. "It is told in the market that you are the master-trader in these parts."

"I am. Pleased to make your acquaintances, Jim, Floyd and Steengo."

"Likewise. If you have a moment I have a picture here I would like you to look at." I hit the high points of our spiel as I passed the pic over. He only half listened, but did put all of his attention on the photo. Turning it around at arm's length, squinting farsightedly to make it out.

"Of course! I thought so." He handed it back to me. "Some markets ago, I forget exactly how many, one of these odorous simpletons traded it to one of my assistants. We buy anything that might be of scientific interest for the specialists to examine. It didn't look like much. But I gave it to old Heimskur anyway."

"Well that takes care of that then," I said, tearing the photo up and dropping the pieces. "We're doing our concert tonight—I can get you a ticket if you want one."

The artifact was instantly forgotten—as I hoped, although it took some time for us to extract ourselves from the attentive embrace of our fans. Only by saying that it was rehearsal time did we manage to break away.

"Don't we look for the thing any more?" Floyd asked worriedly. A good musician, but I think drink was eroding his brain cells.

"We have the man's name," Steengo said. "That's what we look into next."

"How?" Floyd asked, still suffering from semiparalysis of the neural network.

"Any way we can," I told him. "Make friends. Drop names. Drop Heimskur's name among the others. We find out who he is and what he does. Now, as we stroll, I'll report in."

Tremearne and Madonette listened carefully to my report. He overed and outed but she stayed to chat.

"Jim, it's time I left my hole in the wall and visited the other half of the city. It must be safe . . ."

"We hope that—but we don't know that. And there is no point in your taking any chances as long as the thing we are looking for is here. Enjoy the break. And don't do a thing until we find out more here."

We found lunch waiting in our quarters. Fruit and slices of cold meatloaf on silver plates, covered with crystal domes.

"Great!" Floyd said, chomping down a slice.

"Probably minced sheot shank," Steengo said, suddenly gloomy.

"Food's food and I never consider the source." Floyd reached for another slice just as our golden greeter appeared.

"A pleasure to see you musical Rats enjoying yourselves. When you have eaten your fill I have a request for the presence of Rat Jim."

"Who wants me?" I asked suspiciously through a mouthful of sweet pulp.

"All will be revealed." He put his index finger along his nose, winked and rolled his eyes. Which silent communication I assumed meant something like you'll find out soon enough. I had no choice. And I had lost my appetite. I wiped my fingers on a damp cloth and followed him yet another time.

Iron John was waiting for me at the door of the Veritorium where we had all seen the puzzling holoflic.

"Come with me, Jim," he said with a deep voice like distant thunder. "Today you will see and understand all of the revelation."

"I'll get the others . . ."

"Not this time, Jim." His hand closed gently but firmly onto my shoulder and I had little choice but to go along with him. "You are wise beyond your years. An old head on a young body. Therefore you are the one who will be helped the most by your understanding of this mystery that is no mystery. Come."

He sat me down but did not join me; yet I was aware of his presence close by me in the darkness. The mist roiled and cleared and I was once again by the lake.

THERE WAS ONLY *silence in the forest around the dark pond. As the last ripple died away the young man turned and left without looking back. Trod the dead leaves beneath the trees until be emerged and saw the king before him.*

"There is something I must do," he told the king, nor would he say any more. The king saw that the man's dog was gone—but the man himself was unharmed. He had many questions but did not know how to speak them. Instead he followed the young man back to the castle. In the courtyard the young man looked around, then spotted a large leathern bucket.

"I need that," he said.

"Take it." The king dismissed him with a wave of his hand. "Remember I have helped you. One day you must tell me what you found in the woods."

The young man turned in silence and made his way, alone, back to the dark pond. There he dipped the bucket into the water and hurled its contents into the ditch nearby. Another and another. He did not stop but worked steadily at bailing out the pond. It was hard, slow work. Yet the sun never set, the light never changed, the young man never stopped.

After a great period of time the water was almost gone and something large was revealed lying in the mud on the bottom of the pond. The young man kept emptying the water until he revealed a tall man who was covered with reddish hair, like rusty iron, from head to foot. The large man's eyes opened and he looked at the young man. Who beckoned to him. With a heaving shake the rusty man rose from the pond's bottom and followed the young man away from the pond and through the woods.

To the castle of the king. All of the soldiers and retainers fled when they appeared and the king alone stood before them.

"This is Iron John," the young man said. "You must imprison him in an iron cage here in the courtyard. If you lock the cage and give the key to your queen the forest will be safe again for those who walk through it."

Mist rose and darkened the scene. It was the end.

THE RED-FURRED HAND was heavy on Jim's shoulder—but it did not bother him.

"Now you understand," Iron John said, newfound warmth in his voice. "Now you can release Iron John. Welcome, Jim, welcome."

I wanted to say that I felt more confusion than comprehension. That I was experiencing something, yet not understanding it. Instead of speaking my feelings aloud I suddenly found that my eyes were brimming with tears. I did not know why—although I knew that they were nothing to be ashamed of.

Iron John smiled at me and, with a great finger, wiped the tears from my damp cheeks.

Chapter 16

"What was all that about?" Floyd asked when I returned to our quarters. He was jazzing with his trombonio, a complex and gleaming collection of golden tubes and slides, which made some very interesting sounds indeed. Most of them, regrettably, of an ear-destroying nature.

"More training film," I said, as nonchalantly as I could. I was surprised to hear a certain quaver in my voice as I spoke. Floyd tootled on, unaware of it, but Steengo who appeared to be asleep on the couch opened one eye.

"Training film? You mean more about the pool in the forest?"

"You got it in one."

"Did you find out what was in the pool? The thing that dragged the dog down?"

"A stupid story," Floyd said, and tootled a little fast riff. "Although I do feel sorry for the dog."

"It wasn't a real dog," Steengo said. He looked at me, seemed to be waiting for me to speak, but I clamped my jaw shut and turned away. "Nor was it a real pool."

"What do you mean?" I asked, looking at him.

"Mythology, my dear Jim. And rites of passage. It was Iron John at the bottom of the pool, wasn't it?"

I jumped as though I had been zapped with an electric shock. "It was! But—how did you know that?"

"I told you I read my mythology. But the thing that really disturbs me—not this training film as you call it—is the fact that Iron John is here in the flesh, solid and hairy."

"You've lost me," Floyd said, looking from one to the other of us. "A little explanation is very much in order."

"It is," Steengo said, swinging his feet around so he sat up straight on the couch. "Mankind invents cultures—and cultures invent myths to justify and explain their existence. Prominent among these are the myths and ceremonies of the rites of passage for boys. The passage from boyhood to manhood. This is the time when the boy is separated from his mother and the other women. In some primitive cultures the boys go and live with the men—and never see their mothers again."

"No big loss," Floyd muttered. Steengo nodded.

"You heard that, Jim. In all cultures mothers try to shape sons in their female image. For their own good. The boys resist—and the rite of passage helps this resistance. There is always symbolism involved, because symbols are a way to represent the myths that underlie every culture."

I thought about this; my head hurt. "Sorry, Steengo, but you left me behind completely with that one. Explanation?"

"Of course. Let's stay with Iron John. You have just said that you didn't understand it—yet I think that it affected you emotionally."

I started to protest, to lie—then stopped. Why lie? I tried not to lie to myself, ever. This was a good moment to apply that rule.

"You're right. It got to me—and I don't know why . . ."

"Myths deal with emotions, not facts. Let's look at the symbols. Did the young man bail out the pool and find Iron Hans, or Iron John at the bottom?"

"That's exactly what happened."

"Who do you think Iron John is? In the story I mean, not the one walking around here. But before you answer that—who do you think the young man in the story was?"

"That's not too hard to figure out. Whoever the story was aimed at, whoever was watching it. In this case, since I was there alone, I guess it must have been me."

"You are correct. So in the myth you, and every other young man, are looking for something in the pool, and have to work very very hard with the bucket to find it. Now we come to Iron John, the hairy man at the bottom of the pool. Is it a real man?"

"No, of course it couldn't be. The man at the bottom of the pool has to be a symbol. Part of a myth. A symbol of manhood, maleness. The primitive male that lies beneath the surface in all of us."

"Bang-on, Jim," he said in a low voice. "The story is trying to tell you that when a man, not a boy, looks deep inside himself, if he looks far down and for long enough, works hard enough, he will find the ancient hairy man within himself."

Floyd stopped playing and his jaw gaped. "You guys been smoking something I don't know about."

"Not smoking," Steengo said. "Sipping at the font of ancient wisdom."

"Do you believe this myth?" I asked Steengo. He shrugged.

"Yes and no. Yes, the process of growing up is a difficult one and anything that helps the process is a good thing. Yes, myths and coming-of-age ceremonies help prepare boys, giving them the assurances they need in the transition from boy to man. But that is as far as I will go. I say *no* resoundingly to a myth manifest as reality. Iron John alive and well and leading the pack. This is a fractured society here, without women and without even the knowledge of women. Not good. Quite sick."

I was uneasy at this. "I don't agree all the way. I was affected very strongly by watching that story. And I am a very hard guy to con. This got to me."

"It should have—because it was dealing with the very *stuff* of personality and self. I have a feeling, Jim, that yours was not the happiest of childhoods . . ."

"Happy!" I laughed at the thought. "You try growing up on a porcuswine farm surrounded by bucolic peasants who are not much brighter than their herds."

"And that includes your father and mother?"

I started to answer warmly, saw what he was doing and where this was going. I shut up. Floyd shook the spittle from his so-called musical instrument and broke the silence.

"I still feel sorry for the dog," he said.

"Not a real dog," Steengo said, turning away from me. "A symbolic dog like everything else you saw. The dog is your body, the thing you order around, *sit up, beg.*"

Floyd shook his head in amazement. "Too deep for me. Like that pool. If I could change the subject from theory to fact for just a moment—what's next on the agenda?"

"Finding Heimskur, of course, so we can find out if he still has the artifact," I said, happily putting this other matter aside. "Any suggestions?"

"Brain empty," Floyd said. "Sorry. That hangover never really went away."

"I'm glad some of us didn't drink," Steengo said, a sudden edge of irritation to his voice.

For personal reasons I was happy to hear it, glad that he was still human, he came on pretty strong with the myth stuff. Forget this for awhile. I ticked off on my fingers. "We have only two choices. Hint around about him and gather what information we can. Or blurt right out that we want to see him. Personally, I'm all for the blurting since there is a kind of time limit on this investigation." Like ten days to the grim reaper. "Let's ask Goldy, our major-domo. He seems to know everything else."

"Let me do it," Steengo said, standing and stretching. "I'll talk to him like an old buddy and work the conversation around to science and scientists. And Heimskur. Be right back."

Floyd watched him go, tootling a little march in time with his footsteps. "This Iron John stuff sort of gets to you," he said after the door had closed.

"Yes—and that's the worst part. I don't know why I'm bothered."

"Women. I had six sisters and there were two aunts who lived with us. I had no brothers. I never think about women except one at a time in the right situation."

Before I had to listen to one more boring macho tale about the right situation I excused myself and went for a jog. Returned sweating nicely, did some push-ups and sit-ups, then went for a wash. Steengo was there when I came out. Shaking his joined hands over his head when I lifted a quizzical eyebrow.

"Success. Heimskur is head of the bunch who Labor in the Cause of Science, or so Veldi says."

"Veldi . . . ?"

"The doorman here. He does have a name after all. From what he says I get the feeling that this is a pretty stratified society with everyone in their correct place. Great respect is given to the scientist. Veldi was more than respectful when he talked about them because they appear to be the ones pretty much in charge."

"Great. How do we get to meet Heimskur?"

"We wait patiently," Steengo said and looked at his watch. "Because any moment our transportation will be here to take us to his august presence."

"Not the Chariots of Fire again!" Floyd groaned.

"No. But something that sounds just as ominous. A Transport of Delight . . ."

Before we had time to dwell too long on that thought there was a brisk knocking and gold-clad Veldi threw the door open.

"Gentlemen—this way if you please."

We walked heads high and strong. Hiding any qualms we might have had. Though we shuddered to a halt when we saw what was awaiting us.

"Your Transport of Delight," Veldi said proudly, waving magnanimously in the direction of what could only be a landlocked lifeboat.

It was snow-white, clinker-built, with a stub mast festooned with flags, white wheels just visible tucked under the keel below. A uniformed officer looked down from the rail above, saluted, gave a signal—and the rope ladder clattered down to our feet.

"All aboard," I said as I led the way.

Cushioned divans awaited us while attendants beckoned and held out jars of cool drink. As soon as we were seated the officer signaled again and the drummer in the bow whirred his sticks in a rapid drumroll—then shifted to his bass drum. As the first, methodical boom boomed out, the Transport of Delight shuddered. Then began to roll slowly forward.

"A galley—without slaves or oars," Floyd said.

"Plenty of slaves," I said as a wave of masculine perspiration wafted up from the funnel-shaped vent beside me. "But instead of oars they are grinding away at gears or some such, to turn the wheels."

"No complaints," Steengo said, sipping at his wine. "Not after the Chariots of Fire."

We rolled ponderously between the buildings, nodding at the bystanders and occasionally giving a royal flick of the hand at some of our cheering fans. We moved on through what appeared to be a residential quarter and beyond it into a parklike countryside. Our road wove between the trees, past a row of ornamental fountains to ponderously stop before an immense glass-walled building. A party of elegantly dressed ancients awaited us. Led by the most ancient of them all, white-clad and standing firmly erect. But his face was wrinkled beyond belief. I clambered down the ladder and dropped before him.

"Do I address the noble Heimskur?"

"You do. And of course you are Jim of the Rats. Welcome, welcome all."

There was plenty of handshaking and glad cries of joy before Heimskur broke off the reception and led me into the glass building.

"Welcome," he said, "doubly welcome. To the College of Knowledge from whence all good things flow. If you will follow me I will explain our labors to you. Since you gentlemen come from the surging, mongrel worlds outside our peaceful boundaries you will surely appreciate how the application of intelligence makes our society such a happy and peaceful world. No strife, no differences, a place for everyone and everyone in their place. Down this way are the Phases of Physics, the Caverns of Chemistry. There the Avenues of Agriculture, next to them the Meadows of Medicine, while just beyond is the Museum of Mankind."

"Museum?" I inquired offhandedly. "I simply love museums."

"Then you must see ours. It charts the difficulties through which we passed before coming here, a rite of passage and of cleansing, before we found safe haven on this world. Here we grew and prospered and the record is clear for all to see."

And pretty boring if not just downright preposterous. Cleaner than clean, whiter than white. The only thing missing were the halos on the saints who had accomplished so much good.

"Inspirational," I said when we finally reached the end of the exhibition.

"It is indeed."

"And down this way?"

"The museum for students. Biologists can examine the plant life of our planet, geologists the strata and the schist."

"Archeologists?"

"Alas, very little. The crudest of artifacts left by the long-dead indigenes who first settled here."

"May we?"

"By all means. You see—fire sticks and crude pottery. A hand ax, a few arrow points. Scarcely worth preserving were we not so faithful to our role as recorders and archivists."

"Nothing more?"

"Nothing."

I dug the photograph from an inside pocket, took a deep breath—and passed it over.

"You may have heard that the warders in the Pentagon promised us favors if we helped them find this?"

"Did they indeed? I would believe nothing they said."

He took the photograph and blinked at it, handed it back. "Just like them to lie and cause trouble for no reason."

"Lie?"

"About this. It was brought here. I examined it myself. Not indigenous at all, couldn't possibly be. Probably something broken off an old spaceship. Meaningless and worthless. Gone now."

"Gone?" I fought to keep the despair from my voice.

"Discarded. Gone from Paradise. Nonexistent. Men have no need of such rubbish therefore it is gone forever. Forget the worthless item Jim and we shall talk of far more interesting things. Music. You must tell me—do you write your own lyrics . . . ?"

Chapter 17

We were very silent on our return trip, scarcely aware of the manifold pleasures that rode with us in our Transport of Delight. Only behind the closed doors of our quarters did we let go. I nodded appreciatively as I listened while Floyd swore blasphemously and scatologically; he had a fine turn of phrase and went on for a long time without repeating himself.

"And I double that," I said when lack of breath forced him to subside. "We have indeed been hard done by."

"We have," Steengo agreed. "But we have also been lied to."

"What do you mean?"

"I mean that Heimskur was selling us a line of old camel cagal. More than half of his so-called history of science and nature was pure propaganda for the troops. If we can't believe him about that—how can we believe him when he shovels a lot of bushwah about the artifact? Do you remember his last words?"

"No."

"Neither do I. But I hope someone does. I imagine that you didn't notice it—but I was doing a lot of head-scratching and nose-picking while we were doing that tour."

Floyd wasn't being bright today and gaped at the news. I smiled and put my index finger into my ear. "Come in, ear in the sky. Do you read me?"

"No but I hear you," Captain Tremearne said through my fingernail.

"Good. But more important—did you listen in to our guided tour?"

"All of it. Very boring. But I recorded it anyway, the way you asked."

"The way Steengo asked—credit where credit is due. Would you be so kind as to play back the last speech about the artifact."

"Coming up." After some clattering and high-pitched voices whizzing by, our aged guide sounded forth.

"Discarded. Gone from Paradise. Nonexistent. Men have no need of such rubbish therefore it is gone forever."

I copied it down and got it right after a couple of repeats. "That's it. Thanks."

"There," Steengo said, tapping the paper. "Weasel wording. That tricky old devil was playing with us, knowing that we had some reason to be interested in the thing. He never said destroyed, not once. Discarded? That means it might be still around someplace. Gone from Paradise—could be anywhere else on this planet. But I particularly like the bit about men having no need for the thing." He smiled a smile like a poker player laying down five aces.

"If *men* have no need for it—what about women?"

"Women?" I felt my jaw hanging open and closed it with a clack. "What about them? There are only men here?"

"How right you are. And right on the other side of the town wall is—what? I'm betting on women. Either that or an awful lot of cloning is going on in this place. I'll bet on nature and some kind of connection through the wall."

My jawphone buzzed and Tremearne's voice echoed inside my sinuses. *"I agree with Steengo. And so does Madonette. She's already on her way along the wall to the city and will report as soon as she finds out anything."*

I started to protest, realized the futility, kept my mouth shut. "It figures," I said. "The gang in charge here lie about everything else—so lying about the artifact just comes naturally. We'll have to wait . . ."

I shut up as Veldi knocked quietly, then opened the door. "Good news!" he announced, eyes glowing with passion. "Iron John has chosen to speak to The Stainless Steel Rats—in the Veritorium itself. An honor above all other honors. Hurry, gentlemen. But first brush your clothing and, with the exception of heroically bearded Floyd, diple the five o'clock shadow now gracing your musical jaws. What pleasures do await you!"

Pleasures better lived without. But this was a royal command and no way to get around it. I took a bit of diple-fast and rubbed my jaw smooth, combed my hair and tried not to scowl at myself in the mirror. I was the last to emerge and we boarded the Transport of Delight in silence, rolled ponderously to our destiny.

"I wonder why all three of us?" Steengo said, sipping his glass of chilled wine. "Last time it was you alone at the training-film session, wasn't it, Jim?"

"I have no idea," I said, wanting to change the subject. Nor was I too pleased with his light-hearted attitude. I tried to think about Madonette going in alone to the other city, but my thoughts kept trundling back to Iron John. What was going to happen now?

When we entered the Veritorium I was surprised at how big it really was. It was better lit now and I saw that rows of seats reached up in a semicircle. They were all filled now—with the oldest collection of Paradisians I had seen so far. Bald heads and gray hair, wrinkles and toothless jaws.

Iron John himself stepped forward to greet us. "You are all truly welcome here—and these seats are for you." They were three of the best in the front row—separated from the others. "You are our honored guests, musical Stainless Steel. Rats. This occasion is a special one—specially so for young James diGriz. You are the youngest man here, Jim, and very soon you will find out why. Your companions will, I am sure, watch with pleasure. Not only pleasure but I sincerely hope that they will learn by observation. Now we begin . . ."

Cued by his words the lights died and darkness filled the Veritorium. Footsteps sounded in the darkness, and there was a small laugh. Light appeared and I saw the small boy hurry forward, stumbling a bit under the weight of the box he was carrying. He put it down and opened the lid, took out a top that started spinning when he touched its switch. Then he took out a tray of blocks, started to build a tower with them. When it was high enough he turned to take another toy out of the box. He was a very concentrated, very intense young boy, about eight years old. He rummaged deeper in the box, then looked around with a childish frown.

"Don't hide, teddy," he said. Looked behind the toy box, then into it again and then—with sudden determination—turned and hurried off. He vanished from sight but I could hear his footsteps going away, stopping. Then coming back. Carrying a teddy bear. A commonplace, slightly worn, very ordinary teddy bear. He propped it against the toy box and started building a second tower from the blocks.

The scene grew lighter and I realized we were back in the castle courtyard. The boy was alone—or was he? Something was there in the darkness, a shape that grew clearer.

It was an iron cage and, sitting silently, inside it was Iron John. The boy shouted and knocked over the block towers, ran to pick up the strewn blocks. Looked at Iron John, then away. The cage and its occupant must be a familiar sight to him.

Nothing else happened. The boy played, Iron John watched him in silence. Yet there was an electric tension in the air that made it hard to breathe. I knew that something vitally important was about to happen, and when the boy reached again into the toy box I found myself leaning forward.

When he took the small golden ball from the box I realized that I had been holding my breath; I let it out with a gasp. Nor was I the only one for around me in the darkness there were echoes of my gasp.

The ball bounced and rolled and the boy laughed with pleasure.

Then he threw it once, harder than intended, and it rolled and rolled. Through the bars of the iron cage to stop at Iron John's feet.

"My ball," the boy said. "Give it back."

"No," Iron John said. "You must unlock this cage and let me out. Then you will have your golden ball back."

"Locked," the boy said.

Iron John nodded. "Of course. But you know how to find the key."

The boy was shaking his head *no* as he backed away.

"Where is the key?" the man in the cage asked, but the boy was gone. "Where is the key? But you are only a boy. Perhaps you are too young to know where the key is. You must be older to find the key."

There were murmurs of agreement from the invisible audience. It was very important to find the key, I knew that. The key . . .

It was then that I became aware that Iron John was looking at me. He was there in the cage, it wasn't a holoflic. He looked at me and nodded.

"Jim, I'll bet you know where the key is. You are no longer a boy. You can find it—*now*."

His voice was a goad. I was on my feet, walking forward to the box of toys. My foot touched a block and it rattled aside.

"The key is in the toy box," I said, but I didn't believe the words even as I spoke them. I looked at Iron John who shook his head *no*.

"Not in the box."

I looked down again and realized that I did know where the key was. I raised my eyes to Iron John and he nodded solemnly. "See you *do* know where the key to the cage is. You can let me out now, Jim. Because you know the key is there. Inside . . ."

"Teddy," I said.

"Teddy. Not a real bear. Teddies are for children and you are no longer a child. Inside teddy."

I reached out, blinked away the tears that were blurring my vision, seized up the toy, felt the soft fabric between my fingers. Heard a loud voice that slashed the silence.

"Not quite right, Jim, not right. The key is not there—it has to be *under your mother's pillow*!"

Steengo had come forward to join me, had to shout the last words to be heard over the roar of voices.

"Mother doesn't want her son to leave her. She hides the key to the Iron man's cage under her pillow. The son must steal the key . . ."

The shouting voices drowned him out. Then it went dark in an instant and someone ran into me knocking me down. I tried to stand, to call out, but a hard foot walked on my hand. I shouted aloud at the sudden pain but my voice went unheard in the clamor. Someone else jarred into me and the darkness became even more intense.

"Jim—are you all right? Can you hear me?"

Floyd's face was just above mine, looking worried. Was I all right? I didn't know. I was in bed, must have been asleep. Why was he waking me?

Then I remembered and sat upright, grabbed his arms.

"The Veritorium! It got dark, something happened. I can't remember—"

"I'm not much help because I can't either. It seemed like a good show. Hard to follow the plot but you were in it, do you remember that?" I nodded. "Seemed to be enjoying yourself, although you didn't look happy about tearing the stuffing out of the teddy bear. That's when Steengo joined you onstage and all the fun started. Or stopped. It all gets vague about that time."

"Where's Steengo?"

"You tell me. I saw him last on the stage. I was sleeping myself, just woke up. Looked around, no Steengo. Found you here snoring away and I gave you a shake."

"If he's not here . . ."

A muted knock sounded at the door, and a moment later it opened and Veldi looked in.

"Gentlemen, a happy good morning to you both. I thought I heard your voices and hoped you would be awake. I bring you a message from your friend . . ."

"Steengo—you've seen him?"

"Indeed I did. We had a friendly chat before you awoke. Then, before he left, he made this recording. Told me to give it to you. Told me you would understand."

He placed a small recorder on the table, stepped back. "The green button is to play, red to stop." Then he was gone.

"A message?" Floyd asked, picking the thing up and staring at it.

"Press the button instead of fiddling with the damn thing!"

He looked startled at my tone, put it back on the table and turned it on.

"Good morning there, Jim and Floyd. You guys are sure sound sleepers and I didn't want to wake you before I went out. You know, I'm beginning to think that this city is not for me. I need some space to get my thoughts together. I'm going to take a walk back down the wall, get some air to breathe, some space to think in. You hang in there and I'll be in touch."

"That old Steengo," Floyd said. "What a character. That's him all right. His voice, sure enough, and his way of thinking. Some guys!"

I looked up, looked him in the eye. His face was as grim as mine. He shook his head in a silent *no*. I did the same.

Steengo had not left that message. It was his voice all right. Easy enough for the electronic technicians to fake that.

Steengo was gone.

What had happened?

Chapter 18

I really slept," I said. "Like a rock. Thirsty."

"The same. I'll get some juice and a couple of glasses."

"Great idea."

I had scribbled the note by the time he came back, slipped it to him when I took the glass. He opened it behind the pitcher, read it.

Place bugged. What do we do?

He nodded as he passed me my glass of juice.

"Thanks," I said, watching him turn over the note and write on the back. I don't know if there were optical bugs as well as the audio ones. Until we found out we had to act as though there were. I kept the note in my palm when I read it.

Steengo much concerned. Left these for you before we went to the show.

I finished the juice, put my glass down, lifted my eyebrows quizzically. He pointed quickly at his closed fist. When he stood and passed me he dropped something small into my lap. I waited a minute before I poured more juice, drank it, sat back with my hand in my lap. Two small, soft objects. Familiar. I rubbed my nose and glanced at them.

Filter nose plugs. For neutralizing gas. Steengo had known something—or guessed something. He also knew how affected I had been by the sessions in the Veritorium. He had suspected that something physical, not just the training session itself, had gotten to me.

Of course! Obvious by hindsight. I knew of a dozen hypnotic gases that lowered the ability to think clearly, that left the brain open to outside influences. So it hadn't been emotion but plain old chemistry that had carried me away. Steengo had suspected this—but why hadn't he told me? Depressingly, I realized that the state of mind I had been in, probably caused by drugs in the earlier session, rendered that impossible. He knew he couldn't tell me. But had been suspicious enough to wear the plugs himself.

And when he saw me getting deeply involved in the ritual he had interrupted before it was too late, had brought the whole thing to a screeching halt. I felt my teeth grating together and forced myself to stop.

He had talked about mother and the key under her pillow—to these people who denied that women even existed!

With the realization of the enormity of his crime in the eyes of the Paradisians I felt a sudden overwhelming fear for his safety. Would they kill him—or worse—had they killed him already? They were certainly capable of anything, I was sure now of that.

What next? Communication with our backup team in the spacer above was very much in order. I had to get into the open, away from the bugs, and contact Tremearne. Bring him up to date. Something had happened to Steengo. And the rest of us surely were in danger as well—and Madonette, this might affect her. This entire affair was getting a nasty and dangerous edge to it.

And thinking about dangerous, there was the other *dangerous* always hanging over my head. My computer flashed me the highly unwelcome message of a flickering red nine. I had been asleep longer than I had realized.

Artifact or no I was just nine days away from my personal destiny. When I had first heard the thirty-day deadline on the poison I had not been too concerned. Thirty days is a lot of time, I thought.

Nine days was definitely not a lot of time at all. And with Steengo suddenly vanished I had more problems, not less.

"Going for a run," I called out to Floyd, leaping to my feet in a spasm of fear-sponsored energy. "Feel logy after all that sleep. Got to clear my head."

I slammed out the door and down the road even as he was answering. Taking a different route from my usual one—then changed direction at random. Up ahead was a field of polpettone trees, laid out in neat rows and bulging with fruit. I jogged into a path beside the trees, looking around as I ran. No one in sight. There was little chance the Paradisers would put bugs in among the trees.

But they could have. I turned into a freshly plowed field and ran between the furrows. I should be safe enough here. I clamped my jaw twice.

"Hello, Tremearne, are you there?"

"Very much so, Jim. We have all been awaiting your report. Can you tell us what is happening—the recorder is running."

I jogged in position for a bit, then bent to tie my shoe—then gave up and just sat on the ground while I finished the detailed report. I was tired, the chemicals still kicking around in my system had not been kind to me.

"That's it," I finished. "Steengo is gone. Might be dead . . ."

"No. I can reassure you on that score. A few hours ago we had a radio

message from him, just a few words, then contact was lost again. He must be somewhere deep in the city, behind walls the radio signals can't penetrate. He might have been moved from one site to another, was in the open long enough for a brief transmission."

"What did he say?"

The recording was brief and scratchy. Beginning with static and dying in static. But it was pure Steengo all right.

". . . never enough! When I get my fingers on you, you . . ." The next word was hard to make out—but I could think of a half dozen that filled the bill.

"What do you think we should do? Break out of here?"

"No—go along with everything. You will be contacted."

"Contacted? By whom, what, which? Come in, Tremearne."

There was no answer. I rose and brushed off my shorts. Very mysterious. Tremearne was up to something—but he was not talking about it. Must be worried about eavesdroppers. Maybe he knew something that I didn't.

I started back at a slow run, changed that to a fast walk. To a slow walk, then a crawl. If there had been any farther to go I would probably have done it on all fours. As it was I stumbled into our quarters and collapsed, gasping, onto the couch. Floyd looked astonished.

"You look like you've been dipped and rolled."

"I feel even worse than that. Water, quickly, lots of it!"

I drank until I was sloshing, then sipped a little bit more, handed the glass weakly back.

"Knocked myself out. Be a good buddy and get my pack. I got some vitamin pills there should pick me up." When he handed me the pack I clicked out a couple of Blastoffs, super-uppers, and swallowed one. "Vitamins, good for you," I said as I passed one over. Floyd was a little faster off the mental mark lately and did not ask any questions.

Our timing was pretty good. The wave of good feeling and energy was washing away my almost-terminal fatigue when Veldi threw open the door.

"On your feet!" he called out. I did not move.

"Veldi," I said. "Old and trusted servant. No soft knock? No sweet tones . . ."

"The word is out that you Stainless Steel Rats are just plain rats. Trouble-makers. Just get going."

There was the quick thud-thud of marching feet and Sergeant Ljotur came in with an armed squad of soldiers. Armed with wicked-looking spears with gleaming points and barbed shafts.

"You are to come with me!" he ordered. He did not look happy about it.

"No longer a musical fan, Ljotur?" I said, climbing slowly to my feet.

"I have orders." Orders that he obviously did not like. Which of course he would obey since independent thought had never been encouraged in the military. Floyd followed me out and the squad formed up. Four in front, four in back of us. Ljotur checked the formation, nodded, took position in front and raised his spear.

"Forward—*burtu!*"

We burtued at a slow trot down the road and turned right at the corner. Which put us directly on the route to the red brick lodgings where Iron John lurked, as I remembered from our first visit. Trotted down the road and into a tunnel under a row of buildings. One of the guards to the rear tapped me on the shoulder.

"Give me a hand, will you?" he asked in a hoarse voice.

Then swung sideways and planted his fist in the stomach of the guard next to him. Who folded and dropped without a sound.

This was easy enough to understand. I had turned when he tapped me so I kept turning to face the rear. I reached out and got a hand on the other two guards' necks. Squeezed as they turned their spears towards me.

"Floyd!" I gasped out, putting all my energy into my throttle grips so these jokers would pass out before they harpooned me. "The others!"

One of the guards dropped but the other one, with a stronger neck, kept his spear coming. Into my stomach—

No, not quite. The first guard, who had called to me, gave him a quick chop under the ear. He and I whirled about, ready to jump to Floyd's help. And stopped.

The four other guards were lying in a silent, tumbled heap on the ground. Floyd had a spear pressed firmly under Ljotur's jaw, was holding him up with his other hand.

"You want to talk to this guy?" Floyd asked. "Or you want him down there with the others?"

"I've nothing to say . . ."

"No talk. Drop."

Before I could finish speaking a limp Ljotur joined the rest of the sleeping patrol.

"What about this one?" Floyd asked, fingers arced, pointing to the soldier who had called to me.

"Wait! He started this thing. There has to be a reason for it."

"There is," the soldier said in the same hoarse voice. "I am going to tell you a few things. You will not laugh at anything I say—understood?"

"We're not laughing!" I said. "Great, guy, thanks for the help. And what's the plan?"

"First off—remember about the laughing! I'm not a guy. I'm a girl. Do I see lips bending?"

"Never!" I called out, to disguise the fact that a little flicker of emotion *had* appeared. "You saved us. We are in your debt. We are not laughing. So tell us about it."

"All right. But let's drag these so-called soldiers out of the way first. Then we go on. The orders were to bring you to Iron John and that is what I am going to do. Your friend is in danger. Do nothing precipitate. Forward."

We went. Disbelieving perhaps, but still forward. Floyd started to talk but I raised my hand.

"Save the discussion. Explanations will be useful after we make sure Steengo is all right. But Floyd—stop me if I am wrong—did I see you take five guys out while I was just about managing two?"

"You didn't see it. It was over before you turned to look." He was the same old laid-back Floyd—but was that a new touch of firmness to his words? It was a day of surprises. And he was right—I had not seen him at work, just the results.

The brick palace jogged into view ahead. Apparently not all of the troops had been told that we were no longer heroes, for the guards at the entrance did a snappy jump to attention and salute as we trotted past.

"Halt!" our newfound friend (girl . . . ?) called out and we stopped before the guards at the door. "Orders to bring these two to Iron John. Permission to enter?"

"Enter!" the officer in charge called out. The doors opened and closed behind us as we trotted by. There was the large room ahead and inside it was Iron John. And just one other person.

Steengo. Collapsed against the wall, covered in bruises and blood. One eye swollen shut. He started to speak but could only rasp out something incomprehensible.

"You are all here now," Iron John said. "Soldier—guard the entrance. No one to enter or leave. I have a score to settle with these interlopers. Because I have changed my mind about keeping this thing quiet. I listened to my advisers and I am sorry that I did. Secrecy is at an end and justice will be done to the blasphemers. Here is what will happen. First I will kill this aged devil who spoke such filth. You two will watch.

"Then I will kill you as well."

He started towards Steengo, a red giant of unleashed power. Hands extended to kill.

Chapter 19

Let me have your spear." I called out to the soldier at the door. She shook her head in a silent *no*, then said, "I have my orders." No help from this source.

Iron John had turned and was walking towards Steengo. I ran two silent steps in his direction and launched myself into a flying kick to his back. Heel punching out, a killing blow.

Then I was batted from the air. As big as he was—Iron John was just as fast. He had turned while I was in the air and had swung one hand. Knocking me aside, sprawling me onto the floor. His voice was as deep and ominous as a distant volcano.

"Do you want to be first, little man? You wish the others to watch your destruction? Perhaps that is only fair since you are their leader."

He came slowly towards me and I found myself trembling with fear. Fear? Yes, because he was not human, more than human. He was Iron John a part of the legend of life, I could not hurt him.

He wasn't! I scrabbled to my feet, my leg ached, moved away. He was much bigger, wider, stronger than I was. But no, he wasn't a legend. He was a man.

"A big fat red slob!" I shouted. "A hairy conman!"

His eyes were wide, red, angry. His arched fingers reached for me. I feinted a fist at his jaw, saw him move to block it. Kept turning in an unstoppable kick to his knee.

It connected—but he made no attempt to avoid it. My foot hurt. His knee, his kneecap, looked unhurt.

"I am Iron John!" he shouted. "Iron—iron!"

I fell back, there was no escape. I swung a twisting punch that he took on his biceps. It felt like striking stone. Then his fist to my ribs sent me skidding down the room.

When I gasped in breath it hurt. Felt like something was broken there. Stand up, Jim! I got as far as my knees and he came on.

I blinked as I saw two arms encircle his legs, send him staggering. Kicking out. It was Steengo who had crawled behind him, tried to trip him. Who was now sent crashing back into the wall. To fall and not move again.

I was barely aware of this because the instant Iron John's attention had wandered I had jumped. Getting an arm around his neck, grappling my own wrist. Pulling my forearm tight against his throat to crush his larynx, to cut off blood and air. The armlock that kills in seconds. My face was buried in his rank red fur as I tightened hard, harder than I ever had before.

To no avail. I could feel the tendons in his neck stiffen like steel bars, taking the pressure that should have been on his throat. He lifted one hand slowly, then sank his fingers deep into my flesh—

—hurled me across the room to crash into the wall, fall.

I realized that the voice wailing in agony was my own. I could not move. The soldier at the door looked at me, looked away. Steengo had lain, motionless, since that single, terrible blow. Nor could I do much better myself, just able to crawl.

At least Iron John had felt my hold; he was rubbing at his neck. The smile had gone and frothed saliva now coated his lips. Death would be a single blow . . .

"Iron John—you have forgotten something. You have forgotten me."

Floyd was speaking. Thin, black-bearded, uninvolved. He must have stood and watched while Steengo was stricken, I was felled. Only now did he move.

Quietly forward. Hands extended, fingers lightly bowed. Iron John was in a rage. Leaped and lashed out.

And missed because Floyd was not there. He was to one side, kicking the red giant in the ribs so that he stumbled and almost fell.

"Come here," Floyd said in a voice so low I could barely hear it. "Come and be destroyed."

Iron John was cautious now, knew how fast his new opponent could react. He opened his arms wide and came slowly forward. A force of nature. Implacable and inescapable.

Two quick thuds, two blows sounded and Iron John staggered. Floyd was out of his reach again, circling him slowly. A sudden kick, a blow, then away again.

Nothing Iron John did seemed to affect the outcome. He was wary, he attacked suddenly, reached out and struck. Touched only air. Floyd was before him, behind him—striking him. Wearing him down.

They circled for minutes this way. And Floyd was still just as fast, striking with impunity. But the red monster was going slower and slower, arms lower and lower as the endless blows drove the strength from them. He must have realized that there could be only one end to this battle, on these terms. But he was still dangerous. Almost by chance the struggle moved towards me.

He was after me I realized! I had only the shortest instant to draw my leg back before Iron John spun about and dived towards me.

And caught my kick full in his face. He dropped—but his hands closed on my ankle, pulled me towards him. Reached up . . .

Then Floyd struck. No science now—raw power. Pile driver blows to the giant's back and kidneys that opened his mouth wide with pain, forcing him to release me as he struggled to get away from his tormentor.

More blows to his head. He tried to rise, his legs were kicked from beneath him. The thudding of quick strikes like some terrible machine at work. Then a sudden silence.

A moment for balance, no expression showing on his face, then Floyd swung a terrible kick that terminated on the side of the giant's head. Who fell over and did not rise nor move again.

"Dead?" I croaked. Floyd knelt and felt the pulse in his neck.

"No, he wasn't supposed to be. He'll survive. But I think that he will remember he has been in a fight." He flashed a quick smile, then his face became calm again. "If you're all right I'll look at Steengo."

"I'm great. Knocked about but great," I croaked as I climbed painfully to my feet.

"Pulse good," he said, kneeling beside our friend. "He has taken a lot of punishment but nothing seems to be broken that I can find. He will come out of this fine."

I was groggy, now even weaker with relief, blurted out the words without thinking. "He's fine. I'm fine. However we would have been a lot better if you had waded into this fracas sooner."

I saw him wince at the words, wished I could take them back. You never can.

"I'm sorry, I really am. I had to wait, see what he could do. I know that you're good, Jim. I knew you could at least hold him. I'm sorry but I had to see how fast he could move before I took him on. I had to wear him down, not get touched. I knew I could do it—and I moved as soon as I knew. Sorry . . ."

"Reporting," our guard-guy-girl said. "The Red One is unconscious."

She lowered the small, coin-sized communicator as I stalked towards her, hands out and ready to strike.

"Who were you talking to? Whose side are you on? What's happening here? Speak—or get demolished."

The guard, spear lowered and pointed at me, stood her ground. "The answer to your questions is arriving now. There." The point of her spear moved to indicate a spot behind me. A ruse? Who knew, who cared. I turned and looked at Iron John's giant throne.

Which was slowly turning on some invisible axis. Floyd and I both faced that way, hands raised automatically on the defense. A black opening was revealed and, as the throne stopped moving, there was motion in the darkness beyond. Two figures appeared, walked out into the room.

Both women.

One of them was Madonette.

"Hi, guys," she said, smiling and waving. "I'd like to introduce a new friend, Mata."

The woman was about my height, regal of bearing in her dark robe touched with gold embroidery. Her expression was composed, peaceful; small wrinkles at the corners of her eyes, a touch of gray to her hair, were the only signs of age.

"Welcome to the other side of Paradise, Jim," she said—and held out her hand. Her handshake was firm and quick. I opened my mouth but could not think of anything relevant to say.

"I know that you have many questions." Her words filled the gap. "All of which will be answered. But it would be wisest to postpone our little chat until we are out of this place. A moment, please."

She took a very efficient-looking hypodermic from the reticule hanging at her waist. Uncapped it and bent to brush aside the thick hair on his leg to give Iron John a quick injection.

"He will sleep the better," she said. "Bethuel—will you lead the way?"

The guard raised her spear in a quick salute, then marched resolutely past the throne and into the opening. Madonette touched Steengo's cheek, then waved Floyd to her. "Help me carry him. Jim will have enough to do just moving himself."

I resented the remark—a blotch on my masculine pride?—but before I could stumble over they had lifted him and were following the guard, Bethuel.

There were no lights in the tunnel behind the throne. At least none until Mata had entered behind us and sealed it once again. Pale illumination flickered into existence. More than enough to see by. Nor was it a long walk to the open door at the far end. We emerged into a large, red brick room that could have been a mirror-image of the one that we had just left.

Just in physical size, though. Here the walls were covered by pleasant hangings, tapestries of sunshine and floral landscapes. Instead of the swords and shields that adorned the other. The stained-glass windows here depicted scenes of mountains and valleys, villages and forests. Unlike Iron John's windows, which featured the clash of battle, spackle of gore. This was altogether more civilized.

As was the murmur of concerned voices from the women in attendance here. They tenderly carried Steengo to a couch where another woman, dressed in white, ministered to him. I dropped into the nearest chair and scowled around at all the female bustle. My voice, louder and more censorious than I had intended, cut through the peaceful scene.

"Now would somebody, anybody, tell me just what the hell is going on."

The way I was ignored was comment enough in itself. Though a smiling girl did bring me a glass of cool wine—on the way to serve the others. Madonette sat next to Mata, where they put their heads together for a moment before Madonette spoke.

"First—and most important now that you all are safe—is the fact that the artifact is here and is being looked after. In addition there is—"

"Excuse if I interrupt," I said. "A matter of priority." I clamped my jaw twice. "Did you hear that, Tremearne?" His answer buzzed in my jawbone.

"I did, and . . ."

"Priorities, Captain." I spoke quietly so only he could hear. "Mission complete. Alien artifact returned. Antidote for me on its way down. Nine days is close enough to come. Do you understand all that?"

"Of course. But there is a complication . . ."

"Complication!" I could hear the squeak of fear edging my voice. "What?"

"I sent for the antidote to the thirty-day poison as soon as I heard about it. I had no intention of waiting until the deadline to administer it. However there was an accident in transit." Sweat suddenly beaded my forehead and my toes tapped anxiously on the floor. *"These things happen. I've sent for a second batch and it's en route now."*

I cursed viciously under my breath, then realized that I was the object of more than one concerned glance. Smiled woodenly and snarled my answer.

"Do it. Get it. No excuses. *Now*. Understood."

"Understood."

"Fine." I stopped whispering and called out. "I'm most cheered to hear that the artifact has been found. Now, if you please, an explanation of what all this is about."

"Seems obvious," Madonette said undoubtedly miffed by my surly behavior. "It looks like the ladies have saved your bacon and you should be grateful."

Which did nothing to clear the air. "As I recall," I recalled. "It was the gentlemen—at some physical cost I must add—who polished off that russet rottweiler before you all came onto the scene. I also remember that we were watched all the time during the life-and-death struggle by one of your lot who did nothing to help."

The tough answer sprang to her lips and I snarled around at the female company. Tempers flared on all sides but Mata cooled things down.

"Children—there has been enough tribulation and pain, so do not cause yourself any more." She turned to me. "Jim, let me explain. The soldier who aided your escape, Bethuel, is one of our spies who keeps us informed about all the masculine meanderings beyond the wall. I ordered her to help you escape your guards, which she did. I also ordered her not to reveal her presence to Iron John. The men beyond the wall have no idea that we watch them closely and I wish it to remain that way. She aided your escape and you should be grateful."

I was, and I should have admitted it, but I was still bull-headed and angry and settled for a surly mutter and growl. Mata nodded blithely as though I had communicated something of importance.

"See how well everything has worked out? You are here and safe, your friends safe as well, and that for which you seek, the strange artifact, is secure and close by."

I only half listened. Fine for the troops. But there were other forces at work that did not bode well for my future. Accidents in transit did not happen by accident. Someone in the bureaucracy was manipulating me—did not like me. Perhaps had never liked me and never had any intention of supplying the antidote. I would certainly be less trouble to them if I were safely dead. And there were only nine days left to sort the whole thing out.

I had touched my computer controls automatically while these thoughts were whizzing about my tired brain. The number glowed before me. I really had had a longer sleep than I realized.

Eight days to go.

Chapter 20

I looked around at the peaceful female bustle—and suddenly felt very, very tired. My side hurt and I felt sure that a couple of ribs were broken. I sipped the wine but it didn't help. What I really needed was a couple of Blastoff pills to restore me to something resembling life. In my pack—

"My pack!" I shouted hoarsely. "My equipment, everything. Those masculine momsers have all our gear!"

"Not quite," Mata said in soothing tones. "As soon as you left we saw to it that the porter, Veldi, was rendered unconscious and both your packs are here now. Your associate Steengo's equipment was not in your residence so we can assume that it is now in the possession of Iron John or his associates."

"Not good." I worried a fingernail with my incisors. "There are things there they shouldn't see . . ."

"Might I interrupt," Tremearne's voice spoke through my jaw-a-phone. *"I was waiting until things quieted down to tell you. Steengo's pack is safe."*

"You have it?"

"Rather I should have said 'made safe.' All of your packs are booby-trapped with a canister of rotgrot. Which, when released by a coded radio signal, causes the contents of the pack to instantly decay to their component molecules."

"Nice to know. A lot of secrets are being revealed of late, aren't they?"

There was no response from my jaw. I held out my wineglass for a refill.

"Some simple answers to some simple questions, if you please." My anger had been blasted by fatigue, excoriated by fear of imminent death. Mata nodded in response.

"Good. On a historical note—how come guys over there, girls here?"

"A union of convenience," Mata said. "Many years ago our foremothers were forcefully relocated to this planet. This inadvertent transplantation had a sobering effect on them. Whatever excesses of zeal they had displayed on other worlds were not repeated here. Peace, cool reasoning and logic prevailed. We became then as you see us now."

"Women," I said. "A society of women."

"That is correct. Life here was a running battle for a good long time, or so it is written. The Fundamentaloids tried to convert us, while our next-door neighbors tried to wipe us out. The inferior sex they called us, a threat to their existence. When we first came to this planet we found that those macho crazies were already well established. Our group was forced to spend a good deal of effort just staying clear of them. This was time and energy wasted, our founding mothers decided, so they sought ways to bring about peace. Eventually they convinced the male ruling clique that they could prosper by utilizing their energy in a more positive manner. It was a completely selfish appeal, arranging ways for the males on top in their society to stay on top, while providing absolute control of the rest of the men."

"Sounds pretty terrible," Madonette said. "Turning all those men into slaves."

"Never say slaves! Willing collaborators is more like it. We showed those in charge, and in particular the one now called Iron John, how much easier it would be to rule by brain rather than muscle. We demonstrated to their satisfaction how a great deal more could be accomplished. With our intelligence and knowledge of science, and their muscles, two separate societies were born. In the beginning there was much hatred and clashes between the groups. This died away when it was decided that only the male leaders would know of our existence. This suited the leaders to perfection."

"That was when the two cities were built—and the wall?"

"Correct. This planet is rich in red clay and fossil fuel so the males soon became manic brick makers. After we showed them how to build kilns, of course. There were contests to see who could mold the most bricks, or fire the greatest number, or carry the most. The champion was named brickie of the month and achieved great renown. This went on until you couldn't see the trees for the mountains of bricks. We quickly researched brick laying in our data bases and put the men to work on that."

She sipped her wine delicately and waved her hand in a circle. "Here are the results—and quite attractive they are too. While our physical scientists were sorting out the males this way, our cultural engineers were looking at the sloppy mucho-macho theories that had been keeping them going up to this point. The Iron Hans myth was only a part of their pantheon. We simplified and altered it. Then used genetic biology to modify the physical structure of their leader, so he is as you see him now. At first he was grateful, although gratitude has long since vanished."

"How long?"

"Hundreds of years. Cellular longevity was part of the treatment."

I was beginning to catch on. "And I'll bet that you remember this firsthand—since you and the other lady leaders have had the same treatments?"

She nodded, pleased. "Very adroit, James. Yes, the authorities on both sides of the wall have had the treatments. This makes for continuity of leadership—"

"And the need for secrecy of each other's existence that keeps the powerful in power?"

Mata shook her head in wonder. "You are indeed most perspicacious. How I wish you were in charge next door rather than that hairy halfwit."

"Thanks for the job offer—but no thanks. So the men beyond the wall don't know that you women are here. The same must be true of your women—"

"Not at all. They know about the males—and just don't care. We have a complete and satisfactory society. Childbearing for those who wish it, a fulfilling intellectual life for all."

"And religion? Do you have a female equivalent of Iron John?"

She laughed merrily at the thought, as did all the other women who were listening to our conversation. Even Madonette was smiling until she saw my glare, turned away.

"That's it," I snapped. "Enjoy yourself. And when you are through, if you ever are, you might kindly let me know the joke."

"I am sorry, James," Mata said, laughter gone and really quite serious. "We were being rude and I apologize. The answer to your question is a simple one. Women don't need myths to justify their femininity. All of the myths about Iron Hans, Iron John, Barbarossa, Merlin and other mythological men with their salvation myths are all purely male. Just think about it. I am not making a value judgment, just an observation. Such as the observation that men are basically combative, confrontational, insecure and unstable—and appear to need these myths to justify their existence."

There was a lot to argue with there, maybe not a lot but some. A good deal of jumping-to-conclusions and more than a bit of rationalization. I sidestepped for the moment, until I knew more about how this society ticked. I raised a finger.

"Now let me see if I have this straight. You ladies have a comfortable existence on this side of the wall. You provide the scientific backup to the males on the other side. To keep them chuntering along in their locker-room paradise. Correct?"

"Among other things. That is basically correct."

"Dare I ask what they supply in return?"

"Very little, if the truth be known. Fresh meat from the nomads. Who not only won't trade with us but now heartily deny our existence, though they secretly would love to wipe us out. Then there is an occasional supply of sperm to top up our cryogenic sperm bank. Little else. We watch them and keep them going mostly by habit—and for our own safety. If the man in the street doesn't know that we exist he can't cause us any trouble. The men also get a lot of pleasure in bashing the nomads when they start bothering us. Altogether a satisfactory relationship."

"It certainly sounds that way." I finished the glass of wine and realized that I was beginning to feel the effects of the alcohol. Which was better than feeling the bruises and sore ribs. Which should be looked at soon—but not too soon. The unfolding drama of cultural mish-mash was just too interesting. "If you please—a question or two before we call in the medics. First is the most important question. You mention sperm banks so I assume that pregnancy and motherhood still exist?"

"They certainly do! We would never consider depriving women of their hormonal, psychological and physical rights. Those who wish to become mothers become mothers. Simple enough."

"Indeed it is. And looking around I see that they are lucky enough to all have female babies."

For the first time I saw Mata less than completely relaxed and calm. She looked away, looked back—took up her glass and sipped some more wine.

"You must be tired," she finally said. "We can finish this discussion some other time . . ."

"Mata!" Madonette gasped. "I think that you are avoiding the topic. This cannot be. I have so admired you and your people here. You are not going to tell me that I am wrong?"

"No, never!" Mata said reaching out and taking Madonette's hands in hers. "It has just been so long since we discussed these things. Decisions were taken that seemed excellent at the time. Some of us have had reservations since, but, well nothing much can really be done at this point . . ."

Her voice ran down and she emptied her wineglass. She was upset and I felt sorry for pinning her down like that. I yawned.

"You're right," I said. "I think rest and recuperation come first."

Mata shook her head in a firm *no*. "Madonette is right. These decisions must be faced, discussed. Approximately half of the pregnancies are male, male fetuses. This is determined in the first few weeks." She saw Madonette's worried expression and shook her head again.

"No—please hear me out and don't think the worst. All healthy pregnancies are brought to term. In the case of the males the bottle banks are used—"

"Bottle banks! Isn't that an unfortunate term?"

"Perhaps in your society, Jim. But here it simply signifies highly perfected artificial wombs. Technically superior if truth be known. There are no spontaneous miscarriages, no effects of bad diet and so forth. And at the end of nine months the healthy male babies are—"

"Decanted?"

"No, born. As soon as they are viable the men take over. Specially trained nursemen who supervise the healthy growth of the boys. Their education and assimilation into their society."

"Very interesting," I said, for it certainly was. I hesitated about the next question, but curiosity was gnawing away and could not be suppressed. "Even more interesting is where do the men think the babies come from?"

"Why don't you ask them?" Mata said coldly and I realized that this interview was at an end.

"Now I really am tired—to be continued," I breathed, dropping back into the couch. "Is there a doctor in the house?"

This kicked a lot of maternal instinct into gear and extracted a great deal of attention. I didn't feel the injection that knocked me out. Or the one that brought me to much later. The women were gone and we were alone. Madonette was holding my hand. Which she dropped with slow deliberation when she saw that my eyes were open.

"The good news, stalwart Jim, is that none of your bones are broken. Just a lot of bruising. Better news is that the treatment for the bruises is underway. Best news is that Steengo is in pretty good shape, all things considered, and wants to see you."

"Bring him in."

"In a moment. While you were sleeping I talked to Mata. She told me a lot more about how things work around here."

"Did you find out about the babies?"

"She really is a nice person, Jim. Everyone here has been very nice to me and . . ."

"But you are beginning to have some reservations?"

She nodded. "More than a few. Things look so nice on the surface—and maybe they are. But it is the babies that bother me. I am sure that they are well taken care of physically, even mentally. But to believe a stupid myth!"

"Which one of the stupid myths going about is the one that bothers you?"

"Spontaneous creation would you believe! All the males gather around Iron John's pool for a ceremony of life. The golden balls drift up through the water and are seized. And each one contains a healthy happy baby! And grown men believe that nonsense!"

"Grown men—and women—have believed worse nonsense down through the ages. This myth was a common one for the so-called lower forms of life.

Flies being spontaneously created in manure heaps. Because no one bothered making the connection between grubs growing there and flies laying eggs. All of the creation myths of mankind, all the gods dropping down and molding clay and breathing life, the virgin births and the like. They are all nonsense once they are examined. But we have to start somewhere I suppose. I'm just not happy where some of these people are ending up."

There was a rattle and a thump as the door was opened. Floyd pushed in the wheelchair and Steengo lifted a white-wrapped hand.

"Looks like you did it, Jim. End of mission. Congratulations."

"And the same to you—and Floyd. And since it is The Stainless Steel Rats together, perhaps for the last time, would you mind making a few things clear. I have long felt that there was more than random chance in your selection. Dare I ask—just who are you three people? I suspect that you were chosen for more than musical ability—right Steengo?"

He nodded his bandaged head. "Almost right. Madonette is just what she appears to be . . ."

"Just an office drudge—singing for a hobby."

"The office's loss is music's gain." I smiled and blew a kiss her way. "One down, two to go. Steengo, I have a feeling that you really aren't retired. Right?"

"Right. And I do take some pride in my musical abilities. Which, if you must know, was why I was suckered into this operation by my old drinking buddy, Admiral Benbow."

"*Drinking buddy!* He who drinks with an admiral . . ."

"Must be an admiral too. Perfectly correct. I am Arseculint . . ."

"I didn't quite catch that."

"Arseculint is an acronym for Area Sector Commander Cultural Intercourse. And you can uncurl your lip. Perhaps, in context, 'intercourse' is not quite the right word. Cultural Relationships might express it better. My degrees are in archeology and cultural anthropology, which is what attracted me to the civil service in the first place. Sort of hands-on application of theory. I followed the matter of the alien artifact with a great deal of interest. So I was ripe for the plucking, you might say, when Stinky Benbow asked me to volunteer."

"Stinky?"

"Yes, funny nickname, goes back to the academy, something to do with a chemistry experiment. Which is completely beside the point. I thought enough of this assignment to take a leave from my desk. Great fun. Up until the last, that is."

"Which leaves young Floyd here? Also an admiral?"

He looked sheepish. "Come on, Jim, you know better than that. I even washed out of college, never graduated at all . . ."

I pointed an accusatory finger. "Putting academic credits aside you must have some value to the Special Corps."

"Yes, well, I do. I really am sort of an instructor . . ."

"Speak up, Floyd," Steengo said proudly. "Being chief instructor in charge of the unarmed defense school is nothing to be ashamed of."

"I agree completely!" I said. "If you weren't a whiz kid in unarmed combat, why none of us would be here. Thanks guys. Mission complete and successful. Let's drink to that."

As we raised and clashed our glasses together, drank deep, I thought of my mother. I do this very rarely; it must be all the male-female myth dredging that brought her to mind. Or what she used to say. Very superstitious my Ma. Had a superstition for any occasion. The one that I remember best was when you said how great things were, or what a nice day it was. *Bite your tongue* she used to say.

Meaning don't tempt the gods. Keep your head down. Because saying that something was good would surely bring about the opposite.

Bite your tongue, good old Ma. What a lot of malarky.

When I lowered my glass I saw a woman stumble in through the open door. A young woman with torn clothing, dusty and staggering.

"Sound the alarm . . ." she gasped. "Disaster . . . destruction!"

Madonette caught her as she fell, listened to her whispered words, looked up with a horrified expression.

"She's hurt, babbling . . . something about . . . the science building, destroyed, gone. Everything."

That was when I felt the cold tongs grab tight to my chest, squeezing so hard they made speech almost impossible.

"The artifact—" was all I managed to say.

Madonette nodded slow agreement. "That's where it was, they told me. In the science building. So it must be gone too."

Chapter 21

The mutual decision of The Stainless Steel Rats was a simple one: we had had about enough for one day. We were alive, if not too well. We had found the artifact so our mission was accomplished. The fact that it had also been destroyed was beside the fact. I hoped. They would have to supply me with the poison antidote now. I kept that thought firmly before me as I went to sleep. This was a time for rest. Wounds had to heal, tissue had to mend, fatigue had to be alleviated: medication and a good night's sleep took care of all of that.

The sun was shining brilliantly upon the garden of our new residence when I dragged myself there next morning. Sleep had banished fatigue, which meant that I felt all the bruises that much more enthusiastically. My medication was beginning to override the pain and I dropped into a chair while I waited for beneficence to take place. Steengo came in soon after, swinging along on crutches and looking very much like I felt. He eased himself into the chair opposite me. I smiled a welcoming smile.

"Good morning, Admiral."

"Please, Jim—I'm still Steengo."

"Then, Steengo, since we're alone for the moment, let me express my heartfelt thanks for breaking up the brainwashing session with Iron John. For which, unhappily, you paid quite a physical price."

"Thank you, Jim, I appreciate that. But I had to do it. To save you from being programmed. Also—I really did lose my temper. Teddy bear indeed! A complete corruption of history."

"No teddy bear? No golden ball?"

"The golden ball, yes. That represents innocence, the pleasures of childhood without responsibility. It is lost when we grow up. To regain this freedom the myth tells us we have to find the ball under mother's pillow—and steal it."

"But in a society without women you can't have a mother—so the myth had to be rewritten?"

Steengo nodded agreement, then winced and touched the bandage around his head. "Retold as nonsense. In the original story Mother never wants the boy child to grow up, sees him as young and dependent forever. Independence must be stolen away from mother—hence the golden ball under her pillow."

"Pretty deep stuff."

"Pretty fascinating stuff. Mankind depends on its myths to rationalize existence. Pervert the myth and you pervert society."

"Like Big Red and his mates on the other side of the wall?"

"Exactly. But what was happening there was far more dangerous than just editing a myth. I had suspected that there would be some strong narcogases in the air—and I was right. You and Floyd were glassy-eyed and practically hypnotized into immobility. So it wasn't just a matter of listening to one more story about the magnetic field of the deep masculine. This was about having a very pernicious and demented theory punched deep into your mind, into your subconscious. You were being brainwashed, thought-controlled—and this sort of crude forced suggestion can do infinite harm. I had to stop it."

"Risking your own life at the same time?"

"Perhaps. But I am sure you would have done the same for me if the circumstances were reversed."

There was no answering that one. Would I? I smiled, a little grimly. "Can I at least say thanks?"

"You can. Greatly appreciated. So back to work. Now, before the others come, to more pressing business. Since I am now in the open, so to speak, I am relieving Captain Tremearne and taking command of this operation. I am in a better position to kick the cagal out of the chain of command and make sure that your antidote is here instantly. Or sooner. My first imperative order when I took command was to send for it."

"Then you know about the thirty-day poison? If I might be frank—I can tell you—it has had me pretty worried. Thank you—"

"Don't thank me yet. Because I want your assurance that you will stick with this assignment, thirty-day poison or no."

"Of course I will. I took on this job, got paid, and gave my word I would finish it. The poison was just some bureaucratic moron's idea of a completion bond."

"I was sure you would say that. Knew that you would carry on regardless, threat of death or no threat of death."

Why was I uncomfortable when he said this? This was my old mate Steengo talking. Or was there a strong whiff of the admiral behind his words? Once the military, always the military . . . No, I would not think ill of him. But I better remember that the poison was still churning away. He was smiling widely and I let my smile mirror his. Although, deep inside, the worry and fear still nagged and scratched at my thoughts. Find the artifact, Jim. That is the only way to be sure about the antidote.

I laughed and smiled. But only on the outside. "Carry on, of course. The artifact must be found."

"Must be found, you are right. The search must go on!" He looked over my shoulder and waved. "And there's Floyd—and Madonette. Welcome, my dear, welcome. I would stand to greet you, but only with difficulty."

She smiled and kissed his forehead below the bandage. Of course she was the last one to arrive, woman's prerogative. Though I had better abandon such male-chauv-pig reflexive observations. At least while I was still a guest of the ladies this side of Paradise.

"I have been talking to Mata," she said, seating herself and sipping a bit of fruit juice. "The science building was empty when the explosion occurred, so no one was injured. Since then they have sifted the ruins and found that there is no trace at all of the artifact."

"Positive?" I asked.

"Positive. They have been eavesdropping on the other side of the wall, so they knew about all our interest in the thing. They waited until they observed that all the male scientists had looked at it and prodded it enough. As expected those noble gentlemen—referred to here as 'the geriatric incompetents'—had discovered nothing. Having no further interest the scientists had it transferred here. A study program had been drawn up to examine the artifact but was just beginning when the explosion occurred. End of report."

So the artifact might have been stolen, might still be around. I could help look for it. But I could also stop counting the days. Earlier, when I had been woken up by my computer, it had been flashing a glowing seven for my benefit. Now Admiral Steengo had relieved me of this chronic worry.

But I had taken three million for this job—and I still wondered what the thing really was. So the artifact-chase would continue. Minus the pressure of the days. I looked around at my musical rats and realized that nothing had changed for them. The search for the artifact was still on. Well—why not!

"What do we do next?" I said. Steengo, now more of an admiral than a musician, toted up the possible options.

"Was the explosion an accident? If it wasn't—who caused it? There are really a lot of questions that must be asked . . ."

"Mata told me to tell you that you were to ask Aida if you had any questions," Madonette said brightly.

We considered this seriously for a moment, then realized we hadn't the slightest idea of what she was talking about. Still the admiral, Steengo spoke for all of us.

"Who is Aida?"

"Not who—but what. An acronym for Artificially Intelligent Data Assembler. I think that it is the central computer here. In any case, here is the access terminal."

She put what looked like an ordinary portaphone on the table and switched it on. Nothing happened.

"Are you there, Aida?" Madonette said.

"Ready to be summoned at *any* time, darling," the voice said. In a rich and sexy contralto.

"I thought you said computer?" was my baffled response.

"Do I hear a male voice?" Aida said. Then giggled. "It has been such a *very* long time! Might I ask your name, sweetie?"

"Jim—not sweetie. And why did you call me *that*?"

"Training and programming, dear boy. Before this present assignment I ran an exploration spacer. Male crew, *endless* years in space. It was felt by my creators that a female voice and presence would be more efficacious morale-wise than a machine or masculine presence."

"The last exploration spacer was junked centuries ago," Steengo said.

"A lady does *not* like to be reminded of her age," Aida said huskily. "But it is true. When my ship was sent to the breakers I was made redundant. Since I am basically a computer program I am—every woman's dream—eternal. I had, shall we say, a rather varied career before I ended up here. Mind you, I'm not complaining. I find this *such* a pleasant occupation. There are charming ladies to talk to, as well as additional memory banks and data bases to access whenever I wish to. Most pleasurable—but I do chatter on. I have been informed that you have a problem. If you would identify yourselves by name it would make conversation that much easier. Jim and Madonette I know. The name of the gentleman who just spoke?"

"Admiral—" Steengo said, then broke off.

"Let us *do* keep it on a first-name basis. And your first name is Admiral. Others?"

"Floyd," said Floyd.

"And a great pleasure to meet you all. How may I help?"

"An item, referred to as the artifact, was recently brought to the science building. Do you know about it?"

"Indeed I do. I was studying it, so am therefore quite familiar with the strange construction. In fact I had it under observation at the time of the explosion."

"Did you see what happened to it?"

"Taking the literal meaning of *see*, dear Jim, forces me to answer that question in the negative. I had no photo pickups operating at the time so I did not physically see what happened to it. The only information I had was the direction that it left in. That was thirty-two degrees to the right of the zero north-polar latitude."

"There is nothing at all out there in that direction," Steengo said. "No settlements, no nomadic tribes. Nothing but empty plains right up the polar cap. How do you know that the artifact was taken that way?"

"I know that, *mon Amiral*, because this artifact emits tachyons and I was observing it with a tachyometer. Keeping count, so to speak, and most interesting it was too. It did not emit many—after all, *what* source does?—but a few are much better than none. Let the record show that it emitted one tachyon, from the direction I have given you, just microseconds before the explosion that destroyed the equipment I was using."

"You weren't—injured?" Madonette said.

"How sweet of you to ask! I wasn't, because I wasn't there. As soon as I could I constructed a new tachyometer, conveyed it to the site of the explosion with, unhappily, no results. Now there is just background radiation."

"Do you know what caused the explosion?"

"Welcome to this easy give-and-take of social intercourse, friend Floyd. To answer your question—I do. It was a very powerful explosive. I can give you the chemical formula but I am sure that you would find that immensely boring. But I can tell you that this explosive was manufactured quite widely for the mining industry at one time. It is named ausbrechitite."

"Never heard of it."

"Understandable, Admiral, since it was found to grow unstable with the passage of time. Manufacturing was phased out and ausbrechitite was replaced by newer and more stable explosives."

"When was this?" I asked.

"A bit over three centuries ago. Would you like the exact date?"

"That will do fine."

We blinked at each other in silence. Not knowing what to do with this weird historical-scientific evidence. Only Madonette had the brains to ask the right question.

"Aida—do you have any theories about what happened?"

"Simply *thousands* my dear. But there is no point in telling you about them until I gather some more evidence. Right now you might say that we are in the early moves of a chess game with millions of possibilities for the rest of the game. But I can give you some figures. Chances of an accidental explosion, zero. Chances that the explosion was tied in with the theft, sixty-seven percent. What happens next depends upon you."

"How?"

"Consider reality. You are mobile, *cher* Jim while I am, so to speak, tied down to the job. I can give advice, and accompany you in transceiver form when you leave here. But what happens next—that decision is up to you."

"What decision?" Aida could be exasperating at times.

"I will supply a new tachyometer. If you take it in the direction I have indicated you might be able to track the artifact in this manner."

"Thanks," I said and reached out and turned Aida off. "Looks like us humans have to come to a decision. Who follows the trail? Let us not all speak at once but let me speak first because I am top rat. I have the feeling that it is now time to thin our ranks. I say that Madonette does not go any further. We needed her for the music—and wonderful she was too!—but not for crawling around looking for nutcases planting century-old bombs."

"I second Jim's motion," Admiral Steengo said.

"I third it," Floyd said quickly as Madonette tried to speak. "This is really not your kind of job. Nor is it Steengo's either."

"Isn't that for me to decide?" Steengo snarled in his best admiralish mode.

"No," I suggested. "If you wish to be of assistance, you can really help us by organizing the base operation from here. I declare that the motion has been seconded and passed above all objections. This is only a democracy when it suits me."

Steengo smiled and the admiral's scowl vanished; he was too smart to argue. "I agree. I am well past my sell-by date for fieldwork. My aching bones tell me that. Please, Madonette, give in graciously to the thrust of history. Are you nodding—albeit reluctantly? Good. Above and beyond any aid given by Aida, I will see to it that the Special Corps will supply any equipment needed. Questions?" He glowered around in a circle but we were silent. He nodded with satisfaction and Madonette raised her hand.

"With that decision out of the way—may I pass on a request? In conversation I have discovered that everyone here is a true musical Rat fan so . . ."

"Could we do one last gig before the group breaks up? You betcha. All in agreement."

There was a rousing cheer from all except Steengo, who looked unhappy at the thought of all of his instruments reduced to a pile of particles. But Madonette, ever resourceful, had done a bit of work before she mentioned the gig.

"I've asked around among the girls. They tell me that there is a really nice chamber group here, as well as a symphony orchestra—they must have at least one instrument Steengo can play."

"Any of them, all of them—just unleash me!" he said and now it was smiles and cheers all around.

Due to the miracles of modern medicines, curing and healing drugs, painkillers and a large shot of booze for Steengo, we were ready to do our performance later this same day. A matinee, since night here was still a couple of our days away and not worth waiting for.

There was quite a turnout at the sports stadium. Cheers and shouts of joy greeted us and no one seemed to mind that Steengo was not only out of costume but playing from a wheelchair. If this was to be the last curtain for The Stainless Steel Rats we meant to make it a performance to remember. Leaving the more militaristic and macho songs aside for the moment we launched into a mellow blues number.

Blue world—
Hear me singing my song.
Blue world—
What's it I done wrong?
Blue world—
You gonna help me along
Blue wor-r-r-ld.

Here we are—
We ain't goin' away.
Here we are—
On this planet to stay.
Blue wor-r-r-ld.

Landing was easy,
Plenty of fun.

Down came our rocket—
'Neath the blue sun.
Landing was great—
Everything swell.
Now it's all over,
Living is hell,
Down here at the bottom of the gravity well.

We did many an encore this day. Finished finally with the feeling of exhaustion and happiness that only comes with an artistic job well done. Sleep came easily but, unable to resist, I took one last peek at the days remaining before closing my eyes.

Still seven. Still a week. Plenty of time for my good buddy Admiral Steengo to kick butt and come up with the antidote. I think I was smiling when I closed my eyes which, when you think about it, was quite a change from the preceding twenty-three days. Yes it was.

Then why wasn't I going to sleep? Instead of lying there tensely staring into the darkness. An easy answer.

Until the happy moment when I pulled back the plunger and shot up with the antidote I had only seven days to live.

Nighty-night, Jim. Sleep well . . .

Chapter 22

Either I was a slugabed or the admiral, released from his role as a musician, was a workaholic. Or both. Because by the time I had appeared he had single-handedly organized our expedition down to the last detail. He was muttering over the heap of apparatus as he punched the checklist into his hand-held. He glanced up, waved vaguely, then finished off the last items.

"This is your new backpack. It contains a number of items you will probably need—and here's a printout of what's inside it. I assume that you have a good deal of illegal and possibly deadly items in your old pack which you can transfer after I leave. Aida is assembling another tachyometer and I'm going to get it now. Floyd will join you shortly—and here is Madonette, welcome, welcome."

Steengo made as graceful an exit as he could on crutches. Madonette, a picture of good cheer, swept in and took both of my hands in hers. Then discovered that this wasn't an enthusiastic enough greeting so she kissed me warmly on my cheek. My arms embraced her in automatic response, but closed on empty air since she had already whirled away and dropped onto the couch.

"I wish that I were coming with you, Jim—but I know that it's impossible. Still, I'm not looking forward to getting back to the stuffy old office."

"I'm going to miss you," I said. Meaning it to be a calm statement but listening to myself in horror as it came out all dewy-eyed and smarmy. "All of us will miss you, of course."

"Same here. There were some hairy moments—but you took care of everything, didn't you?" The warmth and appreciation were such that I could feel myself blushing. "All in all I think it was an experience of a lifetime. And I am definitely not going back to all those files and staff meetings and sealed windows. It's fieldwork from now on. Out in the fresh air! Isn't that a good idea?"

"Wonderful, yes indeed," I said, missing her already. I don't know where all this might have ended if Floyd hadn't made a disgustingly cheerful entrance.

"Morning all. Good day for the expedition. Hi and unhappily goodbye Madonette, companion of many an adventure. It has been fun working with you."

"Could you teach me unarmed defense?"

"My pleasure. Easy enough if you work at it."

"Then I could train to be a field agent?"

"Probably not. But I'll sure look into it."

"Would you! I'd be ever grateful. I was telling Jim that I don't want to work in an office anymore."

"Nor should you! A girl with your talents can find much better occupation."

They smiled at each other from opposite ends of the couch, knees almost touching, wrapped up in each other. I was forgotten. I hated Floyd's guts. Was more than happy to hear the thud of crutches and the dragging footsteps approaching.

"All here," Steengo said. "Very good. The tachyometer is ready."

The thing that was following him now trotted forward. Walking, stiff-legged, was the ugliest fake dog that I had ever seen in my life. It was covered in black artificial fur with handfuls missing, had beady black eyes like buttons, stuck out a dry red tongue as it barked.

"Bow-wow."

"What do you mean 'bow-wow'?" I gasped aloud. "What is this repulsive object?"

"The tachyometer," Admiral Steengo said.

"Bow-wow," it barked again. "And for convenience sake the tachyometer is mounted within this mobile terminal."

"Aida?" I said.

"None other. Do you like this disguise?"

"I have never seen a more artificial artificial dog in my life!"

"Well don't get *too* insulting about it. Fido is state of the art—and that is *modern* art if you are thinking something nasty. For one thing the dear little doggy communicates with me by gravimetric waves which, as I am sure you know, cannot be blocked like radio waves. They penetrate the most solid buildings, cut through the most gigantic mountain ranges. So we are always in communication, always in touch. Admittedly Fido here has seen better days. But you know what they say about beggars?"

"I do. But we're choosers without being beggars and I choose a better mobile terminal."

"Your choice, handsome. Give me two days and you can have whatever you want."

Two days? And I had like maybe six and a half to live unless the antidote arrived. I took a deep breath and whistled.

"Here Fido. Nice doggie. Let's go walkies."

"Bow-wow," it said and began to pant most artificially.

"This is the plan," Admiral Steengo said. "I will monitor this operation from the orbiting spacer along with Captain Tremearne. Jim and Floyd will head north in the direction taken by the missing artifact. Aida will be in contact with this terminal, which will also be searching for a tachyon emission source." He appeared to run out of words and rubbed his jaw.

"A nice plan," I said, but I could not keep a certain tone of derision out of my voice. "Cooked down to essentials it means that we just trot north until something happens."

"A satisfactory interpretation. Good luck."

"Thanks. And you will keep the other and most pressing matter of a certain injection on the top of your agenda?"

"I shall query the people involved hourly on the hour," he said grimly—and I think he meant it.

We filled our packs, kept the goodbyes as brief as possible, loaded up and followed Fido out without a backward glance. I liked Madonette. Perhaps too much while I was on an assignment like this. Go, Jim, go I cozened. Follow your wandering tachyon.

We followed the flapping black nylon tail through the streets and onward to the outlying farms. The women we met waved happily, some even whistling bits of our tunes to cheer us on the way. The last farm fell behind us and the open plains opened out ahead. I clacked my jaw-radio.

"Are you there, Tremearne?"

"Listening in."

"Any tribes of nomads around—or up ahead?"

"Negative."

"Any buildings, farms, people, sheots—anything visible on this heading?"

"Negative. We've done a detailed scan as far north as the polar ice. Nothing."

"Thanks. Over and out." Wonderful.

"Empty on all sides, nothing at all ahead," I reported to Floyd. "So we just stay on this heading until our plastic retriever detects any tachyons—or we reach the north pole and freeze to death."

"I've been meaning to ask. What's a tachyon?"

"Good question. Up until now I thought it was just a theoretical unit that the physicists dreamed up in order to explain how the universe works. One of the subatomic entities that exist either as waves or particles. Until they are observed they have no real existence. It has been said, and who am I to doubt it, that they exist in a probabilities limbo of many possible superimposed states." I noticed that Floyd's jaw was beginning to drop, his eyes to glaze. He shook his head.

"You are going to have to try harder, Jim—you lost me a long time back."

"Right, sorry. Try this. There are various kinds of units in physics. A photon is a unit of light energy and an electron is a unit of electric energy. Okay?"

"Great. With you so far."

"A graviton is a unit of gravity and a tachyon a unit of time."

"Lost me again. I thought minutes and seconds were units of time?"

"They are, Floyd, but just to simple people like you and I. Physicists tend to look at things in a different manner."

"I believe it. Sorry I asked. Time for a break, five minutes in every hour."

"You're on." I unstuck my canteen and took a swig, then whistled to our dogtrotting terminal that was almost out of sight. "Come back Fido, breakies."

"You're the boss," Aida said. The dog scrambled back, barked and sniffed my pack where I had dropped it next to me on the ground.

"Not too much realism!" I shouted. "Don't have that plastic canine lift its leg on my pack!"

The day went on like that. Apparently forever. We crawled across the landscape: the sun crawled across the sky. When we had been walking for over five hours fatigue began to strike. Floyd was striding ahead at a great pace.

"Tired yet?" I called out.

"No. Great fun."

"To those of us who weren't bashed about by the red peril."

"Just a bit more."

The bit more went on a bit more than I appreciated and I was just about to toss in the towel when Fido spoke.

"Bow and wow, gentlemen. Just detected a couple of tachyons as they went whizzing by. Wasn't sure of the first one but—there it is, another—and another!"

"Coming from where?" I asked.

"Directly ahead. Let's just stay on this course and we'll track the source down. With, perhaps, yes I'm sure, there is the strong possibility of a course deviation later."

"Aha!" I ahaed. "I recognize equivocation when I hear it. Even from a plastic dog mouthpiece for an ancient ship's computer."

"The word *ancient* is so hurtful . . ."

"I'll apologize when you tell me about this complication."

"Apology accepted. Allowing for the curvature of the planet, gravitic anomalies and other factors, I am still forced to believe that the tachyon source is not on the surface of this world."

"The thing is underground?"

"Underground is the very word for it."

I bit hard on the jawphone. "Tremearne, would you put the admiral on the line."

"I'm here, Jim. Aida reported this possibility a while back and I have been monitoring developments since then. Didn't want to bother you, for all the obvious reasons."

"Yes, like we forgot to bring a shovel. Anything else you haven't told me?"

"I was waiting for data, just coming in. I sent a low-flying probe to look for the gravimetric anomalies that Aida had found. Looks like there are a number of them and they are being plotted now."

"What kind of anomalies? Metal deposits?"

"Quite the opposite. Caverns below the ground."

"It figures. Over and out. At least we now know where the artifact is."

"Where?" Floyd asked, since he had only heard my side of the conversation.

"Underground. There are caves or caverns of some kind up ahead. Nothing visible on the surface—but they are there all right. Our technical observers seem sure that the artifact is down there somewhere. Can we take that break now and wait for the reports?"

"I guess so."

Floyd guessed right, which was a good thing since an instant after we dropped to the ground a stream of bullets was fired at us. Zipping through the empty air where we had just been standing.

Floyd had a large and ugly pistol in his hand now which didn't slow him down as he wriggled on hands and knees beside me to the shelter of the mounded earth around a polpettone tree.

"We're under fire!" I shouted into my jawphone.

"Source not visible."

Fido stood on its hind legs—then jumped high into the air despite another burst of bullets.

"Bow-wow. Perhaps not visible to *others* but clear enough to me."

"What is it?"

"Some sort of apparatus at ground level. Want me to take it out?"

"If you can."

"Grrr!" it growled and retracted its legs, then zipped off at a great rate at ground level, so fast it could barely be seen. Moments later there was a muffled explosion and bits of debris rattled down into the shrub.

"That was quick," I said.

"Thank you," Fido said emerging from the undergrowth with a jagged bit of metal in its jaws. "Just follow me if you want to see the remains."

We followed the thing to a smoking pit with a jumble of crumpled apparatus in its center. Fido dropped its bit of debris, lifted one front leg. Extended its head, straightened its tail and pointed.

"Remote-controlled gun turret. Note that the top of it is camouflaged, concealed by dirt and sprouting plants. Hydraulically operated—that's red oil not blood—to lift the apparatus above ground level. Remains of an optical finder there. Note the four automatic guns, Rapellit-binetti X-nineteens. Rate of fire twelve hundred rounds a minute. Eighty rounds a second, explosive and armor piercing."

"Since when have you been an armament authority, Aida?" I asked.

"Since a long time back, sweetie pie. In my heyday I was required to know this sort of thing. I also know that these particular guns have not been manufactured for over five hundred years."

Chapter 23

I took another sip of water, wished that it was a stronger liquid. Was glad that it wasn't since a clear head was an important asset at this time.

"How old did you say these guns are?" I asked. There was no answer because our fake dog was digging away like a real dog throwing dirt behind it at a great rate. Burrowing down under the gun turret.

"Five hundred years old," Floyd said. "How can that be? Why use something that old?"

"You use it if that is all that you have. There is a mystery here that we are about to solve. Remember the ancient explosive that blew up the lab? It was also antique. So consider this. What if this planet had been settled before they started dumping societal debris on it? What if there had been settlers here—only they were hidden away underground? It's a possibility. And if it is true, then it has been five centuries since they arrived. That's how long these mysterious migrants have been hiding away up here. Or down here, really. They must have been settled well before the League ever found this planet. That's why there is no record of them."

"Who are they?"

"Your guess is as good as mine . . ."

"Yarf!" our dogbot said, yarfing through a muzzle covered with dirt. "There is a fiber-optic cable going into the ground, obviously controlling this turret."

"Going down to the caverns. So, the next question—how do we get in . . ."

"Jim," my jaw said. *"There is an interesting development taking place about three clicks away from you, in the same direction you have been walking. We've got image amplifiers on the electronic telescopes so we can see quite clearly . . ."*

"*What* can you see quite clearly?"

"A group of armed men has emerged from some kind of opening in the ground. They appear to be dragging along one of their number who is bound. Now they are erecting a metal post of some kind. There is a struggle going on—apparently they are securing the bound man to the post."

Memories of a thousand ancient flicks flooded my forebrain. "Stop them! It could be an execution—death by firing squad. Do something!"

"Negative. We are in orbit. Short of launching an explosive torpedo, which is contraindicated at this time, there is nothing we can facilitate that will get there inside fifteen minutes at the very quickest."

"Forget it!" I was digging into my pack as I whistled to the houndbot. "Fido! Catch!"

It jumped high and grabbed the gas bomb out of the air. "Go. Thataway. You heard the message—get to those guys and bite hard on that thing."

My last words were shouted in the direction of the tail that was vanishing among the shrubs. We grabbed up our packs and followed. Floyd easily outdistanced me and by the time I got to the scene, staggering and panting, it was all ancient history. Our faithful friend was barking and, foreleg lifted and tail outstretched, was pointing at the sprawled bodies.

"Well done, man's best friend," I said, and easily resisted the impulse to pat its plastic fur.

"For the record," I said for the benefit of my radio. "All males, all armed with shoulder weapons of some kind. There are twelve of them wearing camouflage uniforms. Thirteenth man—surely an unlucky number—tied to the post. No shirt."

"Is he injured?"

"Negative." I could feel a steady pulse in his neck. "We made it in time. Interesting, he's young, younger than the rest. What next?"

"Decision made by the strategic planning computer. Take all weapons. Take the prisoner and remove him to a safe distance, then interrogate."

I sniffed disdainfully as I unknotted the cords on the man's wrists. "Don't need a strategic planning computer to figure that one out."

Floyd caught him as he slumped free, threw him over his shoulder. I grabbed up the packs and pointed. "Let's get to that gully and out of sight."

The bomb that the ersatz hound had exploded was a quick in-and-out gas. One breath and you were asleep. For about twenty minutes. Which was all the time that we needed to hump our loads through the mud of the rain-eroded gully until we found a dry spot under an overhanging bank. Our prisoner—guest?—began to roll his head and mutter. Floyd and I, and our mascot, sat down to watch and wait. It wasn't long. He muttered something, opened his eyes and saw us. Sat half up and looked very frightened.

"Fremzhduloji" he said. *"Amizbko mizb."*

"Sounds like really bad Esperanto," Floyd said.

"Just what you would expect if he and his kinfolk have been cut off from any outside contact for hundreds of years. Talk slow and he'll understand us."

I turned to him and raised my hands palms out in what I hoped was a universal sign of peace. "We're strangers, like you said. But what else did you say? Sounded like 'my friends'?"

"Friends, yes, friends!" he said, nodding like crazy, then shied away when Fido began barking.

"Aida, please. Will you shut your plastic poodle up. He's frightening our guest."

The thing stopped barking and spoke. "Just want to report that I am in contact with the watchers above. They report that the others who were rendered unconscious by the gas have regained consciousness and have retreated."

"Great. Just file everything and report later." I turned back to our guest—who looked very impressed by the talking-dog sequence. "Well, friend. My name is Jim and this is Floyd. The furry fake is Fido. You have a name."

"I am called Dreadnought, son of Impervious."

"A pleasure to meet you. Now—can you tell us why you were about to be wasted by that firing squad?"

"Disobeyment of orders. I was on Watch. Saw your group approaching. I fired the Watchturret at you—but do not yourselves anger! I aimed to miss. To fire demands permission of Watch Commander. That is why I was to be executed. I sought not his permission."

"Accidents happen."

"No accident. Fired because of orders."

"Are you following this?" Floyd asked.

"Not too well. Tell us, Dreadnought, who gave the order to fire if it wasn't the Watch Commander?"

"We all decided together."

"Who is *we*?"

"I can not tell you."

"Understandable. Loyalty to your friends." I clapped him on the back in a friendly manner and felt him shiver. "Getting cold. I'll get you a shirt."

I dug through my pack and took advantage of the opportunity for a muttered conversation with my jawphone.

"Any ideas? From you—or your indispensable strategic planning computer?"

"Yes. If he won't talk to you perhaps the associates he referred to might be more communicative. Try to arrange a meeting."

"Right." I went back with the shirt. "Here, Dreadnought, get out of the cold." He stood up and put it on. "Good. Now I've been thinking. I don't want you to tell me things that you are not supposed to. But maybe your friends, the ones you just told us about, maybe they can let us know what is going down. Can we meet them?"

He bit his lip and shook his head.

"No? Well let's try something else. Can you get back to your friends? Tell them about us. Talk about it. Find out if someone is prepared to tell us just what is happening. Okay?"

He looked from me to Floyd, even down at Fido who wagged its tail, before he made his mind up.

"Come with me."

He was young and strong and trotted along at a mean trot. Floyd and the mechanical mutt kept up fine but my aches and pains were coming back. I trailed behind and was going to call a halt when Dreadnought stopped at the edge of a grove of polpettone trees.

"Wait this place," he said when I had puffed and blown up to them. He twisted away among the trees. He didn't notice that Fido, legs folded, tail and head retracted, had slipped silently after him in the guise of a black floormop. The cessation of physical activity was welcome—as was the instant-heating meal I dug out of my pack. One porcuswine burger with gravy. Floyd popped his mealpak as well and we were licking the last drops of yummy from our fingers when the shadowlike mop reappeared. Legs, tail and head popped out and it barked. I scowled at it.

"Report first, bark later."

"Your new associate never saw me. Within the wood is a slab of rock that levers up with an opening beneath it. He went that way. Shall I show you where it is?"

"Later—if we have to. Right now let us take ten and see if he passes on our message."

Fatigue sat on me. I closed my eyes and took a lot more than ten. The sun was balancing on the horizon when I surfaced again. My computer obliged me by clicking the red six to a five when I checked the elapsed time. Don't worry, Jim—Admiral Steengo is on your side! This feeble reassurance didn't help and I was sure that I could feel the thirty-day poison beginning to bubble and seethe in my bloodstream.

Floyd was snoring lightly, sound asleep. Yet his eyes were open the instant Fido reappeared, disturbing some stones as it slid down the embankment.

"And a good-morning bow-wow to you gentlemen. Your new friend has emerged from under the lifting rock, along with an associate, and is coming this way. Remember—you heard it from me first."

Fido sat and waited, then barked a welcome when the two men appeared. They were nattily dressed in camouflage uniforms and steel helmets, each helmet sporting a shiny spike on top. Bandoliers of bullets were draped over their shoulders, while there was a large and impressive handgun on each hip. But the guns were holstered and held in place by a buttoned strap. I relaxed knowing that with Floyd there the touch of a hand to one of those buttons would bring instant unconsciousness.

"Welcome back, Dreadnought," I said. "Welcome as well your companion."

"He is named Indefatigable and is the Area Commander. That is Floyd with the beard, the other is Jim."

Indefatigable did not shake hands but instead hit his closed right fist against his chest with an echoing thud. We did the same since it never hurts to learn the local customs.

"Why did you come here?" Indefatigable asked in a most cold and quizzical manner. I took slight umbrage.

"You might say we came to save your companion from certain death by the firing squad—your thanks are appreciated."

"If you had not come he would not have fired and have been condemned to death."

"Good point. But I do remember that he fired because of a group decision. Are *you* part of that group?"

I saw now that Indefatigable's brusque manner was a cover-up for the fact that he was very nervous. He chewed his lower lip and his eyes flicked from one to the other of us. He even looked down at the fake dog, which barked. Finally, with great reluctance he spoke.

"I cannot answer that. But I have been instructed to take you to those who may answer your question. Now—you must answer my question. Why did you come here?"

"No point in keeping it a secret. We came here to find those who blew up a certain building and stole from it—and from us—an object of great importance."

This news seemed to relax him a bit. He stopped the lip chewing and Dreadnought almost smiled; leaned forward to whisper something in his companion's ear. They both nodded, then remembered where they were and snapped into a military brace.

"You will come with us," Indefatigable said, making it sound like an order.

"Perhaps," I said. I hate orders. "But you must tell us first—will it be dangerous?"

"We are born into danger; we leave it only when we die."

It sounded like a quotation of some kind—particularly since Dreadnought's lips moved along with his.

"Yes, well, that is a pretty general philosophical statement. But I was speaking specifically about like right now."

"You will be protected," he answered, trying to control the sneer at our feeble physiques and his obvious superiority.

"Oh, thank you," Floyd said with eye-popping sincerity. "With that kind of reassurance of course we will go with you. Isn't that right, Jim?"

"Absolutely, Floyd. With their protection we need not feel insecure." He could eat them—and a dozen more—for breakfast, but there was no point in bragging.

We reached for our packs but Indefatigable stopped us. "You bring nothing. No weapons. You must trust us."

Floyd shrugged agreement since he was always armed. "At least some water first," I said. Picking up my canteen and drinking a bit. Palming a number of small bombs as I put it back. "And of course our companion, our pet dog goes with us."

Fido played its role by barking, sticking out its tongue and panting. Then overplayed its role by lifting its hind leg on my pack. Though this bit of canine ham acting may have convinced our new militaristic mates, because they nodded agreement.

"We must cover your eyes," Dreadnought said, pulling out two black scarves. "So you do not discover the secret of the entrance to Shelter."

"If you mean the slab of rock under the polpettone trees that swings open, you can forget the blindfolds."

"How do you know this!"

"Just say that we do. Now—do we go with you?"

They looked stricken by my revelation, stepped aside and conversed in quick whispers. Returned reluctantly, all scowls again.

"You will come. Quickly."

We dogtrotted, including the dog, to the grove, then followed Dreadnought down the ladder into the tunnel beneath the slab. Fido barked, and when I looked up launched itself down at me. I caught it, then dropped it. Looked gloomily into the darkness as Indefatigable closed the lid.

I just hoped that we had made the right decision because my days were still running out. Going underground like this was a little too reminiscent of the grave.

And it would be my grave if I didn't get the antidote in time.

Chapter 24

Once my eyes had adjusted to the darkness I saw that a thin line of light ran along at shoulder height on each side of the tunnel. The floor was smooth and hard, as were the walls when I brushed my fingers against them. We walked in silence for some time until we came to a cross tunnel.

"No talking now! Breathe silently—do not stir," one of our guides whispered. "Back against the wall."

We stayed that way for long minutes. I saw that there were glowing numerals on the walls where the tunnels crossed. I added to my store of useless knowledge the data that we were in tunnel Y-82790 at the place where it crossed NJ-28940. I leaned against the wall, and was thinking seriously about going to sleep, when I heard the thud of marching boots from NJ-28940. I woke up and remained silent and unmoving as a squad of about twenty men exited from the tunnel on our right and marched straight across and into the same numbered tunnel on the left. When the sound of their footsteps had almost died away we moved out to the whispered command.

"Turn left, after them. Quiet as you can."

This was apparently the only dangerous part of our journey, because once we had left this tunnel for another our companions whispered together again. I wondered if Fido was still with us.

"Don't bark," I said as softly as I could. "But if you are still there, man's best friend, and hearing this with your super hearing, a tiny growl is permitted."

A guttural grrr sounded from somewhere around my ankles.

"Great. A double growl now if you are reading the tunnel numbers and memorizing same."

A quick grrr-grrr reassured me. So I did not have to keep track of our many turnings. After this we marched in silence for a tiresome period; my strength still wasn't what it should be. I was more than grateful when I saw a glow of light ahead; almost ran into our new companions when they stopped.

"Silence!" Dreadnought whispered. Floyd and I silenced and listened—then heard the running footsteps as well. They thudded close, then stopped suddenly.

"The sounds of deadly battle—" the newcomer said.

"Echo with the cries of the dying," Dreadnought answered. Password and countersign. Pretty depressing though. "Is that you, Irredeemable?" Dreadnought asked.

"It is. I was sent to warn you. A message was passed on from you-know-who that you were detected exiting and reentering the tunnels. Search parties are out and you must avoid them."

"How?" Indefatigable asked. With just a touch of hysteria to his voice.

"I do not know. I was sent only to warn. May the God of Battles go with you." With this blessing the footsteps thudded again into silence as he ran back the way he had come.

"What do we do?" Dreadnought asked unhappily. His companion was just as assertive. "I don't know . . ."

I swear that I could hear their teeth chattering. Whatever else they were, these two young men were not plotters or planners. Time for a pro to step in.

"I will tell you what we must do." Speaking as an unhumble old plotter and planner.

"What?" They spoke the word together.

"If they are searching the tunnels—then we must leave the tunnels."

"Wonderful," Floyd muttered. It may have seemed pretty obvious to him but these lads welcomed the idea as they would have orders from the God of Battles himself.

"Yes! Leave—before they find us!"

"Out of the tunnels!"

Good so far, I thought. When the silence lengthened, and I realized that was the end of their contribution, I asked the vital question.

"Out of the tunnels, right. But *where* do we go? Above ground again?"

"No—all exits will be watched."

"Only one other way," Dreadnought said, with rising enthusiasm. "Down, we must go down!"

"To the Cultivastings!" his companion added, just as filled with enthusiasm.

"Let's do it," I said wearily, not having the slightest idea of what they were talking about. "The God of Battles wants it that way."

They double-timed and we followed. Around the bend into the next tunnel, where a glowing outline revealed that there was a metal door inset into the wall. Neither of our hosts tugged at the handle so there was a good chance that it was locked. Indefatigable stepped forward to face the illuminated keypad set into the wall beside it.

"Avert your eyes," he said. "The access code is top secret."

"Get it, Fido," I whispered. Aida reacted instantly, our plastic pet extruded sharp toenails, leaped high then climbed up my clothes, scratching my ear painfully as it jumped onto the top of my head. I resisted the temptation to say *ouch* and stood steady so it could read the punched-in numbers. The door creaked open and the creature jumped back to the ground.

A gentle breeze blew out through the doorway as we passed through it, smelling fresh and summery. Here underground? We stumbled in the darkness until the door clanged shut and the lights came on. We were in a small chamber facing a spiral staircase. Our hosts instantly started down it and we followed.

I was beginning to get dizzy from the round-and-round when we finally got to the bottom. The open door here glared with light. Blinking my tired eyes, I followed the others. Outdoors into a field of ripening corn. Startled birds flapped away when we emerged, while something small and furry disappeared among the stalks.

I knew that we couldn't possibly be outdoors, not after all the cave crawling that we had been doing. So this had to be a really giant cavern, with some kind of brilliant light sources above. These people really were independent of the surface—no wonder they hadn't been spotted before.

Dreadnought led the way between the rows of corn and we followed. It was hot and dusty, my fatigue was still there—and some species of tiny gnat kept trying to fly up my nose. I sneezed and rubbed and walked into Indefatigable's solid back when he stopped.

"Hail the Home and Joy in Survival!" he called out.

"Hail, hail and welcome, brave Defender," a voice answered.

A sweet and high-pitched woman's voice.

We started forward again and I stepped out from behind my guide's massive form, rubbing my nose and sniffling. I had a quick glimpse of a woman and three or four children working with hoes. It was a very quick glimpse—for the instant that she saw me she screamed.

"Invasion Day!"

It all happened incredibly fast. The children dived to the ground and she grabbed at the heavy pistol that hung from a lanyard around her neck. Raised it and began to fire at us.

We all hit the dust faster than the children had. Dreadnought was shouting, the gun was banging, rounds screamed by and exploded among the crops.

"Stop! No! No invasion! Enough, enough!"

I don't think she heard him at all. I tried to crawl down through the topsoil while I saw her squeezing and squeezing on the trigger, her eyes round and terrified, white teeth sunk into her lower lip. The only thing that kept us alive was the fact that the gun kicked hard and the muzzle rode up into the sky, with the last shots vanishing into the zenith.

It ended just as quickly as it had started. The children had disappeared. Indefatigable had grabbed the gun away from her and was patting her on the back as she sobbed hysterically.

"Well trained," Dreadnought said approvingly. "Irreproachable is a fine woman, a good mother . . ."

"And thankfully a rotten shot," I said. "Would you like to tell us what all that was about?"

"Training. Survival. For lo these many generations. With the galaxy at war we seek only peace. We survive. They will kill themselves, but we will survive!"

He was winding himself up into a rallying speech so I broke in before he got into full spate.

"Stop! One minute—enough. The galaxy's wars and the Breakdown ended centuries ago. There is no more war."

He lowered his clenched fist and sighed, rubbed his knuckle across his nose. "I know. Some of us know. Most won't face the knowledge—cannot face it. We are too trained for survival and nothing else. Nothing in our programming and our lives has ever prepared us for a time without war. Without the threat of invasion. Some of us assemble, we talk, make decisions. About the future. We have a leader—I dare not tell you more!"

He broke off as Indefatigable came running back.

"The message has arrived—it is time to leave. The search has widened. If we move now we can stay behind the searchers and get to the meeting place. Quickly!"

We quicklied—and I was beginning to get very tired of it. The circular staircase had been a lot easier to come down than it was to climb up. Floyd saw my condition and if he hadn't half dragged me I doubt if I would have been able to make it. Once more into the black tunnels. I was only vaguely aware of our two guides, Floyd and the scuttling form of Fido. The next time we stopped I sagged against the wall. Enough was enough yet already.

"You will both stay here with Dreadnought," Indefatigable commanded. "You will be sent for."

Nor would our watcher answer any questions in the few minutes that we waited. "Proceed," a voice commanded and we did. Into a dimly lit chamber that appeared glaringly bright to our dark-adapted eyes. A half-dozen young men, garbed like our guides, sat on the other side of a long table.

"Stand here," Indefatigable ordered, then joined Dreadnought and sat down with the others.

"No chairs for us?" I asked, but was ignored. Fido felt equally irked, jumped up onto the table and barked. Jumped back to the floor to dodge the swing of a fist.

"Shut up," one of the men suggested. "We are awaiting orders. We are here, Alphamega."

They all turned to look at a red box on the table. It was made of plastic and was featureless except for louvers on one side.

"Are the two Outsiders you told me of present as well?" the box asked. The voice was flat and mechanical and obviously cycled through a speech occulter.

"They are."

"I speak to you, Outsiders. I have been told that you come here seeking an object taken from you."

"That is correct, speaking-box."

"What is the function of this object?"

"You tell me—you stole it from us." I was beginning to get teed off at all this cloak-and-dagger stuff.

"Your attitude is unacceptable. Answer my question or be punished."

I took a deep breath—and reined in my temper.

"I'd like that," Floyd said cheerfully, as fed up as I was with all this nonsense.

Where the discussion would have gone from here would never be known because at that moment running footsteps sounded and a wild-eyed young man burst into the room.

"Alarm! Watchpatrol coming!"

The sound of a number of thudding feet added a note of urgency to his warning. But at least our captors were prepared for the emergency. A door opened in the wall behind them and there was a rush to get through it. The newcomer, who must have known what would happen, was the last one in the crowd to jump to safety.

The table was in the way. I launched myself across it just in time to have the concealed door slammed in my face. I kicked it but it didn't budge. I looked at the now silent box.

"Speak up, Alphamega. How do we get out of this?"

The red box crackled—then burst into flame. Melted into a pool of plastic. "Thanks," I said.

"Any other way out?" Floyd asked.

"Not that I can see."

The rapid footsteps were just outside. Before I could dig out a gas bomb the scrum of armed men burst into the room.

Things got busy. Floyd dropped the first three who came through the door while I tackled the next two. Then the going got tough because more and more kept pushing in. Some had body armor, all of them had transparent riot masks attached to their spiked helmets. They didn't try to shoot us, but rather enjoyed clubbing us with their guns.

Something hard got me on the back of the head and I staggered and fell. Before they jumped me the last thing I saw was Fido going up the wall like a spider and vanishing in the darkness there. Then I got thudded and had a nice darkness of my own.

"Feeling any better, Jim?" a distant voice said and I felt something wet and cool on my forehead.

"Shbsha . . ." I said, or something like that. Chomped my dry mouth and opened my eyes. Floyd's face swam blurrily into view. I blinked and saw that he was smiling. He put the cold cloth back onto my forehead, which felt very nice.

"You got a bad one on the back of your head," he said. "They didn't hit me quite as hard."

I started to say *Where are we?* but figured that was a pretty dim question with an obvious answer. I could see a barred door which was hint enough. It hurt when I sat up on the bunk. Floyd handed me a plastic cup of water which I gurgled down and passed back for a refill. I patted my pockets and the seams of my trousers hopefully—but all my concealed weaponry was gone.

"Seen any dogs around lately?"

"Nope."

So that was that. Hit on the head. Imprisoned. Deserted by man's best friend. Somewhere underground so my jaw radio probably wouldn't work. Just in case I clacked hard and called for attention, but couldn't even get any static.

"Well—it could be worse," Floyd said in a repellently cheery fashion. I was about to curse him out when he got just the answer he deserved.

"And it will be. You will be dead," the man said from the other side of the barred door. "Instantly. If you attempt to touch me or the Killerbot behind me. Is that clear?"

He was gray-haired, stern-faced, dressed in the same combat fatigues and spiked helmet as everyone else whom we had seen here. The only difference was that his spike was gold and had stylized wings on it. He moved aside and pointed at the very deadly looking collection of mobile military hardware behind him. All guns, clubs, wheels, knives and metal teeth. Teeth for tearing out throats?

I had no intention of finding out. "Follow me," our captor said, turning and walking away. The cell door clicked and swung open. Floyd and I shuffled out and followed him at a discreet distance. Clanking and rattling, the Killerbot rumbled along behind us.

The hallway, while being a depressing and drab tone of gray, was at least well lit. At regular intervals were framed photographs—apparently all of the same individual from what I could see as we walked past. Or of a number of scowling military types differing only in the braid and the medals on their camouflage suits.

Our host turned into a doorway that was flanked by studded steel columns. We followed—all too aware of the clanking apparatus just behind.

"Impressive," I said, looking around the giant chamber. Black marble floor and walls. A large window looking out onto a military camp filled with flapping flags, marching troops, rows of armor-plated vehicles. Since we were deep underground it was obviously a projection—but a very good one. These militaristic themes were also carried through in the interior decorations, light fixtures made of aerial bombs, machine-gun flowerpots, draperies assembled from tattered, ancient banners. I found it horribly depressing.

Without looking back our captor marched around the gigantic conference table and sat down in the single, high-backed chair there. With a wave of his hand he indicated the two smaller chairs before us.

"Sit," he commanded. Behind us was a clank and rattle, a hiss of escaping steam. We sat.

Something brushed my ankle and I looked down and saw that padded clamps had swung into position to secure my legs; motors whirred and they tightened.

I threw my arms into the air just as clamps from the chair arms swung out and clicked shut on empty air.

"Not wise," our host said. There was a clank-clank close behind me and what could only have been a gun-muzzle ground into the back of my neck. The wrist clamps snapped open. I sighed and dropped my arms. I didn't have to look to know that Floyd had been imprisoned the same way.

"Leave."

When his master commanded, the ambulatory war-machine clanked and rumbled out of the room and I heard the immense doors close.

"I am The Commander," our captor said, leaning back in his chair and lighting a large, green cigar.

"Is that your title or your name?" I asked.

"Both," he said, blowing a ring of blue smoke towards the ceiling. "I have imprisoned you since I do not wish to be attacked—nor do I wish to have anyone or anything present while we talk." He touched a button on his desk and looked at pulsing purple light. "And now we are secure against eavesdropping."

"Going to tell us who all you guys are, what you are doing here and that sort of thing?" I asked.

"Assuredly. We are The Survivalists."

"I think I heard a reference to your mob before."

"Undoubtedly. During the years of the Breakdown there were a number of groups with that name. We are the only ones who deserve it since we are the only ones who survive."

"Survivalists," Floyd said, and went on as though reading from a book.

"Groups who believed in the inevitability of the coming war, as well as the inability of their own governments to protect them, who then withdrew from society into underground bunkers equipped with food, water, ammunition and supplies adequate to survive any catastrophe. None survive."

"Very good—you are quoting from . . . ?"

"*Handbook of Historical Nuts, Cults and Saviors.*"

"Very good—except for the title and the last line. *We* survived."

"A little too well," I said. "The Breakdown Wars are long gone and the galaxy is at peace now."

"I'm glad to hear that. Just don't tell anyone else here."

"Why not? But let me guess. You want to keep them stupid and in line because you are onto a very good thing. For as long as there is war or the threat of war those in charge tend to stay in charge. Which, of course, is you."

"An excellent summation, Jim. Though there are those who are unhappy with the state of things . . ."

"We've met them. Youngsters who perhaps aren't too happy with the militaristic status quo and war forever. Who perhaps prefer a future in the bosom of their families. That is assuming you do have families?"

"Of course, safe and secure in the residential caverns. We guard them and protect them—"

"As well as having a generally good time playing soldier and bossing everybody about."

"Your criticism is becoming tiring."

He looked quizzically at his cigar ash, then tapped it into the ashtray before him. Which was made from a shell casing of course. Something black stirred at the very edge of my vision but I made no move to look that way. It was about time Fido made an appearance.

"So what do you want us for?" Floyd asked.

"I thought that was obvious. I want to find out who you are and how much you know about us."

There was a quick movement from under the table to my chair, out of The Commander's line of sight. The thing must have then climbed the back of my chair because Aida's voice whispered in my ear.

"I have done a voice analysis of a recording I made during the interrupted meeting. I stripped away the interference of the voice occulter and now know who the speaker who called himself Alphamega is . . ."

"I already know," I said.

"Know what?" The Commander said. "What are you saying?"

"Sorry, just speaking my thoughts aloud. My thoughts being that you are playing some kind of complicated game, aren't you? You called me by name—and we have never been introduced. Of course if you were present at the meeting of the young dissidents you would know who I was. And now I know who you are."

I smiled and let the silence stretch before I spoke.

"The Commander—or Alphamega—which name do you prefer? Since you are both of them rolled into one."

Chapter 25

I can kill you—quite quickly," The Commander said coldly and calmly. But at the same time he was stubbing and crunching his cigar out in a most agitated manner.

"Temper, temper," I said. "Since you appear to be in charge of both sides in this internal conflict, and you obviously got us here for a reason—why don't you just tell us all about it?"

He was scowling now, angry and dangerous. As my mother always said—why was her memory still popping up?—you catch more porcuswine with honey than you do with vinegar. Gently, gently.

"Please, Commander," I pleaded most unctuously, "we're on your side, even when no one else is. You know exactly what you are doing—while none of your troops has the slightest idea what is happening. Not only are you in charge here, but it looks as though you have managed a mild insurrection on your own terms. You have done an incredible job that no one else was capable of doing. We can help you—if you will let us."

The scowl faded. Floyd followed my lead, smiled and nodded agreement and said nothing; another cigar was produced and lit. The smoke rose up and the smoker nodded beneficently.

"You are right of course, Jim. The responsibility has been great, the pressure continuous. And I am surrounded by morons—*stulteguloj, kretenoj!* Centuries of interbreeding and hiding underground has done little to improve their brain capacity. I am amazed that I alone have the intelligence to see this. I'm as different from them as if I had been born on a different planet, the child of superior parents."

This was sounding familiar. There has never been a strongman, dictator, military ruler, who did not believe that he somehow came from superior stock.

"You are different, sir," Floyd said, almost humbly. "I knew that as soon as you spoke."

We had both obviously read the same textbooks. Though I thought he was spreading it on rather thickly. I was wrong.

"You could see that? The difference is obvious I suppose, to someone from Outside. It hasn't been easy, I tell you. In the beginning I even tried to talk to the senior officers, explain some of the problems and suggest solutions. I could have had more communication talking to a wall. Not that the younger ones are any better. Though they are restless, I give them that. When you get down to it there isn't much joy in just plain surviving. In the beginning maybe, it must have been a challenge then. But after a couple of centuries the pleasures begin to wear pretty thin."

"Was it the restlessness of the younger ones that gave you the idea to supply a leader for them to follow?" I asked.

"Not at first. But I began to see that the young were losing respect for the old. About the only people they looked up to were the scientists. From their point of view the scientists were the only ones who at least appeared to be doing new and important things. That's when I hit on the Alphamega role. They think that I am one of the younger scientists. A rebel who is unable to make any progress against the old ideas, the familiar ways—therefore I have been forced to enlist others of like age and mind."

"My arms are getting stiff," Floyd said, smiling. "You wouldn't mind taking off these clamps for a bit?"

"I would. I want you two just where you are."

Mercurial, our friend. All warmth gone in an instant, he dragged so hard on the cigar that it crackled and sparked. "We Survivalists watch events pretty closely—all over this planet. With a surveillance network set up before anyone else arrived. Amplified and spread ever since. Not a bird craps, not a polpettone fruit falls that we don't know about. That *I* don't know about. Because I watch the watchers. I watched and saw that a lot of energy and plenty of high-powered work was going into recovering that artifact. There is something very important about it—and I want to know just what. I had a squad steal it and destroy the building, hide their tracks. It was impossible to follow them. Yet you did. I want to know how you did that too. So talk—and talk fast."

"My pleasure," I said. "My friend here knows nothing about the artifact. But I do. I am the one who found it first, then tracked it and followed it here. I am the only one who can tell you how it operates—and what incredible things it can do. If you can take me to it I will be happy to show you how it works."

"That is more like it. You will come with me. Your associate remains here as a guarantee—don't you agree?" He stood and buckled on a large and offensive-looking sidearm.

"Of course. Sorry about that, Floyd," I said as I turned my head to face him. Winking with my left eye, the one our captor couldn't see. "I know that you would come after me and help me if you could. But you can't. So stay here and you will be safe. You have the word of James Fido diGriz on that."

"I'll be okay, Jim. Look after yourself."

I only hoped that this mixture of innuendo, hints and suggestions had delivered my message to him. I could only cross mental fingers and hope. The door opened and there was a hiss, rumble and clank behind me as my bonds snapped open. I rubbed my stiff arms and stood up slowly and carefully. The Killerbot blinked baleful little orange eyes at me and waved a smoke-stained flamethrower in the direction of the door. I followed Commander Alphamega out, leaving Floyd prisoner in the chair. Not for long, I hoped, if Fido-Aida had understood my suggestions.

We walked side by side down the wide hall with its framed portraits of heroes. My companion smiled warmly in my direction. Pulling his gun a bit out of the holster at the same time, then letting it slide back.

"You do understand that if you breathe one word about our conversation you will be no more than a grease spot on the floor?"

"Completely aware, thank you. Absolute silence on that topic, yes, sir. I will look at the artifact and explain its operation. Nothing more."

Maybe I was smiling on the outside—but I was pretty gloomy on the inside. Jim, you are getting yourself in deeper than a porcuswine in a mudhole. A depressing thought—and a true one. But I really had no choice.

It was quite a long walk and I was getting tired again. When all this was over—*if* it were ever over—I promised myself a nice long holiday. Head-up, Jim! Think positive and get ready to improvise.

A last door opened and we were in what was obviously a laboratory. Complete with control boards, power cables, bubbling retorts and aged scientists in white smocks. There was a lot of loyal fist-smacking on chests when the leader appeared. Salutes that he returned with the merest tap of his own loosely clenched fist. They moved respectfully back to give us access to a lab bench. On it, now sprouting wires and connections to the surrounding test gear, was the alien artifact. I clapped my brow and staggered.

"What are you cretins doing with the cagleator!" I shouted. "We are all dead if you have actuated it!"

"No, no—not that!" an elderly scientist cackled. Then shut up and looked fearfully at the Commander who sneered in return.

"You are all morons. Now tell this Outsider what you have done," he ordered. "He is the one who knows what the device can do."

"Thank you, thank you! Of course, as you have ordered." The wrinkly turned back to me with shaking hands and pointed a quavering finger. "We have only X-rayed the device and charted the circuitry. Very complex, as you know. There was, however . . ." he began to sweat, looking about unhappily, "a reaction of some kind when we attempted to test the circuitry."

"A reaction? If you have made a mistake the world has just ended! Show me."

"No, not a big reaction. Just that it absorbed electricity from our test circuit.

We were not aware of this at first—and we instantly terminated the test when we saw what was happening."

"And just *what* did you see happening?" The Commander asked, voice like a file on rough steel.

"That, sir, we saw that. A cover of some kind fell away disclosing this recess. And the lights. That is all. Just lights . . ."

Fascinated, we all leaned forward to look. Yes, there was the recess. And inside it there were four little blobs of light. Green, red, orange and white.

"What is the significance of this?" my inquisitor asked, fingers strumming on the gunbutt.

"Nothing important," I said, stifling a yawn at the unimportance of it all. "The test circuitry is simply testing the circuits of your test circuitry."

I poked out a casual finger towards the glowing lights and found the barrel of his weapon grinding into my side.

"That sounds like absolute waffle to me. The truth, *now*, or you are dead."

There are seconds that sometimes appear to stretch for a length of time bordering on eternity. This was one of those occasions. The Commander glared at me. I tried to look innocent. The scientists, slack-jawed, looked at him. The Killerbot waited in the doorway and clanked to itself, hissing steam and probably wishing that it was killing something. Time stood still and eternity hovered close by.

I had very few options open.

Like none.

"The truth is . . ." I said. And could not go on. What could I possibly say that would impress this maniac in any way? At this moment there was a great explosion and pieces of Killerbot clanked and rattled in through the door.

As you might imagine this really did draw everyone's attention. As did the voice that rang out an instant later.

"Jim—drop!"

And there was Floyd at the open door, brandishing an impressive weapon of some kind. Fido had done its job and freed him. He had polished off the Killerbot and was now taking the action from there.

The Commander swung his weapon around, raised it, ready to fire.

I did not drop as instructed because I was possessed by a hallucinatory moment of madness. I had been pushed around too much of late and suddenly, overwhelmingly, felt like doing a little pushing back.

The lights in the artifact glowed their welcome and my finger punched out in their direction.

To do what?

To touch one of the beckoning colored lights, of course.

Which one?

What color meant what to the ancient aliens who had built this thing?

I had no idea.

But green had always meant *go* to me.

Cackling hysterically I stabbed down on the green light . . .

Chapter 26

Apparently nothing happened. I pulled my finger back and looked at the lights. Then at The Commander and his drawn gun, wondering why he hadn't used it.

Then looked at him again. And saw that he wasn't moving. I mean just not moving in the slightest. I mean like paralyzed. Petrified. Glassy-eyed and frozen.

As was everyone else in the room. Floyd stood in the doorway, gun raised and mouth open in an endless shout. Behind him, for the first time, I noticed an unmoving Fido.

The world was a freeze-frame and I was the only one not trapped in it. I was surrounded by people stopped in the act of speaking, walking, moving. Off-balance, hands raised, mouths gaping. Now stilled, silent—dead?

I started towards The Commander, to relieve him of his gun—saw that his finger was tight on the trigger! But with each step I felt the air resisting my movement, growing firm, then more solid until it was like walking into an unyielding wall. Nor could I breathe—the air was a thick liquid that I could not force into my lungs.

Panic grew and grabbed me—then died away just as quickly when I stepped back. I felt normal again. Air was air and I breathed in and out quite nicely.

"Put the mind in gear, Jim!" I shouted at myself, my words loud in the surrounding silence. "Something is happening—but what? Something happened after you touched the green light. Something to do with the artifact."

I stared at it. Tapped it with my knuckles. Groped about for inspiration. Found it.

"Tachyons! This thing emits them—we know that because that is how Aida tracked it in the first place. Tachyons—the units of time . . ."

The device was now functioning—I had turned it on when I had pressed the light. Green for go. Go where?

Stasis or speed. Either I had been speeded up or the world had slowed down. Or how could I tell the difference? From my point of view everything seemed to have slowed and stopped. The artifact had done something, projected a temporal field or stopped the motion of molecules. Or had created an occurrence that froze the surrounding world in a single moment of time. Time had come to a stop everywhere that I could see—except in the close vicinity of the device. I moved even closer and patted it.

"Good little time machine. Time mover, slower, halter, stopper—whatever you are. Neat trick. But what do I do next?"

It chose not to answer me. Nor did I expect it to. This was my problem now and I had to force myself to take the time to think it out. For the moment I had all the time I needed. Though eventually I would have to do something. And that something would probably mean touching another one of the colored buttons. Either that or I could stand looking dumbly at the device while I quietly died of thirst or starvation or whatever.

But which light?

Green had been obvious enough—even more obvious by hindsight. And the decision had been made at a moment of life and death. Now I was not so sure. I reached out, then dropped my hand. With plenty of time to decide I had become the master of indecision. Green had meant go, turn on, get started. Did red mean off, stop? Maybe. But what about white and orange?

"Not an easy one, Jimmy boy?" I said in what I hoped was a jocular voice—which came out very mournful and doom-laden. I wrung my hands together with indecision. Then stopped and looked at them as though I might see some answer printed on my fingers. All I saw was dirt under the nails.

"You have got to do it sooner or later—so do it sooner before your nerve fails completely," I told myself. Reached out a finger—drew it away. It looked like my nerve had indeed failed me completely.

"Take yourself in hand, Jim!" I ordered. Reached back and took a handful of collar and shook myself as violently as I could.

It was no help at all. Random choice then? Why not, just as good as guessing. I put the finger out again and promised myself that I would push down on whatever color was under the finger when the jingle ended.

"Eeeny, meeny, miney, shmoe, catch a . . ."

I never found out what I was going to catch because at that moment I heard the dragging footsteps coming from the hall.

Sound?

Out there where nothing moved!

I jumped about, hands raised in defense. Lowered them and waited as the footsteps grew louder, came closer and closer to the doorway . . .

Slipped past Floyd's immobile body.

"Aliens! Monsters!" I gasped, pulling back. Trying to run although I knew there was no place to go.

Two hideous metal creatures. Bifurcated limbs, many-angled skulls, glowing eyes, claw-fingered hands. Coming towards me. Stopping. Reaching out—

No! Reaching up to twist their own heads off. I could hear a gurgling scream, was only dimly aware that it was my own voice.

Twisted and turned and lifted—

Lifted off the helmets. Two very human faces looked at me with a good deal of interest. I stared back with the same emotion. Realized that, despite the close-cropped hair, the one on the left was female. She smiled at me and spoke.

"Wes bal, eltheodige, ac bwa bith thes thin freond?"

I blinked, didn't understand a word. Shrugged and smiled in what I hoped was a winning way. The second visitor shook his head.

"Unrihte tide unrihte elde, to earlich eart thu icome!"

"Look," I said, having enough of this and very much needing a few questions answered. "Could you please try Esperanto? That good, old, simple intergalactic second language Esperanto."

"Certainly," the girl said, smiling a winning and white-toothed smile. "My name is Vesta Timetinker. My companion is Othred Timetinker."

"Married?" I asked for some incomprehensible reason.

"No, stepsiblings. And you—you have a name?"

"Yes, of course. James diGriz. But everyone calls me Jim."

"A pleasure to meet you, Jim. Our thanks for activating the temporooter. We'll take it off your hands now."

She started towards the artifact—which I now knew was a temporooter. Though I still knew little else. I stepped in front of it and said:

"No."

"No?" Her rather attractive forehead furrowed while Othred's face suddenly looked grim. I turned a bit so I could keep an active eye on him.

"If *no* is too abrupt," I said, "then I will ameliorate it and say hold on just a moment if you please. Didn't you just thank me for finding this thing?"

"I did."

"Finding means that it has been lost. And has now been recovered because of my intervention. In return for this favor I believe you owe me at least an explanation."

"We're dreadfully sorry. But it is strictly forbidden to pass on information to temporal aborigines."

Not too flattering, I thought. But I was thick-skinned enough to take it. "Look," I carefully explained. "This is one aborigine who already knows a good deal about what is happening. I now have in my possession your temporooter, a device that has been constructed for burrowing through time. It seems that you or your associates not only lost control of the device but actually lost it in time and space. This is very worrying because you are forbidden to reveal your operations to people living along the time tracks you explore."

"How—how do you know this?" she asked. Well done, Jim. They may be long on linguistics but are certainly short on extrapolation and imagination. Keep going.

"At first, when we aborigines discovered the device, we thought it was an alien construction from the far past, built by long-lost, millennia-dead aliens. Of course the real explanation is much simpler. It was sent from the *future* and through a malfunction got out of control." Now I was just guessing—but their shocked expressions meant I was still doing well.

"Got so far out of control that it just kept going back in time until it ran out of power. Without power you could not locate it. You thought it might have been destroyed. Which is why there was such consternation when it signaled its presence. And you two were sent to retrieve it."

"You—you read minds?" She spoke in a hushed voice. I nodded firmly.

"The science of mental telepathy is well advanced in this era. Though it is obvious that all knowledge of our abilities has been expunged from your records in the future. But I will cease my mind reading now. I know how embarrassing it is to have one's secret thoughts revealed to strangers." I turned away, pinched my forehead, turned back. "I have stopped the function. We now communicate by words."

They looked at each other, still dazed.

"Speak, please, for now I do not know what you are thinking. Only by speech can we understand each other's thoughts."

"Knowledge of time travel is forbidden," Othred said.

"That's not my fault—you're the ones who lost the thing. You must understand that now I know all about it—as do all of my brothers in telepathekinesis who have been listening to my thoughts. But we are sworn to silence! If you wish your secret to remain a secret it will be secret. But you must aid us in keeping this secret secret. Look about you. See this ugly-looking type in the horned helmet? He is just about to kill me. And when you entered you probably stepped over the wreckage of a very armed and deadly machine—you did?, nod yes—good. That thing was going to kill me and my friend, but he got it first. So just turning off the temporooter and skedaddling is out of the question. You will leave behind a deadly and destructive situation."

"What must we do?" Vesta asked. Palm of my hand.

"First, you will help me by permitting myself and my associates to escape before the time stasis has been turned off."

"That should be possible," Othred said.

"Then that's agreed. Second, I will need another temporooter to take back with me . . ."

"Forbidden! Impossible!"

"Hear me out, will you please. Another temporooter to take back that *does not function*. A realistic fake that will disguise the fact that you and your machine have been here. Catch on?"

"No."

They sure bred them dumb in the future. Or without imagination or whatever. I took a deep breath.

"Look. I want you to remember that all the scientists here, in this time, know that there is a device of some kind that looks like your temporooter. Only they think that it is an alien artifact from the far past. Let us convince them that their assumption is true. If we do that, why no one will ever know about you and your lost equipment. Just have your technicians get some million-year-old rock and carve out something that looks like this. We'll pass it off as the original, the secret will be kept, honor satisfied, all's well that ends well."

"Excellent idea," Vesta said, and pulled a microphone from her armored suit. "I'll have one constructed now. It will be here in a second or two—"

"Wait. I have another small favor to ask. I will need certain functions built into the duplicate to convince our scientists that it is not a dummy. Just a simple device that will destruct after a single operation. This will pose absolutely no difficulties for your techs, I am sure."

It took me a bit longer to convince them of this necessity, but in the end they reluctantly agreed. The duplicate was an exact physical duplicate of the original. It blinked into existence floating in the air before us. Othred reached up and tugged; there was a popping sound as he pulled it down and handed it to me.

"Wonderful," I said, tucking it under my arm. "Shall we go?" They nodded agreement and put their helmets back on.

I had my temporal companions first release the stasis field on Floyd's hand so I could disarm him. Like our mutual enemy his finger was also tightening on the trigger. What a world of nascent danger we do live in! I tucked the gun into my belt and nodded to the tempotechs.

Give Floyd that—his reflexes were great. He was twisting and chopping towards Othred's neck the second he moved—stopped when I called a halt.

"Friends, Floyd. Down boy! Ugly-looking monster friends who are getting us out of here. If you look around you, you will see that all our enemies are paralyzed with indecision—and will stay that way until we are gone. Don't trip over the pieces of the Killerbot on the way out. And, Vesta, if you please. Tap that fake ball of fur with your magic wand so it can join us."

"What the hell is going on?" Floyd said, blinking in confusion as he tried to understand what was happening.

"I feel that some explanation is in order," Aida said, and Fido barked with exasperation.

"Second the motion," Floyd said.

"Forthcoming. As soon as we are out of here. Will you be so kind as to lead the way back to the surface."

I turned to thank my temporal saviors, but they were already gone. Not only short on imagination but bereft of manners as well. And when they had vanished they had taken the time stasis with them; I could hear our footsteps for the first time. I looked back with a sudden feeling of horror but, right, the stasis was still working for the enemy as the silent form of the gun-toting snarling Commander indicated.

"Time to leave," I said. "Since I have no idea how long the nasties are going to stand around that way. Go!"

"Explain!" Floyd shouted. Not in the best of moods.

"In a moment," I equivocated—and stopped dead. For I had suddenly been possessed of an even more horrifying idea. All this playing with time—what had it done for my personal poisonous deadline! I groped for my pendant skull-computer but of course it was gone with the rest of my equipment. How much time had passed? Was the poison now taking effect? Was I about to die . . . ?

Sweating and trembling I dropped the replacement artifact temporooter and grabbed up the plastic poodle.

"Aida—is Fido transmitting?"

"Of course."

"What time is it—I mean what day? No cancel that command. Get on to the Admiral now. Ask him how much time I have left. When is the deadline? Now—please. Don't ask me any questions. He'll know what you are talking about. Do it! And fast!"

Time dragged by on very sluggish feet I will tell you. Floyd must have heard the desperation in my voice for he stayed silent. A second, a minute—a subjective century crawled by before I had my answer. Aida must have done it—and made a good connection. Because the next voice Fido spoke with was that of Admiral Steengo.

"Good to hear from you, Jim . . ."

"Don't talk. Listen. I don't know what day it is. How much time is there to the deadline?"

"Well, Jim, I wouldn't worry about that if I were you—"

"You are *not* me and I am worried and answer the question or I will kill you slowly first chance I have. Speaking of killing . . ." I found that I couldn't go on.

"I meant it when I said don't worry. The threat of the thirty-day poison is over."

"You have the antidote?"

"No. But the thirty days are past. Two days ago!"

"*Past!!* Then I'm dead!"

But I wasn't dead. My brain spluttered and clanked and slipped back into gear. Thirty days past. No antidote. I was alive. I could hear my teeth grating as I spoke.

"Then the thirty-day poison—the whole thing was a fake from the start, wasn't it?"

"I am afraid that it was, and I do apologize. But you must realize that I did not know about it until now. Only one person had that information, the instigator of the operation."

"Admiral Benbow!"

"I'm afraid that information is not mine to reveal."

"You don't have to—it reveals itself. That lawyer who gave me the drink was just doing as directed. Lawyers will do anything if you pay them enough. Benbow was in charge and Benbow invented the poison plot to keep me in line."

"Perhaps, Jim, perhaps." His voice, even when transmitted through the agency of a plastic dog, reeked of insincerity and equivocation. "But there is nothing we can do about it now. A thing of the past. Best forgotten. Correct?"

I nodded and thought—then smiled. "Correct, Admiral. Why don't we just forget about the whole thing. All's well that ends well and tomorrow is another day. Forget it."

For now, I thought to myself, but did not speak that important little codicil aloud.

"I'm glad you understand, Jim. No hard feelings then."

I dropped the dog, turned and clapped Floyd happily on the shoulder, bent and picked up the replacement artifact.

"We did it, Floyd, we did it. I will explain everything as we walk. In great detail. But as you can see we are free, in possession of this artifact. Mission accomplished. Now—lead on, faithful Fido, since you have memorized the entrance-and-exit path. But go slowly, for it really has been one of those days."

I was hungry and thirsty. But even more thirsty for—what? Revenge? No, revenge was a dead end. If not vengeance—what then?

The time had come for a little evening up, a little sorting out of the record. I had been taken in completely by the poisonous con job. So before the last *i* was dotted, before the last alien artifact was laid to rest, I was going to see that a little justice got done.

On *my* terms.

Chapter 27

"Carry this for a bit, will you Floyd," I said, passing over the replacement temporooter. We were leaving the last lit tunnel behind and would depend now on Aida to remember the way. "I'm a little on the tired side."

"I don't wonder. But you have to understand—my patience has just run out.

So work hard and see if you can dig up enough energy to tell me just what happened. I am now completely confused. I remember that I wasted the Killerbot with that gun you now have tucked into your belt, the one Fido brought to me. Then I jumped through the door and told you to get down so I could blast the Commander as well as anyone else who was looking for trouble."

"That's just the way I remember it."

Fido barked and turned a corner from one dark tunnel into another even darker one. Floyd sounded worried.

"I remember pulling the trigger—then suddenly you are holding the gun, not me, and right next to me there are two creatures, people, robots, something like that. I blink and look into the lab and everyone is standing like they are frozen. Nothing moves—but nothing. Then when I look back I see that the two metal things have vanished. So I am beginning to feel like I am going around the mental bend. Therefore I would appreciate it if you would kindly, and quickly, tell me what happened."

"I wish I knew. I saw the same things you did. I don't know what happened."

"But you *must* know—you were talking to them!"

"Was I? I don't remember. Everything is still kind of fuzzy."

"Jim—don't do this to me. You *have* to remember! And what were you shouting at the Admiral about? Something about poison and another Admiral."

"That's easy enough to answer. Certain individuals blackmailed me into this operation by telling me I had been poisoned and that I had thirty days to live if I didn't get the antidote. There was no poison—therefore no antidote. So all the time we have been rushing about I have been thinking about the poison and counting the days before I curled up my toes and keeled over."

He was silent a moment, then he spoke.

"That's pretty heavy. You are sure about that?"

"I am. And I am also terminally tired so can we please put this conversation off for a bit. I would just like to concentrate on putting one foot in front of another for awhile."

Like it or not Floyd had to settle for that for the moment. Because I needed some time for deep cogitation, to dream up some sort of reasonable story for him—as well as the rest of the troops. Stumbling with fatigue I was grateful that we made our way through the tunnels without meeting any opposition. Though I had the gun ready just in case. When Fido actuated the escape hatch and it opened to reveal the blue sky—I sighed with relief. Gave the gun back to Floyd and used my remaining strength to crawl out onto the ground. Dropped with a groan and leaned back against a polpettone tree.

"You have the gun, Floyd," I said. "So pass me back that ancient artifact if you please. Aida—is there any transportation on the way?"

"There should be. I sent out your position as soon as you were aboveground and I could get a triangulation. Help is on the way."

As indeed it was—for a black spot in the sky grew quickly into the launch from the good old *Remorseless*. It landed with a shuddering thud, which bit of flying I recognized, so I was not surprised when Captain Tremearne exited through the open door.

"Congratulations," he said, and stuck out his hand. "You did it, Jim."

"Thanks," I said, as he gave my hand a good crushing handshake. "And don't think that it was easy."

"Never! I was there—remember. Can I relieve you of that thing?"

"No!" I shouted—and was shocked to hear the fine edge of hysteria, or incipient madness, to my voice. Well why not! "I'll hand it over—along with a detailed explanation of just what it is—at the meeting."

"What meeting?"

"The meeting that you are now going to arrange at the Pentagon. I'll want all The Stainless Steel Rats there. A last reunion so to speak. Has Madonette gone back to her imprisoning office yet?"

"She was supposed to. But she would not leave the planet until you came back."

"Faithful to the end! So in addition to all the Rats I would like a few other friends present."

"Friends?" He looked baffled. "Like who?"

"Well that macho fat thug Svinjar for one. King of the Machomen. Then you can invite Iron John and his opposite number, Mata. Ask yourself to come along as well. It will make an interesting gathering."

"Interesting—yes! But impossible. None of the exiles on this prison planet is permitted inside the Pentagon."

"Really? I thought that you were the guy that was going to see that Liokukae was cleaned up and cleaned out?"

"Yes—but—"

"Now is the time, Captain. For at this meeting I am not only going to turn over the alien artifact and reveal its secret—but I am going to tell everyone just how the situation here is going to end."

"How?"

"You're invited to the meeting. You'll hear then."

"This will not be easy to arrange."

"Yes it will." I pointed to Floyd. "Ask him about the strange things that happened when we were back there with the Survivalists. Admiral Steengo will verify his reports. There is a lot more to be cleaned up on this planet than you ever realized. Get your arguments together, consult your superiors, look after this." I passed over the artifacted artifact. "And don't wake me up until it has been all arranged."

I climbed wearily into the launch. Pushed up the armrests on the back row of seats. Stretched out and fell instantly to sleep.

The next thing I knew Floyd was shaking me gently by the arm. "We're back in the Pentagon. The meeting is on just like you said. I have breakfast and some clean clothes waiting for you. They'll be ready when you are."

The shower blasted out warm water and heated air and I stayed under it far too long. But it did wonders not only for my disposition but for my sore muscles as well. I did not hurry. They had arranged the meeting—on my terms—only because they had no choice. They would have informed me to get stuffed if they could. But the labtechs would have found nothing when they examined the artifact. Floyd would have told his confused story about what had happened when he had jumped in with his gun ready. Very confusing. In the end they would have been forced to the reluctant conclusion that the only way they could ever find out what had happened in the underground laboratory was by having me tell them. After which, knowing their record for veracity, they probably felt that they could do whatever they wanted with me.

"Well, Jim," I said to my smiling and sleek image in the mirror, as I carefully combed my hair, "let's give them what they want."

Floyd was my guide. Stamping in step with me along the corridors and into the conference room.

"Hi, guys!" I said in cheery greeting to the far-from-friendly faces.

Only Madonette returned my smile, waved a tentative hand. Admiral Steengo was stern, Tremearne uncommunicative—as was Mata. Floyd was grim-faced—but winked when I glanced his way. Iron John and Svinjar were chained to their chairs or they would have killed me instantly. As it was they strained forward, eyes bulging with homicidal rage. I was most pleased to see that my hairy red friend had a bandaged skull and an arm in a sling. The aged artifact lay on the table before them and I went and sat on the edge of the table next to it.

"Tell us about the device," Admiral Steengo said in a reasonable and friendly voice.

"Not quite yet, Admiral. I assume that your techs could make nothing of it?"

"They say it is over a million years old. That's all."

"There's more to it than that. But first a few introductions. The bruised guy with red fur is Iron John. Leader of a cult which you are now going to abolish. You can ship him off for treatment at an establishment for the criminally insane. Along with the fat man next to him. I have them here because I wanted you to see just what your policies of benign neglect had forced on the human beings out there on garbage world."

I smiled and waited for the cursing and the spitting to die down, then nodded pleasantly at the unwholesome twosome.

"Would anyone here like to live in the kind of societies that you are subjecting the helpless people on Liokukae to? A committee must be appointed now. Plans drawn up to free the women and children from their bondage. You will find that Mata will be able to advise you on that. I think the various males on the planet will have to be interviewed separately. I'm sure that a number of them like their world the way it is. They can have it. The others deserve something better. But all that is in the future. First let us look at the past. I'm sure that the others on my team will grieve the passing of The Stainless Steel Rats. We have played our last gig, sung our last song. And we did pretty well for a bunch of amateurs. One juvenile criminal. An admiral, an unarmed combat expert, and a—what are you really, Madonette? And don't embarrass both of us by talking about the imaginary office job again. That's not your style. Everyone else has come clean—so how about you?"

She drew herself up, looked grim—then smiled. "You deserve the truth, Jim. My office really is out there. But it is in the Galaksia Universitato, where I teach in the department of archeology. The university has so much money involved in this operation that they insisted on a representative."

"I'm glad it was you, Professor. Been fun working with you." I blew her a kiss, which she snatched out of the air and blew back.

"I didn't know about this!" Admiral Steengo said, more than miffed. "I am beginning to find out that there are levels of secrecy and duplicity in this so-called artifact retrieval operation that no one seems to know anything about. The more I discover about it—the more it stinks. And more and more it appears to bear the stamp of Stinky Benbow."

"That nickname is classified and will be stricken from the records," a loathsomely familiar voice grated from the direction of the suddenly opened door. "Fun and games are over. Sit down diGriz. I am in charge now."

"Well as I live and breathe!" I turned, filled with great pleasure, to face the ever-scowling countenance of Admiral Benbow. "This is almost too good to be true. The old poisoner himself—in person."

"You will be silent. That is an order."

Steengo was shocked. "Benbow, you bastard—have you been going over my head with this project? Are there other things about it that even I don't know?"

"Plenty. But your need to know is plenty far down the knowing chain of command. So, like this crook—shut up."

"No more orders, Benbow," I broke in. Reluctantly since there is nothing I enjoy more than a brace of admirals slanging each other off. But this was a time for work, not fun. "Now tell the truth, just for a change. It was your idea to give me the fake thirty-day poison, wasn't it?"

"Of course. I know how to deal with criminals. No trust, just fear. And complete control." The lizard lips bent into a frigid smile. "I will show you how it works."

He snapped his fingers and an aide hurried in with a familiar package. He held it up and the serpentine smile broadened. "You didn't really think that I would let you get away with this, did you?"

It was the package with the three million credits that I had mailed to Professor Van Diver for safekeeping. My fee for putting my life in danger, money well earned. Now in the hands of the enemy. Not only wasn't I bothered by seeing it—I was overjoyed.

"How kind of you, dear Admiral," I chortled. "The circle is complete, the ring closed. The play ended. The alien artifact retrieved. The last song sung. Thank you, thank you."

"Don't sound so cheery, diGriz—because you are in the deep cagal. Although you will not be executed for robbing the Mint you *will* get a well-deserved prison sentence for that crime. This fee, which you extorted from the university, will be returned to them. Along with that artifact . . ."

"Oh—so we have remembered it at last. Don't you want to know what it is, what it does?"

"No. Not my problem. Let the university worry about that. I was against this entire operation from the first. Now it is over and life will go on the way it was."

"Including life on this despicable planet?"

"Of course. We are not going to let the do-gooders interfere with the sound administration of the law."

"Admiral—I do admire you," I said, standing and turning to the intent audience. "Hear that, Iron John? You can go back to your old job at the bottom of the pond as soon as your bones heal. Svinjar, more killing and general swinery on your part. There will be the return of the rule of law and justice—on Admiral Benbow's terms."

"Arrest this man," Benbow ordered, and two armed guards entered and marched towards me.

"I'll go quietly," I said. Turned and touched the alien artifact as I had been instructed to. "But I'll go alone."

It was so quiet you could heard a pin drop. But, of course, a pin could not drop.

Nothing could move, was moving. Would move for quite a while.

Except me, of course. Strolling over, cheerfully whistling "Nothing's Too Bad for the Enemy," relieving the Admiral of my hard-earned fee. Smiling benignly into his glaring, frozen face. Due to stay that way for quite awhile. I turned and waved at my statuelike audience.

"The best part was working with The Stainless Steel Rats. Thanks guys. Thanks as well to you, Captain Tremearne. In fact—not only thank you—but could you give me a little help?"

I walked over and touched his arm as I said this, enclosing him in the stasis-resistant field that enveloped me.

"Help you do what?" He looked around at the motionless scene, turned back to me. "What's going on here?"

"What you see is what you get. No one is hurt, but no one is going to move for some time. Temporal stasis. When they come out of it they will never know that they have been in it."

"This is what happened to Floyd?"

"Exactly."

"Exactly what?"

"Time travelers. The alien artifact is not alien at all—but a human construct from the far future, sent back and lost in time. I promised the time travelers not to tell anybody. I'll make this single exception since I need your help."

"Doing what?"

"Getting both of us out of here so we can start the job of cleaning up this putrid planet. Here is what we have to do. Admiral Benbow has just arrived, as you saw, which means there is an interstellar spacer up there now in orbit about this planet. You and I will grab some transportation and get up to it. Once there you will use your rank, guile and forceful manner to see that we get aboard and far away from Liokukae. Then, when we get back to civilization, we will generate plenty of publicity about the evils men do here on this planet. It will be a scandal and heads will roll."

"Mine will be the first. Along with a court-martial, possible flaying and certainly life imprisonment."

"It shouldn't be that bad. If we get the forces of light on our side, why then the forces of darkness won't be able to lay a finger on you."

"It will take time . . ."

"Captain—that's the one thing we got plenty of! A good six months of it. That's how long this stasis will last. They won't know it, will not even realize a single second has passed. But, oh, will there be consternation among them when they discover how things have changed while they have been dozing! When I leave here the stasis will seal itself, impenetrable and impermeable. By the time it lifts the reform campaign will have succeeded and this prison planet will be nothing but a bad memory."

"And I will be cashiered, out of a job, will have lost my pension—the works."

"And many a human being will be alive and happy who would have been miserable or dead. Besides, the military is no place for a grown man. And with a million credits in the bank you can buy lawyers, live the good life, forget your past."

"What million?"

"The bribe that I am going to pay into a numbered account for you to make all of this worth your while."

He shook his fist. "You are a crook, diGriz! Do you think that I would stoop to your criminal, crooked level?"

"No. But you might be the administrator of the Save Liokukae Fund, which has been set up by an anonymous benefactor."

He scowled, opened his mouth to protest. Stopped. Burst out laughing.

"Jim—you are something else again! What the hell—I'll do it. But on *my* terms, understand?"

"Understood. Just tell me where to mail the check."

"All right. Now let's get you a uniform while I forge some shipping orders. I have the feeling that I am going to enjoy being a civilian."

"You will, you will. Shall we go?"

We went. Marching in step in a most military manner. Marching into the future, into a better, brighter future.

The blues had been sung. A page turned, a chapter ended. Tremearne would do a good job of sorting out this repellent world. I would do equally well as I slipped away between the interstices of society.

In six months I would be far from here, my trail cold, my bank account filled, my life more interesting. Once rested and restored—it would indeed be time for The Stainless Steel Rat to ride again!